S0-ADT-945

AFTERWARD SHE LAY VERY STILL, HOLDING ME.

I kissed the warm softness of her neck and shoulder, the smell and taste and feel of her. She lay looking at the ceiling, she took a big breath that trembled, and she said,

"They want me to be a spy."

I stopped breathing. I could feel myself go white, my heart lurch suddenly. Then I sat up and stared at her.

"I see."

She was staring at me, tense, dry-eyed. My heart was thudding.

"I see. The Public Security Bureau in Canton?" I said. I felt white.

She nodded, yes yes.

"I see. So they know all about us." My voice sounded loud.

"DID YOU TELL THEM?"

**Are there paperbound books you want
but cannot find in your retail stores?**

You can get any title in print in **POCKET BOOK** editions. Simply
send retail price, local sales tax, if any, plus 35¢ per book to
cover mailing and handling costs, to:

MAIL SERVICE DEPARTMENT
POCKET BOOKS • A Division of Simon & Schuster, Inc.
1 West 39th Street • New York, New York 10018

Please send check or money order. We cannot be responsible
for cash.   *Catalogue sent free on request.*

Titles in this series are also available at discounts in quantity
lots for industrial or sales-promotional use. For details write our
Special Projects Agency: The Benjamin Company, Inc., 485
Madison Avenue, New York, New York 10022.

YEARS
of the
HUNGRY TIGER

———◆———

John Gordon Davis

A KANGAROO BOOK
PUBLISHED BY POCKET BOOKS NEW YORK

YEARS OF THE HUNGRY TIGER

Doubleday edition published 1975

POCKET BOOK edition published March, 1977

This POCKET BOOK edition includes every word contained in
the original, higher-priced edition. It is printed from brand-
new plates made from completely reset, clear, easy-to-read type.
POCKET BOOK editions are published by
POCKET BOOKS,
a division of Simon & Schuster, Inc.,
A GULF+WESTERN COMPANY
630 Fifth Avenue,
New York, N.Y. 10020.
Trademarks registered in the United States
and other countries.

ISBN: 0-671-80939-3.
Library of Congress Catalog Card Number: 73-83623.
This POCKET BOOK edition is published by arrangement
with Doubleday & Company, Inc. Copyright, ©, 1974, by
John Gordon Davis. All rights reserved. This book, or por-
tions thereof, may not be reproduced by any means without
permission of the original publisher: Doubleday & Company,
Inc., 245 Park Avenue, New York, New York 10017.
Cover illustration by Roger Kastel.

Printed in the U.S.A.

To Patzi Gordon Davis

Years of the Hungry Tiger

PROLOGUE

In those days there was the Emperor, who was called the Lord of Ten Thousand Years, who ruled by the Mandate of Heaven from the Dragon Throne in the Great Within in the Forbidden City of Peking, and China was called Chung-kuo, which means Central Country, the Hub of the Universe, the Celestial Kingdom, and all other peoples were outer Barbarians, Foreign Devils. And voyages of discovery and emigration were forbidden, because there was surely no suitable food in Barbarian lands, only roots and insects, and no silver, and supplying emigrants with these things would cause a drain on the Celestial economy; and it was forbidden to trade with the Barbarians, there being nothing the Celestial Kingdom wanted of them anyway, having everything already in abundance. But the Barbarians of the English East India Company, and the Dutch and the Russians and the Americans wanted tea and silk, and there was one thing the Barbarians taught the Celestial people to want of them, and that was opium.

For a hundred years the forbidden opium trade went on from Canton, on the river Pearl, with everybody getting their squeeze in the Chinese way, until it became a severe squeeze on the Celestial economy and finally the Emperor appointed Commissioner Lin to stamp out the trade in opium and teach the Barbarians to heed the Vermilion Decrees and to "tremble and obey." And Commissioner Lin held the Barbarians in Canton to ransom for twenty thousand chests of opium which they had in their godowns, and they did tremble, but it was in rage.

Trembling with rage the Barbarian retreated in their clipper ships from Canton to the nearby virgin island called Heung Keung and resolved to wage war to get their twenty thousand chests (and faces) back, and to blast open the wall of China to their trade. Meanwhile, Commissioner Lin wanted the Barbarians to come back to Canton for other trade, so he sent some junks to stop them getting fresh water on Heung Keung, and the Barbarians gave

1

them two broadsides and blew the junks-o'-war clean out the China Sea. And sixteen British men-o'-war sailed from Calcutta, and up the Pei-ho River to the very Heavenly Gates of Peking, demanding trade treaties for Queen Victoria and the twenty thousand chests of opium back. The astonished Lord of Ten Thousand Years appointed Kishen to seduce the Barbarians back to Canton, there to weary them with negotiations while assembling more Celestial warriors to subdue them. But when Captan Elliot got weary of the negotiations he threatened to blow Canton clean out of the Central Kingdom unless he got the twenty thousand chests of opium back, plus the island of Heung Keung as a colony for Queen Victoria. And thus the harlot harbor of Hong Kong was born on twenty thousand chests of opium, a face to launch a thousand ships.

After the Opium War there followed many Unequal Treaties, and there were many foreign settlements, particularly Shanghai, and they all bled China white. Then there was the Boxer Revolution, the rebellion of the Society of Harmonious Fists, to drive the Barbarians back into the sea, and the foreign legations in Peking were beseiged and bombarded for fifty-five days before the combined foreign armies crushed the Boxers; and the Foreign Devils extracted further Unequal Treaties and concessions and imposed heavy war indemnities, and to ensure the payment they seized control of China's customs, railways, and communications, and levied heavy duties to protect their own products manufactured by sweated Chinese labor; and because of these things there was little captialism for the Chinese in China, no prosperous middle class came about, only millions of coolies and feudal peasants and a few comprador-middlemen and corrupt Chinese Imperial officials, and warlords. And China was bled whiter. Then came the Revolution of 1911.

It was democratic revolution, to throw off the corrupt Emperor's government and to break the power of the feudal warlords and to bring China into the twentieth century with a strong Western-style capitalist democracy; but the Foreign Devil capitalists did not want any democratic nonsense from China because they wanted to keep their Unequal Treaties and their extraterritoriality and taxes and war indemnities and cheap Chinese labor just like it was, and they supported the feudal warlords; and the Foreign Devils and the warlords and the military satraps bled China whiter: and every year many died of starvation and froze to death in the streets of the golden city of Shanghai, and small children slept beneath their factory machines and worked eighteen hours a day for a bowl of rice, and the landlords took 70 per cent of the peasants' crops in rental and the warlords terrorized the countryside and extracted taxes fifty years in advance.

Then came World War I, and the United States of America persuaded China to join the Allies in exchange for persuading the Allies to end the Unequal Treaties, but at the peace conference in Versailles in 1919 the Allies did not terminate their valuable Unequal Treaties; they traded them among each other and divided Germany's Unequal Treaties up among themselves, and they bled China whiter. And the Chinese saw that "no sun rises in the West for China," and there followed the May 4 Demonstrations.

The Western newspapers called it sporadic rioting. For two years they rioted and made strikes. But they were not rioting for wages or benefits; they were rioting in outrage. Outrage against Western exploitation and injustice and the exsanguination and against the warlords; it was a new democratic stage in the evolution of China, the first mass action. Two years later, in 1921, a young librarian called Mao Tse-tung and eleven other angry men formed the Chinese Communist party.

They had to be communist.

Then the Japanese invaded China to consolidate their Unequal Treaties and to turn northern China into a Japanese colony.

In those days the government of China was in the hands of the Kuomintang party, led by a wealthy young military gentleman called Chiang Kai-shek, who was supported by the United States of America. Now, when Japan invaded China, the young Chinese Communist party offered to form a coalition with the Kuomintang to fight the Japanese Dwarfs; and together they held the Japanese. Then Chiang Kai-shek turned his guns on the Chinese Communist party and massacred them. Maybe a few thousand survived to flee. They fled up into the great Chingkiang Mountains and established their first Red base. And the Japanese invaded on. And Chiang Kai-shek, supported by the United States of America, did not turn from his massacre

3

to fight the Japanese; he launched his first Communist extermination campaign.

Extermination.

Altogether there were five extermination campaigns. For five years Chiang Kai-shek's soldiers, supported by American bombers and advisers and money, beseiged and bombarded the Red base in the great Chingkiang Mountains, and each extermination campaign was called the final. And all the time the Japanese consolidated their colonization of China. For five years, five campaigns, but all the American aid and all Chiang's men could not exterminate the communists. Because they were dedicated men, and honest, and the peasants trusted them. They were Robin Hoods. And their creed was called the Thought of Mao Tse-tung.

The Fifth Final Communist Extermination Campaign was very bad, and the communists had to retreat out of the Chingkiang Mountains. This retreat was called the Long March.

Two thousand miles the Red Army marched over the mountains and valleys and rivers of China, for two years, two freezing winters and two broiling summers, with their women and children and farm animals and their armory and their printing presses for making their own Red money and newspapers and books; two years, and Chiang Kai-shek's army, supported by the United States of America, bombarded them all the way, and all the time the Japanese invaded and consolidated. One hundred thousand started off on that Long March and only twenty thousand reached the safety of the caves way up there in the mountain province of Yenan, two thousand miles from the mountains of Chingkiang.

And all the way the Red Army were Fish Swimming in the Waters of the People. And the people had never seen such a good and disciplined army, they did not beat the people to make them join up, nor rape their women nor loot their rice bins nor seize their property in taxes as the armies of the warlords did, not a grain of rice did they take but they paid for it, not even a needle did they borrow without returning it. And the Long March was called a Great Seeding Machine, sowing the Thoughts of Mao Tse-tung.

Now way up there in the caves of Yenan they established the first government of the People's Republic of

4

China: towns, farms, factories, banks: and all the time the Red Army were the Fish Swimming in the Waters of the People, and all the time they fought the Japanese and all the time Chiang Kai-shek, supported by the United States of America, fought them. Then World War II broke out: the Japanese were on the side of Hitler, they redoubled their invasion of China. And the Red Army guerrillas kidnapped Chiang Kai-shek from his bed and trussed him into a stolen airplane and flew him to the Yenan caves. And Mao Tse-tung said to Chiang Kai-shek: Why do Chinese fight Chinese when Japan invades China? Let us stop this civil war, and my army will join yours to fight the Japanese first. And Chiang Kai-shek, who had very little option, agreed.

So the Red Army joined forces with the Kuomintang Army, with the advice and consent of the United States of America, on account of the Japanese were bombing Pearl Harbor and occupying the British colony of Hong Kong, and Formosa, and the American colony of the Philippines, which was very bad news indeed in Wall Street. And together they fought the Japanese for four years and drove them back into the China Sea. And when the World War was over, after the Americans dropped the atom bomb on Hiroshima, the Chinese turned their guns back on each other again, and now the Red Army called itself the People's Liberation Army.

For five more years the Red People's Liberation Army fought the armies of Chiang Kai-shek, supported by the United States of America, across devastated China. Five more years, and then the People's Liberation Army drove Chiang Kai-shek into the China Sea, and across it to the island province of Formosa. And drove the Foreign Devils out of their sweatshops and factories and fat International Settlements and extraterritorial concessions. And many of the Foreign Devils and the Chinese industrialists and middlemen fled down the China coast to Hong Kong, and many poor people too who did not want to be liberated. The People's Liberation Army marched down the length of China, the size of all of Europe, carrying the Liberation, right down to the border of Hong Kong, and they could have marched right through Hong Kong and liberated it also, but they did not; they stopped at the Shamchun River.

Altogether the Liberation had taken twenty years.

And in Hong Kong there was the chaos, the harlot stag-

gered under the weight of people, the unemployment and the squatter shacks and the people sleeping in the streets, no land to hoe, not even enough water to drink, no natural resources except sweat and sangfroid. And now it was that her raison d'être of opium was at last outlawed, and she was nothing but an entrepôt, a commercial pimp for China. And now the Americans, fighting the Korean War, blockaded the China trade and she was not even a pimp any more. It was her China refugees who picked her up out of the gutter, and put her to work in backyard Chinese sweatshops, making anything you like; and her stagger became a swagger.

In those early days of the Red bases in the Chingkiang Mountains, and throughout the Long March, fighting all the way, there was always struggle inside the Communist party, argument and debate about the Correct Line of Marxist thinking and the incorrect or Deviationist Line, and it was Mao Tse-tung's policy to promote such Thought Struggle to keep the comrades pure. And in the days of the Yenan caves, fighting the Japanese and the Kuomintang all the time, Mao launched the Great Rectification Movement to expose and correct the Deviationists, and the Correct Thought was called the Thought of Mao Tse-tung. And now, after the Liberation, there began the Great Study Movement to educate the people in Marxism and the Thought of Mao Tse-tung.

And now, in those same days, there began the Great Land Reform Movement, to liberate five hundred million peasants from feudalism, and the party cadres went out across the decimated countryside, the size of all of Europe, and they called great meetings and they explained about the Revolution and Marxism and the Thought of Mao Tse-tung, and each person was encouraged to stand up and speak out his bitterness against the Kuomintang and the warlords and the landlords and the moneylenders and the rich peasants in a loud voice, to tell who had extracted exorbitant rents and usurious interest, and extorted taxes years in advance, who had cheated, who had carried off their daughters into concubinage and dragged off their sons to fight, and peasant courts were formed there and then to try these people, and each was punished according to his deserving, and many were shot. And the lands of the warlords, landlords, moneylenders, and the rich peas-

6

ants were distributed among the five hundred million poor peasants as their very own land, and there was great rejoicing, and the comrade party cadres were good and zealous men.

And all the time there was the re-education.

After the Land Reform there came the First Five-Year Plan, and the Collectivization, which was the second step of what the Revolution was all about, and the party cadres called all the people together and said that it would be better if the peasants of this place joined hands with the peasants of that nearby place, each man sharing his water buffalo and hoes and labor with his neighbors, for thus they would share in greater profit; and the people agreed that this was a good thing.

And all the time there was the Thought Struggle for party purity and unity and discipline, and the Great Study Campaign for re-education of the masses in the principles of Marxism and the Thought of Mao Tse-tung. And now there was the Teachers', Artists', and Writers' Study and Thought Reform Campaign to re-educate and remold the intellectuals. And now there was the Three Antis Campaign, which expanded into the Five Antis, the massive purification campaigns against official corruption, Kuomintang sympathizers, spies, capitalism, smuggling, black market, secret societies, prostitution, all the antis in the big Red black book, and the Mao Mass-Line Technique of Chingkiang Mountains and the Yenan caves was unleashed upon one quarter of mankind in the land the size of all Europe. Trust the Masses! Let the Masses Awake! Let the Masses Make Revolution! And in each city, town, village, street, each person participated in the mass investigations, denunciations, accusations, meetings, trials, the mass exposure of suspects, brother denouncing brother, children denouncing parents, neighbors denouncing neighbors, the dictatorship of the proletariat, and a lot of old scores were paid off, and nearly one million people died. Then there was the great Counter-Revolutionary Campaign. Then came the Hundred Flowers Campaign.

"Let a Hundred Flowers Bloom and Schools of Thought Contend." Let the intellectuals stand up and freely criticize the Communist party and its administration, help the party along its road to socialism by critical debate, tell the party where it has erred, air legitimate grievances. And no intellectuals stood up. And the party repeated its call,

7

Let a Hundred Flowers Bloom! And cautiously, hesitantly, the first one stood up, then another, then one by one they took courage and many spoke out, including party members, against the principles, policies, and leadership of the party, and then so many spoke out so loudly that the Hundred Flowers turned into a challenge to the party; and they were crushed. And many, many intellectuals were sentenced to Thought Reform Labor Camps. That year the Anti-Rightist and Party Rectification Campaigns began.

And meanwhile, out there in the massive countryside, where there had been first the Land Reform and then the Collectivization, there came a new order, the third step in what the Revolution was all about; now the comrade party cadres said that it would be even better for the farmers of this place who had collectivized if they joined hands with the collectivizaiton of that nearby place, and thus formed much bigger lands with many people to help each other, for thus would the land yield even more and the profits be even greater. And these new greater collectivizations would be called co-operatives.

But now there were many people who were worried about this new thing called Collectivization and even more worried about this newer greater thing called Co-operativization, and who did not like to share their good land, in respect of which they had brand-new title deeds, with people whose lands were not so good, or to share the fruits of their labor with people who did not labor so much, and other things. And the comrade party cadres knew that you do not remold a man in a day, and so they said at these meetings that the whole matter of co-operatives was voluntary, and that any man could withdraw his land and his labor from the co-operative after one year if he was not satisfied with the profit. And so the people agreed to these co-operatives. Then, in the summer of that year, there came the Great Leap Forward and the communes.

Now China would make a Great Leap Forward, 700 million Chinese people, one quarter of mankind in a land the size of Europe would be mobilized and the economy would be revolutionized and militarized, as if in battle, making "More Better Cheaper Faster!" And the lands of

500 million peasants which had first been distributionized and then collectivized and then co-operativized must now be communized, organized into 26,000 mighty farming communes owning all their land, buffalo, livestock, tools, 500 million peasants must march into the fields acting as if in battle shouting More Better Cheaper Faster! And for this revolutionary Great Leap Forward there must be revolutionary techniques, there must be deep ploughing to bring the subsoil to the surface, and never must a mou of land lie fallow, and the rows of crops must be planted closed together to yield More Better Cheaper Faster. Dare to Struggle, Dare to Win! We can order the Sun and the Moon to Change Places! And querulous nature must be overcome, there must be irrigation as never before, and 77 million Chinese were mobilized and militarized to dig and dam across the length and breadth of the mighty mountainous motherland, acting as if in battle. And in the towns and cities there must be communes also manufacturing More Better Cheaper Faster, as if in battle also. And for the factories there must be steel, so every man must build a furnace in his backyard and smelt down all the iron he can find and deliver it to the factories. And for the furnaces there must be fuel, so the trees must be cut down. And the women of the motherland must march into the fields and factories and act as if in battle also, so they must deliver up their children to the commune nurseries and no family may eat in their own houses any more, only in the commune mess halls and each only according to his deserving. And everywhere there must be production targets, More, Better, Cheaper, Faster! Unleash the masses and their creative capabilities will bloom! Trust the masses! Let no man with superstitious Western learning say we cannot do that this new way just because he is an engineer or an accountant or an old peasant who has farmed for many years. All such people must be revolutionized and they must be stripped of their authority and made to act as if in battle also. And every night after working as if in battle there must be the Struggle Meetings to revolutionize the thinking, the Mass-Line Technique of the accusations and self-criticisms and confessions, let any man accuse his neighbor of errors, bad thinking, negativism, defeatism, bourgeois tendencies, so that the people learn to think only of the people, in everything must this new thinking dominate and the potential of the people be unleashed. And there was great frenzy in the land and

9

much martial singing and loudspeakers and marching into the factories and the fields, acting as if in battle. That was the beginning of the Great Leap Forward.

That year there were many victories.

PART I

CHAPTER 1

In Hong Kong in the summertime the sun burns down humid maddening hot on the South China Sea and the harbor with the ships from all around the world and the junks junks junks and on the narrow teeming streets and alleys and ladder streets and the gracious spacious apartment blocks and the tenements and the cocklofts on the rooftops and the squatter shacks on the mountains and the people people everywhere and the noise and the vehicles carbon-monoxidizing everywhere and the rickshaws and the coolies and the hawkers and the markets and the cooked-food stalls and the restaurants everywhere and the bamboo scaffoldings on the buildings going up on the mountains that are chopped down to reclaim more land for the teeming people and the factories and the workshops and the sweatshops and the great taipan trading houses and the banks from all around the world and the import-export agencies and shops shops shops and the money-making everywhere and the lucky Chinese names on the signboards and neon signs everywhere and the sweatpots and fleshpots and the bars bars bars and the many many smells. Out there the islands are hot mauve and there is a haze upon the South China Sea, glaring misty blue, and the beaches burn your feet and you have to dive down to reach the cool; and in the winter there is ice on top of mountain Tai Mo Shan. In the summer when you kiss, you taste her and her flesh is warm, and when you make love you both are wet and slippery and the hair on your chest sticks a little to her breasts and afterward you lie flat out flaccid side by side on the wet crumpled sheet and you do not care to touch and hold each other too much because of the sweating, and the matches will not strike readily on the matchboxes, and your fingers wet the cigarettes. And your beer turns warm quickly in the glass.

In the summer the big monsoons come, warm fat rain as thick as your fingers, falling furling crashing down, and lashing with the wind, and the landslides and the floodings and the roads and boulders come crashing down the steep jungled mountains and many people are killed by the rain. There are too many people. And then in the late summer the *tai-fungs* come, the great typhoons, roaring across the China Sea, and the sky is black black black and the sea is smashing and flying and crashing down the waterfront streets, and out there great ships are smashed up on the beaches and whole fleets of junks are smashed to pieces, the steep mountains come crashing down and a lot of people die. And afterward there is the digging for the bodies, and the grief, and the stench of them. There are too many people.

In those days, before the Great Leap Forward, I was put into Special Branch of the Hong Kong Police Force because of my Terrorist Experience, acquired fighting the communists in Malaya, and because of my degree in political philosophy. Terrorist Experience was considered a valuable qualification in those days of the Winds of Change when there were fewer colonies each year to serve in, when as fast as you broke your heart and covered yourself in blood gaining the Terrorist Experience, and just about at last had the terrorists beaten, Her Majesty's Government handed the colony over to the terrorists. Back in Hong Kong, in Special Branch, my Terrorist Experience was thankfully of no assistance at all, but it sounded good to the promotion board. Somebody-up-There-Likes-Me McAdam, they called me. That somebody was supposed to be the Old Man, the commissioner of police, who had also served in Malaya at the same time and who had served under my father in the British Shanghai Police Force in the bad old days before the Liberation.

I did not like Special Branch much. In those days China was very busy with the Korean War, and trying to consolidate and feed her 700 millions. Mostly we were concerned with keeping the Kuomintang agents of Chiang Kai-shek and Mao's communist agents from fighting each other. The American CIA backed the Kuomintang and the Russians backed the communists and all four gave us information about what the other two were up to, to make us do their dirty work for them, but Hong Kong was small leagues in those days. Our work was mostly this kind of routine, keeping the protagonists apart, raiding their premises and confiscating their arsenals and deporting them back to China and Taiwan respectively, and keeping routine tabs on the Bank of China and the fat cats, the wealthy communist businessmen who do routine espionage and pressure work for China in exchange for China's business; but we tried not to antagonize anybody. The Bank of China and the Chinese Chamber of Commerce and the fat cats were most important to Hong Kong, for without China's business there would be no capitalist business, and therefore no Hong Kong. Hong Kong is China's shop window on the world and communist big business and the Bank of China are the foundation of the pyramid, with Her Majesty's Government sitting uncomfortably precarious on the top by tacit consent of Peking, and the Colony was governed, it was said, by the Hong Kong and Shanghai Bank, Jardine Matheson, the Hong Kong Club, and His Excellency the Governor, in that order. Business is Hong Kong's business, and it is Communist China's business first and foremost. The rest is a case of symbiosis. In Special Branch we understood it very well, and in those days we were mostly only concerned with keeping the status quo, and keeping routine intelligence tabs on the fat cats, their investments in compromising ventures such as girlie bars and brothels and massage parlors, and on their mistresses and sex lives in case it should ever become useful. But it was live and let live. There was more to it than I saw, for in Special Branch the left hand does not know what the right is doing, and I was only an inspector, but China was too preoccupied to give us much trouble and Whitehall was too nervous to give anybody any trouble. I did not need my Terrorist Experience at all.

Nor did I use my B.A. in political philosophy, but when I was made aide-de-camp to the governor I wrote a book called *The Story of the Chinese Communist Revolution.* It started off as a novel and ended up as an armchair history. I wrote it to pass the time in Government House, and because I could not bring my easel and paints to the office, whereas writing a book actually looked like work, and because China had been my major subject in my degree and therefore I found it very easy to regurgitate it all predigested for the reader. It did not surprise me that it was published, because the publisher was an Old China Hand who had known my father in Shanghai. What did surprise me was that it became a local best seller, that I was invited to speak at businessmen's luncheons, and the bloody police board wanted to transfer me back to Special Branch to their Political Analysis Section. I strenuously resisted the transfer, pointing out that my book was very nearly procommunist, at least pro-Mao Tse-tung, and I went fishing with the Old Man and persuaded him that I needed general police work to further my career, not furtive back-room stuff, and I thereby got myself posted to the Special Investigations Office of the Criminal Investigation Department. The SIO is supposed to be the elite of the CID, and I had a few very lucky investigations indeed, and the name Somebody-up-There-Likes-Me McAdam stuck.

It is not very difficult to be a good policeman. All you must do is know your criminal law thoroughly, and the law of evidence, leave no stone unturned, compile your files meticulously, take chances but few shortcuts, know your town and know the right people, on both sides of the law. And have a little luck.

The next year the Great Leap Forward started.

In those days we lived in a fine old terraced house above Happy Valley that looked across the harbor. We had four big bedrooms with high ceilings and the passage was long and wide and the floors were wood. There was a large verandah with bamboo blinds which you rolled up like sails, and Catherine grew flowers in pots on the verandah, and there were flower patterns on the bedroom ceiling, and big overhead fans which were always turning slowly in the heat.

From the verandah the harbor was magnificent. Below there was Wanchai, the world of Suzie Wong, and Causeway Bay and the bars and the narrow streets of the thousands of the old Chinese apartment blocks with the laundry handing out the windows on bamboo poles, and the cocklofts on the rooftops and workshops and the sailors, and the Cantonese music and hammering and the yammering and clattering of Mah-Jongg. On the north side you could see the thousands of squatter shacks crowding up

14

lorries and drove them down to Hong Kong, and when they came back they had seen all the Wonders of the World. And we had a Takwuling police football team, the captaincy of which I inherited from my predecessor in office. Every Wednesday afternoon we played against the village teams and sometimes we even traveled as far afield as ten miles down to Tai Po and Sek Kong and Yeun Long to play, just to show we weren't yellow. Nearly every team beat us, which gave the villagers a ton of face.

It was nice up here in the country. Sometimes I went to the police mess at Fanling and to the Gurkhas' officers' mess, and to the Country Club and sometimes I drove over to Shataukok to drink with Nondrinking Jack. Once a week I went into Hong Kong to see Susan. I took her to the beach or the botanical gardens to ride on the swings and to fill her up with ice cream and Seven-Up, and to love her. After I took Veronica Brown out to dinner, if it was her night off from her club. Sometimes Veronica Brown came and spent the night up at Fanling, and we stayed at the Country Club. I could have smuggled her into the Closed Area, back to Takwuling, but it would have set a bad example. And sometimes I went with Nondrinking Jack or one of the other inspectors or with Cecil the magistrate to the Better Hole, near the Golf Club, to eat and drink and dance to the jukebox with the Chinese waitresses and the British army wives.

Sometimes we went to Kam Tim, to the bars outside the old walled village where the army boys stationed at Sek Kong drank: those were nice quiet little girlie bars, and the girls still had the mud of the paddy fields between their toes, they did not go to bed with you very easily, or they had steady army boyfriends; the British army wives were better for the other thing and of course they cost you nothing, except those army wives who operated out of the big hotels in Hong Kong. Sometimes I went into Kowloon, to the girlie bars. Sometimes I went to Mr. O's for a Filipina, "Hundred per cent absolute guarantee no vee dee, Bomban." Those were the days before the Vietnam War.

Before that fourth summer of the Great Leap Forward it was quiet up there in Frontier. Our Chinese were patriotic toward China, as all Chinese are patriotic, but they saw the hungry refugees and they knew what was happening, despite what the communist newspapers and Radio Canton said, and a Chinese knows a bargain when he

29

sees it. Mostly they were law-abiding, and always they were friendly. Mostly they came to us first with their troubles. Occasionally somebody chopped somebody's head open with a meat cleaver, there was a lot of petty gambling and a little bit of prostitution which we turned a blind eye to, and a little opium traffic, but it was all small leagues up here in Frontier. There was little crime.

But that sunset I rode up the trails into the mountains, then I tethered my horse and I climbed on foot because it was too steep. I climbed maybe half a mile, then I saw a Chinese peasant defecating. He had not heard me, he had his back to me and I would have walked past him. Then I saw he had his thumb and forefinger in his anus and he was extracting a small metal cylinder. Then I ducked behind a bush. I pulled out my gun and leveled it on him. He picked up the cylinder and then walked to a tree, still pulling up his pants. He picked up a stone at the base of the tree, placed the cylinder under the stone. Then he saw me.

He stared at me, horrified, then he scrambled. He turned and crashed off downhill still clutching up his pants, crashing through the bushes. I ran flat out after him, crashing dodging through the bushes down the steep mountain. He had a twenty-yard start on me but I could run faster because he was pulling up his pants. We ran a hundred yards down the mountain, then I got him by the collar. I wrenched him around, panting gasping stumbling, jabbed the gun against his jaw.

"Make one sound and I blow your head off."

He stared, panting terrified, face screwed up gasping at the gun digging him. I wrenched his hands and snapped the handcuffs on him.

"Now get back up there fast!"

We scrambled back up the mountain, panting. Back to the stone under the tree. "Sit down!" He sat down in a heap, terrified. I lifted the stone. And in the hollow underneath, the metal cylinder. I picked it up carefully with my handkerchief, unscrewed the top. I thought I was going to see heroin inside. I saw a small roll of film.

He looked at me trembling. Jesus. I tipped the film into my tunic pocket. I screwed the cap back on the cylinder, put it back under the stone.

"Get up!" He clambered up, shaking. It was almost dark now. I looked around. "Up there." I jabbed him in the back.

30

We scrambled ten paces up the mountain, to the edge of a gully. It had thick bush.

"Get in there."

He scrambled down the bank into the bushes, hands manacled behind his back. I scrambled down behind him. I was shaking. The excitement.

"Stop." I looked around for a suitable stout bush. "Kneel down at that bush. *Kneel down there!*"

He knelt, terrified. I undid his handcuffs, panting, held the gun at the back of his head.

"Take off your shirt."

He took it off, shaking. Then I grabbed his wrists and wrenched them around the bush's trunk so he was embracing it. Then snapped the handcuffs back on. Now he was anchored. I held the gun back at his head and hissed at him, "What time will he come and fetch it?"

His face was screwed up, terrified of the gun. "I do not know, firstborn—"

I jabbed him: "Who is he?"

"I do not know, firstborn—"

Again. "Where do you come from?"

"China, firstborn, Shamchun commune—"

"Are you Public Security Bureau?"

"No, firstborn, I am only a Man Bing messenger." I jabbed him, he winced: "Truth, firstborn!"

"How often have you come in the past?"

He hesitated. "This is only my fifth time." I jabbed him. *"Truth, firstborn!"*

"We'll soon find out." I rolled his shirt up into a tight long roll. "Open your mouth." I rammed the shirt tight across his mouth as a gag and tied it tight at the back of his head.

I crawled up the bank and lay under the bushes with my gun out and tried to breathe quietly. I wondered how long I would have to wait.

I waited two hours. The moon came up and the mosquitoes knocked hell out of me and I was thirsty as hell. After two hours I saw him.

He came down the path, a peasant following a path he knew well in the moonlight. Then he veered off to the tree. He picked up the stone, picked up the cylinder, put it in his pocket. He started back to the path. I was crouched now, my gun resting on a branch trained dead at him.

"Halt or I shoot!"

He jerked, aghast, then ducked and ran, and I fired. Fired at his legs, he kept running flat out downhill. I scrambled out of the gully and charged downhill after him. Flat out after him crashing through the black bushes in the moonlight, I fired again wildly, there was a crash of a pistol, then he fired twice more and I felt a blow on my arm which I thought was a tree branch, then I fired again wildly and I saw him fall. I crashed flat behind a tree, gasping, and shouted in Cantonese, *"I shoot to kill if you move!"*

I could just see the heap of him down there in the moonlight. I shouted above the thudding in my ears: *"Stand up!"*

He shouted, "I am wounded!"

I shouted, *"Get your hands above your head or I fire!"*

He clambered to his feet, twenty yards down there, and stood crouched with his hands up in the moonlight. My heart was thudding. I came out panting from behind my tree, holding the gun on him. He stood there, arms up, one leg bent painfully. Then I noticed he had winged me in my bicep.

"You're covered," I panted. I clambered down toward him cautiously. He had lost his gun, face grimacing. His thigh was very bloody. I came to within six feet of him. I stared at his face in the moonlight.

"Good God! Superintendent Chester Wu."

He panted in his impeccable Oxford accent, in pain, *"What the devil do you mean by firing at me!"* he lowered his hands and held his bloody thigh. I held the gun on him, panting, astonished.

"What the hell are *you* doing in the Closed Area at night picking up microfilm from communist dead-letter boxes?"

He panted, "I don't know what you're talking about! Get me to an ambulance, you'll hear all about this!"

I said, "You're the one who'll hear about it. Put your hands back up!"

"Stop being damn silly, Jake!"

"Get your hands up or I'll clobber you! *Sir!*"

I frisked him but I could not find the empty metal container. He had thrown it away. The next day we found it.

That night we limped into Takwuling police station at midnight with Superintendent Chester Wu of the Hong Kong police on my horse because of his wounded leg, with his hands strapped behind his back with the peasant's belt, the peasant handcuffed to the horse's bridle with one hand and holding up his pants with the other, and me bringing up the rear nursing my arm with my good hand and holding the pistol with my bad one.

I never did find out what was on that microfilm. I called in headquarters as soon as I got back and it and Chester were spirited away. But I did know that Chester Wu was quietly deported across the Shamchun into China. I never did discover how he had gotten into the hands of the communists in the first place, nor did I discover what had happened to the peasant. The whole thing was hushed up.

It was several years before we heard of Chester Wu again, and he had done very well for himself. He was the head of the People's Security Bureau in Canton, using his expert inside knowledge of the Hong Kong Police Force.

It was nice up here in the country. I did not try to paint big things any more, I tried to not think big things, only of the simple peaceful things up here in Frontier. Sometimes in the evenings, after dinner, I drove down to Tai Po to drink wine and play chess with Father Ambrose. He had an old Chinese house attached to his church, with a courtyard full of subtropical plants, birds, rabbits, stray dogs, cats, and a turnover of furtive undernourished Chinese. "How many illegal refugees are you unlawfully harboring today, Ambrose?" I always said.

"Illegals?" Father Ambrose said. "I do not know what they are, they are just God's children who say they are hungry."

"You know where you'll go when you die if you break the law, Ambrose?" I said.

"Have some illegally home-brewed wine," Father Ambrose said, "and worry about your own soul. Arresting all those refugees and handing them back to those Red sonsabitches, indeed. Those heathens. At least I have some love for my fellowman."

Father Ambrose was full of love for his fellowman all right, except communist heathen Red bandit sonsabitches. Ambrose spent forty Jesuit years in China before the Liberation, and Mao had allowed him to stay for five years after the Liberation, and then they had had enough of Father Ambrose stirring it and they kicked him out. "On my arse," Father Ambrose said. "Those heathens."

"What were you up to, Ambrose?" I said.

He held the edge of his hand to his lower lip: "Up to here! Anybody who does not agree, anybody who argues" —he cocked his finger like a revolver at my eyes— "bang! No arguments. The communist cannot take argument. Only bang. I saw too much. Thousands. And that is only what I saw, one man. And the Christians? They got plenty of bang-bang. From my mission? Hundreds. Oh boy! That is why they kick me out on my arse. Because I am always arguing with the comrade commissar and the Security Bureau bandits. How many nights I spend in jail? How many times they threaten to bang me?" He glared at me: "I don't know how you can like the communists."

I said: "I just happen to think they're the best administration China has ever had, and the only administration that could have pulled China out of the shit she had been in for a hundred years."

"Shit?" Father Ambrose appealed: "What about the Land Redistribution? They shoot the landowners and give each man a piece of land and everybody is very happy with the communists. Oh yes, kiss-kiss the communists! Then the next year they start Collectivization. And the next year they start the communes! And then nobody owns anything again! And anybody who argues—bang. That is not shit? And then the Hundred Flowers Campaign!" Father Ambrose gave his Mephistophelian beam and threw his arms wide. *Let every person come forth and criticize the party and tell us where we are going wrong!* And when they stand up—" His beam disappeared, he sat back. "First kiss-kiss, then bang-bang." Father Ambrose liked that. "Like James Bond: Kiss-kiss, bang-bang!"

But what about before the Liberation, I said, the complete lawlessness and corruption and exploitation, people dying of starvation in the streets and the boys dragged off in rope gangs into battle for the warlords, and the children sleeping under their factory machines, at least the Reds are organizing 700 million people into a society that gives everybody a roof and a job and a full belly.

"What about the Great Leap Forward?" Father Ambrose demanded. "What about the refugees?"

To catch the illegal refugees was my job. There was not enough space for all the millions who wanted to come to Hong Kong, neither houses nor schools nor hospitals

34

nor jobs, not even enough water to drink. It was a problem of people, and these were other people's people.

Many came via Macao, the tiny Portuguese province forty miles away on the other side of the river Pearl. At the neck where the Macao peninsula joins the mainland of China there is an old arched gateway called the Barrier Gate. The People's Liberation Army and their gunboats shot down the people trying to swim across the big mouth of river Pearl to Macao but regularly the long lines of the old and the sick and the lame and the halt were marched through the Barrier Gate into Macao by the People's Liberation Army. They were the Useless Mouths whom China did not want. They were pitiful to see, hot and ragged and hungry, each person holding on to the person in front. The Portuguese Government of the Maritime Province of Macao, six square miles, never turned away any person. And in Macao there were the snakeheads, the smugglers of human contraband. They called themselves names like Love-the-Masses Travel Service, and Vacations in Happiness and Tranquillity. The snakeheads loaded them down into the holds of their junks and set sail for Hong Kong at dead of night, to run first the Chinese gunboats then the launches of the Hong Kong Marine Police. And down the China coast in stolen People's junks came the refugees, making for the Golden Mountain Where Men Eat Fat Pork and its 223 islands in the night. They tried to land on an island or somewhere on the jigsaw coastline of the New Territories in the night. Then they tried to make it overland to teeming Kowloon. Then they were safe. Every now and again a snake boat sank from overloading, or in bad sea, and the bodies washed up on our islands. Every year thousands were caught. Every year many thousands got in. Up there in the mountains at Takwuling it was not easy for them to cross, on account of the People's Liberation Army guards and their dogs, but every night my patrols caught at least a dozen all the same. They could not believe it when they saw all the rice we gave them. They shoveled it into their mouths with their chopsticks ravenously, and they were very grateful and very polite and very nervous. Then we questioned them and filled in the forms. If they had had jobs of "special interest" in China we passed them on to Special Branch. The next morning we told them that we were deporting them back to China. Then the weeping started and the pleading and the groveling.

It was very hard on the Chinese policemen, it was very hard on all of us. When we got to Lowu post, where the Kowloon-Canton Railway crosses the Shamchun, we shuffled them across the bridge to the halfway mark and the People's Liberation Army guards came forward to take them over. The guards never even nodded a greeting to us, although we saw them every day, they were very stern young men and they took over the prisoners without any change of expression, for it was loss of face that refugees wanted to run away from the People's Republic. The guards marched them off to the police station under the big red flag, and what happened to them then we did not know. There was no way of knowing from one day to the next what would happen to them, and it was no concern of ours. For they were not refugees in the legal sense of the word, seeking political asylum. They were only hungry.

PART III

CHAPTER 5

Now in that first year of that Great Leap Forward there had been frenzy in the land, and all the people mobilized and militarized and marching into the fields singing martial songs and working acting as if in battle, *More Better Cheaper Faster*. And more lands were ploughed than ever before, and deeper than ever before, and more crops were planted earlier and closer than ever before so there would be more yield than ever before; and when the old peasants shouted at the party cadres in the late evenings at the meetings, such people were made to stand and criticize themselves and confess their wrong thinking, that the party knew best. From before the dawn through the long hot day under the China sun and late into the moonlight and the lamplight the Production Brigades worked, acting as if in battle, men and women and children over ten years. And across the mighty motherland the comrade party cadres and the millions were digging the canals and building the dams feverishly by hand, and in the cities there were the urban communes under the comrade party cadres, and the nurseries and commune mess halls and the liberated housewives working, and in the factories there was the frenzy also, *More Better Cheaper Faster* late into the night, and here the party knew best also. The native genius of the masses must be unleashed, they must change this and that technique if it does not work More Better Cheaper Faster, let no man gainsay the party because he has superstitious Western learning, let no such mechanic or engineer say that this machine or vehicle must not be driven so fast, or this machine must be stopped to cool it or to give it oil or to overhaul it, and thus and so, never must a machine be stopped, only must it work More Better Cheaper Faster, such people must be stripped of their authority and work side by side under the masses: and no accountants and administrators must think that only they understand management, they also must be made to work under the masses, it is the masses under the party cadres who must control the management of everything, only the native genius and the party and the masses know how to make More Better Cheaper Faster. And all over mighty China night and day there was the red glow of the backyard furnaces making the pig iron for the factories out of all the metal the people could lay their hands on, burning all the wood they could lay their hands on. And all the time the martial singing and the loudspeakers and the Big Character posters, More Better Cheaper Faster, and the banging of gongs, and the frenzy, and the many triumphs.

In the second year of the Great Leap Forward there were no more victories. For the comrade party cadres were not farmers and the deep ploughing had made the subsoil sterile, and the close planting made the crops small and sickly, and the comrade party cadres who drove the people to build the dams and canals acting as if in battle were not engineers, and because of all the frenzy there were no over-all regional plans for all the water in all the dams and all the canals, and the dams and the canals broke and half of the water tore away and there were great floodings in many places where there had never been flooding before; and the comrade party cadres did not understand the principles of drainage and the fields turned alkaline and now the crops could not grow in them. And the comrade party cadres did not understand machines, the matter of maintenance and spare parts and the right work for machines, they only knew about More Better Cheaper Faster, the machines were driven too hard too fast too long too hot, and across the mighty motherland the machines burned out and ground down and seized up. And the comrade party cadres did not understand the matters of co-ordination and supply of raw materials and demand and transportation like the accountants had understood it, and now all across the mighty motherland there were the mighty bottlenecks, factories without raw materials shouting More Better Cheaper Faster and factories with no transport for their products, all shouting

More Better Cheaper Faster: and the pig iron made of the doorknobs and cutlery and fences and the railway lines smelted in the millions of the backyard furnaces was too bad for rendering into steel and too soft for the making of anything, even of a hoe.

And now, further, in the second and third years of the Great Leap Forward there were great floodings and then great drought and then great bitter winters, and there was no more marching into the fields acting as if in battle any more; and the party told the people they must go out into the mountains and find herbs and roots and berries to eat, and there was great suffering, and sickness, and no strength for work, and many people died. And there was great fear of the winter that was coming, and they called it the Year of the Hungry Tiger.

And now there came a new order from the party in Peking: that there must be a thinning out of the people in the cities, that all people who came to the cities since the first year of the Great Leap Forward to work More Better Cheaper Faster must return to their native villages, and they would not require travel permits. And the city people were very afraid of this order, and the country people were very afraid of the millions of city people who would descend like a mighty cloud of locusts. And there was great confusion on the highways and byways and railways, and many were the people who turned about and set out while they still had the strength to try to get to the Golden Mountain Where Men Eat Fat Pork.

Now, before that fourth summer of the Great Leap Forward, the gunboats and the border guards of the People's Liberation Army shot them down. But now there spread the incredible word, so extraordinary that not even the comrade party cadres knew if it was true or false: the story that whoever wished to visit dear friends and relatives languishing in the decadent city of Hong Kong might do so without travel permits and the border guards would not shoot you down.

At first, at Takwuling, we noticed that we did not hear any shots across the river in the night any more, and there were more people arrested every night, squatting in their tatters in the China heat in the dust of our compound, the hunger and exhaustion deep on their faces. They all had the same story. It was the Year of the Hungry Tiger, Bomban.

Now I put out extra patrols, tramping over the hot rugged hills and beaches and through the fishing villages looking. Then there were too many prisoners every night at Takwuling for them to sleep in the cells and I had tents erected in the compound, and late into the hot night my constables processed them. It was always the same story. It is the Year of the Hungry Tiger, Bomban, there is drought and the land is finished and the people are starving. And no shots fired in the night other side the Shamchun. And the hollow hungry faces and the queuing for the steaming rice and fish and shoveling it ravenously into their mouths with the wooden chopsticks, and in the morning the weeping and the beseeching. And now there were many young people, and children, very thin and very hungry but good strong people once they had a gutful of rice. Not Useless Mouths.

CHAPTER 6

That hot sundown I sat on my verandah above the police station drinking a beer and watching the commune peasants in the paddies across the river, and I was thinking of Susan and I knew that I was nearly all through with the Shamchun Valley and the Frontier, and I wanted to go home. It had done me good up here in the country, and now I wanted my child, and even maybe my wife again. And oh Christ yes I was beginning to understand how men take their women back. After a long time the outrage and the hate wear off. After a long time your mind doesn't reel red-black with outrage any more when you think about it, about all the Christ-hateful things, the taking off her clothes and the look in their eyes at each other, and the coming together clutching ravenously feeling pressing breasts flattened against his bastard chest groping kissing sucking, oh Jesus Christ you can see every hateful outrageous thing, you know every inch of her and you see it all and what her face looks like at this time and what she says and her breasts covered in his saliva and her arms clutching—oh Christ you somehow cease to feel yourself go white with hate and outrage when you think about it,

40

after a long time you have thought and felt so much that you have gotten used to it, and your heart does not break any more. After a long time you feel tired, and a little old, and you can think of the good things again, and then maybe you want to go back again, and oh God yes you always want to go back to your child child child. In the mornings when you wake up it can be very bad, and in the evenings when you are finished work you want your home and child all right in spite of everything. That is how I was feeling that hot April sunset, and I just had to get up and go for a walk.

It was almost dark. The day's refugees were squatting outside the tents, tonight there would be more. They were very well behaved, I was probably the first foreign devil they had ever seen. The P.C. on guard at the gate came to shuddering attention and saluted. I walked through the gate and down the dirt border road. I was not thinking, I was only feeling.

I walked a mile from Takwuling, to the old abandoned Lin Ma Hang police post on the knoll. There was a row of bullet marks along the wall, where some Kuomintang bandits had shot it out with the police once upon a time. Half a mile ahead, on the slopes of Robin's Nest, was our Pak Fa Shan post. The searchlight was sweeping along the border fence.

I leaned against the old wall. The hot China sky was full of stars and in the west was the deep glow of the sundown. The searchlight swept slowly along the fence below me. When it was gone I saw the dark shapes emerge.

I shoved myself off the wall and crouched down. They were jumping down into the riverbed and scrambling across the rocks, then up into the black bushes at the fence. They were in the shadow of the knoll. Fifty of them. I cursed and started along the top of the knoll, crouched behind the bushes.

There it was. Down on the bank, a hole under the fence, the dark shapes scrambling through. I was swearing, crouched low in the bush. The bastards. They had it all figured out, this was not opportunism. I watched them scrambling through the dark bushes at the fence and up the gully, trying to count. Fifty if there was one, Christ knows how many had got through already, scrambling like a silent fire crowd up the ravine. Then I leaped up.

"*Mo yuk!*" I shouted.

They all sat down with a crash. Suddenly it was dead

41

still, only the night insects and my own breathing. Now I could hardly see any, down there in the scrub.

I shouted in Cantonese, *"We are police! I am bomban! Hands on your heads!"*

I could see arms go up in the gloom.

"People outside fence come through hole now," I shouted down the ravine. "Must come through now!"

There was a moment's silence then a big rustle other side the fence, black shapes shuffling up. Down in the riverbed they stood up, black shapes, clambering up the bank.

"Faster!" The searchlight swept past again but we were all in the shadow of the knoll. It was a good place to cross. I followed the light across the paddies other side of Shamchun. *Not a sign of a Chinese border guard.* Last month the bastards were shooting anything that moved and asking questions afterward. *"Faster,"* I shouted. They scrambled faster through the hole under the fence, jostling each other. *"Sit!"* I shouted. *"Mo yuk!"* They scrambled through the fence and scrambled to sit down. *"Everybody hands on heads."*

I did not know how many were down there now.

I shouted, *"Let no person dare to run away!"* I wished that I had my gun to wave around. "Otherwise police will shoot. There are many police hidden in this place. We are going now to the police station. There you will be well treated. You will be fed. As much as you wish to eat. No person will be beaten. Now every person must stand up. *Stand up!"*

There was a big movement down in the dark shallow ravine, the crackle of brush. Fifty, sixty, maybe seventy forms rose up out of the bushes down there in the scrub under the China stars. Christ.

I shouted up on the knoll in the darkness, "Now every person walk slowly up to the road. If I shout *No movement,* everybody instantly obeys! When you get to the road, stop and stand in two lines! Let no person who thinks to elude the watchful foreign devil police! Start walking—*now!"*

I stood there, trying to peer hard through the starlit night, ready to roar, *"Mo yuk!"* If they made a break for it I would catch one, maybe two. *Mo yuk* usually worked. They were very disciplined people. Very afraid of what the foreign devil police would do to them. They were plodding up the ravine, up toward the road. I waited, hands on hips, at the top of the ravine, trying to look an imposing silhouette of colonial authority.

"*Faster!*" I stood there, arms akimbo. They scrambled faster. "*I see you,*" I shouted at the night. "*I see you all, keep moving! You there at the back,*" I shouted. "*I see you! You will be fed!*"

The first people came scrambling up out of the ravine, stumbling in the dark. "Sit! Sit down on the road! Faster!" Scrambling and stumbling. "No talking! Any person who talks will not be fed!" They came scrambling up out of the ravine, and sat down as soon as they reached the road. Not daring to look at me. "Good, good," I shouted. "Now everybody stand up."

They all scrambled up.

Thus we marched, in two long lines back down the dark dirt road through the bushes toward Takwuling. I walked at the back, sometimes I ran up alongside them. Nobody spoke, often I shouted. When we were four hundred yards off Takwuling the sentry saw us, and some constables came running down the road to us. But nobody tried to run away.

CHAPTER 7

At first, they came only in their hundreds, and only in the night, they dug holes under the fence and then dashed up into the dark mountains and valleys and ravines and thickets and jungle patches. More police were sent up to Takwuling and we set up roadblocks and checkpoints in Laffans Plain and in the villages along the mountain and foothills and valley paths, and all along the border road along the Shamchun, showing the flag and repairing the fence. In the broad hot China daylight we could see them in the valley other side the Shamchun, trudging along the paths toward Lo Fong, I looked through the binoculars at the People's Liberation Army border guards and the border guards did not even look at them! Jesus. And in the night our searchlights swept the fence and the paddy fields beyond, and we saw them swarming across the Shamchun, creeping scrambling through a score of

43

new holes in the fence, scrambling across the road up into the jungled foothills of the Hong Kong Mountains. And our police patrols crashed running shouting sweating grabbing tackling yelling after them, *Mo yuk! Mo yuk!* through the bushes up the mountain trails and ravines and down the valleys. And across the Shamchun not a border guard to be seen.

That is how it was in the last days of that long hot April, in hundreds. Then they came in thousands.

In May it was very bad. Now we had our Nepalese Gurkhas up there in the mountains, hiding in the jungle to lay ambush to the thousands. Now I had thirteen inspectors and five hundred men under me and one superintendent above me. Now every policeman who could be spared was up there in the patrols along the Shamchun and in the mountains.

Hidden way up there in the mountains was the second line of defense, Gurkhas and police. We were the first line of defense, down along the border road and in the jungled paths and valleys and ravines and villages of the foothills. Now they came in their thousands and thousands all the long hot sweating night and long hot burning day, the reckless swarming and scrambling and running; and the policemen shouting chasing crashing through the bush and jungle after them, the heat and the sweating and the running and the cursing and the crying and the weeping and the stink and dust of them and the recklessness of hunger, and exhaustion, and the heartbreak. And down there in the valley on the communist side the Shamchun, the chaos.

The chaos of the thousands, the hunger and the weakness and the recklessness in the great China heat, tramping down out of the distant mountains, streaming through the communist villages, scavenging for food, fearful hungry people fleeing from the Hungry Tiger, making for the mountains other side the valley, the Golden Mountain Where Men Eat Fat Pork. Lying by the roadsides and in the village streets, waiting for the night, no food, and the dust of them tramping. And the border guards of the People's Liberation Army who last month were shooting them down were waving the thousands on—*Keep moving, keep moving.*

Kept moving milling trudging streaming reckless fearful hopeful through the paddies down to the banks of the

Shamchun, the thousands and thousands every broad hot dry China day staring hungry hopeful pitiful at the fence and the Golden Mountain Where Men Eat Fat Pork. And there all along the long winding buckled barbed-wire fence of the Golden Mountain were my policemen under the burning China sun and policemen hiding in the jungle foothills and the soldiers, policemen marching and driving up and down the long hot winding dusty road showing the flag, and the dust and the shouting. And the look upon the people's faces, the face of poor bloody China. Waiting for night to come. And when darkness came, over they swarmed.

Creeping swarming down the China Mountain and across the paddies and over the dry Shamchun, swarming along the fence in their thousands, reckless hot dirty tattered dusty exhausted and mobbed the fence in a hundred places and heaved and the high stout fence heaved and buckled and crashed and the people crashed with it then swarmed scrambling over. Young and old and children and mothers with babies on their backs. Scrambling stumbling running clawing up the banks and across the road and scrambling crashing up into the bush and jungle of the foothills. And our Chinese and Pakistani constables ran up and down shouting and beating the fence with their batons, and the people ran to new places and when the constables ran after them they split and formed new mobs, and the fence came crashing down and the constables scattered back and the hundreds and the thousands swarmed and scrambled over. In the jungled foothills the policemen lying in ambush leaped out and yelled *Mo yuk* and the people who were near sat down and the rest ran scrambling on into the night up the mountain, into the second line. All the night the shouting and the crashing and the running and the ambushing and the torches and the Very flares and the yelling of *Mo yuk* and the heat and the stink and the heartbreak of them. When the Very flares went you could see them running past you all around. And when the dawn came you could see them way up there, toiling straggling up the mountains, the thousands that we did not catch in the night. And there across the flattened fence were thousands more. We caught thousands every day and night, and thousands got through, and they were hiding in the jungle. That was in the early days in that May.

Then in broad hot daylight they were swarming over the Shamchun and the flattened fence.

I got back to Takwuling in the Land Rover at dawn from my tour of the posts. The compound was full, on their faces was the hunger. I went through the charge office to my office, my legs had no spring in them. There was the superintendent, waiting for me. On my wall was our new map of the area with the flags making our patrol bases. There were many flags, the superintendent studying them. "Morning, Jake," he said.

"Sorry I'm late." I loosened my Sam Browne.

"I had some coffee. It was nice just to sit. You need some sleep."

"We all need some sleep. Like a drink, sir?"

"No," the boss said. "You go ahead."

I went across the corridor to the kitchen. There were Ah Seung and Mrs. Seung surrounded by steaming pots all over the place. It was very hot in the kitchen. *"Jo-san,* Bomban," they said. I went to the fridge and got out a big San Miguel, snapped the cap off. I went back into my office and shut the door. "What's the score?" I said.

"Last night and yesterday, five thousand three hundred and twenty-seven."

"God."

The helicopters say it's going to be worse today. They've seen Christ knows how many in our mountains."

I took three long swallows and it went down like a mountain brook, *aarh* into my empty stomach. "And Peking?" I said.

"Peking hasn't said a bloody word. Not a bloody word, don't even acknowledge us. And last month they were shooting them."

I took another swallow. I was very tired and hot and irritable. Right now I didn't care about anything, I just wanted to get rid of the super. "What's the story?" I said, and added, "Sir."

I finished my beer while the superintendent discussed the day's plan with me. It was the same every dawn. It was no bloody good putting more men along the fence. The fucking fence was flattened most of the fucking way now. We would need to put men six deep along the fence to stop them. The best places to catch them were in the foothills and at the second line. Now the Army was laying a big barbed-wire entanglement right across the top of the mountains up there at the second line. The entanglement was four feet in circumference, three layers, twelve feet deep. But it would take weeks to finish it. The Army had employed hundreds of Hakka women to help them lay it. My office windows were open and you could hear the distant shouts on the mountain. The sun was coming up now, the first rays hitting the tops of the mountains, golden mauve. I could see half a dozen troops of people toiling up the steep slope, perhaps a total of four hundred. They would be challenged over the top by the Gurkhas and then they would run for it. Maybe two-thirds would be stopped. I forgot about the four hundred and I blinked hard and brought my mind back to listen to the super. I said we should leave all our men where they were for today. Big deal. The super agreed. He got up to go. I said, "I'd like to go into town tomorrow afternoon if we can manage it to see my child."

The super said, "We'll arrange something. You haven't been off duty since this thing began."

"Thanks," I said.

"You're doing a good job, Jake."

"It's the P.C.s who're doing a good job," I said. As I looked up through my window I saw a dozen heads dashing past. A new bloody hole, right there under our noses! "Hey!" I jumped up. *"Mo yuk!"* we bellowed. They had reached the road and were running flat out for cover.

I jumped over the windowsill, ran flat out for the gate. I saw another group dashing up past the compound fence. I ran to intercept them, they saw me and ran off to the side. *"Mo yuk!"* I bellowed and four promptly sat down but three kept running. *"Stop,"* I bellowed, *"or I'll shoot,"* and I yanked my revolver out. They kept on running and disappeared into the bush. The super and a P.C. came running up behind me. My heart was thudding.

"It's no good," I panted, furious. "They know we don't shoot."

"Jesus Christ! The bloody cheek of it, making a hole in the fence right next to the police station! *Foki,* go and investigate that hole!"

The super turned. He had lost weight these last few weeks. We had all lost weight. "Get some sleep," he said and he started back for the gate. I led the four prisoners back to the compound. I handed them over to the P.C at the gate and I tramped into the charge office. "I'm going to sleep now," I said. "Wake me in four hours."

47

I tramped up to the first floor, taking off my shirt. I knew I stank but I was too tired to care. I would shower when I woke up. On the first-floor landing was the P.C.s' dormitory, the rows of double-tiered bunks, some P.C.s in underpants sprawled out, exhausted. I opened my gray door and walked down the short passage past the two bedrooms and looked into the sitting room. Two men were asleep in their underpants, stretched out on camp beds. There were nine more camp beds scattered about with crumpled sheets. I hardly knew half the inspectors who were camping in my sitting room. I had allocated them their areas and there was a Movement Diary, but everybody forgot to sign in and out and I had never once checked it. We were all too tired to remember. It made no difference because we were all working twenty hours a day, sometimes twenty-four. Sometimes thirty-six. If they weren't at their posts it was because the poor bastards were running round the mountains like blue-arsed flies after some mob they had seen. The helicopters and the radio lookout posts reported their observations to H.Q. who correlated them and radioed them to me and I radioed instructions to the men at their posts. Everybody was goddamn radioing everything all over the sixteen goddamn miles of goddamn mountains and valleys of hot dry jungle that came under Takwuling. At first it had made me feel like a general running the battle. Apart from the heartbreak. The heartbreaking exhausted dashing when we ambushed them the frantic scrambling before they surrendered, and the look on their faces, the frightened cowering and crying out and weeping and imploring and the cringing and the despair, old men, young men, women. And the thin and hungry children clinging panting to their frightened desperate mothers and the desperate fathers humbled by the sweating panting barbarian policemen towering panting over them. And the mothers crying out to their children and the children screaming for their mothers and mothers screaming to their husbands. And the old man who had nobody or who had lost the person whom he had, scrambling as best he could up the mountain all by himself and the younger people scrambling past him. It was pretty bad up there in the mountains. And the long exhausted straggling lines of people under arrest being marched back across the mountains by the Gurkhas and policemen to the collection posts, where the lorries from Fanling would come grinding up the trails for

48

them. And load them up stinking humbled frightened despairing and rumble them grinding jolting frightened off to the Police Training Camp at Fanling. Oh Christ, the heartbreak. It was very hard on the Chinese policemen.

But now I just felt exhausted. I stepped over the camp beds out onto the verandah. I could hear the shouting far away. The sun was clear of the mountains now. There other side the river were the people coming. The slopes of China Mountain these days. And not a People's Liberation Army border guard to be seen. I thought, "Tomorrow you will be with Susan. And Catherine," and I felt my heart thump. Then I went back to my bedroom and fell down on my bed.

CHAPTER 8

I heaved myself up and went and stood under the cold shower for a long time, then scrubbed myself till I glowed red, then stood under the shower until I felt cold. When I had dried myself I was already sweating again. I radioed the super while Ah Seung made my breakfast. Then I went out into the compound. It was blinding burning hot, full of the people. I shouted for the sergeant and the P.C. and we got into the Land Rover. The P.C. drove, I sat in the back. As we churned out the gate I picked up the radio microphone and switched in.

"Calling all posts, calling all posts, this is the SDI, I'm on my way. Come in one at a time in numerical order and report your situations, over—"

Behind the station, Laffans Plain jigsawed out in little valleys like tentacles into the jumble of high foothills and mountains. Throughout the plain, right down to the township of Fanling and Sheung Shui there are the old villages and farmers' shacks, China brick with twirled roof ends. And around the villages and the paddy fields and farms were the bamboo glades and jungle thickets, and all the paths. Other side Fanling rose the high jumble of jungled mountains again, all the twenty miles down to the sprawling teeming concrete jungle of Kowloon. There were thousands hiding in the mountains and the valleys and villages, trying to make it over the mountains down to Kowloon.

And now very many of the villagers had turned snake-head, the smugglers of human beings into Hong Kong. And now there were the reporters and the television men mobbing the boundaries of the Closed Area, the eyes of the world were turned on the Shamchun River. And now there were the well-intentioned Hong Kong Chinese looking for their kinsfolk from behind the Bamboo Curtain, thousands coming up from Hong Kong on buses and trains to tramp over the mountains and the valleys wearing placards and shouting, *"Looking for clansmen of Sun"* and *"Looking for kinsfolk of Wong Chee-fat,"* carrying food, and if they could not find their kinsfolk they left the food lying on the ground for the hungry people to find. And many were the villagers and farmers who took pity upon the starving people and hid them from us. And many were the running stumbling desperate young girls who were taken by a village man into his house and made his *tse-mui,* his servant-concubine.

The Land Rover bounced up the trail into the foothills, the radio speaking all the way; it was hard to hear on the crackling radio and with the bounces my sweat dropped. The Chinese were not sweating like me. The sergeant said, "People run away, Bomban." I looked up and there were half a dozen people scattering for the bush and the bamboo.

"Keep going," I said.

I listened back into the radio. I could not care about half a dozen refugees, I was trying to run the goddamn madhouse show, trying to correlate what was happening in a dozen posts at once in a mixture of radio-atmospheric English and Cantonese.

We stopped at the village, the P.C. took over the radio, I climbed out, slamming the door. The sun hit me again.

The village at the base of a foothill, bamboo jungle behind, paddy fields in front. How many were hiding in that jungle, right behind the village? You would need a big team of policemen to beat them out. The village houses were joined together, the roofs of slate with twirly ends. And chickens and ducks and dogs and naked children, a temple, gods of doorways painted on the houses, joss sticks burning, straw and chicken droppings and cow dung. And the heat. And the passive Oriental faces looking at me and the children running out to stare. The village road was too narrow for the Land Rover.

The sergeant and I went down the road between the black brick houses. *"Jo-san,"* we muttered. *"Jo-san—jo-san."* We were heading for the village representative's house, where our base was. The biggest house in the village, for he was the richest. I could hear the police two-way radio bleating from outside. The base was in the front room. The P.C. at the radio set stood up. "Sit down," I said. It was stifling hot inside. "How many prisoners in the backyard?"

"The lorry left two hours ago, Bomban. Now we have sixty-three new ones." The radio was crackling.

"When last did the patrols go out?"

"Last one left twenty minutes ago, Bomban." P.C. Chang looked at his watch.

"Everybody in the village co-operating?"

P.C. Chang smiled and shrugged. We did not like to rub the villagers up the wrong way too much by searching their houses too often. There were too many people at large out there in the mountains for us to burst a blood vessel over a few hundred being hidden in the villages. The best way was to put the responsibility on the village representatives. The village representative came in now and stood silhouetted in the doorway. "Good morning, Ng Firstborn," I said.

"Good morning, Bomban," Mr. Ng said. "Did you sleep soundly?"

"Soundly, Ng Firstborn," Mr. Ng was a good village representative but I would not have put it past him to make a few dollars on the side or to take a *tse-mui* if he could. He could do so very easily. Mr. Ng had many relatives in many places who would all swear that the new *tse-mui* was the niece of a distant aunt who lived somewhere in Kowloon. I stood so the light shone in on his face.

"Ng Firstborn," I said, and he looked at me with friendly, steady, hooded eyes, "are you satisfied that your people are co-operating with police in this matter?"

Mr. Ng's eyebrows went up. "Of course, Bomban!"

"Mr. Ng, I want you to give the following message to your people. Tell them that I intend personally investigating any suspicions that cross my mind. If I see or hear of any strange faces living in these parts, I personally will investigate any story that such person is a distant relative who formerly lived elsewhere in Hong Kong. I am a very energetic policeman, Ng Firstborn."

Mr. Ng nodded in deep approval.

"Good day, Mr. Ng."

It was sweltering, burning hot. My legs were sweating wet as if I had waded through water, my tunic stuck wet to me. There was no wind, even on the ridge high above the village. The sergeant and I were panting from the climb up the steep trail. From here we had a good view. I wiped the sweat off my eyes on the shoulders of my wet tunic and glared through the binoculars and cursed. Every day I cursed when I looked through the binoculars from this ridge.

There they were, the hundreds and hundreds straggled across the high open mountain slopes far away, climbing, scrambling, long lines and groups and bunches and twos and threes toiling. There were my patrols dotted running scrambling to cut off this group and that before it reached new jungle. And down the mountain in the valley the people plodding across the paddies toward the river, along the fence, like an army coming any way they liked. And on the slopes of China Mountain in hundreds, waiting for their chance to come swarming down and across. And along our flattened border fence my constables running dashing shouting along the fence waving their batons. And across the flattened fence they swarmed and scrambled and the constables ran and shouted and grabbed, but they only grabbed one or two per man. *Mo yuk* did not work any more down there at the fence. *And not a fucking People's Liberation Army guard to be seen.*

I cursed and started down the trail toward the valley. We were doing a spot swoop check of the area of the base to check with the patrol. If we met the patrol. The patrol ran about like dogs on a tennis court. We were back in jungle again. It was even hotter in the jungle. The sergeant pointed. And there, off the path, was a notice in Chinese on a piece of cardboard: *Food here,* with an arrow. A few paces into the bush was a big packet.

"Buns." The sergeant handed it to me. About four dozen. It was almost impossible to buy a loaf of bread or a bun in Fanling or Sheung Shi these days.

"Put them back," I said. "Let the poor devils eat."

We tramped down the trail into the ravine. As I came to the bend I saw the line of people. For an instant they stared poised, straggled on the path, then they scrambled. *"Mo yuk,"* I roared. They dived into the jungle in one big scramble, great crashing of bushes, and they were gone. *"Mo yuk!"* I was shouting, running down the trail, the sergeant was running behind me shouting also. There was crashing in the bushes. We stopped, panting. I glared around into the jungle, panting and the sweat running off me. Not a sign.

"Come out!" I shouted furiously. *"We are the police!"* As if the bastards didn't know.

Not a movement. I glared around into the bushes. Dark shadow, brown and green and black in the China sun.

"Come out!" I shouted. I undid my holster. "Pull out your gun," I said to the sergeant. "Come out!" I shouted, and I held my revolver up, "or we'll shoot into the bushes."

The sergeant had his gun out too now. We glared around at the jungle hopefully, panting. Not a sound.

"You shout it," I panted at the sergeant.

"Come out," the Chinese sergeant shouted. "Do not allow your celestial blood to be shed so uselessly!"

Not a sound in the hot burning sweating jungle. I could see sweat on my eyelids. I took a big breath.

"All right!" I shouted. "This is your last chance. Come out and you will be fed and conducted to safety."

We glared, waiting, panting. The bastards knew now we did not shoot. Not a sound. Nor would there be. Short of charging in there and getting our eyes scratched out by jungle and overpowering maybe one man each. We were too tired and too busy and too important elsewhere to do that. "We lose face, Bomban," the sergeant whispered.

"Fuck face." I shoved my revolver back into its holster. I turned and swung on down the trail, sweating and angry.

And all the time the heat and dust and heartbreak. The people across the fence watched us come in the Land Rover, waiting for us to go by. The constables were panting up and down, each man waiting for a rush at his piece of flattened fence. Sweating. The Land Rover went around the bend and an old woman was hobbling out of the bush to cross the road, a boy and a girl with her. The old woman screamed and the boy grabbed her arm to make her scramble back and the girl ran for it. She dashed across the road and into the bushes on the foothills and she was gone. The old lady screamed and tried to dash after the girl and the boy was trying to tug her back, they were all shouting, panic-stricken. The Land Rover skidded to a stop and we jumped out. The old lady was still struggling with the boy and screaming for the girl. *"Chase the child,"* I shouted at the constable. I ran to the old woman and got her skinny wrist and she screamed and wrenched. *"Mo yuk!"* I shouted and I grabbed at the boy and he let go and dashed across the road. The sergeant was pounding after him and the boy dodged screaming, *"Save life!"* He leaped off the road across a ditch. The old woman was screaming tugging and wrenching trying to get after the children. *"No movement, grandmother,"* I shouted at her, *"we will find your grandchildren!"* She was still screaming and pulling. The sergeant was running flat out, but the boy was gone like a rabbit into the bamboo. The old woman was still screaming hysterically, I tugged her to the Land Rover, screaming weeping all the way.

"Get into the vehicle, grandmother!"

She hung onto the door screaming and the tears running down her face. I cursed and picked her up and I bundled her into the back seat handcuffed her flailing wrist to the door handle. I ran back down the road to help the constable and sergeant chase her grandchildren.

But we did not find them. When we came back she had stopped screaming, she was just weeping hysterically to herself. I got the names of her grandchildren and I radioed the patrols to look for them. But we did not find them, or if we found them we did not identify them.

I kept the old woman at Takwuling for three days, and she wept all the time. Then I sent her to Fanling for deportation. There are very many people in the teeming chaos of Hong Kong surnamed Ching.

CHAPTER 9

And across the Laffans Plain and through the villages farms paths paddies there were people and the reporters and television men of the world and the snakeheads, and the Hong Kong people looking for their relatives and the mountains resounded with their cries. And all over the mountains the old discarded commune blue clothing lay littered like a battlefield. And all the time the roar of the helicopters overhead and the bleating crackling shouting of the radios and the weeping and imploring and the mothers shouting for their children, and the long lines of people marching under arrest and the people squatting lying weeping in the base camps waiting for the lorries to come to fetch them, and the heat heat heat, and the despair.

The sergeant halted the Land Rover up the winding jungle road, behind the second line. There were big dense ferns and bamboo along the road and many footpaths leading off. I left the P.C. to stand by the radio, and the sergeant and I set off down the trail to locate the patrol. There were many paths going down into the valley. The sweat ran off me, nerves tight tight, tunic sticking, Jesus Christ it was hot. Legs, back, arms wet as if I swam. I swung down the trail and came to a cross-trail. And there, coming along this cross-trail was a young Chinese woman, and a dog.

She was carrying a big China Products shopping bag. I stopped and glared at her, hands on hips. She stopped quickly. I said angrily in Cantonese, "What are you doing here, madam?"

She stood fifteen paces off. She wore jeans and a blouse, pigtails. She looked guilty but she tried to look haughty. She said deliberately in English, to impress me that she was no peasant to be shouted at, "I am just going for a walk. I often come up here, is that a crime?"

I was angry. "Yes, it is a crime, madam! You're in the Closed Area."

She came toward me. The dog followed her, tongue slobbering happily, tail beating at everybody. She pointed uphill. "The Closed Area starts up there."

Jesus. "The Closed Area has been extended down to the Shataukok Road, madam, to keep people like you out of the bloody way, and you know it! What's your name?"

She looked at me, not so haughtily now but still trying it on. She pulled out her Hong Kong identity card. "Tsang Ying-ling," she said.

It said, Occupation: Student. She said, "I am a teacher."

"Where?"

She looked me in the eyes.

"The Tai Ping Middle School. Yes, that's a communist school, Inspector."

"I know that, madam. What are you doing here?"

She looked at me. She was tall for a Chinese girl, with a squarish face and she had big slanted deep brown eyes.

"I am surveying the situation, Inspector."

Jesus Christ, surveying the situation.

"What's in that bag?" I took it.

"Buns." I held out my finger at her. "Now look here, madam! People like you are a bloody nuisance! We've got enough to contend with without you running around surveying the situation quote unquote scattering bloody buns to succor illegal bloody immigrants!"

She said, "Kindly watch your language, Inspector."

"Jesus Christ." I jerked my head. "Come with me." I started on down the trail.

She stood where she was.

"Are you arresting me?" she inquired.

I turned back on her and held my finger out at her, exasperated.

"Not yet! I've got enough to do arresting illegal immigrants from the paradise across the border! But I bloody well will if you don't do as you're told."

I started on down.

"Where are you taking me?" she called. She stood there up on the cross-trail.

I turned, sweating, furious. I said under my breath, "To the woods to the woods, where do you think?" I said aloud angrily, "You're coming with me and I'm taking you out of the Closed bloody Area back to where you belong! And if you're not very careful I *will* arrest you and put you in a very different Closed Area!"

I turned and strode on down the trail. I did not look back, I knew the sergeant was watching her. The bloody dog came bounding joyfully down the trail and jumped up at me like a long-lost friend, flailing the bushes with his tail, I was in no mood for a dog either. I came around a bend in the jungle and there was the patrol base tent. The P.C. sat at the radio. Two P.C.'s and an inspector were flung out on camp beds, sleeping, sweating. The P.C. at the radio got up to waken the inspector. "Don't!" I said. "How long have they been asleep?"

"Half hour, Bomban."

"Let them sleep. How many people arrested this morning?"

56

The P.C. looked at his note. "Three hundred and seven, Bomban. The lorries left one hour ago. The rest of the patrol are out."

I had had an idea. I went to the table and picked up his pad.

"Write half a dozen notices in Chinese saying 'Food this way.' With an arrow. The sergeant and I will cut some sticks."

Back up the trail was a bamboo thicket. I left Miss Tsang Ying bloody-ling with the P.C. The sergeant broke two young bamboo canes and sliced them down. When we came back the P.C. had the notices ready. We sharpened the ends of the bamboo and stuck a *Food this way* notice onto each. Miss Tsang was watching us. I turned to her.

"Miss Tsang," I said in English, "would you care to donate your buns to the cause?"

She looked at me. "What cause?"

I said, "They're going to follow the notices. Into the big bad wolf's den."

Miss Tsang looked first surprised, then indignant. "Certainly not."

I shrugged.

"All right, Miss Tsang, they're your buns. They'll just have to eat nothing till they get to Fanling. And you can take your buns back to the Tai Ping Middle School. Let's go."

Then I spoke to the P.C. in Cantonese: "When they come looking for the food, wave your gun and make them sit down quietly until the inspector wakes up. Give him a nice surprise."

Miss Tsang said in Cantonese, "And give them the buns."

"Yes," I said. "Miss Tsang's nice buns."

I turned and tramped sweating back up the trail carrying the bundle of sticks and notices. When I got to the cross-path I planted them, all pointing downhill to the tents around the bend. Miss Tsang stood watching me. The dog followed me beating his tail.

"This way, Miss Tsang," I said.

I started sweating back up the trail through the jungle to the Land Rover.

The sergeant sat in front, Miss Tsang sat in the back with me. Staring haughtily with badly concealed interest out of the window. The dog bounced and slipped joyfully on the seat behind us. I listened on the radio, then slung the microphone down on the seat. I looked at her. Her jeans had paint on them, all the colors. She was very pretty in a somewhat severe sort of way. Twenty-three? Two short pigtails. Wide full mouth. Good nose. Tall for a Chinese girl. Big breasts for a Chinese. Northerner, Shanghai way. She felt me looking at her and ignored me. She said, "Where are we going?"

"To check the posts. Then to get rid of you, Miss Tsang."

She ignored that.

"Cigarette?" I said.

"No thank you, Inspector."

I lit one, my fingers wet it. I felt my chest grate. I looked at her legs, the jeans, the paint. She had long full legs. She didn't look much like a communist schoolmistress.

"You paint?" I said.

She did not look at me.

"Yes. I teach it. Among other things."

I said, and as soon as I said it I felt foolish, "I must congratulate you on your English."

She did not look at me. "Why not? You speak good Cantonese."

Go to hell, I thought.

I sat back and let the Land Rover take me, sweating. We were grinding bouncing flat up toward Robin's Nest, behind the second line of defense. We stopped on a ridge, overlooking the huge valley. I said to Miss Tsang, "You will kindly wait in the Land Rover."

She looked at me. "Can I get out, please? As I am not under arrest. It's very hot."

I said, "I've noticed, Miss Tsang. Yes, you may get out but you will remain right here. In the custody of the constable. And your dog will remain *in* the vehicle. As the hostage."

I turned and set off along the slope with the sergeant.

Down below was the whole jungled valley. Up here on the high ridges there was little bush, just coarse grass. I looked through the binoculars along the second line.

The army trucks were unloading the barbed-wire entanglement two miles away, the Hakka women spreading it across the hard brown-green ridge hot under the China sun. Spaced out along the ridge were the Gurkhas and the police patrols. And down the long steep wide fluted hilly ravined jungled hard-grassed slope, right down through the foothills and ravines, right down to the jigsawed valley and the villages and paddies, was the scrambling and dashing and toiling and marching. Spread in streaks lines groups patches sprinkles right across the convoluted jungled mountains were the desperate hungry people coming, as wide as the eye could see, and the police and Gurkhas running chasing shouting ambushing. And the helicopters droning and the radios crackling and the faraway shouting of *Mo yuk* and the chasing and the grabbing and the crying out.

I swept the binoculars and I saw the mob run out of the ravine, cutting across the mountain half a mile down, over a hundred of them. There was not a policeman or a soldier within a mile of them. They were making for a shoulder. Then another mob ran out from a different place in the jungle, running after them. Then another crowd ran out. They had all been hiding in the big ravine, now they had taken courage from each other swarming out, young and old and children scrambling. Now there were two hundred of them altogether.

We ran across the slope, toward the shoulder. As hard as we could, jumping over bushes, stumbling panting cursing. We were only six hundred yards from them now, running in the open, then they saw us. They stopped and began to mill. Some men in front turned around facing the rest, shouting and waving their arms. I slowed down, watching them as I ran. The leaders were turning around and shouting at the people and the people were marching on.

They were three hundred yards away now, marching up straight for us. Two hundred, more, the leader still shouting. I could not hear above my own panting. The sweat was running off me, glaring at them. Then I heard the leader shout, *"We are all marching to Kowloon!"*

"Hear that?" I panted.

"We are all marching like this to Kowloon," the leader shouted to the sky, looking straight at me.

"He may be right," I panted.

"If we stay together they cannot stop us," he shouted, *"for we are many."*

They were two hundred yards below now. Now there was shouting from the people behind also.

The leader shouted, *"This is the soil of China. We shall*

59

march in the open down the roads all the way to Kow-loon!" He was shouting it at me.

"Get out your gun," I panted at the sergeant. "Open the breech as if you're checking that the magazine is full —now!"

We reached for our guns simultaneously and pulled them out. We broke open the breeches elaborately and looked.

"They don't shoot!" the leader shouted. *"Keep march-ng, they do not shoot!"*

I snapped the breech closed. They were seventy paces off now, still coming. They were all taking courage from the men in front. I said to the sergeant, "That didn't work. All right, put your gun away."

We put our guns away and there was derisive shouting from the front.

"Take out your baton."

We took our batons.

"We've got to knock down the front four. I'll take the leader. Baton charge position."

We both put our left feet forward and raised the batons elaborately. I filled my lungs.

"Mo yuk!" I bellowed.

"We are many," the leader bellowed, *"and you are two! We are marching to Kowloon!"* They were fifty paces down the slope now.

I said to the sergeant, "Seven paces forward!" We marched down the slope straight at them, one two three four five six seven, *halt*. There was much shouting and they were still coming. They were thirty paces off now.

"Charge!" I bellowed.

Charged down the mountain at them, batons raised, left forearm raised, yelling *Aaaaaahhh*.

Charged down the mountain at the leaders, and the shouting stopped, and the scream went up, and the scram-bling and the arms thrown up.

Charged batons up straight at the front men and straight into them teeth bared batons wielding cursing hating in the moment of the charge *swipe swipe swipe one two ramattheguts*, shock and khaki and black stick flying swiping stinking sweat and scrambling cries and disbelief and crack and thud of stick on flesh, *one two across the shoulders then ram at the guts* and down he goes and spin around and *swipe swipe and ram at the guts*, the flailing and the shouting and the screaming and the shock.

"Stop!" I bellowed at the sergeant. I spun around, reeling panting gasping. The mountain was spinning and I staggered and tasted sweat and dirt in my mouth. I glared around, reeling, five men were down clutching themselves, writhing, the sergeant reeling panting and people scattering shocked in all directions.

"Mo yuk," I roared. *"Mo fucking yuk!"*

And they crashed down onto their buttocks scattered crashing astonished spread-eagle over a hundred yards, and the dust and the sweat under the blazing China sun.

Then we marched them to the nearest base camp. None of them tried to run away.

It was midafternoon when we got back to the Shataukok Road. We drove through the police checkpoint in sweating dirty irritable silence. I had a cut over my eye which stung. Only Miss Tsang looked moderately clean and unsweaty. The Land Rover stopped on the road outside the Closed Area. I said, "Good day, Miss Tsang. And please stay out."

"Good day, Inspector," she said. She smiled for the first time. "Thank you for your tour," she said sweetly.

"Don't mention it."

The Land Rover turned around on the road and ground away, heading back to the Closed Area.

I wanted to look back at Miss Tsang standing there on the road with her dog, but I did not, in case she was watching. She was certainly very nice-looking.

And in the hot China night the Very flares shooting up and then you by Jesus saw them all about you in the dancing silver light, running scrambling past you all about and you roar *"Mo yuk!"* and maybe twenty people fall down and the scores kept crashing on into the night, and another flare goes up—*"Mo yuk!"* the panting cursing grabbing chasing shouting and the crying and the wailing and the hunger and exhaustion and despair and the heartbreak. The backbreak and the heartbreak. And the searchlights sweeping along the buckled broken flattened border fence, there were the people scrambling panting hungry pushing desperate running coming.

We came around the bend of Pak Fa Shan in the shadow of the foothill where the searchlight could not reach, *and there right there for Christsake other side the flattened fence on the China side came another Very flare.*

61

I jumped out of the Land Rover and ran crashing through the bushes toward the fence and another flare went up on the China side and by Jesus Christ there stood the People's Liberation Army guard with the Very pistol in his hand. *He was showing them the place in the fence, last month he was shooting them down! Oh by Jesus Christ!* "Stop that!" I roared at him. "Stop shooting fucking flares!" I crashed on down the slope. "Stop, you bastard!" I roared running crashing to the fence and the people were running everywhere scrambling for the fence in the light.

"Stop!" I shouted. "Stop shooting fucking flares!" He was five paces from me on the other side the fence, he turned to me without a flicker of expression and reloaded his Very pistol. "Jesus Christ, you bastard," I roared. A row of people were scrambling up the riverbanks in the silver light, they hesitated when they saw me standing shouting there. "Come—come," the guard shouted at them. "Jesus Christ, you sonofabitch!" I raved at him, more people were running over the paddies, "Come on this way!" The People's guard was shouting, "Mo yuk!" I roared and the flare fizzed out again, "Mo yuk!" I roared and flung about me in the blackness. "You are all under arrest." There was another whoosh of light in the sky and more people jumping over the fence all about me. "You bastard!" I screamed. "You fucking two-faced bastard!" and I saw another rush coming across the paddies jumping down the bank into the Shamchun, fifty of them at least by Jesus Christ and the People's Liberation Army guard was launching and loading another flare. "I'll shoot that fucking flare right up your communist arse!" I roared at him in Cantonese. "Mo fucking yuk!" and I lunged and seized a man by the collar and slung him to the ground. I lunged after another man screaming "Mo yuk!" and slung him down with a crash and sprawled on top of him and there was stink of sweat and dust in my face, I scrambled up and charged after the next one and got him by the neck and slung him wide as I ran and he reeled and fell sprawling. "Mo yuk!" I screamed and I was running at the next one and I kicked between his running legs and he sprawled onto the dirt and I sprawled onto the fence, somebody was leaping over me and I seized his foot and he came crashing down with a thud and I scrambled up reeling after the next one and got him by the belt and slung him as I fell, I saw the sergeant and the P.C. lunging about also. *"Mo yuk!"* I was still roaring blind with sweat and dust and fury and exhaustion. And another flare whooshed up brilliantly silver into the night and the border guard was laughing at me. *"You fucking bastard!"* I roared and I flung myself at running figures and I hit the leaping line of them with all my roar and fury and hate, flung and threw and grabbed and crashed into the leaping desperate scrambling, and there was nothing in the world but the crack and thud and crash of bone and sweat knees and shins and feet and legs and bodies crashing sprawling thudding in the reeling dust and stink and sweat and crashing stars and sprawling rolling scrambling shouting dizzy hitting and the China sky and fence and the Shamchun and the mountains and the people were reeling black and bright and crazy hateful. I staggered up reeling hate-filled dizzy with dust and sweat and exhausted gasping hating every one of the starving hateful pitiful bastards—*"Mo yuk!"* I roared and I lunged at a man's knees and brought him crashing down under the reeling China sky, I scrambled up hanging onto my sonofabitch and staggered drunk with rage and hate and in the last reeling staggering brightness I saw no more people coming for the fence, and there was the sonofabitch of the People's Liberation Army guard walking away.

"You fucking bastard!" I shouted at him but it was a croak and I was reeling, in the roaring panting heaving China night, and the border guard thirty yards away was shouting back at me, "You fascist imperialist grandmotherfucker."

CHAPTER 10

On Friday I came in from my patrol late. I had my tunic off and my back stuck wet to the Land Rover seat and my hair was matted to my forehead. I had not yet slept. Tonight the whole bloody border could collapse for all I cared. I slammed the Land Rover door and I hurried into the station and up the stairs two at a time without checking in my office. I stuffed clean clothes and shaving gear into a holdall and I clattered back down the stairs before the telephone could ring, before the duty officer came running to tell me something had happened. There were the people squatting all over the compound, they scrambled out of my way. I revved the old Opel savagely and rammed her into gear and churned out of the compound. I swung right, along the frontier road toward Lowu. Maybe I was asking for trouble going to Lowu, but it would be the quickest inspection of a post on record. I was pretty safe without a radio in the Opel.

Now I was safely out of Takwuling I was grinning. I drove hard, bouncing over the corrugations and churning up the dust. Across the river I could see the people. Streaming up the valley. I could see the constables all along the fence now, every fifty yards. I honked and they waved. Poor, poor bastards. Then Lowu came into sight, the Kowloon-Canton Railway bridge and our police and immigration posts, and on the other side the buildings of the People's Republic of China with the red flag with the five gold stars.

I ran up the steps into our post. Outside was the roar of voices, inside the clatter of typewriter and telephone and radio, police and people everywhere. I pushed through the report room to the O.C.'s office. He was shouting into the telephone. He waved, I pointed to the roof and ran up the stairs. I came out into the hot blinding China sun and screwed up my eyes.

The shambles. There was the Kowloon-Canton Railway bridge over the Shamchun, wide and sluggish and the banks thick with reeds and jungle. Down below in our compound sat the hundreds of the people in their batches of forty, as they had been trucked up from Fanling, squatting hot and thin and ragged under the China sun, waiting. And over the bridge in the hot ragged columns of forty the P.C.s marched them back to hot dry starving China. Halfway across the bridge stood the expressionless People's Liberation border guards, faded baggy uniforms, carbines over their shoulders, the colossal impregnable unsmiling Chineseness on their hood-eyed faces under their stark baggy caps. I watched. The column of forty people shuffled to pathetic halt and the P.C. handed over the written list of their names to the PLA guard. The People's Liberation guard took the list and started shouting out the names. One by one they answered, shamefaced, frightened. I counted them from up on the hot roof of the post. I counted again. Thirty-nine, *thirty-nine,* for Chrissake!—not goddamn forty! Oh Jesus. The next batch of forty was already marching onto the bridge. It was wild burning glaring hot on the roof of the post. The PLA guard was still shouting names. And coming down the hot dusty green-brown-mauve valley and trudging past right there two hundred yards away were the people coming. All along the goddamn Shamchun and the fence and the jungled mountains were our P.C.s and inspectors and the Army and the helicopters and radios and Christ knows what running chasing sweating and cursing. And here was this moonfaced bastard shouting out the names as if they were doing us a fucking favor, just dying for the opportunity to turn thirty-nine people back because we were one short because one terrified half-starved poor communist had escaped out of the lorry on the way in the bedlam. The guard shouted out some name and to his delight no one answered. I stood there glaring sweating cursing hating on the rooftop. "Chan Ming-kit!" the People's guard shouted and his hooded eyes came alive.

No reply. We were all waiting, watching helplessly. He did not shout it again. "Right!" he snapped. "No person answers!" he shouted and waved his gun. "Every person in this batch go backward, *backward*—go back!"

Oh *you two-faced swine.*

He was thrusting the list at my P.C. *"Go backward!—quick!—quick!"* The column of people were milling backward, the sun beating down. *"Go away,"* the guard was shouting as if suddenly they all stank unbearable. *"Backward—go!"*

"Oh you bastards," I whispered.

And across the river the hordes coming. Helpless, sweating, fuming under the burning sun.

"Next!" I roared at the top of my lungs so the People's Liberation Army guards started. *"Bring up the next batch of poor hungry people who have run away from their motherland to the Golden Mountain Where Men Eat Fat Pork!"*

The guards looked up, astonished. My throat was dry and I was wild: *"Next!"* I roared. *"Bring up the next lot of poor people!"* The P.C.s were scurrying, the next batch broke into a scramble across the bridge, the P.C.s hustling them.

The People's Liberation guard snatched the list and started shouting the names. If there is one thing that rattles a Chinese it is being shouted at. I glared down at the People's Liberation guards, sweat running down my neck. I was dog-tired. I hated my job and myself and the Chinese People's Liberation Army. I counted the people in the batch. It was difficult, they were all shapes and sizes. I was still heaving from my fury. There were forty, all right. The People's Liberation guard was still shouting the names, savagely now. It seemed the whole world was full of sweat and shouting. I was screaming tired. Each time the People's Liberation guard shouted he made a savage mark on the paper. And beyond the bridge the people were milling everywhere. The guard shouted to the end of the list, and they were all present, so he jerked his arm and shouted them through. They hurried forward, heads down, hurrying. The guards just looked at them. Then a guard at the end of the bridge stopped a man.

They spoke and then the guard pointed down the riverbank, the man gave a salute and scurried. The guard looked up at me and smirked. The man scurried along the riverbank through the bushes. The guard was watching him go, with interest. The man was scrambling down the bank fifty yards away, then crashed through the reeds and jumped into the water up to his knees.

"*Hey, you bastard!*" I roared at him. "*Mo yuk!*" Then I shouted at a P.C. below, "*Get that man!*"

Constables started running everywhere. The man was splashing across the river. "*Mo yuk, you sonofabitch,*" I yelled from the rooftop. Three constables running flat out down the bank, the People's Liberation guards were laughing. The man crashed across the river and scrambled up the banks into the jungle, out of sight, and a cheer went up from the bridge. The People's Liberation guards were laughing. The P.C.s on the bridge were looking embarrassed.

I wanted to shout *Hum kar chaan*, may your whole family perish! But I stopped myself. My throat was dry with fury. If I had it would have created an international incident and they knew it, grinning up at me, as though to say that if I shouted at them they would be delighted. They would look all shocked, start stamping their feet and waving their guns and drop the barrier and refuse to accept back any more illegal immigrants until Whitehall had unreservedly apologized to Peking for the insult to the celestial people of China. My P.C.s were watching me, embarrassed. It was great loss of face for them. I took a huge breath and clamped my mouth shut, sweating and furious. I swallowed hard and then forced on my biggest best smile. I lifted my palms and shrugged elaborately at the People's guards.

"Ah well," I yelled elaborately in Cantonese. "You cannot blame him for trying to better himself!"

I drove the Opel hard down the road toward Fanling. The big gray police lorries were rumbling up the road through the patchwork of Laffans Plain, carting the people back to China. I waved to the drivers. Carts and bicycles and people clogged the road. I came around the bend and I was in the outskirts of Sheung Shui, a mumble of buildings signboards bicycles carts buses dogs chickens hawkers markets shops cocklofts shacks people everywhere. A hundred yards ahead was a great mob of people milling in the road, over their heads I could see another convoy of police lorries coming.

The mob was shouting and milling. I leaned on the horn. People scattered in front of me, a man shouted, "Fuck your mother!" The mob did not give way. The front police lorry was slowed right down, honking. I slammed on the brakes, and climbed out.

"Give way!" I shouted. *"Give way to the police vehicles!"*

I shoved through the mob, hot and furious. *"Give way!"* Now the mob was throwing things at the police lorries, shouting and jumping. Buns and bread and biscuits beat down at the lorry, people jumping and throwing and shouting. It was *Good luck!* and *Come back!* and *Fuck the police!* the mob was shouting. The refugees were grabbing and shouting, reckless defiance of the police in the sweat and heartbreak, bread and arms and curses were flying against the great hot lorries rolling like tumbrels back to China. I shoved through the mob shouting, "Give way, clear the road, give way!" A woman shouted, *"Fucking police!"* I shouted, *"The lorries must go through, it is not the fault of the police that these people must go back! Give way!"*—pulling people aside. I had pushed my way shouting through to the front lorry, I saw a Chinese man with a camera, then several men with cameras, reporters. *"Jump!"* a reporter shouted to the refugees. *"Jump down from the lorries and run!"*

"Shut up!" I roared. *"Make way."*

But now other people were shouting it. *"Jump—Jump!"*

There were children all over the place, jumping up and down in glee, and a reporter shouted at some children, *"Get in front of the lorry!"* and I lunged at him. The reporter scrambled backward, the other reporters snapped their cameras up to get the shot of the SDI Frontier Assaulting the Press, I swung on them. *"Get the hell out of here!"* I turned and lunged to the front of the lorry to drag the children out of the way and a constable was jumping down out of the car to help, I grabbed two children by the scruff of the necks and a new roar went up, and four refugees jumped out the lorry.

They leaped down in a shout into the roaring crowd and the P.C. and I lunged after them, and a piece of timber hit me. Hit me from nowhere with a crack of thunder and stars across the neck and the world went bright black and I crashed against the lorry. I scrambled up fighting mad and the world was reeling shouting bright. The P.C. was shouting something in front of me, I saw the reporter with their cameras, I saw the reporter who had shouted at the children and I leaped at him and he scrambled back and I got him by the collar and wrenched him around roaring, *"You're under arrest for obstructing a police officer,"* and gave him a savage wrench. *"And it's another offense to try to escape from lawful custody."* I dragged him to the car and handcuffed him to the steering wheel, everywhere there was great shouting. I ran back to the lorry and scrambled up onto the hood with my gun out and I filled my lungs staggering wild with fury:

"Silence!" I roared.

Suddenly there was shocked silence.

"Get out the way of the police," I roared at them, *"or there will be very big trouble!"*

And there was a great surging backward away from the mad barbarian policeman brandishing his gun, scrambling off the road in all directions and suddenly, miraculously, the road was clear.

I jumped down off the hood and waved the lorry forward. And the shocked staring of the crowd was strangely contrasted with the roaring of the engines. The road was trampled thick with bread and buns and biscuits.

My head was thumping and my neck stung. My mouth was dry. I turned and strode back to my car. The handcuffed reporter was standing at the door, I unhandcuffed him. "Get in."

"The freedom of the press—" he began.

"Get in!" I roared.

He scrambled into the front seat and I got in and slammed my door furiously. "What's your name?"

"Chan Wai-ping," he began in English. "I am the editor of the *Heung Keung Po*."

"Yes and you wanted pictures of police brutality for Peking and your pitiful public," I shouted. "Jesus Christ," I shouted, "do you think we like this job? Do you think we like working our guts out to send starving people back to China?"

"You have no right—" Chan Wai-ping began.

"You are under arrest," I shouted, *"for obstructing police by inciting prisoners to escape and inciting children to stand in front of the lorry!"*

The *Heung Keung Po* was the most virulent of the Hong Kong communist newspapers.

I handed him over at the Fanling station and drove on to the Police Training School to check out with my superintendent. I was still furious and my head thumped. I had not slept for twenty hours and I had been working like this for five weeks. There were more laden police lorries. I bounced over the tracks and on up the road to the training camp. Ahead was the high barbed-wire fence with the Nissen huts among the trees. And inside the fence the people, everywhere, and the roar of them and the blaring of the loudspeakers marshaling them. I drove up to the admin building, hurried down the cement corridor to the super's temporary headquarters, telephones and typewriters and radioes and policemen all over the place.

"Where's the S.P.?"

"Down on the parade ground, sir," the P.C. said.

I slammed the door as if the S.P. had no goddamn business at the parade ground and it was all the P.C.'s fault for letting him go. Out into the burning sun, up the curving road between hot lawns and the Nissen huts, the muted roar of voices throbbing in my thumping head. The loudspeakers were shouting. The burn of the tar came through my boots. The lorries were coming in empty and rolling out full. And there was the parade ground. And the shambles.

And the heartbreak and the stink and the heat. Four thousand people waiting squatting lying standing crouching stinking and hot on the huge concrete parade ground.

And the policemen with megaphones shouting, children crying. Four thousand people jam-packed in batches of forty, shuffling across the playground through the big Nissen hut to be processed, name, age, commune, last occupation. Other side the parade ground was the row of the great vats of rice and fish and vegetables stewing up and the stacks of bowls and chopsticks and on the opposite corner the temporary latrines. And the policemen with the megaphones marshaling the people from the lorries to the Nissen hut and from the hut to the food tents, from the food tents back onto the lorries in the batches of forty. The thousands of hot hungry Chinese faces, young and old and women and children and the babes on backs, waiting to be sent back to the hot dry famished China they had run from, and the winter coming, the Year of the Hungry Tiger.

CHAPTER 11

The taxis and buses and trucks were carbon-monoxidizing all down Nathan Road, Kowloon, a heat haze hung pale blue on the harbor. I was very tired and hot but I was happy. I turned into Tsimshatsui and parked the Opel. Bars everyhere, Cupid's, No-Tell, Mermaid, Texas, bars bars bars, and neon lights and jukeboxes blaring and good-looking girls standing outside, and the shops and the signboards scrambling on top of each other. And sailors, tourists, pimps, shopkeepers, and the Chinese music bleating. Signboards fighting each other everywhere. Steam bath and massage parlors, Japanese, Korean, Swedish, Dutch, French. I came to the signboard that said French and Shanghainese Steam Bath and Massage Second Floor. I climbed the dark staircase. Dr. Yip had a dental surgery behind one door and the Beautiful Perfume Company had a sign on the other. I climbed to the second floor. There were joss sticks burning outside the door.

She who answered the door hesitated when she saw the uniform, then she stood aside nervously. The waiting room was empty, the early afternoon is usually the best time.

There were rattan chairs, some old *Playboys,* some Chinese scrolls on the walls. The girl disappeared through the bamboo curtain, her *cheongsam* split up to her thigh. Another girl put her head through the curtain and disappeared. The air conditioning was soaking through my tunic. Mr. Woo came anxiously through the curtains, then his gold teeth beamed.

"Inspector Mak! Long time no see!"

Mr. Woo flustered me through the curtains with a clunky rattle of bamboo, between the rows of cubicles, gushing welcomes. He swept back a thick curtain with dragons on it and there inside were the couch and the robes and towels and slippers. *"Girls,"* he shouted. Five girls came from nowhere, suddenly I was surrounded by girls in *choongaans* in the dim light. Mr. Woo waved a beaming hand. "Which one you like, Inspector Mak, sir?"

"Any one," I said. "That one."

"You like two?" Mr. Woo suggested brightly.

"One's okay, thanks," I said in English.

The others turned around and filed away. My girl came forward smiling nervously, Mr. Woo was backing out the room beaming gold rotundly devilish in the red lamplight.

"Hello." The girl stood smiling. "My name is Sound of Bells."

"That's a pretty name." I just sat there, too tired to stand up. I just wanted to sit there. To fall back and lie.

"You want beer?" the girl said in English.

Oh Christ, did I want a beer. I had a thirst I would not sell.

"Later," I said. "After the bath." I heaved myself up, she came forward to unbutton my tunic and I let her.

She took my clean clothes out of the holdall and hung them up, I draped a towel around my waist. "Okay," I said. She led me down the corridor to the steam room. The place was very quiet. I went into the hot room and sat down heavily and looked at my feet. They were very dirty from twenty hours' patrolling. I dragged my hand across my chest and the sweat was dirty also, my fingernails black. It felt good to know I was getting clean and then cool whenever I wanted. I was slippery with sweat now. I lay back on the bench. I stuck it for ten minutes then I swung up off the bench and walked out.

"So soon?" The girl opened the next door into the bathroom. It was cool and tiled. She switched it on, the cold shower. I handed her the towel and stepped into the cold stinging spray.

"Ah!" The hard spray stung, beating me cold and clean, I put my head under the jet and the cold hard stinging rang in my ears. I leaned against the wall and let the cold spray beat my chest and face with my mouth open, beating into my mouth, then I let it beat my back and shoulders. Then I came out and I was tingling. Sound of Bells wiped my face dry. The bath was ready, full of soap suds, steaming. There was a place to rest my head. I lay down deep in the hot creamy water and closed my eyes and it caressed deep down like a sigh.

"I wash you?" the girl said.

And I just wanted to lie there and not move a muscle and feel her washing me, the gentle scrubbing of the brush and her smooth soft hand slippery and soaping, and the sly-careless passing of her hand that you know is coming, the sly-shy tentative intimacy under the soft warm suds, the knowing she is going to do it and the waiting for it, and when it comes the voluptuous surrender, all good intentions forgotten. I shook my head and sat up.

"No thank you, Sound of Bells, better I wash myself. But I want you to scrub my back."

I scrubbed myself till I glowed red. Sound of Bells scrubbed my back. It all felt very good.

"You very big and strong," she said. "Not like Chinese boy. You like Chinese girl?" She giggled behind me.

"Very much."

"Why you like Chinese girl?" She stopped and peered over my shoulder at me.

"Chinese girl," I said, "very beautiful. Very polite. Very smooth skin."

She said, while she scrubbed:

"You marry?"

"Yes," I said, to keep her quiet.

I wanted the cold San Miguel very badly now.

She washed my hair and scrubbed my fingernails then she put me back under the shower, then she rubbed me dry. Now I felt woolly with tiredness, good and tired and clean and a roaring thirst. We went back down the corridor, glowing clean and tingling, into the pink-glow cubicle. I slumped down on the couch and just sat there, eyes closed, listening to my fresh clean tiredness tingling all over me. It was good, so very good, and the great dry clean thirst, just sitting there on the clean crisp sheet on the soft cool couch. The girl was pouring a big green cold bottle of San Miguel, it went *glug glug glug* and mounted sparkling golden red and long and marvelous up the glass and I took it from her and I did not even look at it, I put it to my mouth and poured it in. It oh God scoured cold deep blissful through my mouth, and went rumbling frothing long and deep and sparkling clean strong fresh down my long hot dry throat into my hot dry empty gut. I drank the whole long beer straight down down down and then I sat slumped there, then I fell back on the couch.

I felt her soft cool warm hands begin to knead my shoulders. I lay spread-eagle on the couch with my eyes closed feeling her massage me and I knew through the great tiredness that when the time came I would not be able to resist, and I said, "No Special today."

"No Special?" she said.

"No," I said. "Just wake me in one hour."

Outside the hot thick air hit me again. It was still light but the neon signs were on, all the colors, the shops and the bars. It felt very comfortable and informal to be in civilian clothes again. The girl standing outside the Cupid Bar had her *cheongsam* split right up to her red scanty panties and she wore black diamond-mesh stockings and red stiletto heels tapping the pavement to the time from the jukebox inside. I slung my holdall in the car and locked it. I walked back down Nathan, Kowloon's Golden Mile. It was thick with six-laned traffic, cars and taxis and growling red London omni-buses and neon lights scrambling over each other. It was Catherine's birthday next week. I turned into the Chungking Arcade. You can get almost anything in the Chungking Arcade. Upstairs in the many, many apartment houses you can get women, almost any kind you like. They are usually clean. On one floor they did a very good line in Australian and American girls. I went into Hassin's Goldsmiths and I had a hurried look around and I bought Catherine a carved jade bracelet with a gold clasp. I did not think she had a jade bracelet when we were together. Maybe she's got one now from this foreign correspondent I hear about. Oh Jesus, I thought: Don't think that. Why think that? You are happy tonight, you're going home to Suzie, we've been through all that, you've figured all that out now after a year. Now, after a year, the thought did not drive me mad with jealous outrage any more. Bitter sometimes, a little grief sometimes, when I was sitting alone in the sunset up at the border and I thought about my child, and the house, and the things still in it, our big deep soft bed and the rugs and the dinner table and her things I knew so well hanging in the cupboard, and the soft woman smell of them, and the feel of them, and in the bathroom all her things. And waking up in the morning and Ah Chan bringing in the tea and the first cigarette which is the best and she leaned over the edge of the bed and began to brush her long hair a hundred strokes. Oh God, it was so good in the mornings. And Radio Hong Kong telling the news and the competitive ritual for the bathroom, Catherine organizing up her hair while I showered, sitting before the mirror, long thin back and her breasts bulging out her bra and woman hips rounded out with childbirth, and the dull stretch marks on her belly and her footprints in the body powder on the floor. The mornings are the best time. Mostly these days up there at Takwuling I had stopped thinking, I had stopped myself for if you do they drive you mad, and her long slim legs and her stockings sheening and the sweet soft secret smooth woman thighs where it is so sweet and secret smooth, to make you want to cry out mine *mine* and never any other bastard's unthinkable hairy fingers fingering and hairy outrageous sacrilegious loins spreading these thighs if you thought about these things it would drive you mad.

I crossed the harbor on the Star Ferry. I liked the Star Ferry crossing, it made you feel you were going somewhere in claustrophobic Hong Kong. All down the harbor were the freighters buoyed, derricks out, and the cargo junks clustered about them in the sunset. Many sampans and junks. A big junk was sailing up the fairway, all sails spread, red and patched and heavy, great batwings against the sunset, the big blunt nose ploughing heavily slow. Some tourists were taking photographs of her with "oohs" and "ahs." Three American sailors were sitting with three bar girls. Later they would have a good time. It would cost them but Americans don't mind. American tourists spoil it for everybody but usually they are pretty well behaved. There are three prices in Hong Kong: one for the Americans, one for the Europeans, and one for Chinese. Hong Kong was looming, the grand old waterfront buildings along Connaught Road, the Hong Kong Club and the Supreme Court and the Post Office.

The ferry's engines went astern and we eased up along-side the pier. I was excited now, that feeling in my gut. I hurried through the ferry crowds and the rickshaws to the taxi rank. Between the old Supreme Court and the gracious old Hong Kong Club and the communist Bank of China, in the heart of this tiny crowded taipan land, was the Cricket Club. Hong Kong is a rather unusual name for a place to have but then Hong Kong is a very unusual place.

I took a taxi to Happy Valley.

There was the old familiar double door with the spy hole and the new Yale I had put in a year ago. I looked at my fingernails. I rang the bell. The door opened and there stood Ah Chan. "Master!" Little old Ah Chan beamed gold-toothed. "Welcome, *Master!*"

"Good evening, Ah Chan." I walked into the hall. "You good, not good, hah?"

"Good, Master!" Old Ah Chan beamed. "Very good see Master!"

The lounge door opened and some voices came out and there was Catherine, bringing the light in with her. "Jake!"

"Hello." She put her arms half around me and gave me her lovely wide mouth to kiss. I smelled her again, the sweet Cathy smell and the feel of her slim arms and the heart-breaking feel of her mouth.

"Happy birthday for next week," I said.

She was smiling, shaking a little. "Thank you, darling —what can I get you to drink?"

"Who're the people?"

"Just some of the mums who played bridge here to-day."

"Well, let's go through to the bedroom," I said.

She took my hand and led me quickly down the old wood passage. And there was our bedroom, almost ex-actly as when I used to sleep in it. The double bed and wardrobe and the rugs and the dressing table and the curtains and the bedside lamps. Through the big old win-dows were the lights of Happy Valley and the harbor and Kowloon.

"Hello," she said.

"Hello."

And the slender familiar feel and smell and taste of her in my arms, as if I had come home—oh Christ, it felt I had come home. She was shaking a little also. I put my hand into my pocket.

"Happy birthday for next week," I said.

"Oh, thank you, darling." Suddenly she had tears in her eyes. She looked at the little parcel. She pulled off the wrapping. The bracelet lay green and gold in the white cotton wool.

"Oh, it's lovely, Jake!"

She held me and I could feel her cheek a little wet. "I've got you a present, too!"

"Have you?" I said, surprised. She opened my side of the wardrobe and there were a few suits of mine still handing and it crunched my heart to see them there. She pulled out a packet.

"It's nothing much. But you always need socks the way you tramp around."

"Thank you for thinking of me," I said.

"I think of you every day, Jake."

"I want to see Suzie," I said.

"Of course, she's so excited you're coming. I'll be in the lounge."

I walked down the familiar passage and opened the door and looked in. And there was my child scrambling off the bed and running squealing across the room jumping into my arms laughing and hugging. I held her up high and clutched her close laughing, "Hello, my darling, darling, darling!"

"Daddy?"

"Yes, darling?" We were sitting on the bed.

"Are you going to sleep here now?"

My eyes were burning.

"Not yet, darling. I'm very busy up in China and so I've got to sleep up there yet."

"You catch all the robbers, don't you?" she said.

"That's right," I laughed.

"You've got a real gun, haven't you, Daddy?" she said.

"Yes, I have," I said. "But it's only to frighten them with."

"Don't you shoot it sometimes?" she said, disappointed.

"No, sweetheart, I never have to shoot at anyone."

She looked at me earnestly. "All the same, you're jolly brave, aren't you, Daddy?"

I hugged her close. "Oh yes, darling, I'm jolly brave."

"You're the bravest policeman in the whole world, aren't you—that's what Mommy says."

I laughed, that made me happy. "Did Mommy tell you that?"

"Daddy, when can we go on the junk again?"

"Well"—I hesitated—"maybe soon. When I'm not so busy." She looked very disappointed. "You see," I lied, "it's got a hole in it now and I've got to fix it when I'm not so busy."

I held her tight and kissed her neck and smelled her.

"You're prickly, Daddy!"

"Am I? I had a shave."

"Daddy, you've got hairs on your chest too, haven't you?"

I smiled at her. "Yes, darling."

"Can I look?"

"All right." I undid two shirt buttons. She peered at my chest closely.

"Do all men have hairs on their chest?"

"Most men," I said.

"Why?"

"Because they're strong. Like Popeye."

"You're jolly strong, aren't you, Daddy?"

"Oh yes, I'm jolly strong. But not as strong as Popeye."

"You're stronger than Mr. David aren't you, because you've got more hairs on your chest," she said.

My pulse tripped hard. "Who's Mr. David, darling?" My fingers were fumbling with the buttons.

"Mommy's friend," she said.

There was a hollow feeling in my chest. "Do you mean Mr. Burton, darling?"

"Yes," she nodded.

"Does Mr. Burton come here often, darling?"

She nodded and the hollow feeling pounded.

"Where have you seen his chest, darling?" I said. I thought: *God, let her answer be the right one.* "On the beach?"

She nodded. "I can swim now, Daddy!"

Relief pumped through me. "Can you, sweetheart?" I was thinking oh Christ don't torture yourself, this is not the way to do it. But I had to ask her now. Out of the mouths of babes, and I hated myself.

"Does Mr. Burton sometimes sleep here, Suzie?"

"I can swim from here"—she pointed—"to the door," she said proudly.

"Jolly good!" I could hear the knocking in my ears. "Lovey? Does he? Sometimes sleep here?"

"Sometimes," she said simply.

Oh God Jesus Christ. I took her finger from my mouth. My hand was shaking.

"Darling—you mustn't tell me any stories!" *Oh Christ, let her be telling stories.* She shook her head, big blue eyes hesitating. "Now—have you seen him?"

She nodded. I closed my eyes—oh Christ oh Christ. I squeezed her hand hard. I said, "That's all right, darling. He's only looking after Mommy."

She stared at me. "Mommy said I mustn't tell anybody because it's not their business, is it?"

I closed my eyes.

"That's quite right, darling, you mustn't ever tell anything to anybody what happens at home. Suzie?"

Oh Christ, I hated myself for using her like this, for all the wrong I had done her, for leaving her, my very own perfect child. My eyes were burning, self-hate outrage in my guts.

"Do you like Mr. Burton, darling?"

She looked at me. She knew what answer I wanted her to give. She shook her golden perfect head unconvincingly. It made me want to sob for love of her.

"Why not, sweetheart? Isn't he nice to you?"

She looked at me worriedly. She nodded. Christ, I hated him. "Sometimes he tells me a story," she said.

Oh Jesus Christ.

"That's lovely, darling." I looked at her and I just wanted to sob out loud. I held her tight, so much love I wanted to crush my girlchild in my arms, my very own perfect girl-child my Suzie darling daughter. I could not get enough of my girl-child and I had left her to see another man sleeping with her mother in my bed, oh Jesus Christ the hate.

"All right, darling. I've got to go to Mommy now."

"Daddy? Who do you love best, Mommy or me?"

I squeezed her. "I love you both the same, sweetheart."

She was quite satisfied with that answer.

"And Daddy?"

"Yes?"

"When you come back from China I can have a baby brother, can't I?"

I could feel tears. "How do you know, darling?"

"Mommy told me," she declared.

Oh Jesus Christ. "I must go, darling," I said. "Into bed now." I hugged her close and kissed her neck so she squealed, my sweet child smell, and swung her down onto the pillow, she was laughing. "I've got to go to Mommy now, sweetheart." I tucked the sheet in around her chin. "Good night, my lovely girl."

I walked back up the passage. I was a stranger in my own house. I turned back to the kitchen and told Ah Chan to call the *tai-tai* to the bedroom. I closed the bedroom door and sat down on the bed. The door opened and Catherine came in, holding a drink. "What's the matter, darling?"

"Close the door."

She closed it and stared at me.

I took a big breath and it trembled: "Burton is not to sleep in this house! Suzie is not to see him in your bed in the mornings or any other time! Go to his place to do your screwing!"

"We're not—" she began indignantly.

Jesus my mind reeled red-black. I hated the beautiful bitch. "Don't lie!" I pointed savagely at the wall: *"Suzie told me what's going on."*

She stared, furious: "Do you mean to tell me you've been poisoning Suzie's innocent mind by questioning her about me?"

"How innocent is she if she sees things like that!"

"You left me," she cried. *"You have no right—you left me—"*

I grabbed her arms and shook her.

"I left you because you were fucking my best friend and lied on oath—"

"Why did I do it?" she shrilled. *"Because you're such an impossible uncompromising bastard who thinks nobody's good enough for him—the great Jake McAdam refused to have anything more to do with the colonial bullshit—well I did—I like my friends—"*

"I'll take you to court and get custody of her myself!"

"That's a laugh. What would she see in your bed in the mornings, pray?"

I let her go. She was holding her face crying, just the sound of my panting.

"We're finished, Catherine. I didn't know we were but we are! Finished!"

She cried into her hands, "I know. . . ."

I leaned against the wall. I was shaking. I wanted to roar and stride down the passage and throw everybody by their necks and slam the door and lock it forever and fall down and weep for love and hate, my child my hateful wife oh Jesus Christ.

"Good-by. Thanks for a wonderful visit."

CHAPTER 12

I took a taxi to Wanchai, the bright hard glare of the neon signs. The Tokyo Bar, the Pussycat, Winner Horse, Lucky Strike, Ocean, United States, the Carnival, the Suzie Wong, and many many more bars and the shops, workshops, apartments, massage parlors, tattoo parlors, hawkers, and the rickshaws, taxis, children, bar girls, pimps and the thump of jukeboxes and the blare of Radio Canton, and the heat. I went into the dim cool of the Seven Oceans Bar.

"Brandy," I said.

There were bamboo cubicles. A dozen American sailors were dancing with girls in front of the multicolored jukebox, a lot of sailors sat with girls, cuddling and talking and making jokes through the thump of the jukebox. There were also some merchant seamen and resident Europeans, some of them had girls also but they were not as possessive as the Americans. It costs to cuddle. It costs in girlie drinks at four dollars eighty cents Hong Kong a throw for a wine glass of Seven-Up, which doesn't last very long at all. The Americans are very nice and sentimental people and they can afford to be, which pisses everybody off except the bar girls. The tune was "Cruising down the River." The girls wore *cheongsams* split right up to the hip or little tunics which only covered their buttocks, and they all wore high heels. And the lights of the jukebox on their legs and thighs, the reds greens yellows and the shadows between the moving thighs and the hips pressed forward and the long hair hanging down their backs and the moving buttocks against the tight dresses. The Yank on the other side of me said, "Excuse me, sir. You a resident British?"

"Resident Jewish," I said. The inevitable friendly Yank.

"What work do you do here, sir?"

I said, "I'm a laboratory technician in the V.D. clinic."

He looked at me. "No shit? What you actually do?" the Yank demanded, fascinated.

I said, "I'm the guy who looks through the microscope at all the slides."

"No shit?"

"No shit."

I tossed back my drink and stood up to go. The Yank put his hand on my arm, snapped his fingers at the barman. "No, really," I said.

"Go on," the Yank said. "I like talking to you—" The barman already had the brandy bottle poised.

"Okay," I said. "Thanks."

I took the brandy and lifted it to him. "What ship're you on?" I did not want to know.

"The *Dreadnought*," the Yank said, "the big aircraft carrier out there."

"Are you engaged in Vietnam?"

"Right," the Yank said.

"What do you think of the Vietnam War?" I said. It was only a polite question.

"The Vietnam War," the Yank said firmly, "is a crusade. For Democracy," the Yank said with a capital *D*.

I nodded.

"And it's our solemn duty to protect the people of Vietnam against communist aggression."

I nodded.

"Will you win?"

The Yank said, "Justice always wins."

"How do you like being a sailor?" I said, to change the subject.

"It's a tough life," the American said. He wagged his head and looked down at his boots.

"What do you do aboard the ship?"

"I'm a mail's clerk," the Yank said. "Look at these hands," he said. He held the palms out. "You know where I get them callouses?"

"Vietnam?" I said.

"Carryin' mailbags," he said.

"No shit," I said.

The Yank looked confidential. "Say, sir, would you mind telling me something. The symptoms of V.D."

I was sick of this Yank.

"Undress!" I said.

He stared. "Whadyasay?"

"Drop your pants and I'll tell you if you got it."

"Kee-rist, the British sense of humor! I mean, just advise me."

I said, "We V.D. people have an agreement with the liquor trade: they don't sell beer in our clinics and we don't treat V.D. in their bars."

The Yank threw back his head again in a scream. "Say fellas—"

"Hello, Bomban," Mi-mi said.

"Hello, Mi-mi," I said. Oh Christ.

"Long time no see," Mi-mi said. She was very pretty, wide mouth, slanted dark eyes shining, black hair long. You could see the top of her breasts. Her breasts were very good. If you looked underneath each breast you would see a small scar. That was where Joseph So had injected the silicone. He just gave his patients a local anesthetic, filled his big syringe with silicone, like a grease gun, then he drove the big needle up into the breast till he reckoned he had gone far enough, then he pumped the silicone in, it tore the tissue apart, and it just had to find a home for itself, and the breast swelled up. When he had pumped up one he would say that the girl was taking up more silicone than anticipated, so the fee would have to be double or else he could not proceed. Joseph So's fees were higher than the best F.R.C.S. in Hong Kong. Sometimes Joseph So did the same thing halfway through the eye operation, while he was cutting out the wedge of fatty tissue in the eyelid to create the fold in the upper eyelids of Chinese girls who wanted eyes like European girls. The girls always agreed, with one eyelid Chinese and the other European. Joseph So was not a qualified surgeon. The girls never came to the police to complain because of the loss of face. I had raided his surgery several times, but he was never engaged in an operation at the moment and the girls we found in the waiting room would never give evidence, for the loss of face. Then one day a Filipino girl came into my office. Joseph So had given her a left breast that bulged out almost to her armpit; it had turned septic and her husband hated her now and if there was one bastard she hated it was Joseph So. I arranged for her to make an appointment with Joseph So to have the other breast blown up farther, to try to make it match the other. As soon as he pricked her with the syringe she was to scream as loud as she could. She was prepared to have her breast pricked, she was prepared to do anything to get him. I was waiting outside with my detectives and a doctor and when she screamed we charged the door and broke it down and there was Dr. Joseph So, very surprised, with all his instruments, and there was the prick of blood on our witness's breast. But Joseph So had done a good job on Mi-mi.

"I sit down?" Mi-mi smiled her creamy smile.

The barman leaned over, girlie drink in one hand. "You buy Mi-mi drink?" I flipped over a five-dollar bill.

"Thank you," Mi-mi beamed. She crossed her lovely legs on my barstool, long and plump and very smooth and they made you groan under your breath. "Why you no come see me?" Mi-mi said. It didn't mean a thing.

"Say," the Yank said, "she your girl in this bar?"

"Just a friend of the family," I said.

I off-loaded Mi-mi and the Yank on to each other and walked out the bar back into the hot night.

I walked down the waterfront to the old Go-Down Nightclub. I carried my jacket, and my shirt was wet a third time. There were many people sleeping on the pavements, men, women, children, illegal immigrants, mostly. They were safe now, there was neither time nor heart to find them all and send them back. Soon they would climb the old buildings and build their cocklofts on the rooftops, and climb the mountains and build their shacks of cardboard and flattened tin boxes. And late in the long hot China summer the mighty typhoons would come with dragons' roar in the black black sky and lashing rain as thick as your fingers. And when the typhoon is past there would be the digging for the bodies.

I came to the Go-Down the sounds of "Build a Stairway to Paradise." There was the big phony warehouse door with the small door cut into it. I stepped through into **the dim thumping air conditioning and the mass of tables** pretending to be made of old crates and the dim bar made out of wine kegs. There were many Americans, smoke and noise, and above it all the thump of the band's amplifiers and Veronica singing. I got myself a seat at the bar and called for a brandy. I took a big sip, then turned around and looked at her, Mrs. Veronica Brown, legs all the way up, and I could feel the dry tears on my eyelids.

Oh yes, some Veronica Brown. And she did nothing for

me tonight. She was a well-nourished woman. Singing into the microphone, giving me her wide Veronica smile, I waved. Veronica Brown, army wife, separated, one child, schoolteacher, no money, Sergeant Brown gone to the dark island of Malta with his regiment after screwing all the Yeun Long whores, the whole god-awful story. And no money. Veronica Brown was a captive of Hong Kong. Government did not pay her enough to enable her to save the money to get the hell out of it to where rents were cheaper. To make ends meet, Mrs. Veronica Brown—schoolmistress—sang and played the guitar in Wanchai bars four nights a week and shared a flat with another schoolmistress in identical circumstances who worked as a barmaid six nights a week.

She had her brown leather dress on and her bare arms and her strong soft legs were golden. Her thick hair was bleached blond and it was tied back in a demure black bow on her strong shoulders, and she was gorgeous. She came to the end of "Stairway to Paradise" and the applause broke out, shouts and whistles and yoo-hoos, every man was lusting after her. She struck a chord and then she started singing "Foggy, Foggy Dew" and the bar went quiet. She came down off the stage and started walking between the tables as she strummed, singing and grinning, and every man in the bar was watching her face and her legs. Veronica had it, all right. The spotlight followed her. She stopped in front of me and I was grinning.

"Now here's another bachelor—"

I shook my finger sideways at her, she gave me a wink. I watched her go, the back of her legs and the leather shining on her hips and waist. Some Veronica. She finished the song and beamed at them applauding, then the spotlight clicked out. I saw her making for a table of Yanks. She sat down and picked up a drink. They were all laughing.

I swallowed my brandy and I turned back to the bar. I needed Veronica Brown tonight. I lit a cigarette. Then I felt a hand on my shoulder. "Hello, sad man," she said.

"What are you drinking?" he said.

"Whatever you're having," she said.

"I'm drinking an undertaker's joy. Two brandies," I said to the barman. "Doubles."

"I've got to get back to my charming Americans," she said. She looked at me. "What's up, Jake?"

"I saw Suzie," I said. "That's all."

"And Catherine?"

"Yes."

"Yes," she said. "I can see it."

I held her hand hard. "What time will you be finished tonight?"

She hesitated. She looked sorry for me.

"Jake, I haven't seen you for five weeks. I've got a date."

Oh Christ, please.

"Tomorrow?" I said.

She looked very sorry. "I'm going out tomorrow on a boat picnic at ten."

Oh God, Sunday. Sunday is the worst day to be alone. "Have you got a place to sleep? You look exhausted."

"There're plenty of hotels."

She made up her mind. "Go home to my place. The amah will let you in."

"Vero? Who is this furtive sonofabitch you're meeting?"

"Just a furtive sonofabitch I'm meeting."

"Vero?"

"Yes?"

"Oh God, I need you."

"Tonight," she said sadly. She squeezed my hand. "I must go now."

I took a big breath. "Vero? As soon as this mess on the border is over I'll take some leave and we're going on the junk. And drink cold beer and wine and swim bare-arsed and make love on the beach."

She smiled sadly. I said, "And sleep. Sleep sleep sleep. Stay in bed all day if we want."

She said, "Jake, have one more drink, and then go and sleep. I must go and sing now."

I went to the Pussycat for one drink, and there supporting the bar were Teetotal Tank and Mini-Max Popodopolos drinking San Miguel as if it were going out of season. Teetotal Tank was six-foot-four with a chest like a barrel and a gut like a barrel and a fist like a ham. Mini-Max was a short, large, detribalized Portuguese lawyer whose biggest dread in life was the Law Library. "The Seldom Seen Kid!" Teetotal said to me. I bought a round of drinks and then Teetotal bought a round and then Max bought a round. Then it was my turn again. Teetotal and Max were very funny men, and they had learned to get along with the San Miguel. The rest is a bit unclear. Two sailors had a big fight next to us and we picked up our drinks and moved further down the

85

bar and advised the *mamasan* to telephone the police. I remember Mini-Max announcing he had a terrible yen and he went off and did a little dance with a bar girl and he looked very good with his chubby beaming Portuguese face and his twinkling legs. I remember Teetotal Tank saying, "Whose turn is it?" and I said, "It's your turn, Teetotal," and then for no good reason we were riding in three rickshaws through Wanchai, neon lights taxis sailors people everywhere, and then we were upstairs in some bar with many bamboo cubicles and beaded curtains. A Chinese girl was sitting next to me pouring my beer and she took my hand and put it inside the top of her dress on her small Chinese breast and I pulled my hand away and slumped back in the dark corner and then I was just crying and I remember there were no tears any more just the heartbreak crying up out my throat, the drunkenness and the exhaustion and the whole red pink dark glow of the bar was reeling and I was just crying. The girl was saying somewhere, "Whatsamatter, Joe, you drink too much, hah?" and then I remember the girl's head was down and I got a handful of her hair and pulled her head up and she cried "Aiyah!" and the *mamasan* was saying, "You no like this girl?" and I said, "She's beautiful, just take her away," and I was slumped back in the corner with my eyes closed and the blackness was reeling big bad black around me and all I wanted so big bad reeling heartbreaking badly was home home home oh God give me my home and sleep sleep sleep—and then another girl was with me and I screwed up my eyes and it was no good, no good in the world, and I hated Catherine the girl myself everybody and I scrambled past her and the whole rotten bar was reeling and I was making for the door to go I don't know where and then there were Teetotal and Mini-Max suddenly and Teetotal said, "Whose turn is it?"

"My turn," Mini-Max reeled loud red. I remember the hot China night and the orgasm of Wanchai lights again like a blow in the face, I remember another bar and the face of a *mamasan* close saying, "Hey, Joe?" When I woke up I was on a couch.

I sat up and my head pounded and nerves cringed. Through the windows was the harbor and the hot mauve Mountains of Nine Dragons in broad hot sun, and it looked terrible. I was in Max's flat. I remembered Veronica, that I was supposed to be in her flat that I had told her I was going to love her. I remembered Catherine, oh Jesus Christ, and Veronica did not count. I got up off the couch. Oh God, why do I drink brandy? I only drink brandy when I'm drunk. I walked through Mini-Max's bedroom to the bathroom. Among many things I needed was to brush my teeth and I didn't care whose toothbrush I used, even Mini-Max's.

"Whatsa time?" Mini-Max croaked, very bad.

"Sun's shining," I said. It seemed after a long time I saw his toothbrush and then the toothpaste tube was the same. Then I was brushing my teeth and my head pounded worse.

"After you with the toothbrush," Mini-Max said.

I went back to his kitchen to the refrigerator. There was no food in it, only beer and wine and olives and caviar. I got a big bottle of San Miguel out and held it against my forehead to get the cold. It was a bad business getting the cap off the bottle, then I went and sat in the lounge: I closed my eyes and drank it straight down. At first I could not taste it, then it started getting through. I drank half the bottle, then banged it down and opened my eyes. Mini-Max was standing there all hairy and horrible and his head back drinking from another bottle, straight down. We sat there drinking slowly. After a long time I said, "Thanks for bringing me home."

After some time Max said, "I thought you brought me home."

I tried to think about this.

"Maybe Teetotal brought us home," I said.

Mini-Max tried to think about this. Then he said, "Sunday. Thank God for that. I couldn't bear another Saturday."

We just sat there. The beer was going straight back to my head but it hadn't made me feel much better yet. My chest felt tight from smoking. "You look horrible," I said.

"Compared to how I feel," Mini-Max said, "I look truly beautiful."

I looked at my watch and it was eleven o'clock. Too late for Veronica, she would already have left on her boating picnic. I went to the telephone anyway and dialed her. I could imagine it ringing in the empty carpetless flat, the Veronica mess, Mary-Anne's half-broken toys everywhere, and her flat-mate's child's toys, the hardupness everywhere. No reply. Well, I thought, this will be the end of that romance, you ruin everything, McAdam.

I had a very hot shower, then a cold one. I scrubbed the booze and Catherine and bar girls and self-hate off my skin till I glowed red, then I just stood with my head under the cold spray and felt nothing except how bad I felt.

I took a taxi down the mountain to the Star Ferry. The hot air blew into the taxi and every corner shouted *Susan* at me. Sunday is a bad day. I crossed the harbor. There were many yachts and pleasure junks and big launches with girls lying on deck and the young men making jokes, making jokes. At the Kowloon terminal I got into a taxi to a certain building in Tsimshatsui. I rode up in the elevator and I was determined not to think. I got out at the tenth floor and there down the passage were the big lucky red double doors of the Oriental International Apartment House in big red letters and then in Chinese characters, and bamboo beads hanging. In the hall were two small godshelf altars with joss sticks smoking strongly. One altar was to the god of brothels and the other was to the goddess of fornication. There was a light burning over the big mahogany desk. Mr. O stood up, gold teeth beaming. "*Jo-san*, Bomban!" Mr. O beamed.

"*Jo-san*, O-san," I said. "Do you have a room for me?"

"The Heavenly Border Room?" Mr. O beamed gold teeth.

"No," I said, "any room except the Heavenly Border Room. And the Gondola Room."

Mr. O beamed effusively: "First you wait Heavenly Border Room then I take you Japan Room, okay-okay?"

I followed Mr. O down the lucky red-carpet passage. I smelled the joss sticks all the way. There were the doors of the Taj Mahal Room, the Bangkok Room, the Peking Room, the Hong Kong Room, the Gondola Room, the Paris Room, the San Francisco Room, and several others. Each room was furnished according to its name. The walls of the Gondola Room were painted with murals of Venice and the bed was a wide gondola that rocked back and forth while you made love on it. That was why I did not want the Gondola Room. Mr. O opened the door of the Heavenly Border Room and beamed as I went in. "What you like to drink, Bomban?"

"A bottle of Mateus rosé. Cold."

"What kind girl you like?"

"Filipina. Tall. Happy. Clean."

"Guarantee," Mr. O said.

"O-san, if I get sick I'll break this house right down."

"Guarantee, Bomban," Mr. O said.

I sat down on the big Heavenly Border bed. The headboard was an angel with big silver-spread wings. The walls were painted in clouds and stars and moons and sunsets. When you switched out the lights, moons shone and the sunsets glowed and a multifaceted lamp in the ceiling rotated, spreading moving celestial lights all over the place, and the bed rose up to the ceiling on a hydraulic jacking mechanism, like the garage ramps for servicing cars. That was the reason I did not want the Heavenly Border Room. Mr. O's *foki* brought the wine in with an ice bucket, opened it, filled a glass. I lit a cigarette and I saw my hands were not shaking so much any more. I sat back on the bed, waiting. It would take about five minutes for them to arrive. Most of them came from middle-class Manila families and they were just taking their two weeks' vacation and paying their way. They did well in Hong Kong with the Europeans, because they were so happy about it, but probably not as well as the American and British girls, who were particularly popular with the Chinese, who will pay big money for a white woman, even if only out of curiosity.

The door opened and there stood four Filipina girls. They filed along the wall, smiling. Mr. O introduced them one by one. They all had Spanish names. I looked at them, each one quickly. They were all pretty but I like my whores to be substantial. That's what you're paying for, womanflesh. "That one, O-san," I said in Cantonese.

"Good-by," I said to the others. "Thank you."

"Good-by," they said, all smiles. Mr. O closed the door behind him, beaming.

"Do sit down, Maria," I said.

She crossed her legs very prettily and smiled as if she were at a party. I poured her some Mateus. "What's your name?" she said.

"Jacob," I said. "I am Irish."

"I am Indonesian, Spanish, Chinese, very mixed up." Her teeth were very white against her gold-brown face and her eyes sparkling black. She was very pretty. "Come in," I said. Mr. O opened the door.

"Japanese Room ready now, Bomban."

We walked down the red-carpeted joss-stick-smelling

corridor. I looked at the girl's legs walking ahead of me, long gold legs and high heels and her crisp summer frock above her knees and her hips swinging. Mr. O opened the Japanese door. There was the bed on the floor, the *futon*, the *tatami*, and the tiny dressing table, and the Place of Honor with the flowers and the scroll. Leading off was the *ohura*, the Japanese sunken bath. The walls were lined with the paper windows. The girl sat down with a big smile with her ankles crossed and the lanterns shone red-gold on her. Mr. O filled our glasses then he slid the paper windows back, and behind the windows were the mirrors, on all four walls. And suddenly we could see ourselves sitting, reflected off into infinity in all directions. There was a mirror on the ceiling.

She gave me her wide Filipino smile.

I grinned at her. "Get undressed, Maria."

She kicked off her shoes and unzipped the zip down the back of her dress with one zip and there she was in just her small white panties and her smooth Filipino skin, red-gold naked in all directions at all angles off into infinity. We sat cross-legged on the *tatami* at the low table and her skin shone red-gold and she was grinning, delighted with the mirrors. She got up and inspected the bathroom. "You want a blow job?" she said brightly, as if the two ideas were unassociated.

When I woke up that evening everything seemed to have happened a long time ago. I was late for duty but I did not care. Outside the hot night and bright lights hit me. The world seemed a little unreal. There were thick heavy clouds, no stars. I bought a newspaper and read the headlines as I walked up Cameron Street to where I had parked the car yesterday. It was still all going on up at the border, yesterday we had caught 4,800 odd. Yesterday was like a bad dream. I drove up Nathan Road, lights and shops and the traffic all the way, and the hot China night blowing in the window, and I tried not to think of last night, but it was a long way out of Kowloon and over the Mountains of Nine Dragons.

Outside Shatin I met the first police roadblock. There was a long line of vehicles from the opposite direction and they were checking them one by one. The inspector came across.

"How're things up there?" I said.

"Like a madhouse," he said.

All the way the vehicles were coming down from Fanling, moving very slowly because of the police roadblocks. It was a very black night. On the faraway mountains the Very flares were popping off up into the night. As I drove into the compound of Takwuling there was a big fork flash of lightning over China and you could see the people in the paddies other side the Shamchun in the long flick-on-and-off flash. I ran upstairs to my quarters and I read the latest sitreps, the situation reports, while I got dressed into a clean uniform. Then I went down to the report room.

That night there was a lot of thunder and lightning and at midnight the rains came. They came down suddenly, first slowly, then with a whoosh as thick as your fingers and a loud beating on the Land Rover so you had to shout and the windshield wipers were going *slosh-slosh, slosh-slosh* and the headlights shone silver and the rain swamped the Very flares and the mountains ran in mud and water and our uniforms stuck wet to us. It rained for two days and nights, and the Shamchun swelled up and broke its banks, and there were many bodies floating in it. On the twenty-eighth of May we caught three thousand people and on the twenty-ninth of May we caught one thousand people and on the thirtieth we caught maybe a hundred. On the last day of May Peking advised Whitehall that it believed that the "incidents on the border would quickly pass." That day we heard many shots fired by the People's Liberation Army other side the Shamchun.

That was the beginning of the summer of that year.

PART IV

CHAPTER 13

The Hermitage was a misnomer. It was a large elegant new block of one hundred furnished serviced bachelor flats for unmarried government servants, male and female. On the eleventh floor was the cheapest bar and restaurant in a colony full of bars and restaurants with the best all-round view of a colony renowned for spectacular views. When the Hermitage first opened, Government made a rule that no officer might have a person of opposite sex spending the night. Nobody took flats at the Hermitage and Government was losing money, always a serious matter. Then Government announced, sotto voce, that any officer who wanted another bed in his or her quarters would have to pay thirty Hong Kong dollars per months extra. Government never looked back.

I rode up in the elevator to the eighth floor, let myself into my flat. Everything was clean, new, the government furniture smart and uncomfortable and identical to every other flat in the Hermitage. There was nothing of my own except the hi-fi and the books and my portrait of Suzie. I had not read a book for a long time. There was a haze on the bright harbor. I rang the bell for room service and went into the bathroom and ran a hot bath. I heard the front door open and I draped a towel around my waist. It was the amah, the young one, Ah Moi. Most of the Hermitage amahs were old dragons. It's best that way. Ah Moi was not pretty but she had this bedroom stare and this dumpling walk which made you want to tear off her baggy trousers and she knew it, all right. Ah Moi knew what she was doing, working at the Hermitage. She still had paddy mud between her toes and she wanted to marry a European and get away from it all. Eric or Bottle-by-Bottle, who lived two doors from me, was screwing her now, or Ah Moi was screwing Eric or Bottle-by-Bottle. I called him after the schoolboy classic novel called *Eric or Little-by-Little*. Eric or Bottle-by-Bottle was in the Legal Department and did not get around much in Hong Kong on account of the Hermitage Bar on the eleventh floor was the cheapest bar in town. One night Eric or Bottle-by-Bottle comes down from the bar to find Ah Moi tidying his flat, at midnight, in her dressing gown. Eric or Bottle-by-Bottle finds nothing strange in this, says "Hello, amah" and passes out on his bed fully clothed. Next morning he wakes up to find Ah Moi in bed with him telling him he's a number-one lover and drawing his attention to the smear of chicken blood she had applied to the sheet and her loins. Eric or Bottle-by-Bottle was too hung over to figure it out. After a while Eric or Bottle-by-Bottle just got used to it and didn't try figuring it out. I told Ah Moi to bring me steak, eggs, and coffee and I got into the hot bath and lay there with my eyes closed feeling the sweat on my face and shoulders and concentrated on thinking and feeling nothing. I was getting quite good at it.

I got to the Supreme Court at ten. It is a big old building, the ground-floor walls tiled white like a public lavatory; to get to the third-floor courts you had to walk across the roof between the water tanks and air-conditioner outlets, the acoustics were very bad everywhere and there were furtive little corridors and stairways that would suit a Dracula movie. Witnesses and jurors were always lost. I found my court first go and went in and up to the bar. Mini-Max was the prosecuting counsel on an attorney general's fiat. He had cut himself shaving and he had a big piece of pink toilet paper tucked between his neck and his butterfly collar. The jury were already in their stand, waiting inscrutably. I did not like the look of them. There was only one European, a woman, the rest were Chinese. Chinese juries hate making up their minds. *"Not my segon,"* not my business. Today was the last day. This case had meant a trying three weeks. The dear old Acting Honorable Mr. Justice Charlie Kwok was on the bench. Bonapart Ng was defending. Anything could happen. Many things had happened. On the third day of the trail, at lunchtime, a happy smiling old gentleman on the jury had accosted me in the corridor. "Excuse me, Inspector," he said.

"I'm sorry, sir," I said, "but I cannot speak to you because you are a member of the jury and I am a Crown witness."

"I'm very happy to be here," the old gentleman beamed.

"I am afraid I'm not allowed to speak to you at all until the case is finished, sir," I said.

"The jury system is a grand institution," the old gentleman had said, "and I am only too happy to do my duty."

"Good, sir," I said, "but I'm afraid I must not talk to you—"

"I beg your pardon?" the old gentleman said. He put his hand to his ear. "I'm sorry, you'll have to speak up."

I stared at him. "You're deaf?"

"Hey?" the old gentleman said.

"Oh no. *Are you very deaf, sir?*" I shouted.

"Deaf?" The old gentleman's face lit up. "Yes, stone-deaf, that's me. I'm pretty good at lipreading, though, and I speak Cantonese very well, been out here since before the war, y'know, but you can't lipread Cantonese too easily."

We had had to impanel a new jury and start all over again. It had been a trying three weeks. Bonapart Ng did not know English too good and he was a bit short on the law. The Acting Honorable Mr. Justice Charlie Kwok was a grand old man and I loved him to bits but a little of him went an awful long way. Old Charlie Kwok had been acting Supreme Court judge for years; whenever a fully fledged puisne judge went on leave old Charlie Kwok acted puisne because he had been a magistrate so long. He had been an excellent lawyer in his day, but at seventy years old a little of him went an awful long way. The clerk gave a long mournful cry of "Court," and dear old Charlie Kwok came in, beaming in his red robes. We all bowed. "Good morning, good morning," the Acting Honorable Mr. Justice Charlie Kwok beamed. So help me, not all Hong Kong trials were like this, but this one was.

"Good morning, my lord," we chorused.

"Lovely day," Kwok A.J. beamed. "Lovely day, do sit down. Did you cut your neck shaving, Mr. Pop—er . . . ?"

"Popodopolos, my lord," Mini-Max said wearily.

"Quite, quite, thank you, I always have trouble with

your name, forgive me, we older-generation Chinese have trouble getting our tongues around some of these English names."

"Your Lordship can call me Pop, for short," Mini-Max shouted.

"Thank you, thank you, lovely day if a trifle hot. It's not"—Kwok A.J. suddenly turned earnestly to the jury —"that I don't know Mr. Popper very well. He is a very learned and able counsel, a veritable decoration to this honorable court. He knows, as the English say, his stuff. You have seen how ably he has prosecuted this case and I'm sure that, as taxpayers, you are well satisfied that you are getting your money's worth in Mr.— er— Pop. I always have trouble with that name. Once a Chinese, always a Chinese, you can't expect too much of us," he nodded beaming at the jury.

"To answer Your Lordship's question," Mini-Max said. "Yes, I did."

"Did what?" Kwok A.J. turned to Mini-Max kindly, cocking his ear.

"Cut my neck, my lord."

"Oh, I am sorry."

"I was trying to cut my throat, then got cold feet, my lord."

Only the European lady juror, Mini-Max, and I were laughing.

"I beg your pardon?" Kwok A.J. craned forward beaming.

"Nothing, my lord," Mini-Max said. "I was only making a little jest."

"Good—*good,*" Kwok A.J. beamed. "I approve of little jest in court from time to time. You see, members of the jury," Kwok A.J. beamed at them, "a court is a very human place. And as such it is often a humorous place. Indeed it is often a *happy* place! Oh, the funny stories I could tell you about funny things that have happened in my courts over the years. Nearly forty years I have been in courts, members of the jury, excluding the Japanese occupation of course—those were trying times indeed— forty years and believe me I am full of stories. No, members of the jury, a court is a human and happy place. All men are brothers. You, me, this poor man in the dock here—"

"And the deceased in this case, my lord," Mini-Max said loudly.

"I beg your pardon?" Kwok A.J. blinked around expectantly. "Mr. Shorthand Writer, what was that please?" Kwok A.J. leaned over the bench.

" 'And the deceased in this case, my lord.' " The shorthand writer stood up with his notebook.

"What about him?"

"He is—was—also our brother, my lord," Mini-Max said happily.

Kwok A.J. blinked blankly around looking for somebody to enlighten him, then his face lit up. *"Of course,* Mr. Pop—the deceased, also! Never forget the deceased, members of the jury, poor man also. No, members of the jury, all men are brothers so naturally a court is a brotherly, happy place. Should not justice be a happy business? We should all be happy that British justice is being done. British justice, members of the jury, is the greatest gift to mankind. You have seen the noble impartiality of Mr. Popper, learned counsel for the Crown, you have seen the valiant defense by Mr. Caesar Ng. Mr. Caesar Ng has been assigned by the Honorable Chief Justice to defend the accused for a mere pittance from the public purse, but have Mr. Caesar's efforts been any the less strenuous? . . . What?" The clerk was standing up whispering to Kwok A.J. *"Bonapart* Ng—of course, I am so sorry, Mr. Ng," Kwok A.J. beamed. *"Bonapart,* members of the jury. I'm sorry, I do have difficulty with some names. I'm getting old and one does tend to become forgetful, one's tongue less nimble. My wife is the same. Oh to be sixty again, members of the jury, aha-ha-ha!" The lady juror, Mini-Max, Kwok A.J., and myself were all laughing. "Now then, where were we?"

"British justice is et cetera, my lord," Mini-Max said wearily.

"Thank you, Mr. Pop. I shall direct the jury more fully later. Let us proceed. Now then. We have concluded all the evidence and counsel are about to address the jury, not so?"

"Quite so, my lord," Mini-Max sighed.

"Excellent. Capital, as English say. Now, Accused, will you please stand up." The interpreter told the accused to stand. "Now, Accused, and members of the jury, you are about to witness British justice in action. And you good people there in the gallery"—Kwok A.J. wagged his finger at them benevolently—"you should pay close attention also, you are about to see British justice at its best,

97

the fairest system devised by man. You are indeed a lucky man, Accused"—the interpreter was translating rapidly —"there are many places, and not very far away, where trials are not so fair, where, indeed, there may not be trials at all. You should be happy to be here today. Yes, happy, I say." Kwok A.J. stood up and stretched up his hands. "We are all brothers!" He sat down happily. "You people in the gallery"—Kwok A.J. stopped speaking English and broke into Cantonese—"you should be happy that you live in a place where British justice prevails, where men are presumed innocent until proved guilty, hah? Do you understand that, hah?" The gallery shifted uneasily. "Accused, do you understand how lucky you are, hah?" The accused nodded miserably, on trial for his life. Everybody had a straight face except Mini-Max, the European lady juror, and me. "Good." Kwok A.J. reverted to English. "Capital. Let us proceed. Mr. Popper, are you prepared?"

"For the worst, my lord," Mini-Max said.

"Capital. Now, members of the jury, pay close attention to the wisdom that falls from the cherry lips of learned counsel. That is an expression which learned judges in England are fond of using about themselves. When it comes to language, and justice, you can't beat the English. Chinese cooking is infinitely superior to English cooking, but British justice is best. Thank you, Mr. Pop, please proceed."

"Thank you, my lord," Mini-Max said.

"Will you be long, Mr. Pop?" Kwok A.J. asked anxiously. "Today is Friday, and tomorrow are the races. I would like us all to finish today if possible so that we will all be free tomorrow to go to the races at Happy Valley. I know you enjoy the races, Mr. Pop, I have seen you there often. And Inspector McAdam. Mr. Ng, do you have a flutter on the nags, as the English say?"

Bonapart stood up worriedly, looking around for the interpreter. "My lord?"

"Capital," Kwok A.J. beamed. "Then we shall all do our best to be succinct. To the point." Bonapart sat down, relieved. "Yes, Mr. Pop? Listen carefully, members of the jury."

Mini-Max stood up heavily, straightened his wig, and turned to face the jury.

"Members of the jury, I am now going to sum up the case for the Crown." Kwok A.J. nodded encouragingly.

"But before I address you on the law and the facts, I must first deal with the matter of proof." He took a heavy breath. "Members of the jury, the burden of proving the guilt of the accused lies on the Crown. The accussed must be presumed innocent until I have proved to you beyond all reasonable doubt, satisfied you, that he is guilty. Throughout the web of English law, one golden thread is to be found: It is for the Crown to prove the accused's guilt, *not* for the accused to prove his innocence—"

"*Capital!*" Kwok A.J. cried joyously. "Capital! You hear that, members of the jury? You hear that, you good people in the gallery? Accused, you hear that? Only in a British court will you hear that!" He repeated it in Cantonese. "This honorable officer"—he wagged his finger at Mini-Max—"is the prosecutor and yet he is the one who is telling you this. Only in a British court! . . ."

At five o'clock the jury retired to consider their verdict. Mini-Max and I adjourned across the road to the Dragon Bar to wait it out. We were very happy the case was over. Anything could happen. We did not talk about the case, we were sick of it. We were sick of Bonapart Ng and dear old Charlie Kwok. I did not care what happened. Mini-Max was feeling pretty good. At seven we were both feeling pretty good. Neither of us cared what happened. At seven o'clock the detective-constable came hurrying into the bar. "Jury ready, Bomban."

"Right," I said. "Let's go."

"With a hey-nonny-nonny," Mini-Max said, "and a hot cha-cha."

We hurried back to court. The jury were waiting in their stand. Mini-Max slapped on his robes and wig. The clerk shouted "Court" and Kwok A.J. came back in beaming. "Good evening, good evening."

"Good evening, my lord," we chorused.

"Delightful evening, if a trifle warm. I am so sorry this case has kept you here so late tonight, members of the jury. Never mind, in a few moments we can all go home to our dinners. Now, Accused, will you please stand up."

The accused stood up miserably.

"The jury have considered and arrived at their verdict, and we are about to hear what it is. It is these seven good people who have been your judges, not I, not Mr. Popper, not the police. This is the shining beauty of British law, that it is kept out the hands of lawyers. Like a breath of morning breeze, their minds pristine and un-cluttered with the lingo and mumbo-jumbo of the law, the jury has come to consider your case. You must appreciate this. Do you appreciate it? Ask him, Mr. Interpreter."

The interpreter spoke to the accused and then said, "I appreciate it, my lord."

"Good. Capital. Then shall we proceed?"

The clerk stood up.

"Mr. Foreman, will you please stand up?"

The foreman looked around nervously. The European lady nudged him, he stood up uncertainly. This had to be the worst jury I had ever seen, but so help me it happened like this.

"Have you arrived at your verdict?" the clerk said.

"Yes," the foreman said.

"Are you unanimous?"

The foreman looked at the interpreter. The European lady tugged the foreman's sleeve and nodded.

"And how say you? Do you find the accused guilty or not guilty of the crime of murder?"

"Yes," the foreman said.

The foreman took a breath.

"Guilty," he said.

There was a shout, a flurry, and Bonapart Ng was on his feet shouting. *"Object!"* Bonapart Ng shouted. *"Object, he didn't understood English!"*

"Hah?" Kwok A.J. leaned forward, cocking his ear at Bonapart.

"Foreman not understand English very good!" Bona-part shouted. *"Clerk ask to him and this lady tell him sometimes I see it with my very own eyes!"*

The foreman was looking horrified, blushing. Kwok A.J. was looking worriedly at Mini-Max. "Mr. Popper, what's Mr. Ng saying?"

Mini-Max clambered to his feet. "My learned friend is complaining that the foreman did not appear to under-stand English when the clerk spoke to him, my lord." He sat down, holding his head.

"Who didn't understand?" Kwok A.J. leaned forward.

"The foreman, my lord," Mini-Max and Bonapart shouted.

"Didn't understand what?" Kwok A.J. cocked his ear encouragingly.

"English," Mini-Max and Bonapart shouted.

"English?" Kwok A.J. said brightly. "Oh, I see! Doesn't understand English, eh? Well well well, this is a new development, isn't it? You see, members of the jury, you must speak English if you sit on a jury. Most important. If jurors don't speak English sufficiently well, they should speak up. Now, Mr. Pop, you say the foreman doesn't speak English?"

"*I* don't say so, my lord, my learned *friend* says so."

"I also say." Bonapart beat his breast.

"It is noteworthy," Mini-Max said loudly, "that my learned friend did not see fit to protest *before* the foreman spoke the fatal word "guilty." Perhaps if the verdict had been "not guilty" my learned friend would not now be protesting about the foreman's English?"

"*European lady tell him!*" Bonapart shouted.

"Dear dear dear." Kwok A.J. put his hands on both ears. "Such a noise! And so late. Really this is a great pity, such a waste of valuable time. Mr. Ng, what do you suggest we do now?"

"You acquit him!" Bonapart shouted.

"Only the jury can acquit him, Mr. Ng, and they have convicted him," Kwok A.J. pointed out.

"*This jury no good!*" Bonapart shouted.

"Tut tut, Mr. Ng," Kwok A.J. said. "You mustn't say things like that—"

"European lady tell him!" Bonapart stamped his foot.

"Well well well, Mr. Pop, what do you suggest?"

"Well, I'm only a lawyer, my lord," Mini-Max said, "but as I see it the jury have returned their verdict and you are bound by it. Whether or not there has been a mistrial because the jury haven't understood the English is a matter for the appeal court."

"*Ask him big words,*" Bonapart shouted. "*Tell European lady shut up and ask foreman big words—*"

"Well well well . . ." Kwok A.J. said. "Dear dear dear! Members of the jury, this is most unfortunate. Accused, will you please stand up?"

The accused stood up.

"My man, the jury have found you guilty. There has however been an eleventh-hour development, an allegation the foreman has not understood English sufficiently well to follow your trial, to do your case justice, as it were this means that the appeal court will order that you will have to be tried again, before a new jury. Never mind. These things are sent to try us. Aha, ha ha! In

the meantime, however, the jury have returned their verdict and I am legally bound to act upon it and sentence
you to death. Where's my cap?" Kwok A.J. peered around
the bench shortsightedly.

"Ask him big words!" Bonapart shouted.

The clerk was on his feet.

"Hear ye, hear ye, hear ye—" he intoned.

Kwok A.J. stood up. He slapped the black cap on top
of his wig.

"The sentence of the court is that you be returned to
wrathful custody, there to be hanged by the neck until
you are dead." The interpreter translated it. The accused
looked stunned. Everybody looked stunned. Bonapart
was speechless. "Now don't you worry about that," Kwok
A.J. beamed at the accused. "The appeal court will look
after you. Good luck!"

"Ask big words!" Bonapart screamed.

"Good night," Kwok A.J. beamed at us. "Good night
and thank you all. We'll all meet again at the retrial.
Good luck!" he waved to the accused. "Good luck!"

CHAPTER 14

I left Mini-Max crying into his beer at the Dragon Bar
and walked through the plush hotel foyer. In the Pearl
Room there was a Rest and Recreation Party for American officers on a visiting aircraft carrier from Vietnam
and European girls were filing up, all dolled up and self-
conscious, into the beaming crew cuts. There was a naval
band in the background and the officers all wore little
plastic name tags. The girls had it made; each one was
surrounded. The boys dearly needed some white womanflesh for a change after all the sloe-eyed Vietnamese girls,
and the grinning Filipina girls of Subic Bay, and those
slant-eyed Japanese girls in Yokohama and Okinawa.
The European girls had it made, all they had to do was
pitch up at the R. & R. Party and the Yanks spoiled them
rotten, wining, dining, pearls, watches, cameras. And a
new carrier in every fortnight. The Yanks had it made.
They were loaded with their danger pay and they all had

rooms upstairs. If they didn't get fixed up at the cocktail party the room boys would fix them up. Everybody was happy at the R. & R. Party. Outside I got a taxi down the waterfront to the Luk Kwok Hotel, to the wedding reception I was going to. After that I was going on to the Shanghai Mess Party.

On the ground floor of the Luk Kwok Hotel was the bar where the Suzie Wong of Richard Mason's book used to hang out. It was still living off it. They said the real Suzie was still there. She charged twice as much as any of the other girls. All the girls said they were in the book. I walked in. The guests were standing, cocktail-party style. It was an informal wedding with a difference. An official from the American Consulate had wed a bar girl. It was big news in Wanchai. "Local Girl Makes Good." I was a guest of both the bride and groom. There were American consular officials, whores, *mamasans*, and pimps all being polite to each other everywhere, all dolled up in their cocktail gear. I went up to the bride and groom. "Mac, ya ole bastard!" Harry shouted.

"Congratulations, Harry." I grinned; I turned to Mi-mi. "Congratulations, Mi-mi my dear, and everything of the best."

"Ain't she somethin'?" Harry said, getting along with the Johnnie Walker.

"She's beautiful." Mi-mi was quite a girl. I guess most of us had screwed Mi-mi. I nearly said, "We'll all miss you, Mi-mi."

"Foki, bring this sumbitch a drink chop-chop," Harry shouted to a waiter.

"Harry darling!" Mi-mi said demurely.

I got a glass of champagne from a waiter. "Good luck." I toasted them.

"Where's the happy pair, hey?" The consul came beaming over rubbing his hands. "Congratulations Harry baby, and Mrs. Harry J. Pikestone Junior!" He gave the blushing Mi-mi a big kiss. "Welcome to the Yoo Ess Ay!"

"Thank you, sir," Mi-mi blushed happily.

"Now, now"—the consul wagged his finger—"none of this sir crap, you're an *American* now, yessiree, you call me Al!"

"You know Jake McAdam, Al?" Harry said.

"Howdy, Jake." The consul shook hands. "Call me Al. Say, haven't I met you someplace, Jake?"

I said, "I once assisted in an investigation of yours into an immigration racket— I think we met then."

The consul put his finger on his nose. "What case was that, Jake?"

Mi-mi and Harry were welcoming the consul's wife. "Chinese applicants for immigration to the States," I said softly, "have to supply a stool specimen for laboratory examination?"

"Oh *yeah!*" The consul slapped me on the back. "The 'Shit Case,'" he whispered, delighted. "There was a typhoid scare, right, and there were guys who were clean who were selling their shit to the applicants and the applicants were presenting it to the lab as their own shit— right?"

"Right," I said.

"Boy." Al slapped my back. "That was some case! It sure put the wind up them in Washington, ha ha ha!"

We were both laughing.

"That's when I met Harry," I said.

"Harry passed through!" the consul screamed.

"Al honey!" the consul's wife said behind him.

I turned to circulate. There were whores everywhere, I didn't know half of them. They were all smartly dressed, looking demure. I saw Vice-Consul Tommy talking to the *mamasan* from the Night and Day. I believe Tommy was a real vice-consul. I can't believe Tommy was a CIA man, like most of the vice-consuls up at the embassy, Tommy was too genuine a soul to be anything other than a nice vice-consul. Tommy was a slight forty-year-old bachelor with wavy gray hair and the most earnestly interested expression and soft gentle voice, not an unkind thought in him. "And how's business with you these days?" he was saying earnestly to the *mamasan* of the Night and Day.

"Pretty good, hah," the *mamasan* was saying. "Thank you."

"Good, good," Tommy said, genuinely pleased for her.

"Hello, Tommy," I said. "Hello, Mama."

"How are you, Jake!" Tommy beamed. He really wanted to know.

"How's the cloak and dagger business, Tommy?" I really liked Tommy.

"Bloody." Tommy wagged his head laughing at my little joke. "Oh so bloody, Jake! I was just asking this good lady how business was."

"Pretty good, thank you," Mama said.

"Plenty of ships?" Tommy said encourgingly.

"Pretty good, thank you," Mama said. She took a sip of her drink, little finger stuck out.

"Good, good," Tommy said. He turned to me. "You know this lady, do you, Jake?"

"Certainly," I said. "The bride worked under Mama."

"She very good girl, you know," Mama said loyally.

"I'm *sure*," Tommy said, meaning it.

"She not same like other bar girl, you know," Mama said. "Just like to talk, dance, maybe have drink, you know," Mama said. "She number-one girl. . . ."

"Uh-huh," Tommy nodded encouragingly.

King Winky passed. "Hello, Jake."

"Hello there, Winky." Winky was called King Winky because his name was Kung Wing-kai and because he was one hell of a big noise in Tanchai because he owned the best six girlie bars. King Winky had a very good time indeed. He was also a partner in a big gambling casino in Macao. He also had an interest in two communist girlie bars and he played Mah-Jongg with the fat cats. King Winky was a good man to know. He was a stout smooth man with a perpetually happy face. Mi-mi had been one of his special mistresses for a long time. He had given her away at the wedding ceremony today. "Sad to see her go, Winky?" I said.

King Winky beamed. "Now I got plenty friends at American Consul," he beamed and we both laughed.

We were walking toward Shandy and Suzie Wong. "Evening Shandy, Suzie," I said, stopping.

Shandy gave King Winky a hateful look and turned and walked away. Shandy had been one of King Winky's favorites for a long time and he had made her a *mamasan*. Recently he had got fed up with her and demoted her back to ordinary girlie. It was a great loss of face for Shandy. She looked better in the darker lights of the bar, but she was still in very good condition. King Winky grinned at me sheepishly. "She okay," he apologized. "Still pretty good give, six years, make plenty money."

"Sure," I said. Shandy had more money than I would ever have.

"Excuse, Jake," King Winky beamed squeezing my shoulder. "I go talk my friend—anytime you go Macao, tell me, I fix you up there."

I turned to Suzie Wong. "And how're you, Suzie?" I said.

"Pretty good, okay," Suzie said. She looked very unhappy.

"What's the matter, Suzie?" I said.

She turned and hurried out of the room into the foyer. I caught up with her hurrying up the stairs.

"Suzie, what's the matter?"

She turned on me and burst into tears. "I *am* Suzie Wong!" she cried. "I *am*, I *am!*" She twisted out of my hands and ran away up the stairs.

And then, that night, I went on to the Shanghai Mansions Mess Party, over on Kowloon side. The Shanghai Mess girls were stewardesses. I arrived at about nine, alone.

It was a hot night, full of moon and stars. The front door was open and all you could see were heads all talking at once. I found a glass and poured myself a big scotch. There was a lot of noise, music, talking. I looked for one of my hostesses, to pay my respects. You were never sure who your hostesses were at a Shanghai Mess Party because at any given date half of them were flying, or shacked up elsewhere or both, and another girl had moved in. There were many people I did not know. Hong Kong is a crossroads. There were many good-looking women I hadn't seen before. Shanghai Europeans. It was a happy hunting ground. They were all out for a good time. Olga waved, she was one of my hostesses. I started toward her, somebody shouted "Jake!" and there was Fred, of the American Secret Service, Washington. Fred flew through town frequently, chasing counterfeit American currency. He and I had worked together on two big cases. Counterfeiting is big business in the East, and U.S. currency is the easiest: all U.S.A. bank notes are the same size so all you do is bleach the print off one-dollar bills, print one hundred dollars on them, and you're in very big happy business indeed. It was a good business for Fred too. From Bombay to Tokyo ole Fred was known as the Upholsterer. "On a job," Fred grinned happily, shaking hands. "Man, am I shagged out."

"I don't know why you bother to stop it," I said. "You give away so much in foreign aid. Why not let them print their own? What's the U.S. up to in Vietnam?"

"We've only got six hundred military advisers there," Fred said. "That's the limit of our involvement."

106

"Like hell," I said, "the French with all their colonial know-how couldn't beat the Reds, how do you think the Yanks can do it, you'll be involved in a full-scale war before you know it, like Korea. You guys better let them hold their general election."

"Money is my business," Fred said, "not politics."

"Same thing," I said, "same players."

"Would you believe this one?" he said, and told me a story. Last week the police found a guy in a hut on an island happily turning out hundreds of thousands of bank notes of a certain Far East country which shall be nameless. At the trial they asked him if he had any witnesses to call and he said yes, one witness. "Who is he?" the judge said. The accused says, "The Minister of Finance" —of the aforesaid unnamed country. "What will he say?" asks the judge. And the accused says, "He will tell the court that I was legally commissioned by him to print this money." And damn me if it wasn't true! We were both laughing. The goddamn Minister of Finance printing his own money; the whole goddamn Far East hangs together with string, corruption everywhere, Fred said.

"Not Hong Kong," I said.

"Ho-bloody-ho," Fred said. He looked around the room: "Who's an easy lay for me tonight? Must try to get myself a piece of ass before I leave for the wilds of Tokyo."

"Plenty of that in Tokyo," I said.

"Yeah, but it ain't *white*," Fred said. "See ya, Jake."

Olga had disappeared. There were many people I had never seen before. I could have just gone up to somebody and started talking, but I am not good at that sort of thing. Like trying to pick a girl up on the beach. Like so many Hong Kong parties. Why had I come? Because you're lonely, I said, so snap out of it and get unlonely, find yourself a girl, like Fred. Like everybody else. Maybe somebody to love. Christ. That's really self-pity. That's really the cuckholded husband rebounding, looking for somebody to kiss it better; fight your own goddamn battles. God, I hate this party. I saw a girl who looked alone and went up to her.

"Hello," I said. "I'm Jake McAdam."

"Hello," she said. "I'm Sonia."

Oh Gawd, the inevitable question but I could think of nothing else to say: "Do you live in Hong Kong or are you passing through?"

She said it as she had said it a thousand times, "Six months. I'm here on a government contract."

Next question: "Which department?"

"Health. I'm a physiotherapist." Seems they're all either school-teachers or physiotherapists. Her question: "How long have you been in Hong Kong?"

I said, "I was born in Shanghai. I've been out here ever since, on and off."

"What department? Or is it the bank?" A man handed her a drink. "Thanks, darling," she said, then turned to me: "I'm afraid I've forgotten your name?"

We introduced ourselves.

"How long have you been in Hong Kong?" he said.

"Let's dance," she said to him.

I saw Derek Morrison getting himself a drink at the bar and I made my way over to him. Derek was my young bank manager.

"How's business?" I said.

"Bloody booming," Derek said. He asked after Catherine, then quickly asked how I liked being back in town and did I have any interesting cases, to cover up. I said I had only one good murder and one bloody awful abortion case worth mentioning. It was the ugliest abortion case I'd ever done: the accused had operated on this girl for seventeen hours and finally killed her, but I was wasting my time compiling the case because a Chinese jury would not even convict Jack the Ripper of abortion. "Because Chinese feel that other people's abortions are not their business," I said. "The only way I'll get a conviction is if I get five whites out of seven on my goddamn jury."

"Nice job you've got," Derek said.

"What's the stock market going to do?" I said.

"God," Derek said, "it's artificially unrealistically maniacally sky-high. Everybody, every *foki* and amah has gone money-mad, buy buy buy, it's bound to crash and when it crashes, oh boy."

We talked money for a while. The Colony had gone money-mad. If there's one thing a Chinese can't have enough of it's money. Make hay while the sun shines. In thirty-six years the New Territories lease expired and the whole bloody caboodle except Hong Kong Island reverted to Red China. But Red China could claim the whole place back tomorrow with a telephone call and as soon as the disaster of the Great Leap Forward was over China was likely to do that small thing and Britain could not fight for it, and everybody knew it, so why the hell was the sun shining on all this hay-making? Everybody should be shit-scared. And real estate? Jesus. All right, you can maybe understand the public having get-rich-quick fever over local industry-shares, but *real* estate? In a place that Mao Tse-tung could take with a telephone call tomorrow? All these goddamn buildings going up? And goddamn rents going up all the time. And it's all luxury stuff, apartments. Land changing hands half a dozen times a week—the same piece of land bought and sold over and over, going up up up before it's even goddamn conveyed. Where's the money coming from?

"The banks," I said. "It's all your fault, Derek."

"Not my bank, mate," Derek said. "Not the Hong Kong and Shanghai Bank, nor any of the big established banks with economic know-how, we're not encouraging this madness: no, it's the goddamn Chinese banks. The one-eyed pisspot family banks, have you seen how many have opened up? Have you seen the new swanky marble entrances? And have you seen the interest rates they're offering, to get the coolies and amahs and the little Chan Fat white-collar workers to deposit their money with them? Ten, eleven, even twelve per cent," Derek said.

"And the bank relends this money out at fourteen, fifteen per cent to these maniacs to buy and sell land and build half-arsed luxury apartment blocks, and what does the bank take as security for the loan? Mortgages on this overpriced land. So what's going to happen when the boom's over, when saturation point is reached and there're too many buildings? What's going to happen when these depositors want to withdraw their money from the bank? I'll tell you," Derek says, "the bank won't be able to repay the depositors because the builders can't repay the bank because they can't rent their buildings. Everybody will go bankrupt at this rate," Derek said.

"So what's the solution?" I said. "The banks must stop lending money. Or the banks must ensure that they have sufficient cash in the vaults to meet all likely demands by depositors, instead of lending it out to every Tom, Dick, and Harry."

"Precisely," Derek said. "But will Government pass the necessary law to make the banks do it?"

Not on your life.

Government would never interfere with anything that makes money as long as it's half legal. That's all Hong

Kong is for—that's all Government is interested in. Take education. Take social welfare. Fuck you Jack I'm all right. Derek was started. Nothing would stop him now except his wife. She appeared and took him off to dance.

I got myself another drink. I saw Pills Carter with his new Chinese wife, Perfect Jade. Her English name was Marianne Carter. Pills was Government doctor at one of the civil servants' family clinics. Anything could happen if you went to see Pills Carter. Even the nurses called him Makee-Learnee. Pills had only come out to Hong Kong a year ago and he had taken to the Wanchai bars like a duck to water. Then his nurse, Perfect Jade, had got hold of him. "Hello, Pills," I said. "How's married life treating you?"

"I am like the first Maori who sighted Captain Cook's man-o'-war," Pills said. "That Maori didn't know what to make of it."

We were both laughing. Perfect Jade had not followed it, her English wasn't good enough. I guess Pills was pretty happy because he didn't stay sober enough to be miserable very long. I wondered what they talked about because Pills didn't speak Cantonese. But he was learning. Because his Chinese Mother-in-law and grandparents-in-law and Perfect Jade's two sisters and young brother had all moved into Pills's and Perfect Jade's government flat, and they didn't speak any English.

I saw Shirley.

"Hello, Shirl, how're you?"

"Hello, you awful man, all the worse for seeing you," Shirley said in her aggressive-plaintive Shirley way. She was tall and leggy with small breasts and an earnest Anglo-Saxon face. "I'm surprised to see you, I thought the police force couldn't function without you."

"The other guy and I take it in turns," I said.

"I didn't believe half those emergency calls you got, I'm sure you used to fake them so you could go off to your other mistresses."

"Not true, Shirley," I said patiently. "How's James?"

"He's very well, thank you. He doesn't cough in the morning from oversmoking or snore at night from over-drinking like *some* people I know."

"Say that a bit louder," I said, "not everybody heard it all."

She put her hand to her lovely mouth and giggled. Then stopped. 'James is gorgeous! All the things you're

110

not. You're just like every other dreadful Hong Kong person. You think you're different but you're absolutely typical. Hard-arsed, insincere, out for number one only."

"Am I?"

"It's true. This town is rotten to the core. Look at them in this room. All the women are on the pill, you can look at them. Sizing up, licking their chops. Bed. A party is *supposed* to be a pleasant gathering where you meet friendly people and have *in*teresting conversations and *wi*den your ho*ri*zons." Shirley glared accusingly.

"I take it you're not going to come back after your government contract is finished?"

"As if you care! Like hell I'm coming back. I'm going home to have a baby by the best all-round man I can find. I'll choose a good specimen and ask him to give me a baby. You think I'm crazy, don't you?"

"No," I said. I had heard all this too. "But you'll get married, Shirley, love."

"I won't get married in this rotten town," Shirley said. "They're all here for a few years just to have a good time. Who wants to marry a pain in the arse like stupid old shapeless me anyway—*you* didn't want to."

"Darling," I said, "I'm married already."

"You didn't even want to give me a baby! You *aren't* married, anyway, you've deserted your wife. I wouldn't mind if you'd left me to go back to *her*. She's beautiful and she's your *wife*, she has a *right*. But no. You left me for fat Veronica Brown."

"All right, Shirley," I said.

"All right, I'll go now. Now I've made you mad. I say, I am an ass. 'By."

I thought, Dear Shirley. I hope she gets a good baby. I saw Monica, the American black woman, talking to Sylvia. Sylvia was another schoolteacher, hard as nails. She was in big with the Americans. Often at cocktail bars. She got lots of presents from American officers, cameras, watches, pearls, radios. Sometimes she took money for it. But she only did it with a man she fancied, unless he was a Chinese taipan. Chinese pay big money for a blonde. I favored her myself. Black Monica was a model, or something to do with television. She was in with the pot-smoking crowd. Mattresses on the floor, candles, psychedelic lights, way-out music and everybody ended up screwing each other. Her teeth were very white. She was very loud and vivacious. I saw Hymie Rubenstein.

"How's things in the pig-bristle business, Hymie?" I said.

"Hello, Jacob," Hymie beamed. He was a good little fat happy Jew married to a little fat happy Chinese Jewess, called Rebecca. Hymie had converted her, her real name was Ming-ping. She was a very good Jewess now. "I know she don't *look* very Jewish," Hymie said, "but for a Chinese to give up pork, man that's *faith*." Hymie ate pork. "Moses never came to China," Hymie said. "Moses never tasted sweet-and-sour pork." Rebecca got very mad with Hymie about the sweet-and-sour pork. "He's a rotten Jew," Rebecca said, "that Hymie of mine is a no-good Jew." Hymie's family had been in the pig-bristle business in Shanghai, before the Liberation. Hymie had expanded the business to include wigs. Chinese hair is excellent for wigs. Four times a year Hymie went into China to buy communist hair and pig bristles.

"How's business in China?" I said.

"Chairman Mao's put the *oo* in shampoo," Hymie said. "The poor bastards have got to export something."

"Are things that bad?" I said.

Hymie shrugged, Jewish. "After the Great Leap Forward? Chairman Mao is letting the peasants farm small private lots after they've finished their day's work on the commune paddies. King Pig is back in business, each family is allowed to keep one pig now," Hymie said.

"For the time being," I said.

Hymie shrugged. "Make pig bristle while the sun shines, that's my motto. That's the Chinese motto too. Boy, are they working on those little after-hours private lots and King Piggy."

I said, "I wonder how long they'll be allowed to keep them."

"Who knows what's going on in China? I don't even understand my wife and she's *Jewish*, for Chrissakes!"

We went to get another drink and talked about China. Some China. Hymie knew a lot about China, he loved it like I do. China gets in your blood. Poor dear old China. Communism was still the best thing that had happened there, Hymie said. Mao Tse-tung was still the best thing that had happened to China. Even the Great Leap Forward was the right idea, it had failed because they had attempted too much too soon, too grand a vision. It would come right, the communists had learned their lesson. They had to compromise with the acquisitive instincts, provide incentive, *some* measure of private property. Like these private lots. There were also some free markets, now, where the peasants could sell their private produce, as well as state markets. Communism in China is going to take a middle road, Hymie said. I said I did not think so. The relaxation of the communes, these little private lots, was only a stop-gap measure, I thought. To placate the peasants and to help production. When the crisis was over, the private lots and King Pig would be confiscated again. Chairman Mao was too much of an idealist to compromise Marxism for long.

Hymie disagreed. You can't push a Chinese peasant too far, he said. The Chinese are bigger businessmen at heart than even the goddamn Jew, Hymie said. The communists will organize the Chinese into a socialist country, which is what it needs, but there'll be plenty of private enterprise in the end. Once a Chinese, always a Chinese. Not the youth, I said, Chairman Mao will work on the youth, propaganda, Mao thought, the young Chinese won't be like their parents. Christ yes, Hymie said, there's propaganda going the whole time up there, day and night. Last week I was staying at the state hotel in Canton, Hymie said, and my young waiter and I got along pretty well. When I was leaving to come back here he comes up to my room with a packet of rice. It was his own rice ration and he was giving it to me because he knew there was starvation in Hong Kong, it was a gift for my family. I tried to tell him there was no starvation in Hong Kong, but he didn't believe it, the communist propaganda machine told him Hong Kong people were dying like flies of starvation. Nothing would convince him. So eventually I had to take the rice, to give him face. I tried to give him something in return, but he refused it absolutely. When I got to the railway station the hotel clerk comes running after me with three cigarettes I had forgotten in my room. Hymie and I had had another drink and I was getting along with the whiskey. "We better get back to the party," Hymie said. "See you, Hymie," I said, "my love to Rebecca." "Come and have dinner sometime," Hymie said, "you're a goy with a few brains."

The party was swinging, a lot of people in open-neck shirts now. I made my way through toward the big patio. There were people standing everywhere in the hot night, clamor of voices, out there were the harbor lights. The women all looked very smart, very poised, very with it. Christ, what was the matter with me? I had half a dozen whiskeys inside me and there were women all over the place, good-looking bed-worthy women and say what you bloody like, McAdam, they aren't all hard-arsed, there are plenty just looking to meet people like you, somebody to like and be happy with and even to love, why the Christ can't you just walk in there and get with it and talk and be gay and you'll find somebody nice, why are you standing here leaning against this goddamn wall watching and feeling that nobody loves you. For Christ's sake, snap out of it and *try.* All right I shoved myself off the wall to go up to the first hard-arsed woman and say Hello I'm Jake McAdam I'm a policeman I've lived in the Far East nearly all my life How long have you been in Hong Kong How do you like it Please please please let's get the bullshit over——and I saw Mini-Max talking to Splinter Woodcock and Norbert and I made my way over to them.

They were talking about squash and losing weight. Norbert played squash to keep himself a perfect specimen. Norbert was, he said frankly, exactly according to the books. Spot on. Height, chest, waist, hips, thighs, calves, weight. He measured them frequently. And only two fillings in his teeth. Norbert was beautiful. Splinter Woodcock's superior officer had once written of him in his annual report: "This policeman is admittedly a policeman," because he could think of nothing else to say. He was a very thin policeman. Norbert's superior officer had written of him, "As a policeman he is conscientious, as a man he is insufferable." It was said that the only good thing about Norbert was he only went after Chinese women. If Norbert slept with more women then anybody he deserved it because he worked on it harder than anybody. Norbert never went for a drink with the boys, read a book, or went to a cinema because he simply did not have time. Norbert never drank alcohol nor smoked, because, he said, he needed to keep in perfect condition with a schedule like his. Mini-Max was needling Norbert, saying that he was surprised to see him here tonight, with a schedule like his.

"As a matter of fact I must be going," Norbert said, unembarrassed, for nothing embarrassed Norbert, "I have a rendezvous at eleven-thirty."

"Nothing here you fancy?" Mini-Max waved his hand.

"No *gwailo* women for me," Norbert smiled.

"Why not?" Mini-Max encouraged him.

"They can't hold a candle to the Chinese," Norbert said.

"Why not?" Mini-Max egged him on. Maybe once a year Norbert appeared in European public and we heard this.

"Examine even the best European woman," Norbert said, "and what do you find?"

"Insects?" I said.

"No. Norbert smiled patiently: "Hair."

"I'm crazy about bald women, myself," Mini-Max said and we were all laughing.

"Seriously," Norbert said, bringing the conversation to a serious note. "We're a hirsute race." He held up his finger: "But Chinese have the most smooth skin. This is what makes Chinese men unattractive to European women, by and large, and why Chinese youths are so attractive to European homosexuals. And why Chinese women are the most beautiful in the world. Smooth skin from top to toe. Whereas you take any European woman and what do you find?"

"Hair?"

"And another thing." Norbert held up his immaculate finger. "European women smell."

"Hirsute and malodorous?" Mini-Max encouraged him.

"They do," Norbert insisted. "It's the dairy products we eat. Chinese think we smell."

"Do they think *you* smell?" I said.

"No," Norbert said, "I don't eat dairy products any more because of that."

"Can you smell us now?" Mini-Max said, interested.

"Frankly, yes," Norbert said. "But I'm used to it."

"Jesus," Mini-Max said.

"Principally their fannies," Norbert said seriously. "You show me a European woman who doesn't smell down there a few hours after a shower—but a Chinese girl? You can send her on a route march for a week, their whole metabolism is superior——"

"Let's get another beer," Splinter Woodcock said. Maybe he said it to change the subject, Splinter being a good Catholic, but that was about all Splinter ever said. If Splinter Woodcock didn't smell of dairy products it was because Splinter only ate every second day or so. Splinter didn't even have a can of beans in his refrigerator, only San Miguel. Splinter owned shares in San Miguel Breweries. Buying those shares was probably the only sensible thing Splinter had ever done, because his money came back to him. Splinter did not go to a bar to chat with the boys or to look at the girls, he went there to drink San Miguel. Splinter liked sitting near the cashier's till. Not a Wanchai bar girl knew Splinter, but every cashier gave him a big hello. When he had drunk so much of his company's fine product that he could not say good-by properly, Splinter got laid. Splinter was a good Catholic. Fornication is a mortal sin; fornication blind drunk, however, is only a venial sin. In every way his money came back to him. Those shares were very important to Splinter. I followed him back toward the kitchen, where the beer machine was. Splinter particularly loved beer machines, all you did was pull a handle and out came wonderful beer. I was surprised he was so far from the machine as the verandah. I was feeling pretty good now. As I passed through the lounge, I looked around for some woman to go for. I looked straight into the eyes of Catherine across the crowded room and I felt my heart lurch and for a moment everything stood still. She came toward me and the party noise came back in my ears.

"Hello," she smiled nervously.

"Hello, Catherine."

My heart was thumping. I felt people were watching us. "I didn't expect to see you here tonight," she was saying, but it was apologetic.

"I still have some friends," I said. "Is he here?" Oh Jesus Christ, I didn't want to see them together.

"Darling, can I talk to you a moment?" I could feel my heart and the anger in my guts. "Let's go to the bedroom."

I turned and walked down the passage, she following me. The bedroom was dark and the bed was full of coats. I closed the bedroom door behind her and then leaned against the door, in the dark.

"Yes?" I said. "Catherine."

She hesitated in the dark.

"Jake? I just want to tell you something before you hear it from anybody else."

My heart was pounding. "What?"

She took a breath. "Darling? I'm going away. Suzie and I."

I stared in the dark. "Going away?" Oh God Jesus. *"Where,* for Godsake? You can't take Suzie away." "I wanted to shout it. "You can't take Suzie away from Hong Kong where I can't see her!"

"Darling"—she squeezed my arm—"it's best for all of us, especially for Suzie. Jake? Please listen: David's newspaper has posted him to London, and we're all going together."

I stared at her. "You want to marry him?"

She nodded in the half-light, yes yes. "Oh Jake, don't you see, it's much better for all of us, specially for Suzie to have a proper home again—"

Oh God, *home.* I heard myself say, "He's married already."

She said: "He's going to get a divorce when he gets to England."

Oh God. I heard myself say, "And you? You'll want one of those too."

"Darling?" She squeezed my arm in the dark. "Don't be bitter."

"Oh no, I'm not bitter! I'm only Suzie's father!" My voice felt thick.

She still held my arm. "Jake, I'm sorry. Let's talk about it sensibly on Monday."

"No." I was angry, hate-filled. "How can we leave Suzie till Monday, for Godsake! You've just told me you want to take my child far away, for Godsake. We'll talk about it right now! Oh God!" I walked to the window and I wanted to sob out loud. "When, for Godsake?"

She said hesitantly across the room behind me, "Possibly Christmas. New Year at the latest. It depends on his head office."

"Christmas." Oh God, *Christ*mas. I turned around to face her. Her eyes were glistening too. I was shaking, my throat thick. I heard myself say: "And will his bloody wife give him a divorce? Or are you going to live in sin forever? With my child?"

"I'm not living in sin," she quavered.

Jesus, I hated her. "You will in London. Or do you intend living in an Earl's Court bed-sitter with a goddamn gas ring? With my child?" She didn't say anything. Oh God Jesus, I hated her. "Well? Will she give him a divorce?"

She took a big breath. "He thinks so. They've been separated for four years."

117

"He *thinks* so. Christ, I've seen plenty of those."

Oh God oh God oh God, I took a big breath and felt it quiver. "And you?"

She said urgently, "Jake? Isn't this better for Suzie? And us? You're still her father, she can come out here to you every school holiday when she's bigger and you can always see her in London, darling. . . ."

Oh God, my child. "Supposing his wife doesn't give him your precious divorce."

"She will."

"He thinks."

"Darling, don't make it harder than it is. You can't stop me."

"Can't I?"

She pleaded, "No, darling, you can't. Please don't let's talk about lawyers. . . ."

"But you've been to see one, haven't you? And how much of the truth did you tell the good man? And what did he advise?"

Oh God. I sat down on the bed in the dark and held my head and I wanted to cry out loud. Love and hate and fight and pity. It was very confused. Fear and love and oh God Hong Kong for ever and ever and no more Suzie and no more Catherine, no more no more Suzie not even once a week no more ice cream no more Daddy Daddy no more Christmas and the house in Happy Valley all empty and I would sell it empty *empty*—. She put her hand on my shoulder and I wanted to sob out loud. I took a deep breath and held it hard to squeeze back the tears. "Answer my question: What do you propose trying to do about your precious side of it? Your divorce?"

She stood in front of me in the dark.

"Let's cross that bridge when we come to it, after David's divorce."

I said, "A clean break. Now! That's the only way, for Godsake!"

She said cold-bloodedly, tender, "Will you divorce me, Jake? You're the one with the grounds."

"You've also got plenty of grounds now, Mrs. Mc-Adam."

She said in the dark, kindly, unhurt, "Two wrongs don't make a right."

That she could talk like that, that I hadn't hurt her! "Is that what your bloody lawyer told you?"

"I haven't been to see a lawyer, Jake. David has, unofficially, just a friend."

David. I hated the sonofabitch. I hoped they suffered, that his wife would not give the bastard a divorce—I said, "Yes, I'll give you a divorce. Gladly."

God, I could feel her relief, her gratefulness and Jesus I hated her, I had not hurt her with that "Gladly." I had only made her happy.

She said quietly, "Thank you, darling."

"Don't call me darling." I wanted to shout and fight and cry. I stood there.

She said hesitantly, "I'm sorry, Jake. When will you start? Proceedings."

Proceedings.

"Never. *You* can proceed against *me* if that's what you want. Proceed against me in England or Timbuktu or wherever his bloody newspaper is. When you do, I'll give it to you on a plate, I'll give you all the evidence your bloody lawyer wants. Just don't ask me to do your dirty work of going to court for you as well."

I could hear her relief, oh how I hated it.

"Darling, let's cross that bridge when we come to it," she said.

Oh, God, this is what it feels like, and I thought I was ready for it.

"Jake?" she took a breath. "You won't have to pay for anything."

I turned on her. "I'll pay! I'm not having him pay me for my woman." I went for the door. I said harshly: "And I'll pay for Suzie. I'm not having her call any other man father."

I flung open the door. I looked back at her. The noise of the party flooded in. I was trembling.

"Jake, I'm sorry."

I pressed my thumb and forefinger on my eyes. I wanted to run and sob out loud. She was crying.

"Good luck, darling," she cried.

CHAPTER 15

Now I do not remember many of the details of that long bad summer. I took some leave and Mini-Max and I flew to Manila for a week. Their police looked after us very well and showed us the town, where anything goes, even more than Hong Kong. Another time Max and I and Teetotal took a week and went to Pattaya, down on the Gulf of Siam, which is a lovely place and it also has some good bars, but we agreed there's nothing to beat the Filipina girls. Another time I had to fly to Singapore to bring back an accused who had poisoned his wife and cemented her body behind the kitchen sink, a very messy investigation. There was an international police conference held in Tokyo which my superintendent and I attended representing Hong Kong police, which was a bloody good booze-up, and the Tokyo police really showed us around. A couple of weekends I went with Max to stay with his family in Macao, the Portuguese colony forty miles away across the river Pearl, in their gracious old colonial house upon the knoll. A lot of weekends I went out on the junk and I always took a girl. It is not hard to get a girl to come out with you on a junk for a weekend, all you have to say is, "I'm going fishing, bring a book and come." Sometimes I took several couples. We had a pretty good time.

After work I went to have a drink. Mostly I went first to the girlie bars. I wanted the noise of the jukebox and the sailors and the girls. I liked the first few drinks alone. Later I went to the other bars, when I wanted people to talk to. I never went to the Foreign Correspondents' Club any more, which is the best club in Hong Kong for everything, for conversation and meeting people and hearing what the China-watchers thought was happening, in case I saw her there with him. Nothing much was happening in China anyway, they were still pulling themselves up by their bootstraps after the Great Leap Forward. There was going to be famine this winter. The people were still being told to find out what roots and grasses they could eat. The Hong Kong Marine Police were still engaged on their massive defense blockade to arrest the Macao snake boats, and the loaded stolen People's junks, and the swimmers, and the People's Liberation Army gunboats and border guards were still shooting them. It would go on a long time.

Sometimes I went to the Dateline or the Seventh Heaven, where a lot of newspapermen hung out and we talked China, but when they adjourned on to the Foreign Correspondents' Club I stayed behind. Later I had some dinner. I do not mind drinking alone, but I do not like having dinner alone. When you have dinner alone too much you really begin to think. At the least you think, What is this, what have you become that you eat alone, that your life is such a mess that you end up eating alone? And at the worst you think of home, where eating should be done. When you dine alone it really reminds you of many things.

Sometimes I went over to Tsimshatsui to Mr. O's Oriental International for Filipina girls, or to the Aunt Lilly Ng's, in Causeway Bay, which was very exclusive and very expensive. Aunt Lilly Ng's establishment was run on the lines of a high-class Western cathouse out of the twenties, very high heels and diamond-mesh stockings and red frilly garters and bustles and orchestra and all, no *cheongsams* at Aunt Lilly's; it was check your coat, go to the bar, take your choice, and absolute satisfaction guaranteed at Aunt Lilly Ng's: it was more exclusive than the Hong Kong Club.

And sometimes I had a date. Some of them were very nice indeed, and we laughed and joked and I turned on the McAdam charm, and I suppose we had a good time, and sometimes she let me into her bed. Sometimes we went out several times. And an analysis would show that I had a pretty good time, and that I could have had a very good time indeed if only I had pursued the right opportunities and played it right, and forced myself to straighten out and lived harder somehow and more thoughtlessly; I do remember that almost every girl I met I thought: What would it be like to be married to you? And God knows I wanted to find such a person to love and sometimes for a short while I tried, and then it was no good.

What I remember well is the waking up early. No matter how late I went to bed. Outside it was still black, the lights of the Kowloon across the harbor, ship lights, stars, dead quiet. And suddenly I was wide awake and I was thinking. I got up straightaway and I could not shower because of the water rationing, but I tipped a bucket of water over myself, I made coffee with the hi-fi blaring and got dressed and I went down to headquarters while it was still only reddening in the east, and started work. It was nice driving down the mountain in the dawn, the streets so quiet. I did not like my apartment, identical with every apartment in the Hermitage, same layout, same view, same furniture. I had nothing of home in it except Suzie's portrait and the hi-fi. I had not done any painting for a long time.

At the office I made coffee and I had done most of the day's paper work before ten o'clock. I would have preferred to have my own police station again, where there is always some investigation to supervise, even if it's just a robbery of a wristwatch, but at least in Special Investigations you get the unusual stuff, abortions, a bit of counterfeiting, the odd swindle, unlicensed medical practice, the odd homicide, gambling racket, confidence trick, tax evasion, unseaworthy ships. In Special Investigations we were supposed to be the experts who could be called in by any station or any government department to take over any unusual investigation, but usually I had caught up as far as I could go with the paper work by ten o'clock. Then I gave my junior inspectors a hard time, demanding to see their work. I went out on almost every officer's investigation personally. It did not make me very popular and I did not care. It is not hard to be a superbly efficient policeman when you cannot sleep. I made my bastards superbly efficient because I could not sleep. We did not get one single acquittal that summer.

When I had finished the paper work I read the newspapers. I got all the Hong Kong papers, and the London *Times* and *Time* and *Newsweek* and the *Oriental Economic Review*. I did not want to have time to think, and maybe I was succeeding but what I remember most about that summer is thinking that I was no good at it. The worst part was the knowing when they were going. Not knowing when, and the waiting for her to telephone to tell me it was next month, that I only had another month to see my child.

The summer went like that. I met Catherine once for lunch, to discuss Susan, for her to impress upon me, satisfy

122

me, that Mr. David Burton was a good man, a kind man, that he was very good to Suzie, really a very suitable step-father for Suzie, I mustn't worry about Mr. Burton and Suzie. In September she telephoned me to ask me to sign certain forms for a separate passport for Suzie, and I felt the panic.

"When are you leaving?"

"I don't know yet, darling."

"What does she need a separate passport for? She's only four, she's on your passport, I'm not having her going anywhere without you. I'm not allowing her to be sent off to friends and relations while you live it up in the Riviera—"

"Jake, dear," she said, "please be reasonable. How is she going to fly out to Hong Kong to spend her summer holidays with you without a passport?"

On Tuesday and Friday afternoons I saw Suzie, on Catherine's bridge-club days. Usually I took her to the beach and we played in the sand making castles and we put seashells and seaweed on the battlements and moats, and we talked all the time. I tried to teach her to swim, holding her under her belly, little skinny chest in my hands, she kicked and thrashed her arms and twisted her face all screwed up from side to side puffing and blowing; and I swam with her on my back and carried her on my shoulders, splashing. Sometimes she wanted to go to the botanical gardens instead, to play on the swings and merry-go-rounds, but I preferred to take her to the beach. At the botanical gardens she was always on the swings and merry-go-rounds and I could not talk to her so much, and touch her and feel her breath. She was always over-excited and she had no time to talk and play with me at the botanical gardens. On the beach she was always close and I loved to hear her talking, how her mind was working, and I could easily reach out and touch her, feel her little arm and skinny back and shoulders, and I could take her in my arms and hug her and feel her breath panting on my face, there is no grander feeling than your child in your arms, your very own child. And afterward we sat at the beach café and I drank a beer and she ate ice cream and Seven-Up as she wanted, and I encouraged her to talk about all the things that went on in her head, I loved to hear her talk. When it was sundown I had to take her home again, to Happy Valley. I kissed her good-by, and she was all excited now about getting home, sticky ice-cream mouth and sweet little breath and the feel of her arms around my neck, and then she was gone. Scrambling happy out the car, running home to her mother. I watched her run up the steps into the old terraced house, full of ice cream and beach and sunshine, and she was no longer thinking of me.

In October the cooler days came. In October the People's Republic of China opened the sluice gates and filled our reservoirs, in terms of our contract with them, and we could bathe every day again, and then the last day of October Catherine wrote me a letter. She wrote because she did not want to confront me: She told me they were leaving on the second of January.

The next day it was November, and the summer was over, and already the shops in Central were putting up their reindeer and Bethlehems and Wise Men and Santa Clauses and it was getting bleak, and next month it would be Christmas.

CHAPTER 16

At the end of that November I noticed the tail following me one evening. I went into the Mandarin Hotel and telephoned Catherine, shaking. Ah Chan told me Missie had gone to the Foreign Correspondents' Club with Master. *Master!* I telephoned the FCC. I could hear a carol being sung at the bar. I was shaking. "What do you mean by having a tail follow me?"

"Tail?" she said.

I had to keep my voice down and it shook. "A small inefficient Chinese gentleman with spectacles from some shyster private detective agency, he sticks out a goddamn mile."

"Oh Jake, I'm sorry."

"Why, for Christ's sake, Catherine? I told you I'd give you a divorce when you wanted it, I'll give you a bloody confession affidavit of adultery, who do you have to put a sordid private eye on to me?"

"Darling," she said, "where are you?"

"At the Mandarin, just answer me!"

"I'll call you from another phone."

I waited, shaking. She called back in half a minute.

"Jake? Will you listen to me, darling? Without interrupting? I'm sorry but I went to see a solicitor— "

"Who?"

"Please, Jake. And I explained everything, and he said I should get evidence *before* I leave the Colony because a confession from you is not enough, there has to be other evidence to corroborate it—"

I shouted, "You said we'd cross that bridge later—"

She cried urgently: "Jake—I'm *not* starting a divorce now, David isn't even divorced yet! All I'm doing is what the lawyer said, that I should just get the formal evidence so that if you chuck in your job here or go to Fiji or something it's not difficult, that's what the lawyer said—"

The next night I went for a drink at the Ocean, then at the Pussycat. At nine o'clock I took a cab down to the Star Ferry.

I took a seat at the back. When we got to Kowloon side, and the gangway was lowered and everybody began filing off the boat, I sat where I was. Everybody filed over the gangplank except one man. I waited till the last passenger, then got up. He got up also. I walked toward the gangway. I heard him following me. Then I sat down again. That threw him.

He didn't know what to do. He sat down suddenly in another seat. The new passengers were coming aboard now. I got up and walked back to my man, stood over him. He looked at me, very embarrassed, then looked away. He was young, skinny in a teddy suit and dark glasses. I said, "Which private detective agency do you work for?"

He ignored me, blushing. Passengers were coming toward us. I sat down beside him. I said quietly: "I'm going to make it easy for you. I've got some very valuable information for you. But I want to tell your boss first. What's the name of your agency?"

He looked at me worriedly. I was very much bigger than him.

"We are not supposed to say, sir."

"To whom can I give this vital information?" I plucked off his dark glasses.

He blinked. "Please tell me, sir."

"I will tell you when I'm satisfied who it is you work for."

He said, agonized, "Sincere Detectives Limited, sir."

"Thanks." I got up and walked for the gangplank, leaving him astonished. He hurried after me. I stopped at the rail till the gangway went up. I could feel him standing agitatedly behind me. The bell went and the moorings were cast off. As the ferry began to move, I vaulted over the rail and down onto the quay. It was as easy as that to get rid of him.

The next day it was raining, mean cold fine seeping misty China winter rain.

I took the elevator to the seventh floor. There was a short corridor. The signs of doctors Pang and Sui, the Good Wind Trading Company, the Fook Lee Import-Export Agency. And a red door, with two bright circular shields above it. One read *Association of British Detectives*, around the Union Jack, and the other said *World Secret Service Association*. On the door was written: *Sincere Detective Agency, Director Ho Fook-sing, Governor, Southeast Asia*. I opened the red door. There were three small desks. Some framed testimonials written in Chinese, some photographs of Chinese people beaming at each other shaking hands. There was a big red wall altar to Kwan Dai, the martial god of valor, with some mandarin oranges as offering, and joss sticks burning. At the end was a bamboo screen. Two detectives were sitting doing nothing.

"May I see the Governor, Southeast Asia," I said.

They motioned me to the bamboo screen. There, behind a desk with an empty in-basket and an empty out-basket and two telephones and more framed testimonials and photographs and two more shields, sat the Governor, Southeast Asia. He looked up at me round-faced, blankly. I said, "You have got one of your *fokis* following me."

The Governor, Southeast Asia, stared. I said, "You're going to save your time and my money. Your detective couldn't catch a cold."

The Governor, Southeast Asia, stared at me.

"McAdam is my name," I said. "Well here is your information. Tonight at eight o'clock I will be at the Lotus Hotel, Room Twenty-two, seventeenth floor, Chungking Mansion, Nathan Road, Kowloon. Do you think you can remember all that?"

He stared at me.

"Make a note!" I snapped.

The Governor, Southeast Asia, grabbed a pencil. "I'll repeat that," I said unkindly.

"Thank you," the Governor, Southeast Asia, said.

I repeated it. "I will leave my door unlocked. At eight-fifteen sharp your detective will fling open the door. He will see me with a young lady in bed. The door will then be slammed in his face. Your detective will then go away. Do you understand all that?"

The Governor, Southeast Asia, nodded quickly.

"And if you make a mess of it, Christ help you. And if I catch you following me once more after tonight, Christ help you."

The Governor, Southeast Asia, blinked at me flatly. Blushing.

"Tonight," I said. "And Kwan Dai help you if you're not there." I slammed the door behind me.

When I got back to the station I telephoned King Winky. I told King Winky what I wanted. White, and she had to understand. King Winky said she would understand, all right. I said to lay on a bottle of whiskey, I did not feel like going through this sober. King Winky understood. Everybody understood.

CHAPTER 17

The arcade was all lit up with Christmas lights. Everything is sold somewhere in Chungking Mansion, anything at all. The walls were crammed with signboards.

I rode up in the elevator with three American sailors and three Chinese apartment girls. The girls wore false eyelashes. The sailors were probably on a ten-day package deal. They could drink as much as they liked free, and change their woman every day, depending on the deal. The elevator stopped and the three sailors and their girls got out, for the April Blossom Apartment House. There was a bamboo curtain and pink concealed lighting.

The doors opened on the seventeenth floor and there was the Lotus Hotel. I went to the reception desk.

"I have a reservation," I said to the *foki* in English.

He led me down the passage to Room 22.

"I'm expecting a lady to call at eight o'clock," I said. I tipped him ten dollars.

There was a good view of Hong Kong Harbor. There was the Peak with its yellow lights. I could see Happy Valley mid levels. I turned from the window and went to the bathroom. It was tiled. I looked at myself in the mirror and my face was taut and I could feel my heart thudding, sick. I opened the half-jack of whiskey and poured a glass half full, took a big gulp and screwed up my eyes to stop thinking. There was a knock on the door. I scrambled in my pockets for a cigarette. I opened the door. The *foki* was standing with a blonde. "Lady to see you, sir," the *foki* said.

I said, "Good to see you, come in."

"Hello." She walked in. I shut the door. She was looking around. She was quite tall and she wore a two-piece suit and high heels.

"Sit down," I said. "Miss—?"

"Sheila."

"Would you like a drink?"

"Ever met an Aussie who wouldn't?" She was about twenty-eight and she was not bad-looking, dyed blond. She sat down on the bed and crossed her legs.

I was pouring the drink shakily.

"What part of Australia?"

"Shall we say Sydney?"

"Okay, Sydney."

"And you're a pommy, right? What are you, a copper or something?"

"I'm in the import-export business," I said.

"Oh sure," she said. "They're all in the import-export business."

"What made you think I was a copper?"

"You look like a goddamn copper. All cops got that same look." She tapped my chest. "And you're wearing a gun, yeah. You're either a copper or a crook. But then all cops are crooks."

"Yes?"

"You should see them in Sydney." Her smile was nice. I looked at my watch.

"You understand about tonight?"

"Relax. You want a divorce."

128

"I don't want to compromise any of my friends," I said. I felt sick in my guts.

"That's the British for you. An Aussie would compromise *all* his friends."

"You realize you'll be mentioned in court?"

"I'll be far away when the shit hits the fan."

"It'll be a very quiet case." I pulled out four one-hundred Hong Kong dollar bills and gave them to her. My hands were shaking. "Tonight is just a formality." It seemed unreal.

"How formal do you want to be? Is he going to catch us before, during, or after?"

"Before."

"Suit yourself. I don't suppose you exactly feel like performing. What do you want me to do?"

"Take off your clothes and lie down."

"Okay, action, stations." She took off her coat and turned her back on me; pulled her blond hair off her neck. "Unhook me, please."

I unhooked the eye.

She stepped out of her dress and put it on the chair. She unhitched her bra, kicked off her shoes, and pulled down her panties. I took off my shirt, trousers, shoes, and socks.

"Right," she said. "Let the show begin. How much time we got?"

"Five minutes, about."

She stepped onto the bed, jumped up and down once to test the springs and lay down, arms and hair outflung. "How do I look, sport? Like the Other Woman?"

"Fine." I felt sick right in my heart.

"You better come to bed, Romeo."

I took a breath, then lay down beside her.

"What?"

"I said shouldn't you take your underpants off?"

"No," I said.

"Have it your own way, sport. No extra charge."

I lay there.

"Hey." She turned on her side and put her hand on my chest. "You feel pretty bad, don't you?"

I didn't say anything.

"Why do you do it then?" She said it kindly. "You haven't got to do anything, you know."

"I know."

"Don't do it if you don't want to. Just get up and lock the door, as easy as that."

Oh God. "It's got to be done."

She lay on her side and looked at me.

"Too much water under the bridge, huh?"

She lay back. "Keep talking," I said. I felt my voice shake. "Anything. How long have you been in Hong Kong?"

"Everybody in Hong Kong asks that question. Doesn't anybody here regard this place as home?"

"I do."

"Dinkum? Where were you born?"

"Shanghai."

"Old China hand, huh? I've been here six months."

"Where do you work?"

"I'm in the import-export business."

"Really," I said.

"Really. Mornings only. Typist. It makes me a legal resident."

"Isn't the money any good?"

"The money's perfectly good. Not much of it but what there is is perfectly good legal tender. *There.* I made you smile."

"How long you been doing this?"

"As soon as I found out how much money there is for a bum Aussie typist in this town."

"How did you get on to it?"

"A nice girl like me. Just lucky, I guess."

"Really." I smiled.

"Easiest thing in the world. Hang around the bars and coffee shops and pretty soon some Chinese gentleman will offer you a job as a hostess in his club."

"How long are you staying?"

"Next month. Going home. Spent a year in England. Hitchhiked around Europe. The usual."

"Enjoy it?"

"Europe's beaut. You can stick London."

"Where do you live?"

"In a flat."

"Alone?"

"Come on. You know rents in this town. A few of us."

"Where's your flat?"

"Come on. I don't mind talking to an unhappy customer but I'm not going to blow all my cover to a cop I just met."

130

"I'm in the import-export business," I said.

"Sure, they're all in the import-export business. You'd be surprised who's in the import-export business in this town. Half the top government brass are in the import-export business it seems."

"Yeah?"

"Come on. Half the top communists too. Everybody's in the import-export business."

"You meet lots of interesting people," I said.

"You'd be surprised."

I looked at my watch.

"Stop thinking about it, just let it happen," she said. "Talk."

There was a knock on the door, I stiffened. She put her arms around me quickly. "There he is," she whispered.

I shook my head. I was shaking. "No, he'll throw open the door. It must be the hotel *foki*. Go away!" I said loudly in Cantonese.

There was another knock.

"Jesus." I swung off the bed. "Cover yourself." I went to the door angrily. I flung it open. "Yes?"

There stood the detective. He took a step back nervously and tried to smile.

"Good evening, sir," he whispered.

I stared at him. I was shaking angry.

"You aren't supposed to knock, you idiot!"

He took another step back. "Sir?"

"You fool!" I hissed in Cantonese. "You're supposed to burst in the door!"

He looked ready to run. "Thank you," he blushed.

I was shaking. "Come here." I grabbed him by the shoulder and pulled him back to the doorway.

"You see that lady!" I pointed. She was laughing. "Stop laughing, for Chrissake!"

"I'm sorry," she giggled.

"You see that lady." I glared at the detective. "She's my girl friend! She's naked under that bedspread! Pull the bedspread down a bit and show the fool!"

She pulled it down to show one nipple, and waved at him.

"And I'm in my underpants, notice that! Now get out there"—I shoved him out the door—"and in ten seconds burst in, take a look, and get the hell out!"

I slammed the door on him and strode back to bed. She was lying there with her hand over her mouth, shak-

131

ing. "Cut that out." I ripped back the bedspread and got down beside her. "I'm sorry," she giggled, she put her arms around me.

"All right, sir?" the detective whispered outside the door.

"Oh Jesus—*yes!*" I shouted.

The door flew open, a head shot in, shot out. "Thank you," it gasped and the door slammed shut.

I lay there. She was holding me tight, shaking, trying not to laugh. "God," my voice shook, "would you believe it?"

She burst out laughing into my shoulder. I swung my legs off the bed and sat up. I took a gulp of whiskey and my hand was trembling. I lit a cigarette, inhaled deep and blew it down to the floor hard. She got onto her knees and put her arm around my neck.

"Come on, sport. It's over now."

I didn't say anything.

"Tell me about it if you like."

I took a big breath and shook my head.

"Shall I get dressed?"

"If you like."

"It's if you like. Do you want to get drunk?"

"No. Thank you."

"Come on," she said, "it's Christmas."

"Christmas," I said.

"All right, I'll go now, if that's okay."

"Okay," I said to the floor. "Thank you very much. You've been very kind."

"It was easy. Thank *you.*"

After she had gone, I got dressed.

Outside it was cold and sleeting. There were Christmas lights everywhere in Nathan Road and the taxis were all full because of the rain. I did not know what to do or where to go. I did not want to go to a bar alone and think. I had drunk over half a bottle of whiskey and it did not feel that anything would make me drunker, and I did not want to go back to my cold naked government bachelor flat. I started walking down Nathan Road for the Star Ferry. I was going to the office, to work. It seemed like the office was all I had. The sleet soaked my suit and I did not care and maybe it was tears running down my face.

Of course, a lot of other things happened that December night, the Year of the Hungry Tiger. Twenty-three

132

Freedom Swimmers set out into the cold China Sea across Mirs Bay and Deep Bay and nineteen made it. A taxi driver got robbed by three squaddies from one of Her Majesty's regiments. An average of 2.9 people committed suicide as usual. Eleven Chinese ladies, eight Chinese men, and six Chinese courting couples were robbed at knife point by a total of forty-seven youths of twenty-one wristwatches and $532.40. Mr. Wu Ho-ping was killed by a bus. An American serviceman paid $190 Hong Kong instead of $1.90 for his taxi fare and thought, "How much is that in real money?" Mui Sai-sai who was seven, was sold by her father into concubinage for $1,000 Hong Kong. One jewelry shop, one goldsmith shop, and two Chinese restaurants were held up at gunpoint, a total of nearly $750,000 taken. Narcotics Bureau knocked over seven opium divans and caught six proprietors, ten *fokis*, and sixty-one addicts diving out of windows and legging across rooftops. Six snake junks carrying a total of 327 illegal immigrants set sail from Macao, having paid between them $320,700 Hong Kong for the forty-mile trip, which is nice work if you can get it. Mr. Chan Fu-wai smote his wife's head open with a meat cleaver. Some $5,800,000 dollars were lost and won illegally at Mah-Jongg and fan-tan. A woman jumped off the top of a re-settlement block, bringing the annual average up slightly above 2.9 a day. An Australian tourist ordered sweet-and-sour pork and got sweet-and-sour cat and said it was beaut tucker much better than Melbourne. There was a landslide at Ma Toi Squatter Area, eight huts and twenty-nine people were buried. A syndicate of five communist fat cats had a bachelor night for some gentlemen of the import-export business in their syndicated Causeway Bay Penthouse, consisting of French champagne, Shanghainese food, and English blue movies, followed by one live lesbian exhibition by two American girls, one heterosexual exhibition by two Chinese, and one bisexual foursome from the Philippines. A shipment of seventeen hundred-weight of raw opium hidden in a cargo of refrigerators arrived on the M.S. *Patel* from Calcutta and the Narcotics Bureau and the Preventive Service both missed it. They also missed two million dollars' worth of low-grade heroin concealed in a shipment of one-pound pickle jars and toothpaste tubes. One of the six snake junks from Macao was fired on and sunk by the People's Liberation gunboat. Two of the others were arrested by the Hong Kong Marine Police and were towed back to China waters and handed over to another People's Liberation gunboat. Another snake junk dumped its seventy-three passengers on a remote colony island at gunpoint and told them that sampans would be sent for them in one hour to take them safely to the Golden Mountain Where Men Eat Fat Pork. On one chicken farm in the New Territories, in one godown in Sai Ying Pun, in one cockloft in Cheung Chau, and in fourteen heavily guarded upper- and lower-middle- and middle-class apartments a total of twenty-two tons of sticky black raw opium was being processed over cooking stoves into heroin and a total of eighty-seven girls were putting it into half-ounce cellophane packets worth an average two dollars Hong Kong a throw on the streets. Pang Wai-kit waited for Sing Mui-po to come up in the elevator and threw a mug of sulfuric acid in her face because she had jilted him. Divisional Detective Inspector Jacob McAdam went back to his Special Investigations Office. Miss Tsang Ying-ling, communist school-mistress of the Tai Ping Middle School, walked into the Heavenly Restaurant and then dialed 999.

CHAPTER 18

By the time I got to the Heavenly Restaurant, there were Uniformed Branch constables everywhere. On the third floor more constables, a lot of nervous *fokis* and customers, a very nervous manager, an outraged young Chinese woman, my young Chinese inspector. I looked into the kitchen to make sure constables were guarding it, then I turned to the inspector. "Where're the monkeys?"

"Over there." The young Chinese woman pointed angrily at a screen.

"Are you the informant, madam?"

"Yes," she said emphatically.

I recognized her. The communist schoolmistress surveying the situation quote unquote up in the Closed Area with her dog six months ago. She did not appear to recognize me.

"Is the monkey still alive?"

"Yes, sir," the inspector said. "But two dead already."

I went behind the screen. A dozen Chinese men were sitting around a circular table. In the center of the table was a hole. Through the hole protruded the monkey's shaved head. It looked at me with big frightened eyes and blinked. Next to it lay the little silver hammer for cracking its skull open, the jug of hot oil for pouring onto its brain, the teaspoons for scooping it out. There were bits of skull and blood from the first two monkeys. An expensive dinner party. "Is this how they were seated when you arrived?"

"Yes," the inspector said. "I ordered them to remain seated. That one is the host."

I said to the photographer, "Get some wide-angle shots from four different positions, showing everybody, including the monkey. Then get some close-ups of the monkey plus"—I pointed—"the hammer, the oil, the teaspoons, and these bits of skull."

The host said to me in Cantonese, "We do not wish to be photographed, we want to get up."

"That's too bad, Firstborn. You're all liable to be charged." I said to the photographer. "Quickly." There was a bright silver flash as his first picture went. I said to the inspector, "Got all their names?"

"Yes, sir."

"After the photos, go around the table clockwise and collect each one of those bowls in front of each one, label them one, two, three, et cetera, same with the teaspoons, for laboratory analysis, we want to be able to prove they all ate some of it if we can. Collect the hammer, the oil, all the chips of skull, the tablecloth, and the table. Then get them around to SIO. Plus these people."

The photographer's flashes were going off, the monkey was struggling in terror at them. I lifted the corner of the cloth and looked under the table. There was the rest of the monkey, trussed into the cage under the hole.

"And photograph the cage under the table. Then unscrew the cage, but keep the monkey in it until we've got somewhere to put him."

"I'm a member of the SPCA." Miss Tsang spoke up loudly behind me. "We have a twenty-four-hour service."

"Thank you, that's a good idea." Miss Tsang was smoldering brightly.

I said to the inspector, "Which were the waiters involved?"

"Out there, sir."

"Have you arrested them yet?"

"No, sir."

"Good, we may want one as a Crown witness. Take them back."

"You must arrest them all," Miss Tsang said hotly right behind me. "They are all criminals in this case." —

I looked at her. She was following me everywhere to make sure I did the job properly.

"Thank you, Miss Tsang." I said to the inspector, "This is the restaurant owner?"

"Yes."

"Have you arrested and cautioned him?"

"Yes, sir."

I looked at him, a small fat Cantonese, looking at me sulkily nervous. "Barbaric," I said in Cantonese. I heard Miss Tsang seethe with agreement behind me. "Where are the dead monkeys?"

"In the kitchen, sir," the inspector said.

We went into the kitchen. It was small, hot, steamy, odoriferous, cooking everywhere. Off the kitchen were the toilets. In any other British territory the Medical Officer of Health would have condemned the restaurant for that, but in Hong Kong it is said the closer the toilet is to the kitchen, the better the food. The two dead monkeys were lying on a tiled table, guarded by a constable. Their skulls were opened up like emptied boiled eggs. First the monkey's head is shaved, then it is installed on the table alive. The waiter cracks the skull open with a silver hammer, peels open the brain. The hot oil is poured on the brain, the diners dip their teaspoons in and eat, like a boiled egg.

"Photograph them. Get a few general shots of the kitchen too. Then put the monkeys in plastic bags, then take them to the mortuary and stick them in the fridge for the government vet."

"Yes, sir."

"Any more?" I walked through the kitchen. Miss Tsang followed us. I wanted to tell her to stay back in the restaurant but decided to let it go. There was a wire cage with seven black chow puppies in it. They were three or four weeks old, plump, gamboling.

"Oh God. Seen this?"

"Yes, sir."

A puppy yawned squeakily, wagging his tail, then they

136

all started yapping. I stuck my finger through the wire and they were all over it. I opened the cage and picked one out and it wriggled in delight, trying to lick my face. The inspector grinned at me nervously. I thought, You like to eat dog too, don't you, Inspector; you think the British are crazy, don't you? "You like dog, Inspector?" I said.

"Yes, sir."

"I mean, eating dog."

He blushed. I haven't eaten it since I joined the police, sir."

"Good. You know how they kill them, don't you?" I said pointedly.

"Yes, sir," he said.

I put the puppy back in the cage. They beat them to death with a short stick to make them tender. "Photograph them. Then take them back to the station in their cage. Have you searched for dog skins?"

"No, sir."

"Well *search!* Every kitchen. Anything that looks like a dog hide. Label it, photograph it. Search every garbage can and gash bucket. Tip them onto newspaper. And go around every table in the restaurant and look for dog dishes. Do you know what dog meat tastes like?"

He blushed. "Yes, sir."

"Then taste it. Take half a dozen uniform boys to help you or you'll be here all night. Any dish that tastes like dog put in plastic bags, label it, take it to the mortuary, and refrigerate it. Draw a plan of the floor of the restaurant. Draw in the tables. Number each table. Get the names and addresses of every person seated at that table, take them back to SIO. Also collect any bones that don't look like chicken or duck or fish, and label them the same way, the table they came from. We're going to charge every single person we can. Have you seized the invoices?"

"Sir?" the inspector said.

"The invoices. The dinner bills, they'll state on them what each customer's meal consisted of."

"No, sir."

"Well do so! Grab anything that says dog or monkey on it. Or 'Special.' And find out who wrote each one. Documents are only any good as evidence if you can establish who wrote them."

"Yes, sir."

"Are dog dishes listed on the menu?"

"No, sir," the inspector said.

"Have you checked every other kitchen?"

"Is this the only floor in this restaurant which serves dog and monkey?"

"Yes, sir."

I turned to the monkey cage. There were only two. Shaven heads, like prisoners about to be electrocuted. They were huddled close together, staring. I scratched the cage and they both bared their fangs at me.

"The same with these. Photograph, label, back to SIO." I went on to the next cage. "What's this?"

"I don't know, sir," the inspector said.

"That is a civet cat," Miss Tsang said loudly. "It is a rare wild animal."

"A civet cat."

"Yes. Nearly extinct."

The cage was not big enough for it to turn around.

"The same with that," I said. "Are there any more animals in the kitchens on the lower floors?"

"No, sir," the inspector said.

"Yes!" Miss Tsang said vehemently. "There are pigeons."

I said, "I am afraid eating pigeons is not an offense in this Colony, Miss Tsang."

"The cages are too small," Miss Tsang said.

"All right," I said. "I'll look at them on the way out, perhaps there's a cruelty charge."

"Yes, cruelty," Miss Tsang said.

CHAPTER 19

She sat the other side my desk and smoked Red Victory cigarettes and drank black coffee intently, answering my questions very much to the point. Sometimes she made a note on a pad to remind herself of something she wanted to say. She was determined to get the whole story down exactly as it should be, indignant, impatient that justice be done. I worked straight onto the typewriter:

Name of witness: Tsang Ying-ling
Sex: F. Single

Age: 26, Western reckoning
Race: Chinese
Occupation: Schoolmistress at Tai Ping Middle
School
Nationality: Chinese, Hong Kong resident
Residential address: Room 18, 4th Floor, 97 Tai
Ho Street, Causeway Bay
Telephone: Residence: None. Office: 743211
(Tai Ping Middle School, Causeway
Bay)
Statement recorded by: J. I. McAdam
Rank and station: S.I.P.   SIO   HQ
Telephone: 243111   927
States in English:

1. I am as above recorded.
2. Antecedent history: I was born in Chungking,
   where my father was a medical doctor. In 1949,
   on the Communist Liberation of China, my family moved to the Philippines. I was four years old.
   My mother died the following year. My father
   returned to China in 1951 because his medical
   qualifications were not recognized by the Philippine authorities nor by the British authorities in
   Hong Kong. Since that date he has been working
   as a doctor at the People's Hospital, outside Canton. I remained in the Philippines in the custody
   of my paternal aunt, now deceased. When I finished high school my father had me sent to Hong
   Kong to attend the Teachers' Training College,
   from which I graduated in 1956. First I was employed by the Hong Kong Government at the Wo
   Hop School in Mongkok. After one year I went
   to the Tai Ping Middle School where I still am,
   teaching all subjects to Class 6.
3. I am a member of the Society for the Prevention
   of Cruelty to Animals.
4. Tonight. 7th December 1962, I received cer-
   ain information concerning the Heavenly Restaurant, 182 Ming On Street, Causeway Bay.
   As a result I proceeded immediately to that restaurant to investigate, arriving at about 2105
   hours.
      I did not invoke the assistance of the police at
   this stage because I preferred to do this my own
   way.

139

I secured a seat at a table on the third floor of the restaurant, three tables away from the third-floor kitchen doorway.

I noticed one corner in the restaurant was partitioned off with portable screens to make private dining areas, as is common in Chinese restaurants. I am now shown a drawn plan of the third floor, Exhibit no. 0. Position marked 1 was the areas so partitioned off. I ordered some food.

At approximately 2115 hours, when the waiter had gone off to comply, I left my table and entered the kitchen on the pretext of looking for the toilet.

5. I passed unchallenged through the kitchen, marked on the plan, into the backyard area. There I saw, at the position marked 2 on the plan, a cage containing seven black chow puppies.

Next to the puppies' cage, in the position marked 3 on the plan, I saw another cage containing three monkeys. I am certain there were three. Each monkey's head was shaved.

Next to the monkey's cage was a cage containing a civet cat, in position marked 4 on the plan.

I now see the cage, Exhibit no. 0, and the puppies, Exhibit nos. 0, the monkeys' cage, Exhibit no. 0, and two monkeys, Exhibit nos. 0, the civet cat's cage, Exhibit no. 0, and the civet cat, Exhibit no. 0. These are, or are identical to, those I saw.

6. I immediately hurried back out through the kitchen. I had spent no more than half a minute there.

En route I saw one dead monkey lying on a kitchen table, in position marked 5 on the plan.

Its skull was opened and the contents appeared to have been removed. I only glanced at this monkey.

7. I immediately hurried down the stairs and out of the building, found a telephone in a shop immediately opposite, and telephoned 999 to summon the police. I looked at my watch: it was 2120 hours.

I then waited outside the restaurant doors until

the police arrived at approximately 2125 hours, led by the officer I now know as Inspector Hu.

I then ran up the stairs to the third floor, leading the police party.

8. I led Inspector Hu into the third-floor kitchen, and first indicated the table marked 5 on the plan where I had earlier seen one dead monkey, mentioned in paragraph 7.

There were now two dead monkeys there, both in the same condition as the first. The dead monkeys, Exhibit nos. 0, are, or are identical to, those I saw.

9. I turned to investigate the monkey cage, marked 3 on the plan, and saw there were now only two monkeys in it. I indicated this to Inspector Hu.

10. Inspector Hu and I then ran back to the screened dining area marked 1 on the plan and looked behind it. This area had been guarded since our arrival by a constable, on Inspector Hu's instructions.

There I saw twelve Chinese male adults seated around a circular table, through the middle of which protruded the shaved head of a live monkey, identical in appearance to the monkeys I had earlier seen in the cage in the backyard.

I also saw a silver hammer, a jug of hot oil, and a number of teaspoons and a number of pieces of what appeared to be bone.

I now see the photographs, Exhibit nos. 0. Those show everything that and whom I saw.

Inspector Hu ordered everybody at the table to remain seated and to touch nothing. I saw him post uniformed policemen at a number of places on guard.

Shortly thereafter, a matter of probably five minutes, members of the CID arrived to take over the investigation.

Signed————————
TSANG YING-LING

It was quarter past eleven. I pulled the last sheet out of the typewriter and handed it to her to read. She read it with pen poised, like a schoolmarm, ready to correct anything.

"Ten out of ten?" I said. "Your cigarette's about to burn your hair."

"Do I sign now?"

"No," I said. "Not until you've actually seen all the photographs and exhibits referred to in the statement. That statement is drawn up as the public prosecutor will want to read your evidence in court. If you would come back tomorrow when we've got everything together and all the exhibits numbered, and sign it then."

"Very good." She stood up, straightened her skirt over her flat belly and thighs. She had ink on two fingertips and her plaits were a bit ragged and she looked tired now it was all over. Her lips were full and her face was square-ish and purposeful and she smiled at me for the first time. Her eyes were large and the eyelids had the double fold like a European's, which is unusual in a Chinese, and they were softer now she was satisfied I had done the job properly, and when she smiled at me like that briefly I thought she was beautiful. I had already reminded her of the incident at the border. "When is the court case?" she said.

I said, "They'll be remanded tomorrow morning. They'll probably plead guilty, thanks to you."

"What sentence will they get?" she demanded.

"The maximum for a first offense is five thousand dollars and/or two years' imprisonment."

"First offense. They have been doing it a long time."

"We will check their fingerprints tomorrow with Criminal Record Bureau for previous convictions," I assured her.

"Why can't you stop it everywhere?" Miss Tsang demanded.

"Because not enough public-spirited people like you help us, Miss Tsang."

"Yes. We must do something. The SPCA. And Government."

I said, more to talk than to challenge, "Don't they still eat dog and monkey in China?"

She shot me a dirty look. "Yes. I do not approve." She went on, "I went to Macao. In Macao it is terrible, much worse than here. I saw puppies there too. I called the police. You know what? They laughed at me. Those Portuguese."

I nodded. "Macao."

"Those Portuguese," Miss Tsang said.

"Won't you have some more coffee?" I said.

"No thank you, I must go now. Thank you." She gave

me her beautiful brief smile. "You have been very efficient."

"Thank you."

"It is true. You should see those Portuguese."

I hesitated. "Miss Tsang, you didn't eat anything at the restaurant, did you?"

"No."

"Would you like to come and have some dinner now? I haven't had anything either."

She dismissed the invitation politely, impersonally, as if it were only the sort of thing police do for their witnesses. "No thank you, I had my dinner already. I must go and take my dog for his swim before it is too late."

"For a *swim?*" I said.

She grinned. "Oh yes, he is half spaniel, you know."

"Even in the winter he swims?"

"Every night," Miss Tsang assured me, "even if it was Iceland. I think he is really a seal."

I grinned, it seemed the first time I had really grinned for a long time. "Where does he swim?"

"Here at Causeway Bay, at the Yacht Club."

"Well," I grinned, "I'll give you a lift home?"

She shook her head politely. "No, not necessary, I like to walk, thank you."

I said, in case she was afraid of me, "I'll get a constable to drive you."

"No, not necessary, thank you," Miss Tsang assured me, then said, businesslike, "Tomorrow I want to go to the court, to see if they plead guilty. What time must I go?"

I said, "Ten o'clock at Causeway Bay Magistracy. But I don't know what time their case will be."

"Ten o'clock." She frowned. "I must be at school."

"I can send a car for you."

She shook her head. "No, not necessary, thank you. I will try." She looked at me brightly, then extended her hand. "Good-by, Inspector McAdam."

I took her hand, she pumped mine once.

"Good-by, Miss Tsang, and thank you—it was admirable."

"It is my duty," Miss Tsang said. "Good-by."

"Good night, Miss Tsang," I said.

She pumped my hand once more and gave me her brief soft smile and turned and walked out of my office without looking back. I watched her go, the flash of skirt and straight back and her legs and no-nonsense walk, and I thought, What a lovely clean girl. What lovely legs. And a goddamn communist.

CHAPTER 20

That Christmas it was very overcast. The winter in China was going to be very bad. There were Christmas decorations everywhere, lights strung across the streets saying Happy Christmas in English and in Chinese characters, strung up and down the big commercial houses, and in the harbor the ships were slung with lights from stern to stern. It was cold, and beyond the Mountains of Nine Dragons and the Shamchun River Valley it was colder, and this winter many people would die.

That week the formal Christmas cocktail parties started. Some I had to go to, some others I went to because if I did not go I would drink anyway. Christmas is a very bad time to drink alone. After the cocktail parties I went to the bars in Wanchai. The bars were pretty empty because most people were at their parties. I did not see Catherine at any of the parties, our mutual friends invited only her, and now she moved in different circles to myself anyway. I spent a lot of time buying things for Suzie. The toy shops were very good. There were many beautiful things to buy, so ingenious, and very cheap. Every time I passed a toy shop I ended up buying her something more. I liked to think of her playing with them.

On Christmas Eve, I threw a cocktail party in my flat for Special Investigations' Chinese policemen and their womenfolk. It was very crowded in the bachelor flat. I hired a caterer. The party began with some difficulty. We spoke in Cantonese. The womenfolk stood uneasily, toying with a glass of Seven-Up, smiling uncertainly. Then the liquor started going to the men's heads, for Chinese are usually not strong drinkers and their faces get flushed red very quickly, and they started to *yum-sing*. If a Chinese says *yum-sing* to you, you must drink your beer down in one go; it is a challenge and you lose face if you cannot do it. They were *yum-singing* each other all over the place, very loud and red in the face. I had to *yum-sing* three times, which is thrice too often. They had a good time and I liked them all very much. They left, flushed and noisy and happy. I looked around the empty flat, cigarette butts and dirty glasses. The waiters were cleaning. I had drunk a lot but I was completely sober. I was saturated from the succession of cocktail parties. I did not know what I wanted to do. I did not want to stay in the empty flat alone on Christmas Eve. She fast asleep in her bed now with her pillow slip hung excitedly over the end of her bed, and early in the morning she would wake up and come running through to our bedroom excited, oh Christ. I turned and walked out of the flat into the cold dry China night.

I went down to Wanchai. I realized I was not going anywhere for Christmas dinner tomorrow. It was the first time I had thought of it. There were few people on the streets. Tonight most of the American sailors would be at R. & R. Parties. I looked into the Ocean Bar and there were only a few sailors there. I went down into the Candlelight Bar. There were quite a lot of sailors. I sat up at the bar and got a San Miguel. The *mamasan* came and asked me if I wanted a nice girl and I said no thank you. I felt heavy and sour with all the liquor I had drunk over the past ten days and I did not feel as if anything I drank would make me drunk, and it felt very bad to be alone in a girlie bar on Christmas Eve in my own hometown. The sailors were pretty drunk and noisy and the jukebox thumped. I sat at the bar and watched the dancing and I tried not to think about Christmas.

On the big day I woke up early. It was cold and overcast, the harbor gray and the Christmas decorations cheerless. I tried to go back to sleep but I was wide awake. I went through to the kitchen and put the hot plate and the kettle on. I switched the hi-fi on loud, Brahms. There were no decorations, only Suzie's Christmas card on the bookshelf. She had drawn it herself, bright scrawly figures with round heads and stick arms and legs. I went to the bathroom and turned the shower on hot as I could bear, scrubbed myself hard then rubbed myself dry hard. Brahms flooded through the flat, I hummed loud as I shaved. The sun was coming up, cold bright China red and orange on the cold mauve Mountains of Nine Dragons and the gray cold harbor. I finished dressing and I wondered what to do. The record came to an end and there was complete silence in the flat. I lit a cigarette and I inhaled it deep over the ache in my throat. I turned and walked out the front door into the cold cheerless Christmas morning.

The Hermitage was dead quiet. I rode down in the elevator and out into Kennedy Road. My breath made steam in front of me. The decorations in the flats' windows. There was nobody else out yet. I walked on down Garden Road. A tram rumbled by at the bottom. I walked through the big glass doors of the Hilton into the big bright empty foyer and into the coffee shop, open twenty-four hours a day. There were decorations hanging from the ceiling and the stereo was playing "Good King Wenceslaus." I sat down at the long bright cold Formica counter and drank San Miguel beer and ate a steak sandwich and smoked cigarettes and tried not to think of Christmas.

At half-past nine I took a taxi back to the Hermitage to get the presents. I was excited now. There were quite a lot of people going to church. The presents were wrapped in Christmas paper, it felt like Christmas now. The radio was playing "Noel"; I sang "Noel" all the way to Happy Valley. My heart was knocking as I climbed the steps to the old house. There was the sprig of real holly on the old front door. We had picked it years ago from a hedge near Canterbury. The berries were painted red with her nail polish. I rang the bell, I heard her footsteps coming. "Jake!" She was beaming. "Happy Christmas, darling!" She put her arms around me and kissed my cheek, kiss kiss, the familiar Catherine feel and smell. She looked beautiful, wearing her mauve ski pants and bulky sweater. "How lovely to see you! And all those lovely presents, come in!"

She was pleased to see me but she was not sad. There were some of Suzie's new toys on the floor, Christmas string, a big plate of walnuts and raisins and chocolates on the telephone table, decorations. The stereo was playing "Jingle Bells." I followed her through into the lounge. There was the golden fire in the big brass grate, a pine tree in the corner, along the mantelpiece dozens of Christmas cards. The booze cart was standing ready. Home.

"Well! Is it too early to have a drink?"

"No. Where's Suzie?"

"She's outside at the back. Relax a few moments, darling. I haven't seen you for ages either."

I sat down. It felt so so good to be here, instinctive. The same old armchair. "The same old armchair," I said. She smiled at me and brought me a beer. I thought, You're so goddamn beautiful.

She smiled. "Remember these ski pants?"

"Yes," I said. "We bought them in Kitzbühel." *"Kitzbühel."*

She said, "You must go and see Ah Chan in a moment. Old Ah Chan, she adores you."

My heart was breaking. "What's going to happen to her when you leave?"

She was lighting a cigarette, it shook. "Oh Jake, don't talk about it, let's be happy."

"Happy," I agreed.

She looked at me. "Oh Jake. Christmas is a bad time, isn't it? But let's be happy," she appealed. "Didn't we have lots of good times together?"

I nodded. "Don't let's talk about that either."

"But didn't we? So many places. It seems there isn't a place left."

Cathy said, "Jake, have you had some breakfast? You're very white."

"Yes. It's these damn Christmas parties. I'm pretty fit, don't worry about me."

"Of course I worry about you."

There were many things I could have said to that.

"Were you at a party last night?"

"Yes. My staff. And you?"

"Yes," she said. "Good? Your party."

"The usual," I said.

"You never used to have your staff party on Christmas Eve. It used to be earlier."

"I left it a bit late."

She looked at the fire.

"Who was your hostess?"

"Nobody. I left that too late as well. Where did you go?"

She looked at the fire. "The Foreign Correspondents' Club."

I hated the name of that place.

"Where did you go afterward?" she said.

"Friends."

"Really, Jake? Not propping up a bar alone in Wanchai? I couldn't bear that."

"Don't worry, Cathy."

"All our real friends are married. And they've got to ask only one of us, and they seem to ask me. Jake?"

"Yes?"

She looked at me. "Are you going to somebody for Christmas dinner?"

"Yes."

"You sure? You're such a lone wolf. You're not going to be alone? I couldnt 'bear that."

"No, Cathy." I smiled at her. I took a big drink of beer. "I've brought you a present."

She wiped her eye with her wrist. "Have you? Thank you. I've got one for you too."

She wiped her cheek and got up. She went to the Christmas tree and picked up a parcel. I looked at her long full body bending, the long lock of hair falling over her face. "I hope it's the right kind."

I opened it.

"A sextent! Oh thank you, Cathy!"

"Is it the right kind?"

"It's the *best* kind."

She looked at me. "And when you shoot a star or a course or whatever it is, you'll think of me?"

Oh God oh God.

"Yes," I said, "I will."

She wiped the corner of her eye.

"I'll call Suzie now," she said.

She went to the lounge door.

"Ah Chan," she called, "call little Missie, please."

"Okay," Ah Chan shouted.

"How long can I have her?"

"Oh Jake. Don't talk like that."

"But you want her back for lunch?"

"Oh Jake. Yes, darling. Isn't this awful?"

I heard her footsteps come running up the passage. There she was running, gold hair bouncing blue eyes joyfu—"*Daddy—Daddy—Daddy.*"

She brought the walkie-talkie doll, half as big as her, she wanted to bring the tricycle Burton had given her as well. She was very excited about the tricycle. She was clean and rosy and sparkling and happy and perfect, my beautiful perfect girl-child. She never stopped talking all the way down to the cathedral about Christmas and the tricycle and the Three Wise Men and Mommy and all her presents, she was very excited and I loved to hear her talk. I parked the Opel, took her hand, she lugged the big doll and we walked down to the lovely old Catholic cathedral and I was very happy. As we came down the steps the beggars came running, lucky red plastic begging mugs outstretched calling, "Chisimas, Chisimas." A tall cassocked priest was beaming at us in the big doorway. "Hello!" he beamed down at Susan. "Did Father Christmas bring you that lovely dolly?"

"No," Susan beamed up at him. "My daddy did. And Uncle David brought me a new tricycle!"

"My—wasn't that nice of Uncle David?" the priest beamed, red-gummed.

We sat down near the back. The priest was addressing himself to the children about a certain glowworm which was rewarded for its effort to touch the glowing baby Jesus by being made hereditarily incandescent. Suzie listened, spellbound, little moist hand holding mine, big blue eyes, mouth a little open, clutching her doll on her lap. Then the priest said he wanted a song from all the children. Did they want to sing "Away in a Manger"? Yes, chorused the children, including Susan. Jolly good, then let all the children stand up on their seats. They scrambled up including Susan, still clutching her doll. I was delighted but I didn't think she knew "Away in a Manger." I took the doll away from her and she stood waiting twisting the hem of her frock around and around her finger, breathless with anticipation. A-one, a-two, a-*three*, the priest said. A-*way* in a-ah *man*-ger—a hundred little voices piped up uncertainly. I was watching Susan, she took a big earnest breath and piped, "No-oh *crib* for His *bed"* —*she knew the words!* I wanted to throw my arms around her and hug her tight, *she knew the words!* She was oblivious to me. They sang it right through and when it finished I wanted to break into applause but I managed not to. She sat back down, glowing, and took my hand. I gave it a big squeeze, feeding on her. This time next year —oh God, there would be no this time next year, this time next week she would be in London. The priest was praying, I closed my eyes tight. I tried hard to concentrate on the prayer I did not believe in, but I could not, I was thinking about Suzie far away in London I fiercely shut my mind to it and I tried to make up my own prayer, very rusty, I could feel her breathing beside me, her eyes were screwed up tight but I did not believe she was really praying, she was probably thinking of her tricycle, trying hard to keep her eyes closed. There was a loud Amen and everybody was shuffling up. The sepulchral organ, the cresting swell of voices. I sang loud, the ache in my throat, I held Susan's little hot hand tight. *Ah-mennn* . . . I led her out of the big old church, among the first. The cold overcast sunshine.

"Daddy?" She was hurrying beside me, clutching her doll.

"Yes, darling?"

"Can I go and ride my tricycle now?"

I looked down at her and I thought my heart would break.

"Presently, angel. Wouldn't you like to have some Seven-Up and cakes with me first? Some ice cream?"

She considered, arm upstretched to my hand, other arm clutching the doll. "Yes."

"Yes."

"Yes, what?"

"Yes please, Daddy."

"Do you love me, Suzie?"

"Yes."

"Lots?"

"More than a hundred," Suzie said.

"I love you lots too, darling." My throat felt thick.

"More than a hundred?"

"Yes, darling, much more than that, more numbers than you can ever think about."

We walked down to the Expresso, she skipped beside me, holding my hand and clutching the doll, happy, excited, looking forward to ice cream and cakes and then the tricycle. The Expresso was warm and empty, tables, cakes, we sat in a corner, ice cream for Suzie, beer for me. I listened and answered, loving every hair of her golden head, watching her eat and chatter, drinking my San Miguel, eating salted breadsticks. Daddy? Yes, darling? Is it true about the glowworm? I'm sure it is, darling, or the priest wouldn't have told us. Daddy? Yes, my angel? You still live in China, don't you, catching all those robbers? I nodded, Yes, darling, that's right. You're a famous policeman, aren't you, Daddy, Mommy says so. My eyes *burned*. Do you want another ice cream, darling? Yes please, Daddy, we're having Christmas pud for lunch, arent we? My throat ached: Yes, darling, I'm sure we are. And turkey, aren't we, hey, Daddy? Yes, I said, the Asia Company's big fat turkey too. And fifty cents in the Christmas pud! she exclaimed. I saw Mommy washing them yesterday, lots and lots. My eyes burned hard: Did you, darling? Fifty cents is half a dollar, isn't it, Daddy? That's right, sweetheart, and how much is two fifty cents? *One dollar!* Quite right! And four fifty cents? *Three dollars!* delighted with herself. I hugged her: No, no, angel, but I love you so much I could eat you up!

Oh Jesus, I hated myself:

Angel?

Yes, Daddy?

Was it lovely opening your presents this morning?

Yes, she remembered happily.

I hated myself: Where did you open them, darling?

In bed.

In whose bed?

In my bed. Mommy came into my bed and we opened them all.

Oh thank God.

Daddy?

Yes, my darling daughter?

Can I go ride my trike now?

Oh my sweetheart.

Wouldn't you like to go for a ride on the swings first, just you and me? Then you can go back to the trike.

We went to the botanical gardens. There were only some Chinese children playing, with their amahs. I pushed her high and low and her gold curls flew, and her little frock, and her big blue eyes laughed and sparkled and her little legs swung and I fought the big ache in my throat. It was nearly time for Christmas dinner. I took her off the swings all laughing and panting and I carried her close to me to the bench. I sat her on my knees facing me, gold hair all over her pink flushed happy face.

"Darling?"

"Yes?"

I took a breath. "Sing me a song. Before we go. Will you?"

She looked at me, all sparkly wide-eyed pink and gold and shy.

"What song?"

"Sing 'Away in a Manger,' darling. Just once. For me."

" 'Away in a Manger'?" she blushed happily. I squeezed her.

"Yes, please. Go on."

"Will you sing too?" facing me close astride my knees, cold in the botanical gardens.

"Yes, I'll sing too, but you must teach me."

She blushed, all shy.

"Go on. A-*way* in a *man*-ger."

She took a big blushing coy breath.

I held her tight and sang slowly with her, looking into her eyes and I felt the tears spring. She sang, looking into my eyes, earnestly, I was half a word behind her, looking into her big baby blue eyes and they were no longer coy they were all earnest, and the tears burned and my voice was thick, sitting on the bench in the botanical gardens on cold Christmas Day singing "Away in a Manger" with my child and I wished it would never end, and I rocked her and held her tight against me before we had finished singing.

I carried her tight back to the Opel, then I swung her up astride my shoulders, and I pretended to play games so she would not see my eyes, and she thought I was playing and she laughed. I drove her back to Happy Valley, and it was almost time for Christmas dinner. She was all excited now about riding her tricycle, and she wanted to scramble out of the car, I put my arms around her and squeezed her and rocked her tight and kissed her golden little girl head and neck, and then I let her go. "Aren't you coming to Christmas dinner?" "No, my lovey," I said and my eyes were burning. "I've got to go back to China." She looked at me, disappointed, then resigned, then thinking of her tricycle. She was used to me not coming home. "Good-by, my angel," I said, "and have a very, *very* happy Christmas!" "Good-by, Daddy!" She turned and ran up the old wide stone steps, little legs and frock and golden hair bouncing, running to her tricycle, and she did not look back.

CHAPTER 21

The best thing to do when you are unhappy is to walk.

I walked along Kennedy, back to the botanical gardens. I wanted to go back to them. There were only a few Chinese. I walked slowly around the aviary. She had learned the names of most of the birds. She particularly loved the flamingos. I stood a long time, watching them. I had read up about birds, to be able to tell her everything. Maybe when she went to the zoo in London, perhaps she would think of me.

I walked down through the botanical gardens, then along the waterfront toward Wanchai. A pimp said, "Hey Joe, you wanna massage, special Christmas offer?" Most of the shops were open and empty, Happy Christmas decorations. Way ahead was the Royal Hong Kong Yacht Club. I would go there for a drink. I came to the causeway out to Kellet's Island where the club building was. The typhoon shelter was full of junks and yachts and sampans.

A young Chinese woman was sitting alone on the causeway wall, very still. She had cat's-eye spectacles, and her hair was in two tufty plaits that stuck out a little and her face was a little square. She had a pad and pencil in her lap and I could see a drawing. I stopped in front of her.

"Hello, Miss Tsang," I said.

She looked surprised, then smiled and took off her glasses.

"Good afternoon, Inspector McAdam."

"And Happy Christmas."

"Of course." She was blushing. "Happy Christmas, I was not thinking."

I said, for something to say, "You got the results of your case?" I knew she had got the result.

"Yes," she said. She said, for something to say, "I must thank you for handling the case very well. I remember now, I have seen your name in the newspaper quite

153

often. And you are also the person who wrote that book, *The Story of the Chinese Communist Revolution*."

I was pleased with that. "Were you satisfied with the fine?"

She said emphatically, "No. Do you think it was because the magistrate was Chinese?"

"No," I said loyally. "Just one of those things."

She shook her head. "An English magistrate would have sent him to jail. The English are very fond of dogs —that is why I was very glad when you came to the restaurant. And that magistrate was Cantonese. I asked."

I said, to change the subject, "What are you doing here?" I looked at the closed notebook.

She said, "To give Mad Dog a swim. I usually come at night but today is a holiday."

"Mad Dog?" I said. "Is that his name?" I sat down on the parapet and she shifted up as if there was not much of it. "Why is he called Mad Dog, is he mad?"

She grinned. "He has no brains at all. He is among the junks." She took a big breath and yelled in Cantonese, *"Mad Dog! Come here! Mad Dog!"*

A wet golden head came paddling around the bows of a junk, gold fur sleeked, big spaniel eyes. He swam a few yards toward us, then tried to turn around furtively to have a bit longer. "Mad Dog!" she yelled and he turned guiltily toward us. He picked up a floating bottle en route and came slobbering up the stone embankment carrying it, long tail sweeping. He was a cross between a spaniel and a chow and the result is not impressive. He shook himself, his feet slipped all over the place, then looked at her with adoring eyes.

"All right," she said in Cantonese. "Go."

He spun and charged back down the embankment tripping over his feet, then leaped into the water, spaniel ears flying.

"See? Mad."

We were both grinning. "Where did you get him?"

"From the SPCA."

"He's a grand dog. Will you have a cigarette? 'Texan,' " I said. "Smoke Texan and cough like a cowboy."

I laughed at my own joke, she smiled politely.

"No thank you, I prefer these." She produced her packet of Red Victory, thought, then grinned widely, "Smoke Red Victory and cough like a communist."

I laughed out loud. It seemed the first time I had

laughed for a long time. She was giggling at her joke and I thought she was beautiful. When we stopped I said, for something to say, "So now you are on school holidays?"

She tried to be serious. "Yes, ten days. Fortunately, the government stipulates the holidays for all schools; otherwise we poor communists would not get Christmas."

We were both still amused. I said, for something to say, "But you don't celebrate Christmas, I mean religiously."

"Oh no. Do you?"

"Yes. But not very religiously."

"Yes, Christmas seems to be a time when Europeans drink too much."

"Were you never brought up as Christian? Even in the Philippines?"

"My aunt tried to convince me. But failed."

I said, "My father was very devout. We lived in Shanghai. We came here after the Liberation too."

"The 'Liberation'? Do you really regard it as a liberation?"

"In many ways."

She looked at me with interest. "Oh. Good." She hesitated, then decided to change the subject. "Aren't you celebrating Christmas today, Mr. McAdam? What were you doing down here?"

"I was just going for a walk. Going to the Yacht Club, for a drink."

"Aren't you married, Mr. McAdam?" she said.

"Yes," I said. "But I'm separated." I went on, "Do you like boats?"

"Boats?" she said. "Yes. I am very fond of the sea. In the summer I go underwater diving."

"Do you? Where do you go?"

"I go," she waved, "on the ferries. To Lautau Island and Lamma. And up in the New Territories, from Tai Po Kau. There are many empty beaches and nice places there."

"Do you use an aqualung?"

"No, they are too expensive. And very heavy to carry. But maybe I will buy one. I have got a very good snorkel and goggles and frog feet," she said.

"I like to dive sometimes," I said. "I have a boat and sometimes I go over the side."

"Where is your boat?"

155

"Over there. You can't see it from here. It's a converted deep-sea fishing junk."

"Do you sail it?"

"Yes, it sails very well. But I have two big diesel engines."

She looked at me. "So you are very lucky to have such a boat."

"Would you like to see it? We could go out to her now?" I said.

"No," she said politely. "I must go soon, thank you."

I did not want her to go.

"Are you enjoying your holidays?" I said.

"Yes." She smiled at me. "We teachers work hard, I think. But we have more"—she thought for the word—"outside duties?"

"Extracurricular." I knew about them. "Oh? What?"

She said, "Political education, discussion groups. Children and adults. And some social welfare work."

"No, our teachers don't do any of that."

"And they're paid *much* more," she said with a touch of indignation.

"Why did you leave government schools?"

She said simply, "I want to do it. I am Chinese."

"Do your extracurricular duties take up much time?"

She said simply, "Three nights a week."

"That's a lot."

"Yes. But it is the communists' strength. That people work for the community." She looked at the junks and sampans. I looked at her closed sketch pad.

"I paint a bit," I said.

She looked at me with interest. "Do you?"

"Well, I haven't done any for some time now."

"Why not?"

I said, "I've been busy. And changing my job and so forth."

"What do you paint?"

I wondered too. "I suppose anything that takes me. I used to do impressionistic stuff, then I went on to abstracts. Then I went to simple things. I don't know," I said, "what I paint. I'm not very good."

"But the important question is *Why* do you paint?"

"To create. Impressions. As they seem to *me*."

She nodded earnestly, and her eyes were elliptical and deep brown and intense and I thought she was beautiful.

"Have you ever taken lessons?"

"No. If there's a lecture on, or an exhibition, I go."

"What paints do you use?"

"Oils. Sometimes acrylics. They're convenient, dry quickly. But not the same depth."

"You should take lessons, you know."

"Maybe you would give me lessons," I said blandly.

She smiled. "Oh no, I am not good enough for that." She wasn't getting herself involved.

"What do you paint?"

"Oh. Anything. Now I am having a spell of doing anything."

"What were you drawing just now? May I see it?"

She looked at the closed sketchbook. "It's not good."

It was a sketch of the typhoon shelter, fishing junks and sampans bashed close together, crowded, and beyond them, in clear spacious lanes, the pleasure yachts and junks and launches. Beyond the shelter were the crowded tenements with the squatter shacks on their rooftops. Down one tenement wall was a gigantic bottle of Coca-Cola. Behind the tenements rose the great new blocks of middle-class flats, and the neon signs.

"It's very good," I said.

"No," she said. "But it will be better when I have painted it in. Tomorrow early if it is fine I'll start." She smiled at me. "Well, I must go now."

I said, "Won't you come and have some tea with me, Miss Tsang?"

She smiled politely. "Thank you, but I must go now, really." She shouted, "Mad Dog."

He turned reluctantly and paddled for the causeway. We watched him come. We were both self-conscious because I had asked her to tea and she had refused.

"Good-by, Mr. McAdam," she added, "and thank you again for your work on my case."

I did not want to let her go. "Are you sure you can't come and have something to eat with me?"

She smiled. "Yes, quite sure, but thank you." Mad Dog was standing there dripping. "Good-by, Mr. Mc-Adam."

"Good-by, Miss Tsang."

"Come, Mad Dog."

"Good-by," I said.

I watched her walk along the causeway, her tall clean figure, hair parted severely down the back of her head and I thought, What a lovely girl.

I walked on down the causeway to the Yacht Club on Kellet's Island. There was not one car. It was nearly three o'clock.

I sat at the big empty teak bar and looked out on the cold gray harbor and drank a row of San Migs and ate three plates of beef sandwiches, and maybe it was just because I was doing my best not to think about Christmas but I wished very much that Miss Tsang had come with me and we were talking now about many things and I could look at her face. At sunset I had drunk enough and I did not know what I wanted to do: I did not want to go back to my empty flat and I did no want to go to empty bars; and took a sampan out to my junk: I put *The Mikado* on the record player and went straight to sleep.

I woke up just before dawn; it was dark and absolutely quiet and I felt wonderful. I had slept almost twelve hours. I went up on deck and there was a sliver of moon and still some stars and the beautiful harbor silent and clean, the whole world was asleep except me, I felt young and strong and I knew what I was going to do today and it felt like a delicious adventure. I clattered down below to the saloon and I put water on for coffee and *H.M.S. Pinafore* on the record player.

"When I was a lad I served a term—"

I had a hot shower singing *H.M.S. Pinafore* and I looked at my unbloodshot eyes in the mirror and said, "By God, you're beautiful!"

The sun was well up when I rowed ashore in the dinghy and went to the Wanchai Market and bought a fresh duck, singing "The Surrey with the Fringe on Top." I had everything else aboard. Then I went back to the junk. I snapped the cap off a bottle of cold San Miguel and it went down good and clean and sparkling into my empty gut, then I took the bottle and the binoculars and I climbed up the mast to the crow's nest and sat down to wait and drink beer and sing "Oklahoma."

I saw a golden spaniel chow come running all by himself out of Percival Road, out onto the causeway, big ears flapping, big tongue flopping, then he took off. All fours spread-eagle and big ears flying and crash-landed into the water.

"Good morning, Mad Dog!" I shouted.

I watched her through the binoculars, tall Chinese girl with the no-nonsense walk and cat's-eye sunglasses, canvas and easel under one arm, a brown wooden case, head up in the cold sunny China morning, swinging along the causeway.

She came to her place of yesterday, put her gear down on the parapet, started putting up her easel. She put the framed canvas on the easel, opened her sketchbook. She compared it with the canvas critically. Opened her paint box, took out a dozen tubes, a pallet, a Seven-Up bottle, a tin, and half a dozen paint brushes. She sat down on the parapet, showing a good deal of communist leg. She rubbed her chin with the back of her wrist nervously, sighed, then lit a Viceroy cigarette, and coughed once. She nipped the end off the cigarette irritably to keep it for later. she picked up her pallet, straightened herself determinedly, then looked straight into my binoculared eyes, and stiffened.

I swung out of the crow's nest, down the guys, down the swimming ladder and dropped into the dinghy, grinning all the way. I could not see her now. I rowed through the sampans, past one water-logged Mad Dog on the way, up to the causeway and clambered up.

"Good morning, Miss Tsang!"

She was grinning, blushing. "Mr. McAdam, why were you spying on me?"

"We policemen never sleep, Miss Tsang."

She was blushing.

"So. And isn't it a lovely day?" I was nervous.

"Yes, it is," smiling, blushing.

"You get started very early," I said.

"Yes, it's such a lovely day, I thought I'd better."

"I thought you would."

She was still blushing. "What are you doing here today, apart from spying? Are you going out on your boat?"

"Actually," I put on my most charming smile, "I came down here at crack of dawn especially to see you."

She flushed afresh.

"Oh," She added. "You want to see me?"

I soldiered on. "I woke up and it was such a beautiful day. And I was determined to come here and invite you to come out with me on my junk. To share the beautiful day."

She was blushing hard.

"I came to paint my picture."

"I know. That's how I knew how to find you. You can paint your picture tomorrow, it'll still be here tomorrow. So will you, you have a holiday tomorrow too but I have to go back to work. . . ."

She started to say something; I said, to deny her the commitment of refusal, "We can go anywhere you like. Just around the harbor if you like, then I'll bring you back and you can carry on with your picture." I was going to say bloody picture. "One hour, two hours, or all day, I'll bring you back whenever you want. It's just to enjoy it."

She looked embarrassed. I zeroed in on her cunningly, "Unless you don't like me."

She said hastily, "Of course I like you, Mr. McAdam, that is not the reason. . . ."

"That's settled then! Miss Tsang, does anybody in this typhoon shelter know who you are, apart from being the lady with the crazy dog?"

She grinned. "No, I don't think so—"

"Then that's settled. There is no reason in this beautiful world why a beautiful emancipated schoolmistress should not enjoy this beautiful emancipated China Sea with a fine upright clean-cut clean-living intelligent—"

She was giggling.

"—beautiful, bourgeois—"

She laughed out loud.

"Capitalistic?" I soldiered on, encouraged.

"Yes!"

"Imperialistic?"

"Yes!"

"Unrealistic?"

"*Yes.*" She was laughing and so was I. It all seemed terribly funny.

CHAPTER 22

That day was wonderful. Mad Dog stood barking on the bows, quivering with pure joy and suicidal desire to plunge over the side. It all seemed very funny, it all seemed a great adventure. We steamed down the fairway in the winter morning sun, through the unloading freighters and the cargo junks, cold fresh blue early morning sky and the sea sparkling blue and the strong thump of the diesels and the big smooth frothing churn of our wake and out there the great blue open China Sea, and the feel of the wheel in my hands, God but it was a beautiful day. I looked at her and she was grinning, and we were both grinning. For the joy of it, and happy-nervous of each other. She climbed up out the saloon deckhead and hung onto the big mast, the wind blowing her wool skirt and her tufty plaits and laughing at Mad Dog and loving it. We were out of the fairway now, heading straight into the wind.

"Do you know how to steer?" I shouted and she turned beaming and shouted, "I think so," grinning all over her lovely face.

"Hold her there, I'll put the sails up!"

I unlashed the mainsail then heaved on the big wooden winch. I heaved with both arms and the old sail came clattering unfolding up a foot and the wind wrenched the big canvas-bamboo-mess outboard and the big mast creaked and I felt the bows lurch, I heaved with all my might and there was the great cracking flap of bamboo and canvas and then she came up. The bows were coming around, I lashed the sail rope down and scrambled back as she shrieked as the big junk keeled, grabbed the wheel from her and heaved it over and we were both laughing, and the big bows swung around and the big bamboo canvas wrenched out full.

We were both laughing. The great bat-winged sail wrenched straining full, and the big *shh-shh* of the sea, I looked down at her and laughed and she laughed up at me, we were close together, almost touching and for all the world I wanted to kiss her.

"Oh," she said, "this is lovely!"

Mad Dog was barking joyously.

"Take the wheel again and I'll put up the other sails."

I hoisted the flapping foresail, then the mizzen down off. She was under full sail now, straining Chinese rigging. I killed the engines. Suddenly there was dead quiet. Then the *sh-sh* of the sea under the bows and the big creaking swell of the big bat sails in the winter sunshine, and the swelling sea. Then Mad Dog barking again up forward.

"Oh," she said, "isn't it fantastic! Can I please keep holding the wheel?"

"Certainly. You like it?"

"It is such a feeling!" Grinning.

"Shout if the wind changes direction."

I clattered below to the galley. I poured a bottle of red wine into a pot on top of the gas stove. I threw in brown sugar, some cloves, cinnamon, singing. When it simmered I poured it into two thermos mugs and took them up to the wheel deck, grinning.

"Have you ever drunk *Glühwein?*"

"What is that?"

"Hot wine which skiers drink, a winter sports drink. We should really have eggnog at Christmastime."

"You do winter sports?" she demanded, hair blowing. "Skiing?"

"Skiing, yes."

"Oh, you are so lucky," she declared, looking at me, hair blowing.

"Do you like winter sports?"

"Of course I have not done it but it must be fantasitc. Is it fantastic?"

"The sport of kings."

She grinned. "And communists too. In Russia there is good skiing and they are very good at ice hockey. And in northern China we have ice skating and one day we will have proper skiing too. Oh, I would go crazy if I could ski. Where do you go?" she demanded.

"Austria. And Switzerland."

"Oh, you are so *lucky.*" She was sparkling enviously, her big almond eyes and her wide mouth grinning.

"Try your *Glühwein*, be careful it's hot."

She sniffed it energetically then took a big sip. Then rubbed the top of her head.

"You like it?" I was delighted with her.

"So this is what the skiers drink." She took another and patted her stomach. "Will it make me drunk?"

"It's only wine, not nearly as strong as Chinese wine."

"Soon I will go red in the face. Chinese cannot drink like Europeans."

"Europeans drink too much."

"Yes, it is their national weakness. And Chinese like to eat too much—that is our national weakness."

"Do you like Chinese wine?" I said.

162

"No. It is too strong. My father likes it very much—he is a great drinker."

"Is he?"

"He says a dinner is not a dinner without wine. I cannot drink with him; after three glasses I am red and getting drunk. He is very impressive, he never gets drunk; I always try to take him a bottle of vodka when I go to visit him."

"Vodka?"

"He is very fond of vodka. He learned to drink it from his Russian friends."

I said, "He hasn't got any Russian friends any more, has he?"

"No, they have all gone home."

"Do you approve of that? The argument between the Chinese and the Russians?"

She took a breath holding the wheel, breeze in her hair. We were getting serious again and we both liked it.

"It is a long question. But the important thing is that they are communists, we should all be friends, helping each other. Unite."

I thought I better let it go.

"And you the only child in your family?"

"Yes. Favorite daughter." She grinned.

"Ah yes, I have one of those."

"You have a daughter?" she said, surprised.

"Four years old."

"Is she in Hong Kong?"

It was the first time I thought of it all day, and it was ten o'clock already. "She's going to England next month with her mother. To live."

"Oh, I am sorry."

"Drink up your *Glühwein*, then I'll make some more. You like it?"

"Am I red in the face, Mr. McAdam?"

"Not yet, Miss Tsang."

"Then I like it very much. Real *Glühwein*, for the winter sports."

The big blue China Sea was swelling in through Lamma and Lantau now and the wind in our faces and the hot wine in our gut. I took over the wheel and heaved her onto the right tack and the big junk lurched with the new power and the bows went up and crashed down and the cold spray flew, Miss Tsang held onto the hatch with both hands, legs astride, grinning and Mad Dog was beside himself with joy up there on the bows. A big swell was coming, cold blue looming right up at us, then we ploughed broadside up the big seething wall of cold blue sea up up, then *crash,* swooping down the other side, and the big sails wrenching and the big deck plunging and the feel of the wheel in your hands, and the big rush of the big old teak junk and the big rush of the sea and canvas and the crash of spray.

"*Will you get seasick?*" I shouted.

"*No!*" she shouted. "*It's magnificent.*"

—*down* into the trough and you cannot see the horizon and it is only you and the junk and the big swelling sea, the next swell is swelling coming over and there's a big creak of the rigging—

"*Take the wheel,*" I shouted and she took it legs braced grinning and I heaved the big sail in closer. Now we were ploughing as close into the wind as the junk would go and there was the big new swell coming at our bows, up up up the big blue China swell was coming and there was nothing in the world but the big rush *shh* of the sea and the bows rearing up, up the high running swell, the whole big bows rearing out of the sea at the top in a rush, then crash whoosh and the spray flying and *down,* into the trough and the high stern swoops up in the air—and the next swell coming, and the next and the next. And the spray flying and the crashing of it and the wind in our faces and the big surges and plunges, and the bright cold sun, we were laughing, and Mad Dog was rejoicing all the way.

CHAPTER 23

I took her into a long cover on Lantau Island, on the engines. There was no wind or swell at all in here. Way up ahead there was a very small fishing village, some sampans at anchor. The mountains were steep and tough green rocky and rocks all along the long jagged waterline. Mad Dog was at his station on the bows, tongue slopping, panting hoarsely at the sea. Miss Tsang was loving every minute of it. I was feeling very good for the first time in a long time, the *Glühwein* a warm glow in my gut and the glow of the sea on my face and Miss Tsang. I put the engines into neutral, went up to the bows, and threw the anchor over. It was more than Mad Dog's flesh and blood could stand, he gave one strangled bark and plunged joyously overboard, bug ears flapping. She shouted at him in Cantonese, "Go and urinate!" We were both laughing.

We went down to the saloon because it was too cold on deck, and Miss Tsang put the duck in the oven.

Now I do not remember much of what we talked about except that we laughed a great deal. We were still a little nervous of each other. It was lovely out here on the cold China Sea, warm in the cozy saloon with the wood all varnished shiny. It was a holiday. We drank another bottle of *Glühwein* and Miss Tsang began to flush in the face and she thought it was terribly funny and declared that she was beautifully tipsy, and it all seemed terribly funny. She said, "I have never had a funnier day."

We had a good time. She chopped up the duck and we ate it with chopsticks, dipped in soy sauce. It seemed I had never been more gay and charming in my life but I was still nervous. It was a lovely day and I thought Miss Tsang was lovely. She was beautiful. She had this strong smooth square face and her eyes were large and dark and wide apart and her thick black hair was shiny and her lips were full and soft and she looked completely happy.

After lunch we were quieter, after all the wine and the hot food and the warmth down here in the saloon. We were both pleased with the lovely day, I looked at her and she seemed to me to be the only clean honest un-adulterated person in this rotten town that I had met in a long time, she had made me laugh and I was happy for the first time in a very long time, I was very pleased with her and I did not want to take her back to the Yacht Club tonight and put her ashore and watch her walk away, I wanted to keep her here, it felt urgent and happy and good and I did not care what she was or who she was, I looked at her in the warm cozy saloon and I wanted to touch her, a tactile hunger in my hands to lean across the table and touch her face and mouth, feel her arms around me and telling her that I was going to love her; it seemed a long time I sat there, screwing up the courage, then I felt my pulse trip and I saw my hand stretch out a long long way across the table and my heart was beating hard, and I touched her cheek. She felt beautifully soft and smooth and strong, she looked at me, startled, then she was blushing and she smiled, then moved her head away slightly. My voice felt thick: "Are you happy?" I said.

She was flushed. "Yes. Thank you."

She didn't look at me. "What did you do that for?"

I said, "Because I wanted to. Because I want to kiss you."

It was dead quiet. I had my hand on hers across the table. She said, looking down, "Do you always do what you want to do?"

"No."

She looked at me. "Yes," she said. "I think you do." She said it kindly, but solemnly. "You can have any girl you want. You bring many girls on your boat and do as you want with them."

"No."

She had not moved her hand but it did not yield to me.

I said, "I went to Causeway Bay because I especially wanted to see you."

"Why?" she said to the table.

"Because I like you."

She said to the table, "Of course I also like you. Or I would not be here today. I would have said, 'Thank you, but I am painting my picture today.'" She looked away. "I like you but that is no reason to kiss."

"Maybe it is," I said. "Because you make me happy."

She was blushing again. "Yes, of course we are happy."

I said, "When you agreed to come, did you think you were in danger?"

She said, blushing, "No. I thought why should I not go on his boat with him, we are two adult people." She looked at me. "But that is no reason to make love."

"I only ask to kiss you."

She said earnestly to the table, "That is the same as making love." She said resolutely, blushing, "I mean, when two people kiss, like we are here now, they will want to make love. And that is impossible."

I was delighted with her. I wanted to laugh at her and I was very earnest. "Why?"

"Because of many reasons. You know them very well."

"Tell me them."

She took a big breath across the table. "Because I am Chinese and you are English. Because you are a government policeman and I am communist. Because our lives are very different in every way."

166

I said, "The English and the Chinese are not enemies or else how could we have Hong Kong? Are we at war?"

"No, of course not."

"In Hong Kong we live together side by side?"

"Yes, but that is not the point."

I did not want to talk about all that, all I wanted was her. I felt my heart thump as I got up. I did not know what was going to happen, I only knew I wanted to do it because I was not going to let it get away and if I did not do it now it might never happen again, tomorrow it might be too late. She looked at me, and her big eyes were nervous, then she straightened up. I came at her to bend down and kiss her and I was shaking, she had her face to me watching me coming, she almost let me touch her lips then she turned her face. She sat there rigid.

I straightened. I was trembling a little.

"I am sorry," I said.

She said nothing.

I said it again, in Cantonese, "Opposite you I not live."

"M'sai." Not necessary.

She sat there what seemed a long time. I did not touch her. She turned her head and looked up at me. She said in Cantonese, "Mr. McAdam, is it possible that I could sleep for one hour? Your wine is too strong for me."

I did not know if she meant it. "Of course. Sleep in my cabin, aft. I won't disturb you," I added.

She looked at me. "It is nothing personal, Mr. McAdam, I have really enjoyed today."

"Good." I smiled.

She hesitated.

"Thank you. You do not think I am rude?"

I grinned. "For refusing me, or for going to sleep?"

She grinned, relieved. "Both."

"Of course not, it's a holiday. Allow me." I got up and opened the cabin door for her.

"Thank you, Mr. McAdam." She was blushing again, but grinning now. "Good afternoon."

"Good afternoon," I grinned, and I wanted to laugh and kiss her wide mouth. She closed the door.

I went up onto the wheel deck and looked for Mad Dog. He was slobbering around the rocks happily. I went back down to the saloon and lay down on the beach and looked up at the deckhead.

CHAPTER 24

When I woke up she was shaking my foot and saying, *"Mr. McAdam, we are shipwrecked!"*

I sat up. The saloon was tilted. The whole bloody junk was at an angle.

I hurried up the steps onto the tilted sundeck. It was nearly sundown. I looked over the side, I could see the bottom, three feet down. She was staring worriedly at me.

"We're aground," I said. I was awake now. "The tide's gone out."

She stared.

"It's my fault," I said. "I didn't know we were in such shallow water."

"What about the ship?" she said.

I felt fine now.

"The junk's fine," I said. "She's only sitting on the sand. No rocks down there."

She looked at me. "What do we do now?"

I grinned at her. "We must wait. The new tide will float us off."

"What a predicament!"

I said, "I've done this before. There's no danger."

"When will the tide take us off?"

"A couple of hours." I did not know the tide times.

"Then it will be dark when we sail back."

"Yes, but I know the way. Let's go below, it's cold up here."

We went below. I went to the refrigerator.

"Will you have a drink? It's after sundowner time."

"The colonialists and their sundowners! Can I make some tea?"

"The Chinese and their tea!" I said.

I poured a San Miguel carefully into a mug so as not to get a head. It went down cool and sparkling and clean after the feeling of having slept off wine. I felt good. I was delighted this had happened. "I'm sorry about this, Ying-ling," I said.

She smiled over her shoulder. "Mr. McAdam, it is exciting, I have never been shipwrecked before. We Chinese are philosophical."

She sat down at the table with her tea. I lit the paraffin heater. It was cheerful down here in the angled saloon. We were a little self-conscious now without the glow of the *Glühwein,* but I felt very good. She was looking for something to say.

"So your Christmas is nearly over. Did you go to church?"

"Yes. I took my daughter."

"But you are not a good Christian?"

"No. Do you have any religion?"

"No. I don't believe in gods."

"Why not?" I was enjoying her.

"We are masters of our own destiny. How can a god permit such human suffering?"

I nodded encouragingly. She said, "Why are you not a good Christian, Mr. McAdam?"

"For many reasons. Except when I'm frightened."

"What are you afraid of?"

"Unhappiness."

She said, smiling, "Are you afraid of the communists?"

"Not of beautiful ones."

She smiled. "Seriously."

"No."

"Why not?" She was enjoying it too, now. "Do you know many communists?"

"A lot. Hong Kong's full of communists in every walk of life."

"But do you know any well?"

I did not want to mention my time in Special Branch. "A few."

"And what do you think of them?" She had a twinkle in her eye.

But I wanted to handle this carefully. "There are many kinds of communists."

She waved her hand. "Of course, in Hong Kong you will meet plenty of fat cats. But they are not important."

I said, "They're very important to China. China's export business, that's how they got fat."

She didn't want to talk about that kind of communist. She said, "I mean, the communists as a whole, what do you think of them?" She really wanted to know, cheerfully.

I said carefully, to give a short answer to a long question, "The communists are the best thing that happened to China. Because their energy and determination, and idealism, have swept China clean of the massive corruption and exploitation of the people and have brought social improvement. And I doubt whether a capitalist system, however well intentioned, could have achieved it. Because the problem was so massive." She was listening intently. "I think it had to be a new broom to sweep it clean."

She waited intently, then said, "And in Hong Kong?"

I was enjoying it. I would have enjoyed talking about anything to her.

"Hong Kong exists by mutual consent between the communists and the capitalists. For one reason only: Money." I held up my finger. "China's money. Hong Kong only exists because China wants it to exist, for money and trade. Everybody here is concerned only with money, even the communists. So the communists in Hong Kong are rather different to those across the border. So?" I looked at her. "Hong Kong is a money-melting pot. Everybody is concerned with money, so we all mix together and get on with business and tolerate each other." I smiled at her. "We all get on pretty well together, don't we?" She nodded.

I was enjoying the sound of my own voice but I waited to see where she was heading.

"And the Hong Kong Government?" she said.

"What about it?"

"Is it busy making money for Britain?" Like the communists are for China?" She said it with a determined straight face.

"No. That's a popular misconception about our government. The British Government gets none of our taxes. It all belongs to the Hong Kong Government. Tax is low anyway. That's why there's so much business here. Duty free. The government just provides an administration, and lets everybody get on with making money, and doesn't interfere. Nor does Peking," I added.

"But the Hong Kong Government is still very rich," she murmured.

"Sure."

"What does it do with all its people's taxes?"

I said cheerfully, "Builds resettlement blocks to house all the poor people." I cut off, *who have run away from China.* "Hospitals, civil service, education . . ."

"Social welfare?" she murmured, with a wisp of a smile.

170

I smiled. "Not much, I'm afraid. The government's policy is laissez-faire."

"Yes." She smiled. "They spend more on salaries for social welfare officers than they do on social welfare, I believe?"

"I believe so." I smiled at her.

"Do you approve?" She cocked her eyebrow.

"No. Every country should have strong social welfare services. A strong measure of socialism."

She liked that.

"Are you a socialist at heart, Mr. McAdam?"

I said, "Every sensible person must be a socialist up to a point. How far it should go depends on the country, its people, and its economics." I was enjoying Miss Tsang sounding me out. "But for most countries private enterprise is the most effective economic system, likely to produce the best national results. Because it provides incentives to work hard."

She pulled a noncommittal face at that. "And for China?"

"Communism," I said, back to square one. I cut off, *at least for the time being.* "Because there are seven hundred million Chinese in a country poverty-stricken by massive exploitation and disorganization under the Nationalists. But the communists need incentives too, and now they're getting it, after the Great Leap Forward. King Pig is back. Small private lots, two ducks—"

She said defensively, "The Great Leap Forward failed mostly because of bad weather, Mr. McAdam, admit it."

Jesus. But I decided to let it go. It was something that she admitted it was a failure. "Don't you agree that some incentives are necessary?" I said.

"Yes," she said, as if there could be no argument. "As long as there is strong basic socialism."

I wondered how good a communist Miss Tsang was. Not very.

"And," I said conversationally, "do you know many noncommunists? In this melting pot?"

"Quite a few."

"Who?"

She said, "A lot of students at my Teacher Training College. My professors. A lot of people at the Graphic Arts Center. Some friends of my father's."

"The Graphic Arts Center?"

"It is a small art school helped by the university. I

171

go there sometimes to try to learn something. The teacher is my friend, Mrs. Day, do you know her?"

"No." I was interested.

"She is a very nice American." She added, "Maybe you should join the Graphic Arts, it only costs ten dollars a month and you can use the facilities and get good advice."

"Maybe I will," I said, interested.

"Yes. And some of Mrs. Day's friends. And some others I know."

"Do you meet these friends often?"

She shrugged. "No. Yes, sometimes."

I thought, Probably that accounts for the milk in the coconut. I said, "And? What do *you* think of the Hong Kong Government?"

She grinned at me as if she had been expecting it. Mr. McAdam, you have been very polite about my people and you are my host so I must not be rude about yours."

I loved her when she grinned like that. "Be my guest at the expense of the Hong Kong Government."

She shook her head, determined to be polite. "Except this. Naturally I do not like colonial governments. But this one is not too bad?" She grinned at me. "Except for a lot of things."

"That's not good enough," I said. "You cross-questioned me."

"You spied on me with binoculars!"

We were both laughing.

"All right," I said. "One more. Are *you* a good communist?"

She looked at me with a twinkle in her eye.

"Very good."

It seemed funny.

"Seriously."

"Seriously. I am going to swim back to Hong Kong right now."

When we stopped laughing she tried to be serious. She had her head on one side and contemplated her tea.

"No, I am not a good communist. I am a rotten one."

"Why?" This was interesting.

She considered. "Because I am too selfish. I am not dedicated enough at all. I am too interested in my own life, the things I like."

"What do you like?"

"Painting. Good books. Good movies. The usual things."

She shrugged at her teacup. "I want to go to Europe and see all the beautiful art galleries and places. And go to one of the art colleges. The London School of Fine Arts. Or Paris. And really learn." She grinned at me. "And have fun."

I was testing her, enjoying it.

"And why can't you do that and still be a good communist? I'm sure the young Russian artists have a pretty good time."

She smiled. "In Russia, yes. This is China." I waited. "In China we are more revolutionary." She smiled. "And conservative."

"Anti Western?" I said.

She corrected me with a smile: "No. Anti Western culture."

I nodded. "Are the Russians such bad communists?"

She smiled. "In Chinese eyes, yes. They are revisionists. Taking the capitalist road. Like Yugoslavia."

"And in your eyes?"

She shrugged, smiled. "In my eyes they are all right. They are good enough for me. But not for China. And I am Chinese."

I smiled at her. "So you are a rotten Chinese communist?"

She grinned. Then said more earnestly, "But not only for that. I would actually like to live among artists. Widen my horizons. Do bourgeois things." She was grinning. "Go to Austria and do expensive bourgeois winter sports."

"Drink *Glühwein.*"

"Oh yes, the *Glühwein* was very good."

"Dance?"

"I am not a very good dancer."

"Clothes?"

She smiled. "No. Yes, I suppose so. All women like that. But not so important. It is *me.*" She tapped her head hopelessly.

I was grinning, delighted with her. "Then why are you a communist at all?"

The corners of her mouth twitched. She was having a good time for little reason and so was I.

"Because my heart rules my head."

"Seriously."

"Seriously. I am Chinese." Then she sat back and was more serious and her face was equally beautiful. A beau-

173

tiful Chinese-woman strong face. Such eyes. "I am Chinese so I love China. The communists are good men doing their best for China. They are the first good, honest government China has had for centuries." She grinned at me: "I am a patriot."

I said, "So am I, but that does not mean I belong to the political party in power in England at the moment."

She held up a finger: I am not a member of the Communist party." She grinned: "I'm sure they wouldn't have me." She shrugged. "But there is only one way for China. China has problems which only communism can cure. And they are curing them, you cannot deny it."

"What about the Great Leap Forward?"

She said, a little on her mettle, "It failed this year. All right, maybe it was too rushed. There was also a lot of bad luck. But two steps forward and one step backward is still progress."

"*One* step backward?"

She said quickly: "We have not yet seen the full economic results of the Great Leap Forward. Are you an economist?"

"No," I admitted.

"Nor am I. But in principle the idea of the Great Leap Forward was sound. The only capital asset China has to work with is its labor, *man*power. And so she used it to the full. The principle was sound. And what about men's minds? What a fantastic success that was!"

"Yes," I admitted.

"What a victory! Seven hundred million Chinese all working so hard for the common good! Seven hundred *million! Chinese.* The Chinese used to be terrible for co-operation. Can you imagine seven hundred million English working so hard for their country?"

"No," I admitted.

She sat back, intently. "Fantastic. It shows what Chinese can do in the future. And it was the principles of communism that enabled them to do it."

I said, "Not just the strength of Mao? And his party machine?"

She shook her head emphatically. "No. Capitalism could not have done it. Because it is selfish. Communism is sel*less.*"

I said, "You don't sound too bad a communist to me."

She smiled at me: "What is a communist, Mr. McAdam?"

I said, "There aren't any. They're only socialists at this moment in history. State capitalists. The first Marxist phase, the dictatorship of the proletariat. Although they call themselves communists."

"Exactly," she said. "Do you believe the real Marxist communism is possible? Where there is no state, only communal property and brotherly spirit and each man gets according to his needs?"

"No," I said.

"No," she said, almost sadly. "Nor do I."

"Cheer up," I said. "The Russians don't either."

She smiled at me: "And Mao Tse-tung?"

I said, "Mao believes it's possible."

"You think so? In his heart?"

"Yes. Particularly in his heart. Mao is an idealist. Through and through. He believes, all right."

She said: "Does he believe it's possible in his lifetime?"

"He'll try to make it possible. He's such an optimist the old bastard will probably live longer than Moses."

She thought that was screamingly funny. She threw back her head and laughed. Then we were both laughing. When she stopped laughing she shook her head.

"He can't do it. Nobody can. It is only an ideal. Utopia!"

She certainly wasn't a very good communist, I thought. I said, "He'll have a very good try. He'll start shaking up the people again. Pretty soon. As soon as he can afford to do it. He's done it before. It's inherent in his theory of contradictions. Each revolutionary step forward is followed by a conservative reaction. To make the revolution succeed the reactionaries must be exposed and corrected. China will get reactionaries after this Great Leap Forward. People who want to stick in a rut, be conservative, say, This is far enough. King Pig. Take the capitalist road, as the saying goes, like the Russians. Like the Yugoslavs. Goulash communists. Rice-bowl communists." I was enjoying the sound of my own voice. "Mao will shake them up. Then he'll be off on another Leap Forward. Then another shake-up to get rid of the new reactionaries. And so on. He won't sit still like Uncle Khrushchev. Mao's too much of an idealist!"

"But he won't succeed?" She was listening intently.

"He'll succeed in shaking them up, all right. In making them toe the line like nobody's business. All seven hundred million of them."

"But the ideal? Marxist communism, will he achieve that? Utopia?"

"No," I said. "Mao will die. China will go conservative after that. Like the Russians. Goulash King Pig again. That's what he's afraid of. That's why he'll keep shaking them up while he's alive."

She said sadly, "It's a pity he won't succeed. Such a wonderful ideal. Such a wonderful man."

"Yes," I said politely. I agreed about the man. I wasn't so crazy about the ideal, utopia or no utopia. I said, "So that's why you're a communist? Even though you don't believe?"

"I believe in the principles. Or most of them."

"Which ones?"

She sat back and contemplated her hands on the table.

"Communal property. The world is so small now. And so many people. Seven hundred million Chinese. Five hundred million Indians. Just for example. And so little property. The property is getting less and less to share, because there are more and more people because of the population explosion. If the property is shrinking, it is impossible, unjust, to have a few people owning it and all the rest going without. It is unnatural. It is natural to share it. Isn't it? If you don't share it," she said, "people will fight for it. Like if you had only one pool of water among the people on a desert island. They must share it. Or they will kill each other. Capitalism was all right in the old days when there was so much and so few people. Before the population explosion."

That's some definition of communist principle, I thought. But it made the point.

"And it is the only way for China," she said intently. "Especially after so many centuries of bad government and colonial exploitation." She added, "Exsanguination."

She didn't seem about to go on. I said, "So that's why you work at a communist school?"

"At least I am helping China in my small way. Doing my duty." She added, "I love teaching. Watching them grow up educated people because of me."

I liked the way she said that. "What are the rest of your teaching staff like?" I said.

She smiled. "Dedicated and dull. And most communist ones are *very* dull." She put her hands at the sides of her eyes like a horse's blinkers. "Like that. I like them, but

I lead my own life, I don't have much to do with them after school."

Interesting. "How would you like to go to China to work?"

She considered. "One day, maybe. But not yet." She grinned broadly.

"O Lord, make me good, but not yet? St. *Paul*."

She liked that. "That's good! O Lord, make me good, but not yet." She nodded soberly at herself. "Yes, I suppose that is me."

I wanted to laugh.

"And? How do you like China when you visit your father?"

"Fantastic," she said. "Truly. Everybody so clean. So honest. Hard-working."

I wanted to say, So happy? "And how does your father like it? Is he a staunch communist?"

"My father practices medicine. He wouldn't care if the sky fell down tomorrow. No, I am joking. Are you spying on my poor father too?"

We were both laughing.

"What about my dog?" she said suddenly.

"Is he a good communist?"

We were both laughing.

I climbed up onto the wheel deck with the flashlight. The tide was coming in, the junk had leveled out a lot. There was not much moon. I heard Mad Dog thrashing. I looked through the binoculars, with the flashlight.

"He's got a big cork float from a fisherman's net in his mouth," I said. "He's trying to drag the whole net in."

"The fool!" She took the binoculars.

We shouted at him but he would not let go of the float. He was going to bring the whole works in or else.

"We'll have to bring him in by force of arms," Miss Tsang said.

I lowered the dinghy and we rowed out to him. It was cold and lovely in the moonlight, the sea silver black, she looked beautiful in the moonlight and she was loving it. We laughed a lot getting Mad Dog to let go of the big cork float, thrashing with his paws and growling in his throat, we nearly capsized the dinghy several times. Finally we got him pulled into the dinghy and he shook himself all over us. When we got back to the junk he wanted to jump back into the sea and nearly pulled Miss Tsang in. We manhandled him aboard, then I put on a pair of shorts and tennis shoes and climbed down into the water to investigate the boat.

I walked slowly around the boat, feeling the sand with my feet, shivering. There were no rocks. The tide had come in, now she was only just resting on the bottom. In half an hour she would be off. I climbed back up the swimming ladder, aboard. Miss Tsang was down below making *Glühwein*, at my instruction. Mad Dog was leashed, he thumped his tail at me hopefully. I looked out to sea.

I did not want to go home tonight. Oh no I didn't want to go, I was happy. I could easily just tell her that it was too dangerous to go home in the dark. I went down into the saloon.

"Hello," she said brightly, making the *Glühwein*.

I said, "We're almost off the bottom. But would you like to stay the night out here?" I added quickly, "You'll sleep in there and I'll sleep here."

She looked at me, wide-eyed, considering.

"Is it dangerous to sail in the dark?"

Oh damn me: "No," I said. "Unfortunately. I know the islands well."

She smiled at the "unfortunately." She said, "Then I think we better go back tonight." She grinned: "Please do not think I am ungrateful, I've had such a wonderful day."

After supper we steamed back to Hong Kong. The moon was bright silver, and then the rainbow lights of the neon signs far away, and the lights on the Peak, and the islands steep and black, and the ships, and Miss Tsang beside me at the wheel all the way. It was lovely and I did not want it to end.

PART V

CHAPTER 25

It was supposed to be a secret rendezvous, lest her school found out. Nothing much could have happened to me, except promotion, because the communists were no trouble in those days. I did not consider her a real communist anyway. I parked the Opel in the Yacht Club parking lot and waited for her in the dark. First I always saw Mad Dog coming loping along the causeway out of Percival Street, then her. Stepping it out, skirt swirling, head up, no-nonsense walk. When she was out of the lamplight she skipped to the car.

"Hello."

"Hello, my darling!" We were both grinning holding each other tight. She felt absolutely wonderful in my arms. "Your face is cold!"

"But my heart is so warm! Mad Dog is scratching your paint."

"To hell with my paint."

We went for a drive. Often we drove up to the Peak, the long winding road cut into the steep jungled mountains, the harbor lights beautiful. She sat very close to me and when I did not need both hands I held her thigh. Even to touch each other a little made us excited. Her skin was incredibly smooth and soft and her legs were beautiful, it seemed I had never felt such young beautiful womanflesh. Way down there were Aberdeen and Deep Water Bay, lights twinkling, and then Lamma Island and then the open China Sea, and then the Communist Islands, the Lemas, guarding the International Shipping Lane with their garrison and very fast P.T. boats with cannon mounted on the bows; the whole China Sea was silver in the moonlight from up here, and the islands black, and the lights of the fishing junks. Along narrow Luguard Road, around the Peak, it was so narrow that I had to be careful not to wipe the sides of the car against the rock. There were no more houses along here and it was very quiet. I pulled off down the dirt track a way, to our place in the tall grass. And there far below was the fairyland glow of Hong Kong and Kowloon, and the harbor.

From way up here the many colors of the neon signs looked like jewels. And the moon and the stars. It was always my favorite view, but I had gotten used to it and now I saw it through new eyes because I was in love. It is a wonderful place for lovers. Nobody came this far up, except us. It was our own place, our second home. Our first home was the junk.

Sometimes we made love outside in the tall grass, on a rug, under an eiderdown. Sometimes we lay in the back of the Opel station wagon on a foam mattress I had filled. It was good lying in the back of the station wagon, like lying snug in a warm tent, like a tent gets to feel like home, she stretched out beautiful beside me, the moonlight coming through the windows. I had installed a heater. We called the Opel home. Sometimes we went to Repulse Bay and parked alongside the beach. There was nobody about, because it was winter. We walked along the beach in the dark moonlight, warm with the chill on our faces. Sometimes she wanted to run. Just to run, for the joy of it. It was lovely to be out in the open with her, to feel her in my arms. Sometimes we did not talk much and sometimes it seemed we never stopped talking.

Sometimes we went to the Driftwood, after walking. It was a small restaurant near the beach, it was always empty in winter. We seldom saw anybody there except the waiters. It was dark and warm and we sat in a corner by candlelight. I told them how to make *Glühwein*, of which she was very fond, but afterward we preferred their Irish coffee, which she also liked. She did not like any other liquor. We did not mind there being no other customers. It seemed that everything was great fun and I loved to see her eyes shining in the candlelight and her face a little flushed from the Irishes. Her eyes were beautiful, large and dark and slanted at the tips, and her eyebrows were perfect. It was a strong, lovely face. Her hair was very black and shiny and I wished it were longer.

"Grow your hair for me."

"I can't grow it much longer than this, that is supposed to be very bourgeois. It is nearly down to my shoulders anyway."

"This is Hong Kong, not Peking. You said your principal was a good sort."

"My principal is very jolly, but the others are stick-in-muds."

"Tell them to go to hell."

"All right, darling, I'm busy growing it now."

But I wished there were other places we could go. I was happy and wanted to walk hand in hand with her in the open and show her off. She had a lovely figure. We could have done it and nobody would have known, or cared, all over this town people were having affairs, fat cats and all; but it was early days yet for her. And I did not like leaving the warm restaurant and going back into the cold to drive her back to the Causeway Bay. One night I said, "I must get another flat."

"Why?"

I said carefully, "For us. We can't go on living in a station wagon. I want to be with you properly."

"But I am with you properly. I could not be more with you properly. Or improperly." She grinned.

I said, "Not my flat at the Hermitage, I agree it's too conspicuous. Though most of them are shacked up with somebody. Somewhere where you won't feel apprehensive."

"A government flat?" she said.

"All right, not a government flat, I'll find something else."

"No. All that money."

"I've let my Happy Valley house, that rent will pay for it."

She didn't like it.

I said, "You needn't sleep there. Just a place where we can go. And have our own things. Like an artist's studio, perhaps. Have dinner together there sometimes. Like any other pair of lovers."

"Maybe we aren't like other lovers," she said.

"What do you mean?" I knew what she meant.

She avoided it. "We have each other. That is enough for us, we have more than other lovers."

I said, "Ying, all over this town there are people having love affairs. Including many communist officials. And they don't have to do it in cars. It's not bourgeois to be comfortable."

But she didn't like the idea of being a kept woman. All that money spent because of her. I went easy on her. It was early days yet. I did not know what was going to happen. I did not care, as long as we were happy. I had been unhappy a long time and I was not going to stop being happy now by crossing any bridges before I had to. I would look for a place anyway.

She said, "It's only two nights a week."

The other nights she had extracurricular duties. Mondays was night school for the Transport Workers' Union, Wednesday was political discussion night. The Transport Workers' Union was very Red, but nobody was making any trouble in those days. The communist schools were only trying to give a decent education.

She did not mention her political discussion night much, and I did not care to ask her much. I knew it was the usual stuff. I knew from my days in Special Branch that we had infiltrated most of the discussion groups and it was normally very dull and harmless stuff indeed. It depended on the group, but mostly they read from the *Collected Works of Mao Tse-tung* and distributed roneoed newssheets, every week one member had a turn to deliver a little talk about some aspect of progress in the motherland or of the turpitude of capitalism, supported by platitudinous quotes from the *Ta Kung Po* or *Heung Keung Po* or one or other of the local Red newspapers, or from the *Red Flag*. Occasionally some real grievance against some department of the Hong Kong Government or somebody's employer was discussed, followed by stout resolutions and letters to the newspaper and threats of strikes which never came off. Nobody went on strike because everybody was too busy making money to pay off their hire-purchase television sets and furniture, the wages in Hong Kong were the second highest in Southeast Asia, and many many times higher then in the motherland twenty miles away, across the Shamchun. The comrades who belonged to the discussion groups were all settled people, certainly not the poor squatters who had just made it at great personal risk to the Golden Mountain Where Men Eat Fat Pork from China. Her political discussion nights were of no significance. One Thursday night she mentioned that, apart from the committee members, only herself and two other people had shown up. And one of them was probably our agent, I thought. She mentioned that the secretary was a fat little Cantonese who was always touching her in a comradely fashion and she had to be careful how she sat because he was always looking at her legs.

"He's got good taste," I said.

"Such a little smooth Cantonese!"

"I like the Cantonese," I said.

She was going to say something, then changed her mind. "They're okay." She was a Northerner.

"But not peeping up your legs?"

"Peeping? They always try to touch your breasts! They bump into you in the street to feel them!"

Every woman I knew complained of that, it was a bad Hong Kong joke.

"What else?"

"They are money-crazy. Money money money! Even in Canton, my father told me. And corrupt."

"Corrupt in Canton?"

"No, here in Hong Kong. So many government departments. You know, you're a policeman."

"I beg your pardon, madam?"

"I don't mean you! I don't think you are corrupt."

"But the Hong Kong Police Force is?"

"Now I have made you angry."

"Not yet."

"Yes, I have. But isn't there corruption in the police?"

"Some," I said shortly. "There is some in every police force the world over."

"But in the Hong Kong police it is worse?"

"Possibly," I admitted, grudgingly.

"Why? Because they are Chinese?"

I avoided that. "Because the three big Chinese vices of gambling, prostitution, and opium are illegal now. And you'll never stamp out those three. So those people try to buy off the police. Some succeed," I said shortly. "If gambling and prostitution were legalized you would eliminate eighty per cent of the corruption. But you cannot legalize opium."

"And in the other government departments?"

"Which?"

"So many. Hawker Control. Squatter Control. Resettlement. Immigration. Building. Even Ambulance! I have even heard of ambulance drivers who say, 'I will not take your son to hospital unless you give me ten dollars tea money.' "

"Yes," I admitted.

"The corruption here is terrible!" she declared.

I didn't like that. "We do our best to stamp it out. It's mostly petty stuff, among minor officials and clerks and so forth." That wasn't quite true at all, but I wanted to defend the government, it was a pretty good government of a very difficult place. And a pretty damn good police force.

"Not very petty. Why is it so bad? Because they are Chinese?"

"Because it is Hong Kong," I said.

"Like Shanghai?" She was trying to tease me now.

"No, not like Shanghai. Shanghai never even tried to get the mud out from between her toes. The Hong Kong Government tries. It just never washes its feet properly."

She smiled, enjoying it.

"Will the Hong Kong Government succeed?"

"Probably not."

"Why not?"

I didn't like saying it. "Because corruption is a fact of life with Chinese. Almost a way of life. People expect to have to give and take corruption just to get along with government officials."

She was not offended in the least, I had said exactly what she wanted. "But," she pointed out happily, "there is no more corruption in China! And no more drugs. The communists achieved it. That shows it is not the fault of the Chinese. So it must be the fault of this imperialistic colonial Hong Kong Government!"

Quod erat demonstrandum.

I grinned at her. "There's no more drugs in China because they shot all the addicts and pushers. You can't be an addict if you're dead. You can't be a corrupt official if you're dead either." I left out, "and nobody's got any money to gamble and go whoring with."

She didn't like that but she couldn't deny it. "There must be the greatest good for the greatest number," she said. "Maybe shooting is the only way."

"For narcotics, maybe."

She didn't like it but she said, "Why don't you shoot them then?"

"Because we English are too softhearted."

She nodded; nod nod nod. but defensively. "Narcotics

184

are vicious. It is better for a few men to die quickly than hundreds of thousands die slowly. In China we have got rid of them. No other country has achieved that. And no corruption," she added.

I thought, With fifty thousand escapees every year? And one quarter of Hong Kong's currency circulating in Kwantung? I let it go. "How do you know I'm not corrupt," I said.

"By your big beautiful barbarian blue eyes!"

"You're the one with the beautiful eyes," I said.

We had a good time. I did not consider her a real communist. I knew many communists in Hong Kong, and I had known a good few in England at university, and I had fought them in Malaya, and she was nothing like any of them. She was an intellectual communist, or a socialist like most university students are liberal. Except that she was twenty-six and not nineteen. Except that she had been doing it all her adult life. Except that she intended doing it indefinitely. Except a lot of things maybe, if I analyzed them, which I did not, not very much. She was just a patriot. China was her motherland, Mao Tse-tung and his communists were doing their best for China with their socialism. Socialism was the answer for China, therefore it was her duty to work for them by teaching in their schools, to do her bit, to inculcate in the young in this dubious city the correct awareness, sincerities, and loyalty to the new China motherland. It was as simple as that: of course she was a communist.

"Wouldn't you be?" she said.

I said, "England hasn't got the same problems."

"Of course you would. You are an intelligent, sensible man. Who could not admire Mao Tse-tung and all the big things he has done for China?"

"But he's made a few big mistakes," I said.

"You mean the Great Leap Forward, hah?"

"He did it against all advice," I said, trying to sound reasonable. "Of the farmers. The engineers. The economists. The Russians."

She had a lot of time for the Russians. "Yes, but China's problems are not ordinary, darling! We have great problems so we had to try the great solutions. It nearly worked. If it had worked it would have been wonderful for China, hah? What other mistakes?"

I said, "First Mao gave the peasants all the land. Then he took it all away and made the communes. Then he

185

gave them small private lots to keep them happy. Then he took them away. Now after the Great Leap Forward has failed he's given them back again. And when the food crisis is over he'll confiscate them back again."

"No." She shook her head firmly. "I don't think so."

"He's done it before. Do you approve of the peasants having small private lots as well as working the communes?"

"I think so, yes. Because it increases production. A peasant needs an incentive. There is no harm in that provided there is no exploitation, no unfairness. And provided he is re-educated, to think of China, first, not himself."

"That's why I think Mao will take the private lots back when the crisis is over. Because he's an idealist. And private lots is not quite communism. It's a little too like capitalism, revisionism. Russian."

"Oh, you are a pessimist! Communism is so that everybody will have justice and good wages and good houses and some money in the bank and holidays, not to take away their things!"

As simple as that. Communism was the best for China, therefore a communist she was. She did not think that everything the communists had done was successful, they had made mistakes, not all their opinions were sophisticated, not all their attitudes to the outside world reasonable. "They are getting old now, Mao and Chou and Liu and Chen," she said. "All their lives they have been fighting as guerrillas for survival, for China, with nothing. And now at last they have won, and now they have so many new problems, so of course they are a little old-fashioned. But they are achieving wonders for China."

"Still got the mud of the Long March and the Yenan caves between their toes?" I said.

She was quite unabashed by the exodus from China. "Every country has people who want to emigrate. Why do so many people leave England every year for Australia and America, hah? Okay, because they want to go away. That does not mean England is a bad country, hah?"

"It might," I said. "But England doesn't stop them leaving." I stopped myself from saying, Shoot them.

"Yes," she said. "I agree. Let them go, I say. We do not need such people, we need people who want to stay and work for China."

"Why does China stop them leaving?"

"For discipline. To make them do their duty. So they do not set a bad example. Like in an army. We are fighting an economic war, you see, against all our natural problems. But I say we should let the unwilling ones go, they are not good communists."

She was not a good communist either, in my book, not Mao's brand of communist. She had too much *joie de vivre* and too many interests. Hong Kong had a good many communists like her. There had been plenty like that at my university.

So I was not worried about her political discussion nights and her Transport Workers' Union night-school nights nor about her working at the Tai Ping, Great Peace, School. What worried me was that two nights a week I could not see her, and she would not telephone me from school, and she would not spend the whole night with me. After a while it seemed that more than anything I wanted to sleep the whole night with her and wake up beside her in the mornings, the morning is the best time to be with your woman. She was my woman now. My tall smooth beautiful clean-cut slender dark-eyed woman, and her eyes were the most beautiful I had ever seen. And when she came back to me, along the causeway on Tuesday and Thursday nights, head up, no-nonsense walk, then skipped over to the car and flung open the door and swung her hips in beaming, it was as if she had been away a very long time.

CHAPTER 26

We had a great time that winter. Sometimes she wrote me a letter in the early mornings, even when she was meeting me that night, and posted it on the way to school and I got it at lunchtime. She wrote:

> I was doing my exercises on the roof and the sun came up over the Mountains of Nine Dragons, over China, all asleep, the whole world was still asleep but me and Mad Dog. Truly the East is so magnificently red and I was so joyful I wanted to wake you to see

it with me. Good-by, I am running to post this now before school.

And she wrote:

Yesterday a little girl in my class was dreaming during art lesson. She was staring out the window and the look in her eyes was so beautiful, and her whole little face, I wanted to run to fetch you to come and see her! But alas I will not see you until tomorrow.

One day the telephone rang as I was leaving for the station for lunch. "*Wei?*" I said.

"*Wei,* is that the Big Bomban McAdam?"

"Yes!" I was grinning. "Where are you?"

"In a telephone booth. You know what?"

"What?"

"I was buying an orange and a butterfly came and sat on my hand. Wasn't that beautiful!"

I wanted to laugh I loved her so much.

"That was beautiful," I said.

"I was just picking up the orange and the pile of oranges was big and golden and the sun was shining on them and just suddenly the butterfly came down all by himself and sat on my hand. Wasn't that good?"

I was grinning, I could feel tears it was so good. "That was very good. He went and sat on the most beautiful thing in China, he knew what he was doing."

"But his colors! And he just sat there, flapping his wings a little and I kept my hand still and people came around looking and there was a lot of noise and he just sat there. Then he flew away. Wasn't that beautiful!"

"You're beautiful!"

"No, but wasn't that good? I just wanted to tell you. Good-by, sir."

"Do you love me?" I shouted.

"Yes, Inspector! Good-by."

In the early mornings she did her Chinese slow-motion exercises on the rooftop, and watered her flowerpots. She was fanatical about both. "Good for the body and good for the soul." *I have just done my exercises and there was a junk setting out to sea in the sunrise and he had his red sails up. . . .* I imagined her doing her graceful Chinese shadowboxing in the dawn, slow motion, more like a ballet dance, watching for sunrise, and the look in her eyes; and singing as she watered her flowerpots with a mixture of her urine and water from her red chamber pot which she kept under her bed for this purpose. She was quite unabashed about telling me such things. She even considered collecting urine from other people in the house where she lived, but decided against it because she didn't have enough flowerpots or chamber pots. She considered getting more of both, lying with me in the back of the station wagon. "It is a pity to waste all that urine."

"Oh, quite."

"It just goes into the sea. But it is so good for flowers."

"Indeed."

"In China everybody must save their urine and shit, you know, to put on the fields, it is the law."

It shook me when she said this in English, though not in Cantonese. The Chinese swear a great deal.

"And a very good law too."

"It is very important because we have not yet got factories for fertilizer. If we had always done this, under the previous governments, China would be a rich country today."

"Seven hundred million Chinese," I said, "that's a lot of urine."

"And shit," she said.

"*And* shit. The mind boggles; terrifying."

She broke into peals of laughter. She thought that was very funny.

"Do you think we Chinese are funny?"

"I think you're a laugh a minute. All seven hundred million of you."

She had a mouse called Puku. A nice ordinary Chinese house mouse, not a white barbarian one. Percy was her cockatoo. Shouted a lot. Loved his head scratched. Could chew up a cotton reel in thirty minutes. Spoke in English and Cantonese. Terrorized the mouse. Very jealous of Mad Dog, shouted at him. Mad Dog was always trying to get a mouthful of old Perce. I knew all about old Perce and the mouse and how they all lived together in her room and I knew all about her flowerpots on the roof, what kind and how many, but I had never seen any of them. I wanted to know everything about her to be able to imagine her in her home, but I could not go near her lodgings. Nor would she come to my Hermitage flat, because it was government quarters.

"We aren't committing any crime," I said. "Half my colleagues have their girl friends living with them. And half the schoolmistresses have half the American Navy half the time."

"No," she said, "everybody talks too much in Hong Kong. And it is only for two nights a week we must make love in your car."

I had already rented out my Happy Valley house, accommodation was very difficult to find. Hong Kong was bloody booming. Anyway, I did not want to live in my old house, with all the memories: I was in a new life and I was happy and I would probably have to keep on the Hermitage flat officially, for the sake of appearances, but the rent from the Happy Valley house would cover the rent for our new place, when I found it. It would not have to be big, just sort of artist's studio, just someplace where we could go.

The junk was our other home in those early days, the winter. Every weekend we went out on it. We hardly ever saw any other pleasure craft for it was too cold for ordinary people. We were no ordinary people. We were in love and we loved the cold China Sea and the warm junk, and we called it home. Because for two whole days and two whole nights we were alone and free, to go where we liked and make love when we liked, and to sleep the whole night together, warm and deep in the big double bunk.

On Fridays I went down to the Yacht Club in the sunset and my look-see boat boy had everything ready, full water tanks, full fuel tanks, everything shining. I steamed out of the Yacht Club to the small public jetty, tied up, and waited for her. As soon as it was dark she came swinging along the causeway, Mad Dog bounding ahead slobbering with anticipation.

It was always a great adventure. We had not seen each other since Wednesday night, it was as if she had been away a long time. While we steamed down the fairway it seemed we could not stop grinning and talking, we were very happy to be together again. And the knowledge that we had a whole weekend together. The first night we anchored off one of the nearby islands. First thing in the early morning she put my dressing gown on and ran up on deck to report on the sunrise.

"Oh, it's magnificent, come and see!"

The whole eastern sky was flaming red over the mountains, and the mountains and the islands were early morning mauve and green and the sea was dead calm cold and there was not a thing moving but Mad Dog swimming, and no sound. And her standing in my dressing gown with the sleeves below her fingertips and her hair mussed and her eyes shiny at the big red silent sunrise; and the sun coming huge and red-gold over the mountain, and her face and the whole junk was bathed in the early morning golden red, and we cast a long shadow on the China Sea.

"Now come back to bed," I said. She threw back the blankets for me grinning and clutched me as I got in and gasped because I was cold and her nakedness was always already warm. And we had breakfast very late and she always sang while she cooked it.

In the middle of the day we rowed ashore, Mad Dog barking along behind us. She splashed up onto the beach, sometimes she did a cartwheel. "We're *free!*" And running along the beach, hair flying, eyes sparkling, running for joy of being in the open together, without a soul to see us, and Mad Dog racing along delirious with excitement. And walking along the beaches and rocks slowly, happily, heads down looking at seashells and driftwood and seaweed and stones, stopping to examine them, calling me to come and see. She made a great collection of such things. And I had never known how beautiful they were till she showed me.

And in the late afternoon we climbed the island mountains to watch the sun go down over the great China Sea. The air was cold and sometimes it was swirling misty and the steep mountains were rugged mauve and green, and the silence ringing, just our breathing, the islands were as deserted as in the days of old Cathy. And the healthy glow in our faces. "There's our home." There far below was the beautiful junk at anchor in the beautiful sea, way down there quiet, and the sea was deep sparkling mauve and the sea red afire and in a deep column all the way from the horizon up to her gunnels, and the gunnels glowered teak red, and the rocks were black-red-golden and the whole mighty horizon of the China Sea was quiet, and we were the only two people in the world.

And, when the sun was gone down, we came climbing back down the mountain. Good and quiet and happy. Walking hand in hand along the darkening beach, back to the dinghy, and usually she was singing very quietly. The junk lay there quietly in the sundown, big and silhouetted, and the sundown flamed out behind it. We rowed out to her, and even Mad Dog was looking forward to coming aboard. And lighting the lamps and opening the beer and making the *Glühwein*, good and glowing and happy, and the lamps shone golden on her face and gleamed in her hair and flickered deep brown on the teak, and it was warm.

CHAPTER 27

Whenever I listened to music, I thought, I wish she could hear this with me. Whenever I read something I liked in a novel or a book of verse, I thought, I must remember to tell that to Ying. Or if I saw something I liked on television. Or in the street. Or in a shop window.

But more than anything I yearned just to live with her, have her there always. Coming home to me in the afternoons from school, all happy and inky and chalky from a day in the classroom, happy to come home, slinging down her books and making tea and telling me what happened at school today and about the nut case she saw on the tram, then maybe us going out for a drink and some supper, or just staying home and letting the amah get on with dinner, and then after dinner just sitting and reading or listening to music or maybe going to a movie or maybe just watching television, until bedtime, and the the ritual of preparing for bed; the bathing and her things lying around, and her things in the wardrobe and the sweet smell of knowledge of them there, and then her coming to bed, oh God yes I just wanted to live with her. To live with my woman. I did not think of her as a communist any more, I just thought of her as my woman.

She was not a real communist anyway. I even liked it. When I thought about it, and after a while of loving her I did not think about it much, but when I did I even liked the fact that she called herself communist. That she had ideals. That she got her knickers in a knot about something. That we sometimes argued. That she cared. That she was a patriot. And an artist. And got all steamed up.

"Bullshit, darling!'"

Her big dark eyes lit up. "Not bullshit! Britain does make money from this colony!"

"Britain doesn't take one cent of our taxes."

"Oh yes? And what about our sterling reserves?"

"What about them?" I said.

She pointed at England, twelve thousand miles away. "Hong Kong must keep so much of its money in the Bank of England, hah! So that the English pound is strong. Where does that money come from, hah? Taxes!"

"It still remains Hong Kong's money in the Bank of England, for Christ's sake, Hong Kong gets *interest* on that money."

"But does China do that, hah?" She pointed. "Does Russia?" She pointed. "Does Japan? No, they keep their *own* money in their *own* bank and they can invest it in the *people!* In houses and schools and roads and hospitals, for the *people!* But Hong Kong? No, so much of their money must -go to stay in England. So Hong Kong Government cannot use its money properly to build houses for the people!"

"Ying, the Hong Kong Government's doing a pretty good job of building resettlement blocks," I said.

"But not enough, Jake. And all these people living in squatter shacks on the mountain. And no social welfare. What happens to all those people or when typhoon comes, hah?"

"And where do all those people come from?"

"I know what you say, 'The paradise across the border.' Okay, it's not paradise in China. But that is not the point, sir! The point is they are *people*. And where is the Hong Kong money? *In the Bank of England.*"

And Hong Kong was bloody booming. The steaming gushing stamp of the pile drivers, and the squatter shacks and the people sleeping in the streets. I looked in the newspaper every day for a place for us, but it was not going to be easy.

On her work nights I usually went out for a drink. Sometimes I went upstairs to the Hermitage Bar. They were mostly the Hermitage Old China hands. Sometimes it could be very funny late at night up in the Hermitage Bar, when the boys were solving the problems of the

193

world. Late one night some of the boys were sitting in a row thrashing out the truths of medieval history, and more particularly whether it was possible to skin a man alive. The argument ranged loudly back and forth in deadlock until Doc Greener came in. Doc Greener was the quack at the Civil Servant's Family Clinic. "Doc," Freddie Buxton shouted, "is it possible to skin a man alive?"

"Anything could happen at the Family Clinic," Ernie said.

Doc Greener registered the question focusing on his beer with difficulty. "Skin a man a-what?"

"*Alive,*" they chorused.

Doc Greener contemplated his beer with difficulty, unsurprised.

"Well," he decided, "first you should tie the chappie down."

"There you are!" Freddie Buxton shouted happily. "What do you say, McAdam?"

"I say what Doc Greener says," I said. "Every time."

"There you are!" Freddie Buxton said. "What you gotta do is tie the chappie down."

Dismay and bad sportmanship at Doc Greener's decision.

"Doc Greener is a makee-learnee horse doctor," Ernie said. Ernie was in the fire department and he lived with a fat Chinese whore called Blossom. "What they should have for the family man who visits the Family Clinic," Ernie said, "is life-insurance machines like at the airport. Doc Greener should also have some life insurance for all the chairs the family men throw at him. You know they throw chairs at him?"

"Issa goddamn lie," Doc Greener said.

"They do," Ernie said. "I've thrown three chairs at him myself and I'm not even a family man."

"You've got Blossom," Teetotal Tank said.

"Blossom doesn't count," Ernie said. "I'd throw chairs at Blossom too, except so far she's broken all our chairs, haven't you, Blossom?"

"Hah?" Blossom said.

"When I want to get rid of Blossom I'll send her down to Doc Greener at the Family Clinic to skin alive."

"What you gotta do," Freddie Buxton said, "is first tie the chappie down."

"Teetotal should send his girl friend down to Doc Greener to get straightened out," Dogs Barker of Colonial Secretariat said. "The one that walks like this." He walked down the bar doubled up holding his back like an old man. We were all laughing.

"Why does she walk like that?" I said.

"You haven't heard about Teetotal's girl friend?" Dogs Barker of Colonial Secretariat said. "You know Teetotal's got that big strong Shantung girl from the Ocean Bar, eats barbed wire for breakfast?" He indicated her size. "Well one night Teetotal's shacked up with a whore from the Winner Horse Bar when this big Shantung one arrives at the flat to see why Teetotal's not drinking at the Ocean, and she beats on his door shouting, *You got Winner Horse whore there, you no good butterfly, lemme in I gonna kill her—*"

We were all laughing.

"So Teetotal's lying there trembling with the poor little Winner Horse whore pretending he's not home." He demonstrated Teetotal in a fetal position. "But he knows this Shantung whore's going to wake the whole Hermitage. So he hides the Winner Horse whore in the built-in cupboard, see. But not in the ordinary part where the clothes hang. He lifts her up and rams her into the upperpart where you stash the suitcases." We were all laughing. "So the poor little Winner Horse whore's all doubled up like this between Teetotal's suitcases, and then he lets in the Shantung whore before she breaks the door down, and she starts ransacking the joint. She throws open the cupboards, looks under the bed, down the toilet, even in the drawers." Dogs Barker demonstrated. We were all laughing. "And the poor little Winner Horse whore's lying up their doubled up like this terrified. Finally the Shantung whore stops throwing Teetotal's things about and flounces into bed for the night. And to this day Teetotal's poor little Winner Horse whore walks like this—" Dogs Barker demonstrated.

We were all laughing.

"Send her down to the Family Clinic," Ernie shouted. "Doc Greener will jump on her spine. I'll send Blossom down at the same time to be skinned alive."

"Hah?" Blossom said.

"What you gotta do," Freddie Buxton said, "is first tie the chappie down."

"How're you doing?" Teetotal grinned sheepishly at me. "We don't see much of you these days."

"He's doing fine," Ernie of the fire department shouted.

"McAdam's the boy they're running the police force for, you seen his picture in the paper?"

"What do you know abut the fucking police force?" Happy Glaum of Marine Police said, "you skouse-louse in the fire department?"

"Watcha language." Ernie jerked his head at Blossom. "There's ladies present. I know all about the Hong Kong Police Force, they're all fucking corrupt."

"You watch your language," Teetotal said.

"If we're so corrupt why is the Anticorruption Bureau part of the police force?" Happy Glaum shouted. "So we could investigate the corruption in departments like the fire department!"

"We all got our eye on you! Dogs Barker of Colonial Secretariat shouted, "letting all those fires burn so the owner can give you a kickback on the insurance money—"

"There's no smoke without fire!" Happy shouted happily.

Ernie shouted, "Putting the police in charge of anti-corruption is like putting a rabbit in charge of a lettuce!"

"All you gotta do," Freddie Buxton of Immigration said, "is tie the chappie down."

Sometimes there were a few women up there, resident school-mistresses or a couple of girls from the Helen May; the language was better then but usually nobody paid much attention to them. It was hard on a girl in Hong Kong who was not obviously very attractive, because there was so much Chinese womanflesh. When I ate in the Hermitage restaurant I usually sat with Gwendoline, who was a schoolmistress from Glasgow and who was very nice. "Eighteen months I've been here," wee Gwendoline said, "and not one man's asked me out! And every night that bar's full of single men!" I wanted to say I'd ask her out if I could. "Is it any wonder that we go out with American servicemen?"

I sympathized.

"Somerset Maugham got it right about the East," wee Gwendoline said. "Young man goes to the East. Learns to prop up the mahogany bar next to potted palm under slowly turning ceiling fan in hot night. Sleeps with the native girls"—she pronouced it *gorrls*— "dies at fifty with a colonial whiskey tan. I'd like to write a book about this place."

"What would yo call it?" I said.

"You Only Need to Knock but Do You Hell?" wee Gwendoline said.

Sometimes I went down to the Hong Kong Club. Good and quiet and gracious. I was the only policeman below the rank of superintendent who was a member, because of my father. No Chinese allowed. A lot of wealthy old China hands who had known my parents in Shanghai and Peking, a lot of stories. I sat in the deep leather armchairs and had a drink and caught up on the overseas newspapers and the *Oriental Economic Review,* and China. China was picking itself up out of the ruins of the Great Leap Forward. The mighty communes were not disbanded but the emphasis was now on encouraging the performance of the work teams of each village rather than on massive bureaucratic communes as a whole. The comrade party cadres had been instructed by Peking to harken to the old peasants on farming matters, and to be more respectful. "Some cadres were overzealous," the *Red Flag* was quoted as saying euphemistically, "and did not have the right attitude to their elders." The food situation had improved since Peking had decided to allow the peasants to cultivate small private lots in their spare time. The *Review* editorial pointed out that this reversal of policy came embarrassingly close to the Russian "Capitalist roadism" that Mao had denounced. How long would Mao let it go on, the *Review* wondered. If he took the private lots, pigs, and ducks back after the food crisis was over he might lose great face and credibility with the peasants. But Mao was an idealist, he had shown himself capable of dismissing his mighty Russian allies for the same departures from Marxism. It would not be surprising if, once the mess of the Great Leap Forward was cleared up, Mao launched another of his mass rectification campaigns, like the Hundred Flowers, the *Review* said. Meanwhile, the editorial went on, thousands of Chinese were voting with their feet: the massive influx of illegal refugees which began in May last year was continuing, with the difference that the People's Liberation Army was shooting again. The Hong Kong police were patrolling the islands in unprecedented force with every launch they had. We could not cope. People sleeping on the streets, squatter shacks everywhere, mighty queues at the water taps, fires, garbage. "We have a problem of people and these are other People's people," et cetera, as the Financial Secretary had said . . .

Overleaf there was an article about Macao and the situation there. "This tiny, faded, jaded, former Pearl of the Orient, once renowned as the wickedest city and vice-pot of the world, once a veritable pearl in the Portuguese Empire but now dominated by the local communist Chinese Chamber of Commerce . . ." et cetera. It went on to give a brief rundown on the Portuguese colony, dropped a few names, facts. Stephen Lo, chairman of the Chinese Chamber of Commerce, multimillionaire communist, vice-chairman of the Gold Trade syndicate, unofficially the official representative of the Chinese People of Macao at the People's Congress of Representatives, Peking's communist parliament, was the real power behind the throne of the Portuguese governor and the Leal Senado, had His Excellency and Lisbon under his thumb. Antonio Fok, one of the gambling casino kings, also a communist multimillionaire, was the vice-chairman of the Chamber. Stephen and Antonio and the boys left the day-to-day running of the Colony to Lisbon and the governor, but anything important had to get the okay from Stephen and Antonio. Et cetera. Peking could recapture Macao with a telephone call, like she could Hong Kong for that matter, but she didn't because it suited her purpose as an outlet and window on the world, Macao gave Peking a lever on England and Portugal to behave themselves and fulfill contracts like supplies of arms to communist countries like Cuba and North Vietnam, et cetera, despite American protests, and to make them do the right thing for China in such places as the United Nations. Et cetera. The article went on to describe the refugee situation. They came swimming the Pearl River in the night, floating down the river on logs and pigs' bladders, and the People's Liberation Army gunboats gunned them down. But every month the PLA marched the long lines of the sick and the lame and the halt through the Barrier Gate into Macao, for the six-square-mile Portuguese colony never turned anybody away. The Casa Ricci, the Jesuit Catholic mission in Macao, was like a battlefield. Casa Ricci gave every refugee forty patacas and one month's supply of rice and a benediction. The people sleeping in the streets. Along the waterfront were the premises of the snakeheads, the smugglers of human contraband who smuggled the refugees across the forty miles of China Sea into Hong Kong. Now because of the PLA gunboats and the pressure of the Hong Kong Marine Police the price was one thousand dollars a head. Where did the refugees get the money? From the loan sharks. By relatives in Macao or Hong Kong standing security. By the girls contracting to work as prostitutes. Et cetera. And the snakeheads packed them down into the holds of their junks like fish, set sail at dead of night to run the PLA gunboats and the HKMP launches. The snakeheads dumped them wherever they could, any Hong Kong Colony island. Ordered them up on deck, made them jump over the side, women, children, and all, and swim for it. Very few of these islands had water. There was a photograph of such a group of sixty found on an island, way out, by the Hong Kong Marine Police. They were in a terrible state. They had not had food or water for three days. Two children were dead. Another two had suffocated in the holds. They had been guaranteed a safe delivery in Hong Kong by the snakeheads for their thousand dollars a head, about ten thousand American dollars the snakeheads had made for that little job. It was very big, bad business indeed. Junks sinking at sea because they were overloaded. We picked up bodies. Unseaworthy junks, the oldest and cheapest the snakeheads could find, because the Hong Kong police confiscated them on capture. We used to see them at public auctions, but the snakeheads' agent bought them up cheap, so now we towed them deep-sea and blew them up. The problem of people. And the squatter huts teeming up the mountains, and the cocklofts on the rooftops and the cocklofts on top of cocklofts, and the places that rent bed spaces, and bed spaces under bed spaces and beds that are hauled up to the ceilings to make more bed space, and people sleeping in the streets.

And Hong Kong was bloody booming.

I turned to the business pages. The Golden Mountain Where Men Eat Fat Pork. The stock market was still crazy. I did not watch the market any more, but I had some Textiles and Telephone and some Star Ferries and they were the highest they had ever been. God, the new buildings. Buildings, land, the steaming stamping of the pile drivers and the massive bamboo scaffolding. The great steps hacked out of the steep mountains for the great new blocks of flats rising up on terraces. The great hacking down of mountain to reclaim the China Sea. And the factories factories factories and the shops shops shops. The bazaars and the great emporiums and the alley shops and the barrows and the hawkers and the little backyard sweatshops making everything, anything at all. The money-making everywhere, there had never been so much money, the *Oriental Economic Review* said. And the other People's people sleeping in the streets. And the banks.

God, the banks. You have never seen so many, banks you had never heard of. Springing up everywhere, particularly in the densely populated Chinese areas, shouting to you to come and deposit your money. Great lucky red posters in their windows offering 9, 10, 11, even 12 per cent interest, outbidding each other. Not the big solid commercial banks nor the communist Bank of China, but these small family Chinese joints with the big new marble portals and the gold-lacquered doors with a couple of splendid shotgunned Sikhs outside, were where these banks invested your savings in order to be able to pay you such wonderful interest. Mortgages on land and buildings. Mortgages mortgages mortgages, for buildings buildings buildings.

But what kind of buildings? Not in resettlement blocks for the other People's people sleeping in the streets, that was Government's unhappy responsibility. Christ no, this is Hong Kong. These banks, if you took the trouble to think about it, must be investing in mortgages and loans to builders and speculators and financiers who were subcontracting and financing the mortgagees and builders and contractors and financiers.

Well, for Christ's sake, when you thought about it. Land? This is Hong *Kong*. The festering pimple on the backside of Mao Tse-tung's China, the communist who chucks the Russians out of China because they are wicked capitalist roaders. Who launches all kinds of rectification campaigns? Who internationally proclaims that Power Grows out of the Barrel of a Gun? Hey? Would you invest your life's savings in immovable land in a joint like that? Would you lend your money to a bank that *re*lends your money to the *seco*nd mortgagee who is *re*lending your money to the guy who is *bor*rowing all kinds of money from seven different Chinese-style banks to buy *shares* and *third* mortgages in *build*ings on land in a joint like that? But all over Hong Kong the hawkers and *fokis* and shop girls and richshaw boys and factory workers and boat people were putting their life's savings into these banks at 10, 11, 12 per cent. I sat in the deep leather armchair at the Hong Kong Club and thought, For Christ's sake.

And all this phenomenal building was luxury—and middle-class flats. Now, what was going to happen when saturation point was reached? There would be empty flats. Half-finished buildings would run out of money. What would be the value of the mortgages then? And then would the banks be able to repay the customers their money in the savings accounts? Most countries had a central reserve bank and laws which said that all banks had to keep 25 per cent of cash ready to meet customers' demands. But in dear old cutthroat Hong Kong there was no central reserve bank and no such law. Now, what would happen when saturation point was reached, when land values dropped, if the public came to the banks to demand their savings back on the spot? It was a dangerous situation, the *Oriental Economic Review* said. Et cetera.

I thought, Well, well, well. I put the *Review* back on the table and left the club. It was cold outside. On the steps I met the Old Man, the commissioner of police. "Hello, Jake!" he said.

"Good evening, sir!" I said. "You're working late." He was still in his uniform.

"Won't you have a drink?" His bushy devil's eyebrows were up encouragingly, you always felt that he was really pleased to see you.

We went into the oak-paneled bar. I didn't want to talk about Catherine and what I was doing with myself. "How's Gladys?" I said.

"She's overseas for six weeks," the Old Man said. "It's such a long time since we've seen you you wouldn't know. You must come up to the house soon—"

"I'd like to—"

He hesitated, then said brightly, "Any news from Catherine?"

I hated this. "I've had a few letters, she seems to have settled down well. I get a letter from Suzie twice a month," I said, trying to sound bright.

"Do you!" the Old Man said, as if this were delightful news. "Of course, she's five now, isn't she, I suppose she writes quite well?"

I hated this. "Quite well. Though it's mostly hearts and flowers and princesses with spiky crowns." I felt my heart turn over.

"How nice!" the Old Man beamed. We both felt self-conscious suddenly. "And, Jake? What have you been doing with yourself?"

"Nothing much, sir." I said. "I'm doing a bit of reading. I go out on the junk most weekends, that sort of thing."

His eyebrows went up and down devilishly and his eyes twinkled. "Not alone! Not in the cold winter!"

I grinned. "No, not exactly alone."

He smiled solicitously. "Have you got a steady girl, now?"

Oh Gawd. "Not a steady." I tried to grin. "Here and there."

Back came the devil's eyebrows, then solicitude. He was a grand Old Man to work for. I knew he wanted to ask about Catherine. "How's Gladys enjoying her holiday?" I said.

"Oh, fine," he said, "but I'm not." Then said brightly, "She's seen Catherine. They had tea together in Selfridge's apparently, and a morning's shopping."

It did not hurt me. "Oh, and how was Cathy?"

"Oh, fine."

"Did Gladys go to the house at all and see Suzie?" I said.

"Yes, I believe she did, but Suzie was at school."

That hurt me. My child at a school already.

"Yes," I said. It was only Suzie that hurt me. All right, I thought: "Did Gladys meet the boy friend?"

"No," he said, "no."

"Did Cathy say anything about the divorce?"

He tried to sound casual: "Apparently his wife isn't forthcoming with a divorce just yet, I believe. Something about the children."

"Yes." Catherine had said this in one of her letters. "Did Cathy say anything about our divorce proceedings?"

The Old Man pretended to think a moment. "I believe she said something about there being no hurry in view of the wife's present attitude, something along those lines, Jake." He tried to sound casual but his face was sympathetic.

"Jesus," I said. "Why the hell doesn't she get on with it?"

He tried to keep his face uninquisitive. "Are you in a hurry?"

I said, "We've been living apart nearly two years."

He nodded at his whiskey sadly. He glanced then decided to say it.

"It is a hell of a pity about you two," he said. "She is such a nice girl. Gladys adores her. And you," he added.

I didn't say anything. All I felt was Suzie in that London flat and how often did she think about me and who did she tell her friends was her father. And my God I wanted to go to Ying-ling and stop thinking.

He took a suck on his whiskey. "All right, drink up! Will you have another?"

"No thank you, sir," I said. "I really must go."

I left the Old Man and I went back out into the chill night. It had shaken me talking about Suzie. God knows Cathy did not hurt me any more, I had just proved that, it seemed we had squeezed the orange dry now, just thank God for Ying. I wanted her now in my arms to tell me it didn't matter about Suzie, Suzie was still mine and soon she would come back out here and we would all three be together. And oh God, I wanted to be with Ying in our own place, even if it was just a couple of rooms somewhere, a place of our own to come home to. Home. I was going to go back home to the Hermitage but I headed for the Foreign Correspondents' Club.

It was half full, men and women. The Foreign Correspondents' Club was a good place to meet women. It was there Loverboy and Catherine had met. I only thought about it because I had been thinking about Suzie. I saw Mini-Max drinking with Reginald and Tim. Reginald used to be a Crown counsel. When he had a trial the investigating police officer used to appoint a detective to follow him at lunchtime because Reginald might get among it too much and forget to come back, or fall asleep somewhere. He was an excellent lawyer, if you could get him into court, and in the afternoons he was even better if the detective had stuck close enough. In those days he used to get among it too much because there wasn't enough to do. Now he was in private practice and he got among it too much because he had too much to do. Now he had so much money because he had too much work to do that he was always on the point of going back to being Crown counsel. Where he could get among it too much in peace. "You'd have to put up with all those detectives following you," Mini-Max pointed out.

"It's only at lunchtime," Reginald said. "The rest of the time they left me in peace. It was even quite nice knowing those detectives were following me," Reginald said wistfully. "It made me feel loved. Every month my salary was paid in miraculously, and the detectives to look after me. Now?"

"Now?" I was grinning.

"Now," Reginald said miserably and proceeded to tell us how it was now. Conveyancing. Land mortgages, securities, securities on securities. Options on options. Jesus, it wasn't just the land that was changing hands half a dozen times a week, it was the options to buy land and options to buy bloody options for options. Money, from all around the world. "Like shit hitting the fan." And he, Reginald, stood in the middle of it covered in shitty money. Reginald said miserably, "I can't even leave the office for lunch, even if I did have a detective to look after me. And all I want to be is a little fat happy Crown counsel." Max and I were laughing.

"How's it been with you lately?" Reginald said miserably. "I see in the paper you knocked off a big counterfeiting ring week before last."

"Yes," I said. "We were bloody lucky."

"Somebody-up-There-Likes-Me McAdam," Mini-Max said.

"Now that's the sort of case I'd like," Reggie said, "all those exhibits. How much was there?"

"Twenty-eight million U.S.," I said. "In dollars and Philippine pesos. Two rings. One led to the other."

"Jesus!" Reggie said miserably, "that's nice work if you can get it. Now *that's* the way to make money—make your own. That even beats Crown counseling."

We were all laughing.

"Let's give it a go," Reginald said. "How do I get a job like that? Will you ask your accused for me?"

"It might be a bit late now," I said.

Reginald went home in his chauffeur-driven Rolls to cry into his silk pillow. Mini-Max and I had another drink. He said, "What you been doing with yourself these days?"

"I've been around," I said. "Where've you been?"

He had just come back from ten days' holiday in Manila. "What did you need a holiday from?" I said. Mini-Max had had a great time. There's this twenty-four-hour nightclub down there called the Aquarium in a street full of nightclubs, each better than the last till you get to the Aquarium. Inside there's this big glass tank pretending to be an aquarium and inside are all these happy naked Filipina girls draped around making like mermaids watching television with plastic Venus stuck on their fannies. And each has got a little number on her Venus rear, see. And what you do is the management gives you a little fishing rod and you put a little number on the bait end and drop it into the tank and all the mermaids pounce on it to see who the lucky fish is. And upstairs there's this air-conditioned hotel. And so on. "I phoned you several times to ask you to come with me," Mini-Max said, "but you were never in. Who the hell is she? Some married woman?"

"I've been around," I grinned. "You don't know her."

He looked peeved. "You can tell me—I'm your lawyer, aren't I? Or have you changed lawyers too?"

I was happy. "Listen, Maxie," I said. "This is confidential. I'm looking for a small discreet flat in the Wanchai or Causeway Bay area. Do you know of anything?"

He stared at me. "What's wrong with your own flat?"

"It's not discreet enough."

"So it's a married woman, hey? It's a love nest we want, is it?" He looked at me as if I was out of my head. "Is she *worth* it? It's going to cost you. It's a helluva time to be looking for flats."

I was happy. "This one's worth it."

"Have you got to be that discreet? Who the hell is she?"

I wanted to tell him. "Max, this is confidential."

He waited, agog. "Of course. I'm your lawyer, ain't I?"

I said, "She's a Chinese schoolmistress. At a communist school, the Tai Ping."

Mini-Max stared at me.

"A communist?"

I said, "But not the kind you think. She comes from a middle-class background, she was at the college here. She's really just a Chinese patriot doing her thing."

Mini-Max stared at me. "But for God's sake!"

I said patiently, "She is not a political activist, Max. She's just an ordinary intellectual socialist the likes of which you met plenty of at university. If she was an American she'd be in the Peace Corps. Or working for the Social Welfare Department. There are plenty of communists like that in this town and they're not treated as social lepers!"

Mini-Max said, astonished, "That's not the bloody

point. *I* needn't treat them like lepers, I'm not in government service, but *you're* in the police. Having a communist mistress makes you a security risk!" He was exasperated with me.

"Balls," I said.

"It's not balls! Technically, it makes you a *security risk*. You can be pressured by the communists through your mistress. Isn't that how the bastards work?"

I said patiently, "Pressured into what? Divulging state secrets? Hong Kong's blueprints for the hydrogen bomb?"

"You know what I mean," Mini-Max said irritably. "How the espionage business works is, they get their information through pressuring guys like you who are in a compromising position because they've got a skeleton in the cupboard, like a communist mistress you don't want your police force to know about."

I said, "Technically. But you and I know the setup here. The communists are minding their own business, live and let live. How many communists here have mistresses? Noncommunist mistresses? In luxury apartments. And do capitalist business on the side? And have secret bank accounts? *And*," I said, "how many high-ranking government officials are having furtive little affairs in this town at this moment?"

"Plenty," Mini-Max said. "But that's not the bloody point."

"And there're a good few who are known homosexuals, how's that for being a technical security risk? But has Government got its bowels in an uproar about them? No. Why? Because this is a unique town where we live and let live. And those government officers *are* privy to official secrets. But I'm not privy to any official secrets that the communists would be interested in, Max, I'm a common or garden criminal investigation officer—"

"For how long?" Mini-Max demanded. "How do you know you're not going to be transferred to Special Branch? What'll you do with your communist schoolmistress *then*? And how long before you're promoted?" He held his finger at me. "You aren't such a common or garden CID officer, are you? You know as well as I do that for some reason which escapes me you're the blue-eyed boy of headquarters and you're going to be made up to superintendent just as soon as they can justify it. Then you'll be privy to a lot of official secrets, won't you; you'll be a bloody good catch for the communists *then*, wouldn't you?"

I said patiently, "Max, I've thought all about it. You're assuming that this girl is a dyed-in-wool party-line communist. She's not. For Christ's sake, you've know plenty of girls like her at university, this Foreign Correspondents' Club is full of people with sympathies like hers. She's teaching ordinary academic subjects to Chinese kids so that they can pass the ordinary school examinations set by the Hong Kong Government's Education Department. Her school is inspected by Government's education inspectors."

"Jake?" Mini-Max tapped the bar with his finger. "What would police headquarters say if they knew you had a mistress at a communist school?" His eyes were big. "They'd dismiss you, right?"

"I doubt it," I said. "But it would affect my promotion."

"Exactly! They'd put you in charge of something like liquor licensing or traffic where you can't do any harm. And watch you like a hawk. And"—he held up his finger—"tell you to either marry her—and take her *out* of that school—or get rid of her? Right?"

I said, "And that's exactly what I'm going to do."

Mini-Max stared. "Marry her?"

"Yes. I think so."

Max sat back. "Jesus." He stared. "Well, it takes all kinds. When?"

I said, "When the divorce is through."

"And when'll that be?"

"I don't know. I expected Catherine to have got things moving already, she's been gone four bloody months."

"Have you written to inquire?"

"Not exactly. I will. But the boy friend's wife's not too keen on giving him a divorce, and there're kids. Catherine's waiting for that."

"Playing it safe?" Max said. "She'll come back to you if it doesn't work out?"

"No," I said. "She knows it's finished. But divorces take a long time, especially in England, they've got waiting lists miles long."

Mini-Max shook his head. "Well, it takes all kinds. You love her enough to jeopardize your police career?"

I said, "I'm not jeopardizing my career. If I play it right."

"Not jeopardizing your career? You don't think it'll go against you that your wife used to be a communist?"

"A teacher at a communist school," I corrected.

"Once you're married, would she be prepared to turn her back on the communists?"

I said, "She wouldn't do anything active."

"Have you discussed this with her?"

"It's early days yet."

"Hmm," Mini-Max said. "You better discuss it with her pretty damn quick. And bring the whole thing out in the open."

"I want to bring it out in the open," I said.

He looked at me. "And in the meantime you want a flat. God, I hope you know what you're doing, boy."

CHAPTER 28

It surpassed my wildest hopes. It was originally servants' quarters on the rooftop of a block of business offices. It was eleven stories high, nothing overlooked it, it had a spectacular view of the harbor. The ground floor was a busy shopping arcade and there was parking space in the basement with four entrances and exits. I had the Chinese toilet taken out and replaced by a Western one, installed a bath, had a wooden trellis built to turn the roof into a patio. I installed an unlisted telephone. I did not tell Yingling what I was doing.

That night it really felt like spring. The sea smelled warmer and the sun flamed deep orange-red on the junks and the Mountains of Nine Dragons were mauve and golden. I sat on the verandah at the Yacht Club watching it. At eight o'clock I went out to the car. She came along the dark causeway, grinning.

We drove into Wanchai instead of along the waterfront. I was grinning. I swung down into the basement. "Where are we going?" she demanded, suddenly nervous.

"This place is perfect. It's deserted at night."

"Perfect for what?"

"I've got something to show you."

We rode up in the service elevator, to the top. Then walked up the service stairway to the rooftop. I opened the penthouse door. "Go in." She looked as if she was expecting a practical joke. I switched on the light. She stared. "Go in. There's nobody here."

She entered, wide-eyed. I was grinning. I went to the big window and ripped back the curtain. There was the patio and the great harbor lights. She stared.

"Well?" I said.

She looked around, astonished. "It's lovely. Is it yours?"

"Come and see the rest." She still had the practical-joke expression. I took her to the bedroom.

"The big bed." She stared. "You are going to *live* here?"

"Partly. It's a place of my own, away from damn civil servants."

She stared around. "All this money!" She looked apprehensively into the bathroom. "Bath. And *gwailo* toilet," she whispered.

I led her back into the living room. "The kitchenette," I said.

"Everything new." She stared. "All this money."

"My Happy Valley house is paying for it," I said. "And the patio, see. And I'll plant creepers to cover the overhead trellis. It'll be a roof garden for us. And the view."

She nodded, too surprised to be excited yet.

"Do you like it?"

"Oh yes," she said. "Who would not like this place? And a roof garden!" Her eyes were enthusiastic now. "You must get a creeper that grows fast. You can have so many flowers out here."

"You must get them for me."

"And these paintings?" She pointed at the walls.

"They're nothing," I said modestly.

"Of course, your paintings!" She went to the nearest and peered, then stepped back. "No, quite good!"

"You give me face."

"No, quite good, truly." She examined the next, then stood back. "Not bad, hah." She muttered something in Cantonese, felt the canvas with her finger. "You quite good with the sky, hah? Acrylics."

"Acrylics," I said. "The Art Shop."

"Maybe you should try some China Products oils?"

"Now we can both do some work in the evenings," I said. "This is a good room for that."

"You pretty smart, hah?" She put her arm around my waist.

"I haven't done anything for a long time." I was bloody

209

happy. "Now we're going to. Well," I said, "let's have a drink."

I went to the kitchenette, and got out a bottle of champagne. I opened it and the cork went pop.

"What is that?"

"The police!" I said.

I brought the glasses, grinning. She grinned: "The *police!*"

"*Yum-sing.*" I sat on the sofa. It suddenly felt new and formal. She sat on the edge of the armchair. "Come and sit next to me," I said.

She came.

"Are you pleased with it?" I said.

She nodded, then made herself smile at me. "Of course. Who would not be pleased with it? It is very exciting." She was flushed suddenly.

"But?" I said. She reached for her glass guiltily. "Tell me, Ying."

She pulled out her cigarettes, stuck one in her mouth. I lit a Texan. I knew what was coming. She inhaled deep, then looked at me. Sitting on the edge of the sofa. She suddenly looked very prim and elegant sitting there holding her Red Victory cigarette. She hesitated, then said firmly, "I don't want to spoil it for you. And it's a lovely studio, truly."

I waited. I had nearly had enough of this nonsense. "But you got this flat for me, didn't you?" she said.

"No," I said evenly. "For myself. I detest that civil service Hermitage flat. Soul-less. I've always had my own home and I want one now."

"But—you really got it *because* of me." She held up her cigarette to stop me interrupting. "Will you be honest?"

I had known it was coming. "I got it because *I* wanted it. To enjoy with you. We cannot go on living in a station wagon and a goddamn junk."

"Please don't be angry."

She walked to the window and looked out. Drew on her cigarette, turned and looked at me. "You want me to be honest? You must understand."

"Of course I want you to be honest."

"All right." She looked at me, then waved her cigarette. "It is a lovely place for me. For us. We can come here and paint pictures. Cook chow. Make love. Have a nice bath." She appealed to me. "Do you think I do not know

210

it is better than making love in a car? Do you think I am so stupid I do not say to myself, Here is a nice bathroom! I do not have to keep all my things in that small room, I have this nice place now! A nice garden!" She glared at me honestly. "Of course, I like nice things too. I also want to make love to you in that big fat bed!" She pointed at the bedroom accusingly.

I said, from the sofa, "Do you love me?"

She said impatiently, "Of course I love you too. Even in China they fall in love, you know!"

I said, "Then what appears to be the problem?"

She drew hard on her cigarette. She said, "But for me it is a serious step. Because . . ." She hesitated, looking for the words, then it came out rapidly, "Because I am a communist. I must set a good example." She shook her head exasperated with herself. "I mean, I must be—" She spoke rapidly in Cantonese.

"Faithful to my principles," I translated.

"Yes. It does not matter if I have ten, twenty lovers! That is nobody's business except mine. But it *does* matter if I live like a bourgeoise, then go to school and teach about communism, and outside people are sleeping in the street!"

I said patiently, "You're not doing anybody out of a place to sleep. You are not being unfaithful to your principles because we come here in the evenings rather than go in my bourgeois car. And junk."

"But you did not buy the junk for me. You had it already. You cannot deny you got this flat because of me. And what do we do on the junk—just enjoy nature, the sea. But now this flat is . . . different," she ended lamely.

"Psychologically," I said. "But not logically."

"Logically too!"

I stood up. "Very well. Let's go."

She stared at me. "Where to?"

"To the car," I said. "Where would you like to go, to the Peak, or Deep Water Bay?"

She glared at me. "Now you are angry. You do not want to understand my side of it."

"I understand perfectly. And the logic of it. To be faithful to your principles you must be uncomfortable with your bourgeois lover. Very well, I understand this is a big step for you. So we will leave the comfort and security here where nobody can possibly see you, unless they land by parachute, nor notice you enter or leave the building because of its many entrances and exits, and we will adjourn back to the discomfort of my car and drive through the crowded streets to the bourgeois Peak where anybody who chooses to peep in the window can see you."

"Oh, you make me angry!" She looked at me sulkily. "Sit down, *please.*"

I sat down and waited. She lit another Victory harassedly. She said carefully, "I am a communist schoolteacher and I am in love with a colonial police inspector. What can come of it, hah? I am like any other woman. I want to talk to my friends about you. Walk in the street with you. Live with you. But no, we must keep it secret. At first it was funny, fun. I was just in love. Now it is getting serious."

"Come and sit down."

She came and sat down on the edge of the sofa, erect. Her eyes were very beautiful. She pleaded, "What do you think of me? You do not think I am really a communist, do you?"

I sat back. I said carefully, "No. I think you are a good Chinese doing a good job as a teacher at a good communist school."

She looked at me. Then she got up. "I like to think you are wrong. But maybe you are right." She walked to the window. She said to the night accusingly, "I am weak!"

"Because you love me?" I said carefully. "Do I interfere with your ideals? Do I interfere with your work, your feelings for China? I sometimes argue with you, but I do not corrupt you."

She said to the window, "No. If I meant that I would not be here now. I mean I am weak"—she looked at me —"because it is *forbidden love.*" She said it forcefully, not melodramatically.

I said carefully, "Forbidden? It is a free country."

She turned from the window impatiently. She wanted to put her hands on her hips but didn't. "Of course it is forbidden really! From the beginning I knew it, that is why I am weak. I knew it was wrong, but my heart"—she tapped her breast vigorously—"ruled my head." She thumped her head.

"Why did you do it?"

"Because I was crazy! Like a girl! You liked me. I liked you. I have been to college in Hong Kong, I like to talk and laugh and read books and paint pictures but everybody at my school is such a stick-in-the-mud, all my

212

old friends are gone now working for government schools and big business and where am I? Then you come along. And I think, for a while I will be crazy and happy. Then it will finish one day. But it has not finished. I love you more! But it is still forbidden." Her eyes were pleading bright, standing across the room, I started to speak and she hurried on, "What can happen to us, hah? Can we walk in the street like lovers? Can we go to movies? Can we go to the beach like other people? Can I take you to my school to show you my work? Can I come to your office? What is going to happen to us, hah, Jake? Now we have this secret flat. Like thieves!" She was standing there pleading with me. I said quietly, "What do you want to do?"

She half glared, half pleaded at me. "You know what we must do. *Should* do." Her eyes were wet. "Finish."

"Do you want to do that?"

She shook her head, eyes wet, standing there. "No."

I said from the sofa, "Then there is only one thing to do. We must stop living like thieves. Say to hell with everybody an come out in the open." I took a breath. "And get married."

She stared at me.

"Get *married?*"

God, I had said it. And it felt good. It felt marvelous. I said, "Do you want to marry me?"

She stood in the middle of the room confused.

"I'll be divorced soon," I said.

"But"—she waved her hand—"how can we get married?"

I said, "Just do it. It's a free country." It felt as simple and marvelous as that.

She stood there. Then she walked to the sofa and sat down on the edge and looked at me, her hands on her knees. Then she smiled but her big eyes were wet.

"Oh, *how* can we be married? I am a Chinese and you are English. I am a communist. You have your job and I have my job—"

I pulled her to me and held her tight. "Do you want to marry me?" I wanted to laugh, but I didn't.

"Of course I want to marry you!" she said rigidly against me. "Do you think I haven't thought all about it?"

"You sound surprised."

"Yes, I am surprised. Of course I want to marry you but it is impossible." She held me tight.

"If it's impossible why have you carried on so long?"

"It is not a long time, only four months. Because I love you of course."

I held her at arm's length. "Plenty of people in different political persuasions get married," I said. I knew what she was going to say but I wanted to have it out.

"All right." She wiped her eyes roughly once firmly, got up. She lit another cigarette. Hand shaking a little. She sat down again firmly, farther apart, and looked at me, blew the smoke out hard. "All right. We must talk about this properly. No more surprises."

I nodded. She drew on her cigarette hard, looking at me with deep firm eyes.

"Different political persuasions, yes, darling. But not different *culture and* political persuasions."

"Cultures? You mean the problems of mixed marriages?" I was really surprised at this one. "Good God, how many mixed marriages are here in Hong Kong? Hong Kong is the example par excellence of a mixed marriage all in itself!"

She held up her cigarette impatiently. "I am telling what I *think*. When I use my *head*"—she tapped it—"not my heart." She tapped that.

"All right," I said.

She drew on her cigarette. "I am not just talking about my father and what he thinks. Of course that is also important, because naturally he wants me to marry a Chinese man, even to live in China. And of course I want my people to be pleased with my children, and all that, and not be a . . ." She thought then said it in Cantonese.

"Curiosity. But that does not really matter, because it is my life. But what about *us?* One day we will go to live in England—"

I said, "I refuse to worry about what may happen in twenty years' time when I retire."

She said, "All right. But maybe Hong Kong goes bang tomorrow because of trouble between China and England. Suppose it happened. We would go to England. You already have a white daughter, I am her new stepmother. What does she think? What do your friends think? I am a curiosity. People in England stare at me in the street. When I go into a shop—"

"Chinese live all over this world."

"But what about *me?*" she insisted. "Where is my culture? My people? My books? My songs? My jokes? My

214

language? I am not Chinese any more, I am a yellow Englishwoman! And our children half and half. Please" —she held up her hand to stop me interrupting, then touched my hand once. "Of course I would do it. Because you are my husband and it is my duty, and anyway I love you so it is better to live with you"—she pointed to the north—"in the North Pole than live without you. But I am telling you that this is very difficult for me. I am *Chinese*. I am Chinese here"—she beat her head—"and here"—her heart—"and here"—her belly: "Would you like to leave all your culture and go to live in China where there are only Chinese?"

"No," I said. "But Hong Kong is my home, not England. We're going to live in Hong Kong."

She nodded vigorously, drawing on her cigarette, back straight. "All right. One day England, but now it is Hong Kong. Number one: I disagree with you that most marriages between Chinese and Europeans are successful. I do not think so. Because of culture. The Chinese girl is trying to be a white wife with all her husband's white friends. Conversation. Jokes. Interests.

"But not in our case, for God sake. That's why we're like thieves—furtive. But"—she held up her finger like any schoolmarm in the world—"what about later? This is my head talking, not my heart. My heart is so in love with you I want to live with you in a barrel. And never get out!" It was her first smile since this started. "But my good Chinese head says, What must I do if we get married?"

I waited. She said earnestly, "I must stop being a communist?"

This was it. I said carefully, "You are not a communist now."

She held up her finger. "You are wrong. I am not a *good* communist, I know, but I *believe*. The point is—"

I said very firmly, "The point is that you would *not* have to stop being a communist. Or a Christian Scientist. Or a Chinese. I don't care if you hate America's guts with a maniacal hatred or Adam Smith's or the whole United bloody Nations. I don't care what political, religious, or philosophical views you have. In fact, I welcome them. They're stimulating."

She said, with a wisp of a smile, "That is a better word than amusing. I am a better communist than you think. Not good, I agree, but not so bad."

215

"Agreed." I got back to the point: "I repeat, you would not have to stop having your communist sympathies. But you *would*"—this was it—"have to stop teaching at a communist school. Or take any other active part in any such activities."

She was looking at me, deep eyes, steadily. Then she looked down. Then nodded. Then she stood up and walked across the carpet, very elegantly.

"I know," she said to the window.

I waited.

She said, "Do you understand what it means?" Her face was very intense. "Long ago I made a decision at college. I was young, but it was a right decision. Therefore now all my friends are communist. All my work. All my —loyalties. And I *believe!* I know not everything the communists do is right, but I believe in what they are trying to do. It is my culture *and* my politics I must give up."

"You don't have to stop believing."

She appealed, "But where will all my friends be who I believe in? All right, they are boring people, but I believe in them. And in my work." She implored me to understand. I nodded. "They will be gone. I must have no activity with them, because I am married to you. I cannot go and see them, *talk* even. All right"—she jerked her cigarette impatiently—"maybe talk a little, but I say to them, How is it going now? and they say, maybe, if they trust me still, It is like this and like that. But do they *trust* me? Hah?" She appealed. "Or do they think I am some kind of traitor, hah? What would you think"?

I waited, watching her.

"And who are my friends now? My culture?" She pointed at me almost accusingly. "Yes, you are my *only* friend!" She pointed at the Peak. "Because my new friends, your friends, who are they? Do I respect them? Do I believe in them?" She dropped her arm to her side, shook her head. "No, darling. I do not think I believe in them." She waved her hand again. "Maybe I do not blame them, they are ordinary wives from England and America with their small problems and intelligences and activities worrying about fat children and fat amahs and fat dinners while their fat husbands work for fat money to put in the fat bank *while half the world is hungry!*" She jabbed her finger at the carpet belligerently. I

216

watched her and I loved her very much. She relaxed her shoulders.

"All right," she said. "Maybe they are very nice people really. Maybe we will have some good conversations. Some good dinner jokes. Maybe with one or two I can even talk about politics. *But that is not the same as my culture.* Because what am I *doing?* I am the same as them!" She jabbed her finger at the Peak. "Empty! What do I say when I die, hah? I lived on the Peak in Hong Kong? *And down here I could not even teach school to my own people!*"

I wanted to hold her tight I loved her so much. I sat there, stony-faced. She said softly, "And people sleeping in the streets. And half the world hungry. And what must I do instead of my work? All right." She shook her finger at me once. "I can work for social welfare. Teach in another school. Bake cakes for bazaar." She nodded once glaring, then implored, "But what about my *culture?* My *beliefs!* My heart!"

She glared.

"All right, my heart is with you. But you have your work, hah? Your Queen and duty. And all your friends. What do your friends say about me, hah?" She struck half a pose. "You know this Ying-ling McAdam is quite interesting, quite cute, she speaks English very nicely for a Chinese, but she is a bit communist, you know. And at the cocktail parties I must be very careful. What I say about politics because of your job. And"—she rubbed her forehead—"what about your job, darling, hah?"

I said, "Let me do the worrying about my job."

She cried, "But I want to know, darling. One day maybe you'll blame me!" She appealed, "Don't you think maybe one day they will say, We cannot promote Mr. McAdam to this job because his wife is a communist, she used to be a communist and she still has her father in China? Nowadays everything is happy between Britain and China, but maybe one day they will not be so happy. Maybe there'll be trouble with the Americans or Chiang Kai-shek. Then what? What do they say to Mr. McAdam then and his communist wife? And what do you say to me?" She came and sat down on the sofa again earnestly, back straight, knees together, then shook her head at me. "And please don't say it doesn't matter, because it does. You are a well-known policeman. And you like your job."

I stood up. "I'll take my chances on that."

I walked across the carpet, then faced her.

"You will not be 'accused' of being a communist. Not if we act now." I looked at her. "It is important that we start *now*." I walked across, stood over her. Looking up at me. I loved her very much. I said, "All you said is very sensible. But none of the difficulties are insuperable. If they were, I would still want to marry you. Now, the question is Do you really want to marry me?"

She sat there, looking up at me. Then she gave a tiny nod, then closed her eyes and nodded, yes yes.

I bent and kissed her. I felt her breath tremble.

I said, "That means we must prepare now."

She waited. I said firmly, "As soon as possible you must stop working at the Great Peace School."

She looked at me.

"Of course you must stay until the end of the term, you cannot leave them in the lurch. But next term you *must* get a post at a non-communist school."

She looked up at me.

"When are you getting divorced?"

I said, "About three to six months. Assuming she starts proceedings now. I'll write to her tomorrow and tell her to get on with it."

"Six months," she said. "Maybe a year?"

"I doubt it."

'Why hasn't she started yet? Maybe she does not want to divorce you now."

"She's living with the man."

"But he is also married you told me, he must also get a divorce from his wife, yes?" She looked up at me, troubled, then patted the sofa. "Please sit down."

I sat down. She lit another Victory, blew the smoke out. Then took a big breath. "Darling? Let me wait for your divorce before I stop working at my school. I *must*."

"Why must you?"

"Because *I must*," she pleaded. "That school is my whole life. And it is my security." She looked embarrassed suddenly. "Yes, security. It is my job. I like it. How would you like to give up your job? If you were asking another girl to marry you, would you expect her to give up her job so long before the wedding?"

"You mean in case we never get married?"

She changed it. "I mean in case you cannot get your divorce for a whole year. Maybe even longer. I have heard of people who cannot get divorced. All this time I am not working at my job I like! I *want* to work."

"I'll support you," I said.

"Oh *no,* darling." She shook her head emphatically. "Thank you, but no. Even after marriage I want to work, I am not like those wives up there"—she pointed at the Peak. "But the real point is I *want* to do *my* job as long as possible. How can you expect to stop now when you do not know when we can get married?"

"Because it's going to be important," I said.

"But not *now?*" she appealed. "Going to be, yes, but not *now.*"

I said patiently, "You must, Ying. This furtiveness has gone on long enough. I'll see the divorce proceedings are started before the end of this term."

"But I must give notice. And if the divorce is not started by then?" She pleaded desperately.

I felt guilty.

"You must do as I say."

She cried exasperated, "I will marry you tomorrow and give up my job. Next month! Anytime. I will live with you in"—she groped exasperated—"Taipei even! I will make all the sacrifices. But how can you make me give up my work so long before? Be fair. I refuse!"

She got up and went to the middle of the carpet and glared.

"You refuse what?"

She glared. "I will give up my work the day your divorce starts. Before, I refuse!"

"Come here," I said. She stood in front of me. Then she blinked, then came down beside me and put her arms around my neck.

"Please be fair. It is all right for you. I am coming to your politics and culture. I am making all the sacrifices. I will do whatever you say. But be *fair!*"

I held her. I loved her very much.

"All right," I said...

CHAPTER 29

We had a lovely time that summer. I do not remember much about the days, now, it is the nights and the weekends I remember. The summer was hot and long and the sun shone bright hazy sparkling blue on the Fragrant Harbor and the many ships, and the many more junks. Hong Kong was booming. The newspapers called it the Hong Kong Economic Miracle. Across China the rains came good that year, the second year after the collapse of the Great Leap Forward, and they were talking again about bumper harvests. Thanks to the Great Helmsmanship of Mao Tse-tung, the Reddest Sun in Our Hearts. They were still a long long way from feeding themselves, but you could see the big cargo junks and lighters coming into the harbor from down the Pearl River, low in the water, with rice, vegetables, cattle to sell to the Golden Mountain Where Men Eat Fat Pork, red flags flying and the Big red Character posters on the wheelhouse, *Upward and Onward!* And five times every day the long freight trains coming rumbling across the Shamchun River on the Kowloon-Canton Railway bringing the People's produce to the Golden Mountain. The *Oriental Economic Review* applauded and attributed it to the fact that the peasant was now allowed to keep one pig and two ducks and his private lot of land to hoe after dark. I pointed this capitalistic triumph out to Ying-ling one night.

She said, "I have never said that the peasant should not have private incentives, have I? I think that is sensible. But for China the big things must be communized."

I had a few interesting cases. There was no political crime, everybody was making too much money. In one case a large building contractor was putting only three quarters of the required amount of cement and steel into his constructions, charging the client for the full amount. It amounted to a lot of money. In a few years cracks would appear, the buildings would be condemned. A lot of people were in on the racket, the builders, subcontractors, architects, suppliers, truck drivers, tally clerks. Eventually I had four architects, four building surveyors, three accountants, two forensic chemists, a lot of bank clerks, and thirty detectives assisting me and our investigations led to a whole lot of other new fiddled buildings. A number of gentlemen in the building trade left town in a hurry, but we got most of them. It was very difficult to prove who had participated in which of many fraudulent transactions, it involved thousands of documents, tally sheets, invoices, receipts, books of accounts, bankers' books, all in different handwritings, a lot in Chinese. There was a great scandal in the press. The communist newspapers made a great thing about it. The *Heung Keung Po*, of which Mr. Chan Wai-ping was the editor, the gentleman I had arrested for inciting the mob at Fanling, accused the government in general and me in particular of neglect of duty in not discovering the malpractice earlier. But, after a short shudder, Hong Kong boomed on. Mini-Max was briefed to prosecute the main trial. It took eight weeks. One afternoon I looked up and was surprised to see Ying-ling sitting in the public gallery. At tea adjournment I said softly to Mini-Max, "There she is." She did not acknowledge us, just walked past us out into the corridor.

"Oh-ho," Max said. "I see what you mean. Quite something."

She was standing in silhouette against the Cricket Club, now, her lovely legs, and pretending to read the *China Mail*.

"I see," Mini-Max said. We walked upstairs to the cafeteria. "I see what you mean. What's the latest bulletin on the divorce?"

"I've written to Catherine," I said.

"And?"

And Catherine had written back, urging me not to worry. She sounded very happy. Burton's wife was now being reasonable, though there was still some dispute about property rights and the children. Catherine had been to see a solicitor who was now drawing up her petition: everything was getting organized, but unfortunately the courts were so full that it would be six to nine months before they got a hearing date. Meantime everything was wonderful, Suzie was blooming, very happy at her kindergarten. Catherine wished me lots of luck.

It did not hurt me. Just relieved, though disturbed that the divorce might take as long as nine months; well into

221

next year. Mini-Max said that in England it could take a year. A *year*. But thank God things were starting. I was happy for Catherine. I would not have Suzie out this Christmas, not until things were normal. But the divorce was in sight, soon we would be out in the open, next year Ying, Suzie, and I would have a lovely summer together.

What I remember about that summer is that I was always happy; that absolute certainty that you love one woman in the whole wide world. I wanted to buy her things but it had to be something small, otherwise she felt like a kept woman. The first thing I ever bought her was high-heeled shoes. I brought six pairs home on approval for her to choose from. She was delighted. She tried on each pair and held up her skirt for me to see which I liked best. When I saw her long golden legs in high heels, and she held her skirt up like that, I forgot everything else.

"Come here."

She came, grinning, holding up her skirt, her thighs were golden-shapely and wonderfully smooth, and where they touched there was the long soft secret olive line, her whole long legs were wonderfully naked soft and it was bliss to touch her. "God, you're beautiful. I'll buy you some dresses to go with them."

"No dresses. It is a waste, you only make me take them off."

"Go and buy some dresses. I'll pay for them."

"No dresses. Small sexy things for us, okay, but not big things like dresses."

"Think big!" I said. "Think petite bourgeoisie!"

I bought her a couple of pairs of fishnet stockings and a red garter belt. I loved to see her in such things. She had a beautiful body. She enjoyed wearing them for me, being sexy. Another time I bought her half a dozen pairs of very pretty scanty panties. Some of them were hardly there at all. *"Gwailo* pants!" She jiggled two pairs in front of her, delighted. "I always like barbarian pants!" Quick as a bunny she yanked up her skirt and yanked down her China Products jobs, tossed them over her shoulder and wriggled the Paris model up her lovely legs, wriggled her hips and let the elastic go with a snap. *"Voilà!"* She tossed the skirt from side to side grinning, like a cancan girl.

"Now the back," I grinned.

She flicked up the back of her skirt and shook her

222

lovely bottom at me. *"Hah?"* she laughed over her shoulder.

"Yes. Come here."

"You see! Everything wasted!"

That summer her discretion was still very elaborate. Very seldom would she spend the whole night. If she did she set the alarm clock and left before it got light. She used a different entrance to the building every evening, after taking Mad Dog to the Yacht Club for his swim. You would have thought he was a seal the way he had to get to water every twenty-four hours. Occasionally, after she left me for the night, I made the effort to get up and go back to my flat at the Hermitage, to show my face, but afterward mostly I did not bother. I took my laundry there. Most of my things were at the penthouse now, it was home now. She kept a lot of her things there too now, a lot of her clothes, and a hairbrush and a toothbrush and her bath salts, and the smell of her; and her books and paints and canvases and her carrot top and avocado pit growing in jam jars.

I had never known a sprouting carrot top could be exciting. She bought a big magnifying glass and examined it minutely and I had to look too. She especially loved the roof garden. The carrot top started the vegetable boxes on the patio, among her new flowerpots. We had half a dozen carrots, beans, peas, onions, two lettuces, a potato, and three radishes, and clearly we were going to have an avocado tree. The creepers had grown over the trellises. We already had two twelve-inch pine trees, an eight-inch peach tree, and a miniature mandarin orange tree, which was very good for luck. She bought a little aquarium and stocked it with tropical fish.

A brand-new lucky red China Products chamber pot appeared one night in the bathroom.

"What," I said, "is that for?"

"For urine, of course."

"And what," I said, "is wrong with the big one?"

She pointed at the harbor. "With the big one it goes into the sea. We need our urine for all our plants."

I took a firm breath. "Not on our plants. I don't care what they do in the paradise across the border, if they smother the whole of China in urine. No bloody chamber pots here."

She stared. "Why not?"

She waved her hand exasperated. "All our *plants*, you can't waste urine."

I said, "Next thing you'll be wanting me to do it while you wait."

She was completely confounded by my unreasonableness. "Okay! *Gwailo* urine's no good anyway! All San Mig. I'll use my good Chinese urine!"

"You will not," I said.

"What is wrong with my urine?" she demanded.

"There's nothing wrong with your urine; it's beautiful urine. If I was going to have anybody's urine I'd want it to be yours. But we're not having *anybody's* urine, except Chairman Mao's himself."

The Mao chamber pot got turned into another flowerpot. It had big red China roses painted on the side. She looked at it wistfully every night when she was doing her rounds with her watering can.

"Such a good chamber pot too."

Percy, her cockatoo, was moved in. For a while we had two tadpoles, collected on her class's nature-study expedition to the reservoir, which grew into very happy frogs called Fei-lo and Winifred. Mad Dog had to be locked in the lounge while they had their nightly hop around the roof garden. One night Mad Dog escaped and zeroed in on Fei-lo and squashed his leg and he had to be destroyed, a black night indeed. Winifred was returned to her native reservoir to find another husband. Ying bought some sea horses instead, for the aquarium. She also bought some crickets, in a little Chinese cricket cage, for just naturally all Chinese love crickets to sing to them in the night, and so do I. It was good hearing crickets eleven stories up in the Wanchai sky, while we sat on the roof garden. One evening she came home from her nature-study expedition with a brown paper packet. She would not tell me what was inside it, it was a surprise. She immediately adjourned out to the empty frog tank, but I was not allowed to look yet. "No more frogs," I said. "Please."

"No, not a frog. Turn your back."

"Is that Puku you've got there?"

"Turn your back."

Then I was told to look. At a handful of writhing snake held out for me to rejoice in.

"Take it away!" I recoiled.

"You don't like *snakes?*" She spluttered as if I had

224

been misleading her all this time. "She doesn't bite, she's a *grass* snake!"

"Snakes are my natural enemies, like dragons! We're not having any snakes!"

"She only eats insects! I don't want to keep her forever! Just till she lays her eggs—"

"Pregnant? Get her out of here before we're crawling in goddamn snakes! That snake and all her seed are my natural enemies! It's all in the Bible! She'll bruise my heel! And if she's not out of here tomorrow my heel will bruise her head very severely!" She was clutching her stomach laughing. *"If she's not out of here tomorrow I'll feed her your goddamn crickets!"*

She reeled into the lounge and threw herself onto the sofa and screamed with laughter so the tears were running down her face. Seems it was the funniest thing in the whole world, that snake.

Sufficient unto ourselves. One day she announced that she was going to save me a fortune, like a good communist should, and brew me my own beer. This was the McAdam Relief Campaign. "Splinter Woodcock's not going to like this," I said. "Splinter *who?*" Seems it was the funniest name she had heard. Next evening she came home with the Encyclopaedia Britannica, a ten-gallon glass demijohn, sugar, hops, yeast, malt, and some glass tubes and rubber stoppers borrowed from the chemistry department of the Great Peace School. There followed great work-ups in the kitchen, steam, hops everywhere. "Splinter *Woodcock!*" The next night the demijohn was going bleep-bleep-bleep through the Great Peace test tube. The next week there was bottled beer everywhere. The next few days there were some nasty explosions, to which we grew accustomed. The survivors were called Victory beer and it was not bad at all. The next brew did not explode so much but it had enough alcohol in it to blow your head off. The next brew she got it right and it only exploded occasionally. It was called Famous Red Triumph beer.

After work I went to a karate class, or for a drink, or to the club to read the overseas papers, and I enjoyed my friends again, but after a while I wanted to get back to the penthouse to wait for her. It seems I was always happy that summer; that strength in my shoulders, and I felt very benevolent toward everybody. My junior inspectors wondered what had happened to me. If I saw or heard anything funny, I was grinning at just thinking how she would laugh when I told her. We laughed a great deal. New jokes seemed twice as funny because she started giggling halfway through, even if it wasn't funny yet, just in anticipation, and by the time I got to the punch line her eyes were wet with laughing. When she really laughed she threw her head back. *"The way you tell a story!"* I was a scream, apparently. I was always happy to get home. "Hello," Percy shouted and started bouncing up and down on his perch. There were our two easels standing ready with whatever work we were each doing, and everything, and the woman smell of her in the place, oh God it was good. She always came into the flat as if she had been running, bursting with smiles.

It was great when she came home, Percy shrieking and jumping up and down as soon as she opened the door, Mad Dog bounding all over me. She loved the penthouse. First we had a Famous Red Triumph each while we inspected her roof garden, watered her plants, exhorted them to grow, rewarded them with praise, telling each other what happened today. The stars, the hot China night, the crickets singing, the fairyland glow of the harbor. "Such a good chamber pot too." Then she cooked some chow. I sat in the kitchen alcove with her and we drank Famous Red Triumph while she cooked. She was very fond of cooking. Chinese love to eat. "Why do you think Chinese look so beautiful? The woman don't get so old-looking as your women. Why do you think we don't smell bad, hah? Because we eat good food."

"How badly do I smell?"

"You don't smell too bad because I give you plenty of good Chinese chow. No milk, no butter, only Great Wall cooking oil. You smell quite good."

"Thanks," I said.

"You know why Americans are so clean? Because they bathe so much because they smell so bad. From ice cream and hamburger. Can't you smell them?"

"No," I said.

"Strange," she said. "I'm *very* glad you're not an American, darling."

Usually we had supper out on the roof garden, at the ornate wicker table and the twirly-back chairs by very bourgeois candle-light. I reckoned that as I never spent any other money entertaining her we would become connoisseurs of wines. We tried a great many that summer, and finally we decided that we disliked very few. We tried some Chinese wines but all except the very expensive ones tasted like face cream and had the kick of a People's steel-works. If you can imagine China Products face cream dissolved in vodka. "It's an acquired taste," she said.

"I believe it," I said.

"My father drinks it all the time. You'd like him, he loves stories."

'When I meet your father," I said, "can I bring my own bottle?"

The stars, the Hong Kong lights, the ships, the crickets. Usually we took a long time over dinner. She said it was more beautiful than any restaurant could be. I wanted to take her to real restaurants, the best in Hong Kong, and show her off and dance with her and have extravagant fun. That would come. "We would get tired of it, darling," she said. "This is lovelier than any place and it's our own. I don't feel I want other people. Aren't I a good chef?"

"You're an excellent chef."

"Isn't the wine good? Isn't the view beautiful? Aren't I a good wife to you?"

"You're a wonderful wife."

"We can dance here if we want to."

Sometimes we did dance a little. Just to hold each other that little made us happy and excited, and the knowing we could do what we wanted when we wanted. Sometimes we talked a long time after dinner, sitting out on the roof garden, and sometimes we read or watched television. She was always buying secondhand paperbacks. On her early nights we often painted after dinner. Our easels were always standing. Our walls were full of pictures now. She was much better than I but I did more because I came home earlier. She was doing a lot of abstract stuff now, which I have never much cared for. I was doing real life, realist and impressionist. I prevailed upon her to pose in the nude but she could not lie still long enough when she wanted to do her own work. That ended up with her painting in the nude while I tried to paint her painting in the nude. It didn't work because after a little while I couldn't keep my sticky hands off her. I did a big charcoal of her in high heels, black fishnet stockings, and garter belt. It was very sensuous and it did look very like her.

227

"Do we make love more than most people, you and I?" she said.

"Yes, I think so." We were both working.

"What color is love?" she said to me.

Sometimes I had already bathed, and I sat with her and we talked while she bathed. I liked to watch her, black shiny hair piled up on her head, China Products bubble-bath suds everywhere, shiny golden breasts soapy, sometimes I just had to lean out and feel her, and it was a most beautiful happy rejoicing feeling. Most nights we bathed together. It was very squashed and mostly we sat side by side with our legs hanging over the edge, the bubble-suds frothing right at the rim. You cannot get much bathing done in that position and mostly we read each other poetry. The Poetry Position. "Good for the soul." Two soapy anthologies and two slippery glasses of Famous Red Triumph.

"What does 'sibilant' mean?"

If I did not know the meaning precisely she looked it up in the dictionary at school and told me the next night.

"A brook can sound sibilant. Mellifluous. I looked up 'mellifluous' too, *there's* a good word."

"I knew 'mellifluous,'" I said. "From the Latin *bonus*, good, *melior*, better. Plus *fluo*, I flow."

"*Fluo?* I learned Latin too, big-head, and it's not *fluo*, I flow."

"Absolutely it is. It's like *pronto*, I pront. And *ame*, I am."

She liked modern poetry, it didn't bother her that it didn't rhyme.

"Why must it rhyme, hah?"

"Of course it should rhyme, to be poetry," I said, "otherwise it's just writing printed to make it look like poetry."

"The tyranny of rhyme," she said. "I'm a revolutionary."

I liked Keats, Wordsworth, Longfellow, T. S. Elliot. She bought a new paperback anthology about once a fortnight. Rod McKuen and James Dickie were her favorites. And Mao Tse-tung. She also liked a lot of the old Chinese poets.

"You're a bad revolutionary, then," I said. "They're verboten in China, very bad bourgeois business.'

Squashed up slippery side by side, China Products fragrance in the hot China night, and her, the sound of her voice and the feel of her beside me, oh God it was good.

And half lying in the bath, her silken smooth slippery back against me, her feet on the taps and her long shiny golden legs up, reading, talking, laughing, saying nothing, just loving, I scooped the suds over her breasts, stroking, loving, feeling her wonderfully soft smooth skin silken with the suds, and her brown nipples stood up erect. And she turned her lovely face and her eyes were dark heavy, she twisted around slippery golden glorious and lay in my arms and opened her mouth. And standing, the feel of her slender full soft body slippery loving against me, her arms around me and her belly and her thighs and her buttocks and her breasts, each line and cleft and curve of her, and the joy. And going into the bedroom with the rosy glow and the lust, and the joy, and collapsing into the middle of the big double bed in the China night and she came down beside me and onto me and under me and she whispered, "Do you love me?"

"I love you."

"I love you also."

CHAPTER 30

Every weekend we went out on the junk. Always alone, sufficient unto ourselves. Far away to islands and bays and beaches we called our own.

It always felt like a big holiday. The warm early morning haze on the China Sea, deep blue and sparkling and languid and swelling, white foam seething on the big craggy rocks of the myriad of green islands as silent and empty as in the days of Old Cathay, the big bows gently ploughing, the feel of the wheel and your own big boat and the good strong throb of the diesels, skins brown and strong, the glow on her face, the whole blue China Sea before us and not a soul to see us, and Mad Dog beside himself with joy. Heading just wherever we wanted, we were the only two people in the world. When Mad Dog saw me approach the anchor he went apoplectic with anticipation and as I threw it over, his feet skidded on the deck like a Walt Disney cartoon and he took off over the side, high-dived, paws spread-eagle and long spaniel ears flying, and disappeared with a crash into his native China Sea. That was Mad Dog fixed up for the day.

She was the next one to be fixed up, she was like Mad Dog about the water. It never ceased to excite me to see her taking her clothes off, grinning. The fun in her eyes. I did not always want to go in just yet, maybe I wanted another beer first, but I went in with her because of the fun in her eyes and because she loved it so. Afterward she would do what I wanted to do. Diving, deep into the warm blue China Sea, naked and free, the glorious free satiny feel of nakedness with your beautiful woman, shimmering streamlined naked, black hair streaming behind her, the line of her back and buttocks and legs and her breasts, she turned and swam streamlined toward me under the dancing mirror of the sun-shot surface, delighted grin on her face, soft slippery arms around my neck and soft cold face bubbling kissing and the glorious fleeting satiny feel of her. And coming satiny golden sleek silver wet out of the water, and walking hand in hand along the beach, the feel of her walking naked and free under the sun beside me; sometimes she wanted to run and splash along the water edge for joy, and play the fool. She was very fond of beachcombing. Head down, wandering along, picking her way around the rocks, the sun on her nakedness, looking into the pools, exploring. Some things she took back for her nature-study class, or for the penthouse. A piece of driftwood, a shell, a piece of coral. There was always something beautiful.

If it was an interesting anchorage we dived a long time together, with snorkels. Mad Dog always swam alongside us, delighted. She was very graceful underwater, even if her goggles did not improve her appearance. After a while I swam back to the boat. I lay on the deck with a beer, watching her. Sometimes I fished. Sometimes she swam right out of the bay and disappeared round the point. Swimming along the rocks, head down, snorkel up, her body golden silver in the sun, flippers paddling slowly, looking at her underwater wonderworld. Every now and again her satiny backside came up, then her lovely legs, then she was gone. She could stay under a long time. She said it was the good healthy Red Victory cigarettes. Mad Dog paddled around in circles barking joyously. Sometimes he even stuck his head underwater looking for her. When I was thinking she must have swallowed the goddamn snorkel she broke surface, blew like a whale.

"Oyster!" Treading water desperately as if the oyster might up and run away.

She was very fond of oysters. No oyster was safe where we anchored. Once upon a time she had found half a pearl and she cherished the notion that one day oysters would make us rich and happy.

"How would you like it if you were an oyster, to be terrorized every weekend?" I appealed to her better nature.

I rowed out to her with the screwdriver, Mad Dog delighted to see me as if I had been away on a long journey. I put on my goggles and down we went. It was great fun doing it, gathering nourishment off the land, it sort of satisfied the instinct to provide. And her pleasure. This was much better than providing her with meat, fire, and shelter. We rowed back to the junk. Then the sweat and impatience of opening them, to see if we were going to be rich and happy. She squatted golden beside me, poking her finger into each one. We never found any pearls, but afterward she laid the oysters in their shells on a plate, with lemon and vinegar, and we ate them with cold wine in the sun. We had a good time.

And lying in the deck chairs, drinking good cold sparkling Famous Red Triumph under the hot China sun on the blue China Sea, the big golden junk riding gently, Ying lying there stretched out golden, on her back, on her stomach, propped up on her elbow, talking, thinking, feeling, reading, sketching, reading aloud, saying nothing, flesh getting deeper warmer golden brown, getting full of beer and sun and fulsomeness. We could talk about everything and anything, and always it seemed to get more and more profound and rich and beautiful with the Famous Red Triumph. On about my fourth Famous Red in the sun I was writing great poetry in my head and thinking great best-seller themes for novels: the lines and curves of her glisteny, and the knowledge of the feel and taste of her, flesh brown and drugged and happy from the beer and the sun, oh God it was good. "What about lunch?" I said.

"All right," she said.

She went naked down the hatch into the saloon. The sound of the cutlery, the fridge door, the pull of the wine cork, she always sang while she worked. I brought the deck chairs to the shade of the awning on the aft deck. Sitting, lying, reclining in the warm shade of the after-deck, eating with chopsticks and with our fingers, drinking wine out of China Products cut glass, the sharp sea taste of oysters, and crab and prawns dipped in soy sauce, then soft sweet and salty roasted meat and the good cold wine, greasy fingers, skins glowing from the sun and beer and wine, eating, talking laughing, and the knowledge of what we were going to do. It was a kind of ritual. And then lying stretched out on the deck chairs, full of fulsomeness, the taste of her wide mouth, long sucking animal kisses, the feel of her in my hands, smooth and soft and strong, touching each other, kissing, slow hands loving stroking playing feeling, full of food and beer and wine in the sun on the China Sea. Then, "Come." "Come," she smiled, and we left the debris lying there and she climbed down the swimming ladder and lowered herself into the cool China Sea to wash the sweat off, and I followed her. Then down the steps into the cool of the saloon. She shone satiny golden wet and I took her in my arms, the joy of her, wet happy cool perfect body in my arms, the feel of her wet warm nakedness against me. And wordlessly to the big double bunk and she waited for me to lie down first, and her eyes were happy heavy with love. And she came and knelt astride me and bent and kissed me, and her hair brushed my shoulder, and she offered her nipples to me. And she tasted golden cool warm and sweet and soft and salty from the sea, the taste and feel and warmth of her, the feel of her breath on me, and her mouth, the most urgent desperate joyful feeling in the world I have ever known. And she came over and down beside me and she opened her long soft strong golden legs, and already it could not be told if our slipperiness was the China Sea or our own sweat.

CHAPTER 31

That Friday was the hottest day in sixty-two years. The sun beat down out of a merciless China sky. Still, burning hot, dry hot-haze mad-making still. In the noon the winds came, short hot gusty and dry, and the dust, and then still again, then gusty again. Every half hour the radios reported on Typhoon Wendy, and everybody listened. She was one thousand miles away east-southeast over the South China Sea, and she was one thousand miles wide and her winds were eighty knots, she was heading west-northwest, and she was bringing the first rain of that summer.

Radio Peking broadcast warnings and all down the South China coast the people watched and waited and the junks put back from sea. That long hot afternoon the Number Three Signal went up and all over the sea the junks were coming in full sail and throttle, and the shopkeepers were boarding up their windows and the people were being sent home from work and the buses and trams and the ferries were packed, and the harbor full, and the freighters that did not have a typhoon buoy were putting out to sea. Already the typhoon shelters at Yaumati and Causeway Bay were full of junks, forests of masts. On Kai Tak Airport the airplanes were wheeled around to point to where the wind would come, and lashed down to the tarmac. It was heat-wave glaring hot, and still.

At four o'clock she telephoned me. I had been waiting for her to call all afternoon, I could not telephone her at school. "Hello, Bomban!" she said cheerfully.

"Where are you?"

"In the new place. I'm getting ready for the *tai-fung*. Plants. Windows."

"Good girl. I'll be there in an hour."

"No sweat," she said. She had picked up a lot of my slang.

Never had I seen so many junks and sampans in the harbor, throttling and sailing and rowing to the typhoon anchorages. And the Mountains of Nine Dragons hot mauve brown and scarred and the concrete jungle of Kowloon white and still.

I drove through Wanchai, to the penthouse. All the shops had their windows boarded up already, most of the bars closed, no sailors on the streets, no hawkers, no rickshaws, just Chinese hurrying home, the trams and buses jam-packed. Hot, hot, hot, blazing dry, the sweat. I parked in the basement and rode up in the elevator, opened the door. "Hello," she grinned.

She was in shorts and tennis shoes, hair in a ponytail, hot and cool at once beaming at me and my heart seemed to turn over at the look of her. Her mouth tasted warm and cool at once. I put my hand down and felt her beautiful thighs.

"Such legs. Tell me you love me."

"I love you and I love you and I love you. What about this *tai-fung?*"

"What have you done?"

She had done plenty. The carpet was rolled up, the furniture shoved against the walls, all the small potted plants inside. Now she was sticking long strips of adhesive tape across the windows. "You'll have to help me with the big flower boxes," she said.

We finished taping the windows. Outward from the center to the corners, like stars. To hold flying glass. Then we taped the joints to stop water coming in. Then we carried the big flower boxes in from the patio. "The creepers and the trellis will go," she said.

"Yes. I'll have to build another trellis."

Then we carried Percy in his cage, the crickets, the hamsters, into the bedroom. "Good-by!" Percy said. The television and all the pictures and ornaments into the bedroom. The bedroom was going to be the safest place except for the bathroom. Because it had the smallest windows. All the crockery was stashed in the wardrobe in the bedroom. Then all the pots, pans, beer, wine. "What about the refrigerator?" she said.

We manhandled it through. She plugged it into the wall socket.

"Now we can have cold beer in bed!" Then we carried the stove through.

"It looks like a godown," she said.

"Hello," Percy said.

She said, "I'm staying here tonight."

I thought. "No," I said. "I've got to stay in my Hermitage flat because I'm on Emergency Standby. And this building will be completely empty. I don't want you here alone."

"I *must*. What about all my animals? If the windows break."

"They're safe in here."

"We're so high. If the lounge windows break the bedroom door will break too."

"They won't break. I don't want you staying in this huge building alone in a typhoon."

"If they won't break what is the danger if I stay, hah?" she demanded.

I said, "I'd prefer you in your own room. Where there're plenty of people if anything goes wrong."

"Then I must carry Percy and everybody home to my room. I am not leaving them here."

"Ying, they're safe here."

"Then so am I. Logical, hah?"

"You're going to your room."

"Okay," she said reasonably. "Then I carry Percy and everybody. I am not leaving them here alone to perish."

Oh Gawd.

"Please, I want to stay," she said.

What the hell, I thought. For peace.

"All right," I said. "Telephone me if the slightest thing happens."

"Do you love me?" She grinned.

"Yes," I said hesitantly.

Then I left her and went back to the office. Then to the Hermitage.

All over Hong Kong the typhoon parties were starting. The bring-your-own-bottle-and-bedding-and-something-to-eat-and-let's-have-a-ball parties.

Friday was always a good day to find a party starting at the Hermitage. Off-duty policemen, customs and immigration men, firemen, other civil servants, the boys, anything could happen. But typhoon time at the Hermitage was always a humdinger. Typhoon time really flushed them all out up to the bar, and all their girl friends and boy friends in an atmosphere of jolly air-conditioned siege.

Down there in the streets and across the harbor it was burning sweating pregnant hot and still, people buses ferries trams taxis junks. *Tai-fung lai*, typhoon comes. The transistor radios going all the time, Radio Hong Kong and Radio Canton and Radio Peking.

And in the squatter shacks made of tin and cardboard on the steep jungled mountains and in the cocklofts on the rooftops the poor people waited. They had tied everything down. And down there in Wanchai the staircases of the buildings were crammed with them, and all their possessions. But there were not enough staircases for all of them.

Only the Number Three Signal was up.

CHAPTER 32

At nine o'clock that night the first squall came. In a rush in the hot night and whipped through the harbor and up and down and over the mountains and through the streets and in through windows and tore at curtains and blew over flowerpots and wrenched at neon signs, and with the squall came the first rain. It came in a splatter with wind, so people rushed to slam windows; then *down* it came. In a swirl and hammer and the harbor ran battered with the rain and the lights were hammered, through Hong Kong lashed the squall, whipping and battering and swirling and in a minute there was the rushing of the drain-pipes and the gutters, down off the steep mountains came the beating rain, down over the embankments into the steep roads, brown water rushing carrying mud and rocks and sticks, and the rain whipping down.

But in Wanchai the streets were deserted, all the shop windows boarded up, most of the bars closed down. The squall whipped through the neon signs and it blew open the doors of the Seven Oceans Bar and there was a big squeal from the girls. Two waiters rushed and slammed the doors and the jukebox drowned the clatter of the rain again. The Oceans was the only Wanchai bar which had not closed down yet, over half its girls were still there.

Teetotal Tank and Splinter Woodcock were there. Splinter was staring at the cashier and Teetotal was putting the hard word on the big Shanghainese whore called Mirabelle Wong. Teetotal did not believe in paying for it. Why pay for it, Teetotal argued, when they got it for nothing in the first place? It was un*reas*onable to pay for it. It didn't cost them anything to operate, and you didn't wear it out. It was virtually indestructible. Teetotal Tank never paid for it but he spent an awful lot of money getting it for nothing. Every now and again, over the years, Mirabelle Wong had given it to Teetotal for nothing when business was bad and he had bought her a lot of girlie drinks. Tonight, Teetotal had decided, was to be such a night. Tonight was an ideal night because once in bed they would have to stay there for about twenty-four hours until Typhoon Wendy went on her merry way. Teetotal was working on this theory. Mirabelle Wong was working on the same theory, with the difference that if she was going to be confined to bed with a fat hairy barbarian like Teetotal Tank for twenty-four hours she was bloody well going to get paid for her trouble.

"I very tired," Mirabelle Wong said. "When typhoon come I go sleep twenty-four hours, no wake up."

"Me too," Teetotal said. "I no wake you up, I lie very quiet."

"No!" Mirabelle squealed girlishyly. We sleep alone, you want too much *yum-yum.*"

"I won't." Teetotal raised his hand in blind anxious oath. "So help me I won't."

"No," Mirabelle said, no can do, I know you, tonight I want plenty sleep. Better you sleep your house."

"But Mirabelle," Teetotal pleaded, "I love you."

"You no love me," Mirabelle declared, you butterfly."

"No shit—I love you."

"You butterfly," Mirabelle said, "no shit."

"Have another drink, Mirabelle," Teetotal said.

"Okay," Mirabelle said sweetly. "*Ah Seung—ah!*" she shouted cheerfully at the barman.

The transistor radio on the counter spoke in Cantonese. Wendy was 150 miles away and she was coming at ten knots.

The hot squall rushed over the Nine Dragon Mountains and down into the Shatin Valley swirling great dust, then came the rain. It rushed through the valley, tearing and flapping and shaking the huts and the gardens and the rain tore down off the mountains and the gardens were flooded and the ditches ran full. The people clutched in their huts with their ducks and their chickens and pigs and listened to the rain beating and rushing, and the beat and tear of the wind. And they knew this was nothing compared to the *tai-fung* that would come.

The squall beat through the Tolo Sound on the junks and they swung hard on their anchors and the rain beat down flying, and big black mountains were swinging wild around.

At eleven o'clock the first big winds came. Rushed through the harbor, through the islands, and the sea ran before them, big running swells in the fairway and crash-

237

ing against the waterfront and leaping high and crashing against the typhoon shelters and through the mouths of the breakwaters so the big junks heaved and crashed against each other and the ropes and canvases wrenched; through the streets the big winds rushed and the neon signs wrenched and flew, up and over and down the mountains the big winds tore and the jungle bent and tore and big branches flew, up through the squatter shacks on the mountains and the cocklofts on the rooftops made of boxes and tins the big winds tore and the shacks and the cocklofts shook and wrenched, and inside the poorest people all hung on.

By eleven o'clock Teetotal Tank and Mirabelle Wong had still not reached agreement on terms. At half-past eleven Mirabelle Wong chastely announced she was going home, alone. Teetotal thought cunningly to himself, *Ploy*. He waited a minute after Mirabelle Wong had gone through the back of the bar, then he gave chase. It was intended as chase. Teetotal lurched out the back door with an inward whoop and a holler into the big wind, and newspaper flew into his face and clung. Teetotal reeled clawing it off his face and his suit flapping, he staggered up the alley head down and out into the street, and big wind got him. It spun Teetotal around and threw him down the street reeling astonished and flapping, it threw him against a wall then along it and he fell in a doorway. Teetotal picked himself up in the lee of the door happily. Mirabelle's stairway was just around the next corner. Boxwood and papers and rubbish were flying, a garbage can crashed along the street faster than a man can run, the neon signs whipping.

"*Abate, wind*," Teetotal shouted.

A big neon sign crashed flying down the street, it hit the road and broke and leaped again and smashed through a bar window. "*Abate, wind*," Teetotal howled. A piece of sheet iron flew past and hit the street and sparks flew then it crashed along doing cartwheels for a hundred yards then sliced deep into a parked car with a crash and shatter of glass, then another neon sign flew crashing. "*Abate!*" Teetotal looked wildly skyward for flying objects then hurled himself into the street head down and the big wind got him and swung him and swept him faster than his legs could run. Teetotal hurtled diagonally across the road, jacket and arms flying, a bamboo pole hurtled past him and there was a crash and another neon sign flew over his head and Teetotal Tank tripped and flew also, and hit the road and rolled. The big wind rolled him over and over down the street for twenty yards, into the gutter at the corner. In one huge gasping whimper Teetotal scrambled up out of the gutter, the wind howling in his ears, and scrambled on his hands and knees around the corner into Mirabelle Wong's stairway. Teetotal panted on his hands and knees in the doorway. He was covered in dirt and his hands and face were grazed but Teetotal did not feel it. He felt only triumph. Teetotal rested on his hands and knees for a minute congratulating himself, then he clambered to his feet and started reeling up the stairs. He staggered up two floors counting out loud, then he was on Mirabelle's floor.

"Mirabelle!" Teetotal shouted happily. "I made it!"

Outside howled the wind but Teetotal did not hear it. "Mirabelle darling Wo-ong!" Teetotal shouted and he got out his cigarette lighter and started staggering down the dark corridor examining door numbers happily. "*Mirr-a-belle?*" he crooned happily. It was a middle-class block of flats. "Where art thou, Mirabelle beautiful Wong?" Teetotal sang. He kicked over a little altar of joss sticks and he came upon her door. It had a fancy wrought-iron outer grille. He pressed the bell long and loud, "Oh *Mira-belle?*" he crooned. The door opened six inches and a Chinese girl glared through the grille.

"*What you want—hah?*"

"I want my Mirabelle," Teetotal beamed at her.

"Take your finger off bell!" the girl snapped. A girl's voice in the background in Cantonese, "Tell him I'm not here."

"Mirabelle not herè," the girl snapped through the crack.

"Oh yes she is," Teetotal panted happily. "Tell her it's Teetotal."

`"She know," the girl snapped. "she not here." She slammed the door.

Teetotal's policeman's brain picked up the contradiction. He stabbed at the bell triumphantly and kept stabbing. "*Mirabelle!*" he shouted. "*Mirabelle Wong, I know you're there!*" He kept stabbing at the doorbell. The door opened abruptly, another Chinese girl stuck her head out.

"*I tell you Mirabelle not here!*" She slammed the door.

Teetotal grabbed the iron grille in both hands and shook it. "*Mirabelle, open up! Mirabelle!*" He leaned one hand on the bell and he shook the grille with the other. *"Mirabelle,"* he howled, *"I love you!"*

The passage light went on and a door opened, then another. Teetotal did not even notice them. *"Mirabelle Wong!"* he howled, kicking the door and jabbing the bell. Her door flung open and Big Mirabelle stood there, big and furious.

"Shut up!" she shouted furiously in Cantonese.

Teetotal beamed at her. *"There* you are!"

"Go away, fat barbarian!" Mirabelle shouted. *"Or I call police."*

"I *am* the police," Teetotal beamed happily.

She slammed the door.

"Mirabelle!" Teetotal howled. The door flew open again, and then the grille, and Big Mirabelle heaved Teetotal Tank by his lapels into the room and slammed the door furiously. Teetotal staggered and collected himself, beaming, a big bruised graze down his face, and rolled in dirt. Big Mirabelle stood hands on big hips, her two flatmates standing angrily on each side, a Yank stood behind them.

Teetotal appealed beaming, "Through thunder, lightning, and rain—"

He belched and then vomited all over Big Mirabelle and fell in a swoon.

CHAPTER 33

At 4 A.M. Teetotal Tank woke up, unfed, undressed, and unlaid. On the bathroom floor. They had dragged him in there. He clambered to his feet, switched on the light. He inspected his face in the mirror and saw a long grazed bruised chest and black eye, two happy bloodshot eyes and big bristly cheeks with roses in them. Teetotal knew where he was and he was very happy about it. *"Goodie— goodie—goodie."* He rubbed his hands.

He twinkle-toed through to the kitchen, grabbed a bottle of beer, opened his mouth joyfully and drank it straight down, slapped his hairy gut and said, "Hah!" He twinkle-toed back to the bathroom. He ran the shower, climbed in, started soaping his hairy chest and face vigorously, humming. *"Dum-de-dum,"* Teetotal Tank hummed. The beer in his gut was making him feel even better. He dried himself vigorously, admired his hairy chest, selected a toothbrush, gave his teeth a good brush, sprinkled some Johnson baby powder on his chest, and under his arms. Then he rubbed his hands together gleefully, and twinkle-toed through the flat to Mirabelle's room. He opened the door, took a big happy breath of the smell of woman in a closed room, peeled back the sheet, climbed into bed and enfolded her joyously in his hairy arms.

He also enfolded the American. There was a jerk, a scream, a shout, a flurry, the light snapped on and Teetotal Tank sat up blinking astonished at a furious naked Chinese girl and a furious naked American. She took one hateful look at hateful Teetotal and decided this was it. She filled her lungs, screwed up her face theatrically, and screamed. She screamed and screamed at the horrified Teetotal and on the third scream she clawed at him, and the American leaned way back and gave Teetotal Tank a straight left in the chops. And Teetotal sprawled clean out of the bed onto his back.

He scrambled up and the girl was screaming after him furiously and the big American was lumbering around the bed after him. Teetotal scrambled up apologizing profusely and fled into the lounge, the girl and the American after him. The lights snapped on and Big Mirabelle was coming from another room furiously shouting at him and then the third girl, Teetotal scattered shouting explanations in English and Cantonese and they were after him on all sides shouting, he fell over a chair and scrambled up. *"You no good,"* Mirabelle was screaming. *"You make plenty trouble—we lose face."* And Big Mirabelle had had enough and she got him by the armpit, *"Get out!"* Big Mirabelle shouted and the other girls got him also and in one scramble-fling they heaved Teetotal Tank stark naked out the door into the passage with a shout and slammed the door.

Teetotal Tank reeled across the passage and bounced against the wall stark naked horrified blinking. It had all happened very quickly, it seemed to Teetotal there had never been such a swift rout of so few Englishmen by so many naked angry Chinese. Then he flung himself hairily back on the door, hammering.

"My clothes!" Teetotal hammered. *"Give me my clothes!"*

The door did not open.

"Mirabelle, give me my clo-o-o-othes!"

No response was the stern reply. Teetotal beat the door and filled his lungs with anguish.

"Mirrr-a-belle—gimme my clo-o-othes," he howled from the depth of his barrel chest, *"or I'll call the police."*

The lights went on in the passage and doors opened, faces stared out at him and then laughed and then shouted.

"Miraabellllllllle," Teetotal bawled.

Mirabelle's door opened, but not the grille. *"What do you want?"* Mirabelle shouted.

"Gimme my clo-o-o-o-othes!" Teetotal clutched his family jewels.

Every door in the passage was open, people laughing and shouting. *"Please gimme my clothes,"* Teetotal bawled. Mirabelle lumbered off and came back carrying his clothes. Teetotal was almost sobbing, clutching his family jewels. "You want clothes?" Mirablee shouted gleefully.

"Yes, ple-e-e-ease!" Teetotal sobbed, clutching his family jewels.

"Here!" Mirabelle shouted and she tossed his tie through the grille and everyone screamed with glee.

"Give me my clothes!" Teetotal howled, shaking the grille.

"Put tie on!" Mirabelle shouted gleefully.

"Gimme my pants!" Teetotal howled.

"First put on tie!" Mirabelle shouted, and now everyone was shouting, *"Put on tie!"* and laughing.

Teetotal got the message. He had to let go of his family jewels to a fresh howl of glee and he put the tie around his naked neck shaking with mortification, everybody laughing. *"Now gimme my pants,"* Teetotal howled.

Mirabelle threw him one sock and there was a fresh scream of laughter.

"A joke's a joke," Teetotal howled.

Teetotal Tank hopped around on one leg putting on the sock and the whole passage was screaming with laughter. Then she tossed him the other sock and he hopped around on the other leg, sobbing now. Then Mirabelle tossed him his left shoe, and he had to hop around some more. Then she threw him his right shoe. All the time he

242

was howling, *"Gimme my pants."* Then she threw him his shirt and Teetotal was ready to sob gratitude. He flung on his shirt and then he pleaded for his pants. She made him plead a long time and they were all screaming with laughter, then she threw him his trousers. And Teetotal grabbed his trousers and scrambled into them falling over himself in the laughing and the shouting, and ran down the passage pulling up his trousers.

It was 5 A.M. and outside it was black and the wind and rain were howling and the sheet iron and the wood and the debris flying down the streets. The stairs were full of poor people from the rooftops sheltering. Teetotal sat down on the stairs with them to wait out the typhoon, cursing. He cursed a long time, then he started to laugh. Wendy was seventy miles away.

The Hermitage shook twice as if in an earthquake, I woke up with a start and I knew heart-thudding sure that something was wrong at the penthouse. I looked at my watch—five o'clock. I scrambled out of bed and grabbed the telephone and dialed her. The line was busy.

I pulled on a pair of running shorts and a shirt and a pair of tennis shoes and grabbed my car keys. I wrenched open the door and it flew out of my hand and the wind beat in. I flung out of the flat onto the open access corridor and heaved the door closed behind me. The wind lurched me down the corridor. The wind was rushing up the stairs in a big howl and I had to cling to the balustrade, hair flying. On every floor the wind got stronger and it moaned. The ground floor was flooded, rocks and mud and water off the mountain. I ran sloshing down into the parking basement; it was under six inches of water.

I gunned the big Opel in low gear out the lower exit and she staggered as the big wind and rain hit her. The big rain smashed down and the water tore around the bend moved high off my front wheels, battering off the steep mountain in waterfalls, rocks, branches, mud, I roared the old Opel up onto the level, then the big winds smashed me again, both right side wheels lifted and thumped down and she swung across the road and I swung her back cursing, and the wind hit underneath her again and jerked her off her wheels and she crashed down and I swung the wheel back. I roared in second gear, the rain smashed down on the windshield, the wheels spinning in the rushing water. There was a crack, I hit a rock in the road, hit my head on the roof, the Opel crashed up the pavement, I swung her back. The trees were thrashing, big black branches flew, I roared flat out in second gear, teeth clenched furiously. A car was lying on its side, wheels spinning with the gale, I skewered around the bend at the Christian Science Church, the flood curved up around the church wall, I swung into the water cascading off the mountain, it beat down in a waterfall onto the windshield, the wind beat the car broadside on and I swung her shouting, "Jesus Christ!" A palm tree snapped and flew and crashed over the big beating fronds, and down the road. The wind and rain beat me all the way.

The wind tore up Garden Road in a roaring howl, the floodwater rushed down, mud rocks branches debris. I slammed on my brakes, a forty-foot tree was flying up Garden Road, cartwheeling and rolling and smashing. It flew up the steep road like a shrub, it mowed down a light pole and smashed down a fence and crashed through a big window. I roared down in first gear and the big wind got me broadside and the big car keeled, for a long howling moment I was taking the bend on two wheels, then she smashed down and she was roaring downhill into the roaring typhoon. I had my foot flat, beating down into the big wind. Rocks were rolling downhill past me, rain smashing up the mountain onto my windshield, branches flying, big limbs whirling up the mountain, I was ducking and swerving instinctively, shouting curses at the windshield wipers. A tree flew up from nowhere and crashed over the hood, all I could see was branches flying, then another was coming and I swerved. I beat my way down Garden Road swerving and ducking, then I swung right at the Cricket Club.

Queen's Road West was deep under water, I ploughed into it blindly, the water crashed up over the mudguards with the crashing rain, the sea smashing high over the waterfront, the big spray flying hard. I ploughed along, engine roaring, face pressed to the windshield, cursing, rain flying thick as your fingers, the water flew up from the wheels. The flood was rushing down off the mountain like rapids over rocks and debris, spewing. There were no other vehicles. I gunned into Wanchai. The jungle of neon signs was stripped, the street full of them, lying, skidding, flying. I raced her in second, charged the debris

in the road and jerked and jolted swerving cursing, floodwater flying and the big wind howling beating.

Then a bamboo scaffolding pole flew past me from behind. Thirty feet long, like a javelin high across the road,
smashed through a shop window with a soundless blast
of glass. Then came the others, huge flying cartwheeling
crashing ahead across the road, smashing into buildings
and through shops and smashing down neon signs and
splintering and flying again cartwheeling skidding smash-
in. A huge lattice of big bamboo scaffolding was tearing
off a big building, thrashing bucking crashing smashing
and shattering splintering flying, in a great jagged mass of
gale and rain. I slammed on my brakes, the road ahead
was a battlefield of bamboo. I swung around into the wind
broadside and gunned hard up the side alley.

I roared up the alley teeth-clenched, then swung into
Hennessy Road into the floodwater off the mountain,
rocks and neon signs and debris swirling, I gunned the
old Opel ploughing water and I was two blocks from King-
Ling Building and I hit the boulder. Maybe it hit me, I did
not see it, just the crash. Crashed and jarred and stars, and
the old Opel leaped and the typhoon got her underneath
and flung her.

Flung her, the wheels came up and she rolled big
smashing splashing across the junction glass flying in the
howling rain and roar of the mountain water and there
was nothing in the world but the crashing and the roar,
then she crashed against the traffic lights on her hood and
the floodwater was roaring through the windshield into
the shattered station wagon.

I kicked the door with all my might and it burst open
and the big wind tore it. I scrambled out and the big wind
wrenched me out the door and hurled me and I sprawled.
I scrambled up and ran bleeding splashing down the road
through the floodwater, the typhoon blew me staggering
wildly splashing running toward King-Ling building. The
wind roared up the service stairway, I ran up two at a
time, plastered wet, at the fifth floor I had to rest, heart
thudding in my ears. Typhoon Wendy was still four, five
hours away. My legs were trembling when I got to the
roof. I flung open the rooftop door and the wind tore it
out of my hands.

I flung myself across the gap at the penthouse door,
rammed in the key heaved against the door with all my
might, the wind roared out at me and the door heaved

and fought back and I roared *"Ying!"* and heaved with all my might. *"Ying!"* I roared and I burst the door open and flung into the lounge and all I saw was the howling chaos.

Chaos, glass and water and wind roaring, windows smashed curtains gone smashed trellis and creeper everywhere, plant pots smashed everywhere, the wind crashing smashing roaring, and I saw that thank Christ the bedroom door was still closed. *"Ying!"* I roared and it was nothing in the roar and howl, I staggered crash against the wall and flung at the bedroom door and seized the handle and heaved.

"Ying!" I roared.

The door crashed open two inches against the wardrobe and a new howl of wind roared through the crack. *"Ying!"* I roared and I could not even hear it myself, I heaved, then I saw the wardrobe slide. It slid sideways in a rush and suddenly the door was gone, wrenched away, and I blew in.

Blew in beautifully, reeling crashing sprawling across the jam-packed room and crashed spread-eagle on the bed and there was nothing in the world but arms and legs and Percy screaming and Mad Dog's slobbering all over me in the howling wind and Ying-ling's hair all over the place and Mad Dog barking, arms legs tail Ying-ling Percy screaming and typhoon everywhere, *"Close the bloody door!"* I was yelling above Mad Dog and Ying-ling and Percy and Typhoon Wendy, *"Close the fucking door!"* Then we were fighting up off the bed stumbling clutching and that bloody Mad Dog was trying to scramble out the door into the teeth of Typhoon Wendy and Typhoon Wendy sent him skidding backward on his arse straight under the bed and Ying-ling's face was screwed up laughing, we fought over to the door and heaved and we fell down in a crashing heap of arms legs hair, I heaved her up and I was laughing too now, we threw ourselves against the door with all our might, feet skidding heaving, the door bucked and heaved inch by inch closer, closer, grunting cursing heaving and Typhoon Wendy howled and heaved; and the door closed.

We leaned against it gasping wet awry, and her head thrown back laughing and Mad Dog was pawing up at me slobbering.

"Are you all right?" I shouted above Typhoon Wendy. *"I was until you arrived!"*

And flung herself into my arms laughing and we fell laughing back onto the bed and Mad Dog was all over us, and Typhoon Wendy howled out there.

She was still sixty miles away.

At nine o'clock that morning Typhoon Wendy came. The supreme winds came in a black roar and the rain lashed and smashed and tore, roared across the China coast, crashing through the thrashing islands of Hong Kong, the sea crashed over the breakwaters and crashed into the typhoon shelters and came crashing down the waterfronts, and the jungles of big neon signs came crashing smashing flying down through the howling streets, and the mighty bamboo scaffolding smashing and bricks and gravel flew like grapeshot and cars were picked up and smashed along and trees snapped and flew and windows smashed and roofs tore off and doors smashed in. The supreme winds roared and tore across the cocklofts on the rooftops and smashed away the walls of box and tin, roared smashing up and down and around the jungled mountains and smashed through the squatter huts with the thrashing rain, and the steep jungle mountainsides came sliding crashing killing down.

And we lay on the mattress, in the bathroom, on the floor. With Percy hanging in his cage from the shower spout and the hamster running around in his wheel and the crickets going *crick crick crick* and Mad Dog panting slobbering happily at our feet: we lay together listening to the roar and lash and shake of the typhoon, drinking first cold Famous Red Triumph and, later, a bottle of Mateus rosé, and talking, and often just quiet, listening to the typhoon, then talking again. We always had plenty to talk about. We had moved in here when the first crack came in the small high bedroom windows. Neither of us had slept more than a few hours and now, with the black howling morning, and the wrecking, and the Famous Red and the wine and the menagerie all about us, and the good quiet happy feeling of afterlove with your own true love and now you are lying wide awake next to her again drinking in the morning and you know that it will always be like this and you will never weary of it, of her, listening to the typhoon out there, and there was nothing we could do about it, I said to her, "Don't you want to sleep?" and she said, "I am in the arms of my own true love, why should I sleep?"

And masts snapped and flew like great javelins, and rigging tore away and lashed in the howling and the great armadas of junks crashed and smashed high and low and against each other in the typhoon shelters and the China Sea ran huge and crashed roaring smashing over the breakwaters. And anchor ropes broke and big junks went ploughing smashing crashing through the armadas, and the screams and shouts were nothing in the roar of the sea and the crash of timber and the rain and the supreme wind. And out there in the harbor great ships swung about on their typhoon moorings and many broke the great chains holding them and went ploughing crashing before the howling wind and sea and crashed against the waterfronts and crashed through the other ships and crashed and broke up on the islands. The supreme wind and rain roared over the village of the New Territories and roofs tore off and doors smashed in and furniture sucked out and flew, the supreme wind roared through the tranquil valleys and smashed down the crops and the rain tore down the mountains. And all the time the screaming of the wind gone mad. At nine o'clock the tidal wave came to the village of Shatin.

It came from way out there in the howling crashing China Sea, seething rushing swelling high and wide before the supreme winds down the howling Tolo Sound, three times the height of a man, much faster than a man can run. The junk people saw it coming and there were the screams and bellows in the lashing, but there was no place for them to run. Came swelling rearing high and mighty down the sound so you could not see the mountains beyond, crashing smashing along the shoreline, higher and higher it was swelling rearing bearing down and the spray lashed forward from its long high ridge with the great howling wind, higher and higher coming roaring down the terrible wave looming up up up up and curling over and coming vicious big and terrible and more and more mighty white thrashing churning wall of crashing white coming thundering down and the great wave hit the first junks. Hit them in a thunderous crash that shook like cannon, crashing sea flying everywhere, it lifted them up and carried them crashing smashing plunging skewering. The tidal wave thundered along the Tolo Sound, smashing through the junks and sampans and carrying them along before it, the roar and thunderous crashing and the howling of the wind and the crash of timbers and the screams; it smashed high over the concrete dike before the village and threw the junks high over it and smashed them over the paddies and through the village like surfboards, crashing roaring. The tidal wave roared through the village of Shatin and smashed down huts and concrete walls, crashed through a hundred shops thundering smashing high and terrible through the narrow streets and through windows and smashed down doors and roared up stairways and swallowed up the screaming fleeing people crashed down the villages of Pai Hok Ting and Ng Yuen, and through the stables of the riding school and the screaming horses, crashed flying thundering high and terrible up the valley and over the paddies and the huts and the water buffalo and the dogs and the chickens, the people screaming thrashing flailing over the rooftops and through the streets, dogs chickens carts junks people crashing smashing spewing. And all the time the screaming howling lashing of the wind gone mad.

We heard and felt the supreme wind hit the building, it shook so Percy's cage swung wildly and he screeched, then we heard the bedroom door and windows go in a crash of wood and glass, then the front door went, in a crack like cannon and we felt the suck. The supreme wind roared through the penthouse and sucked the sofa and armchairs and tables out the french windows, hurtling smashing cartwheeling flapping across the patio splintering and over the wall, flying eleven stories high out over Wanchai, it sucked my carpet flying unfurling flapping beautifully through the China sky eleven stories high just like the magic carpet it indubitably was: and we lay on the mattress against the buckling bathroom door and I held her tight and God alone knows why but we were laughing and I remember I said, "You will certainly marry me." And I remember she said, "I certainly will. It is natural."

Of course a lot of other things happened that day, during the eight hours Typhoon Wendy raged across the Colony. Five of the boys from the Hermitage were mercilessly trapped in the Seven Oceans Bar with Nancy Ho, Minnie Wong, Lucy Chan, Isabel Ng, and Miriam Chan. Splinter Woodcock sat at the Hermitage Bar between the till and the beer machine, drank twenty-two pints of his company's fine product, watching his money come back to him and said nothing to anybody. Chan Fat-ho ran amok with a meat cleaver. Fat Cat Wong Man-kit of the Chung-kwok Import-Export Agency spent the day in bed with his American mistress. Wong Ting-tak, which means Wong Man of Great Virtues, found himself swimming in a paddy field. A landslide buried seven squatter huts and forty-two people. A man was blown away off a four-story building. A junk carrying five tons of raw opium from Thailand sank. The roof of the godown of the Sincere Underwear Company blew off and twenty thousand pairs of falsies blew away like a snowstorm. Another tidal wave hit Shatin and drowned 104 people plus two monkeys chained to a pole, two more horses in their stables, five water buffalo, twenty-eight dogs, fifty-one cats, and a large but unknown number of chickens. The tug *Dorothy* sank with all hands on board. A ship being towed to Hong Kong broke its cable and just disappeared. An ambulance was blown away, crew and all. Five thousand nine hundred squatter shacks were blown away. There were eleven more bad landslides. Four hundred elevators jammed between floors. The Fire Brigade went out to 294 fires and rescued a total of 3,281 people from fire, flood, house collapse, and mud. The floating logs of the eight sawmills located at Shaukiwan sank 200 junks and smashed up 1,000. Fifteen thousand telephones were knocked out. Three thousand automobiles were destroyed. For eight hours Typhoon Wendy raged over the Colony, and the winds reached 162 miles per hour. But altogether only eight big ships were wrecked and eleven went aground, and only marginally over 1,000 junks were sunk, only 80,000 people lost their homes, and only 240 people died.

She was the third typhoon to score a direct hit on us in three years. She was a bad typhoon but most of us remembered worse. Why, it was said afterward, in 1932, 11,000 people died!

CHAPTER 34

In September it got cooler. Typhoon Wendy had filled our reservoirs but in the New Year we were going to be on water rationing again, four hours of water every fourth day. Government had decided to build a reservoir at Plover Cove, a long deep bay with a row of islands across the mouth, which would be connected to each other by a wall, then the seawater pumped out. The Hakka farmers and the Tanka fishermen at present around Plover Cove would have to be resettled. Plover Cove had excellent *fung shui*, the two peninsulas each containing a slumbering dragon. The Hakkas and Tankas were demanding massive compensation from the Hong Kong Government for the loss of all that excellent *fung shui*. And all the bad joss the outraged dragons would move like bulls in a china shop. Government engaged a highly paid geomancer to placate the dragons and encourage them to move on. I met Terry Lockhart, one of the district officers, at the club and he told me about it. These two dragons were going to cost the Hong Kong Government a whole pile. The geomancer had been stumbling around over the hills in his golden high-priest robes with his entourage every day for a week at Christ knows how much an hour beating gongs and chanting incantations and still those dragons showed no signs of moving, and now he was talking about there being more than two. We were both laughing. "Nice work if you can get it," I said. That night I told Ying-ling about it, in the bath. "Do you believe in dragons?" I said. She was soaping her face, legs hanging over the bath.

"Do you believe in spirits? In ghosts? And witches?" She soaped.

"I don't know," I said.

"I don't know about dragons either."

"But *drag*ons?" I said.

"But *witch*es?" she appealed through the soap.

"Witches exist. There are thousands of people running

251

around the world claiming to be witches and witch doctors."

"There are seven hundred million people running around China who will tell you there are dragons. Seven hundred million Chinese can't *all* be wrong."

"Who's ever seen a dragon?" I said.

"St. George," I said disgusted. "That dragon doesn't count."

"Then why is he a saint, hah? What did he do except kill that poor dragon most mercilessly, dragons are good luck, you know."

"Not our dragons," I said. "Our dragons are our natural enemies."

"What dragons?" she said. "The dragons that St. George did not kill?"

Government signed a contract with China for the supply of water through the pipeline. China offered us the water free, but Government insisted on paying for it. The communist papers made capital out of it. They were full of China's agricultural triumphs this year, China was having bumper harvests, though no figures had been released since the second year of the Great Leap Forward. The bumper harvests were due to the Great Helmsmanship of Chairman Mao Tse-tung. China had also had bad drought but now she could offer water as a People's Gift to their less fortunate compatriots in Hong Kong, but the Hong Kong Government did not want the unfortunate compatriots to be grateful to the motherland. There was no mention of the refugees coming in every day. It was true that the Hong Kong Government did not want to be indebted to China, but the greatest reason was that our water supply could be cut off, held to ransom, at China's whim if there was no contract. Maybe there was reason to think of trouble with China. Theoretically, China was heading for another change, sooner or later.

There was nothing about trouble with China in the *Oriental Economic Review*, but it reviewed a new book, called *China in Perspective*, by a Professor Milton Barnes. I ordered it air-mailed. I read it at the office, in almost one go. That evening I met some China-watchers at the Foreign Correspondents' Club. They all agreed that, theoretically, Professor Barnes was right: the ground was getting ripe in China for an ideological shake-up, a new purification campaign.

The next evening I happened to meet Dermot Wilcox, the director of Special Branch, at the Hong Kong Club. He was thin and balding, with spectacles, he did not look like a policeman at all. He looked bookish. The Special Branch boys were all bookish, there wasn't a James Bond among them. Dermot knew more about what was happening in China than the Old Man and the governor. In the final analysis, Dermot answered only to Whitehall. Nobody knew how far the Branch went, except Dermot, not even the superintendents under him. To speak to him you would think he had no opinions outside the editorials of the *South China Morning Post*. We sat in the deep leather armchairs and had a drink. I asked him if he had read the book. He said the office copy had only arrived that morning, what was the professor on about?

"In a nutshell, that probably as soon as next year Chairman Mao is going to shake up his communists. The party and the people. With a new purification campaign. Like the Three and Five Antis or the Hundred Flowers. Because since the collapse of the Great Leap Forward the government has had to reintroduce economic incentives like King Pig and the two ducks and the private lots to get over the food problem. And this is the type of revisionism that Mao threw the Russians out of China for. Mao is a purist, he hates this revisionism. And the party hierarchy is now full of it, this mentality. So are the people. The result is that within the highest party echelons there is going to be a challenge to Mao's power and ideals from these 'revisionists.' A power struggle. And it's going to reverberate all over the country. And the outcome is going to affect the whole world. If the revisionists win it could mean a vast change in China's policy to the Western world. To Russia, for one. To America, for example. If the revisionists win, there may well be two Chinas in the U.N., with Communist China in the Security Council with a veto power. He lists a host of the possibilities, affecting the whole world."

Dermot nodded expressionlessly, as if it was mildly interesting. "And if the Maoists win?" He puffed his pipe.

"A harder line," I said. "More idealist, puritanical, holier-than-thou. Uncompromising. A deepening of the rift between Russia and China. More hostility to America. If the revisionists win, on the other hand, you could get a very mild and reasonable brand of socialism. It could change the whole world's power structure, he says. And 'of course this power struggle and the result will have considerable effect on Hong Kong."

"What does he say about Hong Kong?" Dermot said.

I had the feeling he had read the book, all right. I said, "Only the obvious. As a capitalist colony Hong Kong is anathema to Mao, the very opposite of what he stands for. Although it's useful to him, he may kick us out if there is this power side of things."

"Academically," I said. "Not practically. I prefer active police work. I'm happy in Special Investigations," I said.

He puffed his pipe. "Playing cops and robbers," Dermot Wilcox said.

"Not exactly," I smiled at him.

"Cops and robbers," Dermot said. "Cowboys and crooks. You'd use your brain in Special Branch."

"I use it a bit now."

He shook his head quietly. "Not your brain. You use your experience. Your general police know-how, that's all you're using. There's nothing new you can't handle adequately, you've exhausted the challenge. Whereas in S.B.? In Special Branch you'd be thinking all the time, for the long term. Important long-term stuff, international stuff."

"As a superintendent, maybe. But not as an inspector, even a senior inspector."

He said quietly, "And what makes you think you're not going to be commissioned soon to superintendent? You will be. In a year or two."

"It's nice of you to say so."

He pulled a face. "If you applied now as a senior inspector you would grow up with the department," he said. "Grow up with the country."

I smiled.

"The department must grow," he went on. "Hong Kong is becoming increasingly complex and more important internationally. And Special Branch is the most important arm of the police force, no matter what the commissioner thinks. And of Government. And the most powerful." He nodded at me disinterestedly. "I could use you."

"I don't know enough," I said. I did not want to talk about transfers to Special Branch. "I had enough of Special Branch in Malaya."

"Malaya," he said. "That wasn't S.B. work, that was cowboys and crooks again, compared to the way special branches work nowadays. You'd like it." He shrugged.

I shook my head politely. "No, general police work. People."

"Criminals." He shook his head, disgusted. "You actually *prefer* to deal with *that* kind of mind, rather than with thinking, specialized people of your own intellectual and educational standing?"

I nodded firmly, trying to look polite. "Yes."

Christ, he was going on about it. "I'm a policeman," I said. "Not a political scientist."

"Why did you take a degree in political science, then?"

"It was a general degree," I said. "It was more political history."

"So general that you wrote a book on the history of the Communist Revolution?"

"The *story* of it," I said. "It just turned out a sort of armchair history. Because I'm no novelist."

Dermot nodded, nod nod nod. "And," he said, "what do you think about the professor's prophesies? About Hong Kong's involvement in it?"

I said I had to go in a minute. I did have to go, it was Ying-ling's early night home. I wondered what he would say about me joining Special Branch if he knew I was going home to her. But I really wanted to know what he thought, if he would talk. I said that everything that the professor said about Hong Kong was obviously possible, but the most interesting thing, or the most worrisome, was a third alternative, which the professor had not mentioned, and it was obviously this: Instead of Mao kicking us out of China to prove his political purity he might try to make us stay on certain conditions. Namely that the communists control Hong Kong for practical purposes, like they do in Macao, through the Chinese Chamber of Commerce. Make the communists the real power behind the throne, so that Her Majesty and the Hong Kong Government are doing what Peking tells them to bloody well do. Such a situation would give the communists terrific face. And save Mao's face about permitting Hong Kong to exist on the holy soil of China, while preserving the enormous usefulness of Hong Kong as China's window on the world.

I watched Dermot. I really wanted to know what he thought. This was what it was really all about for us. Anybody who thought, who had the savvy to appreciate the real Macao situation, would realize it. But the professor's book had made me think again. Maybe it wasn't so theoretical any more. I had let things slide with Catherine since her last assurance. It was October already and I still hadn't heard from her solicitor. Dermot had his lower lip jutted out looking as if he had never thought of this before.

"What do you think?" I added, "Sir."

He looked at me, then sat up straight, put his pipe in his pocket to go home. "That is what it's all about, old chap. And more."

He was putting his pipe in his pocket, to go home.

"What evidence?" I said. "What straws in the wind do you see?" But I knew he wouldn't talk.

We left the club together. "Cheerio, old chap," he said. "Best of luck at the cops and robbers."

I got into the car and sat there a minute. Then I started driving back to the office, to write to Catherine. Then I turned around and drove to Cable and Wireless. I sent her a long overnight telegram demanding to know when the divorce proceedings were beginning and the reasons for the delay.

The next day she cabled back that everything was under control and that she had instructed her solicitor to write to me immediately explaining the position fully. And I felt happy again.

CHAPTER 35

The next week it was November, and I received her solicitor's letter.

It was the usual hostile stuff that solicitors prefer, advising me, as if this would come as a nasty shock which I deserved, that he was instructed by my wife to institute divorce proceedings against me on the grounds of my adultery with a certain European woman, name unknown, in Room 22 of the Lotus Blossom Hotel, Kowloon, Hong Kong, on such and such. The petition would be served on me in due course. Whereupon I could, if I wished, make a confession affidavit admitting the adultery. If I chose to make the confession, it would greatly facilitate the conclusion of the proceedings. In the meantime please advise whether or not I intended to contest the divorce, as this would considerably affect the trial date. If I did not contest, a hearing date could be secured in June next year. Yours faithfully.

Outside it was a beautiful autumn day. I thought: *June. Why so bloody long?* And why hadn't the bloody petition been prepared months ago? Eight bloody months! Then I calmed down. And thought: Well thank God anyway it was happening at last. In black and white. June wasn't so bad. I thought, We can get married at the end of that school term, July, the beginning of her summer holidays. She can resign at the beginning of the April term, it isn't so bad. And we'll be going on leave at the end of that year. It wasn't so bad, thank God anyway. We would be married in time to go on long leave together, seven months, go anywhere we liked. Passages paid by Government. A long sea cruise. God no, it wasn't such a bad day. Soon it would be Christmas, and then the New Year anyway. I sat straight down and wrote back to her solicitor placing on record that I would *not* be contesting the divorce, that I *would* supply the confession affidavit immediately on receipt of the petition. Which kindly have served on me immediately.

That night I told Ying-ling. We sat on the roof garden in the autumn evening and drank our best bottle of wine. I asked her where she wanted to go on our long leave. *Our* long leave, hell it was good to say "our." "Our" is a beautiful word, like "wife." I could not want a more lovely wife.

"Does Government really pay my fare too?" It seemed too good to her to be true.

"Absolutely. Return airfare for the whole family to England. But we can pay the little extra and make it a round-the-world trip if we want."

"Round-the-world," she said. "Is it really happening to us?"

"Us," I said. That's another good word.

"I have some money saved," she said.

"You can keep it," I said, "for China Products when we get back. In the meantime think big. Think bourgeois."

She was delighted. She couldn't think at all.

I said, "We could fly from here to the Philippines, then to Bali, then Thailand. Spend a week in Bangkok, say a week down on the Gulf of Siam. Then Kuala Lumpur.

Take a train from K.L. down Malaya to Singapore. Then fly on to India. Then either take a boat from Bombay, through Suez, or round the Cape, to England. Or fly from Bombay, through the Middle East to the Mediterranean. Say, Karachi, Tehran, Damascus, Baghdad, Beirut, Constantinople. Then take a train through Europe. And take a boat back, via America. Take Greyhound buses zigzagging across the U.S. to the coast. Catch a boat or a plane in San Francisco or L.A."

"I'd *love* to see America," she said. She couldn't believe it all.

"Or we could go the other way. Take a boat from here to Vladivostok, then take a train across Russia to Moscow. Then on to Europe and England."

"Oh, *Russia,*" she said. "I'd love to see Russia!"

Anywhere in the world. But first it was going to be a holiday in the sun somewhere. Bali or Pattaya or Zamboanga or anywhere, three weeks lying on a beautiful palm-slung beach, the sea crystal-clear blue and the sun shimmering on the coral down there, swimming, floating, playing, goggling, laughing, lying together stretched flat out in the sun getting good and golden and fulsome. And then going back up to our hotel for lunch, the best damn hotel. And drinking beer and *maitais* before lunch, the good glow of the sun on us and sand on our feet, sitting barelegged salty sandy on the bar-stools, talking and laughing, as long as we like. And if we meet somebody we like, we can sit there with them talking and laughing and exchanging ideas as long as we goddamn like because it doesn't matter who sees us any more. And afterward the long lunch on the terrace, good food and wine. And afterward going upstairs to our room, the best room in the best goddamn hotel overlooking the South Sea, happy, and closing our door on the whole wide world and it doesn't matter who knows we are in there, sea sand on the carpet and just leaving our swimsuits right there on the floor where we pulled them off. And the big soft double bed, the joyous glow of the sun on her lovely body and the grin on her happy beautiful face, the sudden feel of her nakedness in my arms and all over me, and the soft feel and taste of her, oh yes. And afterward the long exhausted sleep in her arms, the smooth beautiful exhausted feel of her against me all the way down. And we would walk through the village hand in hand and look at the shops and the bazaar and market, as long as we liked, watching the world go by. And going back to the hotel and lying in the deep languid bubble bath together, and the South Sea sunset streaming in through the windows and getting ready for tonight, cool and fresh, a cold beer and a cigarette, watching my beautiful wife get ready for tonight. And dancing, my beautiful wife in my arms, her happy face and the shine of her long black hair and the feel of her cool warm soft in my arms, the love and the pride for her, and the knowledge that when we wanted we could just walk back upstairs to our room and it doesn't matter who sees us go.

And when we had finished our holiday in the sun we would go on to the white winter of Australia, and ski. A great feather bed, the snow on the windowsill and icicles as thick as your arm, the village lights twinkling. And the crunch of the snow under our shoes and the snow filtering down out of the sky onto her face, the black shine of her hair. "I'm absolutely positive I will learn to ski very well, darling!" And whooping thrilling flashing skidding tumbling crashing laughing down the mountains, the thrill of the speed and the cold wind and the sun and the laugh in her face as she picks herself up out of the snow all covered in it. And stopping at lunch-time at the little log-cabin cafés. And coming down off the mountains in the sunset, good and tired and happy and the good feeling of taking off your heavy ski boots, and then the long hot bubble bath together, the feeling *aaah* as you ease down into it. And then getting warmly dressed up again, and our shoes feeling very loose and comfortable after the heavy ski boots, and going crunching out into the snow hand in hand down to the old Tyrolean *Gasthof* to drink beer and wine in the lovely old noisy *Keller* with the benches and the long wooden tables, and dance to the jukebox, and everybody happy; and going late and happy and full of wine and food back out into the beautiful snow, and all the lights twinkling, hand in hand crunching through the snow back to the *Pension* and the big warm double bed, oh God it was going to be wonderful. And when the summer came we would head south, and would take a villa on the Costa del Sol, and hire a maid and send for Suzie. And the three of us would have a lovely time in the hot Spanish sun, cheap San Miguel and wine and fruit and the hot white beaches and the clean blue sea. That was how it was going to be.

PART VI

CHAPTER 36

Max invited us to spend Christmas in Macao. "Do you want to go?" she said.

"No," I said. "Do you?"

"No," she said. "I do not even know Max. It is very kind of him but I want to be with you. It's a family time, anyway. Do you miss your family, darling?" she said.

"I miss Suzie, that's all."

"Next year we will have her out here. And every Christmas after that. Do you want to go to church on Christmas Day?" she said.

"Midnight mass on Christmas Eve," I said. "Will you come?"

"Yes, if you want me to."

"You must stop worrying about people seeing us. Soon it won't matter any more. Do you really want to come?"

"Yes. Because I want to make it a real Christmas for you."

"Will you pray?" I said.

"Yes, if you want me to. Do you think He will mind if a heathen prays to Him on Christmas Eve?"

"I don't think so. But you better not make a habit of it."

"All right, I won't make a nuisance of myself. I don't think it will be a problem. And I'll sing the hymns too, I like the sound of Christmas carols."

"That doesn't sound very communist," I said.

"I am not a very good communist, you are right. But my heart is all right."

261

"Your heart is wonderful."

"You are the one with the wonderful heart," she said. "I am very proud of your heart."

"You are wonderful all over."

"Our children will have wonderful everythings, with such wonderful parents. What will you pray for?

"Mostly for you."

"Yes, that's good. Will you please say thank you on my behalf for you, darling, in case He doesn't hear heathens on Christmas Eve, Christmas Eve must be a busy time."

"Very well," I said.

"But I will sing the carols very loudly. It will be a grand Christmas. What do you want us to eat for the dinner?"

"Anything," I said.

"Oh no, not anything. I will do my best to make it a splendid Christmas. I know at Christmastime Europeans like to feast and be with their family and friends."

"You're my family," I said. "And my best friend."

"I will do my best to make you a wonderful family and best friend. And I understand about Christmas even though I am not a barbarian. And about Christmas spirit."

Two weeks before Christmas the parties began. I had to go to most of them, and I enjoyed them, sure, because I was a happy man, but I wished very much that she would come with me. I did not care any more, in six months we would be married. Although it would have been embarrassing, professionally speaking, if anybody had inquired about where she worked, but we could have given her an alibi. "They've all got to know sooner or later," I said, "and take us or leave us."

"Darling, when it is all settled I will carry my head up high and say take me or leave me. But now it makes unnecessary problems. And communists are very narrow-minded, they would not understand. We have done very well for one year nearly, it is only another six months."

"I'll come back early," I said.

"No," she said. "You come back when you are full of beer and happy with your Christmas. I will be waiting for you. What do you say, Mad Dog, hah? Will we be okay while the bossman Bomban is out getting full of Christmas, hah?"

Mad Dog beat his tail and looked at us adoringly.

I enjoyed the parties, sure, seeing all the people you only see a few times a year and greeting them like long-lost friends, and the jokes and talking shop and who's doing what to who these days, but I was always happy to leave early and go home to her. I felt in great form at the parties because I was happy and everything was going right for us. People said how well I was looking and I wanted to tell them why. I would have loved to have her there, for all the world to see. And everybody charmed and laughing with her, and the men would say, Christ, no wonder McAdam's not seen around much these days, the lucky bastard doesn't want to get out of bed. This time next year it would be like that.

A week before Christmas was the Old Man's party, up on the Peak. There were Chinese traffic policemen to tell us where to park and a traffic cop to punch the elevator button. It was a very big party, including His Excellency the Governor. I was the only cop below the rank of superintendent. I saw Dermot Wilcox and he waved and grinned and asked how the cops and robbers were getting on. That was the end of his repertoire of party jokes. Gladys, the Old Man's wife, said she had had a Christmas card from Catherine. I said so had I, and one from Suzie, she had drawn it herself. Gladys said how pleased she was to see me so well. The Old Man had said I did a great job on the building case, he thinks the world of you, come and meet some people. There were a lot of people I had never seen before. She introduced me as the man who had written that fantastic book, *The Story of the Chinese Communist Revolution.* Somebody said they had read it a long time ago and somebody else said they didn't think they had read it and somebody said he had never heard of it, weren't the gins a bit weak? I circulated. A number of people had known my father, both in Shanghai and here. When Mao had liberated Shanghai they had come to Hong Kong and started the China trade all over again. Some had lost everything in the Liberation, some had brought it all with them, some had been allowed to maintain branches in China by Mao, but it was they, along with the Chinese taipans who fled with them, with their know-how and sangfroid, who made Hong Kong. A lot of them had originally made their money out of the opium trade, but now they were respectable. Many I had not seen since Catherine and I broke up. I saw Derek Morrison from the Hong Kong and Shanghai Bank talking to old Neil McGregor of Jardine Matheson and an American lady who turned out to be a visiting journalist. It is said that Hong Kong is governed by the Hong Kong and Shanghai Bank, Jardine Matheson, the Hong Kong Club, and the governor, in that order. Derek said he had been very interested to follow my building case. Bloody typical of Hong Kong, he said. Neil McGregor said the building boom was over saturation point, about time too, it was an unhealthy boom, all these luxury middle-class apartments. That's the Chinese for you, Neil McGregor said, the great middle-class Chinese mentality. I said as long as it trails off gradually and not all of a sudden. Derek said Exactly. He had thought the balloon was going to go up with that building case of mine. A lot of people would be in trouble if the building industry suddenly fell through. It only needed a bit of panic, such as my building case, or a spot of trouble with China, or some other sort of loss of confidence, and all hell could break loose. "What would happen?" Mrs. Something Junior, the American lady journalist, said.

Derek said, above the noise, "The building industry works on credit supplied by the banks. The banks get their money from depositors. If the building industry goes broke, where is the people's money? The people come along to the bank and demand their money back. The bank can't pay because it's lent it to the builder, who's gone broke. So the bank goes broke and everybody loses their money. As simple as that. And once a bank goes broke, oh boy."

"Oh boy what?" the American lady said.

"Panic," Derek Morrison said. "Everybody runs to the other banks to draw their money out. No banking system can stand a rush like that."

"There was a leader article about it in the *Oriental Economic Review* a little while back," I said. "It advocated proper banking legislation."

"What legislation?" the American lady said to me.

"You've read the article," Derek said. As a banker, he didn't want to say too much.

I said, "Legislation which says banks must keep a certain percentage of their deposits in *cash*, so that they can pay out when demanded. I believe twenty-five per cent. But in Hong Kong there is no such legislation," I said, "and banks can invest every cent that's deposited with them, and some of them do, particularly the small Chinese banks that have sprung up everywhere, and they've been investing mostly in the real estate boom."

The American lady joked. "But not the Hong Kong and Shanghai Bank?"

"No, madam," Derek said, "not the Honkers and Shankers."

"What about the other big banks?" the American lady journalist said.

"What other big banks?"

We all laughed. I was enjoying it, it was nice seeing all these people again but I was ready to go home soon.

When I got home, as I put the key in the latch, I heard Bing Crosby singing "White Christmas." The whole penthouse was transformed. *"Hello!"* Percy shouted. There were Christmas decorations everywhere, and a Christmas tree and there stood Ying-ling in jeans and sweater holding some decorations grinning at me like a Cheshire cat, as pleased with herself as if she had invented Christmas herself.

"How lovely!" I said.

"You like it?" She beamed, delighted with herself, her pigtails sticking out. I put my arms around her and my eyes were burning and I hugged her and she was laughy and Mad Dog put his paws up on us delighted and his big tail sweeping. "Where did you get the pine tree?"

"Rotary Club. Only ten dollars, and the money goes to charity. And the bells and things I got from China Products."

I was grinning. "I didn't know China Products catered to such bourgeois tastes."

"Oh yes, we Chinese are very practical. And look. She pointed at Suzie's Christmas card stuck up on the wall. We're going to have a lovely Christmas!"

I could not kiss her properly because her lovely wide mouth was laughing like a Cheshire cat.

And we did have a lovely Christmas. On Christmas Eve we went to midnight mass and she sang the hymns as loud as any good-hearted barbarian at the back of the cathedral and we grinned at each other and I loved her very much. On Christmas morning there were all the presents wrapped up under the tree. I woke up to "Good King Wenceslaus" and there she was with a tray of coffee and a bottle of champagne, whichever I wanted, grinning all over her face. It seemed the best Christmas I had ever spent. At dinner we drank a toast to Absent Friends, which she proposed, and it was a happy toast. Everything was going to be all right. She said, "It's nearly New Year already, and that's the year everything's going to be all right. Next year you will have all your friends again, darling."

"You're my best friend," I said.

"And best lover, hah?"

We had a great time. I thought it was the best Christmas I had ever spent, and, indeed, it was so.

CHAPTER 37

In January it was bleak-sunny cold and in the early mornings there was ice on top of Tai Mo Shan. Across there, from the lights of Tsimshatsui to the cold mauve scarred Mountains of Nine Dragons, from Kwun Tong to Laichokoh and from Shaukiwan to Sai Uing Pun there were the factories and the alley workshops and the backyard sweatshops clattering thumping gushing melting welding weaving. But there was no gushing stamping of the pile drivers from new buildings any more. There were still the teeming cocklofts on the rooftops and the squatter huts crowding up and down the mountains, but out there were also many new empty flats.

In the newspapers there was a lot of talk about textile import quotas which had been imposed on Hong Kong by foreign countries to protect their own textile industries. The stock market was down. The Chinese banks were not offering high interest any more, there were no big posters in their windows shouting at you any more. There was an editorial in the *South China Morning Post* saying, with the voice of the oracle, that the textile tariff quotas imposed were a nasty blow to Hong Kong's manufacturers and money might be short for a while but that Hong Kong with its typical sangfroid, resilience, versatility, ingenuity, et cetera would adapt itself and diversify. With the wisdom of hindsight, the editorial said there had been too much speculation in the building sector, too many luxury and middle-class apartments built, resulting in the supply now exceeding the demand. Ying-ling brought her copy of the newspaper home. "That is what makes me *mad* about this government," she said. She had just come

266

in the door. "All this money put into luxury apartments! Rich people trying to get richer out of building apartments and now there are too many and they are empty and meantime poor people are sleeping in the streets!"

"It's not Government's fault," I said. "Government didn't build the apartments, it was ordinary businessmen."

"It is the capitalist system," she declared. "If Government was *for* the people it would be the government's money, the people's money, and they would build sensible places for the *people,* and there would be no more sleeping in the streets, no more squatter huts! *That's* what makes me mad about the capitalist system."

"Government's doing a pretty good job building resettlement blocks. Where do these squatters come from, anyway?" I said. "*That's* what makes me mad about the communist system."

"We are not discussing the communist system," she said. "We are not perfect, I know, and in China we have had many difficulties. Now we are discussing the capitalist system and what makes me mad. Instead of all these empty capitalistic flats there should be houses for the people. And Government must build them. More. Faster."

"More better cheaper faster?"

"Now you are making fun of me. I am *glad* the fat businessmen are losing money," she said. "It serves them right for being greedy."

"They're greedy," I said. "But it's thanks to the greedy businessmen that Hong Kong exists for anybody. Including China."

"That's not the point," she said. "The point is—"

The Chinese Lunar New Year was coming up. The City Council was putting up their colorful street decorations and all the big hotels and banks and shops were putting up their big lucky red Chinese characters, *Kung Hei Fat Choi!,* Happy Prosperous New Year! The great Chinese celebration, four days' holiday and feasting and firecrackers and exchanging presents and settling all financial debts and burying hatchets and paying double salaries, Hong Kong closes down and the fireworks go up, Europeans pay their servants double salaries and go into hibernation for four days with windows closed, the Kowloon-Canton Railway is thronged with Chinese going home to their families in China for the holiday. But Yingling was not going to visit her father.

"No," she said. "I want to be with you. He works a long way from Canton. By the time I have waited in Canton for the other train I will only have a day and a half with him."

"He'll be very disappointed. It's a family time," I said.

"He will probably have to work most of the time anyway. You're my family," she said. "You gave up your Christmas for me."

"I didn't give up anything."

"I want to be with you. Maybe I will have a long visit with my father in April school holidays."

"I wish I could come," I said.

"Oh I wish so too! Going up on the train together? And I would love you to meet my father. He loves to drink and tell stories." She grinned at the thought of it. "He will think you are a good son-in-law if you laugh at his stories."

"I wonder," I said.

"He will be all right. How would your mother have taken it?"

"My mother was old-fashioned," I said.

"So is my father. He will argue with me but in the end he will be all right. What would your mother have said, hah?"

"All the usual arguments," I said. "But my mother is dead. Your father still wants his daughter. And his grandchildren. And not too white about it."

She thought that was hilarious.

"Not too round in the eyes," I said. "And not too unlucky blue."

She was laughing. "You have beautiful blue sinister Occidental eyes, darling."

Two weeks before Chinese New Year we drove up into the New Territories for a picnic and to see the lucky cherry blossom trees. She was very fond of picnics; before she knew me she and Mad Dog were always going off on picnics. The New Territories is not much country but it was all the country we had, and it was very beautiful in all its hills and valleys and winding roads and paddies and ducks and water buffalo and Chinese hamlets. We drank Famous Red Triumph most of the way and Mad Dog hung out the back window barking joyfully at the water buffalo. She pulled the rubber bands out of her pigtails and put them over his snout to keep his mouth closed but he barked through them all the same.

That was a good day. We went slowly through the valleys and walked through the orchards. The young cherry trees had their branches tied up in bunches to prevent them blossoming before the New Year. If there was a warm snap and they blossomed prematurely they would be less lucky and the farmers would lose a lot of money. We did not buy our tree yet because it was too early, and anyway I wanted to come back alone and buy the best and luckiest tree for her.

The New Year was going to be the Year of the Rabbit. And rabbits run.

CHAPTER 38

Ho Ting-tak owned the Ho Choi Bank, which translated means the Good Luck Bank. Mr. Ho was a millionaire, in the sense that his Good Luck Bank owned millions of dollars' worth of mortgages, but owed millions of actual dollars to the people who had deposited the money in his bank. He also owed them 10 per cent per annum on top, compound interest. Ten per cent on savings bank is very good money indeed, but Mr. Ho was only being competitive, only keeping up with the times. Most of Mr. Ho's depositors were people who lived in cubicles, and the boat people, but Mr. Ho was investing their money in luxury and middle-class apartment blocks. Mr. Ho was not a trained banker, but he made a lot of money. So did all the other banks. But the international banks had very well trained managers and their interest rates were not as high and their investments were worldwide.

That late January all the banks were very gay, the great *Kung Hei Fat Chois* written up in lights, crammed with happy Chinese withdrawing their money for the presents, new clothes, big chows, settling of debts, double salaries. The bank with the biggest decorations of all was the communist Bank of China, next door to the Hong Kong and Shanghai Bank and between the Hilton, the Supreme Court, and the Cricket Club. Above their big communist brass doors, with their big stone lions at revolutionary attention, was a great portrait of Chairman Mao beaming across the cricket pitch from a flaming red sunrise and a horde of joyful handsome peasants lugging abundant sheaves of wheat, and on top of the roof were the multitude of big red flags with the five gold stars. And all down Queen's Road Central the big banks had their *Kung Hei Fat Chois* and their house flags and their national flags and their Union Jacks flying. It was all very gay, and all the banks were cheerfully crowded.

That day there was a warm snap. The next day there were newspaper photographs of farmers trying to stop their cherry trees blossoming before New Year. That day I decided to go up to the New Territories to get Yingling's tree, after lunch. I did not know what happened in Hong Kong that afternoon until I got back.

That afternoon a capitalist Chinese gentleman of the import-export business walked angrily innto the crowded Ho Choi Bank clutching a telegram. He shouted to the teller, *"I want to see Mr. Ho!"* He held the telegram up and shook it. Everybody stared. *"I demand to see Mr. Ho!"*

"Why do you want to see Mr. Ho?" The teller stared.

The angry capitalist Chinese gentleman shook the telegram and shouted that his check drawn on the Good Luck Bank agents in Los Angeles had bounced! What had the Good Luck done with his money in Los Angeles? Now he had lost face and business in Los Angeles! Where was Mr. Ho?

Mr. Ho was coming bustling blushing, he bustled the angry Chinese gentleman into his office and he fussed all over him assuring him that everything was all right, the check drawn on Los Angeles would be paid in a few days, please all he needed was a little time. But the Chinese gentleman shouted, Why did the Good Luck Bank need time, where was all his money? Mr. Ho held up his hands pleading *sh-sh-sh* please all he needed was a few days, because it was Chinese New Year and everybody was drawing out so much money, but the Chinese gentleman shouted, Why is this no-use bank short of money, what have you done with all our money? I want all my money now! And outside in the hall all the people could hear him, and the angry Chinese gentleman burst out of Mr. Ho's office shouting, *This Good Luck Bank is no good, I want to take out all my money or I will go to the police!*

And then everybody wanted all their money. Maybe

there were sixty people in the bank and now there were no more queues, just everybody pressing.

The story spread like wildfire, Through the crowded streets, alleys, tenements, apartment blocks, squatter shacks, the cocklofts on the rooftops. Now inside the Ho Choi Bank there was a roar of noise. There was a big crowd on the pavement. Now a traffic constable came to control the crowd, there was a jam of traffic and loud honking.

More traffic policemen came, then an inspector. They got the crowd off the intersection, now they organized a long queue outside the Ho Choi Bank. *"Only customers of this bank in this queue please, everybody else keep moving please.* Then a police superintendent came. The superintendent did not know anything about this kind of alarm, he was only saying what he had been instructed to say, "There is no cause for alarm." In the breasts of all the banks and of the commissioner for banking there was plenty of cause for alarm. In the Ho Choi Bank, Mr. Ho was desperately making many telephone calls, to many banks, trying to borrow money.

All that afternoon Mr. Ho's tellers paid paid paid. At 4 P.M. Mr. Ho had no more money to pay out. His balance sheet showed assets of eighteen million dollars and liabilities of only eleven million. But those eighteen million dollars were all in real estate mortgages. At four o'clock Mr. Ho telephoned the commissioner of banking again. Mr. Ho was weeping. Then he went outside and borrowed a police megaphone. He told the crowd that the government commissioner of banking was taking over the affairs of the Ho Choi Bank. There was silence, then a roar. Mr. Ho fainted on the pavement.

That is what happened that Chinese New Year. It was the beginning of bad times.

CHAPTER 39

Chan Wai-ping had read Marxist economic theory and the *Collected Works of Mao Tse-tung,* and what he did not know he thought he knew. Mr. Chan was the owner and editor of the small communist vernacular newspaper called the *Heung Keung Po.*

Mr. Chan hated all noncommunists. He also hated banks, except the Bank of China, because banks, the moneylenders, epitomize capitalism. In particular he hated the Chinese banks who did only Chinese business. Because they were the ilk who had bled China white in the bad old days, who held a whole countryside in their family clutches with their landlordism and control of money at usurious interest. These Hong Kong banks were the yellow-skinned running dogs of the imperialistic British and the aggressive capitalistic warmongering Americans, and the lackeys of them both, the bandits of Chiang Kai-shek. And why should not the Bank of China have that business which enriched the capitalist Chinese banks? If the Chinese capitalists had to go to the communist banks for their revolving credit, they would be in the sphere of influence of the communists. A man can be told to do a lot of things by his bank manager.

I got the evening edition of Mr. Chan's newspaper at the vehicular ferry, coming back from the New Territories with Ying-ling's lucky cherry tree. I bought the newspaper because of the sensational headlines which took up the whole front page, big Chinese character:

BANKS BANKRUPT!
GIVE US BACK OUR MONEY!
MANAGER FAINTS!

And the story read:

Today capitalism struck a vicious blow on the downtrodden workers of Hong Komg! Today, the capitalist Ho Choi Bank is bankrupt! Many thousands who trusted the capitalist bank lost all their money today! Oh woe! Oh treachery!

Today the inherent injustice and contradictions of the capitalist system were uncovered. Today a poor misguided Chinese went into the tiger jaws of capitalist Ho Choi and requested politely to withdraw his hard-earned life's savings. Cowering, the manager refused because he had squandered all the customer's money in no-good capitalist luxury apartment houses hoping to get rich at the expense of the poor. Such is the folly of this city of imperial decadence! Fortified by the teachings of Mao Tse-tung, crying out in a loud voice against the injustice and inherent contradiction of the capitalist system, the poor customer bearded the tiger. "This capitalist bank is not good! The capitalist system has inherent injustice! Give me and all these poor people all our money at once!" cried he. Greatly angered the other people cried out indignantly, "This capitalist bank is no good! Give us all our money at once so we can put it in the Bank of China!" Greatly frightened the capitalist manager was forced to pay. But of course he did not have enough money! The poor people cried in an angry voice, "Now the inherent frauds, injustices, contradictions, and other weaknesses of the capitalist system are exposed! Alas that we did not harken to the teachings of Mao Tse-tung! We can only trust the Bank of China which is founded on just Marxism economic principles! Oh woe! Give us all our hard-earned life savings at once! Being desperate people we will even try to bring the imperialistic police into this shameful matter!"

But already the imperialist colonialist capitalist police were there. Sensing danger like foxes the yellow-skinned running dogs were trembling ordering the indignant crowds to go away. Soon a red-faced foreign-devil officer arrived with arms to take command of the desperate situation. Hiding shamed faces they tried to intimidate the people, but soon their turpitudinous game was up! Staggering under his guilt and inherent contradictions the manager confessed his crimes and announced that the Hong Kong Government was taking over the Ho Choi Bank. Hereupon he fainted in his great fear. In a loud voice the people cried, "We do not trust the capitalist colonialist Hong Kong Government, we only trust the Bank of China! Give us our money at once! Oh woe! Oh treachery."

How many more of the capitalist banks have done the same thing? How many more banks will the colonialist government fraudulently take over? Once the banks are in Government's hands what will happen to the remainder of the money? Tomorrow we shall see when the poor people hurry to the banks to demand their hard-earned life savings back before it is too late.

The truth is that capitalist banks do not keep the customer's money but lend it out at high interest to other capitalists. When the banks demand the loans back, will the capitalists be able to pay or will they go bankrupt too? This is one of the many inherent weaknesses of the treacherous capitalist system. Today the people who had deposited their money in the Bank of China were rejoicing that they had such wisdom. . . .

Jesus Christ. I bought a copy of every evening paper, English and Chinese. Then I drove straight to the penthouse. There was a long queue right down the block outside the Ho Choi Bank, constables directing traffic. A lot of people had bedding. Two cooked-food hawkers had set up shop on the pavement. There was a big crowd watching. I hid the cherry tree outside on the patio where Ying-ling would not see it when she came home, and went straight to telephone my superintendent at headquarters.

"Where the hell were *you* this afternoon?" he said.

"I went to buy a cherry tree in the N.T., I checked out on the roster."

"Cherry trees!" the boss said. "While Rome burns! A bank's gone bankrupt. Do you know what that means?"

"Yes," I said. "No."

"Nor do I. Nor does anybody. Except tomorrow the shit's supposed to hit the fan. We're all on standby for crowd control, no cherry trees tomorrow!"

"Why are you still at the office, sir? Is there going to be any criminal investigation?"

"Christ knows. Everybody flapping around like hens, the banking commissioner's in a frantic huddle with the governor and the Old Man and Christknowswho. Our's

274

not to reason why. If it's a criminal matter it's Commercial Crime's baby anyway, not ours, thank God. Our only concern right now is crowd control tomorrow if there's a run on the banks."

"Of course there'll be a run on the banks! Read the *Heung Keung.* I'll read it to you." I translated the relevant bits. "How do you like that?"

"Yes," the super said. "Bad."

"He's deliberately aggravating the situation by exhorting the people to run on the banks. The bastard's trying to break them. To the eternal glory of the communist banks. And the terrible thing is what he says is true."

"I'm not an economist," the super said. "I'm a policeman. So are you, remember!"

"But is anything being done about stopping the panic?"

"Like what, for example?" the super said irritably. "How do you stop three million money-mad Chinese rushing to get their money if they want to?"

"Well, is there going to be a broadcast by the governor, for example? To tell the people not to panic? A press conference?"

"That may only make them panic more."

"They'll have to do it when the runs start. We should prosecute any newspaper which makes mischievous statements."

"Then they'd scream that we're interfering with the freedom of the press. And it would look as if Government's *really* hand in glove with the banks to cheat the people and that'll make them panic more."

"Goddamn Government's got to be *tough!*" I said. "Government's always pussyfooting around trying to do the least offensive thing. If we slapped a bloody warrant on this bastard Chan *tonight* for libel or public mischief or whatever, and stop his bloody paper for at least a couple of days, slap bloody arrest warrants on any other paper that deserves it, *make a broadcast* telling the people not to be bloody fools, call a bloody press conference and instill into them that sensationalism is the worst thing —we'd probably stop this run at first base."

"If we start throwing our weight around we'd have a bloody riot," the super said.

"You'll have a bloody riot if a few more banks go under and the communist press says it's a monstrous public fraud! Look, sir—let me try to take out a warrant of arrest on this bastard Chan tonight. That may at least stop his morning edition going out."

"We can't do that," the super said irritably. "For one thing you'll have to take advice from the director of Public Prosecutions first to see if we've got a charge on him. You can't go at it like a bull at a gate."

"If we don't," I said, "you're going to have a bull in a china shop."

The super didn't think it funny.

"Jake," he said wearily, "I'm quite sure the governor and the attorney general and the Old Man are capable of figuring it out. *No bloody action,* McAdam! The DPP wouldn't sanction it anyway, it's a policy decision, not for him alone. Nor us. Not even *you,* McAdam," he said irritably. "Keep your nose out of it. It's Commercial Crime's baby anyway, not ours."

"Commercial Crime," I said. "Those blokes wouldn't know if their bums were on fire."

"They're very good," the super said. "Stop looking for bloody work we don't understand. I've got to ring off now, I'm busy."

"Do you want me to come in, sir?"

"No," the super said. "There's nothing you can do about it. There's nothing anybody can do."

I telephoned Derek Morrison at the Hong Kong and Shanghai Bank. His secretary told me he was in conference. You bet he's in conference, I thought, they'll all be in conference all bloody night. I left for the office."

When I got there I telephoned Derek Morrison again, "Jake," he said, "I've only got a minute, I'm very busy."

"What the hell's happening, Derek?" I said. "Nobody here knows anything."

"We don't know anything either. The boss and the commissioner of banking are running around like blue-arsed flies. We're taking precautions against a run."

"Is a run certain?"

"As God made little green apples. The Chinese and money? At New Year? But it'll be the Chinese banks that get hit more than us, we can probably cope. I've been saying for a long time this would happen! You didn't have to be a financial whiz-kid to see it coming."

"Which banks are going to get hit hardest?"

"Depends how much cash they have in hand and how much is tied up in goddamn mortgages. That's what the commissioner's scratching his little fat head over right now. I've warned them. The whole bloody Colony hangs together by string."

"What's the immediate solution?"

"There's only one solution. Chinese panic about money. So shut the banks. Just shut the goddamn banks and tell them to go home until they got a bit of bloody sense. And in the meantime rush around like blue-arsed flies and borrow some cash. Switzerland, London, New York. Fly the bloody stuff out in jets. Then pay out the panic-stricken Chinese in pounds, dollars, and francs. Until the shaky banks can get their houses in order and liquidate some of these bloody awful mortgages. Then redeem the foreign currency. But will the world's banks lend dough to banks like we've got here on the security of the crappy mortgages they've got to offer? Government would have to guarantee the loans, of course."

"And do you think Government will close the banks? I doubt it myself."

"My dear Jake, you should know by now that Government will do everything too late, Government hates making decisions, these guys are career civil servants, and their policy is laissez-faire, they'll let the capitalists make their own decisions. So that they can't be blamed if they make the wrong decision. Government will play it by ear and keep their fingers crossed. In the same way as they've been procrastinating proper banking legislation. Christ, they would stop this trouble right now if they only withdraw fifty dollars a day until further notice. But will they?"

"And in the meantime the communist press will make confusion more confounded," I said.

"Those communist-press bastards should be nailed right now. What are you chaps doing about it?"

"We're career civil servants," I said. "There's one bastard at least we could probably nail tonight and make an example of. But the rest would scream about freedom of the press."

"Yeah," Derek said, "and Government would rather curl up its little pink toes than risk that. How much freedom of the press is there in China, hey?"

"Chairman Mao would know how to handle this," I said.

"Nobody's got any money to demand in China. Look, I've got to go."

I rang through to the super to tell him what I was go-

277

ing to do, but switchboard told me he had gone home. I called the duty inspector into my office.

I gave him a list of the principal communist newspapers and I told him to have plainclothesmen cover each one. We worked out a plan; it wasn't much but it was the best we could do in a hurry. I also told him to plant men in the queues outside the two branches of the Ho Choi Bank, posing as customers, to mingle and talk as much as possible, particularly to any newspaper reporters, find out the rumors and their sources. Then I contacted a certain friend of mine who shall be nameless and told him I wanted to tap the *Heung Keung Po*'s telephone just for tonight. Which is highly illegal without the authority of God knows who all. Then I telephoned the super at home and told him what I'd done, omitting the telephone-tapping bit.

"Jake, you're making too much of this at this stage."

I said, "The next stage may be too late, sir. If we decide to bump them for anything the evidence will be useful. Do you want me to cancel the order?"

"No," the super sighed. "Can't do any harm. Can't do any good either. As long as you don't start arresting anybody yet. And get some sleep, we're all on standby tomorrow."

"I'm going home now," I said.

"I hope you got a good cherry tree," the super said. "That doesn't blossom too soon."

Ying-ling was already waiting at home. She had read the papers and she was scandalized. "My God! All those people lose their money because some fat greedy banker tries to get rich quick with apartments! And all the time people sleeping in the streets! It is outrageous! How many more banks like this, huh? Will he go to jail?"

"Only if he stole the money. Or committed a fraud."

"He is just as bad as a thief or robber! He took the people's money and he speculated, hah? Trying to get rich quick with other people's money! Isn't that stealing, hah?"

"Morally maybe."

"Of course morally! What is the good of anything without morals? It is just as if he took the money and bet it on the races in Happy Valley." She pointed angrily at Happy Valley.

"Not quite. He was just a bad investor."

"Then it is fraud!" she pronounced. "Of course. He tells

the people, I am a good banker, give me your money, when all the time he doesn't know his job so he gambles and loses. Isn't there any law that says a banker must invest rightly? Keep the money safe? If I am a doctor and I cut you up badly and kill you don't I go to jail, hah?"

"Yes. If you were very negligent."

"So why not for bankers, hah? He was negligent! He was no good and a fraud. A doctor only kills one person at a time, this man kills thousands in one day. Isn't there any justice in Hong Kong?"

"Hong Kong's justice is good," I said wearily. "This is a question of economics."

"*Good?*" she appealed. "Justice *begins* with economics. All men must be treated fairly, hah, a reasonable wage, a house, food, not cheated of his money, hah? That is what justice is all about! That is how it is in China!"

I didn't want to argue about how it was in China. I said, "There is no law here which says a bank must keep so much money ready to pay out to customers on demand. The bank can invest it all if it so decides. That is the trouble here."

She stared, then slapped her forehead. "My God! Why isn't there that law? What is the matter with Hong Kong? I'll tell you what"—she pointed accusingly at Central—"money! That is all this place thinks about. It is mad with money! It started on rotten opium and it is still rotten. They think any way to make money is all right!" She pointed at Central again. "The government does not worry about the poor people who put money in the bank, big fat Government says oh-oh-oh I must not interfere with money-making, no sir! We are capitalists here! We have only laissez-faire here! Hah?"

I got up to get another drink. "It's not as simple as that. There's another facet to this business. Hong Kong has got no natural resources. Yet it provides employment for four million people. And every year scores of thousands more come here from over the border. How does Hong Kong do it? I'm talking, Ying-ling." She was exasperated with this tangent. I said, "Hong Kong does it by guts and enterprise. Now, the banks have made a lot of money out of Hong Kong. But the reverse is also true. Hong Kong has made a lot of money out of the banks. Because it is the banks who lend the industrialists and the builders the money for their businesses which provide the employment for the millions. Most of whom *come from*

China. And when nobody else would lend them the money to try, it is the likes of the Good Luck Bank who stuck their necks out and lent it to them."

She lit a Red Victory impatiently, blew out hard, glaring at the patio. "Laissez-faire. Money-mad. Everybody thinks only of himself. That's what I hate about Hong Kong. That's why I'm a communist," she said bitterly.

I didn't want to argue about that either. She said angrily at the patio, "I'm *glad* the banks are in trouble. And the government. It serves them right for being greedy."

"I beg your pardon?" I said. "That's a bloody foolish thing to say. Because if the banks go broke the people lose their money! Do you know what happened in 1932 when Wall Street crashed?"

She didn't look at me. She drew on her cigarette hard.

I said, "And if the communist press tries to make sensational political capital out of it, it will be not only foolish but political savagery. It will prove that *they* don't care for the people. Just for their political ends."

She said, staring at the patio, "You cannot blame them for telling the truth. The freedom of the press." She looked at me. "You cannot arrest them."

I said slowly, "If I cannot arrest them it is because there is freedom of the press in this colony." I left out *unlike in the paradise across the border,* but she understood it. "The *Heung Keung* goddamn *Po* isn't concerned with telling the truth, it's concerned with attacking the capitalist system and it doesn't care if all the people lose their money in the process. Fuck the freedom of the press in cases like this."

She said sulkily, "I'm just furious with Hong Kong."

I got up and walked to the patio. Eleven stories down there the mob was queuing. After a moment she came out. She wasn't going to give in but she put her arm around me to make peace.

She did not see the cherry tree in the dark.

She went back to her lodgings early because she did not want the crowd to see her leaving in the morning. At midnight the telephone rang, the duty inspector. He said, "The *Heung Keung Po* is putting out an early morning edition at half price and they have raised the hawkers' commission twenty per cent. And they've hired two vehicles to deliver newspapers to Aberdeen and Yeun Long at six A.M."

"Aberdeen and Yeun Long?" Jesus, yes. The two most unsophisticated areas.

"Right," I said. "I'll come in now. I want at least two dozen men to be in Aberdeen at six A.M., who've you got?"

When I got to headquarters I got out the maps of the two areas. At opposite ends of the Colony. Yeun Long, right up in the New Territories, a farming and industrial area. Aberdeen is where most of the boat people live. Unsophisticated as hell. Several banks operated in both areas but the Kwangtung Trust was the biggest Chinese bank. I would have to get Yeun Long CID on to doing the job out there. I told my men what I wanted. Dressed to look as much like locals as possible. Each man cover a section inconspicuously. As soon as the newspaper hawkers arrive, go up, buy a copy, listen, talk, befriend, try to pick up any rumors and the sources. *Anything.* Go down to the boats. If you have to, offer information money, but for Christ's sake, don't blow your cover unnecessarily. If it comes to information money, telephone and we'll send a car to pick him up. I assigned them their areas. You'll just have to play it by ear. Queues are likely to start forming early at these banks here, here, here, I'll have other men covering them. If you get on to *any* kind of witness to a source of a rumor, *grab him and telephone in.* Take him to tea or offer goddamn information money or goddamn arrest him on some holding charge, if necessary, *but don't let him disappear—got it?"*

"Yes, sir," they said.

They could only do their best. We had nothing to go on. I put two radio cars to tail the delivery trucks. And if anybody let a witness slip they would get their arses kicked. All right?

"All right, sir," they chorused. They filed out of my office goodnaturedly.

Then I telephoned Ross, the divisional detective inspector at Yeun Long. He wasn't asleep yet, he was playing poker in the Mess. I told him what I wanted and why. At least two dozen men in whatever positions he thought best in the circumstances, at 6 A.M.

"Simple," Ross said. I knew he would do it right because he was a first-class policeman.

Then I went home to sleep. I didn't know what would come out of it. It was not much of a plan, but at least we might get some useful evidence of some bloody thing which was better than sitting on our arses all night while Chan Wai-ping made hay in the moonlight.

At four-thirty the alarm woke me. I went out onto the patio to look down at the queue. It was longer. I looked at the cherry tree, and swore. The bloody thing had almost blossomed overnight. That was bad joss. Bad luck.

CHAPTER 40

Aberdeen: five thousand registered fishing junks, a forest of masts, fifty thousand boat people teeming living crouching quarreling giving birth and dying in the great Chinese togetherness. The *Heung Keung Po* did not normally circulate among the boat people. The boat people had nothing to do with anybody but themselves and Tin Hau, goddess of the seas.

At six-thirty that Saturday morning the police car called in on the radio. There had been five additional hawkers on the *Heung Keung Po* truck, they had headed off toward the junks, my boys were sleuthing after them. The rest of the newspapers had been picked up by local hawkers, my boys were tailing them. They were already a lot of people on the streets. The hawkers shouting the headlines, *Banks Lose Our Money!* They were selling a lot already. At seven o'clock the first telephone call came in, from Detective Police Constable Ma in a teahouse near a hawker's pitch. D.P.C. Ma was not the brightest I had ever known but he was keen as mustard and he was very excited: The Good Luck Bank crash was huge news, everybody was talking about it, everybody was going to run to the banks today to get their money. "Thanks, Ma," I said, "but tell me something I don't know." "Okay, Bomban," Ma said excitedly. Some other calls came in, two to tell me that three other communist newspapers were now also on special sale in Aberdeen today, the place was buzzing with the news. At eight o'clock there was a queue starting already outside the Kwangtung Trust Bank. I now had all the communist morning newspapers in front of me, they were all sensational. No information had yet filtered down to me about what the hell the governor and attorney general and banking commissioner had decided last night. My super and Derek Morrison didn't know anything new either except that today the shit was going to hit the fan. I got two calls from Ross up in Yeun Long, the same was happening up there. But that was all I got. The phone calls were coming in fast now from Aberdeen but it was nothing we didn't know already. Uniformed constables were keeping the queues orderly, and there were many more on standby up at Aberdeen station. Then at nine o'clock D.P.C. Liu telephoned in: Three men in the queue said they did not have any money in the bank, but they were expecting five dollars and a bowl of noodles if they queued.

Oh yes! "Who promised them that?" I shouted.

"It is just a rumor, Bomban," Liu said. "I cannot find out the source."

Jesus Christ!

The next calls came in fast: Five dollars and a bowl of noodles was the story. But Jesus Christ we couldn't nail down the source of the rumor, everybody had just been told by somebody who was told by somebody. Then D.P.C. Ma called in frantically: He had a boy of twelve who admitted he was spreading the story on instructions of a man he had never seen before who had given him ten dollars to do so, that's all he knew.

"Give him fifty dollars to look for that man and don't let the kid out of your sight," I shouted.

Christ, maybe we're getting somewhere! Ross at Yeun Long phoned in. "Don't tell me," I said. "It's five dollars and a bowl of noodles."

"That's right," Ross said, "but we can't find out who's starting the rumor."

"Tell your staff sergeant to pull out all the stoppers, Ross, now that we've got something specific to go on."

"Roger," Ross said.

At ten o'clock that morning the queues outside the Kwangtung Trust in both Aberdeen and Yeun Long stretched for over three blocks, and the bank doors opened and they flooded in. At five past ten, the super called me and told me that Special Branch was taking over my Malicious Rumor Investigation.

"Because of its political content," the super said.

"They're bloody welcome to it!" I said. I was furious.

"And because they have better resources for this kind of thing," the super said. "Quote unquote."

Jesus, *my investigation*. "Why the *hell* didn't they get their better resources going last night then?" I said.

"Maybe they did start last night," the super said. He added, "The Old Man says you can stay on the case with Special Branch if you want to. Do you?"

"No *thanks*," I said.

That was the last I effectively heard of it. Special Branch grabbed the youngster that D.P.C. Ma had grabbed. I heard they got a number of people in for questioning but apparently they couldn't nail the rumor down even with their superior resources, quote unquote. Or if they could it was policy, quote unquote, not to. You never knew with fucking Special Branch. All I knew was that I ran into the director, Dermot Wilcox, at the club later and he said my "groundwork" had been "useful." But anyway it made no difference, the damage had been done and that day the bank runs started.

They queued all that Saturday outside the Kwangtung Trust, all day the tellers paid paid paid in the great Chinese clamor, thrusting, sweat, fear, stretching and jumping up to see, young women with children on their backs, and outside the uniformed policemen controlling the crowds and traffic. *"Move along please, there is no cause for alarm."*

But there was every cause for alarm. The riot squads were on standby. All over the Colony bankers were making telephone calls to each other and around the world, London, New York, Tokyo, Geneva, Sydney, Johannesburg, Rio de Janeiro, trying to borrow money. This could be the crash of Hong Kong. At four o'clock that afternoon I got the *Heung Keung Po* hot off the press.

. . .while the capitalist policemen tried in vain to persuade them to go home, mendaciously shouting that there was no cause for alarm, in the police stations their running dogs tremblingly girded their weapons for the uprising they knew to be their just deserts. But the righteously angry people had had enough of this double treachery and cried out in loud voice, "We will not be fooled again by capitalists and their running dogs! Why are running-dog policemen here if these are honest banks? We demand our money now so that we can place it in the honest double safety of the Bank of China! Oh woe that

284

we lacked such wisdom before! Oh double treachery!"

At four o'clock a car drew up outside the Yeun Long branch of the Kwangtung Trust Bank and a man climbed out with a loudspeaker into the clamor. The police shouted over their loudspeakers for attention and the man shouted in Cantonese, "I am the manager of the Hong Kong and Shanghai Bank! I come to tell you that the Hong Kong and Shanghai Bank which has plenty of money supports the Kwangtung Trust Bank!" He paced down the queue shouting it over again, "There is plenty of money! The Kwangtung Trust is a very good bank and the Hong Kong and Shanghai trusts it! So should you! There is no need to worry about your money! Go home and stop worrying!"

But the people did not go home and stop worrying. The Kwangtung Trust stayed open all that Saturday paying, paying. The newspaper hawkers were having a field day. The people queued all that night, waiting till Monday. On Sunday morning the Kwangtung Trust opened again to pay out. On Monday morning they were still queuing. On Monday the Kwangtung Trust and all its twenty-two branches went bankrupt.

CHAPTER 41

The pandemonium and the heartbreak, KWANGTUNG TRUST BANK CRASHES! The bannerlines, the cries of the newspaper hawkers, the radios exhorting calm, *Tonight His Excellency the Governor and the financial secretary will broadcast to the people, there is no need to panic.*

The panic, the loud mouth-to-mouth clamoring, running down a thousand streets to a hundred branches of a score of banks, black heads converging crowding struggling angry anxious shouting. Outside the banks there were the police trucks and policemen with their loudspeakers and their cordons, *Quiet please! No pushing! Queue quietly. There is no cause for alarm!* And inside the banks the uproar.

Outside the Hang Tong Head Office the mob stretched

for ten blocks down the waterfront. We held them back at the doors, letting them through in batches. From inside came the roar. Twenty deep down the long counters on both sides of the hall, pushing, shoving, shouting, jumping, stretching, craning, clerks running, tellers shouting account numbers over loudspeakers. Upstairs the administrative offices had been opened up as pay counters also, desks shoved into rows. On each counter gold bars were stacked four feet high, for the crowd to see, and there was another big stack six feet high inside the main door. It was not giving the crowd confidence. I looked over the third-floor balcony down into the main banking hall below onto the clamoring mob. The heat and roar and smell of people resounded up like in a whirring factory. A new batch was mobbing up the stairway to the third floor.

"Quiet and slow!" I shouted. A young man came bounding up the stairs, elbowed, then ducked his head to charge through a gap like a rugby player. I grabbed him by the collar, swung him around, and shook him once. *"Slow!"*

I started down the stairs, around the first corner and nearly fell over a man on his knees, crawling.

"Old man!" I shook his shoulder.

The old man twisted his head up dizzily. His eyes were very old and his gold-shod mouth was open. "I have come to get my money," the old man whispered.

"Can you not walk?"

His mouth opened and closed. "My heart beats very hard."

I hoisted him to his feet, then scooped him up. *"Ah-ah,"* the old man gasped and his breath was terrible. I clambered up the stairs trying not to smell him, then swung him down, panting. "Over there." I turned before he could thank me with his terrible breath and hurried down the stairs again.

In the afternoon the hysteria came. All over Hong Kong swarming, running, jostling queuing in the streets and the police cordons and loudspeakers and linked arms and the clamor and the heartbreak and the cries of the newspaper hawkers. Inside the banks there was pandemonium. In Macao, forty miles away across the China Sea, they were running on the banks also. The radios kept up the bleat in Cantonese and English: "There is no need to panic. There is plenty of money. You must disregard newspaper reports to the contrary. Tonight His Excellency the Governor and the financial secretary will broadcast explaining the situation. In the meantime you are advised to go home." But the people were not going anywhere except into the pandemonium of the banks. Now the banks were plastered with big posters in Chinese: "The Hong Kong and Shanghai Bank gives unlimited support to the Hang Tong Bank!" "The Chartered Bank pledges unlimited support to the Dao Heng Bank!" "The Mercantile Bank pledges unlimited support to the Kwong On Bank!" The Bank of China offered support to nobody.

There were no crowds outside the Bank of China. Next door, in the Hong Kong and Shanghai Bank and the Chartered Bank, the crowds who had been crowding outside the other banks to get their money out were now crowding to deposit their money in the Hong Kong and Shanghai and the Chartered banks. The money clamored in and the clerks rushed it out to the Securicor armored trucks and the Securicor trucks rushed it back through the crowds and the clamor and the police cordons around the corner to the Hang Tong and the Kwong On and the Dao Heng and the other banks to pay out again. The same money was rushing desperately around and around. Across the road, inside the Supreme Court, the petition of the commissioner of banking for the winding up of the Kwangtung Trust was being heard. If the Kwangtung Trust was truly bankrupt, thousands went bankrupt with it and a hundred thousand lost all their money; that hundred thousand and their employees and their families meant one million mouths in a colony of four million. Lawyers for one million mouths were fighting to keep the Kwangtung Trust alive. The Supreme Court was packed, creditors, debtors, shareholders, officeholders, reporters, policemen, depositors, the piles of papers, the judge on the bench, a dozen barristers, two dozen solicitors, wigs, gowns, papers, books, heartbreak, anger overflowing the huge main courtroom, down the corridors, the stairs, swelled out into Statue Square, the heartbreak and weeping and anger of the people who did not understand what was happening in there, all they wanted was their money, weeping and wailing and the shouting and the banners and the placards, *Robbers Must Give Our Money Back!* and *We Are Not Guilty So We Don't Need Lawyers!* and *Down with British Justice!* roaring up to the sky. Somebody shouted into the face of the inspector, *"We want our money not your robber British justice!"* and the inspector shouted, "The court is trying to protect you!" and somebody shouted, *"The British Government is protecting the rich!"* and the roar went up to the sky, the policemen linked arms tighter reeling under the surging, and somebody shouted, *"We must go to see the governor—this British justice robs us!"* and the ragged roar went up, *"Protest to the governor!"* and then the surge. Surged ragged scrambling shouting Statue Square, banners heaving, an old man fell and the crowd trampled over him bloodily, surged shouting crying past the Bank of China under the beaming Chairman Mao and the Stars and Stripes of the Hong Kong Hilton, up Garden Road for Government House.

Marched shouting, crying on the big regal gates and clamored to see the governor to make him stop the Supreme Court, and the governor could only send his sympathies and the message, "We must await the courts decision," and the mob howled in hate and heartbreak and charged the gates and beat and shook them screaming *"Down with British justice"* and mobbed the sentries, and the lorryload of riot police arrived and heaved and shoved them off the gates, and all the time the outrage and the weeping and the pleading and the roar, and then the shout went up, *"Let us go to the Kwangtung Trust to seize our money back!"* and then the roar went up, *"The Kwangtung Trust!"* and they surged back down the road.

We got the message on the Land Rover's radio. The Supreme Court was adjourning, the mob pouring out of the building. We roared down the road, pulled up outside the Kwangtung Trust. You could hear the roar from the Hang Tong and the Square. The Kwangtung Trust was closed, the staff were switching the lights off, Headquarters had warned them. Now we could hear the ragged roar of the Government House mob coming running down and the Supreme Court mob running along, the storming of the bank had spread like wildfire. Another police Land Rover came roaring down the mobbing road and a uniformed superintendent and six constables bailed out and ran to join us to throw up some kind of cordon, then another roar went up and the Government House mob came around the bend.

Came mobbing and shouting across the road in one ragged roar and mobbed our thin police cordon, heaving

288

crying howling hitting fighting, young and old howling Chinese outrage, mobbed right through the dozen of us, mobbed the big steel doors and beat the walls and heaved against the big glass windows, the super bellowed, *"Get them off the windows!"* and the first brick flew. And smashed crashing off the window with a great fracture web and another roar went up and more stones flew, bricks and stones flying everywhere, the constables were struggling to regroup with their backs to the windows heaving and bellowing the mob back, *"Heave! Heave!"* we bellowed, somewhere in the roar there was the siren of the riot-squad trucks coming and then there was a scream and I saw the man I now know to be called Wong. Wong screamed and charged, head thrown back, a big fishing knife up high, bellowed and charged and the constables scattered, he screamed all the way and charged straight at the big window with all his might, and Wong stabbed the bank. Lunged and stabbed the bank in full screamed charge and there was a great smashing crash of glass and Wong crashed right through the window.

Crashed headlong howling into the bank in an explosion of blood and flying glass, face slashed down to the bone, and skidded over the floor and a scream went up in the bank. Blood gushed from his face into his eyes and screaming mouth but Wong did not feel it, he scrambled up bellowing gushing blood and he charged. Charged screaming blood and outrage through the banking hall with his big bloody knife on high, blood black down his chest, blood flapping off him, the bank staff scattered screaming. Wong hurled himself and stabbed the counter. Lifted his body arm on high and screamed blood and stabbed, splashing blood, beating kicking screaming crying through the flying blood, I was charging down the hall with my gun out, I slipped in his blood and sprawled and everybody was screaming, a constable overtook me yelling and Wong scrambled up onto the counter. Scrambled splashing blood screaming, *My money*, blood spraying out of his mouth, he ran down the counter brandishing the knife, leaped down screaming, everybody scattering screaming shouting, he lunged and stabbed into a typewriter and grabbed the chair and swung it around his bloody screaming head and slung it high over the hall and he lashed into the next desk and stabbed the adding machines, screaming, I vaulted the counter after him. The manager was heaving the strong room closed and Wong gave one bloodcurdling scream and charged, I picked up a chair and hurled it, it hit Wong square on the back but he ran screaming bloody murder at the big strong-room door. Flung himself at the strong-room door screaming outraged murder and stabbed it and stabbed it howling blood flying, blood in his eyes, blood spraying from his flapping lip, blood spraying onto the bankrupt strong-room door. The tears were running down his face with the blood and he was choking, *"My money —my money,"* stabbing and stabbing the strong-room door. I seized his bloody wrist from behind and shot my other hand around his neck in a half nelson, and the big knife clattered. I kicked it away.

He buckled under my weight and slithered down the strong-room door, and now he was just sobbing. He sank sobbing dragging blood down the door onto his knees in a heap, in his blood, and I let him go.

"Call an ambulance," I said to the constable.

You could hear the roaring and the fighting outside in the street. Down the road the police were arms-linked bellowing back the howling mob as Hang Tong heaved its heavy doors closed. That day Hang Tong went under also.

That night they slept in the streets. The lights were burning in all the newspaper offices and banks and the Supreme Court and Central Government offices. That night hundreds of armed policemen guarded London Airport as armored trucks from the Bank of England loaded twenty million sterling pound bank notes into a chartered BOAC Boeing 707 bound for Hong Kong. That night the man called Wong became world news. MAN STABS BANK. PEOPLE'S HERO STRIKES DECADENT CAPITAL-ISM was the motif in the communist newspapers. MEN BITES YELLOW-SKINNED RUNNING DOG was the jubilant headline in the *Heung Keung Po*.

The next day there was the running clamoring heaving and the heartbreak and the outrage at the banks again; but that day Government proclaimed that no person might withdraw more than one hundred dollars in one day from their banks, and that day the Boeing 707 arrived with the twenty million pounds: that day the bank runs ended, but it was too late. That day the Supreme

Court ruled the Ho Choi, the Good Luck Bank, and the Kwangtung Trust bankrupt, and 114,000 depositors, representing one million mouths, one quarter of Hong Kong, lost their money.

CHAPTER 42

On the day of Wong's trial the courtyard outside the Central Magistracy was packed with communist-newspaper reporters, clerks from the Bank of China, China Products, communist schoolchildren, banners, copies of the *Heung Keung Po*. As I came up the steps they burst out on a signal, *"Cong-yee!"* Protest! and the newspapers shot up in the air, *"Cong-yee!"*

"Good morning," I beamed my way through them, "lovely morning—"

"Cong-yee!" they clamored and the newspapers rattled in my face. At the door of the courtroom was Mr. Chan Wai Fucking-ping himself, importantly bespectacled, ferociously holier-than-thou, yelling *Cong-yee!* I stopped and cupped my hands at his ear.

"Good morning, Mr. Chan! Lovely morning!"

"Cong-yee!" Mr. Chan bellowed furiously in my face.

"I beg your pardon?" I beamed with my hand to my ear.

"CONG-YEE!" Mr. Chan bellowed furiously.

As I went through the doorway the chant suddenly stopped. I went to the police prosecutor and thumped Wong's file down in front of him. "There it is," I said.

"Isn't the attorney general sending a Crown counsel?" the prosecutor said anxiously.

"No, we want as little fuss as possible, all in a day's work to the bighearted boys in blue. Here are your instructions." I opened the file to the memoranda section and tapped the second-last entry: "Those are my recommendations to the director of Public Prosecutions, read them. And here're the DPP's instructions to you. All you've got to do is call on the case and then stand up and say that you withdraw all charges against the accused."

"With*draw*?" the prosecutor said. "Phew, that's a relief."

"Now listen, this is important. That mob out there thinks there's going to be a trial. And they're going to come in here and create a valiant demonstration as soon as Wong's case begins. Now I want you to give them all the rope they need to hang themselves. Are you listening? As soon as the magistrate comes in, and *before* Wong gets into the dock, just stand up and say *quietly,* so the gallery doesn't hear, 'Regina versus Wong, I withdraw all charges.' Right? Then as soon as Wong appears they'll start *cong-yeeing* all over the place. Then Tommy Fox-Smith will climb into them."

"Okay," the prosecutor said, very relieved. "But this isn't Mr. Fox-Smith's court today."

"Christ!" I said. "Where's Tommy sitting today?"

"In Number Two Court," the prosecutor said. "He usually sits in here but not today."

"Oh *hell!*" I said. "Hold everything. This case *must* go before Tommy Fox-Smith. How much time have I got to switch?"

The prosecutor looked at his watch. "Seven minutes."

I dashed back out the door, bounded up the stairs three at a time up to the inspector-prosecutor's office. "Listen, Mike," I panted. "You've got to transfer Wong's case to Tommy Fox-Smith's court—"

I explained it to Mike. Then I hurried down to Number Two Court and explained it to the police prosecutor there. Then I sent a detective out into the hall to drop the information that Wong's venue was changed. I told the orderly to keep Wong hidden in his office until the magistrate came in. Then I told him to open the court doors and let the Chan Wai-ping mob in.

They came scrambling in eagerly and filled up all the public benches. I had gone to sit beside the prosecutor at the bar. Mr. Chan Wai Fucking-ping sat in the front row where he could give the signals. They were very impressive in their expanse of leashed righteous strength. Each one of them had his copy of the *Heung Keung Po* in his little hot hand, glaring slant-eyed. The orderly's door was open a crack, my detective in there watching me. The clerk had gone to fetch the magistrate. Hell, I thought, it was worth a try.

"Soft and cool," I whispered to the prosecuting inspector.

There was a knock on the door and the orderly shouted *"Silence in Court!"* and we all stood up.

And Thomas Fox-Smith, magistrate, entered importantly, and he gladdened my heart. Tommy was just the boy for Chan Wai-ping mob. Tommy Fox-Smith was stout and handle-bar-moustached and he was an officer in the Royal Auxiliary Air Force, on the committee at the Hong Kong Club, chairman of the Sons of England, he had been a district commissioner in Kenya, pronounced *keenyah,* he called the Chinese the bally natives and Mao Tse-tung that bally fellah across the bordah. Tommy was just the boy. We bowed to each other, sat down, I nudged the prosecutor and he said softly, "May it please Your Worship, the case of Regina versus Wong, the attorney general has withdrawn all charges against the accused . . ." and then I nodded at the orderly's door, and Wong was led out into the courtroom, and it surpassed my wildest hopes, somebody up there likes me, because *"Cong-yee!"* Chan shouted and his mob leaped up with him and thrust their newspapers aloft and bellowed,

"CONG-*yee!"*

"CONG-*yee!"*

And Tommy Fox-Smith surpassed my wildest hopes.

"SILENCE!" Tommy Fox-Smith roared, on his feet fat face red, eyes bulging outraged, clutching the bench, "SILEEEENCE!"

And Mr. Chan Wai-ping bellowed high-pitched red-faced excited, *"Cong-yee! We protest against British injustice, cong-yee!"* and his mob bellowed, *"Cong-yee!"*

And Wong was blushing clutching his face because his stitches throbbed.

"SILEEEENCE." Tommy Fox-Smith roared and smashed both fists on the bench and his eyes bulged furious. *"Seize that man!"* Tommy bellowed, he punched his finger at Chan Wai-ping and filled his outraged imperial breast, "SEIZE HIIIIIIM!"

And two orderlies scrambled and grabbed Mr. Chan Wai-ping in mid-*cong-yee,* newspaper valiantly aloft, and pulled him forward. Mr. Chan Wai-ping surrendered to martyrdom, was pulled in front of the bench shouting *Cong-yee,* then he waved his hand and the *cong-yeeing* stopped. Sudden dramatic eager silence, except for Tommy Fox-Smith shaking with fat imperial outrage.

293

"What," Tommy Fox-Smith bellowed, *"do you think you're doing in my court?"*

Mr. Chan squared himself excitedly. "We—"

"Do you," Tommy bellowed still standing, *"think you're in Outer Mongolia? Or the Belgian Congo? Or Peking?"*

"We—" Mr. Chan began.

"You may be able to behave like that in Peking," Tommy Fox-Smith bellowed at Mr. Chan, *"but we British insist on good manners, by God sir! What's all this infernal* cong-yeeing *about?"*

"We protest—" Mr. Chan began.

"Who's we?' Tommy Fox-Smith bellowed.

"Hah?" Mr. Chan said.

"Hah?" Tommy Fox-Smith bellowed. *"Hah? Hah? Where do you think you are, in Peking? In my court you say I beg your pardon Your Worship, do you understand that—*HAH? *What are 'we' protesting about—*HAH?*"*

"About injustice," Mr. Chan blustered redly.

"About injustice?" Tommmy Fox-Smith roared, insult added to injury. *"What do you know about justice! Don't you dare come to my court and start telling me my job! The cheek of you, sir! The absolute confounded damnable cheek of you!"* Tommy's face was bulging fat red, his moustache sticking up. *"My God! We'll deal with you later! Just tell me what injustice you're braying about, man!"*

Mr. Chan took a red-faced breath. "You are putting this innocent man in jail—"

Tommy Fox-Smith sat down in his chair with a crash and clutched the bench, bulbously red. He took a deep breath and trembled.

"The audacity of you! The ignorant cheek! This isn't Peking, man, where a man is judged guilty before the trial! This man hasn't even been tried yet, how *dare* you presume to tell what I am going to do? How *dare* you, sir! Don't you know that under British law a man is presumed innocent until proved guilty, you *foolish little man?"*

"Hah?" Mr. Chan blushed.

"Hah?" Tommy Fox-Smith mimicked. *"Oh, you* FOOLISH *little man!"* He shook his fat face at him on the "foolish" and tapped his head and his eyes bulged furious. *"Are your ears in order?"*

"Hah?" Mr. Chan blushed.

"Hah? Hah? My goodness what a language! *Oh inter-*

pret it to him, Mr. Interpreter!" Tommy Fox-Smith exploded.

The interpreter said in Cantonese, "Your ears good, no good, hah?"

"Ears?" Mr. Chan Wai-ping blushed.

"Do they function?" Tommy bellowed.

"Hah?" Mr. Chan blushed furiously.

Tommy stood up and bellowed at him delightfully, *"Are they clean?"*

The mob in the gallery was looking mortified.

"Clean ears?" Mr. Chan blushed mortified.

Tommy filled his lungs. *"Because the prosecutor said that the attorney general has withdrawn all charges against this accused!"* he roared.

There was a stunned silence.

"Hah?" Mr. Chan stared.

Tommy Fox-Smith quivered, then sat down furiously. He waved the back of his fat imperial hand at Mr. Chan. "Oh go away! You *foolish* little man! Go away! Go on, shoo! Shoo! *Shoo!*"

Mr. Chan was very red. The whole gallery was red, astonished.

"Accused," Tommy Fox-Smith turned politely to a mystified Wong who had not understood a word except the bit about clean ears, "the attorney general has, withdrawn charges against you and you are free to go. Take this *foolish* little man with you, please. And remember when you read the communist newspapers tomorrow what really happened. And same to you noisy people in the gallery, tomorrow when you read your favorite newspapers, go on, go away——"

It surpassed my wildest hopes. But it was the beginning of the bad times.

CHAPTER 43

The drought was bad that year. That winter was cold and dry. There was no more gushing stamping of the pile drivers for new buildings that year. Among the crowded neon signs scrambling joylessly over each other up to the skyline there were many windows without lights, naked unfinished buildings. "To Let" signs everywhere. The stock exchange was very down. And the people sleeping in the streets, and the people queuing with their cans at the public water taps from midnight on the third day waiting for the four hours on the fourth day.

But we had a good time. Most weekends we went out on the junk. We walked a lot that winter; we anchored and rowed ashore up on the New Territories coast, and walked over the hills and valleys and through the little Chinese villages where they seldom see a *gwailo*, or strangers of any sort. The people were always surprised and pleased to see us. Some of the villages were hundreds of years old. Hong Kong is Instant China. Often we had a picnic; she was very fond of building a fire and barbecuing chops. Some of the fishing villages had eating places, fresh oysters and prawns and crab, and beer, and we always had a bottle of wine in the rucksack. I do not now remember much about the days except that I was working quite hard, I had a number of good interesting cases. In the evenings we read a lot, and painted a lot. She was still on her abstracts, but now she began a study of traditional Chinese art, which I pointed out was very bourgeois and un-People. She was also learning German, in anticipation of the skiing in Austria. We read a lot of poetry and we resolved to write the *Under Milk Wood* of Hong King, but we never did, though we made a lot of notes. We were going to do so many things.

In March Catherine's petition for divorce was served on me, at my office. It cited the unknown Australian girl as co-respondent. I felt, Thank God, at last! I wanted to telephone Ying-ling at school and tell her. The court date was July 10, in England. That was later than I had hoped. That meant I would not be finally divorced until the expiration of the three-month decree nisi thereafter, on October 10. But at least we had a *date*. That night we opened a bottle of champagne. We would still be married in December, before we went on leave.

"Did you really not sleep with that unknown Australian girl?" she said. "Wasn't she pretty?"

"Would you mind if I had?"

"Yes. Because then you wouldn't have gone to your office that night and I wouldn't have met you. I'm really quite fond of that unknown Australian girl."

"She was really quite nice," I said.

"Yes, I quite like that really quite nice unknown Australian girl. And I like Catherine very much for divorcing you. Are you going to get Suzie out here this summer?"

It made me happy to think of it.

"Definitely. I haven't seen her for eighteen months."

"She'll still remember you, darling. We'll have a wonderful time. I'll be an excellent mother to her. We are even going to have the same surname, Mrs. and Miss McAdam; what more could a communist maiden ask?"

That night we started planning our leave. It was only eight and a half months to go, then seven months' leave. Oh yes, we were going to do so many things. Every week one of us came home with a new bright idea. The penthouse was littered with travel brochures. She went to the public library and came home with a lot of geography and history books, like a schoolmarm. We had to go to the Philippines, where the beer was fantastically strong, then it was New Guinea to see the aborigines, then, oh boy, Borneo and Sarawak! There were all kinds of long houses and head hunters and rapids to shoot in canoes. Then Bali, lying in the sun. Then it was absolutely definitely Indonesia, the great object lesson in the Failure of Capitalism after Colonial Rule. Then India, trains and buses up to Nepal and across to Kashmir. Then fly from Bombay to Damascus, Tehran, Baghdad, Beirut. Then skiing in Austria. *Skiing.* She had all the hotel prices all the way and we were going to stay in the best bargains, all right. She had it all figured out. One night she came home with a contraption the size of a beer mug. When she unfolded this wonder it was almost as big as a Gramophone and it was a China Products portable gas stove. She was going to save us a fortune in breakfast bills in places like the Bali Hilton. "Why pay two dollars U.S. for each breakfast, hah? When all I do it, *Voilà!* Coffee. Boiled eggs."

"Who buys the eggs?" I said.

"I do of course. I run down to the village shop. Save four dollars U.S. Lunch we don't eat at the hotel, we'll be sight-seeing. Eat good cheap native food. And so interesting."

"Can I take you to dinner?" I said. "For all the dinners I haven't bought you."

"All right, darling. As long as they're not too expensive. After our honeymoon we're going to stay in cheap native hotels and eat native food and get to know the natives, aren't we? It'll be so fascinating. But we'll do whatever you want, darling."

And that April I received instructions to appear before the police promotion board in May. I did not tell Yingling. There was only one vacancy for the gazetted officer rank of assistant superintendent and only four of us were summoned. We had all sat the written examinations years ago. We sat outside the boardroom side by side and waited. It was the first time I had been in uniform since Takwuling and it felt good. I knew I was going to walk it. I knew my record was better than any of the others. They were each called in ahead of me and they were each in only about half an hour. When the ADC summoned me, I marched in as regulations prescribed, saluted, doffed headgear, and sat down and looked at them. They asked a lot of questions, on law and procedure and Southeast Asian and international affairs, and particularly about current affairs in China, and I walked them. I knew that I knew as much about any of that as any of them. Only one question caused any trouble, and I was ready for it too:

"Inspector McAdam, do you intend to remarry?"

"I am still married, sir."

He said, "I'm sorry to have to press you, in the circumstances, but do you *intend* to remarry? And if so, may we know whom?"

I looked at the five of them sitting there and I knew that three of them at least had mistresses and not one of their wives was a patch on my woman. I had worked ten long years for this board to summon me and I was damned if I was going to let them spoil it.

"I'm a Catholic, sir. However, if I am divorced I will almost certainly someday remarry. Someone, someday, sir."

Charles Frith leaned forward. "Do you have anybody in mind? We do not mean to pry offensively, but it is a standard inquiry and it can be of considerable importance."

"To have somebody in mind is an elastic state of mind, sir."

They all looked at me and I looked them in the eye. "Very well," Charles Frith said. "The answer is 'I don't know.'"

Outside the windows the spring sun shone bright and the harbor was blue, and I knew I had walked it.

John Fellows, one of the other candidates, was waiting for me outside the boardroom. We went to lunch at the Hilton and John said, "I know it's yours. They just got us along so it didn't look too much like a foregone conclusion."

"It's no foregone conclusion," I said.

"Of course it is. I haven't fought the Comrades in Malaya, I haven't got a degree, I haven't written any books, I haven't got your record, none of us has. We're just the best guys they could find in a hurry to make it not look like a cakewalk. We'll see in a month."

That evening I went home to Ying-ling full of beer and wine and brandy and I told her where I had been today and she hugged me, jumping up and down, and she opened another bottle of Grand Mousseaux because she also knew I had walked it. She knew it so definitely you would have thought she had appeared before the board herself.

That May the light early summer rains came, a sort of seeping China mist that hung low over the harbor. Then the clear days came, good bright sunny, and you knew it was almost summer already and soon it would be the long hot days on the junk again, laughing and loving and swimming gloriously sensuously satiny naked again and lying long and golden on the hot deck drinking cold beer and wine in the sun again. But that May morning it was overcast when I got to the office and found Catherine's letter waiting for me. I opened it cheerfully. It began "My darling Jake," and it told me that her affair with Burton was finished, that she had stopped the divorce proceedings, and that she wanted to come back to me.

CHAPTER 44

It was not a very long letter. I reread it, my aghastness had gone, now came the anger, that it had all gone wrong. When everything had been going right at last. Oh Jesus Christ! I grabbed the telephone and booked a call to London. It was 8 A.M. Hong Kong time, midnight last night in London. I drove hard around to Cable and

Wireless to give them a check. How many minutes did I want, the girl wanted to know. Christ, how many minutes do you need to talk your wife into a divorce? I wrote a check for twenty minutes. My hand was shaking. I told them to put the call through to the penthouse.

I drove back to Wanchai hard. As I got in the door the telephone rang and I grabbed it, shaking. "Hello!"

"Hold the line, Mr. McAdam, we're calling your party now."

I heard the telephone ringing a long, long way away. I lit a cigarette and my hand shook. Then I heard a click and a little sleepy faraway voice said, "Hello?" and my heart was pounding and I shouted, "Suzie! Hello, Suzie darling!"—and I had tears—"Suzie, this is Daddy!"

"Hello?" Suzie said.

"Suzie, this is Daddy! Do you remember me?"

"Who?" Suzie said, far away.

"Daddy!" I shouted and I felt my throat thick. "Your Daddy in Hong Kong, don't you remember me?"

"Daddy?" Suzie said and I thought my heart would break.

"Yes—remember I used to take you on the swings in the park and on the beach?" I waited, heart pounding.

"Yes?" she said uncertainly, awake now.

"You sent me a Christmas card," I shouted. "Remember?—you drew it yourself?"

"Yes," Suzie said uncertainly, far away. "Are you really my daddy?"

"Yes, darling!" I was nearly crying now. "Yes! Do you love me?"

"Yes," she said, uncertainly polite twelve thousand miles away in the middle of the night. I took a great breath and I felt it quiver all the way in. "Listen, darling —where's Mommy?"

"Out," Suzie said.

"Who's looking after you?"

"Janet is."

"Who's Janet, darling? Where is she now?"

"Downstairs. I'm sleeping in Mommy's bed."

"Hello?" a voice said. "Who is this?"

"Are you Janet?" I shouted.

"Yes? I was downstairs watching television."

"I'm calling from Hong Kong. Where's Mrs. McAdam?"

"From *where?*"

"Hong Kong. What time will Mrs. McAdam be back?"

"She said about midnight. I'm the baby-sitter. Mrs. McAdam said to watch television."

"All right. Tell Mrs. McAdam when she comes in that Mr. McAdam telephoned her urgently from Hong Kong, all right?"

"From Hong *Kong?*"

"Right. Let me speak to Suzie."

"Hello?" Suzie said.

"Suzie, this is Daddy. Do you love me?"

"Yes," Suzie said.

I felt my chest quiver. "All right, darling, go back to sleep. Daddy loves you."

I put down the phone and took a big breath and I felt the big aching cry come up my throat, the heartbreak, and I dropped my head and cried into my arm. Then I dragged my sleeve across my eye and went and poured myself a whiskey. I lit a shaking cigarette then called Cable and Wireless and told them to keep trying for Mrs. McAdam.

The telephone rang and I grabbed it. I was calmer now. "Mrs. McAdam on the line for you, sir." *"Hello, darling!"* she said.

"Hello, Catherine! How're you?"

"I'm fine, I've been to the theater with Mother."

"Catherine, I've got your letter, what the hell's happening?"

"Darling, Dave and I are finished," she appealed.

"Since when?"

"Since two weeks ago, he's been posted to New York—"

"Who finished it?"

"We both did." She was almost crying.

I did not believe that. "Has he gone back to his wife?"

"Probably." She was crying. "Darling? When it came to the crunch of the actual divorce we couldn't go through with it."

"Neither of you or *he* couldn't?" I said cruelly.

"Both, darling! *Both!"*

"Why couldn't you?" I demanded.

She was crying. "I realized I still loved you—"

I felt hard. "It's not as simple as that and you know it. Were you fighting?"

She was crying. "Yes. Every day, darling, for months. We had such bad a bad time—"

"What the hell were you fighting about?"

301

"*Everything.* He didn't want to go through with it. Oh darling, we've had such a bad time—"

"*He* didn't?"

"*Neither* of us, darling, I've told you I love you—"

"Tell the truth, Catherine!"

"I *am* telling the truth, I *am!*"

She was crying. I felt sick in my guts but I wasn't near tears at all. "Catherine, stop crying, dear."

"Jake?" she sniffed, then a big breath. "I want us to try again."

I took a breath. "No, darling," I said.

She cried: "*Jake, I'm your wife, I have the right to try again*—"

"No you haven't, Catherine, not any more—"

"I *have*, I'm your *wife!* I'm the mother of your *child*, what about Suzie?"

I got angry. "Don't use Suzie against me, you didn't consider Suzie a long time ago."

"You rejected me," she cried.

"You know why I rejected you, Catherine?"

She was crying. I took a big breath.

"Catherine, listen to me, darling. Are you listening? We can*not* try again because I love somebody else. And I'm going to marry her."

There was crying into the phone. "Who?"

"It doesn't matter who."

She cried, "*Darling, before you marry anybody I've got the right to try again just once more.* I *have*, darling, *we* have that right, please please *please* darling—"

"Catherine, it's no good, *my mind is made up.*"

"It can't be made up until you've seen us again, we have that right—don't you love us at all?"

"That's not the issue, Catherine, the point is I love somebody else and so did you until two weeks ago!"

"Jake?" I heard her voice shake. "I'm coming back to Hong Kong."

I felt myself go white. "Catherine, you are *not!*"

"You can't stop me!" she cried. "It's a free country, I'm a British subject."

I was shaking. "You are *not* coming back to Hong Kong! It will serve no purpose—"

"It's my *home*, I have a *right* to defend myself against another woman!"

"It's too late, Catherine!"

"It's not too late, darling," she cried. "You're not married yet, you can't get married until we're divorced, I'm your wife and I have the moral right to try again, darling—"

"No, Catherine! I'm living with her and nothing will move me!"

"*I don't care* who you've slept with—I don't *care*, darling, *I don't care!* You've got to give us another chance—I'll get a flat and a job, I'm not helpless—" She broke down crying.

I was shaking, white. I took a big breath and held it, then I said quietly, "Catherine. Listen to me, darling." She was just crying. "Catherine, divorce me. It's the only way. Go back to David."

"I don't *want* to go back to him! I'm coming to Hong Kong," she wept.

"Catherine! For God's sake divorce me!"

She cried, "I *won't!* I won't until you've given us another chance—"

I was shaking.

"Catherine, if you won't divorce me I'll divorce you! I've also got grounds!"

She cried, "I'll fight it! I'll come to Hong Kong and fight it tooth and nail until you've given me a chance—*I will I will I will!*" She broke into sobs. "It's my life—not just yours! Just give us one chance is all I ask!"

"Catherine—"

"Your twenty minutes are up, sir," the operator said.

"Catherine, I'll write to you! For God's sake don't do anything until you've got that letter!"

"When is your leave?" she cried.

"December, but I'm taking her *with* me—"

"*Darling, I'm coming to Hong Kong*—" she cried.

"I'm disconnecting you, Mr. McAdam," the operator said.

"*Catherine, wait for that letter! Do you hear me?*"

"Yes," she sobbed.

"You're disconnected." the operator said. "Unless you want to deposit more money."

I slammed the phone down. Oh God God *God!* I got up shaking, sick in my guts. I went into the bedroom for I don't know what, then into the bathroom and retched over the lavatory.

Then I went back to the phone and called the office and said I wouldn't be in till much later. Then I called Mini-Max.

CHAPTER 45

Maxime's Bar was empty at ten o'clock. We sat in an oak-paneled corner. "Do you think she means it all?" Max said, big liquid Portuguese eyes.

"She was hysterical at times. But I think she meant it, all right."

"But after she's slept on it?" Max said. "She's panic-stricken. She's had a hard time with this guy, they've broken up, she turns back to you in panic. She must realize she can't insist on this at the stage of the fight. Particularly now after what you've said."

"With Catherine you don't know. I don't know what she's turned into. She sounded desperate."

Mini-Max nodded. "Not so easy, with a kid. To get re-married."

I hated reference to Suzie. I felt sick in my guts.

"What I want to know is, what are my chances if I sue her for divorce here in Hong Kong? If she fights it."

Mini-Max blew out smoke.

"You know what a contested divorce is like. It's hell. All the dirty family linen washed in public. And the outcome depends on the discretion of the good lord judge."

I looked at him, sick in my guts.

"Meaning," Mini-Max said, "that the judge has a discretion as to whether or not to grant you a divorce on the grounds of your wife's adultery if *you* have also committed adultery. And are still living in adultery, for Chrissake. Whereas your wife has at least stopped her adultery, here she is back in Hong Kong trying to come back to you, turned over a new leaf. *With* your child."

I felt sick in my guts. "What are my chances?"

Max sighed.

"It depends on the judge. If you get old Charlie Kwok or Sir Peter you're all right. With old Pottinger J. you're probably all right, he's a misogynist and doesn't approve of women messing us chaps around. But any of the others? If you get the Chief Justice, you've had it. He's a Bible-puncher."

"What about Christie J.?"

"With Agatha," Mini-Max said, "it depends on what he had for breakfast. He doesn't know any law, anyway, and he wants to be Chief Justice, terrified of being upset on appeal."

"Could Catherine appeal," I said, "if I won?"

"Certainly, she could appeal. *If* you won." He looked at me, very Portuguese. "Meaning, Jake, that if Catherine fights a divorce you're in for an awful time. And you could well lose. Christ, how many women could she throw at you if she really wanted, if she was prepared to pull out all her guns and call witnesses?"

"They were all after her first adultery."

"That's not the point. Here you are, standing in the witness box—with all the press in the gallery, incidentally —pleading for a divorce on the grounds of your poor wife's adultery, and how many women can her lawyer throw at you? Christ, I can think of a dozen. Legs, the secretary-bird. Veronica Brown. And Shirley long-legs what's-her-name who was always telling everybody what a bastard you were. To name a few."

I said, "She couldn't prove Legs or Shirley, not as I remember the laws of evidence."

Max leaned forward in his chair at me: "Jake, she wouldn't have to, baby! There you are, the petitioner, standing in the witness box in your own hometown, and you're under oath—*oath*, Jake—to tell the truth, the whole truth, and nothing but the truth, so help me God, quote unquote. And your wife's lawyer cross-examines you and says, 'Mr. McAdam, did you or did you not commit adultery with one Veronica Brown? What do you answer? Under oath."

I didn't say anything, this I didn't care about.

" 'And with one Legs?' " he says.

Max looked at me, liquid-eyed, then held up his finger. "Now remember you're not just somebody appearing in the circuit court in goddamn Sussex where nobody knows you. You're probably Superintendent McAdam whom everybody knows appearing in the Supreme Court in Hong Kong. In Hong Kong you're *news*, man, and the press are in the gallery, you bet your life. What do you say to these questions?"

I felt sick in my guts. Not because of the questions.

"I would have to admit it," I said. "Under oath."

Mini-Max sat back. "Exactly. And you'd be very wise.

Because if Catherine could prove that you had lied, committed perjury, you would be *out* of this police force!"
He looked at me. "This police force cannot afford to have a proven liar, convicted of perjury, on their staff." He nodded at me sadly. "And if you admit half of those adulteries, Jake, I don't like your chances of winning the divorce. At least with half our judges. She's got only two adulteries to her discredit."

Oh God. I didn't care about the questions, all I cared about was the divorce and Ying-ling. "I don't believe Catherine would go as far as that."

"Don't, repeat, *don't* underestimate the wrath of a woman scorned in a divorce court. I've seen a few. And that's only half the god-awful story. The other god-awful half ruins your career. What happens when Catherine's lawyer moves on to the enthralling subject of Ying-ling?"

He looked at me.

"Ying-ling Tsang," he said dispassionately. "The communist mistress for two years of the well-known Superintendent McAdam. I quote: 'Isn't it true, Mr. McAdam, that for the past two years you have been living in a Wanchai love nest with a member of the Communist party?' "

"She's not a member of the goddamn party," I said.

Max winked deprecatingly. "With a communist schoolteacher of a school dedicated to the cause of communism? *Whose parents are communists, living in China,* while she soldiers on the good cause here in Hong Kong, living with you. What would your police force say to that little bit of news?" He looked at me. "You'd be out, wouldn't you?"

I said, "I don't care about that."

"Oh *don't* you!" Mini-Max said. "Don't you hell. You *love* this police force. You could end up losing your career *and* losing the divorce."

"I'll do it," I said. "If I have to."

"What you've got to do is persuade Catherine to go ahead with the divorce."

"I'm writing to her tonight. I'll bloody fly to England if necessary to argue with her. Oh Jesus." I sat back, sick in my guts. "She's withdrawn proceedings, that means she's lost our place in the queue, doesn't it? If she starts again she'll have to apply for a new hearing date all over again."

"I'm afraid so," Mini-Max said.

Oh God *God!*

"Another goddamn year. Oh *Jesus!*" I wanted to shout it. "How long will I have to wait in Hong Kong for a court date?" I demanded.

"About six months."

"Oh Je-*zuz!*"

"Take it easy, boy."

"Take it easy? I've got to marry her and regularize our whole *life,* for Chrissake. We're supposed to be going on leave together in five bloody months! We've got it all planned. It'll break her heart. And bloody mine!"

"Would she go on leave with you unmarried?"

"Christ, she's *got* to. We've *got* to go on leave together, we've got it all planned."

"You've got to make her give up that job of hers," Mini-Max said. "That's dynamite to you."

I took a big angry breath. "Oh Christ, Catherine."

Mini-Max looked at me. "You've got to talk Catherine into it," he said. He looked at me, then said, "You don't want a contested divorce action, Jake."

CHAPTER 46

It rained that afternoon, dark and thick as your fingers. I drank half a bottle of whiskey writing to Catherine, the rain beating down on the patio and you could not see the harbor. It was a long letter. At five o'clock I went out to mail it, and the rain soaked me and the gutter ran dirty full and in the *China Mail* there were headlines of land-slides, and I did not care. At six o'clock she came in, dripping, beaming, Mad Dog shaking himself all over the place and she said, "What's the matter, darling?"

"Sit down," I said.

I took a big breath and I felt tired and white. I had it rehearsed but it was no good, her looking at me expect-antly like that.

"Catherine's broken up with Burton and she's stopped the divorce proceedings and she wants to come back to me." I squeezed her hand. "I telephoned her and told her, No, no a thousand times no and I wrote to her this afternoon reiterating that, pleading for her to reinstate the divorce proceedings."

She was still half-smiling at me, then she looked away, her hand in mine and she tried to sound in control.

"Oh," she said. "Oh dear."

"Ying," I took her in my arms and she was rigid. I told her I was in love with you and that we're going to get married. Everything is going to be all right."

She sat up out of my arms, tried to smile. She wiped some rain off her hair.

"What about Suzie?" she tried to smile.

I said desperately, "Suzie's got *nothing* to do with it."

She tried to stand up and I held her hand down.

"Catherine's your wife," she tried to smile, "she's entitled to come back."

"Oh Jesus. She is not!" I wanted to shout but I controlled it. "Ying, this is not time for goddamn Chinese face. Forget face!"

She looked at me, all wet and trying to smile, then the tears in her eyes suddenly. Then sat back, trying to be bright. "Tell me from the beginning."

I told her, from the beginning. She listened intently, she did not interrupt, trying to look controlled, helpful, I could feel her hand trembling. I told her I had consulted Max. But not what Max had said were my chances. She took a big breath, then said, "Where will she stay? You cannot let your child live in a boardinghouse."

I knew where she would stay. With the Old Man and Gladys. "She can stay in the Happy Valley house when the tenant's lease is finished. She can stay in my goddamn government flat if she has to. But I'm staying with you."

She said, "How can I live with you while she's in Hong Kong? She will surely find out, then what'll happen to you? How can you get a divorce if you are living with me if your wife is here wanting to come back? I do not know law, but it seems to me wrong."

"Well it doesn't seem wrong to me. For God's sake leave the law to the lawyers and cross those bridges as we come to them!" I stood up, walked across the carpet. "But there's a couple of bridges we've got to cross right now." I stopped and looked at her. "The first is that whatever happens you're coming with me on leave."

She looked at me, pale. I said, "The second is you've got to give up your teaching post at that school immediately, darling." She stared at me. "You've got to, Ying. Do you see?"

She sat there. Then she stood up, walked to the window, and looked out. It was still raining.

"Yes, I see."

"Everything is going to be the same, Ying. It's *got* to be."

She nodded at the rain. I took her shoulders. Her eyes were big steady wet, then she tried to smile.

"Except it's not the same, is it, darling?"

Oh God.

"It will be! The divorce will come through, somehow." I squeezed her shoulders. "She's suddenly panic-stricken, that's all." I loved her so much I wanted to shout it. "All this means at the worst is that the divorce is delayed! We're going to leave, Ying! We *are* going to get married. Everything is going to be the same!"

She looked at me, tremulous tearful, then her chin crinkled and her eyes filled up. I clutched her tight. "Oh *Ying*"—and I thought my heart would break, I wanted to bellow *Damn you, Catherine!* She took a big trembling breath, then came off my shoulder and looked at me; she shook her head and tried to smile: "Darling, I cannot come with you." She closed her eyes and shook her head: "I cannot. I cannot give up everything if we're not married—don't you see?"

I felt white, my heart thudding: "Ying-ling, that's nonsense!"

She tried to smile, eyes pleading full. "It's not nonsense!" She stepped back and shook her head. "Please, darling, listen—don't you see—it may be *years* before we are married! All the time I must give up my life. And live like a mistress, a concubine, I want to carry my head up high—"

I felt desperate. "It won't be like that! We'll live together openly. *Now* you're living like a mistress—"

"No, darling. I still have my *work*, I am leading a useful life. I am not your mistress, I am your *lover*, I am *me*, not a fat useless mistress, I have my *own* work and my own friends and my own room and my own money—"

"It *won't* be years before we're married—one year at the most—"

She cried, "You don't *know* darling! How long is it now? Now your wife is coming back. It may be years, darling—"

309

She was wide-eyed, trying not to cry, desperate that I understand. I took a big breath. It was no good arguing with her now, we were both too overwrought but I had to ask it: "And? If it does take years to get the divorce? Will you leave me?"

She took a big trembling breath with her eyes closed standing there rigid, then "No!" she cried into her hands. "It is you who will leave me!"

"Oh God, Ying!" I clutched her tight, my anger was all gone, just desperate. "I will never leave you!" I rocked her, tight against me.

Later we lay on the double bed in the dark. It was still raining. We had smoked a lot of cigarettes. We were calmer now.

She had listened to me without interruption, only the tremulous glow of her cigarette in the dark. Now it was her turn, and I was not to interrupt her either. It almost seemed that I did not care what she said, now. I was calm, deadly reckless calm. Catherine could do her worst. Nobody, not Catherine, not Ying, not Mao Tse-tung nor all the Queen's horses were going to take her away from me. I did not care who I trampled underfoot. Her cigarette glowed as she marshaled her thoughts, I lay there holding her and waited.

"I understand all your points. And what I say is this." She breathed deep. "My career is not important. China will go on very well without me. I am not even a good communist, I know." She drew on her cigarette. "Your career *is* important. You are going to make the life for all of us, you and me and any children." She spoke slowly, her cigarette glowed. "And I want a good life for all of us."

I waited.

"This is what I want to say: If you have to sue her for divorce here in Hong Kong and she fights you I will give up everything." She drew hard on her cigarette again. "Everything, as if we were married. So that at the court nobody can say, 'Your mistress is a communist school-teacher.' And ruin your career."

She waited for me to acknowledge this. I squeezed her hand.

"But. darling? Are you listening?" She took another big breath into the dark. "I do not want to do that until there is a real divorce actually starting. I do not want to give up my life. My teaching. My friends. Everything.

Until it is necessary, when the divorce starts. I am not a good communist but I am *me*."

I waited. She said, "I love you. I will wait for you. But I will not come on leave you as your mistress?"

Outside it was raining hard.

It rained on and off for three weeks. And all the time the heat, and the landslides. The third week I got Catherine's reply to my letter.

Some of the things she wrote were true and some were hard to believe and some were downright incredible. I could not believe all the bitterness and hate. Catherine was crazy, at least she was beside herself with resentment. But the most important thing was what she called her "concession" to me: that she would not proceed back to Hong Kong now, on two conditions: one, that I did not do anything "crazy" like try to institute divorce proceedings against *her;* if I did she would come and "fight it to the death" and "throw the book at me." The second condition was that I come to England to "discuss the whole matter of reconciliation exhaustively" when my leave commenced and stayed in London for at least two months, "to give us a chance."

I telephoned her several times in the ensuring weeks. It was no good. The only good was that she did not come back to Hong Kong. There was not enough time for me to institute divorce proceedings against her, before I went on leave.

CHAPTER 47

It rained a lot that summer. Warm misty Hong Kong rain that seeped. There were some bad landslides. I do not remember much about the days. After work I waited for her to come home, I did not want to go anyplace else. Trying not to think about it. I wanted to spend the weekends at home; there were only nine weekends left, then only eight, then only seven. I told myself, It's only seven months. And you'll be skiing and seeing Europe again, it will go quickly. The divorce will come through when you get back. It will, when you see Catherine and talk sense to each other she'll see that it's no good. I was not worried about the divorce so much any more, I was only thinking about Ying-ling and the going away. Away from my love. She always came in the door smiling brightly but we both knew it was a pretense. "Hello, darling!"

I did not want to let her out of my sight. I followed her into the bedroom and watched her take off her school clothes, shake out her hair, go to the toilet. She chatted brightly about what happened today. She was determined. She kept the bathroom door open matter-of-factly, and I heard the tinkle of her urinating, the most defenseless sound in the world. It was a joke about her going to the toilet as soon as she came home, about it being territorial and her own nice little barbarian toilet. "I'm going to miss that little barbarian toilet!" she joked one day. Then "Oh darling, it was a joke. Don't look so sad. It's only six months."

"It's an international disaster," I said.

Then it was the ritual of inspecting her flowers on the patio. The pine saplings were quite big now, so was the avocado tree. Everything was doing very well. I looked at her bending over them talking to them, weeding, encouraging them. What would we do with them when I left? Suddenly it was very important. "What about the flowers?" I said.

She hooked a lock of hair behind her ear. "I'll keep them on my rooftop. I've neglected my rooftop for two years. I'll think of you every day when I'm looking after them. And in the mornings when I'm doing my exercises."

Oh God, Ying-ling in the sunrise over China, on her rooftop I had never seen.

"The sunrise," I said.

"At least we'll be seeing the same sun, darling!" That was all we had left out of all the things we were going to do.

When we were on the patio I wanted to get the flowers over with so we could go inside and I could have her all to myself. And I wanted to take her to dinner to expensive places and show her the things we had never seen together, candlelight and polished waters, show her off and spoil her, and dance with her and feel everybody looking at her and saying, "What a lovely girl." Now oh God, I wish that we had done it, I wish that I had lavished it upon her and done many things for her, and forced her right out into the open, irrevocably. Maybe it would have worked, and sometimes now in the long night I think so. But she did not want to and after a moment I did not want to go out any more, I wanted to be alone with her in our penthouse again. I know one night I said, "Let's go out. I want to take you to dinner. Let's go to the Mandarin or the Hilton."

She was taken by surprise.

"All right."

"Nobody will know us, in that kind of place there'll be none of your colleagues."

"Of course I want to if you want to!"

I looked at her.

"You don't want to go, do you, darling?"

She sat down on the edge of the sofa beside me.

"No. But we'll go if you want to. I'm not afraid. But I want to be alone with you here. Do you want to go?"

"No," I said. I did not want to go any more, I wanted to stay here. She put her arms around me. "Oh God."

"What, darling?"

"I love you, that's all. And I'm going away."

She looked at me, then smiled. "You must know I love you, don't I look as if I love you? I'll do anything for you! What do you want me to do? Shall we make love?"

I said, "Come on, leave with me."

She smiled: "Darling, as soon as everything is all right I'll go with you to the end of the earth. Don't think about it now! I'll be waiting when you come back! We've still got six weeks. And then it's only six months!"

"It's not six weeks. It's five and a half. And it's not six months, it's seven."

"But doesn't it sound better to say six? That last month will be *nothing* for two wonderful people like us."

I smiled at her. "Big Brown Eyes."

"You're the one with the eyes!" she said.

Except it wasn't seven months, either. That November morning my super called me into his office. He had his hand extended to shake mine, and in the other was the police board's official notification. That on expiration of my leave I would be gazetted as superintendent. And that on expiration of my leave I would proceed to the Police School, Newbury, Berkshire, England, for a five-month course of instruction.

The Newbury Police School was no ordinary academy. It was a high-powered educational division of MI5, where specially selected police officers were given a special high-powered course in what is euphemistically called Intelligence Duties. I was being posted to Special Branch when I came back.

CHAPTER 48

That night I had to put up a lot of drinks at the Police Club. Then my millionaire staff sergeant took the whole of Special Investigations to a Shanghainese dinner. Everybody was having a good time and I laughed and made jokes and all the time all I wanted was her and feeling *Oh God twelve months*. One year. And Special Branch. And *oh Jesus Christ, Catherine!* At eleven o'clock I took a cab up to Mini-Max's flat in Midlevels. He came to the door in his underpants, all hairy and horrible. "Hello, mate," he said, hand stuck out, "congratulations. I heard about it at the club. The youngest superintendent ever."

"Thanks, Max, I've got to talk to you. As my lawyer."

"I gathered." He went to the liquor cabinet and came stumping hairily back with two glasses. I took a breath and said, "I'll be away a year altogether. I'm going on a goddamn high-powered intelligence course. I'm going into Special Branch when I come back."

He looked at me.

"Oh Jesus," he said.

I got up and walked to the window with my whiskey.

"Special Branch," Mini-Max said. "You know what *that* means. It means," Mini-Max said sternly behind me, "that you better get that divorce from Catherine pretty damn quick and marry this girl. Or you're in the shit."

"I know."

"Christ. A superintendent in Special Branch with a communist mistress? Good God, they wouldn't have you in Special Branch even *after* you married her if they knew she was a communist."

"She wouldn't be a communist any more," I said.

"Even an ex-communist" Max said. "An ex-ex-*ex-*

314

communist. Married to a Special Branch officer? You know that?"

I knew it. "She's not a real communist."

"Oh, Jake!" He came beside me and looked at me with his big liquid Portuguese eyes stern: "She works at a communist school, her father lives in Communist China. Even if she never lifts a finger for communism she's politically suspect. Because she can be got at. Pressured. And therefore *you* could be pressured. And always could be."

I knew that, for Christ's sake. I said, "I'm not in the diplomatic corps."

"Jesus," he said. "You're taking a chance."

I walked back across the carpet.

"Supposing the communists put the screws on you through her one day?"

I said, "I'll handle it. Correctly. She'll be very much an ex-communist by then."

"Her family's in China," Mini-Max said irritably. "They wouldn't stop at getting at you through her by putting the screws on her bloody family! You know how this bloody espionage game works."

"There're plenty of Chinese in this police force—and in this government—with family in China."

"Those officers aren't in fucking Special Branch!"

I took a big breath.

"I'm marrying her," I said. "All kinds of people get married in Hong Kong. That won't happen, that's far-fetched."

"Is it?" Mini-Max stumped across the carpet to the liquor cabinet. "What would the police board do if they knew you proposed marrying a communist schoolmistress? They'd keep you *well* out of Special Branch, wouldn't they? But that not *all*. You wouldn't be promoted to superintendent either, would you?" He glared.

I breathed into my glass. "Probably not."

"*Probably?* You know damn well! If they didn't fine you, you'd stay an inspector forever. Without responsible duties!" He glared.

"So what the hell am I supposed to do?"

He walked away, back to the window.

"Give her up," he said. "Now."

I almost wanted to laugh.

"For Christ's sake! That's impossible."

"It's not. Just walk out. Get rid of her." He turned

315

around. "Or walk into the police board tomorrow and confess all and stay an inspector forever."

I wanted to shout it: "I refuse to give up either the woman I love or my career on the theoretical off-chance that one day in the dim and distant future some half-arsed Chinese Red agent who I can run rings around and beat at his own bloody game anyway might conceivably take it into his fat head to try—repeat *try*—to put the screws on me because once upon a time my wife worked for a fucking communist school!"

Mini-Max looked at me. "You wanted my advice? In the middle of the goddamn night. Well, I'm giving it to you."

"Would *you*," I demanded, "give up either your woman or your career on that kind of off-chance?"

"I wouldn't give up my career for a woman," Max said. "That's for bloody sure."

"Well, I'm giving up neither."

He sucked on his cigarette, glaring at me, thinking. Then he nodded; nod nod nod.

"All right," he said. "You're going to marry her. You'll probably get away with it. You're so damn lucky. And as you say all kinds of people get married in this town. East meets West and all that jazz." He stumped back to the window. "That advice I'm giving you as your friend, not as your lawyer. On your head be it. But you'll probably be all right. But"—he turned around and held up a finger—"you've got to marry her pretty damn quick! You've *got* to get that divorce from Catherine. As a Special Branch officer with a communist *mistress?*—you're a sitting duck! You'd be a textbook example of an espionage security risk. You know how the game works."

"I know."

"They zero in on weaknesses like mistresses, homosexuality, vices, and put the screws on you. Blackmail. Co-operate or else!" He was making up for his advice about marrying her. "Christ, the communists would rub their hands in glee if they knew a senior Special Branch officer had a communist mistress with family in goddamn China!"

"I know, Max."

"Christ alone knows how you've got away with it so long already! Both your police force and the Reds must be asleep."

I said, "Exactly. That shows it's far-fetched. There's no

sweat between Hong Kong and China. It'll be all right."

Mini-Max held up his goddamn Portuguese finger.

"But it won't be all right to keep her as a mistress. Remember the Profumo case? And Christine Keeler wasn't a bloody communist, even. She only had a Russian naval attaché for a boy friend."

"I am not a bloody cabinet minister."

"But *Jesus!*" Mini-Max said exasperated. "You'll be in with the MI5 and the CIA and Christ knows who else. You'll probably even be in with the goddamn Russians against the Chinese for all we know. And in with the CIA against the Russians. And in with the MI5 against the CIA, for Chrissake! Hong Kong is the crossroads, buster, and your Special Branch stands smack in the middle of it."

I walked up the carpet.

Mini-Max glared. "You know what they'll do with you?" He jabbed his finger. "You'll be court-martialed. They'll really throw the book at *you*. Police Ordinance and Standing Orders and Official Secrets Act and the Dirty Tricks Act and Christ knows what! And *when* you come out of St. Helena or wherever they send guys like you, you *won't* get another job, except possibly selling life insurance in Mexico City. *If* you can get a visa."

"I know," I said irritably.

"And? If Catherine doesn't give you a divorce?"

"I'll sue her for divorce," I said. I lit a cigarette and my hand shook but I felt better now I had talked to him. "Catherine will give me a divorce. When we talk it out, she'll see it."

"Oh yes?" Mini-Max stumped off the settee. "And if she doesn't? You'll institute proceedings against her when you get back. *One year* from now. By which time you'll be well and truly in the Special Branch cesspool. As a superintendent. *With* a communist mistress. And what if Catherine fights it and you get the wrong judge and lose?"

If I let myself think about it I felt sick in my guts and I was not going to think about it. I had made my decision and that felt cold-blooded right. "I'll cross that bridge when I meet it. But if it comes to the crunch, if anybody ever tries to put the screws on me because of Ying, I'll quit the police. Confess to the board and quit."

"And do what?"

"Sell life insurance in Mexico City?"

"Jesus." Mini-Max got up and stumped over to the

317

liquor cabinet. "For a woman. Does Ying know about this?"

"No. She knows about my being commissioned and about the course, but not about Special Branch."

He poured a shot.

"For Chrissake you've got a brilliant career ahead. And you love it!" He glared at me. "You *love* the bloody police force. Now you're on your way to the top. And you propose"—Max glared—"risking all that—and Queen and country, I might add—for a"—he was going to say Chinese communist schoolmistress—"a woman."

"Queen and *coun*try," I said.

"*Potentially*. You're a security risk and you know it or you wouldn't be here in the middle of the goddamn night!"

"I said if it ever comes to risking Queen and country I'll quit."

"Jesus, Jake. On your head be it."

My nerves screamed for sleep but I was wide awake. I let myself quietly into the penthouse. Mad Dog was lying flat out on the carpet and he just thumped his long tail at me thump thump thump. "Hello," Percy said sleepily. "Tut tut tut."

Her easel was set up, brushes sitting in the can of turpentine. The books of paintings we had bought, Renoir, Van Gogh, Cézanne. Her paintings on the wall. The look in the eyes of the little girl in her classroom. The Canton junks flying the red flag with the five gold stars. Our junk. Dawn over the China Sea. Weekends on the junk, the morning sparkling on the deep blue China Sea, the big creak of the sails and happy look on her face and the warm breeze blowing her hair and Mad Dog beside himself for joy up there on the bows. And the beach white and empty and her golden satiny naked wet swimming like a seal in her underwater wonderworld and coming up plastered wet gasping to shout and tell me what she had seen, oh Christ. Oh Christ, a year. And oh Christ yes I was doing the right thing. I walked quietly to the bedroom. Written in big letters on the mirror was WELCOME TO OUR HERO! And underneath: *Wake me up, hero*.

She was asleep. Long black hair spread out, one arm outflung. She was perfect. I got undressed and I got very gently into bed beside her, so as not to waken her. I leaned over and kissed her outflung wrist very gently.

My woman. I lay back on the pillow on top of the bed in the dark and closed my eyes, listening to her breathing.

When I woke up she was already gone. She had written on the mirror, *Why didn't you wake me, hero?*

CHAPTER 49

I did not want to let her out of my sight. In the mornings I always woke up very early, still tired, but she was already gone. I got up straightaway, drove back to the Hermitage in the dawn to leave my laundry, but I went there just to be moving. The dawns. I did not want to be alone in the penthouse. I went to work very early. I told myself that I was not thinking about it, but all the time it was there, crying out. A *year*. I worked very hard clearing up old files to hand over to my successor and I chased up my junior inspectors, I made work for myself. When I got back to the penthouse, I put the hi-fi on loud while I got myself a beer. All day long I have been waiting for that beer, that first long sharp swallow like food which made the cigarette taste good for a change, balm to my ragged nerves. My nerves were very ragged. Then there was nothing for me to do but wait for her. And when she came I did not want to let her out of my sight.

I took our Famous Red Triumph onto the patio while she inspected her flowers and said encouraging things to them and watered with her lucky red China Products watering can and dug the earth with her China Products trowel, and fed Percy and the crickets and the hamsters, talking to them in Cantonese, but her face was not sparkling like it used to be, then she smiled at me and pretended everything was fine. And the sundown on her shining black hair and the full slender line of her shoulders and her arms and her back and her hips and her strong gentle face talking to her flowers and I raged inside that we should be threatened; by Catherine, by politics, by the bloody Hong Kong police. I refused to choose! I still had not told her about Special Branch and I was not going to, until I came back. She *was* me now, she was grafted onto me now, my very flesh was changed now by her; there was no question, no choice to make, she *is* me, whether they liked it or not, they had no right to impose decisions on me, not the Hong Kong police nor Queen and bloody country had the right to take my woman from me, they had no goddamn right to anything except my loyalty and that they had, *I refuse to choose!* And I was filled with recklessness, I knew that I had made the right decision, an end to running, and I felt strong and reckless, and I wanted to throw my arms about her and lift her up and shake her and tell her that everything was going to be all right. And in the cold light of China dawn when she was already gone, at my lowest ebb, I knew that it was not as easy as that. That everything Max had said was true and real, what I had been avoiding for two years was staring me in the face now. The decision had been made; but what Max had said was real, all right.

She bought a lot of mothballs to hang in my closet. I arranged with a junior inspector to keep my car. I paid twelve months' rent in advance. I arranged with Max to keep an eye on the junk, and to keep my long-playing records and tapes dry. I wanted Ying to move into the penthouse but she said no.

"What have you decided?" Mini-Max looked at me.

I was very tired, even in broad daylight. "Max, this is my concern."

"It's not just your concern! It's my concern as your lawyer because you're going to be a security risk!"

I said, softly, so nobody else in the bar could hear, "I'm not the first man to face this problem, nor the last. Plenty have got away with much worse."

"And plenty have been caught. Ensnared. The espionage trials are all about people like you who thought they could get away with it and got deeper and deeper into the blackmail. If nothing *else*, even for*getting* your goddamn duty, what about the risk to *her!* If you love her so blindly! Supposing they get at her!"

I closed my eyes and said slowly, "She'll be safe in my bed."

"And where'll her family in China be?"

"Only her father. And he's a big-wheel doctor in charge of a large hospital, they wouldn't touch him."

Mini-Max took a big breath.

For our second-last weekend we went to Macao. I

wanted a sort of treat for her, and to get us out of the penthouse. We were going to stay in the most expensive suite and have the best wine. We sailed on the Friday midnight ferry. We had a cabin opening onto the promenade deck. We went aboard separately but the steamer was nearly empty.

"Isn't it exciting! Let's walk around and look!"

We walked down the deck when we were under way. There were a lot of merchant ships anchored, all their lights, cargo junks clustered around them. It was a clear night, floods of stars, the lights of Kowloon and Hong Kong a jeweled glow. A fat Portuguese gentleman came around the corner, she let go of my hand. We walked down to the stern, into the aft floodlights and she let go my hand again. She looked up at the stars, head back, long hair loose and her eyes were glistening. Then she suddenly turned around and leaned over the rail.

"I shall work very hard! Yes. And paint many pictures! And read lots of good books! The year will *fly*."

Oh God. "And write me lots of letters," I said.

"Yes. Letters." She was crying, face turned away from me.

"Ying?"

She didn't look. "What?"

"Look at me."

She turned her face to me, wiping her eyes. "I'm sorry."

I wanted to grab her, and hold her tight but I could not in the floodlights. "What?" She tried to smile, now, eyes blurred.

"I'll be back. And there'll be none of this going away ever again."

She tried to smile. She said, "*Will* you get the divorce, darling?"

Oh God I felt desperate.

"*Ying, believe me!* You've got to do that."

She tried to smile.

"I'm sorry. I do." She closed her eyes.

I put my arms around her and held her tightly and my throat ached. I felt her breathe out and tremble against me then she said, "Not in the light. Please." She moved away. "Let's not be sad." She tried to smile. "Come."

We walked along the promenade deck. There was nobody about. I held her hand and she squeezed it and smiled. We came to the lounge windows. We could see a few people sitting at the cocktail bar. There was a band playing but nobody was dancing. We looked at them, from the dark. She stood close to me. She whispered, "I have never danced with you."

There was no need to whisper. "You have. In the flat."

"But not properly, with other people in the same place, like you're supposed to. People are meant to dance together. Couldn't we go in—and just watch?"

Suddenly I was angry again that we were still living like this. "Of course."

She looked at me.

"No, it doesn't matter."

"Of course we will!" God, I'd had enough of this life. "Come."

She squeezed my hand. "No, let's go back to the cabin, I want to go there."

Oh God. I wanted to do whatever she wanted to do.

"We'll get some champagne," I said, to cheer her up.

When we got to the cabin I rang the bell for the steward, to get some champagne. Then she said, "Can we still go back to the bar?"

"Yes, of course."

Suddenlly she grinned. "Come! Let's go!"

She was grinning all the way. We went through into the bar. It was good and dark. And almost empty. The band was sitting around doing nothing now. I don't know how many people she had expected but I don't think she thought it was going to be like this. This wasn't how it was supposed to be. But she didn't want to let it go. I led the way to a table. She sat down, then leaned across and whispered:

"Will the band still play?"

"*Sure.*" Oh God, all the things we were going to do on leave and now all she was getting was an empty bar and all she wanted was for the band to play. I signaled to the waiter. "Send the bandleader please."

The bandleader came across the floor, beaming. "What tune you like us to play, sir?"

I looked at Ying-ling. She looked at me, grinning. "You choose."

"Play us"—I thought quickly—" 'Slow Boat to China.' "

I looked at her. She was smiling. I just wanted to hold her tight. "Relax," I said.

"I *am,*" she grinned.

The waiter brought the champagne. The cork popped

loud in the empty bar. The band struck up "I'd like to get you, On a slow boat to China. . . ."

"Shall we dance?" I said.

"Thank you," she smiled politely.

I led her onto the empty floor. All the waiters and the band were watching us. She smiled self-consciously as I took her in my arms. She was stiff and formal in my arms. I pulled her close and kissed her eyebrow. "I love you," I whispered and I could feel her waiting desperately for me to lead her off. "Relax."

"I'm sorry, darling."

"That's better," I whispered, "like that."

"Am I doing it right?"

"You're doing it beautifully." I kissed her smooth forehead and I smelled her soft shiny hair and I wanted to cry, this was all she was getting out of the wonderful leave we were supposed to have together. "I love you," I said.

"I love you also."

So we danced in public for the first time on the China Sea, turning slowly in the empty nightclub floor of the Macao ferry with the band playing, just for her, and all the waiters watching us silently.

In that last fortnight she had to take away her plants. One by one she lugged the flowerpots away with her in the dawn when she left. There were brown rings where the pots had stood, each day the patio and I got more desolate. The pine saplings we would have to take to an island and plant, she decided, and the avocado sapling, and I was pleased about that. She said we would plant them side by side on a hilltop and they would be ours forever. But we could not plant the avocado tree all by itself in the world, it had to have a mate.

"I'm sure avocado trees are hermaphrodite," I said.

"But we can't let it grow up without another avocado."

On the last weekend we set out on the junk with the trees and a brand-new avocado pear. She had had a hell of a job finding it in winter and finally she had bought this one frozen at Dairy Lane, come from Taiwan. I chose Kat O Chau Island to plant them on. Because it was the most remote, right way up there east of Shataukok, right on the edge of Communist China water. The island the Freedom Swimmers swam for.

At eight o'clock the next morning we chugged through

the islands into small Kat O Chau Bay. There were several small villages around this large haven of islands, all very procommunist. China junks often put into these villages for water and to show the flag. The sea was heart-breaking clear blue-green and you could see bottom, and the little beach was very white. Up there was a fine ridge on which to plant our trees, overlooking China. We dropped anchor and Mad Dog leaped overboard. We rowed the trees ashore in the dinghy. We climbed the hill with the saplings and planted them.

When we got back we took off our clothes and plunged into the cold China Sea. Then the three youths and the girl came running out from behind the rocks gesticulating.

Ying-ling gave a scream and ducked down holding her breasts. The first youth was splashing out to us, he did not look at her. *"Please,"* he gasped, *"we are hungry—"* He pointed into his mouth.

"Who are you?"

He panted, "We swam from China in the night—" The three youths and the girl had reached us now, panting at me anxiously. They were too exhausted to be embarrassed.

"Come out to the boat," I said. Ying gave a gurgle and disappeared underwater. Then broke surface and swam flat out for the boat. The refugees were all looking away. I pulled on my trousers.

I led the way out in the dinghy, they swam. They climbed up on board and slumped down, exhausted, cold. I went below to the saloon.

"It's all right," I said to Ying. "Make them some rice and open a few cans of meat."

"What are you going to do with them?"

"Get them to the police."

She looked guilty. "Can't you—let them go?"

I said, "No. I'm a policeman. They're illegal immigrants. The Immigration Department will decide if they're to be allowed to stay in Hong Kong, not me."

It embarrassed her to come face to face with refugees from her own country. Loss of face. I pumped a jug full of water and got an armful of blankets and climbed back up to the wheelhouse. The girl lay flat out on the deck with her eyes closed.

"Drink," I said. "My wife is making food."

They were very polite. I watched them drink thirstily. They were very lean. The youths wore short trousers and the girl an old bathing suit too big for her. She had short-

324

cropped hair and a blister on the corner of her mouth.
"Where are you from?"

"Near Lungkong," the first youth said. "We work on a commune."

"Where did you swim from?"

"I don't know the name, sir. We swam all night. We reached this island at sunrise."

Probably about ten miles, I thought. Hell I started the engines and I called Mad Dog in. I went forward and pulled up the anchor.

I steamed down the channel between Kat O Chau and Ngo Mei Chau. I was irritable. I didn't want a bunch of refugees aboard.

I turned to them.

"Why did you run away from China?"

The spokesman looked at me earnestly. "We want to be free, sir."

Ying brought the food up. A big bowl of rice and meat and some chopsticks.

"Eat," I said.

They were ravenous. They sat around the bowl gratefully and shoveled the food into their mouths. Ying watched them soberly. They smiled at her and she smiled. I waited until they were half finished, then I stopped the junk a good way from land.

"Don't be afraid. But I am a policeman and I must now arrest you."

They stared, mouths full, aghast. Then the girl dropped her chopsticks and flung herself onto her knees and her arms around my legs. *Oh please, sir!*

"Get up, girl."

"Please, sir, do not send us back—they will shoot us."
Her face was screwed up crying up at me desperate, clinging to my legs. The youths were talking at me all at once, I raised my hands and shouted, *"Silence!"* Ying-ling looked aghast.

There was a shocked silence. They stared at me. The girl slumped, sobbing. I heaved her up. She stood there hunched, crying, shaking in her baggy swimsuit.

"Now listen to me. To be arrested is the best thing that can happen to you. If you sneak into Hong Kong now you have no clothes, no food, no money, no work, no place to sleep. And you will be illegal people always frightened of being caught. It is much better that I hand

325

you over to the Immigration Department and they will probably permit you to remain."

They were staring at me. Ying looked ashamed. Then the youth who was the leader cried, *"Sir, if they don't permit us we will be shot."*

"I can guarantee the Hong Kong Government would not deport anybody who was going to be shot!"

"Madam!" The girl scrambled to Ying-ling and flung her arms around her legs. *"Oh, madam, don't let your husband arrest us."*

I felt sick in my guts. Ying-ling looked at me, pleading, then she held the girl's head and said something in Cantonese. The youth grabbed my arm, his eyes were full of tears, *"Sir, give us a chance, let us swim and we will get to Hong Kong."*

I had had enough. I didn't like doing this, for Chrissake.

"Eat your food! I promise you nobody is going to get shot!"

They stared at me. They did not trust the Hong Kong Government, they did not trust any government. I turned to the wheel and rammed both engines into forward and rammed up the throttle. I kept my back to them. Ying-ling came beside me. "Get me a beer please, and a sandwich," I said.

"What will happen to them if they are sent back to China?" she whispered at me, pleading.

I said irritably, "Who knows what's happening in China these days to such people? Thought Reform Labor Camp? Take the girl below and let her lie down. Christ knows how she swam all night."

She went below. I hated this refugee business but I was glad she was seeing it. What it's like in the paradise across the border. But Christ, not on our last weekend. She came back with the beer and a corned-beef sandwich. "Jake?" she said. I looked at her. "If they jumped over now, what would you do?"

"Try and catch them of course. But I would only catch one. Then the police would mount a manhunt for the rest. So don't get any ideas."

She subsided. "Where are we going?"

"To Tai Po Marine Police." I wasn't going to venture up to Shataukok police station by sea, sail on the edge of Comrade water, with Ying aboard.

They did not try to jump over the side. It took all

morning to steam them down to Tai Po. I handed them over to the Marine Police inspector at the jetty. I kept Ying-ling down in the cabin. It was only Saturday afternoon but the weekend was over. All I wanted was to forget about refugees and China and the police force and our parting, get her home to the penthouse and stay locked up with her there.

As we came around the point I saw a lot of sails on the horizon. I looked at them through the binoculars. There were maybe fifty, an armada of Chinese junks, all sailing the same way, to China. They were not just a fishing fleet going home. This was political. They were all sailing to some commune in Mirs Bay for a political session.

She looked at them through the binoculars.

"Don't they look grand?"

"Let's go home," I said.

That was our last weekend. Still, we had planted the pine trees. Side by side all alone on the top of the ridge, so that when they grew up their branches would just touch each other. They are still there.

CHAPTER 50

Each morning she took some of the things away in a holdall, plus a painting, each evening she came back with the empty bag, and the wardrobe got emptier and the walls barer. Then she started on her ornaments and all the shells and coral and driftwood. Off the windowsills and shelves they came, dropped into her bag and the penthouse got naked and heartbroken in front of my eyes. I said, "Ying?" She turned and looked at me. Oh God. "Leave them. Leave them here."

"No. I want them in my room. For all our happy times."

Then I wanted her to take them. But the penthouse and I got more and more desolate and heartbroken. "What about your pictures?" she said.

"You take them," I said.

A lock of hair fell over her face and she scooped it behind her ear, legs apart, hands on hips, considering. "Darling, I have not enough space in my room. I will take this one, of Suzie. The rest you must give to Max to keep, darling."

Then she started on the big flower boxes. I took them in the elevator down to the basement and she hired a rickshaw coolie to take them up to her lodgings.

"It's very crowded on my rooftop," she came back smiling.

"I wish I knew what your room and rooftop looked like," I said.

I bought her a fish tank and a little electric air pump. We netted the fish and put them in plastic bags of water and she hurried back to her room to put them in her new tank. It was not a very big tank because she already had Percy and Puku and the hamsters and the crickets and Mad Dog and all her pictures and her chamber pot for her urine for her flowers in it.

"I wish I knew what your room looked like," I said.

Then she started on my clothes. What I would need for which climate and insisted that I take this and that, and she examined them all for darning, buttons. I sat on the bed and watched her and Mad Dog sat on the floor. Every time I looked at him he cocked his big ears expectantly and then thumped his tail once. He knew we were packing up. I thought, Oh, Mad Dog, just you look after her. "How many suits are you taking?" she said. "In the summer they'll go moldy here, give them to Max to look after."

"Two," I said.

"This and this," she decided. "You look good in these two."

"Okay," I said.

"Sweaters," she said. "You'll need them in England. And when you go skiing."

Oh, skiing.

"Two," I said. "The blue ones."

"Better take a brown one too, darling. You cannot wear the same two all the time, people will think 'Here comes old Blue Sweater again.' Even though they go with your eyes."

I thought my heart would break.

"Oh God, Ying," I said.

She looked up.

"What, darling?"

Oh God, I loved her.

"I love you, that's all. I wish you were coming."

She smiled. "I do too." Then she smiled brightly, "Next time!"

"Next time we'll have a child," I said. "We won't be able to do so much."

"A blue-eyed Chinese baby? I'll carry her on my back, we'll go everywhere. Okay?"

The last week was pretty bad. I did not feel like going on long leave, passages paid, at all.

On my second-last night I had to throw a farewell party, the traditional, at the Hong Kong Club. I had arranged my social affairs very badly. It was meant to be just for the people to whom I was socially indebted, but soon a lot of others were coming. Ying-ling had printed out most of the invitations. It seemed very wrong that she could not come to my own party.

"Never mind," she said. "One day we can have a big party and you can introduce me to all your friends."

It was a pretty good cocktail party. The invitations read "6 to 8 P.M.'" but at nine o'clock it was still going strong. There was the big babble of voices. A good few were mutual friends of Catherine's and mine. Most of them avoided mentioning her. After a few drinks I realized how much I liked most of them, and I wished desperately, I wish Ying was here. To say *This is Ying, isn't she something?* She would dazzle them and have them eating out of her hand. Right out of her beautiful Chinese hand. I wanted to be proud of her and I wanted her to like my friends. Mini-Max was there, getting along with the scotch. He said quietly, "Well, Sergeant? Any changes?"

I wished the whole damn lot of them would read their invitations. "Have another drink, Maxie," I said.

"This *is* my another drink, McAdam only throws a party once a decade these days. I said have you decided anything?"

I took a breath. "You know it, Max."

Mini-Max looked at me pityingly. "Listen, Jake, will you do one thing for your ole lawyer pal Twinkletoes Popodopolos? Will you please change your mind about her *before* you start this James Bond course? Because once that course starts, you're committed, mate. You're a goner."

Dermot Wilcox, the director of Special Branch, sidled up to me grinning morbidly under his skinny hook nose. He was also getting along with my whiskey, I had never seen him in such a good mood. "Enjoy your leave," he said. "You're going to need it."

"Thanks," I said. I tried to grin. I added, "Sir."

"Strange things are happening," he grinned hookedly, like a man who thrived on trouble. "Strange things in China."

"Like what?" I said.

He grinned at me as if it was some kind of bad joke he was keeping in store for me. "You'll find out when you go to school. Except it will have progressed a whole lot by then. Oh yes," he beamed evilly at me, "Oh yes."

"Oh good," I said. I can't wait. You mean this Mao-think business that's starting?"

His eyebrows went up and down, delighted with his bad joke.

"It'll keep. It'll keep a long time. No more cops and robbers for you," he said, delighted with himself, "just solid brainwork from now on. Get the most out of your leave, you'll need it."

The Old Man and Gladys were the first to leave, I accompanied them to the stairs. I liked them both very much.

"And congratulations *again,*" Gladys said, "on your appointment. And *give* my love to Catherine and Suzie." She looked at me brightly.

"Yes," the Old Man shook hands and his devil's eyebrows beamed up. "Mine too!"

On my last night my millionaire Chinese staff sergeant threw a farewell chow for me at the Yeung Kee. I had arranged my social affairs atrociously, but I had to give him face. The Yeung Kee is a very unprepossessing back-street Chinese restaurant, and it serves the best Chinese food in Hong Kong. Twenty of us sat at two big round tables. There was plenty of drink. I was feeling very tired from not sleeping properly but I had to pretend to be very gay and happy. Halfway through the dinner the *yum-sing* started and it got very red-faced and noisy. I had to *yum-sing* a tumbler of whiskey, down down down, and I thought I would retch but I got it down. The staff sergeant made a speech wishing me a good leave and good luck and long life and double happiness as superintendent. After the dinner they wanted to take me to a good brothel. "Last time you have Chinese girl for twelve months, Bomban!" Mok shouted.

"Not go Chinese whorehouse!" the staff sergeant said. "We get Filipina girls, much better!"

I liked them all very much and I did not want to go to Dermot Wilcoxes bloody Special Branch.

"Bomban," the staff sergeant said to me confidentially in Cantonese, "I know very good place got American girls. And Australian girls, number one."

"Not necessary, truly, thank you," I said.

After dinner I shook hands with them all and got a taxi back to the penthouse. It was drizzling.

"Hello, darling," she said. My suitcases were open on the bed, she had been repacking for me. I put my arms around her and held her tight and rocked her and I felt her eyes wet against my mouth.

"Did you have a good party, darling?"

"Ying," I rocked her, "oh, Ying."

The cupboard doors were open. Her last dress was folded, on the bed, ready to go. I wanted to shout out, *I promise I will come back to you. I swear it, nobody and nothing will stop me!*

"Come to bed."

I went through to the bathroom. All her things were gone, her dressing gown and shower cap and towels and soap and everything, all gone. Only our two naked toothbrushes on the naked glass shelf.

The next morning at ten we left for the airport. The flat was bare, the carpets rolled up, curtains drawn, aquarium empty, no flowers.

I went out into the street and got a taxi to take us to Kai Tak Airport. While I weighed in she went and waited for me near the bar. As I was checking in there was the first call for my flight. I hurried to find her, I saw her sitting on a bench near the bar. Then somebody called "Bomban!" and there was my staff sergeant and half a dozen detectives at the bar with Nondrinking Jack and Max, come to see me off. "Come and have a drink, Bomban!" I looked harrassedly at Ying.

Max looked at her, then at me. "I must just do something first," I said. I tried to look pleased to see them.

"Sure," Max said. He took the staff sergeant's elbow.

I turned and walked away. I looked back and she was following me. I went around a corner and waited. She came around.

"Hello, darling," she said. She stood a pace apart.

331

"Oh Christ," I said.

Her eyes were wet. "Are they your *fokis?*"

"Yes. And Max, the Portuguese one. And Nondrinking Jack."

"I will wait on the verandah," she whispered. "I can see you on the tarmac. You must give your *fokis* face now."

"No! Wait on the bench where you were. I've got to have one drink with them. Then we'll duck out onto the verandah. Oh, Ying—" I held her tight.

The loudspeakers said, "This is the second call for BOAC's flight five oh eight—"

I walked back through the crowded noise. The loudspeakers were going all the time announcing flight departures, people everywhere. The boys gave me a big hello up at the bar and the staff sergeant thrust a San Mig into my hand. "You lucky bastard," Nondrinking said. They wished me luck, and the usual. Max whispered, "Sorry, mate. I didn't think she'd be out here."

"Thanks for coming," I said.

He whispered: "Stick around a couple of minutes then say good-by and disappear with her. I'll cover up for you."

Ying sat with her hands in her lap, I wanted to cry out when I saw her sitting there all by herself. I took a big gulp of my beer and it was hard to swallow.

"Go on," Max whispered, "fuck off now and say good-by to her properly, I'll handle the *fokis.*"

"Yes," I said. I called the barman and ordered a round of drinks for the boys. "I'll fix it," Max said. "Go on."

"I must go," I said.

"Drink it down down!" the staff sergeant said.

"Good-by." I tried to grin. "Thanks very much for coming out—good-by—" I was shaking hands, saying yes, good-by, as quickly as I could. The loudspeakers said, "This is the third and final call for BOAC's flight five oh eight."

She was standing at the exit to the verandah, she pointed urgently at her watch. The verandah was empty in the drizzle.

"Good-by, my darling."

"Good-by. You must go now."

"Calling Passenger McAdam of BOAC's flight five oh eight to Exit three," the loudspeaker said.

"Good-by." I kissed her wet face. She was trying not to cry.

"I love you," she said.

She cloesd her eyes and nodded, nod nod nod. "Go now, darling."

I was the last one out onto the tarmac, the stewardesses waiting for me. I looked up at the balcony. There were only a few people out there in the cold drizzle. She had her lucky red oilcloth umbrella up. She waved and she tried to smile and I thought my heart would break. At the bottom of the gangway I turned and looked back. She was still standing there under her umbrella all alone waving.

"Come *on*, Mr. McAdam, *please*," the stewardess said.

I turned and climbed up the steps. I had a window seat but it was on the wrong side. When the plane turned around we were much too far away to make out faces. But I could see her lucky red China Products umbrella. .

PART VII

CHAPTER 51

The old Tyrolean room opened onto a verandah that looked over the snow-clad Austrian village and across the valley onto the snow-clad mountains.

In the mornings when the sun was halfway down the gleaming golden-white mountains it was about time to get up. I made tea while I shaved and then I sat down at the table and lit my first cigarette and started a new letter to Ying-ling, every morning I had to make this contact with her. *Good morning, my lover!* It was already her evening, she was taking Mad Dog through the clamor of neon lights signboards coolies pimps taxis rickshaws sailors down to her quiet causeway out to the Yacht Club, and Mad Dog galloping and taking off for his swim while she sat in the dark and smoked her Red Victory and please God longed for me. I longed for her, warm soft smooth in the big deep warm bed beside me, waking up, her black hair down to her shoulders, her warm smooth naked golden back: *Oh look at that mountain!* And the crunch crunch crunch our boots in the snow going down to the Sonne Gasthof, wooden tables and fresh rolls butter strawberry jam coffee for breakfast, oh God the mornings are a bad time to be without your woman. And oh whooping down the flying mountain trails together, the cold sting on your face and the whipping speed, she would be a natural, her black hair flying and her golden nose red from the good bright cold and her wide mouth laughing and the snow in her hair, oh God she would love it. And tramping back to the *Pension* in the late afternoon, good and tired and hungry and thirsty and happy, and getting into the hot deep bath together, the slippery shine of the water on her and the feel of her, and her happy face, and afterward going back to the Sonne or the Stetnerhof, warm and clean, crowded cheery wooden tables and the good gut-glow of the beer and *Glühwein* and the music and the dancing, oh God I wished she were here. I wrote, *Next winter we must go to Japan together to ski. And oh we're going to make so much love. . . .*

I did not write to her about the other matter. I had not told her the whole truth, I did not want her to worry about it until we had to. I had only told her that my meeting with Catherine had been very bad, that I had failed to persuade her, but that I was certain she would capitulate when she was convinced that I was determined to return to Hong Kong without her. While I still had to go back to England for the course she would stick to her guns, but not when I left. Maybe I did believe that. But I did not tell her that, at the end of that bad week in London, after we had been through all the motions from the first confused nervous emotional meeting and Suzie running into my arms shouting *Daddy-Daddy-Daddy* because she had been told her daddy was coming today, not because she really remembered me, and the sweet tearful agony of my child in my arms, and then afterward she began to lose interest in me, just another adult —from that first confused meeting and the astonished strange-familiar feel of Catherine as we embraced nervously and then tried to talk about anything except divorce; down to the seventh meeting when we reached the bottom of the barrel of a relationship, right down to the bitter fight and hate and stormings and she shouted *Never never never!*—no, I did not write and tell her all that. I did not tell Ying that I had been to see Catherine's psychiatrist, what he had said, nor the bitter things her mother, who used to be like my mother to me, had said, nor had I told her much about Suzie, what it feels like to see your child and she is not a baby any more but nearly seven years old and she's got a new life now and doesn't know you any more and doesn't feel and understand what you are feeling and what is even worse your wife crying at you *I'll never let you see her again except over my dead body!* Oh God no I did not want to write and tell her about that now. Now, I had made my decisions hard and clear, and most times I did believe that

Catherine would capitulate, and by Christ if she did not I would do what I had to do. I had made my decision.

In this same *Pension* lived three final-year German medical students from Innsbruck University, down in the valley, and they were living as if it was their final year on this earth. They had the joint figured out. They knew all the barmaids, ski instructors, and ski-lift ticket collectors, they paid for very little. In the mornings it was my job to wake up the one whose turn it was to go down to the university for the lectures and to forge the others' names on the attendance register. They were very tired after their hard day; it is not easy to enjoy yourself so hard, do not think it is not hard work. I met a lot of strange girls, waking up the boys. Then I wrote to Ying, then I went down to the Sonne in my ski gear for breakfast. Sometimes I bought the Tyrol *Tagezeitung*, the local newspaper, for the hell of it to improve my German. There was never anything about Hong Kong or China in it and I was glad about that. I did not want to know about international politics and particularly about what the communists were up to. I did not think of Ying-ling as a communist any more, ten thousand miles away from the nearest Hong Kong policeman, I only thought of her as my beautiful long-legged golden-skinned Chinese girl, the feel of her hips when I kissed her there and her laughing eyes and the golden sheen of her as she dove down like a seal and the taste of the seawater on her breasts, oh no I did not think of her as a communist. I did not want to think of anything except her.

After breakfast I went up the mountains. I skied as long and hard as I could. Every time I saw something beautiful I thought oh Christ, I must tell Ying about this; and it got me right here, that happy conviction that you loved your woman and to hell with everybody and everything. At lunchtime I rendezvoused with Klaus and Oetz and Michel, the medical students, and we got along with beer and the *Glühwein* until Oetz felt strong enough to venture out into the mountains, for Oetz was very afraid of heights. If Oetz had had his way we would have stuck around in the café with the beer and *Glühwein* and got ourselves a flock of fräuleins and then ridden back down the mountains with them in the cable car, none of this suicidal foolishness of skis on these highly dangerous mountains, if God had intended this He would have given us wings, the natural position for *Homo sapiens*

337

was horizontal with a fräulein *Homo sapiens* underneath him. Oetz's main trouble with skiing was that he could not stop. Because he could not stop he found himself going very fast. The only way he could stop reliably was to plough into a tree. Oetz was a great admirer of the great indoors.

In the late afternoon I came down, tired and healthy, and I went to the Sporthotel and I sat by myself and drank beer and finished the day's letter to Ying. *Hello, my lover*—they were love letters; I did not talk of decisions, promotions, China. She wrote me love letters; she told me the color of the sky in the dawn over the east during her rooftop exercises, the reds and the golds and the mauves and the fading glimmer of the stars and the first rays of sun on the Mountains of Nine Dragons and the color of the sails of a Chinese junk full-spread and the golden-silver vermilion of the China Sea and the bright early morning haze and the ships twinkling in the dawn and the clusters of golden-brown junks and the smell of her flowers: *Oh my darling, the mornings are the best time for beauty, and the worst time for lovers to be apart.* She also wrote:

The hullabaloo about the Star Ferry fare increase is still continuing. Now there are many petitions, signed by thousands of people. I agree. The Ferry Company has made good profits for many years and now they say that because of increase in costs we must pay 25 per cent more. But they should be satisfied. The rise in cost of living is bad. Everywhere prices go up. The newspapers say it is a "price spiral" and business is bad. Many flats are empty but the mountainsides are full of the poor people living in shacks and cock-lofts. I agree with you that the colonial government is doing good work with resettlement estates, but it is still true that it is a rich government and it receives a nice royalty from the ferry company for the use of the piers and harbor and now Government and Star Ferry Company must share the extra cost, and leave the poor people alone. That is how it would be in China. If the ferry fares go up then the two bus companies and the tram company will ask for more. Then the electricity company, then the gas company, then the telephone company, and how could Government refuse? Then the factories must put up their prices also, because of the increases and then the shops also. Inflation. Recently water charges and school fees went up. It is a very serious matter to poor people. How can a poor family afford several tens of dollars every month extra? All because a few fat shareholders of Star Ferry are worried because this year they will make less profit. The newspapers are very angry too. I am enclosing some cuttings, my capitalist superintendent. Are you one of the fat shareholders also?

A storm in a bloody teacup. I was a shareholder of the Star Ferry and I did not care a stuff whether they got their fare increase or not. What made me mad was that it was another storm in a teacup like the bloody bank-run crisis, which would blow up into a real storm. Chinese panic about money. It was clear from the cuttings that there was wide misunderstanding about the whole thing, rendered more confounded by press sensationalism. The hard fact was that the Star Ferry Company's overheads had gone up 23 per cent. This left them unviable. How could the company be expected to operate at no profit? It was not a philanthropic organization. The fare increase asked was 25 per cent, but this was only five Hong Kong cents, less than one American cent. The bloody newspapers. The hard fact of Hong Kong's raison d'être and survival is efficient business and Government could not subsidize the uneconomic or inefficient, with fifty thousand illegal immigrants a year from China and not even enough water to drink, for Godsake. Life must go on. The bloody press was largely to blame again. And poor bloody Government getting the blame, and, indirectly, the police, I wrote back to her. Who would bear the brunt of the trouble? The poor bloody police. It didn't take much imagination to see it: Some half-arsed demonstration, a crowd gathers, causing an obstruction, some poor constable has to ask them to move on, nil result, in he has to go to arrest the demonstrator. Who resists. Crowd gets hostile. Police reinforcements have to come. Then anything could happen. In Hong Kong's crowded streets, anything. And all for an increase in first-class (*not* second-class) fares of less than one American cent, for Godsake. This is going to cause "roaring inflation" and "price spirals"? I wrote all that to her, but it was all academic, sitting here in the Sporthotel drinking

339

beer, she was all I wanted to think about. After I had finished the letter, I went down to the Sonne to drink with Klaus and Oetz and the boys.

But ten thousand miles away that day a young man called Chu took up a position outside the Star Ferry concourse. He was on a hunger strike. On his jacket was painted, *Join Hunger Strike to Block Fare Increase! Democratic! Oppose Gambling!* In minutes a big crowd gathered and the press came.

The next day, young Mr. Chu resumed his hunger strike, there was a bigger crowd, and a lot of reporters, and some youthful supporters took up picket positions on the Kowloon side of the ferry.

That afternoon, Mr. Chu was told by the police to move on, because the crowd he attracted was causing an obstruction. He refused. He had to be arrested. He refused to accept bail. His youthful supporters marched on Government House, thence to the Legislative Council. That night twenty of young Mr. Chu's supporters staged a demonstration march from the Star Ferry.

They marched up Nathan Road and back shouting, *"We object to the increase!"* Now there were three hundred youths marching, for the hell of it. They were having a good time. They marched back all the way up to Mongkok and now they were four hundred strong, marching against the traffic, squatting in the road, shouting protests and laughing and having a good time posing for the newspaper photographers and obstructing traffic.

At 1 A.M. the Old Man's second-in-command was called out. He told them not to cause obstruction and to behave sensibly. The march resumed back to the Star Ferry, obstructing all the way. At 4 A.M. the Old Man's number two had had enough. He told them to cut the nonsense and to go home to bed. They refused. He approached the ringleaders single-handed and said, "Now be good boys." Somebody struck him in the back. His men moved to arrest the assailant. Who strenuously resisted. It did not take much imagination to see it coming, even sitting ten thousand miles away in the Austrian Alps writing love letters. There was a communication gap between Government and the people, as usual, and the next night it was through that gap the rioters marched.

For two nights they rioted. There were no more placards saying, *Down with Fare Increase,* no organization, no purpose, just thousands of youths rioting for the hell of it, indiscriminate malicious damage to property, attacking buses, burning cars, shops, hotels, post offices, fire stations, waterworks, parking meters, traffic signs, looting, arson, smashing, gasoline bombs, anything except Star Ferry property. And every policeman mobilized in paramilitary riot-suppression engagements. And the Army. And sticks and stones and bricks and bottles and flowerpots raining down on the police, and cordons and barricades and tear gas and baton charges and, finally, firearms. Up and down Nathan Road and round about and in and out the rabbit warrens of side streets and tenements and stairways, fires and barricades and arson and looting and smash smash smash. For two nights, before the police got them back under control.

And the Golden Mile of Nathan Road in ruins, smoke, broken glass, burned-out cars, looted shops, debris. Nine hundred people arrested. Millions of dollars' damage. And all for five cents on the first-class fares, less than one American cent, less than half one English penny. The newspapers made a lot of money reporting it and they were the first to be shocked and shout *Why?*

That was the beginning of the summer of that year.

That month in Peking there was a meeting of the Standing Committee of National People's Congress, to formally launch a new rectification campaign. Chairman Mao himself was present and the Defense Minister defined its aims as

eradicating bourgeois ideology and establishing proletarian ideology, remolding people's souls, realizing people's ideological revolutionization, digging out the roots of revisionism and consolidating the socialist system! We will crush the authorities in power who take the road to capitalism, the reactionary bourgeois authorities in power and all bourgeois royalists! We will oppose all actions to suppress Revolution and strike down all freaks and monsters! We will vigorously destroy all the old ideas, old culture, old customs, and old habits of the exploiting classes and transform all those parts of the superstructure that do not correspond to the Socialist economic base!

And they called it the Great Proletarian Cultural Revolution.

CHAPTER 52

The academy library had a small fictional section but they were all historical and political novels of educational value for police officers in the cloak-and-dagger business. Even my book was there. If you were going to do any bedside reading, the authorities hoped you wouldn't waste your time. "A police force is a dedicated body of chosen men," the commandant had opened his welcoming speech on the first day, "and you, gentlemen, from several parts of the Commonwealth, are the very carefully chosen few of the already carefully chosen." To us would be revealed the machinations of the most complex and powerful intelligence systems presently operative in this complex dog-eat-dog world. Et cetera, et cetera. If there be any reason why we should not be joined together speak now or forever hold your gun at the ready and your cyanide capsule handy. Officers would please make full use of all facilities, particularly the laboratory and the excellent library which between them contained everything a dedicated, sophisticated intelligence officer needed to use and know in this vale of tears; and it was hoped that we all would, to enable us to tackle our tasks with the success that had hallmarked our careers to date, find it in our hearts to be back in the precincts by midnight; breakfast at seven-thirty. And Christian names only, please. And that was the end of the bullshit. Thereafter it was just solid no-nonsense work. And the library was indeed almost everything a sophisticated police officer needed. There was information in there to make governments tremble. Governments come and go but policemen do not. Politics in there to make your blood run cold.

Next door to the library was the common room, which had big leather chairs, and on the walls were photographs of past classes. There were twelve in our class. I recognized a few Hong Kong faces in the old photographs. Chester Wu was one, the superintendent who spied for China, whom I had arrested at Takwul'ng that night years ago. Next door was the dining room, one long table, the commandant at the head. You were expected to dine most nights and had to give notice if you were not going to. Friday night was informal, you could go away for the weekend.

There was wine at dinner and afterward a not very good port. The commandant was a widower and he was lonely. The Old Man had written to him, telling him I was coming. Damn nice to have me, old chap. He remembered my father, from the Shanghai days. We adjourned through to the common room and sat in the deep leather armchairs and had another drink.

By God, he said, those were some days, Shanghai. Anybody could get anybody bumped off for fifty dollars, half down, the other half when there was a body. The wickedest city in the world. Damn good thing really that the communists came and cleaned it up—*we* couldn't. We all deserved what we got in Shanghai, in the whole of China, he said. At least old Mao Tse-tung put an end to the wholesome crookery, as a policeman you had to admire him for that. We thought he was going to take Hong Kong as well.

What did I make of the recent Kowloon riots, he said.

We had another drink, I told him what I made of it. Did I think there was an underlying political cause? I thought of Ying-ling's long earnest letter in which she had striven to convince me that the communists were *not* to blame. I said No, because most of the rioters were youths, it was confined to the precincts of Nathan Road, and the damage was indiscriminate, not only against government property. I thought of Ying's letter again: "Laissez-faire has failed to solve the many increasingly complex social problems. Especially there is purposelessness and frustration among the youth, a lack of belonging and community spirit, which is so strong in Mao's China." I said, There is a problem of too many people, ever since the "Liberation." Being a purely capitalist refuge there is a lack of community spirit, everybody looks out only for himself. And half those people are under twenty years old. They are only thinking of themselves in the tough Hong Kong rat race. There is a big difference between what they want and what they're likely to get. Unlike their parents, they do not view Hong Kong simply as a refuge or staging post before going on to better things. But there is no other place for them to go. Nobody wants them. And the future of Hong Kong is limited.

Anything could happen. And then there is a problem of housing and recreational space. Children playing in the streets, slum conditions, et cetera. So, join a demonstration for the hell of it.

"So what's the answer?" the commandant said.

I said, "Hong Kong is Hong Kong. It's only this big and it's got no natural resources. Nothing but cutthroat business to rely on. All you can do is the obvious. Keep working on Government's resettlement housing. Provide more recreational space. Youth centers and services and community centers. But Government can't do it all. Industry must help and provide their workers and the Community Chest with facilities. You've got to develop community spirit. Somehow."

"With Chinese?" the commandant said. "Don't they keep their houses clean but throw their rubbish outside their doors?"

I said, "The communists did it with their street communes. We've *got* to do it. The riots show that. Committees for organizing cleanliness and orderly living in the resettlement estates, for a start. Community pride. Give them a recreational center, a basketball team and a football team, something to be enthusiastic about. Encourage Boy Scouts and Girl Guides, send the Marine Police in to start a Sea Scouts Brigade. And smiling policemen to organize a Youth Auxiliary Police Brigade. Build a club on top of every resettlement block where kids can play Ping-Pong and dance to pop music and watch TV," I said, "Laissez-faire is fine, but fifty per cent of our youth are teen-agers, and they are not established in the economic structure, they're absolute beginners. And what background have they got to fortify them for the rat race?"

The old boy nodded, interested, encouraging. "What else?"

I thought of Ying again.

"Education. Number one: There is not enough. The Hong Kong Government is skinflint and has only itself to blame that the communists cash in and provide good cheap communist education. Even so, there are not enough secondary-school places, the examination system is too rigid. Primary school ends at twelve but so-called enlightened Whitehall legislation stipulates that they cannot work until sixteen. Result: a puberty loafer problem. Number two: The education is British middle class, to turn out white-collar workers. The Hong Kong Chinese are bourgeois in the extreme, they *all* want to be white-collar workers. But Hong Kong is a cutthroat industrial dog-eat-dog community, there are not nearly enough white-collar jobs for them. And they know it. So you turn out a yearly crop of bespectacled school swots and potential desperadoes. So we need more *technical* schools. And vocational guidance centers—stick those in your community centers also."

"And what is Hong Kong's future?" he said.

The question bored me, you hear it at every cocktail party. I said, "Two factors. First, Hong Kong will exist as long as it is useful to China for economic and espionage purposes. To the extent that this depends on China's economy, the period is more or less predictable by economists—fifteen, twenty years. The second factor is entirely unpredictable, for it depends on China's emotional condition. A capitalistic colony on the sacred soil of Red China is loss of face. An ideological anomaly. And it only needs some small border incident, say, or some internal squabble or power struggle or a bit of rabble-rousing in Peking, and Hong Kong could be snatched back tomorrow."

"And," the commandant said. "And what about this Great Proletarian Cultural Revolution?"

The Great Proletarian Cultural Revolution. There was plenty to think about. It was perfectly intelligible, if breathtaking, in theory; the trouble was the facts. In theory it was a power struggle by Mao, for himself and his ideals, to remake man: to purge the party from top to bottom of the black poisonous bourgeois revisionist elements, the capitalist-roaders, the Khrushchevites, the scabs, which meant any person who advocated pragmatism, conservatism, rapprochement with the Russians, a united socialist front, economic consolidation, a better standard of living; it was a purge of the party and people from top to bottom by unleashing the spirit of Revolution all over again, the spirit of the struggles of the Chinkiang Mountains and the Great Rectification of the Yenan caves and the San Fan and the Wu Fan and the Anti-Rightist Campaign and the Four Clean-Ups, Smell them out, Point them out, Throw them out with the Mass-Line Technique: and bring the Spirit of Revolution to the Youth, purge them of the poisonous incipient revisionism, make them worthy successors of the Revolution,

make them aware, *make* them make their own Revolution
to tear down the Old Order to build the New Man.

Ying-ling wrote:

Isn't it magnificent? It makes me so proud to be
Chinese! That we can have such ideals and have such
fantastic courage to implement them, to institute a
Revolution against ourselves, a civil war of ideology,
to keep ourselves pure. What a wonderful man Mao
is! What other leader in history has had such ideals
to remake Man, Society, on such wonderful just lines?
What other leader has ever said "Bombard the Headquarters" in order to eradicate revisionism and
stuffiness and high-handedness from the party administration, to keep the party true servants of the People?
—not even your Jesus Christ has done it in thousands
of years! It makes me so proud!

Those were the principles. The facts were chaos.

Chaos and convulsion. The schools and universities
were officially closed for a year, the young Red Guards
had taken over. Many newspaper editors and most of
the top teaching staff of most of the universities had been
sacked, struggled out, hounded out, chased out, professors and teachers hounded through the streets, dunce
caps on their heads, painted black, accused, criticized,
beaten, classrooms smashed up, books burned, walls plastered in the *daizibao* the Big Character posters, there
were seas of posters all over the street walls accusing,
condemning, criticizing, announcing great victories, and
all the time the roar of the shouting beating smashing.
And now Chairman Mao himself had put up his own Big
Character poster reading "Bombard the Headquarters" and
now he issued a sixteen-point directive calling on 750 million people to transform China into a "great revolutionary
school." And now he had held a mass rally of one million
youthful Red Guards in Tien An Man Square in Peking
and praised them for their revolutionary spirit "to act, to
make revolution, to rise up" and the Red Guards swarmed
exultantly out over the cities and towns attacking smashing the Four Olds, old ideas, old culture, old customs,
old habits, and anything foreign, tore down the non-
Revolutionary street signs and shop names, tore the
decadent Western clothes off people's backs and beat
them and hounded them through the streets. Break into

the shops selling non-Revolutionary literature and throw out the books and tear them up and burn them and stuff the shelves with the works of Mao Tse-tung,

Mao Tse-tung!
Mao Tse-tung!

And break into the houses of the people accused suspected named hinted at as being bourgeois poisonous weeds and smash up their furniture and smash the windows and tear out the plumbing and slap dunce caps on their heads and encircle them and shout at them and beat them to confess, *confess!* CONFESS! and paint them black and beat them shouting screaming through the streets, and break into the museums and art galleries and smash up the decadent priceless objets d'art and smash and tear down the paintings and jump on them and tear them up and paint them over and slap up the Big Character posters of the Thoughts of Mao Tse-tung, seas of Big Character posters screaming yelling roaring denouncing announcing, break into the convents and beat up the decadent Christian nuns and paint them black and slap dunce caps on their heads and denounce them chase them defile them and tear up their Bibles and smash their rosaries and smash up their churches and smother them in the Big Character posters of the Thoughts of Mao Tse-tung,

Mao Tse-tung!
Mao Tse-tung!

And smash up the foreign cemeteries and dance on the graves and swarm and attack and besiege the Communist party headquarters smashing yelling screaming that those party officials and those and those are also Black Bourgeois Capitalist-Roaders Poisonous Weeds Black Gang Non-Revolutionaries, smash down the doors and rampage through the party offices and drive the poisonous weeds capitalist-roaders out into the streets and slap dunce caps on their heads and encircle them and shout shout shout and denounce and dance and spit and beat and kick and seize control of the party headquarters in the name of Mao Tse-tung,

Mao Tse-tung!

347

And besiege the Municipal Offices and hound out the mayor and the councilors who are Poisonous Black Bourgeois Revisionists and beat them accuse them revile them and throw them out of office, and besiege the police stations and the Sanitary Works and the Public Health and the Port Authorities and the railways, buses, tramways, and all the civil service offices in the name of Mao Tse-tung. And now the Red Guards were meeting resistance, the comrade party offices and cadres who refused to have this juvenile nonsense, and now there emerged the Scarlet Brigades to fight the Red Guards, and there were pitched battles, running battles in the streets a thousand strong a side, sticks stones iron bars knives blood deaths, and all the time roaring shouting smashing running accusing denouncing, and the blood. And now the Red Guards from the countryside came swarming into Peking to exchange revolutionary experiences, the railways commandeered by Red Guards from all over the bloody place, and there were more mass rallies, Red Guards roaring camping scavenging fighting everywhere, and Chairman Mao told them they were a great grand "Reserve Force for the People's Liberation Army" and they must bombard the headquarters harder and expose the Party Persons Taking the Capitalist Road and hound them out out: Chairman Mao also said the Red Guards must not interfere with the peasants and workers, the peasants and workers were quite capable of making their own Revolution: and the Red Guards must please all go home by November 20. And the Red Guards roared their adulation for Chairman Mao and the Revolution and they swarmed out over the towns and cities rampaging bombarding the headquarters, and all the time the roaring shouting beating denouncing accusing and the seas of posters screaming, and the blood. I said to the commandant, "It'll probably succeed."

The commandant stared at me. "How can it succeed, for God's sake! A shambles like that!"

I said, "It's working already, sir. Mao wants to get rid of President Liu and all the conservative elements he represents. He also wants to shake up the party generally and get seven hundred million people back onto the straight and narrow communist path before he dies. And he wants the youth to realize they're the heirs to a communist society. Like Hitler said, 'Give me the youth.' There're three hundred million young Chinese born since the Liberation who have no firsthand memory of the Bad Old Days or the Revolution. So Mao's using his Mass-Line Technique that he's always used successfully before. He forms the young Red Guards, like the Boy Scouts, with himself as Commander in Chief, arms them with his almighty authority and he tells them to Bombard the Headquarters and they get stuck in and do the dirty work for him—*far* more effectively and unearth far more suspects than his police force or a decorous legal procedure could do. And it's better than shooting them, like the Russians do. And, from Mao's point of view, so what if a few million innocent ones get beaten up? He's running seven *hund*red million people, for Chrissake."

"But what about the economy all dislocated?" the commandant said a little irritably. "Just when things were coming right after the disaster of Great Leap Forward."

I said, "Ideology-in-Command, sir. That's always been Mao's motto. That's the only way to achieve a true communist state—by remaking man. When you've remade him into the true unselfish Socialist Man he will work hard and build a perfect economy anyway."

He nodded at me quietly, like a judge who understands but disagrees with you. I didn't care. I went on, "It's all part of the Marxist law of contradictions anyway. Everything contains two opposites. For every step forward along the road to socialism there will be a conservative reaction, people who will say, Thus far and no farther.' Therefore to consolidate your one step forward you've got to stop and tear down the opposition and if that entails taking half a step backward, too bad. That's been his policy all his life. And look where China is today. From the mess it was twenty years ago."

The commandant nodded.

I went on, "And I think the Cultural Revolution will work seventy-five per cent. You'll have every comrade-official frantically sitting up straight applying the Thought of Mao Tse-tung and being very holier-than-thou about his duties, and every factory manager and accountant and technician and worker frantically confessing and purging himself of all his wicked capitalist tendencies and in the end when the dust is all settled Mao and the Thoughts of Mao Tse-tung will be sitting on top of seven hundred million people all over again. And they won't step out of line again in a hurry."

"And when they do?" the communist said.

"Another Cultural Revolution," I said.

"And the economy in ruins again," the commander said.

"Maybe," I said. "But they'll be one quarter of mankind so on-the-ball and ideologically zealous that the rest of us better watch out. They'll be capable of overrunning us and our economics like machines. Europe, America, Russia. They'll overrun Asia in five minutes."

The commandant nodded, nod nod.

"So what's the answer?"

I knew he was testing me. Suddenly I was sick of the subject. I said, "The only answer is to combat it by giving the poor underdeveloped countries an alternative to the philosophy of communism. By making them economically strong and nationalistically strong and proud. And you *don't* succeed in doing that," I said, "by handing primitive people their independence and giving the political power to half a dozen local political upstarts who're going to abuse their power to their own aggrandizement and personal enrichment at the expense of the people, like the British have mostly done. That is just the situation the communists love to walk into and take over. And you don't do it," I said, "the American way."

"And that is?" the commandant said.

I said, "The big good ole Yoo Ess Ay way, graddammit! Free enterprise and the get-rich-quick economic philosophy work fine in Boise, Idaho, and Washington, D.C., where they've got a twentieth-century civilization of sorts and a fundamental respect for the Constitution and democracy and habeas corpus and the rights of man, and even a basic acquaintance with law and order, but that economic philosophy isn't worth a damn with primitive people whose whole life has been one of feudal despotism and warlords and extortion. But what does the good buddy-boy ole Yoo Ess Ay do? It tries to promote American-style politics which are Christ-awful crooked anyway even in America among a bunch of local bandits and warlords, then supports them with all kinds of gum-chewing American aid, fights their Christ-awful crooked power struggles for them and in the meantime imports their All-American Boy Free Enterprise in the form of American investment in local industries. Which sets up all kinds of factories, exploits the local cheap native labor for a pittance and sends the profits home to Wall Street." I was enjoying myself now. "That's what the communists

350

mean by 'imperialism.' International capitalism. The profit of the development of this new country doesn't go back into the country: it goes into the pockets of American shareholders and a few local wide-boys. And the ordinary people remain the same, worse off even. And then the Americans look all hurt and wonder why communism takes hold. And pour in more aid and soldiers into supporting this setup. They did it in China. Cuba. And now they're doing it in Vietnam. Christ, it's elementary why they fail. But"—I wagged my head—"the good ole Yoo Ess Ay will keep right on doing it because, yes, *sir,* this is democracy, donchaknow."

The commandant nodded, noncommittally.

"The goddamn Yanks have bitten off more than they can chew in Vietnam," I said. "And it serves them right. The stupid arrogance of the nouveau riche."

The commandant smiled. I said cheerfully, enjoying the sound of my own voice, "Capitalism hasn't worked very well in underdeveloped countries, has it? We capitalists haven't been very sensible, have we? We haven't given capitalism a reasonable chance, have we, to put its best foot forward so as to provide the natives with a decent alternative to communism? We've just hit them over the head with capitalism. We've set a rotten example of the political and economic creed we believe in. Since giving them their independence they have suffered nothing but corrupt inefficient governments and exploitation by international capitalism. Supplying us with cheap raw materials and cheap labor. Instead of building them up into strong capitalist systems with a strong middle class who will provide a strong sensible government and political philosophy to oppose communism. We just fucked it up." The commandant blinked. "Like we did in China before the Revolution."

The commandant blinked again. Then said, "So what's going to happen?"

I said, "God alone knows. But one way or another we've let those countries become what Mao calls "the exploited countrysides of the world which must take the Road to the Chingkiang Mountains." And he says that international capitalism will never give up its exploitations until it is militarily beaten. And he's made China into the shining virtuous beacon of world revolution, the 'strong Red base' for the exploited countries to turn to. He says he has taken up the burden of leadership in world justice. Therefore China must remain pure. Therefore there must be the Cultural Revolution. And in *that* massive context, temporary economic setbacks," I said, "and a bit of chaos from time to time are the mere 'buzzing of flies,' as Mao says."

The commandant asked me if I wanted another drink.

"My turn, sir," I said. I called the steward.

"And Hong Kong?" the commandant said. "Where does it stand in this Cultural Revolution?"

"In fear and trembling," I said. "When China breathes, Hong Kong trembles."

CHAPTER 53

On the South China Sea there was a heat haze and on the Hong Kong Peak there was the thick warm mist, so cars drove with their headlights on at noon up there, and the mist came rolling in the gracious apartment windows. That Saturday the Royal Hong Kong Observatory forecast a cloudy night with occasional showers. That night the killer rains came.

With thunder and lightning like cannon, came teeming straight down thick as your fingers out of the blackness and you could not see any lights; came crashing down off the steep jungle mountains in waterfalls, tons of rain rocks trees crashing rushing down the steep roads footpaths ladder streets, came crashing on the concrete jungles and through the basements and parking lots in great torrents tearing at the foundations, rocks and trees mighty tons of water crashing on and on down the steep mountains. And burst the nullahs and tore up the drains and tore great cracks and chunks out the roads and tore away embankments and smashed the cars and swept them crashing skidding rolling down. The big black killer rains came rushing roaring down through the squatter shacks and tore them away crashing smashing splintering tumbling killing down the mountains through each other, bloody muddy screaming men and women children babies cats dogs chickens screaming yelping shouting smothering down the mountains in the black roar of the rain rocks

352

trees mud timber. And roads gave way in great chunks and crash of tar went crashing down the mountains, and in the great bad mad blackness great chunks of jungled mountains gave way, crashing whooshing sliding killing down onto the roads and down through the squatter huts and crashed through the basements of the apartment blocks and flattened cars and smashed down embankments, and with the landslides came the boulders. Great boulders big as cars rolling bouncing crashing down the mountains and through the squatter huts and down the roads, smashed the Peak tram down the mountain and tore up the tracks, the big black killer rains and rocks and mud came crashing down into Staunton Creek and tore two thousand junks off their moorings and swept them splintering floundering out, and tore away the paddies and the vegetable gardens and the fish farms of the New Territories and tore away the Kowloon-Canton Railway and flooded out the Golden Mile of Nathan Road, and tore down off the Peak crashing flooding down into Taipan Central and tore up the roads and tramlines, rocks and mud and trees and water rushing through the bars and shops and down the basements, dogs cats chickens garbage lumber cars. And in the big black crashing madness there were fires, and the screams of the fire engines and ambulances trying to find a way.

That Saturday night Mr. Ng and Miss Lo went to the Great Ruby Cinema and saw *Taking Tiger Mountain by Strategy,* made by the Peking Taking Tiger Mountain by Strategy Opera Company. Next year Mr. Ng and Miss Lo were going to be married, when Mr. Ng had saved enough money. It takes a lot of money for a young Chinese couple to marry because the bridal bed must be grand and new, all the furniture new, and the wedding dinner must make a lot of face. Mr. Ng had also bought a brand-new Datsun car. When they came out of the cinema at eleven-thirty it was raining tremendously. The roads were under sir inches of dirty swirling water.

Miss Lo lived with her parents. Mr. Ng parked in the next street, called Wing-On Street. Wing-On Street is a very steep cul-de-sac. High up above it is a reservoir, built into a gorge in the mountain. There were fourteen other cars parked in Wing-On Street. It was raining too hard to think of getting out of the car and Mr. Ng and Miss Lo did not mind. Miss Lo was a virgin, and had every intention of staying that way until the big bridal night, the morning after which Mr. Ng would have to produce a white bloodstained silk handkerchief to his family to prove it. But they were young and in love and it was very exciting to have the excuse of being trapped in the car by the rain. At one o'clock the reservoir flooded over.

The flood cascaded over the reservoir and tore down the long narrow gorge taking boulders and trees with it, and crashed down on the cars and over them and under them and carried them crashing rolling down, two four six eight ten cars in the smashing frothing leaping wave down Wing-On Street.

Mr. Ng and Miss Lo were kissing. They did not know anything until Mr. Ng's new car jolted, they jolted upright with a cry and the wave crashed over their windshield and the next cars' undercarriage hit them with a deafening crash. Crashed their car upward sideways in a cacophony of water and metal, Miss Lo and Mr. Ng were flung backward shocked screaming clutching uncomprehending and the cars smashed on top of them and the water all about them, crashing down the steep road, and the Datsun crumpled. Crumpled skewering under ten cars down the steep road, they were screaming on their backs under the crashing tons of cars and water, and then the doors buckled and the black water crashed in. On all sides, black roaring swirling spewing gasping strangling, Mr. Ng screamed and twisted and thrashed, his face was just clear of the water, he screamed and grabbed out for Miss Lo and grabbed her hair and yanked her head upward and he felt her retch, he screamed at her but he could not even hear himself. Then the car crashed over again onto its wheels.

It crashed to a stop at the bottom of Wing-On Street jammed under a dozen cars. Miss Lo was jammed on her back, head hanging down. The water was over her ears now, she was kicking bucking screaming but Mr. Ng could not hear her above the roar of the water crashing in, he twisted sideways screaming and kicked at the door thrashing screaming but the door jammed fast, the roaring water was up to his chin now and it was pitch black. Miss Lo screamed and tried to buck her head up out of the water, she smashed her face against the crumpled roof and screamed and the water ran in her mouth and her scream was a strangled gargle. She twisted and thrashed and kicked and crashed and smashed her bloody face up white-eyed, then she crashed back and her head went right under and she took her first strangled scream of water and she contorted. The water rushed in her ears and nose and sucked down into her chest in her scream, she contorted and kicked and thrashed wildly once, then her hair washed about her glazed eyes and her throat just opened and contracted.

Mr. Ng had thrashed over onto his hands and knees, head twisted up against the crumpled roof to gasp the last air, the water was up over his back now, the side of his face underwater, screaming for help in the rushing gurgling blackness, but his scream was nothing against the roaring of the water. The car was almost filled up now. Mr. Ng thrashed gasping screaming and thrust his mouth up sideways into the pocket of air and scrambled his legs and screamed and gasped and thrust, the pocket got smaller and Mr. Ng bashed his face into it hysterically screaming and his face was covered in blood now, then he sucked in half a mouthful, water up his nostrils and gargling in his throat. Mr. Ng screamed his terror and spewed it out and thrashed his bloody face upward sideways again in the blackness, and he sucked in water again, he retched and coughed in terror and gasped and he sucked in more and contorted to turn on his back to thrust his whole face upward, and he sucked in water. He kicked and thrashed but his head hit the hood and he sucked in water again, and he sank back. And the killer rain roared down.

Roared down the steep mountain gorges, in a hundred places the mud and boulders and the jungled mountain went crashing sliding smashing down. The massive avalanche of mud and rocks hit Stobbs Road with a sudden roar and the huge concrete building shook down to its sodden foundations and the sodden earth gave way and went crashing sliding down and the huge apartment block stood naked gaping on its pylons and Stobbs Road cracked and gave way with a massive crash, and avalanched down in the black crashing madness onto the apartment blocks below in a tidal wave of mud and concrete and cars, and the mud poured in. Poured in through the smashed doors and windows and the amah's room of Mr. Chan's ground-floor apartment down onto the amah's head as she lay in her bed under the window, and buried her alive.

355

Poured in through the smashed bedroom windows of Mr. and Mrs. Chan, he woke up to his wife screaming and snapped on the bedside light and all he saw was orange mud pouring in the smashed windows.

"Get out!" Mr. Chan screamed.

He leaped out of bed into the mud and dragged his wife screaming sloshing after him to the door and he wrenched on it and it would not open against the mud in the room. *"Dig mud!"* he screamed and frantically clawed at the mud beside the door and he wrenched the door open and mud three feet high flooded into the room from the passage. Up to their knees in mud and Mrs. Chan screaming, the window was full up with mud pouring in, *"Get out of house,"* Mr. Chan screamed and dragged her screaming by the wrist through the mud, heaved her wrenched her plodding shouting down the passage, he flung open the sitting room door and the mud flooded in with them, he dragged Mrs. Chan to the front door and flung it open. The mud was only one foot deep in the covered concrete drive, but it was coming higher around the corner of the building in the beating rain. There was shouting all over the building in the rain, the elevator was jammed between floors and the alarm bell was ringing, Mrs. Chan was screaming. Mr. Chan grabbed his car keys and stumbled his wife through the mud, he did not know where he was going except he had to get away from this dreadful place, he wrenched his screaming wife down the concrete steps down to the parking lot, bundled her into the car, just screaming hysterically, covered in mud.

Mr. Chan did not know where he was going. He swung the car wildly down out into Kennedy Road, the windshield wipers sloshing, the rain hammering down. The road was running one foot deep in water rocks branches mud rushing water cascading down off the cuttings in thick waterfalls, the rain beat thick opaque silver in his headlights. He could not see any lights of the city below. The flood beat from his wheels up over his windshield, he swung wildly around a boulder the size of an armchair and Mrs. Chan was still just screaming and then there was a crack and a crash like thunder and the road shook, Mr. Chan slammed on his brakes and his wife crashed against the windshield screaming, and the road in front of the car disappeared. Disappeared in one great crash thirty yards wide, went crashing down the steep blackness, and down behind came tons of mud and rocks and trees and concrete flying. Mr. Chan stared uncomprehending terrified and Mrs. Chan was sprawled across the seat screaming hysterically, blood streaming through the mud on her face. Mr. Chan regained his frantic wits, he rammed the car into reverse, then the landslide hit him.

Crashed down off the mountain in a great flash of orange silver and rocks and jungle in his headlights, onto his hood, Mr. Chan screamed and roared the engine and his wheels spun in reverse, then the rest of the landslide hit him. Came crashing down off the mountain with a crack of cannon onto his car, for a split second Mr. Chan heard the crash and felt it, then the car crashed in on top of him. When the landslide stopped you could not see the flattened car.

And the water tore down off the mountain water falling onto the landslide, and the killer rain beat down.

Ying-ling pulled on her shoes and grabbed her flashlight and umbrella and ran up the steps to the rooftop in her pajamas and dashed out splashing into the thick rain, she swung her flashlight around on her potted plants and breathed *ai-yah!* They were flattened. All she could hear was the hammering of the rain and now the muffled wail of an ambulance. Then there was another long crash through the hammering rain, and it was not thunder. She swung her flashlight at the mountainside behind. All she could see was a dim mass of wood, then some lights flashing, then screams.

She clattered down to the ground floor, to the front door, and stopped, astonished. The road was running like a river. Then she ran out, up the cascading ladder steps of the mountain as fast as she could, panting, plastered wet, flashing her light. There were more shouts and screams and lights flashing through the rain up there. There were sodden juts crowded on both sides of the steps above a cemetery and paths leading off to them, she could not yet see where the landslide had occurred. The rain hammered down, mud everywhere. She climbed a hundred yards, then turned along a mud path between the shacks. The rain hammered down, there was shouting ahead. Lights flashing, then she saw the big outcrop of rock towering up out of the rain. Shouts and lights. She shone her light and gasped.

The ground below had given way and the rocks stood poised, overhanging. Thirty feet below the landslide lay. It had buried fifteen huts, a piled swath of mud and rocks and smashed planks and debris twenty yards wide disappeared downhill into the mass of rain, people scrambling shouting screaming. She stared aghast. The rain hammered down. Any second the hanging rocks could go. She heard the ambulance siren wailing. She yelled down to people in the mud below, *"Beware these rocks!"*

It was swamped in the rain. She ran back along the muddy path, down the steps, panting plastered wet. She saw the first police and ambulance men running up with stretchers, ropes, and shovels. She shouted at the inspector, "There are some huge rocks that will fall down and kill everybody!"

"Where, Madam?" The European inspector panted.

"I show you!" She plunged him off down a path. She ran ahead, dodging, skidding in and out of black shapes of people. There was shouting and screaming and crying. She ran them to the landslide. A great swathed mass of yellow mud, sticks planks tin branches mud three times as high as a man. Muddy people clambering wading crying, and the rain teeming down. "There!" she flashed her light upward. The great mass of rocks as big as a tram stood poised in the rain.

"Hell," the inspector said. The rain beat down on his cap.

He shouted to his men and they began to scramble past him into the mud, picks, shovels, ropes, stretchers. He bellowed in Cantonese through a loudspeaker: *"Everybody get away from this area, please. It is dangerous. All the injured will be taken care of. This area will be cordoned off—"*

There were people everywhere, crying. An old lady scrambled past Ying screaming. Scrambling slipping clawing up the muddy mountain screaming, *"My husband."*

"Wait, grandmother!" Ying shouted. The old lady was scrambling uphill on the edge of the landslide through the tottering houses. The rain hammered down. The old woman reached the upper part of the landslide, right below the overhanging rocks. Somewhere in there her roof had been. She flung herself screaming into the mass of mud and clawed up it. Mud piled down on her, she heaved out her scrawny legs and scrambled upward, clawing halfway up the dune of mud when Ying-ling reached

the upper path through the teeming silver rain and pandemonium.

"Grandmother, come back!"

There was a sudden crash, so the earth shook, two tons of mud had fallen out from underneath the poised mass of rocks, crashed straight down on top of the landslide, and everything of the old woman was gone except one foot. One old muddy foot sticking out. Ying-ling screamed and looked up at the mass of rocks above, rain beating down, a big gorge gaping under them. She flung a piece of wood onto the mud and started clawing up it toward the foot. It sank under her weight but she could claw up it, panting gasping reaching out, she was three feet short of the woman's foot, she looked upward crying into the rain at the towering rocks, then the wood disappeared sideways from under her in the mud, she shrieked and came rolling sliding down the landslide. A Chinese policeman grabbed her arm. *"Stand back please, miss!"*

She pointed up into the mud, crying. Policemen and coolies were scrambling past everywhere. "Shine your light, *there is a woman in there, here is her foot.*"

The policeman shone his light up into the mud. *"Where?"* There was no foot. The mud had moved.

"Oh!" She stared, mud running off her. *"You must dig for her!"*

"Is she your relative?"

"No." She was just crying. The rain hammering down.

"We will dig for everybody, stand back please—*stand back!"*

Policemen, ambulance men, flashlights, arc lights, ropes, ladders, shovels, ploughing up through the mud, the rain hammering down. Coolies were scrambling along carrying mud away in baskets slung from bamboo poles across their shoulders. Crying people huddled, scrambling, watching. Men working deep into the mud. Wood and tin and glass and pots and pans unearthed. Two men came plodding carrying a stretcher. They laid the muddy body down beside others. People around. An ambulance man was pouring water on the corpses' faces so they could be identified. A policeman shone his light for a woman to try to identify somebody. Dead muddy faces, bloody mud in the mouths, ears, eyes. The woman tittered, ashen-faced: all around the hubbub and the teeming of the rain. Another body was coming on a stretcher, the ambulance man doused its face, the eyelids flickered, *"This one's still alive!"* He heaved the body over, and pressed on its back, there was a throaty muddy gurgle.

"No, it's gone." He felt the pulse. "Gone," he said. The woman tittered, ghastly white in the lamplight. Another shout through the rain, *"Here is one alive—stretchers—"*

Downhill the landslide went out of sight, a great mass of mud. Policemen and ambulance men and coolies and lamps down there, then blackness. Ying-ling scrambled down the hill through the shacks, across one path, two, three, slipping sloshing scrambling, down to the bottom of the earthfall. There were arc lamps set up, men digging, coolies carrying. More stretchers, more bodies. A police loudspeaker: *All people must leave these houses . . . there is danger of further collapse . . . come quietly . . . come along . . .*

Up the mountain an arc light was now beamed on the poised towering rocks. The rain was silver curtaining down. Firemen were behind it, trying to devise a way of holding the rocks by chains.

"Impossible," a police superintendent said, "there's nothing for them up there to anchor the chains to." The rain splashed off his peaked cap. "How's the evacuation down there going?"

"Pandemonium, sir," the inspector said.

Pandemonium, men women children babies grabbing scrambling clutching slipping sliding crying shouting, pots pans bedding furniture scrambling lugging, slipping sliding, the police loudspeakers blaring.

"Tell them abandon their property. I give those rocks five minutes." He raised his loudspeaker. *"Attention . . . attention. All personnel are to cease digging and retire back behind the cordon immediately—"*

As he spoke a cry went up from the crowd—*The rocks!* The big boulder moved. It creaked down an inch with a shower of mud and the mass of boulders around it shifted, then they stopped.

"Get out!" the superintendent bellowed, *"everybody get out!"*

Police and coolies and people scrambled, a shriek went up. *"Leave your property and get out!"* Scrambling shouting slipping sliding jostling crying muddy bloody pandemonium, *"Get out, Get out,"* the policeman bellowed. *"Get out!"*

A roar *Ai-yah* went up and in the arc light the great rock shifted again. Shifted forward with a slow sucking

360

jerk, the crowd surged back, the rocks sucked forward another six inches in the silver hammering rain, then they stopped, and the gasp hung in the air and a hundred yards below the terrified screaming went up. The mass of rocks poised in the arc lights a long moment, then there was a sucking roar above the rain, and they crashed.

Came kneeling over in great terrible slow motion in the silver glare of the arc lights, then down in an invincible crash so the earth shook and the mud flew in great sheets, and the great landslide slid. Shook and shuddered and crashed off down the mountain, great rocks as big as cars tumbling skewering skidding down in the great mass of killer landslide; slowly at first, ponderously invincible then faster faster faster, skidding skewering tumbling. The first avalanche of mud hit the shacks and swamped them down flat then the great rocks overtook the avalanch and hit the next row of shacks in a crash like cannon and wood flew, without a falter the rocks smashed on down through the huts crashing smashing wood and mud flying through fifty yards of huts and hit the cemetery wall. And smashed through the cemetery wall and brick and concrete and tombstones flew like grapeshot with the crack of cannon, crashed a swath forty feet wide and five feet deep right through the sodden graveyard, down to the bottom, tombstones and coffins and bones and hair and teeth and shrouds smashed flying, muddy sodden, and behind the great rocks came the avalanche of mud and buried the graves again. And when the avalanche was stopped, the hammering of the rain.

It rained for three days without ceasing, and then the seasonal trough of low pressure moved and the sun came out. And all the time there was the digging, and the grief, and the stench. Then the seasonal trough of low pressure moved back, and the bad rains came again; it rained for four weeks but altogether only 14,000 people lost their homes and only 307 people died, and only eighty-two junks were sunk, not counting the junks on Staunton Creek.

CHAPTER 54

The winding lanes and hedges of Berkshire were green but the trees were russet bare in November; soon it would be Christmas and there would be snow. I had bought an old Volkswagen. Most weekends some of us went down to London. I went to art galleries, wandered around and made mental notes of things to tell Ying. The theaters and the galleries were wonderful, I had forgotten how bloody, wonderful they were. I wished she were here, but I was happy. Because it was nearly New Year and in four months I was going back to her, and then soon it would be summer in Hong Kong; summer on the China Sea and wine in the sun, and her. I did not brood about Suzie, Catherine had told me that come hell or high water she would not permit me to see her and they had gone up to the family in the Midlands, I had managed to stop thinking about it and now all I thought about was that it was nearly the New Year.

Then one night I went down to London to a theater and slept in a hotel. At 5 A.M. I set off back to Newbury. I stopped at a transport café and bought a newspaper and read it while I had a coffee. It was still dark outside. On the second page there was an article on the Cultural Revolution in China.

It was only a filler, nothing much we hadn't read before. The Red Guards seemed out of even Mao's control. Powerful provincial party bosses were under fire and offering strong resistance, there was a lot of bloodshed and violence, "Red terror" the Soviet news agency Tass called it. Mao's instruction that the Red Guards return to school by November 20 had been ignored and he had been obliged to extend the deadline to December 20. And there were no schoolbooks any more because they had all been burned and no new revolutionary curriculum had yet been worked out and there was very little school furniture left unsmashed and most of the teachers had fled in terror of their students. Now there was a great deal of alarm about the economy and it seemed only the People's Liberation Army and the youthful Red Guards supported Mao. And now Mao ordered a massive escalation of the attacks of President Liu, China's Khrushchev and Arch Black Weed and Revisionist Scab; and that the Cultural Revolution spread to industry. And now the confusion reached a crescendo, bitter resistance to the Red Guards from party cadres and established administrators, and now the fighting in Peking reached its fiercest and the bombardment of the headquarters was redoubled, and Red Guards swarmed over the factories routing out the Party Persons in Authority taking the Capitalist Road, with dunce caps and shouts and kicks and paint and confessions, doctors, teachers, mayors, engineers, managers, accountants, even party cadres hounded through the streets to the screams of *Yellow-skinned Running Dogs;* and the managers and mayors sweeping the streets and doctors scrubbing the lavatories applying the Thought of Mao Tse-tung. And the factories ground down and the railways clogged up and the docks paralyzed and now workers were going on Long Marches to Peking, and now rival Red Guards were fighting each other in the factories, schools, hospitals, public works, dockyards, in the streets, this Red Guard Brigade says that that Red Guard Brigade are also Khrushchevite Scabs and Yellow-skinned Running Dogs, sticks and stones and knives and axes and firearms, and blood running in the streets. . . . The newspaper didn't know what to make of it. China could not afford to lose one day's industrial production, let alone six months'. And this was going to go on a long time, it was getting worse, not better. And if the prairie fire spread to Hong Kong? If our own communists started Struggle to prove their revolutionary zeal to Mao? I read the rest of the paper, drinking my coffee, trying not to think about it. Then I saw the small headline. *Communists Demonstrate in Macao* and I thought, Oh Jesus.

Macao, Nov. 30: Sixty communist men and women stormed into Government House yesterday in this tiny Portuguese enclave on the South China Coast, forty miles from Hong Kong, and staged a vociferous demonstration in Red Guard style.

They were protesting against the Macao Government's action two weeks ago, when police were sent to put a halt to an unauthorized building of a new communist school and a clash took place and several injuries were suffered by both workers and police. The communist school concerned had applied to the Macao Government for permission to build, but when official reply was not forthcoming they had proceeded without it. Radio Peking immediately accused the Macao Government of "fascist atrocities." The Macao Government immediately promised to set up a Commission of Inquiry to investigate the whole affair.

Yesterday's demonstrators mobbed the governor's doors inside Government House, shouting quotations from the Thoughts of Mao Tse-tung and demanding that the governor come out and bow his head in shame. They also demanded (i) severe punishment for the commissioner of police and other officers; (ii) a public apology from the governor; and (iii) payment of compensations to the injured persons.

The demonstrators left after one hour, still shouting protests, and threatened to return tomorrow. Meanwhile Radio Peking again denounced the Taipa School incident "a premeditated bloody fascist atrocity" and demanded that the Portuguese Government meet the demonstrators' "Just Demands" forthwith. "However the Portuguese have remained insolent and unreasonable and delayed reply," the broadcast said indignantly.

I thought, *Oh goddamn the bloody Portuguese!* Now the bloody Cultural Revolution spreads to Macao. Next is bloody Hong Kong! The goddamn Portuguese with their goddamn mañana, with the Cultural Revolution raging outside their goddamn gates they have the colossal stupidity to start a fight at a goddamn communist school! Now we'll goddamn never hear the end of it: hysterical denunciations from goddamn Red Guards, the valiant People armed with the Thoughts of Mao Tse-tung will not tolerate the bloody fascist outrages of the Portuguese imperialists and their Running Dogs—the Portuguese don't stand a chance, another great victory for the Thought of Mao Tse-tung! Then they have a go at Hong Kong by way of an encore! Oh Je-*zuz*. I went to the pay phone.

The directory pages rattled in my hand. I worked out

the time: 6 A.M England, early afternoon in Hong Kong and Macao. I telephoned Reuter's, got through to the Far East desk, finally the boss. "Are you a journalist?" he said.

"No, I'm a frantic resident of Hong Kong, can you be so kind as to tell me what happened in Macao today?"

"We don't give out news to the public, you'll read it in tonight's newspapers."

"Please," I said.

He said he'd tell me the gist of what he remembered. Yes, riots had broken out in Macao. The Reds had marched on Government House again, en masse this time. All screaming Mao-think. Stopped by the police outside Government House, then the fighting broke out. Burned a police jeep, fought their way into Government House up the stairs, smashed windows et cetera. Governor locked in his office. Mob screaming, "Bow your head!" Beat up television crews. Finally the police turned water hoses on them. "All right?" the Reuter man said. "That's about it."

"That's about it for Macao!" I said. "Tomorrow all hell's going to break loose."

"Good luck!" the Reuter man said.

Back in Newbury I went straight to the commandants' office at breakfast time.

"Have you heard about Macao, sir?"

Only what was in the newspaper; he said he'd get on to Head Office and see what he could find out. Then all he said was to confirm what the Reuter man had told me. It was night in Macao now, the city was tense but quiet.

"The calm that precedes the storm," I said.

"And the Hong Kong police and the Army are on emergency standby," he said.

"You bet they are," I said. I thought, Oh Jesus.

I went down to Registry and booked a call to Mini-Max. It was no good calling anybody in Special Branch. Those bastards will tell you nothing.

CHAPTER 55

There was seven hours' delay on the call. Every man and his dog was telephoning Hong Kong. I got through at 4 P.M., midnight in Hong Kong. "Max, what's happening over there in Macao?" I shouted.

"Everything's happening in Macao," Max said. "Macao's where it's all happening, want to buy some cheap real estate?"

"Be serious, this is costing me a pound a minute."

"I am serious. The ferries are full of Portuguese women and children fleeing to Hong Kong. The Reds stormed Government House today. There's a curfew now and all's quiet except for the Red-Guard-style posters slapped up everywhere denouncing the fascist Portuguese. All the police and Army on standby, same in Hong Kong. The stock market took a dive here today."

"How're the Portuguese going to play it?"

"I've been telephoning Macao all day but everybody's running around like blue-arsed flies. Christ, we're within our rights. Government had not yet given permission for the bloody Taipa School building, so they had no right to start building."

"And you had no bloody sense to forcibly stop them with a goddamn Cultural Revolution raging in China," I said.

"They were defiant," Max said. "Christ, Government's got to show who's boss, you can't have people slapping up buildings without town-planning authority. And we've set up a Commission of Inquiry into the school fight, we've done everything correctly by civilized standards, we're in the right."

"Not in China, you're not! You know what Chairman Mao's letting them do to *his* law and order. And your local Reds want to show Mao that they're on his side, a victory for the Thought of Mao Tse-tung over the decadent imperialist Portuguese. You bastards were *mad* to give them an excuse! It's *face* they want, a decorous government inquiry is no good to them. They want to grind your faces into the dirt, and if you don't give in they'll bloody murder you. Then our Reds will start and Hong Kong will go up in smoke too. You don't have to be a clairvoyant to see it coming."

Max said, "Macao and Hong Kong are too important to Peking—Mao's got his head screwed on the right way."

Jesus. "What are the China-watchers at the Foreign Correspondents' Club saying?"

"The China-watching pundits think the balloon could go up at any moment."

"And they're bloody right! Peking's in the middle of an ideological civil war and a king-size power struggle—if Mao needs to kick the Portuguese off the sacred soil of China in order to appease his Red Guards and save face he'll do that small thing!"

"So what do you suggest we dumb Portuguese who've only been in Macao a mere four hundred years do about it?"

I said, *"Give in. Now*, before the confrontation gets worse. They want you to apologize? Apologize. They want you to sack the commissioner of police? So sack him, put all the blame on him. And pay the goddamn compensation to the injured coolies. You've got to roll a few heads."

Max was astonished. "English sunshine gone to your head, has it? We're in the *right!"*

"What the hell else can Macao do, for Christ's sake? Once you have a riot you'll have Red Guards swarming all over the place and they'll make mincemeat of you in five minutes and you'll lose Macao anyway. And your face. So what's the point?"

"The point is *face*. This is China. If we just give in we'll lose all our face, the communists will swagger through town lawlessly and run the place more than they do, life wouldn't be worth living."

Jesus. "What does Macao think?"

"What I think. We can't be pushed around. We're expecting a bejezuz demonstration tomorrow."

"A riot you'll have. And all your cops on standby armed to the teeth?"

"Of course they're armed to the teeth. How would you be armed, assuming you have teeth?"

"With an olive branch."

"And with no face. We've got to ride it out and show

whose boss in our own colony. You've been talking to Harold Wilson again."

"What about your mother?" I said.

He said, "If it gets worse I'm going over to fetch her tomorrow night. The bloody ferries are crammed but I'll get her on somehow."

"American dollars should do it."

"Yeah, the pataca's not worth a damn at the moment. The Hong Kong dollar's not looking so good either, everybody's buying American dollars at a premium."

"Max—have you seen anything of—her?" I said.

"You mean . . . ?"

"Yes."

"Neither hide nor hair. How're things your end?"

"Pretty grim."

"Is Catherine sticking to her guns?"

"Yes. She'll change though. She's under a psychiatrist now. Sort of nervous breakdown."

"Oh God."

"Yes. I feel bloody sorry for her actually. Anyway I must go, Max, this is costing money."

"Yes—well, you know my opinion. What you should do. It's even more serious now with this political situation."

I didn't want to talk about it at all, let alone on the telephone.

"I hope it works out in Macao. Be bloody careful if you go over there. In and out."

"Just call me Twinkletoes."

"Good luck. Listen, call me here collect if anything develops."

That night I got the story again on the BBC. At five o'clock the next morning I telephoned my man at Reuter's in London again. It was afternoon in Hong Kong and Macao. He said, "Well, it's happened." I felt myself go pale. "They marched on Government House again yelling Mao-think. Mobbed the police guards. Burned a police jeep. Police turned fire hoses on them, then tear gas. Then a baton charge. Repulsed them off Government House but now the mob's attacking the Senate Building, the Leal Senado."

"Oh God," I said.

The roar. Mobbed down the road in outraged disarray roaring outrage and hate and the Thoughts of Chairman Mao, mobbed the Leal Senado with sticks and bricks and iron bars, smashed the windows, smashed down the doors, mobbed up the marble stairs shouting, roaring, smashed the furniture and hurled it out the windows, chairs desks file cabinets, typewriters telephones, mobbed through the Legislative Council Chamber screaming shouting smashing, tore down the curtains, the flags, smashed down the portraits, hurled the chairs out the windows. Mobbed the statue of Mesquita outside and flung a rope around its neck and tore it down with a roar and dragged it down the road. Mobbed the post office, sticks and stones and iron bars flying and mobbed the Catholic Holy House of Mercy screaming shouting smashing, chased the nuns down the streets. Rampaged through the streets fighting police, attacking cars, beating Portuguese, mobbed a traffic policeman and beat him to death with bamboo poles, *beat beat smash hate*, mobbed the City Hall and smashed up the offices and threw the furniture out the windows: for five hours they rampaged, roaring shouting screaming. Five hours, then the governor called out the Army. And the curfew. And the ruins in the streets, and the blood.

That afternoon I went down to London with a toothbrush and bottle of whiskey, and persuaded the Reuter man to let me sit next to his telex machine all night.

That night Ko Ming made a radio broadcast in Macao. I read the translation on the Reuter's telex and I thought, *Here we go!* Ko Ming, uncrowned king of Macao, multimillionaire, president of the Chinese Chamber of Commerce, official representative of the Chinese People of Macao at the People's National Congress in Peking, made his broadcast "by arrangement" with His Excellency the Governor of Macao. *"By arrangement,"* by God! Now we see who the real power in Macao is! Ko Ming appealed to the Great Chinese People to stay calm; then came the punch line: *"pending discussions between representatives of the Taipa Community and the Macao Government about the Taipa School Incident and the Four Just Demands."*

I thought, Oh yes here we bloody go! The governor of Macao has to call in the uncrowned communist king to plead for law and order for him. But at a price; the price is the Four Just Demands, quote unquote: sack the police chief, compensate the injured, apologize, guarantee no recurrence. Or else. The "or else" was contained in the other telex reports that outside the Barrier Gate there were thousands of outraged Red Guards massed. Threatening to march against the Macao Fascist Imperialist Foreign Devils and their Yellow-skinned Running Dogs; Red Guards were landing in Macao by sampans to Hold High the Mighty Banner of the Thought of Mao Tse-tung tomorrow; communist hospitals in Macao gloriously preparing for tomorrow. Everybody preparing for tomorrow. And in Hong Kong?

Oh God, Hong Kong. And oh God, Ying-ling and me. The telex was chattering. Another item from Macao from the Reuter man. It said that the communists were now presenting a Fifth Just Demand to the governor of Macao. Namely, *"the public ceremonial burning of all police truncheons."*

Oh Je-*zuz!*

No Portuguese face at all! What a Victory for the Thoughts of Mao Tse-tung! And what would happen to our Hong Kong police when our Reds tried an encore?

Max Popodopolos hurried down the ferry gangway, through the clamoring crowds of Portuguese, into the building. He had not slept. Inside the babble of voices was a muted roar, women, children, fear, tears. There the crowd was twenty deep around the ticket office, shouting, pressing, jostling, clutching money, clamoring to buy refuge, the smells and noise of fear. There must have been a thousand at the ferry. A chalked notice read *Sailing Full*. Max turned and shouldered back to the immigration officer.

"I bet you one hundred American dollars you cannot get me two tickets for the afternoon ferry!" Max said.

The Portuguese officer looked at him with big liquid eyes.

"It is an offense for officials to gamble. The danger is considerable."

"Two hundred!" Max gritted: "That's twelve hundred patacas, for Christ's sake, for twelve patacas' worth of tickets!"

The immigration officer said: "I would possibly bet three hundred American, señor."

"All right, for Chrissake!"

The little officer led him into the office behind the counter. He held out his hand. "Your bet, please, señor." Max thrust the three big green bills at him. The little man opened a desk, pulled two tickets out of a booklet of fifty. "I am sorry you lost your bet, señor."

370

Out in the street the crowd had got bigger. People hurrying down the road toward the ferry carrying baggage. Max signaled to a taxi driver. He ignored him. Max strode up to the taxi and flung open the door. The driver said in Cantonese, "Fuck off, Portuguese barbarian devil!"

"Fuck thee also!"

He slammed the door. He set off walking hard down the waterfront.

Taxis and pedicabs passed him and jeered. It was a bright cold winter Sunday morning and he was sweating. Soldiers and policemen everywhere, on street corners, patrolling sullen. Soldiers clearing the streets of debris, sticks, stones, glass, bricks, smashed traffic signs, smashed cars, furniture. There were no Portuguese civilians on the streets: they were either locked in their houses or clamoring around the ferry. No face. There was a waiting fear in the air, Max could feel it. Quiet. He passed Government House, then started up the steep knoll to the family villa. He was sweating badly and he had to admit it was not all San Miguel and Johnnie Walker. It was good honest Portuguese fear.

The servants had deserted. He went up onto the villa's rooftop with the binoculars. He had a good view of the tiny city. He could see Taipa Island, where the trouble had broken out, the communist islands beyond. He looked at the ferry. The crowd was bigger, he could almost hear the fear, the shouting jostling milling trying. And more Portuguese hurrying along the waterfront toward the terminal carrying bundles and baggage. And the line of stationary taxis, watching. He swung the binoculars toward the Leal Senado: armored cars and soldiers. There must be plenty more outside his vision and he saw the two communist ambulances, waiting for the new day. The Kiang Wah People's Hospital. Just waiting ready, hopefully. Jesus. Big knots of Chinese hanging around, waiting. He swung the binoculars over Wanstai Channel and his eyes widened.

Communist gunboats, two of the sonsabitches cruising down the Wanstai Channel a hundred yards offshore, red flags flying, all hands on deck! Max stared at them, heart thudding. *What the hell were they doing here!*—there was only one reason they were here! He swung his glass to the east, to the Pearl River estuary. Two more! There was a *whoooop* and the morning ferry was leaving. Decks packed. And a thousand people clamoring at the ticket office. Max clattered down the stairs from the rooftop.

His mother had cooked breakfast for him: he felt sick in his guts but he knew he would get nowhere with his mother until he had eaten a large greasy breakfast.

"You should eat a breakfast like that every day before you go to court, bambino." They were talking Portuguese.

"I will, Mama." Jesus. Five hundred yards down that hill.

Her face puckered in pleasure as he took a mouthful.

"It really is time you got married, bambino, a good wife to look after you."

"Okay, Mama."

Mrs. Popodopolos said, "I don't even mind any more if she is not a Portuguese girl, although why you cannot find a Portuguese girl I do not know. Even an English girl would be all right."

"Thanks, Mama. Please go and pack."

"Do not try to change the subject, bambino. I do not approve of leaving Macao at all, the Portuguese have lost enough face without Maria Popodolpols standing in the queue. Even," his mother said, "an American girl would do."

"Okay, Mama."

"I am sure there are some very well bred Americans. I am sure, for example, that Senator Kennedy is a gentleman."

"I'll find out if he's got a sister," Mini-Max said, "if you'll go and *pack*."

Then he heard the shouting. He shoved back his chair and snatched the binoculars.

"Finish your packing, Mama!"

The roars. They roared and surged outside the Leal Senado confronting the ranks of police and soldiers, men and women and youths and girls and children shouting yelling thrusting fists and their *Little Red Books of The Thoughts of Chairman Mao* up into the air, men with loudspeakers shouting out the page numbers then the roar of the quote and the sea of fists thrust in the air. And the Red Guards come from across the border, red armbands, shouting screaming hating, and the ambulance waiting and the couriers on motorcycles. The quotes roared up in unison, then the shouts and jeers, *"Portuguese*

372

barbarians are paper tigers!" and through the din the police loudspeakers were ordering the mob to disperse, and the answering roars and yells. And youths brandishing shields ,and sticks and stones screaming challenges to the soldiers to fight, and now children were dancing out in front in glee challenging the soldiers out to fight, dancing spitting yelling jeering laughing. And then there was a yell over the loudspeakers: *"Klll the Portuguese devils!"* and the mob took up the hysterical roar, *"Kill the Portuguese devils!"* and the screams of hate roared up above the brandishing, and the first stones flew.

Came crashing through the air, then came in a hail, sticks stones bricks hurtling, the soldiers and police ducked and dodged and arms thrown up in disarray and the mob roared in glee, *"Kill the Portuguese devils,"* and a second hail came crashing and the soldiers were scattering, and the army officer yelled *"Fire!"* and six soldiers who heard him fired a ragged booming volley into the air above the surging mass of screaming heads, and there were the screams and pandemonium. The mob surged backward yelling screaming scattering running outraged down the street.

The motorcyclist roared down the street ahead of the routed roaring mob. Round the corner of the theater another ambulance and crowd were waiting, he shouted a signal and two motorcycles roared off in different directions. The crowd outside the theater took up the roar. The motorcyclist raised his loudspeaker at the mob coming running from the Leal Senado. *"Comrades,"* he yelled, *"reassemble here!"*

On his rooftop Max lowered his glasses, sweating. The mob was outside his line of vision but he could hear the roar. He heard more shots and he swung around. They were coming from the direction of the border half a mile away. He turned and ran down the stairway to the garage to get the car started. Then he heard another roar, like a football crowd. It came from the mob attacking the Nationalist Union premises. Then there was another roar, from the Casa Ricci Refugee Center. And he heard the roar from down there in the town. Another mob was swarming back on the Leal Senado. Swarming shouting yelling following the men with the loudspeakers and the *Little Red Books.*

CHAPTER 56

The mob was surging shouting jeering at the ranks of police and soldiers, flooding into the side streets and alleys, and the loudspeakers chanting and the red books waving and the children prancing in glee. Max swung the car down out of the steep hill and along the waterfront, then slammed on his brakes. One hundred yards ahead was a yelling surging mob; in one swing Max swung the car around and roared back down the road, then back up the hill. Up to the top, then roared through the maze of residential back streets. Not a person to be seen.

"Roll up your window!" he snapped at his mother.

The only way to the ferry was down through Central. He swung down the narrow cobbled back streets. Still deserted all the way, only the sound of the Volkswagen's engine, all the shop windows boarded up. He turned down into Victoria Street. Some people hurrying in both directions, but no traffic, the shops boarded up. He gunned the engine, honking and swinging the car through the people. He came around the bend and braked hard. Ahead was the intersection with the main street and there were hundreds of people running shouting and yelling. He could still turn around. He began to spin the wheel and the brick hit the back window.

Hit the car in a crash of flying glass and his mother screamed. He looked back, a group of men running at the car, a brick hit the hood from the other side, a man running with a bamboo stick, screaming, *"Kill the Portuguese devils!"* Max yelled at his mother, *"Get your head down!"* and swung the wheel and roared ahead teeth clenched and his hand hard on the horn. He roared into the road, a brick beat the car then the crashing of sticks on the body, he swung the wheel screaming, *"Get out of the way!"* people scattering yelling picking up sticks and stones swiping hurling crashing. He roared flat out down the street on the wrong side. Yelling shouting people everywhere running scattering swiping throwing, he swung the wheel dodging, sticks stones people flashing reeling scattering shouting and the crash and clatter, a man was wrenching at his door, he swung the car and shook him off, four men running from the right, he swung and mounted the traffic island in a crash and his head hit the roof. His mother was screaming, blood on her face. He crashed across the traffic island, crashed onto the other side of the road. Forty yards ahead was the turnoff he needed, a hundred running reeling scattering people in between. A man ran at him waving a meat cleaver, Max swung the wheel screaming, *"Jesus, you bastard,"* a garbage can crashed off the hood, his mother was streaming blood, he screamed, *"Keep your head down!"* and swung the wheel. He roared at the last fifteen yards to the turnoff, a stone smashed his window, he swung to miss a girl, her face creased up in hate, and swung at the turnoff. He hit the curb in a crash and bounced over it. Sticks and stones beat the back of the car. And he was out of the main road and roaring down the back street toward the ferry.

His mother sobbing, bloody, the cold air rushed on his bloody face through the shattered windshield, the narrow back streets suddenly empty again, then the waterfront again, then the crowds of Portuguese at the ferry, the clamor. Blood was in his eyes. Women weeping, men shouting, children crying, the clamor and the jostle and the pressing, and the fear. He staggered through the crowd carrying his mother. His heart was thudding hard in his ears and he did not hear the rifle shots from the Leal Senado.

It was after midnight in the Reuter office, I had drunk a lot of whiskey and the cigarettes rasped, I read it on the telex as it came through: "the crowd estimated at three thousand returned to the leal senado comma hurling missiles comma causing considerable injuries stop after repeated warnings to disperse comma the army again opened fire stop initial reports are eight dead communists and thirty-five wounded stop the mob dispersed screaming hysterically stop a curfew was immediately reimposed stop local communist leader ko ming has reportedly just left macao by car into china to confer with kwantung provincial communist authorities stop item ends."

I stared at the machine: "Je-*zuz!*"

I jumped up and strode into the Reuter man's office.

"Those bloody idiot Portuguese opened fucking fire

again and killed eight Comrades and wounded thirty-five! Jesus, are they out of their minds?"

"Close the door," Clive, the Reuter man said.

"What's wrong with bloody tear gas? For Christ's sake, opening fire on China's doorstep on Chinese communists with a bloody Cultural Revolution! Where the hell do they think they are?"

The Reuter man shook his head wearily at me.

I said, *"Baton charges if necessary but not goddamn bullets!* And those goddamn crowds should never have been allowed to collect in the first goddamn place! Disperse the bastards with tear gas!"

"Maybe the wind was blowing the wrong way," the Reuter man said.

"If the goddamn wind's wrong you send a squad upwind to fire tear gas from the back! They could have kept those crowds indoors crying all bloody day in a place as small as Macao with tear gas! And *now* what happened? Ko Ming gone into China to confer with the communist bosses! You know what *he'll* come back with! An ultimatum from Peking itself, we're not dealing with the local Red yokels any more—China! All seven hundred million of the bastards!"

I sat down. Dragged both hands down my face, I felt gray.

"What's Peking going to say about *this?*"

"One guess."

"And then? What about Hong Kong?"

I sat there. Oh God, Ying-ling. What would happen to us if it started in Hong Kong?

I went up to the staff rest room with a hot whiskey-coffee. I looked at my face in the mirror. It was definitely a thirty-year-old face. My Hong Kong tan was all gone, some good lines around the eyes now. Oh God, Hong Kong.

Macao, the Cultural Revolution, Hong Kong, Ying-ling. All I wanted was to go home. Oh God, home, Ying-ling, Hong Kong. I sat down in the armchair and closed my eyes and took a deep drag on my cigarette and it burned my throat and I did not care.

The telephone rang, I picked it up. "Hello" I said.

"It's just come through on the telex," Clive said. "The Macao Government has just announced that they accept *all* the communists' demands."

I stared across the rest room.

"All?" Oh thank God.

"But what about the police truncheons?" I demanded.

"Yes. There will be a public ceremonial burning of all police truncheons."

I sat back.

"Good God!" *No Portuguese face at all.*

"How can they control the place from now on?" I stared. "Has Ko Ming come back from China yet?"

"Doesn't say, presumably not."

"But what about the eight dead communists and the Christknowshowmany injured? There'll be new Just Demands about *them*."

"At least the Portuguese have capitulated on the original issues," Clive said.

I said, "But the original issue of the Taipa School gunfight is *peanuts* compared to the new issue of eight Comrades dead and thirty-five injured! It's not all over by a *long* chalk!"

I sat there.

"We'll see when Comrade Ko Bloody Ming comes back from bloody Comradeland. They're going to eat the Portuguese alive."

"Well," the Reuter man said, "just thought I'd let you know."

I sat there. "Many thanks indeed, Clive," I said.

I sat back in the armchair. *Not over by a long chalk!* Oh God, I wanted to go home. I was deathly tired. Even the whiskey-coffee was cold and tired and I did not care, just oh God, my Ying-ling. I tried to sit up and think.

Jesus, shooting eight Chinese on China's doorsteps with a Cultural Revolution. And oh Jesus, they would have their noses rubbed right in it and there would be no more Portuguese face at all, a great Victory for the Thoughts of Mao Tse-tung. The Comrades want Glorious Victories for the Great Red Proletariat over the insolent fascist imperialists. They won't be satisfied until they've rubbed the Portuguese noses right right *right* in the shit. And then watch out, Hong Kong.

I lay back in the chair.

Oh, to sleep. To wake up and there is no Macao, no communists, no policemen, just Ying-ling.

CHAPTER 57

Now in December it was sleeting cold and in the shops it was cheery and Christmasy. She wrote:

Hong Kong looks very festive, but the Europeans are very nervous. The negotiations between the Macao Government and the Chinese Chamber of Commerce are still going on, with the Portuguese trying to save face. It serves them right. The streets and shops are empty over there, no tourists dare go there. . . .

Max wrote:

There'll be no Christmas in Macao this year, and maybe never again. It's now three weeks since the shooting. Every time we accept their so-called Just Demands, the bastards present us with a new one, each more humiliating than the last. First there were four Just Demands, then five, then six, there'll be more. They're *all* carrots, laughing at us. I have heard that the governor has told China that the Portuguese will just pack up and quit Macao, but both Peking and Lisbon refused. China doesn't want Macao back, it wants to get face for the Invincible Thought of Mao Tse-tung. The fact that tiny Macao doesn't have a chance detracts not a jot in Oriental thought from the glory of the black eye Mao is supposedly dealing the face of Portugal. Another Great Victory for the Reddest Sun in Our Hearts. And Macao is a ghost town. Serves the bloody Chinese Chamber of Commerce right, they're losing a fortune because no tourist will go where communist lawlessness prevails. Hong Kong is very jittery too, the stock market has hit an all-time low, empty buildings everywhere. A lot of business and expatriates have packed up and pulled out. Rents are an all-time low. Our middle-class Chinese are mobbing the American Embassy trying to get visas.

Everybody is scared the Hong Kong communists will attempt an encore to outdo their Macao comrades in getting Victories for Mao. Meanwhile across the border the Cultural Revolution rages to the bafflement of everybody, but you understand that better than we do. . . .

Did anybody really understand it?

Out there, in every commune, village, and teeming city across the mighty length and breadth of teeming China there were the Red Guards swaggering marching with their banners, the shouting and the chanting and the loudspeakers and the oceans of red books: in the factories, schools, shops, communes, streets there were the Struggle Meetings, struggle struggle struggle with the Rightists and the Reactionaries and the Scabs and the Khrushchevites and all the Party Persons in Authority taking the Capitalist Road, and the bandits of President Lin Chan-Shi and all his Running Dogs, isolate, expose, and purge their minds by Struggle and Mass Criticism and Self-criticism and Confession, drag them out of the party offices and the government offices and the factories, schools, shops, docks, buses, paddies, and parade them through the streets to the Struggle Meetings and surround them and scream at them and chant at them, Shame Shame Shame, Struggle Struggle Struggle, make them weep and quake and faint and bow their heads. "Confess! Confess!" beat them bloody black and blue and spit on them paint them black slap dunce caps on their heads paste their confessions on their backs, parade them through the streets in chains shouting chanting roaring the Thought of Mao Tse-tung; hunt them out at every level, inform inform inform to the Red Guards, inform on your brothers sisters parents children manager foreman colleagues superiors inferiors, Bombard the Headquarters, Bombard the superstructure, Bombard the Base, Struggle Struggle Struggle. And the clamor and the in-fighting and the Red Guards of this factory fighting the Red Guards of that factory because these Red Guards are not as good Maoists as those Red Guards—and the bloodshed and the debris and the smashed schools empty and the factories upside down and the economy ground down, and the fear. It was very hard to make out what was happening in China, except that it was bad.

In Macao it was very bad. It was the time of waiting. There were no more curfews, but there were no more Portuguese in the streets either. No more people in the hotels, in the casinos, in the restaurants and bars. No more tourists on the ferries. No more money.

That month the Chinese gunboats were back. Cruising in the harbor, big and gray and blaring the Thoughts of Chairman Mao. Outside the Barrier Gate the Red Guards rallying marching shouting blaring swaggering. And everywhere the posters and the banners: *Down with Portuguese Facist Imperialism—Down with British-U.S. Imperialism—Blood Debts Must Be Paid in Blood—Long Live Mao Tse-tung*. And hardly a Portuguese policeman in the streets. They were all indoors.

First there were Four Just Demands. Then there were Five. They were accepted. Now there were Six Just Demands. They were accepted. Broadcast over the radio by His Excellency the Governor himself: "The Portuguese Government wishes to announce that it accepts in their entirety all six demands. . . ." The gunboats sailed away. That day His Excellency the Governor left Government House to call upon the Chinese Chamber of Commerce to accept their Six Just Demands. No face at all. When he got there he found there were Seven Just Demands.

The next day there was to be a further meeting at Government House. The representatives of the Chinese Chamber of Commerce failed to show up. His Excellency waited in vain. No face at all. That day the gunboats came back.

That week His Excellency the Governor announced that the government accepted all the Seven Just Demands. That week the communist press made the Eighth Just Demand. That week it was Christmas.

The New Year came that way. In the New Year the Chinese imposed the boycotts. No Portuguese allowed in any hotel, restaurant, café, bar, taxi, boat. No food sold to any Portuguese in any shop.

No Portuguese face at all.

It was a cold January day.

I listened to the Cantonese broadcast from Macao on the commandant's radio in Newbury. At one o'clock they started marching through the streets, fifteen thousand in neat columns of six, disciplined, triumphant, each with his red armband of the Great Proletarian Cultural Revolution and his *Little Red Book*. In massive orderly schedule they converged outside the Chinese Chamber of Commerce, and drew up in appointed places to wait. The sea of faces.

From the eaves of the Chinese Chamber of Commerce hung the long thick columns of red firecrackers. From the windows hung the massive red flags with the five gold stars. Above the door hung the massive smiling portrait of Mao Tse-tung. There was very little noise.

Exactly at two o'clock the big black limousine appeared, driving pretty fast, conveying His Excellency the Governor of Macao to the Chinese Chamber of Commerce to sign Portugal's acceptance of the Ten Just Demands. As the limousine appeared the roar went up. The cheering clapping laughing jeering triumphant applause of fifteen thousand Chinese and the square went red with the flurry of the red flags and the red books in the roar.

The limousine halted smartly outside the Chinese Chamber of Commerce, the door opened immediately, and His Excellency the Governor climbed out quickly into the happy roaring waving red. Out climbed the rest of the Portuguese party, equally rapidly. There was a surge of the cheering crowd toward him but the men in Red Guard armbands linked arms and held them back. His Excellency paused a moment, smiled faintly once at the surging roaring crowd and waved politely, once. Then he walked rapidly up the steps followed hurriedly by his entourage.

There was nobody to meet His Excellency the Governor of Macao on the ground floor of the Chinese Chamber of Commerce, not even a *foki*. He mounted the stairs rapidly without looking to left or right. The roar outside was echoing. On the first floor there was nobody to meet him either. His Excellency started up the stairs to the second floor. At the top was a *tea-foki*, waiting. The *tea-foki* led His Excellency into the big room.

There was a long table with a rich red tablecloth, under a big portrait of Mao Tse-tung. There were thirteen Chinese gentlemen in suits standing around talking. As His Excellency appeared, the chairman of General Workers' Union took a polite step forward.

"Good afternoon."

"Good afternoon," His Excellency said. He shook hands shortly, politely, with each gentleman. His entourage shook hands in turn.

The chairman of the General Workers' Union indicated the chairs about the long red table, under the portrait of Mao Tse-tung. They all sat down. The *foki* poured green tea into little Chinese cups. They sat in silence while it was poured. Then the chairman looked quizzically, politely, at His Excellency the Governor of Macao.

His Excellency the Governor of Macao stood up. His aide passed him a document. Without clearing his throat, His Excellency began to read aloud in Portuguese. A member of his entourage translated into Cantonese, sentence by sentence.

His Excellency read aloud for nine minutes. There was no sound in the big red room but his deep Latin voice and his translator's. The Chinese gentlemen listened politely, smiling faintly.

His Excellency read the last sentence in Portuguese. The translator began the Cantonese. The *tea-foki* stood at the window with his hand ready. His Excellency took the pen from his aide to sign the document. As he began his signature the *tea-foki* waved his hand at the window, in Mesquita Square the tapers were put to the fireworks, and the roar of cheering and the cacophony of fireworks went up.

His Excellency walked down the long red table mid the roar of the firecrackers and the cheering and shook hands with a faint smile with each of the thirteen Chinese gentlemen, saying "Good afternoon." Then he turned and walked out of the big red room and down the empty stairs.

Outside the crowd was going mad. His Excellency paused a moment on the front steps and waved once at them. Then His Excellency climbed into the limousine and drove back through the madly gleeful joyful crowds, back to Government House.

That night there were the firecrackers and the singing and the victory rallies through the streets and in the football stadium (rented at a nominal fee by the Portuguese Government for the purpose). "The East Is Red" roared out over Macao and the red flags flew like an ocean and four People's gunboats cruised by with all joyous hands on deck.

That was the beginning of that big bad year. In Hong Kong there were rallies also, celebrating the Victory in Macao.

PART VIII

CHAPTER 58

Coming in low you see the blue China Sea change to green around the dark green silent islands, and the junks are silent diminutive way down there, and then here are the silent freighters and the cargo junks and the *walla-wallahs* and the crammed buildings and go-downs and the junks flying the red flags of China, and mighty taipan Central and the ferries all going on without you silently, and the mauve Mountains of Nine Dragons and beyond the great vast mauve of China; and now the plane is coming in low over the teeming rooftops of Kowloon, cars, buses, rickshaws, Chinese teeming silently just down there and the signboards scrambling over each other and somewhere over there other side the harbor is Ying in her classroom also sick with excitement and oh God I was happy. "Aren't you worried about all those Chinese?" the American lady next to me said.

"Madam," I grinned, "I am Hongkongese."

"I thought you were British," she said.

"Only my parents." Happy, grinning all over as I climbed off the plane, and there were the hundreds of Chinese, Chinese every-bloody-where, and I loved every one of them. I had been away a long long time and it was a beautiful Hong Kong morning and I was back back back and just other side that magnificent harbor was my beautiful woman, oh God it fell marvelous. I got into a taxi and I said, "Star Ferry, Elder Brother!" and I loved every narrow crowded street and signboard and I wondered how the hell the place had survived without me.

I got a coolie to carry my suitcases over on the ferry,

then I took a taxi through Wanchai to King Ling building, and oh God it was good all the way. I rode up in the service elevator to the rooftop and flung open the familiar door. And oh yes the windows were open and the carpets were down and flowers on the table and there was her note: *Darling, I'm crazy with happiness but I can't get here till school finishes at four!* and in the refrigerator was a bottle of champagne and a dozen beers and all kinds of food, and a big card propped up against the beer reading *Welcome to Our Hero!* And the bed made up and everything clean and aired, and I threw myself down on our big soft double bed with a laugh in my throat.

It was a long happy afternoon waiting for four o'clock. I took a cab around to headquarters. I went up to the seventh floor, checked through the security gates into Special Branch, saw the director's secretary, got shown in. "Hello." He shook hands wearily across the desk as if I had been away for the weekend. "You're early, we weren't expecting you till Monday."

"I got tired of waiting."

"Against regulations," he said. "Sit down. Did they teach you anything?"

"Plenty," I said.

"Well," he said, "you've only begun to learn. Your appointment was confirmed in last week's *Gazette*. We'll have to throw a party for you up at the Mess sometime to welcome you officially, next Wednesday all right?" He consulted his diary.

"Fine," I said. "Thank you."

"You'll have to throw one yourself too the next week. Congratulations on your results by the way, I see you got top marks all around."

"Did I?" I said. "They didn't tell us."

"Well, there's plenty for you to do here when you've caught up on your sleep, when do you want to start?"

"Monday. Where are you putting me?"

He pulled his gray earlobe unenthusiastically.

"In Analysis, seeing you're supposed to be so clued up on the Great Proletarian Cultural Revolution now. You'll be working with the relevant MI5 and CIA sections, there's a hell of a lot for you to catch up on, take you a month. Staff meeting's at nine A.M. sharp, none of your Special Investigation hours please, this is nine to five, if you're lucky. You're supposed to be so lucky, aren't you? Well don't bank on it any more."

"How's it been here?" I said. "Since Macao."

"You got it all in Current Affairs at school didn't you?"

"Only secondhand."

"You don't want it firsthand," the DSS said. "You were very fortunate you were cloistered in sunny England. Those goddamn Portuguese nearly gave us heart failure, we were working twenty-four hours a day for six goddamn weeks with out hearts in our mouths. And so little reliable information. We thought Hong Kong was going any moment."

"And now?"

He sighed, weary of that question. "That's part of your job, you'll find out soon enough how little we know. Our Reds have been half asleep but they're all a-twitter now worrying about how they're going to outshine their Macao comrades."

I was too happy to worry. "And? Will they?"

He sighed. "Who knows? Hong Kong, the festering capitalist sore on the backside of oh-so-ideologically holier-than-thou Communist China screaming for glorious victories? It only needs a small excuse."

I did not want to think about it.

"Well, go home and sleep off your flight." He was tired. "Come in on Monday and we'll show you around the think tank."

I would much rather have been coming back to my old stamping ground in Special Investigations, I had had enough of politics but I was too happy to care. I telephoned Max but he had left for lunch. I took a cab into Central and went down into the Malaysia Club, through the bead curtain and there was his broad familiar back. "Good God!" Max said.

"Hello, my champion!"

After all the bullshit I said, "And how's Macao these days?" And Max said Jesus and proceeded to tell me how it was in Macao these days. The communists ran the place now, anything the governor wanted to do he first had to get the okay from the Chinese Chamber of Commerce. Any coolie could complain about anything and the Chamber telephones the governor or the chief of police and says, "Now what's all this?" And the place run down, no tourists, no bloody business. And they've made us close down the Casa Ricci Refugee Center and the Kuomintang headquarters and hand over all Freedom Swimmers. No Portuguese face at all. And the police? Jesus, they're having a time of it, they wouldn't dare charge Jack the Ripper with a parking offense if he's Chinese. "What does a Portuguese call a cheeky Chinese coolie?" Mini-Max said.

"What?"

"Sir," Max spluttered. He wagged his head. "But the Reds are having a Smile Campaign now to try to get the tourists back. The Chinese Chamber of Commerce has realized they can't eat their cake and have it, business was in tears. But the tourists aren't coming back, no sir. Because if some goddamn coolie takes it into his head to pick on you there's not a damn thing anybody can do about it, you can just disappear. And there's nothing anybody can do to help you." He held up his finger. "And don't say I told you so. We had to try to show who's boss in our own colony. If the same thing had happened in America how many would have got shot?"

I did not want to argue with him. "And Hong Kong?"

He rubbed his face. "I think Hong Kong's too important to China. But don't bank on it. And you?"

"I don't want to think about it. 'A single spark can start a prairie fire.' Quote, Mao Tse-tung."

He looked at me. "And Catherine?"

I said, "I don't want to think about that either. I'm going to see Reg tomorrow to start divorce proceedings."

"Is she still going to fight you?"

"She says so. But I don't think she will when it happens."

"Is she still threatening to come back here?"

"After the summer holidays, she says. But I don't think she'll do that either." I didn't want to talk about it. "She's in an emotional mess. This affair with this guy shook her up badly. She's panicky about her age and a lot of things. But I'm going ahead, Max."

He nodded, nod nod. He looked over his shoulder. "What about the security aspect of it? Especially now."

I said, "If it comes to that I'm quite prepared to give up my job for her."

Max's big liquid Portuguese eyes.

"Well—it's good to see you happy anyway."

"I'm happy, all right," I said.

I showered and shaved and all the time I was laughing inside with excitement. I had a stiff brandy and savored the good burn and then its solid feeling in my gut, then I

386

just paced about and gave myself up to the impatient excitement of waiting for her.

At ten to four I heard the key in the door and my heart turned over like a porpoise and as I went for the door it opened. And there she was. Standing nervously grinning in the doorway, she had loosened her hair for me in the elevator, the line of her hair and neck and shoulders and legs and her beautiful nervous grinning laughing mouth and eyes—"Ying!" and then oh God she was laughing shaking clutching in my joyful arms tearful kissing, her hair in my mouth, jerky laughing kisses clutching and the wonderful smell of her, *"Oh my darling darling darling,"* and she was laughing jerkily clutching, *"Let me look at you—so white!"* *"I've been in England,"* I laughed and she cried, *"Are you telling me?"* and oh God the wonderful feel of her and I pulled up her blouse and put my hand on her breast and oh God the laughing bliss.

Later, lying exhausted peaceful happy on the bed with the dusk outside, the feel of her lying in my arm, her smooth knee across mine and her belly against me, and the feel of her head on my shoulder and sometimes the small tickle of her hair, and the feel of her face, the softness, and the incredibly smooth feel of her light-golden skin, her shoulders and arms and hips and thighs, the bliss of my woman in my arms again; I had been away a long time and now I was truly back at last and I knew nothing else mattered. Nobody could touch us. We had been alone all our lives together, it was them and us, and we were never lonely, it always felt good. It is a wonderful feeling, if you ever have it you are very lucky, and there is only one thing you must do about it and that is seize it and rejoice. I was very happy with what I was doing, I knew it was good. We were awake most of the night. I was still functioning on Europe time, when it was Hong Kong midnight it was my noon, I was wakeful sleepy, she was sleepy wakeful, we lay in each other's arms and neither of us wanted to sleep, we wanted to be awake for each other, it was wonderful fun being wakeful sleepy: once I went to sleep and when I woke up she was coming back into the room with a big sandwich and two mugs of beer and I was wide awake again; we talked about a lot of things in little pieces, then we did not want to talk any more or think about anything except each other. I remember once I said, "Were you upset about Catherine?" and she said,

"No, I knew it was going to be like that. I knew a long time ago it wasn't going to be easy."

I said, "It will be all right, I'm seeing a solicitor in the morning to start the divorce," and she said, "Don't let's talk about it tonight. Everything is going to be all right, I know that too."

Another time I said, "What about the Cultural Revolution?" and she said, "Don't let's talk about it tonight. Tonight it's us." She held me tight a little and said, "I am Chinese and the Cultural Revolution is wonderful, but don't worry, I won't let any Cultural Revolution hurt us."

I said, "You're a revisionist, we'll have to send you to Struggle and Thought Reform Labor Camp."

We did not talk about it any more. I remember thinking dreamily that it did not matter because it was completely true that nobody was going to stop us, everything was very clear. What I did not really know, and oh God forgive me I should have known it, is that the world does not care about you and it will destroy you if it feels like it, and it does not care afterward if it was not necessary.

I woke up at dawn, realizing I had been asleep, as if I had had a siesta because I was still functioning on Europe time. She was sitting on the edge of the bed in her short dressing gown smiling happily at me with her long hair loose. "Good morning, come and see the sun." It was wonderful waking up to her.

"How do you feel?"

"Wonderful. We had a wonderful night. Come and see the sun with me?"

The sun was a great red glow behind the black mauve Mountains of Nine Dragons, fanning up gloriously fiery red through orange to yellow into the crisp spring starlit gray, the mountains were on fire on the rim, and below them Kowloon was asleep, quiet gray under its dulling neon lights, and the harbor was quiet mauve clean peaceful and down there on the Wanchai waterfront it was silent empty.

"The East is red," she said.

It glowed golden onto her happy face and shone into her hair in tiny spectrums, and in her eyes.

"I watched it every morning while you were away. I thought, At least we're seeing the same sun."

We went back to bed, she sat cross-legged opposite me, her long legs golden smooth, drinking coffee and smoking

388

our first cigarettes. The night was like a dream, it was wonderful to be together. We talked, we had so much to talk about and didn't know where to begin. I said, "Max says I'll get a date in the Supreme Court by August for the divorce. Then there's only another three months for the decree nisi. We can get married for Christmas."

She grinned at me, "We're already married. Don't I make you a good wife? Chinese ladies are known for it."

"You're an excellent wife. But I want you living with me openly and unafraid."

"I'm not afraid of anything, darling, there's nothing to be afraid, I decided that."

I said, "But there may be. With the Cultural Revolution. And Macao." I said, "I want you to quit your school as soon as possible, Ying."

She said, "Darling, I can't quit until the summer school holidays, I can't desert them at the beginning of a term."

"When are the summer holidays?"

"End of July. That's only three months off."

"It's over three months. Then you will quit?"

She smiled and her lovely eyebrows went up in laugh-frown, sitting there cross-lovely-legged. "Darling, must we talk about it now? What about Catherine? Is she really going to fight you?"

I was calm, happy. "I don't think so. And if she does I believe I'll win. And if I don't you and I are going away somewhere if we have to and live happily ever after. Jamaica. Where de rum cum frum. We've got some money and I've got a goddamn degree." I smiled. "I almost wish it would happen, after my strong diet of goddamn politics for six months. An island in the sun."

"This is our island in the sun, darling, it's the best of both worlds for both of us. Let's just go to Jamaica for a holiday when we're rich."

"When *who's* rich, comrade?'

She thought that was hilarious.

"Let's have some champagne for breakfast." I held out my finger. "The New McAdam does what he wants. The man who went East and grew up with the country."

We sat cross-legged on the bed and drank champagne in the China sunrise. God it was wonderful to be back. I remember I said, "But you must quit the school when the summer holidays begin, Ying."

She puffed on her cigarette then smiled at me earnestly,

she did not want to talk about it now but she had thought about it all.

"Darling? Yes, I will. When I know the divorce is really happening. But must we talk about it now?"

"It will be well under way by the school holidays," I said. "You mean if Catherine fights it you won't?"

She appealed to me: "Darling, I'm not saying I won't do anything for you. I *will,* if it's necessary. But please, I don't want to give up my work until it's necessary. Do you understand that—please understand that!"

"I do," I said.

She appealed to me smiling earnestly: "But do you? Darling, I thought all about it while you were away. And I knew what was going to happen and I decided I love you and I'll give up anything for you, but only when it's necessary. When the divorce really *really* starts I will quit if that is necessary. But maybe it won't start for a long time, how long has this divorce business been going on and it still has not started? I do not want to give up my work and everything and maybe in one year it is still not started; I do not understand why English law takes so long."

I said, "It's starting today. I'm seeing Reggie today."

She leaned forward and kissed me. "Then, darling, if everything is all right I will quit in the summer holidays."

"And if it isn't all right? If Catherine fights?"

"Then if it is necessary for you to win the divorce, or not lose your job, then I will quit, I promise. But please don't try to make me give up my work until we know it is necessary, what's happening. Let me do my work and you do yours. You like your work, don't you?"

"Yes," I said. "I think so."

"Of course you do. Are you a good policeman?"

"Absolutely."

"So am I a good schoolteacher. Do you do your duty?"

"Frequently."

"So do I. Do you give away secrets to the enemy?"

"Only my heart, to a certain communist."

She grinned, "Do you love your Queen and country?"

"With a mad passion."

She grinned. "Same for me. Oh, darling, we have proved that we can both do our work and have each other too, there is no danger. The Cultural Revolution is not for export, it's for the Chinese people in China, to stop the rot of capitalism returning, it is not for Hong Kong which is all capitalism. Hong Kong is too important to China.

Macao deserved it, but Hong Kong is not like that, is it? I do not believe it will happen here. If it was going to, it would have happened months ago."

I wished I believed it. Sometimes I did believe it. Macao was months ago now. I said, "I hope so but a single spark can start a prairie fire. Quote, the Chairman."

She appealed, "Oh, darling, be practical, not theoretical. Theoretically America could drop a hydrogen bomb on China tomorrow. Will you please be happy?"

"I am happy. I have never been so happy."

"Do you want some more champagne? Do you want to make love? I'll do anything you say. It's going to be a wonderful summer, I know."

CHAPTER 59

We had a lovely time that springtime. I had been far away a long time and all I wanted was her and now I was truly back. In the evenings it was still chill and usually we went to bed quite early, and it was wonderful lying deep in the warm bed with her, especially in the early mornings, waking up and finding her there, I like to feel the back of her warm smooth shoulders against my face, and hold her sleeping breasts and feeling her whole long warm smoothness against me, the morning is the best time to be with your love. She made us coffee and brought me the newspaper and left in a frantic flurry of bra and pants and dress and hair-burshing and a grin over her shoulder to go back to her room to get ready for school. I lay in bed and read the paper, fresh from the early night with my love, then went to the office early, and that felt good too.

On Friday evenings we sailed out on the junk. She loved the junk. We anchored in a good bay on an island and then she cooked dinner. Friday night was big chow night and she took a lot of trouble to cook something very exotically Chinese, and I sat and watched her and drank beer and we talked, about anything at all. Except about what happened at the office today, that was her joke. "What can't you tell me about what happened at the office today, darling?"

"Ve vill ask ze questions."

She didn't think the Cultural Revolution was a joke at all, but she liked my jokes about it and it's lovely being in love with somebody who loves your jokes and laughs a lot. It was great down here in the saloon, with the lamps shining yellow on the big varnished beams and the warmth from the stove and the sound of the sea lapping and the knowledge we would sit a long time over dinner and drink a lot of wine and talk about a lot of things. I liked to watch her brush her hair before going to bed, sitting naked on the edge of the bunk, and I made her hold it this way and that to see what she looked like in different styles, and she liked it. "You are a bourgeois reactionary and not a good clean-minded Comrade," I said. "I'm a Comrade-in-arms."

"Really I am very pure and virginal. I only do it because I love a paper tiger."

"When you come to bed you will see this tiger is not made of paper. We'll also see who's virginal."

When she was brushing her hair I liked to lie there and look at her smooth back and stroke her thighs, and kiss her hip, that soft firm very smooth bulge as she sat up straight, it felt wonderful on my face, and she liked me doing that; and lie with my head in her lap and feel her belly against my face, that sweet warm cool smoothness, and she would hang her head down to brush her hair over and her breasts pressed against me. I had been away a long time and all the time she was wonderful like this but I had not been here to love her, and now I was again, and I knew I could not live without her, and her hair and her eyes and mouth and shoulders and breasts and belly and legs, I would not live without the joy of her forever and I was glad with all my heart for what I was doing.

I didn't want her any other way, particularly her goddamn dedications. It is great to love somebody with dedications, who you can argue with and try to bully and tease. I liked her flapping around in the mornings rushing off to do her goddamn thing for China, even if I had to make my own breakfast. And I knew when we were married it would be the same flap in the morning when she rushed off to some nice wholesome middle-class school to do her thing.

Even on Sunday mornings she was always awake suddenly at dawn, and often I woke up to the slow scuffling sound of her Tai Chi Chuan slow-motion exercises on the topside deck. And Mad Dog splashing somewhere. Mad

Dog spent the night on deck leashed to the mast and I don't think he slept at all in case he missed something. Sometimes she swam before breakfast and she came in all wet sleek naked to tell me to come and swim.

"Later, Comrade. Come back to bed and be comradely."

"Comrade-in-arms."

We very seldom saw any other pleasure craft where we went, though we saw a lot of fishing junks and a lot of them were communist. A number of the Colony's outlying fishing villages were very communist. They fished in China waters and they had to get licenses from the nearest commune. Now, with the Cultural Revolution, they had to sail to China once a week for a Mao-think Struggle session, or they were in big trouble. Special Branch had a lot of paid informers among them.

Every weekend we went to different islands. And we climbed over the hills and explored down into the valleys and along the many beaches, and into the little fishing villages. She knew the names of all the grasses, shrubs, flowers, birds, and most of the insects, it was most impressive and I enjoyed it when she crouched down to examine something and identified it and told me about it. Sometimes there were small farms, cut into the valley slopes, farmers carrying water in wooden buckets suspended from bamboo poles across their shoulders, shuffling down the rows of plants watering them. And the wife weeding and Granny and Grandpa and the children weaving ladies' handbags and putting together plastic flowers, piecework for the factories far away in Kowloon. There were always ducks, pigs, chickens, and chow puppies and she always had to spend a time admiring them. If there was a hen sitting on eggs she had to see it all. The hen stuck up her feathers dangerously and pecked but she got her hand underneath making noises chickens like to hear and lifted her up and admired the eggs and told her she was doing a grand job. It was the same at almost every farm. She was particularly fond of the ducks. At one place the farmer had hatched duck eggs under a broody hen. The hen was looking thoroughly disconcerted. The ducklings were quite happy with the hen but the hen was not so sure at all about these ducklings. Ying thought it was terific. When she tried to get a duckling out, the hen scrambled off the nest, calling them. They waddled after her, frantically waving their stumpy wings. The hen headed them down to the pond, for a drink, clucking dangerously. And the ducklings took one look at the water and to a man they swarmed in with a whoop and a holler and the hen nearly had a heart attack.

She squawked up and down the edge of the pond frantically squawking at them to come back, and the ducklings took no notice whatsoever. They were having a wonderful time. We were all laughing, except the hen. Then Mad Dog must needs leap into the pond into the middle of the ducklings and the old hen went berserk. She screeched up and down beating her wings wild-eyed screeching at Mad Dog, Ying was yelling at Mad Dog, everybody was shouting, there was such a hullabaloo that it even got through Mad Dog's waterlogged brain that he was unpopular and he turned to come out, but as he did so a duckling swam past his nose. And it was more than his retriever flesh and blood could stand, with the best will in the world he grabbed the duckling, and all hell broke loose. The hen went mad and everybody was yelling at him and the duckling was squeaking out the side of his mouth, Mad Dog swam apprehensively through the hullabaloo but he could not get it into his thick head to spit out the duckling, he clambered up the bank and we all ran at him but the hen beat us all to it, and Mad Dog did not know what hit him. She flew beak first wings beating and got a fierce beakful of Mad Dog's apprehensive behind and Mad Dog yelped and spat out the duckling, it picked itself up and legged it back to the water flat out, Mad Dog was yelping twisting around and around but the hen hung on, taking all her frustration out on Mad Dog's behind, Mad Dog had been the last straw. She beat up Mad Dog clean through the pigs and chickens, yelping squawking, Mad Dog fled yelping out of the farmyard. We were all laughing and Mad Dog had no face at all.

In the villages we usually like to eat. Eating in public really made us feel it was a holiday. The restaurants had round wooden tables and small backless stools and they always had cold beer. The local people stared at us and we joked with them and soon the whole eating house was happy with us. There was always fresh seafood, crabs, lobsters, prawns, fish, very alive, swimming in glass tanks and big wooden buckets and you chose the ones you wanted. She would never choose. We always had oysters first, then prawns, a big steaming plate of them, you dip them into black soy sauce and mustard and it is almost impossible to get tired of them. We threw the heads and shells to Mad Dog, he snapped them up in midair and gobbled them down without touching sides. That dog would eat anything, orange skins, apple cores, anything, without question. It was very impressive. So help me I never saw him turn down anything. Once I threw him a big tomato and he did not think twice. Another time I threw him a banana, skin and all. Once I threw him a red pepper chile and he did not even flinch, just swallowed and thumped his tail. Those red chiles are hot enough to blow your head off. It was an ambition of mine to keep throwing him red chiles to see how many it took before he caught on but she wouldn't let me. We always had a good time.

In the villages there was a great deal of life and noise, dogs chickens cats ducks children coolies hawkers barbers dentists cooked-food stalls fortune-tellers letter-writers temples tailors jewelers machine shops weavers basketmakers carpenters boatbuilders markets, and grannies and grandpas and all in the great Chinese togetherness. It was the real Old China of before the battles long ago out here. Tourists never got to these villages, and very few Hong Kong people. It was great to walk down the lanes openly together and examine things and buy things together, it felt like a holiday. I wanted badly to go on a real holiday with her, to Japan or the Philippines or Thailand and be really free. Stay in good hotels and go to good cocktail bars, dine in good restaurants, see her all tarted up and beautiful and sparkling, show her off, take her to an amusement park. I do not care for amusement parks but I had this notion that I wanted to take her to a carnival and have a crazy time, ride on the swings and merry-go-rounds and Ferris wheels and go screaming along on the roller coasters with her and have a go at the coconut shies and laugh at the distorting mirrors. And walk the streets of Hong Kong, hand in hand.

We were going to do all these things, when we were married.

March and April went this way and the Cultural Revolution still did not come to Hong Kong.

I usually went to the office early. There was plenty for me to learn about the local front before I was much use to the Branch. Nobody expected any wonders from me that spring. I relied heavily on my inspectors to brief me. Every day the director called a series of meetings to keep abreast of what we were doing, but usually one officer never got to hear what the next was doing, unless there was "a need to know." A lot was happening but it did not seem to me to be anything that wouldn't happen all the time in Hong Kong. There was one potentially dangerous incident where a police constable had to arrest a hawker for obstruction, the hawker grabbed the constable's gun from the holster, they wrestled, it went off wounding the hawker in the leg. We only charged the hawker for resisting arrest, he claimed "compensation" and "apology" from the Hong Kong Government, but the trial was held before old Charlie Kwok who convicted the hawker and merely cautioned and discharged him and wished him "Good luck, good luck." Some communist demonstrators in court shouted *"Protest!"* and old Charlie Kwok beamed at them shortsightedly and said, "Yes, yes, good-by, good luck—" and shuffled out of court happily. And that was that. The next week the *Red Flag* complained that Oppressed Hong Kong Compatriots were asleep because they did not succeed in getting compensation and apology for this Fascist Atrocity, but nothing happened.

Our own communists held some meetings hailing the Cultural Revolution and declaring their undying love of Chairman Mao the Reddest Sun in Our Hearts, but they were too worried about business to risk confrontation with the Hong Kong authorities. Their Macao compatriots had burned their fingers in gaining their Glorious Victory. Business was bad all around, following the bank crisis there were a lot of empty and half-finished buildings, imports from China were way down because of the havoc of the Cultural Revolution. China was in plenty of economic trouble, the Bank of China was feeling the pinch. Nor would a Victory in Hong Kong be as easy as in Macao. Nor was there the excuse. I believed it, I wanted to believe it. At least until the divorce came through and we were safely married.

The border was pretty quiet. One evening I met Nondrinking Jack in the Foreign Correspondents' Club. "How it going up there?" I said.

Nondrinking shrugged with a mouth full of beer. "You see the Red Guard kids swaggering around. They hold their Mao-think sessions regularly, everybody gets into little huddles and reads their *Little Red Books* aloud and shouts Rah-rah-rah for Chairman Mao and Down with All Paper Tigers and Their Running Dogs, then they get on with the job in the paddy fields. A lot of posters denouncing President Liu and Poisonous Weeds, and that's about it."

"What about the People's Liberation Army?"

Nondrinking shrugged. "Justee samee. Shitty. No smilee. No wavee. Fuck offee. Since Macao, more illegals are trying to make it via the Shamchun Valley, there's quite a bit of night shooting. There've been a good few executions on Execution Hill, but nothing extraordinary. What do you think, you're supposed to be in the know?"

"Seen anything of my old friend Chester Wu?" I said. Chester Wu was the spy I had arrested at Takwuling that night years ago.

"Saw him three weeks ago through the binoculars, looking as tubby as ever. I wonder how he's taking the Cultural Revolution, if ever there must be a Capitalist-Roader it's him."

"Old Chester's too bright," I said, "to fall foul of the right people, he'll come out of the Revolution still head of the Security Bureau in Kwangtung."

"If the President of China can be kicked out as a Running Dog I don't like Chester's chances with his record for wine, women and song and Swiss bank accounts. Maybe he'll defect back again."

"I'd love to have him on my payroll," I said.

"*Every*body would love to have him on their payroll. Christ, the Americans and the Russians would pay a fortune for him, you couldn't afford him."

I said, "Old Chester should be grateful to me, I made him a potential millionaire when he decides to defect."

"He was a nice chap, wasn't he, Old Chester."

That night I met Derek Morrison, my bank manager. "How's business?" I said.

"The Honkers and Shankers is all right," Derek said. "But ask the Bank of China. I don't see how they can afford to carry on with this Cultural Revolution nonsense. It's bloody economic madness."

"What do you think's going to happen here?" I said.

"Nothing. They might be mad but they're not bloody stupid. Chairman Mao cannot *afford* to bugger up Hong Kong as well when things are so bad in China."

In China it was bad. Our information from our sources inside China was as confusing and conflicting as it was extraordinary. Mao had had to call in the People's Liberation Army to carry out "Revolutionary Take-overs" of government bodies, and for a while there emerged the

"Triple Alliances" of the Army, Reformed Party Cadres, and Red Guard Workers to replace the Capitalist-Roaders and Liu-ist Scabs who had been purged; the Army was put firmly in control and the Red Guards were ordered to prepare for the spring sowing, and for a while we thought the Great Proletarian Cultural Revolution was nearly all over bar the shouting: then after a month Mao cut back the Army's powers and forbade them to interfere with the Great Proletarian Cultural Revolution, and the chaos resumed. Chaos, bloodshed, gang fights, street fights, the schools closed, the factories upside down. I was supposed to be one of Special Branch's experts on the Cultural Revolution and I did not see how they could carry on. China could not afford to lose a single day's industrial production, let alone a year's. Yet she had done it. Putting the details together was exasperating. Nobody really knew what was happening. Peking did not really know what was happening in Canton, Canton knew less about Peking. The Russians did not know. The CIA didn't. The MI5 didn't. The pundits at the Foreign Correspondent's Club didn't. Perhaps the most reliable information outside the secret services came from the Japanese foreign correspondents based in Peking, because they could decipher most of the Red Guards' Big Character posters. The posters were very competitive and confusing. Claiming ubiquitous struggles and triumphant Victories for the Thought of Mao Tsetung. There were many Victories. And much bloodshed. And chaos. Our communists in Hong Kong were very confused too. They hailed the Revolution but they were never sure from one week to the next who was in and who was out in the hierarchy up there in Comradeland. They only know that it was Glorious and Invincible and Victorious. We tried to piece together the welter of discordant information and keep up with what our own communists were thinking of doing. And they were doing nothing and didn't know what to think. We paid out a lot of money for a lot of information that didn't add up to much. Chiang Kaishek's agents were always coming at us with tales of communist plots to blow us all to kingdom come but they did not check out. The New China News Agency handouts were long on hyperbole and short on detail. The head of the New China News Agency was China's chief intelligence agent in Hong Kong and if he knew much about what was happening in China, except Victories, you wouldn't have guessed it from his handouts. There was nothing we could do about it. The only person who could do anything about it was Mao Tse-tung himself. Mao could have stopped the Revolution. But he wasn't going to, for a long time.

The spring went that way. I was happy. My solicitor had sent off my divorce petition. Sometimes I did wake up in the night, worrying, but there she was asleep beside me. I had made my bed and I would lie in it. After the Revolution everything would be all right.

CHAPTER 60

It turned warm that last week in April. Next week would be May Day, the day the Workers of the World unite and rejoice. In Headquarters we were very relieved: all our information indicated that our Comrades were planning no trouble. No demonstrations, no Chairman Mao glory rallies: just banquets. One hundred and thirty-eight communist organizations had booked out Christ-knows-how-many restaurants for great glory celebration chows with lots of Ching San beer, Ma-tai wine, firecrackers, red flags and portraits of the Chairman, every communist cinema was showing the latest communist extravaganza called *Chairman Mao Is the Reddest Sun in Our Hearts;* and that was going to be that. We had got hold of Chiang Kai-shek's agents and told them that if they tried any funny business to sabotage the Reds' little shindig we'd bloody murder them, and they'd said okay. Live and let live, nobody wanted any trouble, and there wasn't going to be any.

That Friday night was warm and starry. I picked Ying up at the Yacht Club jetty. We anchored off Lamma Island for the night. It was beautiful sitting on deck in the starlight on the China Sea drinking Famous Red Triumph. I could sense she was waiting to tell me something. "What are you so pleased with yourself about?" I said. She puffed her cigarette in the dark, then said, "I know you're not going to be crazy about this."

"What?" I said.

She breathed deep. "I'm going to China on Monday."

I stared at her in the dark. I couldn't believe it.

"You're going *where?*"

She grinned at me.

"I'm going to see my father." I stared at her. Jesus Christ. She said, "That's where he lives."

Jesus! "I know that's where he lives! But what the *hell* makes you thing you're going to China in the middle of the goddamn Cultural Revolution!'

She slid off her seat onto the deck at my feet.

"I'm being *sent*. By my school! With fourteen teachers from other schools, to represent us at the May Day celebrations in Canton! And I'll see my father at the same time! . . ."

"Good God." I stared.

"What?"

"This is no time for you to go to China, Ying!"

"Darling, you forget I am Chinese . . ."

"Like hell I forget it! I'd rather you went if you were goddamn American. How long the hell for?"

She drew on her cigarette. "This is the part you're not going to like."

"I don't like *any* of it! How long?"

She said apprehensively, "Six weeks."

I stared at her. "Six *weeks?* What the *hell* for?"

She said: "Darling, I didn't make a fuss when you had to go away—"

"What the *hell* will you be doing in China for a month and a half?"

She said patiently, "It's an edu*cati*onal tour. We'll be visiting communes, factories, schools."

Oh Jesus. "In short, so you can experience the Cultural Revolution. Come back and teach the kids about it?"

She said, exasperated, "Jake, it's going to be *fascinating!* You yourself say you'd give your eyeteeth to see China now. It's history! And it's my country! And I've been chosen to represent my school! And six weeks off with all expenses paid. *And* I'll be seeing my father who I haven't seen for two years. I don't like leaving you but of course I'm excited, wouldn't you be?"

I got up. Walked across the deck. Good God!

"You're not going, Ying," I said firmly.

She stared after me. *"What?"*

I turned. "Oh Christ, I know. A wonderful experience, history in the making, it's your country, et ectera, I know."

"And your father—"

"*And* a month off school, all expenses paid!

That really impressed her. Scratch a Chinese and you find a capitalist. "Ying, you can't go to bloody China in the middle of the Cultural Revo*lution!* You know what's happening up there, anybody with the *slight*est hint of bourgeois about them is in big trouble, the Red Guards would tear you apart! With us in our situation?"

She took a big breath. "I knew you'd say that."

"Of course I'm saying that!"

"Darling," she appealed patiently, "how would any Red Guard know about us? If *anybody* knew about us I would not be chosen to represent my school. One of *fourteen* teachers. It was announced at assembly this morning and everybody applauded me—I am a People's hero!" She was trying to make a joke. "You know what the principal said to me?"

Oh Jesus, "What?"

"He said it was a great honor. He had recommended me because I am the best teacher!"

I held my finger at her. "But not the best communist! You'd be Red Guards' meat, Ying—"

"Oh. You spoil it!"

I said emphatically, "I'm sorry, Ying! I don't mean to spoil anything for you. But you *must* get out of it!"

She cried, "China! The most fantastic country in the world. In the middle of its history, the Cultural Revolution. This is the greatest political exercise in history! And it's *my country!*" She tapped her breast. "I am Chinese remember! I came here to be *Chinese,* to work for China! *And* my father is waiting for me, I haven't seen him for *two years.* And you tell me I must get *out* of it?"

"I know—and I really am sorry, darling. But it's for your own good, *our* good—"

She cried exasperated, "You imagine the most terrible things about China, you think we are a lot of savages!"

Aw Christ. "I do not! But China is something I know more about than you—"

"You are not *Chinese,* you don't know how important it is to be able to *go* there. And we will be visitors, shown around not ordinary people—we will be VIPs! Wouldn't you want to go there now! Ask your friends at the Foreign Correspondents' Club."

I took a breath. "That's not the point, Ying."

"The point is you think the Red Guards will tear me

apart! Well, *think* about it, darling! Why am I chosen to represent my school if I am not well thought of, hah? It's not the Red Guards' job to attack visitors; what do they know about a stranger? On a *conducted educational tour?*" She smiled, calmer, winningly. "Darling, don't worry about me. Nobody's going to struggle me and I'll come back safe and sound." She put her arm around me. "It's just going to be an absolutely *wonder*ful experience! I am so excited. Darling?" she pleaded, "did I make a fuss when you went away for a year?—*listen* to me please—to your wife? To your police college?"

I said, "I was not going to China in the Cultural bloody Revolution."

She said urgently, "I have been *chosen* for it!" Her eyes were wonderful. "How could I get out of it even if I wanted to? If I said suddenly now I did not want to go they would demand, *Why not?* I cannot say my mother is sick, my father is sick. What can I say? Then they would start asking questions, get very suspicious—hah?"

Oh Jesus Christ. I walked across the deck. Why did this have to happen now? There was only one fucking way out and that was for her to quit the school right this red-hot minute! Just disappear and never go back. Come live with me. Jesus Christ, and *then* the Comrades would be on to her. They'd find out where and why and then our cover would be nicely blown, God alone knows how we've got away with it so long but that would really blow our cover. And the Comrades would really try to put the screws on me, they'd be absolutely delighted. Oh Jesus, why *now?* "There's only one way," I said.

"What?"

I turned to her. "And that is to quit that school *now*. Just disappear. You'd have to quit anyway when the divorce starts."

She stared, incredulous.

"Darling, that's *crazy!* All this time we have been so careful and now we ruin everything by running away? Where to? They would find me! And what about my children at school, their examinations—and what do I do while waiting for the divorce, we agreed—"

Oh *Jesus*—

"And *why?*" she appealed. "Just because I have been chosen to do something I really want to do."

I said, "That's goddamn better than you being eaten alive in China and maybe never coming back!"

She cried, "Oh *Jake*."

"Oh Christ, Ying, *let me think*."

I walked across the deck. Oh God, it was hopeless. I felt my hand shake as I wiped my face. How the *hell* could she get out of it? She couldn't get out of it except by quitting. And that was more goddamn dangerous than going to god-damn China. She followed me and put her arm around me.

"Darling? There is no danger in this schoolteacher going on an educational tour of China." She tried to make a joke. "You'll be green with envy."

Oh Jesus Christ in a teakettle.

"'Six weeks is *nothing* after our one year," she said.

"Anything could happen in this continent in six god-damn weeks!"

She was smiling, pleading with me to see it her way.

I walked across to the deck. She pleaded behind me.

"Darling? It's crazy dangerous just to quit, isn't it? There's no alternative. Is there?"

I thought, Christ *Christ* CHRIST!

Much later, lying in the big double bunk I said, "I am so sick of this. Living like criminals."

She held me happily. "Darling, we've had a grand time. And we won't live like this much longer."

I said, "God speed these six weeks."

She said in the dark, "Of course He will. In no time."

"I thought you didn't believe in God," I said.

She grinned in the dark. "I don't. But I'm so excited I'll believe in anything. Don't let's talk about it any more. Let's just be happy."

Oh God. "Come here," I said.

"I am here, darling. I couldn't be much more here."

"Like that?"

"Yes," I said.

"Is that good?" she said. "Oh yes, darling, you think it's good."

"Oh God, I love you so."

"Oh," she said. "Oh yes, darling. Like that."

"Oh Ying. I love you so."

"Oh don't stop, darling, don't worry about me. I love you, darling, just love me and use me, oh yes, I love you, yes like that oh yes yes yes my love my love my love don't think about me——"

Afterward she lay holding me on top of her. She said, "I love it when you groan."

"What about you?" I said.

"I don't want anything, I just wanted you. Like that."

I lay on top of her.

"It was a groan of fear," I said.

"No." She held me. "There's nothing to be frightened about. I'll come back safe and sound. And full of myself. Don't think about it any more. There's nothing more to think about."

But there was plenty to think about. After a long time she went to sleep. I lay there in the dark, listening to her breathing, thinking. She had to go to China, answer the summons. There was nothing we could do about it. The Comrades did not know anything, or else why would they send her? It was clearly just a Mao-think tour. There was a lot of it going on. They knew nothing. If they did they would not summon her to China, they would not risk taking her away from me, frightening me off her, estranging me from her. And if our Comrades here didn't know, no Red Guards with mud between their toes would know.

She had to go. But oh God, why did it have to happen now?

CHAPTER 61

I put Ying ashore at the Yacht Club jetty, then took the junk into my mooring. I got out a flashlight, went down into the engine room, took out the dipsticks.

The oil was hot and thin. But those Gardner diesels will go forever. But better take their heads off and have a go around. There was quite a bit of water in the bilges. Probably only calking. Anyway the pump was good. She was pretty good all around. As stout as a junk could be. Sure she was. I could sail her almost anywhere, she was built for deep-sea, for typhoons dammit. I could sail her clear to Cape Town or Kingston, Jamaica, if I had to. But Manila's the obvious place.

Fuel, I thought. I carry a hundred and twenty gallons now. About six hundred miles to Manila, say six miles to the gallon, one hundred-odd gallons, therefore one hundred-odd hours steaming, say four and a half days going twenty-four hours a day. Better stow a few forty-four-gallon drums of fuel. More water. Sails? The mainsail is all right but the ropes are old. I sat crouched down in the engine room and thought. That mast's all right, stout as a tree trunk. Get a new jib sail. And a canvas sea anchor. New ropes all around. Hard rations for a month. A two-way radio maybe, three hundred miles' range. We'll see about a radio. Don't know what they cost, and the rest would cost plenty anyway. And overhaul the engines. Everything reground, new bearings, rings, jets. A passport for her. Oh Christ.

Oh Christ, but it's no good pitching up anywhere without a passport for her, I said. And you can't get one of those in a hurry, and she goddamn leaves for China tomorrow. *Goddammit,* why didn't we get her one when we thought we were going on leave together instead of thinking she'd travel as my wife! Well, it's too late for that now. That means a counterfeit job, now. I felt my pulse lurch. Oh God, charming. Absolutely bloody charming. That's a pretty risk. A lovely risk to have to take at this stage, when you're assuming you are not even going to need a passport because you're not going to have to run. Charming, the first actual crime I have ever committed, and a bloody serious one. Five years in jail for that one.

I climbed up out of the engine room, into the dark. I was sweating. But it's no good thinking about refitting the junk without thinking about the bloody passport too. I took a big uptight breath. Getting the passport will be nothing. How many people in this colony are running around on forged passports, for Godsake? Forged identity cards? How much counterfeit currency running around? The passport is the goddamn least of your worries.

I left the junk and went back to the penthouse.

On Monday morning I woke up before dawn and she was making coffee. I got up and brushed my teeth. My face was white in the mirror. I was wide-awake exhausted. I went through to the kitchen. She had her back to me, soft and smooth and bare, her hair loose below her shoulders. She looked around, shiny-faced, trying not to look excited. "Hello, darling!"

"Come back to bed."

"I will. It's nearly ready."

We sat in bed, drinking the coffee. It was still dark outside. She held my hand. I looked at her, she smiled at me apologetically, trying not to look excited. I said, "You're not going to rush off to do your exercises today are you?"

She smiled. "No. Of course not."

I sat there.

"What, darling?" she said.

"You know what."

"Darling? Don't feel sick about it."

I felt sick in my guts. She looked at me pleadingly, then took my coffee from me. She slid down beside me and held out her arms. "Come," she smiled at me. "Please."

Afterward she lay holding me.

"Jake? Don't be worried."

"Sure," I said.

"Oh Jake." She said, "Darling, you know I have to go. There's no way around it."

We lay there.

She said, "Darling, I must go now."

I watched her in the half-light. She got dressed busily. I pulled on a T-shirt and a pair of shorts. "Don't come out," she said.

"I'm coming in the elevator with you."

She went into the bathroom and picked up her toothbrush and paste.

"For God's sake, don't take Colgate's with you," I said. "Buy some Great Wall."

She grinned. "All right." She put the Colgate's back.

"Have you got anything else like that in your case?"

"No," she grinned. "No sexy pants. Nothing."

I said, "Wear your hair in a bun. Or doubled-up plaits. For God's sake, don't let them cut it off."

She grinned, then kissed me on the mouth. "All right, darling."

"I'm bloody serious."

"So am I." She tried not to smile.

I took a big breath.

"All right. And for God's sake, don't say anything foolish. Don't be provocative. Don't get into any ideological arguments."

She smiled. "Don't worry, darling, I won't."

"And shout your Thoughts of Chairman Mao as loud as the rest. And condemn Hong Kong roundly. Tell them it stinks, capitalism stinks to high heaven."

"Yes," she grinned.

"So do the Portuguese. And the Americans. And the British stink worse than both put together."

She held her nose. "Yes, sir." She burst out laughing.

"Oh God, Ying—" I laughed also and hugged her tight. "I'm serious."

"So am I." She giggled.

"I beg your pardon?"

She burst out laughing. *"No! no! I'm not serious—"* She hugged me.

"Have you got your *Little Red Book?*" I said.

"Yes, baby.'

"Read it," I said. "Know it backward."

"Darling," she grinned, "I already do. Better than you."

"Have you got enough money?" I said.

"Yes, I won't need much. I've got a hundred dollars, my ticket's paid for, I've got plenty in the Bank of China if I need more."

"How much?"

"Nearly three thousand."

"Dollars or yuan?"

"Hong Kong dollars! Wish it *was* yuan."

I took a breath.

"Okay. Well, let's go."

We walked through the front door out into the dark, I carried her small case. We got into the elevator. She said, "Remember to water the flowers."

"Yes," I said. "And feed Percy and everybody."

"And eat *properly*. At the Mess."

"All right."

"And dinner at your club, don't mess around here."

"All right," I said. "Remember to write."

"I shouldn't write to you, should I?"

"God no! It was a joke. Don't you dare write from China!"

We got down into the dark basement garage, the elevator doors opened. We stood there. She looked at me, smiled.

"Good-by, darling."

"All right." I took her in my arms. "Good-by, darling." I said. I felt sick in my guts.

She whispered: "Please don't worry."

I held her tight.

"And please don't be sad, it's only six weeks."

"For God's sake, be careful, Ying." My throat felt thick.

"Of course I will." She held me tight. "I'm very sensible. You don't realize what a sensible wife you have."

"All right. Go now."

"Good-by, darling."

I watched her walk out into the dark basement. When she got at the edge of the light from the elevator she turned and waved, and I waved. She pointed upstairs, to tell me to go back to bed. She grinned.

Then she was gone. Just her footsteps echoing.

"God speed these six weeks," I said.

PART IX

CHAPTER 62

But God did not speed them.

That very Thursday two things happened which did not even make the newspapers. At Kowloon Cement Works an Australian engineer had a dispute with a Chinese driver of a lorryload of fast-setting premixed cement, and punched him. At the Artificial Flowers Factory the Chinese manager dismissed ninety employees following a dispute over bad working conditions, and six hundred remaining employees went on a protest go-slow strike.

Next week was going to be May Day, when Workers of the World rejoice. It is a big day in Russia, in China it would be a very big day indeed, with the Cultural Revolution. All Hong Kong police and the armed forces would be on twenty-four hours' standby over May Day. At police headquarters the Kowloon Cement and the Artificial Flowers was very bad news indeed. And oh God, very bad news to me.

The next day was Friday. That morning at the directors' meeting the only thing we discussed was the Kowloon Cement and Artificial Flowers. It had not yet made any of the morning papers, not even the communist. It was 9 A.M., there were two hundred workers on protest at the Cement gates, they were still on go-slow at the Artificial Flowers. We had our boys out there among them but our contacts within Cement Works were thin and they were zero in Artificial Flowers.

There were a lot of opinions at the director's meeting. Some thought it was a storm in a teacup; if the communist press hadn't got on to it by now, it showed there was no organization; the majority of the communist business houses and fat cats did not want a Victory at the expense of their pockets like their comrades in Macao. Most disagreed. Including myself. The fat cats didn't mean a thing if some twenty-year-old zealots in the unions decided to show their revolutionary zeal. Our Labor Department was out there now, trying to get the workers to negotiate with the managements. But the cement workers were refusing to send representatives to discuss their grievances: they insisted that management confront the whole lot of them. Now they were chanting Mao-think at the Clerk of Works.

The day went that way. It was in the noon papers, but only small items. We got very little inside information. The Kowloon Cement management had demanded that the man whom the Australian engineer had assaulted be medically examined before the dispute be investigated further: the workers had refused. Jesus *Christ,* that bloody Australian! Trust a goddamn Aussie to open his big mouth and put his foot in the Cultural Revolution just before May Day. I went up to the Mess too late for lunch and had a beer instead. Sheffield, another superintendent in Special Branch, came in and we talked about it. "Trust a goddamn Australian!" I said. The director joined us at the bar. "What?" he said. I said, "In my opinion, the manager of the bloody Cement Works should be taken down to the factory by the scruff of his neck, told to put on his most charming smile and take the wind out of the workers' sails by apologizing, and fire the goddamn Australian. Kick his arse all the way back to Sydney. But why won't the manager do that? Because he insists on standing on his dignity, having a decorous investigation. Well you can't *afford* the luxury of decorum at this time with these chaps. You can't assault workers a few days before May Day with the Cultural Revolution on and the precedent of goddamn Macao!"

"Quite so," Dermot said shortly. "But it's a free country. The manager is quite entitled to insist on a proper investigation into his own company's affairs, he's the boss."

"That's ex*act*ly what the governor of Macao thought, sir," I said. "There must be a way of bullying him into it."

"Not legally."

"Then let's be illegal! Anything for peace! And there bloody well *should* be legal machinery. Christ, this colony

410

exists entirely by its manufactured exports. It's *mad*ness not to have industrial conciliation legislation which forces people to go to the conference table! It's archaic. Look at Artificial Flowers. The working conditions were bloody harsh. No payment for tea breaks and no payment when overworked machinery broke down and the worker had to wait. When the workers objected, the manager just sacks them and bluntly refuses to listen to anybody, neither to the workers nor the Labor Department or Harold Wilson or the Thoughts of Mao Tse-tung!"

"This colony prospers," Dermot said, "because of laissez-faire. Remember that."

I said, "Thanks to laissez-faire, sir, there's six hundred workers chanting outside his gates. Where's the prosperity in that? And who's going to clean up the mess?"

"The Labor Department isn't exactly idle," Dermot said.

"The Labor Department wouldn't know if its bum were on fire!" I said. "And anyway they're powerless because they cannot force the parties to negotiate because of goddamn laissez-faire."

Dermot said quietly, "And if there was industrial conciliation legislation, what would we do now? The cement workers don't *want* to negotiate, they want to confront the manager en masse and make him lose face. So would we send a squad of policemen in to drag the workers off to the conference table? They would resist and there'd be a lovely fight. What would our friends across the border say about that? On May Day? With a Cultural Revolution? After Macao?"

I said, "With respect, industrial conciliation legislation is only half the point, sir. The whole point is that if we had a little more modern economic legislation and a little less laissez-faire and the laws of Adam Smith the bloody manager of the Artificial Flowers wouldn't get away with working conditions like that, and the dispute wouldn't have arisen in the first place and we would not have six hundred angry Chinese locked outside the gates just before May Day, wide open to agitation."

Dermot listened politely. I went on, "And we wouldn't have had the bank crashes and half our new buildings standing unfinished now and unemployment as a result. It's all an example par excellence of the capitalist system and laissez-faire running riot and breaking down. It's thanks to our riotous laissez-faire that the economy went

411

crazy over real estate, therefore the banks went crazy, therefore they crashed, therefore money's short now, therefore there's a shortage of jobs now, therefore the manager of the Artificial Flowers thinks he can impose his miserable terms of employment on his workers and kick them out if they protest. And we haven't got industrial conciliation legislation to *force* him to be reasonable. Just before goddamn May Day. Therefore we as policemen are worrying ourselves sick right now about the security of the Colony."

"Speak for yourself." Dermot smiled at me with his eyes but not his mouth.

Well, I'm a sad sonofabitch. "Aren't you worried?" I said. I added, "Sir?"

He said, smiling with his mouth but not his eyes, "You've accounted for the Artificial Flowers problem. Would you care to account for the Cement Works? Their management is not money-grubling Chinese. They're British. Those workers have no economic grievances. They're just being bloody-minded Chinese."

I was in no mood for the D.S.B.'s stonewall cynical omniscient silences, my woman was gone to China and we were sitting on a powder keg. I said, "Will you have another drink, sir?"

"My round," he smiled, enjoying it. He snapped his finger at the waiter and said *Hambalang.* "Then I think we should get back to our desks, gentlemen."

I tried to smile at him, and he enjoyed it. I said, "Bloody-minded British too. And bloody-minded Chinese is also right. We saw that in the Kowloon riots last year. Those kids had nothing to riot about except, one, they're kids in a laissez-faire society which because of its political uncertainties offers them little; two"—I held up my fingers—"because there was nothing better for them to do in this concrete jungle because our laissez-faire government does damn-all for them; three, because of our laissez-faire we had had a disastrous bank crisis which left the Chinese panic-stricken anyway because they're crazy about money and our laissez-faire capitalist newspapers cashed in on the sensation; and four, because they're bloody-minded Chinese"—I glared at the director—"who don't like us, never have since time began. Their xenophobia is *that* close to the surface. And Government and the bloody Cement Works management know all this, and they *know* May Day's just around the corner, but when one of their

412

engineers hits a cheeky Chinese, the management"—I pointed at Central—"must needs get all British and bloody-minded, too, sitting on its fat capitalist arse and Government can do bugger-all about it!" I looked at him. I said, "The only thing is for the general manager to go down there and sack the goddamn Australian. And apologize."

"What about company morale?" Dermot said mildly. "The Australian was provoked. That was fast-setting concrete, it had to be delivered right away. And what will happen in other factories?"

"That's just tough," I said. "If we don't settle this we'll have a riot and there won't *be* any factories, sir. That's the price we pay for our precious laissez-faire."

"Without laissez-faire there wouldn't be any Hong Kong," Dermot said quietly. "It only prospers because of laissez-faire, and Mao only uses Hong Kong and permits it to remain because it prospers."

"And if we keep up this rampant laissez-faire attitude there won't be any Hong Kong either," I said. "God, we're living with *Victorian* labor laws! Our trouble is we always have to have a goddamn disaster like the bank crash before we do anything about it."

Dermot smiled at me maddeningly.

"Well, maybe we should get back and do something about the disaster." He smiled, held up his finger. "But as intelligence officers, please. Not politicians. That's not what we're paid for."

I went to the bank and bought five hundred American dollars. At a premium of 11 per cent. The Hong Kong dollar was way down. Thanks to one goddamn Australian.

I left the office at six-thirty that afternoon. The Kowloon Cement and Artificial Flowers demonstrators had packed up for the night. I felt as if I had been awake all last night, uptight. Tonight was probably the last chance for getting her passport. Christ knew what would be happening next week. Tomorrow the communist press would take it up. I felt sick in my guts. My lips tasted salty. Oh God. But it had to be done. Next week it might be too late.

I wanted a drink but I took a taxi straight to Causeway Bay, to Honest Menswear Company. I bought a cream tropical suit off the peg, a color I have never owned. Then I took a taxi to the Sincere Wig Shop, *Special Rates for*

U.S. Personnel, and in an American accent bought a man's blond wig.

I went home and had two stiff whiskeys, while I changed into the Honest suit. I packed a holdall with a change of clothes, a bottle of whiskey. I left my passport, took only my Hong Kong identity card, issued when I was eighteen and which described me as a student. I left my gun. If Customs searched me at either end the gun would blow everything up in my face.

I looked at my face in the mirror. Pale, dark rings under my eyes. But with the whiskey the hollow feeling in my gust was going. I had to put it behind me. The whiskey made it a lot better. I put on the Sincere wig carefully, it fitted perfectly. I put on my spectacles which I used only at the cinema, looked at myself. I took a big breath.

"Are you in the ice-cream business?" I said.

Then I took a taxi down to the Macao wharf. It was deserted. The immigration officer waved me through on my Hong Kong Resident's I.D. card. I caught the eight o'clock hydrofoil to Macao. It was almost empty. Almost nobody went to Macao these days. It was forbidden for government servants to go.

CHAPTER 63

The streets were empty though it was only 9:15 P.M. No other tourists, no Portuguese policemen. The taxi driver was very polite and even opened the door for me outside the Estoril Hotel. I went up to my room and had another whiskey. Then I called for a taxi.

The old tailor shop on the narrow crowded waterfront was still there, but the big Chinese sign, *Vacations in Happiness and Tranquillity,* had been painted out and now there was a large portrait of Chairman Mao hanging inside. But the signboard still said Lo Wingkit was proprietor. I told the taxi to drop me at the Double Happiness Bar, opposite the Hotel Rio Pearl. I sat down in a kiosk in the very back and ordered a San Miguel. The bar was dim and almost empty. I waited a minute then a Chinese girl came over. "Hello," she said. "I sit down?"

"Okay."

"What your name?"

"Kevin," I said. "And yours?" We were speaking English.

"My name Maria Chan," she said. "You buy me drink?"

"Okay," I said.

The shouted for the drink and the *foki* brought it.

"We go hotel?" I said.

"Okay," she said. "Short time, long time?"

"All night," I said.

"Two hundred patacas," she said shamelessly.

"You must be crazy. In Macao? These days?"

"Okay, one hundred okay."

"Fifty," I said. "I pay for hotel."

"*Ai-yah!*" she said, hurt to the quick. "Fifty!"

"Fifty," I said.

"Okay," she said hopelessly.

I took out twenty patacas.

"Go and get room at Hotel Rio Pearl. Room with bath. Then come back and tell me room number. Then I follow you in five minutes. I not want my friends maybe see me."

Marie understood. She was very happy with fifty patacas. I drank my San Mig tastelessly. Maria came back. She was really quite pretty. She wrote down the room number because she could not be sure of the English.

"Okay," I said. "I come five minutes."

I finished my San Mig, then walked out of the Double Happiness into the hot night. I crossed the street to the Rio Pearl, once rather a grand old hotel, started up the stairs. Nobody paid any attention to me. I opened the door of Room 33 and there was Maria Chan.

The room had a bathroom, <u>all</u> right. The curtains were good and heavy. And a telephone. Maria undid her *cheongsam* and there she was in her bra and pants. She had a little gold crucifix hanging around her neck. That was a bonus. She was undoing her bra, once upon a time long ago I would have been very pleased with her but I was far too uptight to feel anything now. I put my hands over my face and slumped down on the bed. "Maria—I am sorry! I cannot do it."

"*Hah?*" Maria said indignantly. She had her pants down to her knees.

I thrust out a hundred patacas at her.

"I'm sorry, Maria. I am married. You are number-one girl but it is a terrible sin. I am a Catholic too!"

She stared, with her pants down at her pretty knees. Then she took the hundred patacas.

"Okay," she said. She folded the hundred patacas and heaved her pants back up. "You come back bar?"

"No," I said. "Tomorrow maybe."

"Okay," Maria said. She got back into her *cheongsam*.

"By-by," Maria said.

"Good-by, Maria," I said. I listened to her footsteps down the corridor. Then I switched out the lights and tested the visibility. I was very uptight. It was dark. Then I picked up the telephone and dialed the Vacations in Happiness and Tranquillity tailor shop.

"Wei?"

"Do you speak English?" I said.

The telephone rapped than another voice came on. "Hello?"

"May I speak to Mr. Lo?"

"I am Mr. Lo."

"Mr. Lo, I want you to make me a special suit overnight. Can you come and take my measurements? Immediately?"

Mr. Lo sounded interested. "Yes, sir. Where?"

"Hotel Rio Pearl. Room Thirty-three. Got that?"

"Yes, sir," Mr. Lo said.

"Do not ask at the reception desk. Just come straight up and knock. Understand?"

"Yes, sir."

"Thank you, Mr. Lo Five minutes?"

"Yes, sir," Mr. Lo said.

I climbed up on the dressing table and took the bulb out of the overhead light. I was shaking now. I switched on the bathroom light and turned on the tap gently. Then I sat down on the edge of the bathtub and waited. My heart was thudding. I did not make a good criminal, for all my experience, but I had done a pretty good job so far. I had covered my tracks as well as I could in the circumstances. I could not afford the convenience of an accomplice, the weak link in any crime, I could not even afford to let Mr. Lo see my face even with false hair. I had to live with the knowledge of Mr. Lo a long time. The knock came on the door. "Who is it?"

"Tailor Lo," Mr. Lo said.

"Come in. I'm just washing."

"The bathroom light shone into the dark bedroom. A man came in. I heard the door click, then I switched off the bathroom light and stepped into the bedroom. My heart was thudding. I said in English, "Good evening, Mr. Lo. Do not be afraid, I just do not want you to see my face." My voice sounded loud. I could see him dimly. "Mr. Lo, I have a problem. A friend of mine has lost his passport."

"Oh yes," Mr. Lo sounded relieved. "What kind of passport?"

"Hong Kong British passport," I said across the darkness.

"Oh yes," Mr. Lo said. "That is all right. British subject."

"When can you replace it?"

"Tomorrow morning, any time," Mr. Lo said, "if you have all details."

I said: "Estoril Hotel. Place it under the carpet on the second-last step of the third flight of stairs, just before the third floor. By three o'clock tomorrow morning. Understand?"

"Yes." Mr. Lo repeated the instructions.

"Your fee is one thousand patacas?"

"Yes," Mr. Lo said.

I held out two notes, I felt my hand shake.

"Two hundred U.S. dollars, Mr. Lo. Here are the particulars"—I handed him an envelope—"including the photograph, date of issue, old visa stamps. All right?"

"Ho-ho," Mr. Lo said. "Very good."

I said, "I will leave now. You will remain here ten minutes, then leave. Understand?"

"Yes," Mr. Lo said. He sounded relieved it was over. "You need not worry, I only want business, not trouble."

"You better, Mr. Lo. Because I have many friends. Thank you. Good night."

"Good night," Mr. Lo said.

At 3 A.M. the next morning, her passport was there. Nobody saw me collect it. I had done a pretty good job. I took the 4 A.M. ferry back to Hong Kong. I destroyed the Sincere wig but not the Honest suit. It was too good.

The next week was May Day.

CHAPTER 64

Across the length and breadth of China there was the mighty clamor of the vast parades, the singing and the roaring and the flags and the portraits of the Reddest Sun in Our Hearts, the massive frenzy. In Hong Kong 130 trade unions made their celebrations and outside the communist cinemas there were the mobs surging to see *Chairman Mao Is the Reddest Sun in Our Hearts,* and all Hong Kong police and Army were on Riot Standby. That day the other six hundred workers at the Artificial Flowers factory went on strike. That day the workers of Kowloon Cement handed in to management their Six Just Demands.

One, sack the Australian engineer; *two,* apologize; *three,* sign confessions of your guilt; *four,* guarantee no revenge; *five,* compensate; *six,* guarantee no recurrence.

That day the left-wing press took up the cudgels.

On the rooftops opposite Kowloon Cement were Special Branch detectives with binoculars, notebooks, telephoto cameras, and walkie-talkie radios. Down there in the street were the crowds, reporters, television men, and over one hundred policemen standing by and keeping the traffic moving. Inside the gates, the Kowloon Cement Works was silent and empty. All the workers had been paid off. The European employees who lived inside the company's compound had been moved out to hotels. Outside the gates squatted the four hundred workers, umbrellas, thermos flasks, pickets, banners, *Little Red Books*. On the factory walls were plastered their Big Character slogans and their Six Just Demands.

They were strictly observing factory working hours. It was now 10:30 A.M., they were just starting their tea break. Three of them left the mob and marched ostentatiously to a public telephone kiosk, clutching their *Little Red Books*. The leader produced thirty cents and dialed. The telephone rang across the harbor in the plush head offices of the Kowloon Cement Company, the demonstrators demanded to speak to the general manager. He came on the line. The demonstrators were crowded around the mouthpiece, they took a big breath and chorused in Cantonese:

"All reactionaries are paper tigers!"

"In appearance the reactionaries are terrifying but in reality they are not so powerful!"

"From a long-term point of view it is not the reactionaries but the People who are really powerful!"

"Hah?" the leader said in the phone kiosk.

"Do you speak English?" He added optimistically, "Speakee English?"

"Hah?" the leader said.

The general manager flicked the call back to his secretary irritably. "Miss Wu, please tell them that what I've said stands, I will meet their representatives here in my office or at the Labor Department offices!"

"Yes, sir," Miss Wu said. *"Wei?"* she said.

They chorused: "All reactionaries are paper tigers! In appearance—"

Miss Wu raised her voice: "The general manager says he will meet your representatives—

"The reactionaries are not so powerful—"

"—in his office or at the Labor Department," Miss Wu shouted.

"From a long-term point of view it is not the reactionaries but the People—"

Miss Wu switched back to the general manager. "Well?" the general manager said, "what do they say?"

"They say all reactionaries are paper tigers, sir," Miss Wu said anxiously.

The leader from the telephone kiosk came back to raise another thirty cents. Two taxis came tooting down the street and pulled up one behind the other. I watched them through Detective Pang's binoculars. Out of the taxis climbed eight Chinese schoolgirls, one man, two women. The man was handsome and very stern, the women were very good-looking indeed. A gasp of recognition went up, the crowd surged forward. The visitors were well-known film stars from the communist Great Wall Film Studios. Carrying big baskets of fruit. The crowd surged, the reporters were jostling, a police inspector waved the two taxis on. The film stars and the eight schoolgirls forged through the crowd, smiling. The demonstrators were beaming, blushing. The film stars thrust their fists aloft and shouted,

"Hail Mao Tse-tung! Hail the Masses!" and the demonstrators thrust their fists aloft: *"Hail Mao Tse-tung! Hail the Masses!"*

The demonstrators were very flattered. The actor made a speech: "Comrades, we bring you a gift, fruit from the glorious motherland, to show our undying support in your righteous valiant struggle against the imperialist paper tiger reactionaries! Dare to struggle, dare to win! Let us seek guidance from the Thought of our Chairman! Page seventy-six!"

Everybody scrambled to open their *Little Red Books,* the communist reporters were getting it down, snapping pictures. The actor quoted, chanting, and they came in in unison:

" 'Lifting a rock only to drop it on one's own feet' is a Chinese folk saying to describe the behavior of certain fools!

"The reactionaries of all countries are fools of this kind!

"In the final analysis, their persecution of the revolutionary people only serves to accelerate the people's revolution on a broader and more intense scale!

"Did not the persecution of the revolutionary people by the tsar of Russia and by Chiang Kai-shek perform this function in the great Russian and Chinese revolutions?"

"Comrades," the actor shouted, *"the so-called managers of the Cement Works are paper tigers lifting a rock only to drop it on their own feet!"*

There was a shout. A noncommunist photographer was getting a picture, three demonstrators grabbed at him, shouting *"Running Dog!"* He wrenched himself free and ran. An inspector shouldered in front of the demonstrators: *"Now—now, gentlemen!"* he shouted in Cantonese.

"No running dog must take picture!"

"He's gone now," the inspector shouted.

The film stars and the eight schoolgirls started singing "Sailing the Seas Depends upon the Helmsman," and everybody started.

Up on the rooftop I looked at the detectives' lists of known communists they had spotted. We knew them all, we knew they were behind the demonstrators now and there was little we could do until a fight started. Jesus, I did like all those uniformed police down there. It dramatized the situation and gave the strikers face and created the opportunity for confrontation. If I had had my way we wouldn't have had a single policeman in sight. We would ignore the strikers, if I had my way, and get hold of the Kowloon Cement management by the scruff of their necks and *make* them compromise. *Let* the goddamn Comrades claim a great Victory. But we were goddamn helpless. The goddamn Labor Department should have brought the two sides together by now, that was their goddamn job but they hadn't succeeded. I came down the back stairs from the rooftop, I was doing no good up there. Nerves. Goddamn the whole rotten stinking business. Goddamn Chairman Mao, the communists, the Cement goddamn Factory, the goddamn Flowers, the Cultural bloody Revolution. Where was our goddamn toothless Labor Department? I got down into the crowded street and there was the Labor Department arriving in a taxi. The film stars were just leaving, the last handshakes, roars of applause.

The Labor Department officer, Mr. Koo Ping-fat, climbed out of the taxi, beaming, and the film stars got into the same taxi. The taxi drove off to roars of applause with the film stars waving out the windows, and Mr. Koo stood beaming fainter and fainter, then not at all. Nobody had noticed him. Mr. Koo straightened his tie and made his way through the crowd toward the demonstrators. He put his beam back on. He held up his hands for silence, but everybody was watching the departing taxi. He lowered his hands and waited till the taxi was out of sight, still beaming but not so wide. Then he tried again.

"Good morning!" Mr. Koo shouted, beaming. "I am Koo of the Labor Department and I have come to help you! To urge you to meet the manager of this factory to settle this matter."

Some demonstrators turned to look at him. "Where?" a man shouted.

Mr. Koo shouted, "The manager has said repeatedly that he will gladly meet six of your representatives—"

"He must see all of us!" a man shouted and everybody began to pay attention. They took up the chorus hurriedly. *"See all of us!"*

Mr. Koo held up his hands, beaming, "He will meet you either at his office or in my office in the Labor Department—"

"He must meet all of us here!" the leader shouted.

"Please!" Mr. Koo shouted. "Be reasonable, the manager is trying to find a solution—"

"The manager is an imperialist paper tiger!" the leader

shouted and they took up the chant: *"Paper tiger! Paper tiger!"* They had gotten over the Great Wall Studios now. The leader shouted, *"Manager must meet all of us here and accept all six demands and bow his head and confess and pay compensation—"*

"Please," Mr. Koo shouted, "I am one of you, I am Chinese like you—"

"You are yellow-skin running dog!" a man shouted and they took up the roar in glee:

"Yellow-skin running dog!

"Yellow-skin running dog!"

and the crowd was surging with delight to see.

"Gentlemen, please let me help you," Mr. Koo shouted, sweating and blushing and the leader shouted a page number of the *Little Red Book* and chanted, *"We must oppose everything of which our enemy is in favor—Mao Tse-tung!"*

And the delighted roar went up, *"We must oppose everything of which our enemy is in favor—Mao Tse-tung!"*

The fists flung up in the air and Mr. Koo was sweating blushing shouting, but you could not hear him and now the front row of demonstrators were advancing on him, shouting, *"We must oppose everything—"*

And Mr. Koo turned about. Sweating, blushing and shouldered through the crowd, fatly disarrayed, to the roar of the Thought of Chairman Mao. The constables were trying to keep the people moving. I turned walked fast down the road, looking for a taxi to take me to the Artificial fucking Flowers.

I sat in the taxi, glaring out the window. Good God! Five days this had been going on and the communists were only just beginning to organize themselves; five precious days' grace we've had and we *still* haven't sorted the problem out to take the wind out of the Comrades' sails, *five precious days wasted!* God, our incompetence was colossal. We *knew* from Macao how things would go, and what was happening in China. We *knew*. Five fucking days to smooth things over, to kick the arses of management into sorting it out before the Comrades collected their wits— and had we? Jesus, are we spastic? There're ways and means. But oh no, we're British. We British don't interfere in the rights of the citizen to sort out his own affairs his way. Constitutional law and all that jazz. Well we're in China now buster where they don't give a *shit* for constitutional law and if we don't forestall them, they'll turn this town upside down! See what good your laissez-faire does then! What good has it done Kowloon Cement, they've closed *down* already, *that's* the good it's done them. This time tomorrow we'll be fighting for our *lives* in this town, let alone our precious laissez-faire!

I could hear the noise from Artificial Flowers two blocks away.

Six hundred workers locked outside the gates, pickets, protests, two thousand people from the factories all about, and three big blue trucks full of khaki policemen waiting, a dozen policemen pacing about with loudspeakers keeping the peace and traffic moving. And the big noise of mob waiting. I watched from the rooftop and cursed. The whole bloody thing was infuriating. Policemen doing management's dirty work for them, while management sat on its fat arse and stubbornly refused to negotiate. The police holding the angry poor at bay at the very gates. Christ, what did it look like? *"Let them eat cake?"* What splendid public relations! How long before some worker picks a fight with a policeman or chucks a stone at a factory window? *Then* what happens? A fight, a riot, communist screams of Bloody Fascist Oppression, and we have another Macao. My corporal tapped my arm and pointed.

A goods vehicle was arriving. And a noise went up from the mob. The policemen were clearing the way for the lorry to go to the Flower factory. For the fat capitalist lorry. Now it was backing up to the gates. The mob was shouting now. Inside the factory compound loyal workers were carrying out crates of plastic flowers for loading. The mob was shouting through the gates. Then the foreman appeared. He unlocked the gates, swung them open, the cordon of policemen held the shouting crowd back. The first crates were loaded onto the lorry, then a roar went up, and the crowd mobbed the gates. Broke the police cordon and mobbed the lorry, seized the crates and hurled them off shouting and wrestling with the police, the constables leaped out of the big blue waiting police trucks and came running and the roar redoubled, khaki and all the colors surging shouting wrestling down there and the crates flying and busting open and plastic flowers showering everywhere and the police loudspeakers yelling at them to break it up. "Oh Jesus," I said.

After five minutes the police got them apart, sweating panting shouting, and formed a cordon to keep them off

423

the gates. Trampled plastic flowers everywhere. Now everybody was shouting at the police, gesticulating in their faces, while the lorry was loaded up again. The superintendent was shouting through the loudspeaker, asking them to disperse and to address their grievances to the Labor Department. They roared back at him.

He was still trying when the hundred riot police arrived in the three big blue trucks, and the new big roar went up. As the constables started debusing the sticks and bricks and cans and stones and shoes started flying, the constables scrambled into riot formation, shields up. The mob was swelled right down the street now, surging and yelling and the missiles flying, and Chinese hanging out of every factory window shouting, a great mass of surging roaring screaming confrontation. The riot squad banner was unfurled, *Disperse or We Charge,* and another defiant roar went up. And the superintendent gave the order and our riot boys ran in. And the yelling and the running heaving swiping hurling struggling scattering surging down the street. And the big roar of hate.

By the time I got down to the street they were loading twenty-one arrestees into the trucks. Struggling and shouting Mao-think. The crowd was roaring down the street, missiles were still flying. The road littered with debris. I ran across to the superintendent. He was sweating, a gash on his cheek.

"We'll want these boys interrogated by Special Branch, please."

"You're welcome to the whole damn lot!" he panted.

"Will you send them to San Po Kong station? I'll make arrangements from there. Can I use your radio?"

"You're bloody welcome."

I called up headquarters. Then I radioed San Po Kong and told them to have a paddy wagon and escorts ready. Then I called up my detectives on the rooftops on the walkie-talkie and told them to stay on observation until further orders, poor bastards. The mob was still shouting at the end of the street, the loudspeakers still blaring. Another Artificial Flowers truck was reversing into the gates to load more crates. Jesus. It was going to look absolutely beautiful in the left-wing press tomorrow. There was no blood on the arrestees but tomorrow the left-wing press would be wallowing in blood and Savage Police Fascist Brutalities on Patriotic Oppressed Workers.

CHAPTER 65

It was after midnight. I paced up and down my office, holding the dictating machine microphone, concluding my covering report for tomorrow's 6 A.M. meeting with the director and the Old Man and O.C. British Forces. I was very bloody tired and I had had enough of the Hong Kong Government. It had been a long report and I hoped it gave them a sick headache.

General, underlined. Although each of the twenty-one persons arrested denied under interrogation—enclosures 1 to 21—that their demonstration was organized by any central body it is clear that various communist bodies are now supporting them, although they may still be unco-ordinated.

I lit a cigarette, went on:

Without any clairvoyance, it is certain that the left wing will not continue to be unco-ordinated in exploiting these disturbances. With the Cultural Revolution in rampant progress, and the precedent of the Victory in Macao, the left wing wants and needs a Victory in Hong Kong to demonstrate its revolutionary fervor. All it needs to galvanize it into co-ordinated action is a quasi-legitimate excuse, and this they now have. Indeed it is extraordinary that they have not organized themselves already, as it is equally extraordinary that Government has not yet organized a settlement of this ridiculous industrial dispute by some means or other.

I wanted to say a hell of a lot more, but took a breath and went on.

The pattern to come is clear.
First: The serious situation that has been allowed, underlined, to develop from these originally petty dis-

putes will first be exploited by extravagant demands, which, because of their nature, and the language in which they are couched, will be unacceptable. The Kowloon Cement workers' demands are significantly phrased: "Confess" and "Apologize" and "Guarantee," the language of the Cultural Revolution and that used in Macao. Doubtless, after today's conflict, much stronger stuff will follow, like "fascist" and "bloody atrocities" and "towering crimes."

Second: A confrontation will be engineered, by the simple expedient of promoting noisy demonstration. This, as happened today, will inevitably lead to police intervention, followed by some violence, this providing new grievances, namely police "oppression" and "bloody outrage."

Third: These enlarged grievances will be loudly taken up by the communist press to inflame public opinion against the capitalist system and against the police: starting tomorrow.

Fourth: Further bigger demonstrations protesting these enlarged grievances. San Po Kong, where Artificial Flowers fester, is so massively populated, so heavily industrialized, so full of workers, trade unionists, and young people, that it is an absolutely ideal locale for the "successful" promotion of such disorders. The maze of streets, the multitude of rooftops and balconies, will make the demonstrations, and the inevitable violence and riots, tactically very difficult for police to contain. We can expect massive trouble there on Monday. Furthermore, Hong Kong labor legislation being what it is, there will be thousands of unemployed teen-agers with nothing better to do than indulge in acts of vandalism. We know from recent Kowloon riots the bloody-mindedness of our people and the infectiousness of disorder in our overcrowded society. This the left wing will encourage and exploit, to create an impression of mass outcry. There will be large demonstrations outside the Kowloon Magistracy on Monday when the twenty-one arrested today are brought before court. We have to be prepared for this, although police presence, with the inevitable ensuing conflict, is precisely what the left wing wants: it is a vicious circle.

I sat down behind my desk. I felt old and tired and angry.

Fifth: There will doubtless follow organized protest marches on Government House. Mass marches are the order of the day in China today, they were also the case in Macao. Their prime purpose will be to confront the governor en masse and make him lose face and to gain a Victory for the Thought of Mao Tse-tung, as was achieved in Macao. The marchers will chant extravagant demands, including "Confession," "Apology," "Compensation."

This stage is clearly the most dangerous for us because:

Firstly, these marches on Government House will have to be contained, which will eventually result in police conflict with "peaceful petitioners," with all the hullabaloo that it will evoke;

Secondly, with this confrontation with Government itself, it is very likely that Peking will feel obligated to make its voice heard, support the demonstrators as compatriots and denounce the Colonial Government. This will inflame the locals. The international repercussions could be extremely grave for Hong Kong, with China in the turbulent, emotional throes of the Cultural Revolution.

And that's putting it bloody mildly! I thought.

Thirdly, if the left wing are thwarted at this stage, as they must be if we wish to avoid the fate of Macao, the demonstrations will reach a crescendo. They are likely to resort to widespread riots, sabotage, strikes, stoppages, boycotts, to achieve their end. Not only will the good order of society be destroyed, but the economy, and, if it escalates to the international level, the Colony itself.

I lit another cigarette. I could feel the dark rings under my eyes. Now was the time to say it. It was not my place as mere bloody policeman to say it but I would bloody well drag it in by the scruff of its neck.

The following conclusions are very obvious.

One. Every effort must be made, illegal if necessary, to get the management and workers of these two factories to the conference table immediately to re-solve their dispute, to take the wind out of the left-wing sails. Although Government is legally unable to force management to do anything, it is astonishing that, with the ingenuity of the Orient, it hasn't found means of coercing these recalcitrant citizens into a more conciliatory attitude. Government has only it-self to blame for not having industrial conciliation legislation to cope with such disputes, and for its abys-mal lack of modern labor legislation at all, the ab-sence of which permits some employers to make themselves unpopular by their working conditions and then refuse to accept mediation. However pros-perous the Colony may be because of Government's policy of laissez-faire, however good the lot of the majority of its citizens especially when compared with China's, Government has only itself to blame if it continues to allow itself to be a sitting duck for com-munist exploitations, distortions, and extremism by not having a modicum of legislation to minimize in-dustrial frictions and injustices in our uniquely crowded, highly bourgeois society, especially now that we have the object lession of Macao and the Cultural Revolution to warn us.

That's enough, I thought. That's as much as I can squeeze into a goddamn S.B. report.

It will all come back at me, like pissing into the wind, but fuck 'em.

Two. Police, whilst in a state of constant readiness, should remain well in the background, preferably un-seen altogether, to avoid confrontation as much as possible. Public relations psychology is vital. Defi-nitely, soldiers should not be seen or used at all at this stage.

Three. Where police are required, the greatest, underlined, restraint and patience should be exer-cised. Every policeman should be so instructed. They must appear as good scouts. Nothing will serve the left wing's ends better than a bit of hasty blood.

I ran my sweaty hand through my hair and lit another cigarette. My nerves were screaming with irritability and tiredness. What I wanted was a drink. I signed off:

Further interrogation of arrestees and other sources continues. A comprehensive index of statements and sources and files referred to in this S.B.R. is contained overleaf. Signed, McAdam, et cetera.

I flicked off the infernal machine and yanked the tape out. I rammed the files inside my safe and slammed the heavy door. Then I took the tape down the passage, into the night typists' room.

It was one o'clock. Outside headquarters I got a taxi. Riding through the bright gay neon lights and bars of Wanchai. I knew I should stop to get something to eat, but I was not hungry. Too goddamn screwed up tight to eat. What it all means to you and her. The only reason you're angry is what it all means to you. Oh Christ, please come back. Bring her back now, that's all, and I'll look after all the rest myself. I don't care what happens just as long as I've got the chance to control ourselves. The worst part is the not knowing what is happening to her, knowing anything could happen, please God bring her back, then I'll know what to do. What will you do? Like hell you know what to do. When she comes back you'll still have to play wait and see and live in fear. Catherine may fight the divorce. Now pull yourself together. You went into this eyes wide open. The only thing to do now is play it hard and cool and ride it out and if the worst comes to the worst you get out. I opened the penthouse and the hot humid silent emptiness shouted "Ying-ling" at me. "Hello," Percy said.

That was the beginning of the summer of that year.

That Monday the riots started.

CHAPTER 66

First there were the workers picketing, holding high the banners: *British Are Paper Tigers!* and *Fascist British Suppress Poor Chinese Labor!* and *Blood Debt Must Be Repaid in Blood!* and *Hong Kong Must Not Forget Macao!* and the loud chanting from the *Little Red Books,* and the singing, "The East Is Red" and "Sailing the Seas Depends upon the Helmsman"; and the left wing coming in handshaking delegations and the synchronized busloads of schoolgirls with their Mao badges, the *Little Red Books* and the vociferous righteous chanting and the cheering. And the headlines in the left-wing press, *Unite and Fight!* and *Hong Kong British Execute Imperial Aggression on Behalf of United States!* and *Cease These Atrocities!* and *Release Our Patriotic Workers Savagely Arrested!* Then came the beating on the factory gates and the screaming of abuse, until the police had to come. And the delighted roar went up from the crowd five thousand strong, and then came the stones flying, sticks bottles cans iron bars hurtling onto the policemen, the battle of the loudspeakers against the roars and the sticks and stones, and then the baton charge. And the running shouting roaring storming swiping struggling through the myriads of streets and alleys and factories and resettlement blocks. And the barricades and the bonfires and wreckage and slashing and smashing and the arson and the burning of the cars and lorries and omnibuses and the stoning of the ambulances and the fire engines.

For two days they rioted. On the second day the twenty-one arrestees, on bail, appeared in the Kowloon Magistracy for trial. Three hundred Comrades massed inside the court, down the corridors, out into the street, chanting shouting stamping singing all day. On the third day the accused did not appear to answer their bail, but the Comrades were there all the same chanting stamping singing, shouting at the police: *Yellow-skinned running dogs!* Then the sticks and stones started flying, they held up a Coca-Cola truck and threw the bottles and smashed the traffic signs, the riots spread right down the golden mile of Nathan Road, smashing hurling burning shouting. There were police, tear gas, and baton charges, but not a bullet was fired, not one person was killed. That day the left-wing press called it *White Terror!* and *Genocide Backed by U.S. and Chiang Kai-shek!* and *Outrageous Provocation of All China!* and Hanoi officially pronounced it *part of the process of turning Hong Kong into a U.S. base of aggression against North Vietnam.*

That day Peking called it *towering crimes and large-scale sanguinary atrocities and fascist outrages engineered by the Hong Kong authorities as the thug of U.S. imperial-*

ism to provoke deliberately seven hundred million Chinese armed with the Invincible Thought of Mao Tse-tung.

That day the Red Guards held a massive rally in Canton protesting against the Bloody Murders by the Fascist British Pigs and they burned Harold Wilson in effigy and screamed to march across the Shamchun and liberate the City of Imperial Decadence run by White-skinned Pigs and their Yellow-skinned Running Dogs.

That day Peking summoned the British chargé d'affaires and denounced the Fascist Barbarous Atrocities Instituted in Co-ordination with U.S. Imperialist War Escalation in Vietnam Making Hong Kong a Base for U.S. Aggression demanded the immediate acceptance of all the demands made by the Hong Kong workers, the immediate cessation of all fascist measures, the immediate release of all compatriots, the punishment of all the culprits responsible for the sanguinary atrocities, apology, compensation, guarantees. And the left-wing press went mad with joy.

That day the Red Guards marched on the British Embassy in Peking and sacked it.

That day the Comrades marched on the British Consulate in Macao and sacked it.

That day the Hong Kong-Kowloon All Circles Anti-Persecution Struggle Committee marched on Government House in Hong Kong.

Came marching four abreast chanting *Governor is a murderer! Governor is a murderer!* Marching up the middle of Garden Road chanting from the *Little Red Book,* fists upflung, marching on the big chained gates of Government House. Stood outside the big gates in ranks chanting fiercely righteously from their *Little Red Books,* chanting at the three Chinese policemen and the governor's aide-de-camp and the immobile Gurkha sentry, chanting for the governor to come out, waiting for the committee to arrive. The Hong Kong-Kowloon All Circles Anti-Persecution Struggle Committee arrived in a motorcade of four big black air-conditioned Mercedes and a roar of clapping cheering, they drove up to the viceroy's gates and shouted out the window to the ADC, *"Open up, we've come to see Governor!"*

"I'm sorry," the ADC said, "you may hand any petitions to me."

"Protest! We drive in!"

The ADC said, "May I see your pass?"

They climbed out of the four big black cars shouting *Protest! Protest! Protest!* And stood in a righteous horseshoe with their *Little Red Books* shouting the Thoughts of Mao Tse-tung and the mob marched back and forth shouting chanting roaring, fists flung up. For one hour. Then the Hong Kong–Kowloon All Circles Anti-Persecution Struggle Committee climbed back into the four big cars and shouted,

"*Tell Trench we'll come back to see him tomorrow! Tell him to be ready!*"

In Kowloon they were still rioting. They rioted till midnight.

CHAPTER 67

The next day there was a desk behind the chained gates of Government House, with a notice: *Petitions Received Here.* And a cordon of policemen at Garden Road to divert traffic and to let the petitioners march through in groups of fifty to do their chanting and postersticking.

That day they marched three thousand strong up Garden Road, chanting, jeering, loudspeakers, banners, posters, paint, glue. Marched through the police cordon in batches of fifty, up to the gates. And beplastered the Government House gates with their Big Character posters, and the sentry boxes and the trees and the telephone poles and the walls, *British Pigs Are Paper Tigers!* and *Apologize!* and *Bow Your Head Trench!* and *Trench Dare You Come Out!* And marched off singing and chanting back through the cordon to give the next batch of fifty a chance, past the other 2,950 shouting chanting clapping. And then counter-marched up and down Garden Road, to have another go. And in the doorways and windows of the communist banks and shops there was the clapping and applauding and the tea to refresh them before they had another go.

They matched and counter-marched through Central all day, then they swarmed. Swarmed on the government buildings and slapped up posters, *Fascism!* and *Bru-*

tality! and *Blood Debts!* and *Murder!* And inside the vast Bank of China there was the hurry, scurry, glee, and the tea-making and the poster-making and the regimenting and the cheering. And now high-powered loudspeakers were rigged to the upper windows, then the voice of the Bank of China came blaring out above the roar:

All reactionaries are paper tigers!—Mao Tse-tung!

The British foreign devil fascist paper tigers are lifting a rock only to drop it on their own feet!—Mao Tse-tung!

Dare to struggle, dare to win—Mao Tse-tung!

We must never be cowed by the bluster of reactionaries!—Mao Tse-tung!

Monsters of all kinds must be destroyed!—Mao Tse-tung!

These imperialists are trying vainly to bully us in such a way that we will have to take them seriously!

And swarmed roaring over the Supreme Court and daubed it in Big Character posters and swastikas and slogans and all the time the roaring and the glee and the loudspeakers bellowing and the hate hate hate. And the roaring frustration because there was not a policeman to be seen.

At four o'clock four truckloads of police drove through Central and a roar went up and the loudspeakers screamed *Fascist brutal murderers yellow-skinned running dogs, dare you come out!* and the policemen on a signal grinned and waved and drove on.

The astonishment. And then the loudpseakers screamed *Victory! Victory!* and the roar went up, *Victory! Victory!* and they swarmed across the road to the Hong Kong Hilton and roared and screamed for the Union Jack and Stars and Stripes to come down. And a Chinese bellboy just happened to be already on his way to do so, because the Hilton always lowered its flags at this precise time, and down they came, and the mob went mad with joy and the bank loudspeakers roared *Victory! Hail the Thought of Mao Tse-tung!* And they swarmed joyfully victorious two thousand strong to the Mandarin Hotel —for another Victory, but alas the Mandarin never flew flags. And so they marched shouting chanting glorious Victory down on Wanchai, armed with the Thoughts of Mao Tse-tung and paint pots and glue and posters, and rampaged through the world of Suzie Wong and fell upon the right-wing Chinese newspaper offices and the Magistrates' Court and slapped up their posters and paint and swastikas and the Victorious Thoughts of Mao Tse-tung.

That day one million Red Guards marched past the British Embassy in Peking, booming chanting and plastered it with paint and posters. That day fifty thousand Comrades marched and remarched past the British Consulate in Macao and beplastered it with paint and posters, and forced the consul to stand eight hours in the sun without a hat or food or water to watch them marching hissing shouting chanting by. That day the Red Guards broke into the British Consulate in Shanghai and dragged out the staff and ordered them to bow down to a portrait of Mao Tse-tung and frog-marched them around the compound and wrecked the consulate and beplastered it. They rampaged till midnight in Wanchai and Causeway Bay. That night the Hong Kong Government announced that only groups of twenty might proceed up Garden Road to present petitions at Government House.

That night the left-wing press called this announcement Frenzied Provocations.

CHAPTER 68

They slept anywhere they could, on chairs, down corridors of the police stations, on the floors. In the canteens there was coffee and tea and chow. It was better than last night and considerably better than the night before when nobody had yet thought to contract for a caterer nor hire extra *fokis* to keep the lavatories clean, let alone think about extra toilet paper and chopsticks and rice bowls, or somebody to sell cigarettes to a man in the middle of the night. There would never be hot water nor enough taps, but now at least their wives and mothers and girl friends usually brought them clean uniforms and underwear. In all the eighty-seven police stations it was the same. In police headquarters almost all the lights were on. All the lights in Special Branch were burning. It was 4 A.M. I said into the dictaphone, "New paragraph."

The Hong Kong–Kowloon All Circles Anti-Persecution Struggle Committee which arrived outside Government House in four Mercedes Benz were telephotographed and have now all been identified (see detailed list enclosure 27).

One of the leaders was Fong Ting-tak (S.B. 257/A/27/62 refers, attached), editor of the vitriolic left-wing magazine *Red Heaven,* a millionaire (see list of business interests, ibid., enclosure 5). He maintains a yacht, two luxurious apartments, and a hectic social life. He has two sons at Shanghai University, and it is rumored that they are under Red Guard fire there for their bourgeois antecedents. These facts should be subtly released to the press via Government Information Service.

Other leading committee members were two Great Wall film personalities, Wu Wai-ping and his wife. Both are very wealthy and had their honeymoon in America eighteen months ago, and have business interests in California real estate. (See S.B. 837/A/37/64.) This should also be leaked to the press.

The committee was yesterday made up of Hong Kong Island personalities only. Notably education, business, and trade-union representation was absent. It can be expected that a bigger, more representative committee will shortly emerge.

The Bank of China is presently the focal point of the committee. This is no surprise. Information has not been forthcoming for two days from our usual sources within the bank, despite all efforts to contact them. Probably the new activity has frightened them and it is not wise at this juncture to press them too hard.

The committee will undoubtedly create subcommittees or groups at grass-root level to carry out "Struggle" activities both on orders from on high and on their own initiative. These unsophisticated Struggle Committees may be easier for us to penetrate, as we have sources well placed in most unions (see enclosure 34.) But conversely these groups will be so numerous and will probably act so much on their own initiative that much information will be misleading and consume a lot of our energy fruitlessly. We can only control them by large-scale deployment of police on paramilitary lines.

The pattern likely to develop from this stage, both on principle and on information received, will be as follows, possibly concurrently:

First: Further demonstrations, marches on Government House, to make Government capitulate and lose face.

I hesitated, then added with a tone of I-bloody-told-you-so which I hoped would be detected by more than only my typist,

The original grievance of the Cement Workers and the Flower Workers being, of course, long since forgotten, now the situation has been allowed to reach this point.

Second: Deliberate rioting when these demonstrations are frustrated.

Third: Strikes by left-wing unions, and by others on their intimidation. Transport, dockers, postal, industrial, electricity, water, etc. (See enclosure 35 for a full list of unions, summary of spheres of influence, activities and office-bearers.)

This will require strike pay. The amount of strike funds available in those unions which publish accounts is listed in enclosure 36. Clearly these are inadequate for a prolonged strike. It is known of two fund-raising methods that appeared today:

Firstly (see enclosure 37) in a number of communist shops, and particularly China Products, "donation" boxes have appeared on shop counters. When a customer buys something the sales staff deposit his change into the donation box. If he protests he is harangued and intimidated.

Secondly (see enclosure 38) today there were three reports of tellers in communist banks withholding part of customers' checks as "donations toward the Struggle Committee's funds": the teller simply refused to hand over the whole amount.

436

Clearly a fund-raising campaign has begun. The possibilities for such unscrupulous "squeezing" of bank customers is enormous. All left-wing enterprises pay all staff salaries directly into communist banks on principle. Furthermore, all importers of goods from China are required by the China authorities to arrange their overdrafts and revolving credit through a communist bank, otherwise China refuses to supply. Such people could easily be squeezed for large sums.

We must exploit these unscrupulous squeezing methods. Traps should be laid by us: we should arrange for the opening of accounts by suitable Chinese collaborators, with funds supplied by us. The propaganda value to us of such prosecutions would be enormous. (Conversely, an unsuccessful prosecution would be disastrous).

Oh Jesus.

I threw the microphone down and picked up my cigarettes. Then picked up the microphone again and said, "Mrs. Aiken, cut out the Jesus." I left the office, locked the door behind me. All down the corridor, Special Branch boys burning the dawn oil. Trying to figure out what's going to happen next, tomorrow, next week, next month. Clutching and chasing straws. The whole bloody joint upside down. I stopped at the typists' room. Full of respectable middle-aged women with earphones typing hard. They were mostly wives of British army officers, pressed into Her Majesty's emergency service. Mrs. Aiken glanced up at me and typed on furiously, then yanked the earplugs out. "Yes?"

"Where are you up to, Mrs. Aiken?" I said above the clatter.

She said, "I don't think any more, Mr. McAdam, I just thump. Halfway through side two."

I said, "I'm going up to the Mess for a drink for fifteen minutes. There's another tape can you knock it off by six?"

"If you don't stand here jawing."

I walked out the pool, down the corridor, to switchboard. I said to the desk clerk, "up in the Mess." I went through the gates, to the elevator, rode up, walked down the quiet paneled corridor. The Mess was quiet, just the barman. "Beer, Mr. Wong," I said. "Beer beer beer."

I sat down in an armchair and leaned my head back and closed my eyes and tried to switch off. I took a big breath, Oh Ying oh Ying oh Ying. She had been gone twenty-three days.

CHAPTER 69

Mary-Anne Wilkinson woke up early that Sunday morning and found herself in bed with two Americans in the Hong Kong Hilton. One on each side. Then she remembered there had been four. *Four!* Champagne bottles and cigarette stubs and clothes everywhere.

It did not seem such fun now, in the cold light of dawn. A gangbang. "Mary-Anne, I promised my wife I'd never be *alone* with another girl, aha ha ha." She had had them in the palm of her hand, and she had to admit she had always rather fancied the idea—but *four?* She had only had two lovers in her whole *life* before she came to Hong Kong. Mary-Anne did feel remorse. Chuck Simpson and Don? Chuck had been her date at the Vietnam Rest and Recreation binge but she had preferred this Don somebody. Snoring now. She tiptoed around the room looking for her panties. Her hangover did not feel so slight now and her mouth tasted terrible. Yes, there too but only one of them and she had spat it out and rinsed her mouth out with champagne afterward —ha ha ha—but she still thought she could taste it. How *sor*did! She got dressed quickly. *Evening* dress!

She tiptoed out the room, hurried down the long carpeted corridor. The room boy on duty looked at her knowingly but without surprise. Nothing surprised the room boy. She rode down in the elevator. God, she had so obviously just crawled out of a man's bed! She hurried through the ground-floor shopping arcade to the side entrance. She stopped at the glass door, wide-eyed. Garden Road was full of policemen. Right the way up.

Before dawn they had come trundling through the city, the big blue police trucks full of policemen in riot kit, helmets, batons, shields, gas guns, gas masks. All roads approaching Government House were full of them. Outside the Hilton they were strung at arm's length, five deep; behind them were four platoons. Relaxed, talking quietly, smoking if they wished. Two Land Rovers, radios talking quietly. Up on the rooftop of the Hilton were Special Branch men with binoculars, telephoto cameras, radios. Likewise on all the surrounding buildings. In every police station, in the Ops Room of headquarters, of Government House, in the Secretariat, of Victoria Barracks, the Welsh Barracks, at Lye Run, Fanling, at every post along the Shamchun, in every fire station, ambulance depot, the officers sat at the radios, the men waited. It was oily pregnant warm already, it had been like that all night, would be so the whole long hot summer.

Mary-Anne Wilkinson scuttled back from the door, aghast. She hurried back to the corner and peeped at the main foyer. God, policemen there too! She was absolutely surro*und*ed! In her evening dress! Mary-Anne Wilkinson did not know what to do, except she was *not* going to face hundreds of grinning, knowing policemen. She hurried back to the elevator, up to the twelfth floor. She knocked sharply on the door. Chuck blinking at her, bristly and naked and horrible. "Keerist, honey! Where you been?"

She walked in imperiously, to the window, pointed down.

"Keer-rist," he said. "Are they for real?"

"Oh no, they're just our imagination."

"Kee-rist. Ain't they something?"

"I've *got* to get another dress! You'll have to buy me one when the shops open."

"Sure thing, honey. Meantime come back to bed."

"Not bloody likely! And don't call me honey!"

She banged the bathroom door and started getting undressed furiously. *Get this muck off my bum anyway!*

"Mary-Anne, will you have some champagne to get the taste of the gorilla's armpit out of your mouth?" Chuck pulled back the shower curtain.

"Do you mind if I perform my bloody ablutions in privacy?

"Out!" she pointed at the door, whipped back the plastic curtain.

Chuck picked up her dress, bra, pants and went into

the bedroom. He winked at Don and stuffed her clothes deep under the mattress.

I came out of the air conditioning of the Hilton into the hot quiet humid morning, through the ranks of men, up to Superintendent Charles Frith. "Want some tea, old chap?" Charles said.

"Yes please. Nothing from Mil-Pol?"

"Nothing that you didn't hear up there on the roof. No sugar I'm afraid, Iris made me cut it out."

"I wish to Christ something would start happening."

"Too early for them yet," Charles said. "They were up late celebrating their victory."

"I believe there was a bit of discipline trouble last night at a few stations?" I said.

"Not exactly discipline trouble, old chap, just a bit fed up, feel they've lost face, allowing all those damnable posters to go up on G.H. and the Supreme Court, they think it's awful loss of face. Which it is, of course."

"Better than a bloodbath and another Macao. At least we've kept ourselves in the right."

"Not that it's going to do any good," Charles said.

"No. They want their bloodshed."

I looked at the ranks of Chinese constables standing there in their metal helmets, quiet, relaxed, waiting. The first row of each platoon was the Baton Squad; slicker shields, long batons. Behind them the European inspector, platoon commander, with a revolver. On his left, the corporal with the loudspeaker. On his right the Bright One, the best marksman, with a carbine. And the banner, folded now, which read on one side, *Disperse or We Charge*, and on the other, *Disperse or We Fire*. The man to whom the platoon commander would say, "That ringleader in the red shirt! Shoot him in the knees." Behind them, the Tear-Gas and Greener Shotgun Squad. Behind them the Arresting Squad, the boys who run in. And so on, all the way up Garden Road. And in the very front of the foremost Riot Platoon, right across Garden Road, stood the five rows of Chinese constables in ordinary soft police caps, unarmed. The frontline boys. To stand there bare-handed and tell the screaming Comrades they could not go farther. To stand there like good flatfoot coppers and take the initial shit.

I looked at them all, the rows of Chinese boys in khaki, stolidly waiting, that nice-looking, stolid, slant-

440

eyed, decent Chinese look, and I thought, Jesus Christ, for three hundred and fifty Hong Kong dollars a month, about fifty American dollars. What about them? Twenty miles up there is China with a bloody Cultural Revolution and Christknowshowmany Red Guards screaming to march over the border. Forty miles over there Macao lies in ruins. Right here in town the Comrades are plotting to make all hell break loose. Anything could happen. With the Cutural Revoution, this time tomorrow the British woud be pulling out of Hong Kong. Or this time next month. Or next year. Remember Kenya. Remember Tanganyika. Remember the Federation of Rhodesia and Huasaland. Her Majesty has got a great reputation for selling her colonies down the river. And what happened to the good loyal black police? And what could happen here? Britain'll ship the whites out, all right. But what about those Chinese constables standing here waiting. And they know it, all right. "No wonder," I said.

"What's that?" Charles said.

"No wonder a few of them are corruptible," I said, "in this corrupt town. Poor bastards."

CHAPTER 70

They came marching out the Bank of China and China Products five hundred strong in three columns, men boys girls women, inscrutable earnest eager righteous, chanting martially, fists upflung in the big roaring chant:

ALL REACTIONARIES!
ARE PAPER TIGERS!

and the Bank of China loudspeakers burst into glorious applause, they marched past the Hong Kong Hilton gloriously chanting, fists upflung, fists upflung, right up to the stolid ranks of soft-hat police, concertinaed to a stop three feet in front of them chanting in their faces, "All reactionaries are paper tigers!" Superintendent Charles Frith came ambling forward, and held up a hand politely.

441

"Good morning," he shouted in Cantonese, "who is your leader?"

They stopped to hear the fun. The foremost cheerleader with the megaphone shouted, "Chairman Mao is our leader!"

And the joyful ragged shout went up, *"Chairman Mao is our leader! Chairman Mao is our leader!"*

"Oh," Charles said, "is he here?"

A moment's astonishment. Then the foremost leader with the megaphone shouted, "Chairman Mao is in our hearts!"

And the cry went up,

"Chairman Mao is in our hearts!"

Charles Frith kept a straight face. "Where are you going, please?"

The foremost cheerleader with the megaphone shouted, "Move paper tiger police! We are going to see the governor!"

And the chant rose up,

"Move paper tiger police!"

Superintendent Charles Frith held up his hands for silence with a pained expression at the noise.

"Certainly you may go to see the governor, ladies and gentlemen," he said. "But only twenty persons may go at one time, I'm afraid. It is a new Order-in-Council issued last night, I'm afraid."

The cheerleader with the megaphone shouted, "We all go see Governor!"

And the shout went up,

"We all go see Governor!"

Charles held up his hand, the shouting stopped, intent.

"You may *all* go to see the governor, certainly. But you can only pass up this road in one group of twenty at a time, you see. When one group returns the next group may—"

The shout, *"We all go see Governor at one time."*

Charles beckoned for a loudspeaker and a constable brought it.

The man shouted through his loudspeaker, "Fascist oppression!"

And the roar went up,

"Fascist oppression!

"Fascist oppression!"

Charles ambled back through the ranks, looking at his watch. The man with the loudspeaker held up his

Little Red Book and shouted, "Page seventy-two" and they all opened their books and shouted studiously,

"In appearance the reactionaries are terrifying but in reality they are not so powerful!

"From a long-term point of view it is not the reactionaries but the people who are really powerful!

"Mao Tse-Tung!"

"Page seventy-five!" the leader bellowed and the studious roar went up, shouting into the stolid faces of the Chinese constables two feet in front, shouting chanting shouting.

It was very hot.

The righteous roar of the Thoughts of Mao and the fists upflung into the policemen's faces, and the hate hate hate. Every five minutes Charles repeated over the loudspeaker that they could proceed up to Government House but only in batches of twenty. Inside the Hilton all the tourists were trapped, hanging out the upper windows, pressed against the big locked glass doors, filming, photographing, waiting for it to happen.

But nothing was going to happen if the police could help it. They had been just standing there for six hours taking it, not lifting a finger in the roaring hate. At lunchtime Hilton waiters emerged through back doors pushing trolleys of tea and sandwiches for the policemen, though not for the front rows of policemen, and the mob roared "Fascist! Fascist!" Then the Comrade with the megaphone pointed upward at the Hilton's flags, the Union Jack and the Stars and Stripes, and screamed, "Remove imperialist fascist flags!"

And the delighted roar went up like yesterday,

"Remove imperialist fascist flags!"

The chant went on for five minutes, then the manager of the Hilton himself appeared on the balcony and started lowering the Hilton house flag. When he lowered the Stars and Stripes the mob went mad with joy. Then the manager hooked another folded flag onto each flagpole and started raising them up to the top, he gave a jerk and two more Union Jacks unfurled and the mob howled in rage,

"Pro—test!"

"Pro—test!"

A mob came running shouting furious out the back doors of the Bank of China, and burst in the big main glass doors of the Hilton Hotel, shouting brandishing their *Little Red Books* rampaging through the arcade and foyer screaming, "Down with British fascism! Down with U.S. imperialism and their running dogs! Stop British bloody atrocities! Bow your heads! Nazis! Nazis! Nazis!" swarming in all directions shoving brandishing their *Little Red Books* scattering astonished Americans, "Monsters of all kinds must be destroyed," red book brandished in the little old lady's nose, *Nazi! Nazi!* chasing bellboys down the foyer, "Yellow-skinned running dogs!" brandishing shouting through the Espresso and the Coffee Shop,

"Mao Tse-tung!

"Mao Tse-tung!"

Charles sent a platoon of policemen running in through the big glass doors to eject them with bare hands, they scattered screaming "Protest! Protest!" back out the doors brandishing their *Little Red Books* screaming shouting spitting *Yellow-skinned running dogs!* and the loudspeakers of the Bank of China boomed out, "People of the World you have just witnessed another brutal British fascist atrocity! People of the World unite against this savage frenzied British oppression!" and the roar went up from Garden Road.

Upstairs on the twelfth floor Mary-Anne Wilkinson lay flat on her back sweating, between Chuck and Don. She dragged a towel down over her messy breasts and belly and said, "Golly."

"I never knew you could have so much fun without laughing," Chuck said.

CHAPTER 71

Outside in the roaring screaming there were the reporters and television men and foreign correspondents. A young television reporter stood in front of a camera: "The police you see behind me are here to restrict demonstration marches to Government House to orderly groups of twenty. The result? Well look at that screaming mob. The foremost five rows of policemen are unarmed, arms linked, face to face with the seething screaming mob thousands strong, screaming yelling abuse right into their faces. The police are refusing to be provoked, the communists are desperately trying so they can claim bloody oppression. A fantastic exhibition of provocation met by iron police discipline and restraint!

"This is the third week of disturbances, the second week of riots. Although not a police shot has yet been fired, and only one youth has been killed, and killed by a stone thrown by a rioter, the communist press is falsely alleging that the police have killed thousands in many brutal ways. The authorities are acting with the greatest restraint, well aware that any move could produce the most irrational reaction from Peking. Peking has already denounced the British conduct as towering crimes, quote unquote, and demanded that Britain accede to the communists' demands. Today's largest communist newspaper put out what it called an emergency edition urging the people to fight to the bitter end, quote unquote.

"Look at them now! That additional booming that you hear comes from the loudspeakers of the Bank of China, blaring out invective, inflaming the demonstrators. Sweltering hot under the China sun here these front-rank policemen are taking it slap in the face with monumental discipline, on their feet now for eight hours, on standby in their police stations for many nights now and they must be exasperated men indeed. And worried. One false move and tomorrow could be gone. Listen to that roar!—it is every vile oath and epithet in the Chinese lexicon being hurled into the policemen's faces."

Screaming yelling hysterical—*"Hum kar chaan!*—May your whole family perish!—Fuck your mothers!—*Hum kar chaan!* Fuck your sisters!—*Hum kar chaan!*—Fuck your brothers!—*Hum kar chaan*—Fuck you ancestors." yelling screaming hate-filled frenzied right into the policemen's faces and Bank of China's loudspeakers blaring "Fight to the bitter end! Compatriots of China unite and fight the yellow-skinned running dogs and the white-face pigs who have the audacity to make themselves the enemies of seven hundred million Chinese people armed with the Invincible Thought of Mao Tse-tung—fight fight to the bitter end!—dare to struggle! dare to win!—deal crushing blow upon blow upon the white-skinned pigs and their yellow-skinned running dogs!—Blood debts must be paid in blood!—the white-skinned pigs and their running dogs have murdered and wounded thousands of

445

our loyal compatriots!—advance wave upon wave!—Monsters of all kinds shall be destroyed! The fascist whiteskin pig-butchers are provoking us beyond endurance but they are lifting a rock only to drop it on their own feet! All these brutal fascist Nazi measures will be repaid—"

The girl screamed into the constable's face, "Death to your whole running dog family!" and spat, the constable tried to wipe the hanging spit off his face on his shoulder and she danced in glee and spat again and the mob went mad and the police loudspeakers roared that the next person to touch a policeman would be arrested forthwith and the Bank of China loudspeakers screamed, "Protest! Protest! You have just made another savage threat against the Chinese people! We must remember this! Such frenzied provocation will not go unchallenged by the seven hundred million people armed with the Invincible Thoughts of Mao Tse-tung! Strike back resolutely at the yellow-skinned running dogs of the white-skinned pigs strike crushing blow upon blow!" and the girl lashed at the constable with her nails screaming and two other girls lashed out, clawing screaming and the mob went mad punching clawing jumping surging heaving screaming shoving to let at the constables and jabbed at their eyes and kicked and punched and clawed and the China Bank loudspeakers roared, "Fight to the bitter end!" and the police loudspeakers barked an order and the dodging constables grabbed for their short truncheons and swiped at the fists and claws, shoulder to shoulder dodging standing their ground and the Bank of China roared, "Armed fascist police have struck our unarmed citizens! We will remember this frenzied provocation! We will fight back to the bitter end!" and the man screamed and kicked the inspector in the testicles with all his might. The inspector bellowed and crumpled and the mob roared its delight and two constables lunged furiously batons swiping after the assailant and the mob roared, "Protest!" screaming hitting kicking and the China Bank loudspeakers roared, "You have seen another savage British atrocity!" and somewhere a sharp whistle blew and twenty Comrades who had not been touched fell down.

Fell down untouched screaming "Help! Murder!" and pulled out bottles of red ink and splashed themselves on the head and lay screaming writhing clutching themselves.

And their Comrades picked them up shouting "Witness! Witness!" and carried them to the sidewalk screaming and writhing and pulled out bandages and wrapped them around the ink stains and the left-wing press photographers clamored to get photographs and the Bank of China loudspeakers roared, "Blood! Blood! You have seen Chinese blood shed by the yellow-skinned running dogs! It must be avenged! Fight to the bitter end! and the mob roared and lashed out frenzied jubilant and the inspector in charge of the foremost platoon raised his loudspeakers roared, "Protest! Protest! Savage thugs of "Disperse peacefully!" then handed the loudspeaker to his Chinese sergeant. The sergeant bellowed it in Cantonese and the mob roared and booed and spat and clawed and punched and kicked and the Bank of China's loudspeakers raored, "Protest! Protest! Savage thugs of white-skinned pigs threaten sanguinary suppression of peaceful workers—we must fight to the bitter end!" The inspector bellowed in English, "Number Two Section fit respirators!" and the second rank rammed on their gas masks. "Number Two Section up!" the inspector bellowed and the second-rank corporal bellowed through the roar, "By the center-quick march!" and as one man the eight gas-masked Smoke Squad marched smartly through the ranks, halted six paces in front. Suddenly there was much less shouting from the mob, except the Bank of China blaring. Everyobdy was watching the disciplined force.

"Number Two Section—draw gas pistols!"

In unison they drew them, *one*-two-three, *one!* and raised them to shoulders. The mob was suddenly silent. The inspector shouted, "Remainder—fit—respirators!" and the rest of his platoon rammed on their gas masks.

"Front Platoon—with-draw!" The soft hats turned about and trotted up Garden Road. Then the inspector bellowed at the mob through the loudspeaker, "Disperse or I use gas!" and the sergeant bellowed it in Cantonese and beside him the constable raised the big banner in English and Chinese, *Disperse or We Use Gas*, and the Bank of China loudspeakers screamed, "Protest! Protest! you have just seen frenzied provocation of fascist Nazis thugs threatening to shoot us down in cold blood! We will fight to the bitter end!" and the inspector bellowed:

"Disperse or we charge!" and the mob broke and ran.

Ran helter-skelter screaming down the hill yelling "Murder! Protest! Atrocity!" even the twenty wounded wearing their red-ink bandages scrambled up and ran screaming "Protest! Murder! Ai-yah!" and the inspector bellowed, "Replace gas pistols! For*ward!*"

And he led his men running down the hill in formation after him, all down Garden Road the platoons came running in formation and the mob fled screaming shouting, the Bank of China loudspeakers screamed, "Fascist bloody Nazis pursue peaceful compatriots to murder—we will remember!" The policemen came to a sweating panting gas-masked halt across the entrance to Statue Square, the other platoons were running to occupy the other approaches. There were three thousand people sealed in Statue Square, roaring, shouting, chanting, and the Bank of China's loudspeakers blared, "Chinese policemen! Turn your guns on your white-skinned pig officers! They will not be here much longer! You will be facing a people's court!"

Suddenly a new sound blared out across the square to drown the Bank of China, it was a Mozart opera from the government loudspeakers in Beaconsfield House, and then there were new howls of "Protest! Protest!" and the Bank of China bellowed,

"You witness another atrocity! The white-skinned pigs have the audacity to think they can smother the voice of seven hundred million Chinese armed with the Invincible Thought of Mao Tse-tung! Chairman Mao said we will never be cowed by the bluster of the reactionaries! Monsters of all kinds must be destroyed!"

CHAPTER 72

The television camera panned the yelling frenzied crowd and focused on the young man with the microphone: "And now you can see workmen at the Bank of China erecting bigger loudspeakers to shout down the government's Mozart. Police strategy is to contain the mob, to demonstrate their strength without using it, and this is driving the demonstrators and the Bank of China mad with frustration. They are bent on provoking a bloody clash. Meanwhile, reports come in of riots in two nearby areas. In each case rioters have been stoning police from upper windows and pelting them with garbage, sulfuric acid, and the contents of chamber pots. When the platoon charges they scatter into the lanes and side streets. There have been riots at two magistracies as arrestees of the last few days were brought to trial, requiring the police to use tear gas.

"But these events must be seen in their international political context. One week ago Peking officially protested to the British Government against quote barbarous fascist atrocities in Hong Kong unquote and demanded that Britain immediately accept all demands made by their Hong Kong compatriots, that is release all persons arrested in the riots, apologize to them, compensate them financially, and punish the policemen responsible. Britain's Foreign Minister George Brown sharply rebuked the Chinese chargé d'affaires for his undiplomatic language and spurious allegations of fascism. Peking has now demanded an apology for the Minister's quote shameful imperialist language unquote and repeated the demands. Meanwhile one million Red Guards have demonstrated uproariously outside the British Embassy in Peking for three days and plastered it with posters. All over China Red Guards are up in arms demanding to quote liberate Hong Kong unquote. In Canton eighty miles away thousands of Red Guards are rallying, screaming to come down here and quote *kill the white pig devils* unquote. In Macao the communists have demonstrated in continuous uproarious marchpast of the British Consulate, covered it in posters, forced the British Consul to stand bareheaded in the sun. The whole of China is in a state of civil war anyway over the Cultural Revolution. Today the communist New China News Agency has officially released false reports that two hundred Chinese have been slaughtered by the police here, while the local communist newspapers say thousands. With such malicious false reports there is no saying what Peking may do, or be forced to do by their millions of Red Guards.

"I can see some stone-throwing now. It is common knowledge that the communists are paying youths and schoolchildren two dollars for each stone thrown, seven dollars for hitting a policeman. From where I stand you

449

can see a concerted attack on a police platoon outside the communist Bank of Communications—now the police inspector is shouting through his loudspeaker—now he has raised a banner reading *Disperse or I Charge.* The mob is going mad. Now his men are charging! The mob is scattering—a great mass of fighting and screams of *Protest!* The police are into them for the first time today! It's very hard not to shout hurrah!"

And the China sun beating down, and the big ache in your feet legs spine neck, standing hungry thirsty sweating and you haven't slept on a bed five days and you've been on your aching legs since fucking dawn. And the roaring spitting screaming in your ears and the prancing right there in front of you to drive you mad with loss of face and still you have to stand your ground under the devil sun in the screaming cacophony, following them up when they move and blockade them from moving back, follow and stand, follow and stand, and all the time the roar and the sticks and stones and shit and sweat.

And outside the post office the bricks and stones and concrete came flying through the air, from all sides onto the platoon of forty gas-masked policemen, the big banner went up high, *Disperse or We Use Gas,* and stones kept coming in a screaming hail, the inspector bellowed his order and there was the sharp thud and the gas canisters shot high spewing smoke and the crowd scattered running screaming coughing gasping crying reeling and the Baton Squad ran in, shields up, truncheons swinging, *one two three four,* and the Arresting Squad was running in behind them, the air thick with gray-blue tear gas and the bellowing screaming coughing and two blocks away in Statue Square they got the stinging whiff of it and the Bank of China loudspeakers screamed, "Protest! Protest! Fascist police fire lethal gas on innocent compatriots and murder women and children! We must fight back to the bitter end! Chairman Mao said if anyone attacks us we must certainly act in self-defense and wipe them out resolutely!" And a man screamed, "Death to your whole family!" and threw the mugful of sulfuric acid right in the policeman's face. The policeman screamed, reeling, clawing at the searing agony of his face, eyes, mouth, ears, down his neck. and a roar of glee went up from the mob, the assailant ran flat out across the square shouting *Protest,* the policeman ran blindly wildly across the Statue Square and flung himself headfirst into the shallow fountains thrashing and clawing his agonized face and the mob howled with delight, the assailant ran flat out for the back doors of the Bank of China screaming *Protest* with two detectives running flat out after him and the bank guards dashed to block the doorway behind him, screaming *Protest* and brandishing sticks and iron bars and *Little Red Books* and the loudspeakers were screaming, "Protest! Protest yellow-skin running dogs trying to break into the Bank of China!" The policeman was thrashing in the fountain and the mob was howling and an ambulance was wailing, the police loudspeakers roared "Disperse or I use gas" and the government loudspeakers were bellowing "Oh What a Beautiful Morning."

CHAPTER 73

In June came really long hot days, and the terrorism.

What do you say about a reign of Chinese terror through the narrow teeming streets of tiny Hong Kong where twenty miles away one quarter of mankind was roaring, raging against themselves, and children denounced parents and flogged their teachers down the streets and students smashed through universities and museums burning books and smashing priceless works of art and Red Guards set fire to embassies and smashed up factories and rival Red Guards fought pitched battles and every day millions of Red Guards roared to march down to the City of Imperial Decadence Run by White-skinned Pigs and Their Yellow-skinned Running Dogs, and every day bodies came floating down the Pearl River; and all the time the fear of three million Chinese people who do not want to be liberated, and the fear of ten thousand sweating exhausted Chinese policemen going into the running battles in the streets, who think that Britain will sell them down the river? A reign of terror that in the end destroyed your woman, your lover, your darling, your life?

That took the great red joy out of the sunrise so

that when you see it you can only weep; and turn your back on it. That took the blue sparkling joy out of the morning sea so the sun and the sea and the morning will never be the same again, so they break your heart. So that you do not want to feel the freshness of spring any more because it breaks your heart, nor ever feel the great golden heat of summer any more because there is no more joy of wine in the sun any more, nor lie deep in your bed in the winter any more because she is not there any more to be warm with. That makes your house and your bed and your heart cry out out, that makes you not want to go home, that makes your footsteps ring loud in your ears in the street. That makes the crunch of snow break your heart because you never took her to the snow and because once long ago when you heard that sound she was waiting for you, far away where the east is red.

Mostly I remember the nights, the work work work, and it seemed that everything had happened yesterday because in the mornings I went home to sleep after the director's meeting with the O.C. British Forces and the political advisers, and when I woke up that day's news seemed like yesterday's. "Hello," Percy said as I walked in the door. First I drank a large San Miguel down. Then I filled her red China Products watering can and watered her flowers. The water supply was only turned on every four hours every fourth day. Then I fed Percy and the rest of her menagerie. Then I bathed, then I threw myself down, wet, on top of the bed, and I was asleep before the air-conditioner dried me. Now I do not remember much about those days, except then began the intimidations and the strikes and the bloodshed and the running battles in the streets.

First there came the flash strikes, the emissaries and thugs of the Hong Kong–Kowloon All Circles Anti-Persecution Struggle Committee going out to the unions, brandishing their *Little Red Books* and weapons to Mobilize the Masses, *"All Comrade unionists will stage important strikes! Any person who does not strike is a yellow-skinned running dog!"*

"Yellow-skinned running dog!"

And the posters and the shouting the beatings and the threats. The flash ferry strike and the bus strike and the tram strike and the dairy farm strike, the dockyard, gas, electricity, waterworks, the fresh produce market hawkers strike; the postal strike, the gangs shouting brandishing chanting beating the bus drivers and the ferry crews and the cowhands and water workers and the gas and electricity workers, and slapping up the Big Character posters and the leaflets dropped from rooftops; and the police patrols tore down the posters and painted over the windows if the posters were pasted inside and the gangs stoned them and threw acid from the rooftops and the communist press screamed *"Police Poster Removal Is Frenzied Fascist Provocation!"* and the New China News Agency telegraphed the governor protesting "Frenzied Fascist Poster-Removals Decree," and now policemen rode on the buses and ferries and trams protecting the crews and passengers from the intimidation and the Hong Kong–Kowloon All Circles Anti-Persecution Struggle Committee screamed *Fascist Intimidation! Fight Violence with Violence! Strike Back Wave upon Wave! Deal Crushing Blows!* And the committee's gangs out there in the streets threatening and bribing people to throw stones, one dollar a stone, five dollars for hitting a policeman, *"Fight Back Most Valiantly, Advance Wave upon Wave!"* and now the posters bore the names of the Yellow-skinned Running-Dog Policemen Who Will Perish, and in Canton twenty thousand Red Guards demonstrated mightily protesting against the Fascist White Pig Removal of Loyal Big Character Posters and Radio Peking screamed it was Hysterical Fascist Oppression and Red Guards screamed outside the British Embassy that Blood Debts Would Be Repaid in Blood: and screamed that the Hong Kong—Kowloon All Circles Anti-Persecution Struggle Committee must all return to China for Struggle and Self-Criticism for failing to Deal Killing Blows on Fascist White Pigs. And the Hong Kong-Kowloon All Circles Anti-Persecution Struggle Committee redoubled their Struggle orders to the unions: *"There must be a great general strike!"* *"Fight the fascist thugs on every front!"* *"Anybody who does not strike is a yellow-skinned running dog!"* and *"Yellow-skinned running dogs will be buried with the British pigs!"* and through the sweating clamorous factories and workshops and dockyards and markets and vast teeming tenements went the gangs and the Comrade unionists brandishing their sticks and choppers and iron pipes and *Little Red Books* shouting and

453

slapping up the Big Character posters, and chased the workers through the streets, beat on their doors in the middle of the night, beat their wives and children, lay in wait for the policemen who came to tear down the posters and set upon them from all sides with sticks, stones, iron bars, choppers, cargo hooks and then ran into unions and the communist banks and stoned them from the rooftops. And for the Great General Strike there had to be Glory Funds to paying the strikers and the Compatriots Advancing Wave upon Wave Dealing Crushing Blows, ten dollars for striking a White Pig employer and fifty dollars for burning a car, so *All Compatriots must donate! Anybody who does not donate is a yellow-skinned running dog!* and the communist banks deducted large amounts from their depositors' accounts for the Glory Strike Fund and the order went out that all compatriot businessmen must advance two months' salary to their staff to buy up rice to create a shortage. And Buy Up Canned Food So There Will Be Shortage! Run the Taps So There Will Be No Water! Burn the Lights So There Will Be No Electricity! Beat the Farmers So There Will Be No Vegetables! Beat the Fishermen So There Will Be No Fish! Action, Comrades, Action! Advance Wave upon Wave!

And now the communist unions and shops were arming and barricading themselves, bows, spears, choppers, knives, acid, barbedwire entanglements and booby traps on their rooftops and fire escapes and stairways, and they drilled for Great Battle. And the orders went out to all the communist schools that they must barricade themselves and drill and prepare for the Great Battle, and lay up arms, and the children must demonstrate in the streets and strike Crushing Blows, all the schools must be turned into Great Classrooms for Applying the Thought of Mao Tse-tung, any principal or teacher who does not obey will be buried with the Fascist British Pigs or be returned to China, and the communist press screamed at the government:

Dare you enter our shops?
Dare you enter our banks?
Dare you enter our schools?
You will be repulsed with double counterattacks
    most fiercely!
We dare the fascist white-skinned pigs!

454

and Peking's *People's Daily* roared *All Chinese Must Stand Ready to Answer the Great Motherland's Call to Smash the Fascist British Rule in the City of Imperial Decadence Run by White-skin Pigs* and in Canton the Red Guards screamed to march across the Shamchun, and all the time across the length and breadth of China, the size of all of Europe, was the roaring of the Great Proletarian Cultural Revolution, one quarter of mankind gone mad.

Anything could happen. We could not touch their premises: those were the orders from London. We could not take a communist building without a pitched battle and a lot of dead Comrades, and if that happened anything could happen. World War III. Mao had sacrificed China's own economy for his ideals; at any moment he could sacrifice Hong Kong even if it was just for face. It was very hard on the Chinese police. There was a standing Emergency Evacuation Procedure for Europeans, but what about those ten thousand Chinese policemen out there in those streets? What were those poor bastards thinking, waiting sweating in their riot kit under strict orders of restraint while communists screamed, *"Yellow-skinned running dogs, your whole family will perish."* At first they understood the need for restraint, but not any more. In particular they did not understand why we did not raid the union premises. After a while they only thought of Her Majesty as a queen who took orders from a prime minister who was a trade unionist himself and who was very frightened of Mao Tse-tung, and made them lose face. At least the Portuguese had tried to fight. There were hundreds, then thousands of Europeans leaving already, empty flats everywhere, furniture, cars, yachts, for sale dirt cheap everywhere, and hordes of Chinese queuing at the immigration and consular offices. In June it was bad. Morale was getting very bad, waiting on Whitehall, which meant waiting on Harold Wilson and Arthur Bottomley.

"I tell you," Teetotal Tank said, "Rhodesia had the right idea. What do I tell my men? What the hell's happening in Transport House or wherever the hell Harold Wilson festers?"

"You can make an educated guess," I said.

"Sure, and I'm sick of educated guesses and so are the men!"

"So are three million terrified Hong Kong, Chinese who don't want to be liberated," Mini-Max said. "And me."

"You know what the men are thinking," Teetotal glared at me. "They're thinking of Kenya. The poor bastards think Britain is going to sell them down the Pearl River."

"She won't do that." Christ I was tired and wished to Christ I believed it.

"Oh won't she! That's what she told the Kenya farmers!" He glared at me. "And what d'you mean 'she'?: It's not *she*, it's *he*, for Chrissake, and you know who *he* is!"

"I don't think you can blame this one on Harold Wilson," I said. "Seven hundred million Chinese screaming the Thoughts of Mao Tse-tung are not the same as tribesman terrorists with mud-ringlets in their hair."

"The principle's the same!" Teetotal clenched his fists. "And for the last ten fucking years the British principle has been to sell out all her loyal colonies whenever it's got hot for pisswilly long-haired English politicians to honor their obligations to their poor loyal subjects!"

"Drop your voice, for Chrissake. This is a public bar not the Police Club."

Teetotal Tank glared around the empty bar then back at me. "What about those poor ten thousand cannon-fodder Chinese *foki* policemen out there sitting in their riot kit twenty-four hours a day! Sir! And their wives and their children. And the three million ordinary honest-to-goodness Chinese out there who don't want to be liberated by Mao's Red Guards thank you very much and half of them put up against a wall and shot, they rely on pisswilly British to maintain British justice and law and goddamn order—*and what do we do? Sir?*"

I said, "And you can for Christ's sake cut out the sir."

"We run around like dogs on a fucking tennis court taking all kinds of *Hum kar chaans* and stones and acid and iron bars and we're black and blue and bloody and exhausted while the fucking communist press screams treason and genocide and fortifies their premises and screams All Reactionaries Are Paper Tigers. And the paper tigers do nothing about it! Do the paper tigers raid their premises where they're plotting treason? No, we skid to a stop at the doorstep and get a faceful of acid.

No wonder the fucking Comrades think there's power in the Thought of Mao Tse-tung!"

I said irritably, "You know what could happen if we put a foot wrong."

Teetotal pointed at the door. "Most of us used to understand the necessity for caution and restraint, *sir.* But you reach a point. You reach a point where you've *got* to strike back, or you lose control of the situation forever. And of your men. And your self-respect. *Sir.*"

Up there other side the Shamchun River there were the peasant demonstrations along the fence and swarming over the crossing-points at Lowu and Man Kam To and Shataukok, chanting, singing, shouting at the Hong Kong policemen reading them the Thoughts of Chairman Mao, slapping up the Big Character posters. They really believed we were White Barbarian Fascist Pigs Perpetrating Sanguinary Atrocities, and because we did not fight back they really believed in the power of the Thought of Mao Tse-tung.

From Takwuling police station you could see the executions of the people who tried to escape into Hong Kong. They were marched up Execution Hill, big white dunce caps upon their heads, and the People's Liberation Army officer read the charges and the sentence of death and all the villagers clapped. Then they all got out their *Little Red Books* and chanted aloud, then there was a loud lecture from the PLA officer, and more cheering and clapping. Then all the villagers filed past the condemned people and spat on them. Then the officer shot each person through the head, and there was loud cheering and clapping. Then the PLA officer urinated on the corpses, and then the villagers filed past and urinated on them also: then they went back to work in the commune paddies.

And stoned our patrols, and the commune peasants who crossed the border every day to work their fields on our side came marching singing chanting with their banners, shouting at the people, and they squatted around and held their loud Mao-think sessions. And now many of our villages near the border were half empty, and Shataukok was a ghost town on the British side of Chung Ying Street. The Army were in their barracks. They did not show themselves along the border lest it be Frenzied Imperialist Fascist Aggression. There were no standing orders for the Army; if anything of a military

457

nature at all happened, it had to be referred to White-hall before a soldier could fire a single shot. Lest it start World War III. The place was indefensible. Better to sacrifice four million Hong Kong people than involve Great Britain in a war. It was very hard on our Chinese police.

Max said to me, "What about Ying?"

"Next month she'll be back. Please God."

"That's not what I meant," Max said. "What about these communist schools arming themselves with acid bombs and high explosives and the Invincible Thought of Mao Tse-tung? What are you going to do about *that?*"

I said, "She'll be getting out of that school the moment she gets back."

"Will she?" He didn't believe it.

"She certainly will. If she doesn't it'll be over my dead body."

"Maybe it *will* be over your dead body. Jesus, Jake, you're playing with fire." He looked at me, big liquid Portuguese lawyer's eyes. "What about the divorce?"

"October," I said.

"Do you think Catherine'll really fight you?"

"I don't care if she does. I don't care about my job. All I want is Ying back here and the devil can take the hindmost."

"Jesus, Jake. Do you really love her that much?"

I did. I had loved her a long time and I had never loved her so much. Sometimes I could see her face, hear her voice, her laugh, often in my sleep I thought she was in bed beside me and I put out my arm. And often I was talking to her in my head. And every day I prayed. I had not prayed for a very long time, but now I did. Please God. Protect her and bring her back. I don't care what happenes as long as she comes back undamaged, just bring her back. Sometimes it took me a long time to go to sleep. Lying in the hot morning on top of the sheet, feeling my sweat, the hot prickle of hot tired nerves on my palms, the red blackness of tight-closed eyes: just bring her back safe so I can love my love forever and, hold her and taste her again, her sweetness and coolness and smoothness again, and re-joice in every line and curve and cleft and dimple of her again and look into her dark eyes again and laugh again and forever for the joy of what I see in there, please God. So the sun will rise in the mornings with its great red joy for another day again, and the magnificence come back into the sunset again, and the joy of another night again. So the early morning mist on the junks and the great blue deep sparkle will come back into the China Sea again, so we can walk up the mountains and down into the valleys again, free and strong and young, and feel the good sweat of summer and the fresh joy of spring again. So we can walk along the faraway island beaches and lie on hot rocks and swim naked again, and feel the glorious freedom of my beautiful woman in my arms again and her joyful laugh on my face again. And just sitting on a mountaintop in the sunset looking down on the mauve valleys and paddies and the water buffalo and hamlets again. And the sun shining satiny silky golden silver on her as she swam slowly face down reveling in her underwater wonderworld, and I dived in after her and came up underneath her shimmering slow-motion nakedness so glorious and free, and we dived under together like seals, diving and coming back up and under again and her long hair streamed out behind her, grinning, oh please God bring her back again.

And now in June the strikes mostly failed; and many people formed committees to support the government. And in Canton twenty thousand Red Guards massed in a great rally roaring that the Hong Kong–Kowloon All Circles Anti-Persecution Struggle Committee were Bourgeois Liu-ist Scabs Who Must Be Returned to China for Struggle and Self-Criticism for failing in the strikes, and the Hong Kong–Kowloon All Circles Anti-Persecution Struggle Committee redoubled their struggles to regain face, redoubled the gangs and the beatings and the acid and shouting and the posters, and now they started the rumors, roared abroad in the Comrade press and the posters and the gangs. That China gunboats encircled Hong Kong with all guns poised for the Great Liberation. That the governor was fleeing in mighty imperialist fear, abandoning all his yellow-skinned running dogs to the Just Wrath of the Oppressed Patriotic Masses. That all the banks except the Bank of China were going bankrupt and smuggling out all their assets so all people must rush to save their money. That there was a great rice shortage and soon everybody will starve unless they rush to buy up rice. And in Peking ten thousand Red Guards stormed the British Embassy and sacked it again. And now five People's officials came down from Canton for Criticism Meetings with the Hong Kong —Kowloon All Circles Anti-Persecution Struggle Committee and ordered the Comrades to make massive infiltration and propaganda in the New Territories among the fishermen and farmers, why wasn't there any Great Struggle among the fishermen and farmers? Why was there no general strike? And the Struggle Committee redoubled their redoubled struggles and beat and bribed the busmen and the ferrymen and the taxi drivers and their wives and children and burned their vehicles and threatened and bribed and beat the stevedore coolies. And the order went out that all Hong Kong fishermen must sail to China for a Great Mass Anti-Persecution Struggle Meeting and then sail back to Hong Kong in a great armada of junks flying high the Great Red Banners and put the fear of the Might of Seven Hundred Million Chinese Armed with the Invincible Thought of Mao Tse-tung into the City of Imperial Decadence, and any Yellow-skinned Running Dog who did not so sail would be buried with the British Pigs and his family would never again fish the China Sea. And in Macao a great China gunboat led five hundred junks in single file in a Great Outrage Armada denouncing Savage British Fascist Genocide in the City of Imperial Decadence. And a great rally raged chanting through the Macao streets dragging effigies of John Bull and Uncle Sam and the Hong Kong Police and the Hong Kong Governor, and held a great People's Court and sentenced the governor of Hong Kong to death and hanged the effigies from lampposts. And swarmed roaring shouting chanting into the Villa Verde Radio Station and chased out the Portuguese and broadcast to the Suppressed Compatriots in Hong Kong to kill kill kill the British Pigs and all their Yellow-skinned Running Dogs. And in Russia the newspapers jeered at China for not liberating Hong Kong from the Bloody Yoke of Colonialism. And from Radio Canton there came broadcasts from Chester Wu to his former colleagues of the Hong Kong police, "Dear Friends, the time has come for you to answer the call of the Great Motherland. Lay down your arms and rally to the great Thought of Mao Tse-tung. Chinese should not fight Chinese. If you mend your ways now you will be pardoned, if you do not you will soon be facing a People's Court. Turn your guns on your white fascist officers. Already the whites are abandoning you like rats leaving a sinking ship." And now from Peking itself came a gift of Ten Million Glory Dollars for the Valiant Struggle Strike Fund. Valiant Struggle Against the Savage Fascist Sanguinary Slaughter of Hong Kong Compatriots —*ten million magnificent Mao Glory dollars!* And in the communist press and the Big Character posters there were the roars of applause and cacophony of praise for the Reddest Sun in Our Hearts, and the Glory battle cries went up, *Advance Wave upon Wave.* And all the time the roaring hating of the press and posters and radio and the great crushing at the immigration offices and the consulates and the banks, and the police riot squads in the running fights, and the heartbreak and the fear, and still the orders to attack did not come from London, and Jesus Christ, it was getting bad in June.

CHAPTER 74

In Canton Road it is teeming, dogs, bicycles, signboards, hawkers, food stalls, children, workshops, coolies, shops. Upstairs on the second and third floors of 210 Canton Road was the Hong Kong Synthetic Fibers Workers' Union. In the upper windows were the Big Character posters, Kill British Pigs and Yellow-skinned Running Dog Police. On the walls at street level there were three new Big Character posters. They were the bait, for the police. There were two Struggle Squads on guard, one squad on the stairway, the other in an alley across the crowded street.

The two Chinese plainclothes detectives had the sense not to try to tear down the posters on street level by themselves, but one photographed the building. Then they passed on down the road, and the two squads screamed and charged out into the street.

Brandishing knives and axes and iron bars shouting *Yellow-skinned running dogs!* and people scattered, and the detectives ran flat out down the street and flung themselves through a shop doorway, and the foremost mobsters hit them. Hit them swiped them smashed them

461

stabbed them from all sides scrambling over each other to get at them screaming *Yellow-skinned running dogs,* swiping shouting stabbing, stabbed the first detective seven times deep in his shoulder and arms and thigh before the second detective got his gun out and fired. And hit a Comrade in the guts and sent him reeling screaming, fired two more shots at the ceiling, and the Comrades scattered yelling falling scrambling over each other fleeing screaming *Murder! Murder!* They fled back down the road and into the Synthetic Fibers Workers' Union stairway screaming *Murder!* At both ends of the street big crowds had gathered, ready to run away. The loudspeakers of the union began to roar: *"Yellow-skinned running dog police murdered our Comrade! You have all witnessed this frenzied atrocity!"* The detective staggered bleeding to the telephone and dialed Kowloon Control.

The big blue riot squad truck got there in seven minutes, with orders to arrest the gang for attempted murder. All the shops had been shut and shuttered, at either end of the road there were big crowds. But nobody on the street. The union loudspeakers roared *Yellow-skinned running dogs come to kill! Strike back wave upon wave!* The riot squad scrambled out, gas masks on, shields up, ran for the cover of the shop-front verandah. The gas-gun squad ran for cover of the shop-front verandah opposite, and the bricks and the acid bottles came flying out the union windows, glass and acid exploding, flying. The inspector ran with the rest of his men to the union stairway, he bellowed up the stairs through the loudspeaker, *"Surrender or I use force!"* and the union loudspeakers screamed *"Death to your whole families! Defy yellow-skinned running dogs enter premises of Mao Tse-tung!"* and the inspector shouted *Fire!* Across the road the constables fired their gas guns, the hissing canisters, smashed the union windows in a crash of glass, and the inspector bellowed *Charge!*

Charged scrambling up the narrow concrete stairway, eight gas-masked batoned men, and they got halfway up the first flight and the bricks and acid hit them. A crashing smashing hail of bricks and concentrated sulfuric acid crashing down on their heads, glass smashing bricks and acid flying splashing down their necks arms legs, the policemen charged on scrambling bellowing up the narrow stairs to the first floor and the bricks and bottles and the acid crashed and smashed them all the way, and they had to turn back. They retreated back down the stairs ablaze with acid and bloody under a hail of bricks and flying bottles smashing crashing after them, and the loudspeakers roared, *"Victory! Victory! You have witnessed yellow-skinned running dog atrocity!"*

The inspector ordered another gas volley up into the windows, then another, then they stormed up the narrow stairs again firing gas up ahead of them, into the roaring crashing smashing, the stairway was black with tear gas but the Comrades had gas masks too and the bricks and bottles and acid came crashing down, and all the time the roaring screaming jeering. Down in the street more Comrades were stoning the police cordon, bricks and stones and bottles flying, then there was the siren of the police truck bringing the commissioner of police and another riot squad; and from Pol Mil to Government House to London and to every news agency around the world the word went out that the Hong Kong police were raiding communist union premises, and in every police station a mighty cheer went up.

You could hear the roar from Canton Road from a long way. Then we came around the corner, there was the mob everywhere and suddenly the Land Rover was rocking crashing under the hail of bricks, mobsters scattering everywhere. The bastards had thrown a barricade of crates and garbage across the road to stop any more police getting through, but the corporal rammed her into four-wheel drive and shoved his foot flat and we hit the barricade and there was nothing in the world but the crashing churning jolting, and debris flying like grapeshot and people scattering and our siren blasting, and we were through. The mob scattering in front of us, the line of gas-masked police, then the open Canton Road and the smashed glass and bricks everywhere and the searing stink of gas, the missiles flying down from the shattered union windows, the road shining black wet with acid and full of glass and stones. We scrambled out of the Land Rover and ran along under the verandah to the commissioner of police.

He tore off his gas mask. "Who's got the knockout stuff?" He had to shout it.

"I have, sir." Teetotal pulled out the little pressurized gas phial, no bigger than an aspirin bottle. One whiff of that would knock anybody out cold. Trouble is you had to do it in their faces.

"When the hell do you want to go in, Jake?" the C.P. shouted to me suspiciously as if I had no business here.

"Not particularly ever, sir, but I want to see what I can find in the first rush, before everything's trampled to death."

"You won't make it up the stairs, they've put six of us out of action already."

"Through the roof?" I said.

"Through the wall next door, sir," Flanagan shouted. "Smash a hole through from the adjoining flat."

"Think you can?"

"Used to be in the Fire Brigade, sir," Flanagan shouted.

"What've we got?"

"Crowbars and axes."

"Give it a go," the C.P. shouted.

We grabbed the tools out of the vehicles, grabbed my four S.B. constables and four others. We ran along under the verandah to the adjoining building, up to the second floor. There was not a soul, everybody locked indoors. We beat on the door of the second-floor flat, bang bang bang until they opened up for us. "Excuse us, we're going to knock your wall down." You could hear the roar from next door and down in the street. We dragged a wardrobe away from the wall. *"Let's go,"* Flanagan and McDougal started smashing into the common wall with crowbars, the dust and concrete flew. It was so old the crow swiped in easily. Dust, concrete sweat flying everywhere. We took turns with the crowbars and pacifying the household. The old bricks came smashing out. You could still hear the roaring in the street, the gas guns and bricks and bottles. We were making good time. The wall was only eighteen inches thick. We hacked down to the last layer of bricks. *"Right,"* Flanagan said: and we smashed smashed smashed together and the first bricks smashed through, we saw the astonished Comrade faces, then they were shouting scrambling for the front door, and we went mad with the crowbars and smashed clean through the wall. Clean through a huge portrait of Mao Tse-tung, the Reddest Sun in Our Hearts, we dived through the hole after the sonsabitches. McDougal got to the front door as the last sonofabitch slammed it. He flung it open and charged down the stairs with Flanagan and the four uniformed constables after him. I ran to the stair landing and saw the last sonofabitch dive into the first-floor flat and slam the door in McDougal's face. A section of U.B.s were charging up the stairs from the street and McDougal was hurling himself against the door and Flanagan was shouting, "Bring axes!" I ran to the windows and bellowed down to the C.P., *"They're in the flat below—we're breaking in—no more tear gas!"* and I shouted to my S.B. *fokis. "Search!"* I heard the first-floor flat door go in with a crash, and then shouting crashing thudding smashing, and I started searching.

Shattered glass everywhere. Under the windows were stacked rows of bottles of acid and big baskets of bricks and stones and the iron bars and axes and spears. In the corner was a big desk and filing cabinet, I flung them open, they were full of papers in Chinese. *At fucking last!* Jesus it felt good to get your hands on something tangible. I went through the room ransacking it. Then checked to see what my *fokis* were turning up in the other rooms. They were as delighted as I was. I shouted to them that we would evacuate everything, in the drawers and filing cabinets we found them in. Search the walls and floors for hidden compartments, label each drawer. I shouted to the sergeant that he was in charge and made for the front door. To get downstairs into the first-floor flat before the boys wrecked everything worth reading. I clattered down the black stairs, into all hell breaking loose.

Dark, shouts thuds bangs crashes hollers, I burst in the doorway and was knocked back by a uniform dragging a Comrade out yelling *Protest,* I edged myself back into the melee, dodging, ducking, something hit me on the shoulder, fists sticks shouting everywhere, I looked for somebody to hit and everybody near me was occupied. I threw myself at a bastard from behind and grabbed his hair and yanked him back and hit him with all my might in his guts and he crashed, some sonofabitch slugged me and I saw black-red stars and went down, I kicked out with all my frenzied fascist might and Jesus Christ it was lovely to feel the sonofabitch disappear, I scrambled up after him through the arms legs bodies thumping crashing everywhere and hit him with all my might on the side of his head, grabbed his collar and dragged him toward the front door, fell on the top step, I wrenched the sonofabitch up by the collar and dragged him down the stairs, straight into the C.P. and we all fell down the acid stairs together.

"Sorry." I picked myself up, panting, burning, heart thudding in my ears, dragged the sonofabitch Comrade down the last steps out into the roaring street. "Somebody give me a flashlight!" I grabbed it and turned and bounded back up the stairs into a battered bloody constable dragging another Comrade down and we all crashed down in a bloody acid heap, arms legs cursing gasping heart thudding, I scrambled up and bellowed, "Sorry," and I ran back up the stairs, I grabbed up a piece of wood and dashed in close to the wall, flashing my light. All the fighting was going on down the long corridor now. It was two flats knocked into one. I dashed into the first bedroom. I saw a pair of legs under the bed and grabbed the ankle and dragged him out the flat screaming *Protest* and gave him to a constable running up the stairs. I dashed back to the room to search. At the end of the corridor was a staircase leading up to a big mezzanine cockloft and a whole flock of Comrades were holed up in there hurling bricks down, and Teetotal's boys were chopping the wooden stanchions down with axes. There were no papers in the bedroom except Mao posters and I went on to the next. There was no fighting near me now, just the hullabaloo of Teetotal's chopping at the end of the corridor and Flanagan bashing down the locked kitchen door bellowing *Open up!* The kitchen door broke open and Flanagan barged into the blackness and I heard him scream *Christ you bastard!* and then *Jake!*

I ran down the corridor to the black kitchen doorway, there was all kinds of fighting inside, Flanagan was reeling out clutching his hand, pumping blood.

"The bastards chopped my fingers off!"

I grabbed his arm and pulled him down the corridor and got my flashlight on it. His face was screwed up in agony, blood everywhere, three fingers flapping by bloody skin, the bones sticking out. *"Pull them off!"* Fingers Flanagan shouted. That's how he got the name.

"No, for Crissake!" I was ripping off my shirt.

"Pull the sonsabitches off, for Chrissake!" He wanted to get back in there and get the bastard who did it. I rammed my handkerchief in a ball in his palm and bent his hanging fingers around it in a shattered fist and

466

wrapped my shirt around it. He was leaning against the wall, blood everywhere. There was the crash of a body falling, some Comrade had taken a flying leap from the mezzanine floor. Teetotal hollered, *"The rest of you come down or I'll chop the last stanchion!"* All hell was going on in the kitchen. I started down the stairs with Fingers. Two uniforms were running back up the stairs. *"In the kitchen,"* I shouted at them. I got Fingers down into the street and the newspaper photographers' flashes went. The street was roaring, down at both ends the riot boys were holding the mobs back. "Jesus," the C.P. said.

"Is an ambulance coming?"

"They say they can't come through the mob without a police escort," the C.P. fumed. "I've sent for another Land Rover."

We were both covered in blood. It looked as if Fingers's whole hand had been chopped off. The prisoners were sitting on the road looking sorry for themselves, six of our chaps were badly beaten up. "Send for more S.B.s please," I shouted. "There's a pile of stuff up there. Good luck with those fingers, Fingers."

"Catch the bastards," Fingers gritted.

I ran back up the stairs. At the first landing I met them bringing the last lot out, under arrest. I counted eleven going past. They were not struggling any more. They looked a mess, we all looked a mess. At the door I met Teetotal, he was exhausted, bloody, grinning.

"That the lot?"

"One dead in there. Jumped out of the cockloft."

We were both panting.

"I saw him, Peking'll love that. Jesus, you look bad." He had a big gash on his forehead and a big graze on his cheek, blood running down his triumphant heaving chest.

"God, that did my heart good."

"Do everybody's heart good. Tomorrow the balloon will go up in Peking though. Nobody else in there?"

"Only our boys. And the stiff."

We went through the shambles. The body was lying, face down, head bloody. We stepped over him, into the kitchen. I could feel the blood sticking to the soles of my shoes. We found the electricity mains and got the lights on. God, what a shambles. The C.P. came up and asked how long I would be. We went through the flat together. I said about an hour, to be sure they didn't have any hidden compartments. He went out and left me alone with my *fokis*. You could still hear the roaring down there in the street. I went through to the kitchen and had a long drink of water and washed my face and hands. It was stinking hot. I looked out the kitchen window down into the littered street.

Thank God. And oh Jesus what happens now? Tomorrow any bloody thing could happen. Tomorrow Peking's Most Vehement Protest Against Frenzied Fascist Outrage, Butchery, Provocations. Tomorrow the Comrade press screaming Bloody Fascist Murder. Tomorrow Red Guards massing screaming on the Shamchun. As from tomorrow the real blood starts. And oh God I don't care, I don't care what happens in this god-awful town on this god-awful continent just so long as she comes back. I don't care what happens to anybody as long as you leave her alone.

The next day Peking lodged their Most Vehement Protest Against the Frenzied Provocation of the Savage Armed Invasion of the Patriotic Hong Kong Synthetic Fibers Workers' Union and the Barbarous Murders and Mass Suppressions and Fascist Atrocities and repeated the Five Just Demands and cried *"Violence for Violence to Overwhelm Barbarous Brutality! All China Stands Alerted! Let the Fascist Barbarians Taste the Iron Fist of the Chinese Workers! Applaud the General Strike!"* And in the Comrade press there was the joyous screaming praise of the Reddest Sun in Our Hearts, *"Fight Violence with Violence"*—*"Fascist White-skin Pigs Must Taste the Iron Fist"*—*"Advance Wave upon Wave!"* And at the village of Shataukok, where the border runs down the middle of the main road, eight hundred peasants massed under the People's Militia and the committee gangs swarmed out with their sticks and axes and iron bars drumming up the Great Glory General Strike applauded by the Thought of Mao Tse-tung and the Great Glory Food Strike also, now: *There Must Be No Food in City of Imperial Decadence Run by White-skin Pigs! Any Black Sheep Yellow-skin Running Dog Who Grows, Sells, Hawks, Unloads Food Will Perish! Deal Crushing Blows! Violence for Violence!* And the Hong Kong–Kowloon All Circles Anti-Persecution Struggle Committee summoned all the principals and teachers to a Great Struggle Meeting and announced that in all schools there must be Great Mass Revolt, and that any principal, teacher, or child who did not obey would be buried with the British, and the Comrade press roared its headlines, *We Defy British Pigs to Try to Enter Compatriot Schools!*

CHAPTER 75

That morning at Shataukok they boarded up the windows of the Chung Hop wine shop, other side Chung Ying Street, the border between Hong Kong and China. We always knew there was going to be trouble with the Comrades when the Chung Hop wine shop's shutters went up. Superintendent McNally and all his men went to the windows of the Hong Kong Police Post to look.

It was dead quiet out there. There were the usual machine guns mounted on the corner outside the wine shop and on the rooftop behind the life-size effigy of the governor of Hong Kong hanged from the lamppost. Then the first radio report came in from our lookout, way up in the mountains overlooking Shataukok. "Large crowds gathering out of your sight on the Chinese side of Chung Ying Street." McNally radioed Shataukok Main Police Station, half a mile back up the road into the hills. "Send down two riot squad platoons to take up position at the Rural Committee Building four hundred yards behind this post." Then they settled down to watch and wait, eighty Pakistanis and twelve Chinese constables, the two inspectors and Superintendent McNally.

They waited for two hours. Then the radio crackled from way up there in the mountains, "Large crowds marching down Chung Ying Street heading for yours." Then suddenly they heard the roar rising up over the hot deserted village, then around the corner of Chung Ying Street they came, one thousand Chinese peasants armed with sticks and iron bars and bottles running across the road into British territory, straight at the fence around the police post, screaming yelling roaring surrounding it, then came the barrage.

From all sides, great hail after hail of bricks stones bottles crashing smashing, McNally shouted at his men to fire tear gas through the gun slits and he yelled for a Pakistani section to follow him and they ran doubled up, ducking out into the rear compound into the hail and they fired a volley of tear gas over the fence, ducking and doging, then the first explosion came. A great crash and shatter of smoke and flying nails, *"Get back inside!"* McNally roared, he ran flat out for cover and another bomb came flying out of nowhere and exploded deafeningly behind him, and another. Inside the post it was deafening, gas guns going off in all directions, McNally ran for the radio.

Four hundred yards back up the road our two riot squads, in the Rural Committee Building, eighty men, fell into their ranks to march down to the post in full formation to break up the mob. Suddenly there was a new sound uproar from down the road. The terrible sudden savage staccato of machine gun. And the front ranks of the riot squad fell.

The machine gun mowed them down, they fell shattered shocked writhing on the road spouting blood, bullets blood dust flying everywhere in the savage clattering, the policemen broke ranks and picked up the eleven writhing wounded and ran scrambling bloody back for the Rural Committee Building under the flying bullets, and a roar of joy went up from the mob. Then the savage machine gun mounted on the rooftop on the China side of Chung Ying Street turned on the police post.

Turned clattering savage murderous, it raked the observation tower then trained on the windows and gun slits *da-da-da-da-da*, bullets flying smashing crashing whistling ricocheting around inside the post and concrete flying, everybody threw themselves flat shocked astonished outraged wild-eyed, the machine gun fired murderously *da-da-da-da-da* straight into the big open windows of the observation tower which was crowded with seventeen policemen and mowed down Constable Mawaz right through the head, blood brains hair skull splattering flying mid the bullets smashing crashing around inside the tower, Inspector White threw himself wild-eyed across the bloody concrete floor and flung himself down the ladder. *"They've killed him!"* White bellowed. *"They've killed him."*

"Then get him down!" McNally roared.

"Yessir!" White scrambled back up the ladder into the screaming ricocheting and raced on his hands and

knees and grabbed Mawaz by his bloody collar and Constable Ahmed screamed and fell clutching his chest and White bellowed wild-eyed, *"Get him down too,"* and all the time the shocked madness of the machine gun and the bullets screaming smashing ricocheting around. Then suddenly the machine gun stopped and the sniper fire started. From the front and rear and side and from the rooftops, sniper fire smashing in the gun slits with deadly accuracy. "Keep your bloody heads down," McNally roared and flung himself on the radio and shouted hoarsely, "N.T. North, N.T. North. Now they're sniping from three sides from hidden rooftop emplacements on both sides of the border—deadly accurate fire they must be PLA not People's Militia—request permission to open fire in self-defense, repeat essential to open fire in self-defense—also essential that the Army be sent down to take over, repeat this is a military operation, do you read me, over."

And the cacophony of the sniping roaring stone bombs came over the radio loud and clear in N.T. North Control and Pol. Mil. H.Q. and around every police and military radio in the Colony it was packed with shocked policemen and soldiers, and they heard the word come back from Pol Mil. H.Q.: "Permission to fire on snipers granted except snipers in China territory—repeat do not fire into China territory—request for military assistance is being referred to London—riot platoons in Rural Committee Building are unable to come to your assistance because they are pinned down under heavy crossfire —two constables are dead and eleven wounded—repeat—

McNally grabbed his M1 carbine, he pressed himself flat against the wall, peeped out the window into the screaming hurling mob, two Chinese were crouched outside the big locked gates placing explosives, McNally rammed his carbine through the window and fired *da-da-da-da-da* and the two men spun away smashed bloody and the mob scattered back screaming falling over themselves shocked outraged that the Foreign Devil Fascist Pigs had dared fire back on the compatriots armed with the Invincible Thought of Mao Tse-tung. Then the sniper fire broke out again, bullets flying crashing and the concrete flying and the mobs came screaming yelling hurling back again and there was nothing in the world but the cacophony of sniper gunfire and the stones and bombs.

And in Pol. Mil. H.Q. in Hong Kong Island mid the tiers of desks and telephones and telexes and maps and stenographers and runners the terrible staccato of the gunfire and the explosions and the roaring came through loud and clear over McNally's staccato voice:

"Pinned down by sniper fire from all sides—impossible to locate them because we cannot look long enough— we must have military help."

Way up the road, behind the mountains, the Army was awaiting instructions from Pol. Mil. H.Q., and Pol. Mil. H.Q. was awaiting orders from London. It was three o'clock in the morning in London, and the right people were fast asleep, scattered to the four winds.

CHAPTER 76

Up in the mountain, in his room in the Shataukok Main Police Station, Nondrinking Jack was asleep, off duty. The machine-gun fire woke him. He bounded out of bed, pulled on shorts and tennis shoes and ran downstairs to the Report Room to find out what the hell was happening. Then he ran out the back and down behind the hill to the Army lines, to the nearest armored car. "Three volunteers!" Nondrinking Jack shouted at the Chinese constables. "Into the car!" The three constables and Nondrinking Jack scrambled into the back of the armored car. "*Go!*" Nondrinking Jack, a policeman, ordered the Pakistani driver, a soldier.

"Please, sir," the astonished Pakistani soldier said, "do you have permission, sir, to take this car, sir?"

"You have my permission!" Nondrinking Jack shouted. "*Go!*"

"Oh my goodness me," the Pakistani private said, "this business I am not liking."

"*Go! I am not liking it either!*"

They drove over the top of the hill, started down the road to Shataukok. Inside the car they could hear nothing. They could see no snipers, no policemen, just deserted fields and buildings. Then, three hundred yards ahead, was the Rural Committee Building and the police Land

Rover abandoned in the road and the policemen lying dead by the ditch. Then they could hear something pinging outside the car. "What's that?" Nondrinking demanded. He had never been in an armored car before.

"Bullets, sir," the Pakistani private said miserably. "Oh my goodness me."

They were glistening with sweat. Fifty yards off the building now. The pinging was heavy now. Nondrinking wiped his forehead.

"Pure San Miguel." He tried to make a joke. "Stop outside the building." As they stopped outside the Rural Committee Building the pinging was thick and loud.

"*Out!*" Nondrinking shouted.

He flung open the back of the armored car and ran flat out doubled up into the shattered building, the three constables running flat out after him. He burst into the main room, there was blood, plaster, bodies, glass everywhere. "*Out!*" he shouted. "*Get the injured out to the car!*" He grabbed the nearest bloody man by his armpits, a constable grabbed the bloody legs and they staggered, stumbling, out the building sweating cursing panting, flat out for the car under the sniper fire, they slung the injured policeman in and ran flat out back to the building. Two other constables were lugging a man out, shot through the ankles. They slung him in the armored car and raced back into the building. There were some wounded lying to the side of the building, pinned down by fire from two directions. Nondrinking ran doubled up around the side, grabbed up the nearest and ran back to the armored car and slung him in on top of the others. They were lying tangled on top of each other, spouting blood, gasping, groaning, bullets thudding against the armor. Nondrinking Jack and the constables ran back and forth between the armored car and the building and lugged out eleven men under the sniper fire, and the car was absolutely full. They were lying two deep on top of each other in the car now, blood everywhere. Nondrinking Jack and the constables scrambled in on top of everyone, they could not close the doors for bloody legs hanging out.

"*Reverse,*" Nondrinking bellowed. "*Reverse like hell, don't turn around,*" and the car went grinding flat out zigzagging backward up the hill, blood and sweat and bodies everywhere, and you could not hear the groans and gasping for the twanging of the bullets on the armor.

Over the hill, they drove like hell for the Gurkha military hospital. Another constable was dead on arrival.

Then, all bloody and sweaty, Nondrinking Jack commandeered a second armored car and the pair of them went roaring back over the hill, back down to the Rural Committee Building, and they got the rest of them out. Altogether it took them three hours and they were under long-range fire all the time. Then Nondrinking Jack said Thanks very much to the Army and gave them their armored cars back. He walked back to Shataukok Main Station and got himself a large San Miguel, seeing he was still off-duty. He could still hear the gunfire down there at McNally's post. But there was nothing anybody could do about that, until London said we could send the Army in to take over.

In London it was 5 A.M. In Hong Kong it was three o'clock in the afternoon, hot as all hell. In Shataukok, four policemen were dead, ten shot up. In London they had woken the Prime Minister but they were still running around looking for the rest of his advisers. In Pol. Mil. H.Q. it was all tense muted British hell, police, Army, Navy, Air Force, telephones, maps, teleprinters, radios, shorthand-writers, typists, runners, and over the radio came the gunfire and explosions from Shataukok and McNally's staccato voice: "Impossible to move about inside the post because of accurate sniper from all sides—richochets are flying around inside—Corporal Ahmed is now also dead—two more snipers located on top of public lavatory to our rear—"

They had not eaten food all day. They had finished the water in the refrigerator, the tap water was unfit for drinking. The bombs were still flying mid the snipers' gunfire and the machine gun. A fire bomb hit the Land Rover in the rear compound, it went up in flames. Then suddenly the sniper fire stopped.

Stopped. On all sides. On a signal from somewhere. Suddenly it was dead quiet.

They lay flat, sweating, dry-mouthed, dry-throated in the sudden sweating silence. McNally waited, then crouched to the window and peered through the bottom corner gingerly. It was dead quiet outside. He could see nobody, just the litter of glass and stones and sticks and concrete. He crouched on to the next window, looked gingerly through his binoculars. The Chinese soldier

474

manning the machine gun was staring over the edge of the sandbags at him. He crouched around the post, window. He could just make out the tips of the snipers' rifles on top of the public lavatory. Then he clambered up the ladder up into the tower.

It was a shambles up there, blood, hair, brains, plaster everywhere. The bullets had gone clean through the steel hatch at the top of the ladderway. Everybody was still lying flat. McNally scrambed on all fours across the bloody concrete, and looked out.

Dead quiet. There were the sandbagged machine emplacements, the tops of the sonsabitches' heads just sticking up. He saw one grin. He rapped at his men, "Keep your bloody heads down." From the north, from Kong Ha village, there came some more sniper fire, he ducked. Then silence again. He crouched all around to every port, looking carefully, heart thudding, dry gut, dry mouth, sweating.

He scrambled back down the ladder. Constable Mawaz's blood was a big red-black sticky pool at the bottom, his face covered with a sack. McNally crouched over to the radio, said dry-mouthed, "N.T. North, firing stopped, obviously on a signal. The mob has disappeared. However machine guns and snipers are still in position. It's just a ruse to make us show ourselves. Expecting all-out attack this time, repeat expecting all-out attack. We badly need food and water, repeat food and water."

Then the three machine guns opened up again.

Opened up flat out from across Chung Ying Street where they knew the Hong Kong police could not fire back, three bigger caliber machine guns than before, *dadadadadadada,* bullets smashing crashing ricocheting flying everywhere again, raked the building from end to end then fired flat out into the tower's big observation ports again and there was nothing in the world but the terribly cacophony. *"Get out of it!"* McNally bellowed up the ladder. *"Get the hell out of the tower!"* —and they could not hear him above the crashing, McNally scrambled flat out up the ladder and screamed, *"Get out of this tower!"* and they came scrambling wild-eyed on their bellies through the blood and hurled themselves down the ladder, and the crashing hammering came over loud and clear in Pol. Mil. H.Q. and McNally shouting, *"Opened up on us full blast with three machine guns—heavier caliber than before—this is the heaviest fire we've been under—they're absolutely smash-ing it in—they're going to wipe out the post—we can't look out the windows—they—"*

The radio went out in a screeching crash. Then silence. In Pol. Mil. H.Q. there was stunned silence, then all hell broke loose.

CHAPTER 77

The hammering of the machine guns filled the hot mountainside, hammering the police post, ricocheting whining off the convoy of armored cars coming down the road: the eyes of the world were on that police post and convoy, waiting for World War III.

Nondrinking Jack walked crouching behind the leading armored car, beside the colonel. Nondrinking Jack had come along with the Army for the ride, and he dearly wished he hadn't. What a way to spend your Saturday off. Nondrinking Jack kept his head down and let the colonel do the looking. "What do you see, Colonel?" he shouted.

"Nothing." The machine guns were hammering.

Nondrinking Jack shouted, head down, "I don't like it. That's what the cavalry sergeant always says in the Western. Then an arrow thumps him in the chest. Right here," he demonstrated.

"Some people running away out of Kong Ha village, about twenty of them," the colonel shouted.

"Away? Thank Christ for that," Nondrinking Jack said. "Oh my goodness me. Oh my goodness me," Nondrinking Jack said, "this business I am not liking." The sun was beating down, burning drythroat hot. How many PLA were waiting for them down there other side Chung Ying Street? If they can attack a virtually unarmed police post for the sake of face what the hell are they prepared to do to this handful of the Fascist British Army, Non-drinking Jack thought. What a glorious Victory for the Thought of Mao Tse-tung that would be, the terror and pandemonium in Hong Kong tonight, what a resounding

Victory over the Fascist Imperialist Reactionary Paper Tigers Lifting a Rock Only to Drop It on Their Own Feet—

The Rural Committee Building was fifty yards ahead now, the machine guns hammering, Kong Ha village was coming up alongside the convoy. Now was the time for the Kong Ha village boys to open up, *now*. And suddenly the firing stopped.

Stopped, and there was crashing silence. And then the tramp of their boots on the tarmac, and Nondrinking Jack thought he could hear himself sweating.

They peeled off the road and headed through the paddies in the new ringing silence, the colonel, Nondrinking Jack, the line of Gurkhas, heading for the back of the police post. The armored cars rolled on down the road, toward the front of the post. Hot and silent. Except the thudding in Nondrinking Jack's chest. The Gurkhas were alert, unsmiling, they carried their rifles ready, stalked confidently along in the wide open across the paddies, they knew exactly what they were doing. If the Comrades opened up now they could mow the lot of them down. It seemed the paddies would never end.

They were coming out of the last paddy now. The police post compound was fifty yards ahead. Now they could see the shattered concrete, the fire bomb chars, the charred Land Rover, the bomb damage. There was not a sound from the post. The colonel was walking upright across the open, as if he was walking across a playground. Nondrinking made himself straighten up. *Now,* by Jesus Christ, *now* was the time for the sonsabitches to open up and kill them all.

They were going through the gate now. Walking normally, upright, not fast, not slowly, dead silence except the crunch of their boots. Nondrinking Jack glanced behind him for the Gurkhas: they had almost disappeared everywhere into strategic positions, crouching behind cover, guns ready, without an order. They knew what it was all about. And the Comrades did not open up. They also knew what the Gurkhas were all about. The colonel went through the back door, shaking hands with McNally.

"If you'd like to get your chappies out, old chap?"

That night in Peking the Deputy Foreign Minister of People's Republic of China thrust a note at the British

477

chargé d'affaires mid the flashing Chinese press cameras. The note read,

> Today people on our side of Shataukok and patriotic Chinese inhabitants of the "New Territories" held a peaceful rally on our side to voice support for our patriotic countrymen in Hong Kong in their just struggle against brutal suppression by the British Authorities. When the Chinese inhabitants were peacefully returning to the New Territories, fully armed policemen and riot police of the British Authorities flagrantly carried out a premeditated sanguinary suppression at them, throwing tear bombs and opening fire and flagrantly firing at the People's Republic of China. The Chinese frontier guards fired warning shots against such atrocities and provocations but in total disregard the policemen and riot police of the British Authorities continued to fire ruthlessly. . . .

That weekend the bombs started.

That Sunday afternoon the telephone rang in my office, I had been working all night on the Shataukok debacle. "Yes?" I said irritably.

"Hello," she said. "It's me."

I burst into the penthouse riotously laughy shaky happy.

"Ying?"

And oh God the laughing joyful clutching hugging, I hugged her tight and swept her off her feet and put her down, oh my darling, laughing clutching her tight against me, long slender body breasts belly thighs shoulders, I held her at arm's length and she was laughing tearful.

"Hello, darling."

"You cut your hair!"

"Yes but not much, it is growing again—"

I laughed. "I don't care if they gave you a bloody crew cut, just thank God you're back! They fed you all right!"

"You look so tired!"

"Oh thank God—" I clutched her tight, her loveliness against me, she laughed jerkily, happy tearful, I kissed

478

her neck and smelled her and she was looking at the big windows.

"My garden."

"I tried to look after it but even they were pining."

She looked around the room at the familiar things, then her eyes were suddenly full of tears and she was trying to smile and she couldn't, she looked away and turned out of my arms. She leaned her forehead against the window, back to me. "Ying?" I put my hands on her shoulders, they were shaking. Her eyes were closed and the tears were running down her face.

"Ying, what's the matter?"

She shook her head, forehead pressed against the window, pressed her knuckles to her eyes and turned away. "Ying?" She walked to the center of the room, I followed her and turned her around.

"Ying, what's the matter?"

She looked at me and tried to smile, tearful. "I'm all right, darling, I am only happy."

She closed her eyes and the tears ran down her cheeks and her chin crinkled up and she burst out into sobs, she took a big trembling breath to say something, then she tried to laugh.

"Love me—just love me—"

And oh God jerky shaky I picked her up, salty tears loving shaking, I picked her up and carried her through to the bedroom and fell down beside her on the bed and clutched her tight and kissed her wet salty face mouth eyes loving rejoicing the sweet blissful feel of her, the tearful joy and oh my love my love my lover my darling my love—

CHAPTER 78

Afterward she lay very still, holding me, I kissed the warm smoothness of her neck and shoulder, the smell and taste and feel of her, she lay looking at the ceiling, she took a big breath that trembled and she said, "they want me to be a spy."

I stopped breathing. I could feel myself go white, my heart lurch suddenly. Then I sat up and stared at her.

"I see."

She was staring at me, tense, dry-eyed. My heart was thudding.

"I see. The Public Security Bureau in Canton?" I said. I felt white.

She nodded, yes yes.

"I see. So they know all about us." My voice sounded loud. "Did you tell them?"

She shook her head vigorously. "No, they already knew! They said they had known a long time, almost since we first started."

"Jesus." I stood up. My heart was thudding, I reached for a cigarette, my hand trembling. The white feeling in my guts. *Oh God, of course they had known! That explains everything! That explains why we got away with it for so long, why we had no trouble from her bloody people, no bloody questions asked, nothing to put us on our guard. The bloody Comrades knew all about it and they were just too delighted to encourage it to get a senior bloody British policeman into their information net with a communist mistress, oh Jesus Christ the bastards have just been keeping me on ice all this time! Until they needed me! And now's the goddamn time, now I'm a super!*

"Jesus Christ, of course they knew!"

I was shaking, sick in my guts. Christ! I strode to the wardrobe and flung it open and threw her dressing gown at her. "Get up," I said. "There's something I've got to do."

"What?" she stared.

I was shaking, my mouth sick dry. *"Just do as I say, darling! Go and sit in the lounge. And don't say a word. Do it!"*

I pulled on a pair of shorts. She got off the bed, went into the lounge. I was sweating. I started to ransack the room. I pulled all the furniture away from the walls, went along the baseboards, the windows, the light fittings. I was looking for their listening device. Then I started on the wardrobe, I pulled everything out and flung it on the floor. I searched every crack and corner. Then the bed. The dressing table. I ransacked the bedroom from top to bottom, sweating. Nothing. I knew how to look for these fucking things, and there was certainly nothing. Then the bathroom. Then the kitchen. Then the lounge. She stared at me, I motioned her not to speak. I ransacked the lounge. I unscrewed the panel of the air-conditioner, the light switches, looked along the curtain pelmets. There was nothing. I was sweating, dry-mouthed, but mostly I had stopped shaking. She was staring at me, white-faced.

"I was looking for hidden microphones."

I went over to her. She was trying hard to control herself, wide-eyed dry-eyed tearful. I looked down at her. Oh God oh God oh God. I said, "Do you love me?"

She closed her eyes.

"Yes I love you! Would I come back and tell you this if I didn't love you?"

"All right," I said. I was still standing over her. "Now you've got to tell me everything, from the beginning."

I went to the kitchen and poured two stiff whiskeys. Still shaking. I thought, "You took a calculated risk, you knew it, you said you had it all figured out so what are you so bloody shocked about! The great bloody McAdam!" But what the hell did they expect *her* to get out of me—goddamn official secrets? Christ no! They know that no half-decent police officer tells his wife or mistress anything she shouldn't know. Christ no, they're after better odds than that! Blackmail. Through her. "Tell us, or else." Or else we blow your story to your authorities. Then it's her. "Tell us or she suffers." Through her father. Christ, I felt sick in my guts. So this is what it feels like to be on the hook. Like they've all felt when the crunch came. She was sitting, hands clutched in her lap, pale, exhausted, eyes swollen. I handed her the drink. She shook her head.

"Drink it, darling. Like medicine."

Her hand was trembling, she took a big breath and gulped it once, eyes closed, and suppressed a retch. She shuddered once at me. Then she tried to give me a sick tearful smile, and I wanted to shout for love and hate for the whole rotten stinking bastard sonofabitch world. She put up her moist hand and held mine for a moment, then I pulled a chair in front of her and sat down. I was still shaky but I was calmer now. I lit two cigarettes and passed her one.

"Now tell me. From the beginning."

She breathed out and said, "We arrived in Canton, fourteen schoolteachers. Eight I knew before, the rest I don't. We were taken to a school. We were given a room to sleep in, a schoolroom." She took a weary breath. "As soon as we get there, two men came and said that I must come with them. That is all, you must come with us, please. So"—she rubbed her wrist across her forehead once—"so of course I go."

"Where to? The Public Security Bureau?"

"Yes." She took a breath. I did not want to interrupt her. "We go inside. They take me to a room. They tell me to wait, sit down. They go into an office and say 'She is here.' That is all. So—I wait. . . ." She looked at me. "And oh I was very frightened."

I squeezed her hand. "Go on."

She rubbed her forehead. "I could not think properly. I knew why they wanted me, straightaway. And all the time I am trying to think clearly, what I must say, but oh darling it seemed like the most terrible crime in the world, I felt sick." I squeezed her hand. She said, "All I could think to say was that you are a good man and you like the Chinese people, you were also born in China, you are not stupid about communists, like the Americans. I did not know what they are going to do, if they are only angry and shout at me and tell me I am a no-good communist that is all right, but then I think maybe they can stop us, and oh darling I was terrified—" She was getting tearful again, I squeezed her hand. "Go on, darling."

She puffed her cigarette hard and wiped her eyes and pulled herself together.

482

"So. Then they come. Two men. They do not look friendly but they are quite polite. They say they are Public Security Bureau—"

"Did they give you their names?"

"No names." She looked at me, then went on, "And you know what the first one says? He says, 'You have cut your hair! What will Mr. McAdam say about that, he likes long hair!'" She said flatly, "I cut six inches off my hair when I left you here."

I smiled mirthlessly. Yes. The Shock Approach. "And?"

She took a big breath. "They have a big file, and he is comparing me with a photograph he has. Before I can answer anything he says sternly, staring at me like this, he says, 'You were born in China but when the Liberation came your father ran away to the Philippines.' Then they say: 'Your father returned to China later, but you went to Hong Kong and finish school and then go to university!' They say it sternly, like that. Then they say, 'After university you work first in a private capitalist school for one year!' Then they say, 'Your father made plenty of money in China and in Philippines and he puts it in the bank before he comes back to China.' I said, 'He came back to work for China, because he loves China, he is a communist!' I say. And they say"—she took a breath—"'There are *two* kinds of communists! Revisionist Poisonous Weed `Goulash com-munists, and there are Maoists!'" She rubbed her fore-head, she looked at me. "Now I was very worried for my father."

I nodded. Oh Jesus yes. "Go on."

"I said, 'He is a good communist otherwise why would he go back to China!'" She glared at me, then went on, "They did not answer me, they said, 'The Cultural Revolution will take a long time but we will'"—she used the Cantonese, then the nearest English—"'we will get rid of all the revisionist scabs and bourgeoisie very well indeed!'"

I squeezed her hand. "Tell it, darling."

She puffed hard once on her cigarette, her eyes swol-len, and closed her eyes to unconfuse herself. "They said more about that, but I do not remember if it was before or after they talked about you again but the mean-ing was clear all the time." She stared at me tremulously and I felt my heart crunch, I knew what was coming. "They were threatening my father about you and me——"

I nodded. "What did they say? From the beginning."

She went on tremulously, "They said, 'Are you a good communist?' I said, 'I try.' They said, 'You are a revisionist capitalist-roader!' I said, 'I will try to be better.' They say very sternly, 'You are the lover of McAdam of the British police in Hong Kong!'" She took a big breath. "So I say, 'Yes—I am.'" She looked at me. "They know all about you! They start to tell me and my heart is going boom-boom. They tell me about your father. Where you born. Your career. Malaya. Your work in Hong Kong. They say you are a senior policeman now." She pulled on the cigarette, trying to remember precisely. I said, "What did they say about my job?"

She rubbed her forehead.

"That you are a superintendent in Special Branch."

"What did they say about Special Branch?"

She said, "Now, nothing. Later, yes. At this time they told me about your wife. That she is in England, and Suzie. That you are a Roman Catholic, and your wife, about the divorce." She looked at me, harassed. "They knew everything, they were telling me to prove it."

I said, "What else?"

She breathed wearily. "That you had this flat. Your car. Your boat. All the time they are talking very sternly, and all I can do is say 'Yes, yes.' What else can I say?"

I nodded.

She took a breath. "They said, 'Every night you sleep in this man's bed! Then you go to school and pretend you are a communist!'" She puffed hard on her cigarette, white-faced, looking at me. "They said, 'In this flat you keep bourgeois clothes! But when you go to school you wear decent clothes and pretend you are a decent young woman!' They said, 'You have accepted gifts! He pays for your food and you save up your money!' They said, 'You read decadent Western literature! You have not attended all the study groups!'" She rubbed her forehead again once. "They said so many things. They said"—her voice took on a note of indignation— "'You keep pets! You have a bourgeois dog and a bird and even a glutton mouse!'"

484

I could not help a smile.

"How did they know about my mouse?" she said.

I said, "What's more important is how they knew about your decadent bourgeois clothes. Did they say they'd been in here? Or describe it?"

She shook her head. I wanted to get up, pace about but I sat still.

"A goddamn guess. They wouldn't risk me finding them in here, that would spoil everything." She was staring at me. "Go on." I knew it all now. First they terrify her. Then they relent and win her gratitude. Then they blackmail her. I still felt sick in my guts. She took a breath. "They said I am a revisionist. A poisonous weed. Capitalist-roader. Many things. Then they said"—she looked back at me—" 'And your father is the same!' "

She stared at me angrily. "And I shouted, 'No! He is not the same! My father is a good communist, I am a revisionist yes but my father is a good communist! If he is not a good communist why does he return to work in China! Hah?' " She appealed to me. Her eyes were hot angry wet. *"Why?"* I took both her hands and she pulled them away and pressed her fingertips to her eyelids hard and breathed out hard, tremulous, then looked at me and breathed, "I'm all right."

She blew her nose. I took her hand and she let me hold it, limp.

"They said, 'Do you know what the Cultural Revolution is for? Do you know what we do to revisionists like you and your father?' " She closed her eyes. "And I was so frightened now for my father I only want to please them, I say 'No sir, but I am very sorry.' But he says, like a judge, 'We hand you to the Red Guards.' " She looked at me red-eyed. " 'Then later send you to Thought Reform Labor Camps. Then' "—she stared at me—" 'if necessary we shoot you.' "

I took her fists and held them. I nodded. "Then?"

She breathed deep, tremblingly. "I forget so many things. They said, 'Tomorrow there is a Great Rally of Red Guards at the Sports Stadium to protest against the Brutal Savage Atrocities of the Fascist Authorities in the City of Imperial Decadence Run by White-skin Pigs and Yellow-skinned Running Dogs, and your lover is a policeman who has committed these barbarous atrocities.' " She looked at me. "He says, 'There will also be

485

a Mass Trial and Self-criticism Meeting of Liu-ist Revisionist Scabs!' And he looks at me like this and says, 'You will go!' "

I said, " 'Barbarous Atrocities!' I must tell you about those barbarous atrocities. What else did they say?"

She said, "Then they put me in a cell."

Jesus, what is a cell! Christ, all my life I've been putting people in cells, what's so outrageous about the bloody Comrades putting her in a bloody cell, so why am I so bloody outraged that they put her in a cell! "And everything was painted black," I said.

She nodded, white-faced. "How did you know?"

"I know," I said. "Yes. How long were you there?" She was trying to be calmer now.

"Twenty-four hours."

I cursed. "Yes. And you were terrified. And when you were a shuddering wreck our two friends took you out to the Red Guard rally."

She nodded.

"How long did that last?"

All afternoon."

"What happened? Were you put on Criticism or Confession or goddamn Struggle?"

"No," she shook her head, white. "I watched."

"You watched. Did you know you were only going to watch? The mistress of a Hong Kong policeman who commits Barbarous Atrocities?"

She shook her head. "No. I thought I was going to be tried."

Jesus, yes. "And what did you see? Were the accused painted black?"

She nodded. "Dunce caps?" I said. "Chains?" She nodded. "Dragged me into the stadium? Beaten?" She nodded. "Spat on. The whole mob howling—"

She nodded, eyes closed, white-faced. "Something like that."

"And afterward what happened to them?"

"They were taken away."

I took a breath. "All right. I'll be very interested to hear it all later. Then what happened?"

She said, "There were speeches. About Hong Kong." She looked at me. "They said twenty-four compatriots had been killed by police in San Po Kong Artificial Flowers Factory."

I looked at her. I said slowly, "Ying, I was there. Twenty-four were *arrested*."

She rubbed her forehead, closed eyes. "All right. I believe you."

She took a big confused breath.

"Then they took me back to the Public Security Bureau. They said, 'Tomorrow there will be more Struggle. That is all.' Then they put me back in another cell. It was also painted black, but it had an electric light."

I took a big breath.

"How long?"

"All night. They brought me food of course."

Jesus. "Yes."

She was tired. "The next day, the same. Another Struggle Meeting in a factory. The managers and foremen were being accused by the workers. They were taken through the streets. The Public Security man explained to me what was happening, what they were accused of."

"Yes. And then?"

She said, "That day I was taken to three factories to see Struggle."

"All the same?"

"Yes." She was tired.

"Then?"

She said, "Back in the cell. They said they were considering my case. And my father's case." She said wearily, "By now I was very frightened."

I squeezed her hand. "Did you see him?"

"No, of course not."

"Did they say he was under arrest?"

She shook her head. "No, he was not yet arrested. They said he was under"—she rubbed her forehead then said it in Cantonese—"surveillance." She looked at me wearily. "They said every day that they were considering his case but first they must consider what to do with me. My father's case depended upon me." Her eyes went wet and she clenched her fists. "But they wouldn't tell me *why*, what I had to do first! I asked them, '*Why*? Why does my father's case depend on me, what do you want me to *do*?' But they would not *tell* me!" She glared at me tremulously, then quoted, " 'We are considering your case!' And in between every day they take me to see the Struggled Meetings in the factories —and at the schools."

487

She was tired now.

"What questions about me?"

She breathed deep. "Your work. Everything I knew about your work." She looked at me, big liquid eyes urgent. "I told them I know nothing. Which is true. They say I must know. I said I know he is in Special Branch. I told them what you told me. 'Special Branch is not spying, it is counter-espionage,' every government must have this. I said, 'It is intelligence only.' They say, 'What is intelligence?' I say I do not know, only what I read in newspapers and books, which is true." I nodded—she went on, "They say, 'Does America spy on China?' I say, 'Yes.' 'How do you know?' 'Because I think so.' 'Did Mr. McAdam tell you this?' 'No.' 'Does Taiwan spy on China?' 'Yes.' 'How do you know?' 'Because I think so.' 'Did Mr. McAdam tell you this?' 'No.' 'What about Macao?' I say, 'I only know what I read in the newspapers and the *Dai Bo Ji*.' 'Didn't Mr. McAdam speak about Macao?' 'Yes of course.' 'What?' I told them what you told me. 'It is in the newspapers and magazines.' They say, 'What else did he say?' I say, 'Nothing.' They say, 'Lies!' I say, 'It is true!' 'What about Vietnam? What about Cambodia? What about Laos? Russia?' I tell them everything I know, I said, 'It is in the newspapers.' They say, 'Lies! What does Mr. McAdam say about his work?' I say he tells me nothing. Which is true." She looked at me tearfully, and I thought my heart would break. "I was so frightened I would have told them if I had known anything, but I did not know." She was trying to remember all the sorts of questions. "They said, 'What does Mr. McAdam thing about communists? About Chairman Mao Tse-tung?'" She looked at me tearfully.

I nodded.

"I told them, 'Mr. McAdam is an intelligent man, he went to university, he likes China, he was born in China, of course he has many opinions.' I told them, 'He thinks the communists are good for China.' They say, 'Why?' I tell them. All the reasons. I say, 'He thinks Chairman Mao Tse-tung is a great man.' 'Why?' I tell them. Then they say, 'What does he think about the Cultural Revolution?'" She looked at me and rubbed her forehead, I waited. "Oh, darling, I can't remember everything now, there were so many questions, every day. And then they change the questions. Then come back again. I told them what you think about the Cultural Revolution, what you told me, that's all right, isn't it?" I nodded she went on. "They were very interested in that. All the time the tape recorder was going." She shook her head. "There were many days of questions, and I wrote a book."

"A book?"

She nodded. "Not really a book, but hundreds of pages. Information on everything I know. Answers to question. But that was afterward."

"After what?"

She breathed out. "After they told me I had to be a spy."

Be a spy! For Christ's sake. That sensation in my guts, oh God. I poured another drink. I was tired, sick in my guts.

"All right. How long after you got there was this?"

She said, "Seven days."

"And all the time you were sleeping in the black cell?"

She nodded. "Yes."

Yes. By now terrified, "What happened?"

She took a big breath. "They took me to the same office. They have my file and my father's. They say, 'You must certainly go for public trial by the Red Guards. Then you must go to Thought Reform Labor Camp.'" She went on flatly, "They say, 'In your case it will take a long time.'" She looked at me. "'Several years, maybe ten.' They said, 'Because you are a very bad case you have many reforms to make.'" She looked at me. "You can imagine how I felt."

I squeezed her hand. *Just thank God she's here.*

She breathed deep and went on, "They said, 'You will never see Mr. McAdam again. And your father's case is very bad also! He must also go for Struggle and Mass Criticism and Thought Reform Labor Camp!'" She stared at me, I squeezed her hand, *go on, darling.* She said, "I shouted, 'Not my father, he is a good communist! Why my father!' They said, 'He has done many crimes.' *'What crimes?'* I shout. They say, 'Not your business.' I say, *'Is* my business!' They say, 'There is nothing we can do with people like you, you are no use to China until you are reformed!' They say, 'If you were a good useful loyal communist to us in Hong Kong we would forgive you and your father but you are no use to us because you are a traitor.' I say, *'But what do you want me to do? You haven't told me what I must do!'* They say, 'Nothing you can do for us in Hong Kong because you do not try to help your motherland, you only think about making love to policemen!'" She flung out her arm pointing, demonstrating, "'Take her away! Tomorrow you go for Struggle to the Red Guards!'"

I cursed: Jesus. "Very subtle," I said. "So they took you away?"

She blew her nose. "To my cell."

I stood up, paced to the window. I said, "Then came the friendly guard who suggested that if you volunteered to spy maybe Chairman Mao would forgive you."

She shook her head. She drew on her cigarette. "Late that night they take me to another office. It is another man, very big. He is very kind."

"He always is."

"He says that he is a junior to the first man who was questioning me. He says he knows my father."

"Ah yes. He knows your father."

"He says he has been reading my file and he feels a little bit sorry for me. He says, 'It is easy for a girl to go astray in Hong Kong. And it is normal for a woman to fall in love, even with a European man.'" She gave me a wisp of a smile. "He says, 'Some policemen are very pleasant fellows.' And he says that he can see from my file that I met you long ago, in 1963, long before the Cultural Revolution, so my problem now is understandable. And I am so grateful to this man I could kiss his feet. He says it must be very sad for me, but I have failed in my duty and we must all love China first. I say, 'I *do* love China, I have always loved China! I do my work at school!' We go on talking like this a long time. He is stern but he is kind. Then he says, Maybe he can help me."

"Oh yes, maybe he can help you."

She went on, "He says, maybe he can persuade his boss to let me go back to Hong Kong and maybe my father will not be arrested. Now I am nearly crying again. He says he cannot promise but maybe he can persuade his boss that I can do work in Hong Kong. 'Oh thank you!' I say. 'What kind of work?' And he says if the boss agrees it would be very simple. I say, 'Please tell me what work,' and he says, 'Information.'"

I nodded bitterly.

"I say, 'What kind of information?' He says"—she waved her hand—"'Just any information about anything affecting your motherland, like a good patriot!' And of course I say I will do it, I am a good Chinese! But then he shakes his head and says, 'I am only junior, therefore you must not hope too much, because your case is very serious and your father's case also.' Then he says, 'Otherwise your father will be arrested in the morning.'" She looked at me. "You can imagine how I felt?"

"Yes," I said.

She rubbed her forehead. "That night I did not sleep."

"I can imagine. So?"

"So. So the next morning they take me to the boss. And I am shaking. I smile at him. He says he is very busy and my father is already arrested! He says, 'My junior has made a suggestion,' but he cannot agree! Because my case is too serious. Now I am crying again. He says, 'You are too unreliable! You have been in Hong Kong too long, you will not do your duty, you do not love China. You must have Struggle and at least three years' Thought Reform!' and so on. And I am shouting, *I love China! I will do my duty!* and he says, *Take her away! She must learn to love China!* and I am hanging on to his desk like this and shouting and he is saying, *It is too late! We do not believe you love China! You only love yourself!*"

She had tears in her eyes and her fists were clenched. I held her hands, I knew the rest, I had known it all long ago. "Go on."

She wiped her wrist across her eyes. "Like that. Many times he says, 'Take her away!' Finally he says, 'Take her away. I will think about it.'"

"Yes? How long did you have to sweat that one out?"

She said, "Till that night. Late that night they fetch me again. Do you really repent?' he says. 'Yes, Comrade,' I say, and I am shaking. I have not slept two nights."

She did not have to make excuses to me. "He says, 'Do you really want to serve China?' I say, 'Yes! Yes!'" She appealed to me. "Which is *true!*" I nodded. "After many questions like this he says, 'Very well. We have decided to give you a chance.'" She was speaking wearily. " 'We will give you a chance to make up for your crimes. And maybe for your father's, also. If you do your duty you and your father will maybe be forgiven.' And I was crying I was so grateful and happy."

I nodded. I was even grateful too. It was the most elementary espionage con job but I was sick-in-my-guts grateful. She said wearily, "For a long time like this. Finally he pulls out a paper and says, 'Then you must sign this paper!' And I signed."

"What did it say?"

She shook her head, "I don't know. It was long, I was so anxious."

I cursed. "I don't suppose it will make any difference."

She went on, "Then they became different. They—were still stern but they were more comradely. They called me Comrade. They told me what I must do." She took a big breath and said, "I must get as much information as possible from you about your work."

I cursed. "Like what?"

She said, "I must encourage you to tell me your work problems. I must ask questions, even"—she smiled faintly—"in bed."

I nodded bitterly.

"They said I must encourage you to bring work home at night and not stay late at office." She looked at me. "I must be here at five o'clock waiting for you, like a wife."

"Sexy," I said. "No aphrodisiacs I don't suppose?"

"Yes, sexy too, they said that. I must"—she looked for the words—"be a very good mistress."

"You don't need their goddamn advice on that."

She smiled, miserable. "I must keep the flat very nice for you because you have not got an amah because this place is secret."

"We can get half a dozen bloody amahs now."

She went on, "I must ask you about your friends. Especially in the police. Their girl friends, their wives. If they have got mistresses."

"Their weaknesses," I said.

She nodded. "And I must encourage you to bring them home here to drink and have dinner so I will hear you all talking."

"As if that's likely! I'm not likely to bring policemen here if you're my left-wing mistress."

She rubbed her forehead. "I was coming to that." She took a breath. "They said that later I must stop working at the communist school and go to work for an ordinary school or else just do nothing, just live with you. To get your confidence."

"Oh."

I looked at her and I thought my heart would break.

"Isn't it a pretty thought?"

Yes. I took a big breath. I felt sick in my guts. It was impressive, but only because it was happening to me. To us. Not somebody in one of those thousands of files all over the world, in the numerous books, in the newspaper reports, *Jesus Christ this is us.* I said, "These files you're supposed to encourage me to bring home: did they teach you how to film them?"

She nodded.

Jesus. "Where is the camera?"

"In my room."

Oh God, I felt deadly tired, sick.

"Who's your contact in Hong Kong? Who do you report to?"

She shook her head. "I don't know. I will be contacted through my dead-letter box."

Of course. They weren't taking any chances on her knowing the identity of her contact in case she talked. They weren't naïve.

"Where's your D.L.B.—your dead-letter box?"

She looked at me, big-eyed, weary.

"Why do you want to know?"

I looked at her. "Of course I want to know."

She stared at me apprehensively. "What will you do if I tell you?"

I stared at her, she said tremulously, "I am only telling you this because I cannot betray you by spying because I love you."

Oh Jesus! This is what happens of course! I said impatiently, "Listen, darling. We're both in this together, we've both got everything to lose. Everything. We have to *trust* each other, for God's sake! How could I use your dead-letter box for any police purpose without endangering *you?* And I love you."

She looked at me nervously, harassed. She said guiltily, "Then why must you know where it is?"

I wanted to shout *For Christ's sake!* "Listen! We've

got to make a plan to get ourselves out of this. To formulate a bloody plan I must know *everything* you know so *I* know what I'm dealing with, so I don't say afterward, If only I'd known! You've got to tell me everything that happens from now on, for God's sake you've got to trust me!"

She cried, "I do trust you! Why do you think I told you all this? Because I love you and trust you and I cannot betray you! But I also do not want to betray my country to anybody! I do not want to be a spy for anybody and I do not want to betray you but also I will not betray my country! Do you think I have not had nightmares about this?" She pointed desperately at China. "And what about my father! He is still in China, if they knew I was telling you this they will get my father! They told me this! Do you think I have not had nightmares about this?"

She was crying suddenly. I sat down and held her tight and I thought my heart would break, the nightmares were just beginning. I said, "You have to trust me *completely* and I have to trust you. Otherwise we will poison our minds with suspicions and then neither of us will know if the other is telling the truth!"

She cried against my neck, "I know I am a bad communist but I will not betray anything! I am only telling you because I cannot betray you either."

I held her tight, "I understand that, Ying, but you *must trust me!*"

She cried, *"In my staff room! In an electrical switch-box behind a filing cabinet! That is my dead-letter box! Now I have told you!"*

I felt her retch, I stumbled her through to the bathroom and held her over the lavatory and squeezed her hot forehead. "Be sick my lover! Vomit it up." She shuddered and retched and there was nothing to vomit up but the whiskey, but she retched and retched, nerve-wracked and nothing came up. Then she straightened, shuddering, red-eyed, and then held me tight so I wouldn't see her face. I held her then I took her back to the bedroom. She lay down, with my arm around her shoulders staring at the dark ceiling. She was shaking. She whispered, "What are we going to do?"

I took a big breath. "I don't know yet," I said.

CHAPTER 79

After a long time she went to sleep. She was dreaming, her breathing changed and she said something in Cantonese but I could not catch it. I lay, looking at the ceiling, trying to think, trying not to think. I needed to sleep. To sleep to sleep, please God. I wanted to take her in my arms and feel her breath, her eyes and lips and hair, to help me but I dared not lest I wake her. I lay, trying not to think any more. But I could not. I got up carefully and went to the kitchen and made some hot milk.

At first it seemed better in the white light of the kitchen, doing something, knowing she was asleep in there, it began to seem that it wasn't so bad. Christ, what could they do to me? I was here and she was here. How did they know I wouldn't use her as a double agent, feed them false information through her and have them running around after red herrings while we knocked the living shit out of them? How did they know that *we* hadn't set this whole thing up, that I hadn't, on instructions of Her Majesty's Secret Service, got myself a communist mistress so that we could feed them false information? What made *them* so sure that I could have gotten away with a Comrade mistress so long without my own force getting to know about it? It even surprised *me* so surely it must be a point for the fucking Comrades to ponder before they started throwing their weight around. Watching the milk heat up I seemed to get my second wind and I felt cold-blooded; *I can play the sonsabitches at their own bloody game.* I have the advantage, I'm in my own territory and I know that they know. I went back to bed with my drink and closed my eyes hard and lay there, and I did not feel cold-blooded any more.

It's clear what the bastards are really doing. They aren't fools, they *know* they're highly unlikely to get any worthwhile information through Ying-ling, except bits of police gossip, they *know* I'm highly unlikely to leave files lying around for her to bloody photograph. No, that's chicken feed. What the bastards are really going to do is extort information *out of me direct*. Blackmail *me*, direct. Under threat of harm to her. Under threat of harm to her father, *get at me through her*. And if that doesn't work, under threat of exposing me to my own authorities as being a security risk, lose me my job and blow it up into a public scandal. *Top-ranking policeman in communist love nest!* That would shake up police and Government and the public if nothing else, frantically worrying about how many official secrets I had divulged. Christ, it would reverberate all the way to Whitehall, it would take a lot of sorting out and the bloody Comrades would love it. Direct blackmail, *that's* what the bastards are after, she's just the hostage.

All right! I swung up off the bed. The night was unreal, the sick feeling in my guts. Oh God, this is me, her, us. Not a case in a file, not Burgess and Maclean, not Vassal, not Houghton and Ethel Gee, this was us, for Chrissake. I was not cold-blooded. That was unreal too. The only thing that was real was the sound of her breathing and the Thank God she was here. All right. There is only one thing to do.

Only one thing. I went to the kitchen and snapped the stove on again. *Face* it! Only one honorable, one sensible goddamn thing, you knew the goddamn risk! All right I am facing it. All is lost.

All is lost.

That is not dramatic—that is the fact. It is no good trying to play it cold-bloodedly, fool them, stall them, you'll only get in deeper. The subterfuge and the double life. No matter how well you play it, your own side will catch up with you. And pay the blackmailer once and he will bleed you white. *So the hard fact is that all is lost and the only thing to do is get out!*

Quit. I breathed deep and I felt old. Like you told Max you would.

And get the hell out of China, the whole godforsaken Far East. Where there's no fucking Comrades. Where there're no bloody politics and cloak-and-dagger fucking intelligence. Get the hell out of it before they can get at you, kiss your beloved bloody China and your beloved police force good-by before one or other of the bastards kills you. While you still have honor and dignity and a clear conscience. While you still got goddamn *time* on your side.

I was thinking clearly now. Yes, I had time. And I needed time because I could not walk into the office tomorrow and simply give three months' notice of resignation. Firstly, it would not be accepted at a god-awful time like this, and secondly because during those three months the bastard Comrades would put the screws on me. Seize her father and say to me, "Withdraw your your resignation and co-operate or else." And for the same reason I could not make a clean breast to the police until her father was safe—the police would start a massive investigation into me, the Comrades would be alerted, her father would be in jeopardy, and Ying would have a nervous breakdown. I need the time to do something about her father. And it is obvious I have time.

Obvious. The Comrades will take it easy on me until they are confident of me. They have to be confident before they can exploit me properly. Christ, I'm a bloody prize. A gazetted officer in Special Branch? An intelligence officer's dream. I'm a textbook example of what every intelligence service wants to get their teeth into on the Other Side. The Russians would *grab* me, the bloody Yanks would fall over themselves to get me. All I've got to do to be rich now is go along to the American Embassy and say, "I've got a communist mistress, the Comrades are screwing me, what am I worth to the United States as a double?" And then go to the Russian High Commissioner and put my feet up on his desk and say, "Comrade, I hate to bother you but I've got a Mao mistress and they're screwing me so I cashed in as a double with the CIA, what am I worth to you in Swiss francs as a treble?"

Oh Jesus. And how are you going to use the time?

Now cut that out and get the calm back. Reckless deadly calm. You know what you've got to do and you cannot think any more tonight, *you must sleep now.* Finish this drink and do not think any more.

Think about Europe.

Or the Caribbean. Jamaica.

That's where we'll go. It's lovely there. Blue sea and white beaches and tropical mountains. We'll get a cottage or a bloody shack on a beach ten thousand miles away from Mao Tse-tung. And a garden and a dog and maybe even a horse and I'll buy a boat. I've got a goddamn degree. Or I'll write a book and tell the world what it's like to love a lovely crazy Chinese communist girl, my wife.

Oh yes, *wife.* Isn't that a pretty word? My wife asleep in there. Singing in the garden under the bright Caribbean sun. Swimming with me in the blue-blue Caribbean Sea. Nobody is going to take my wife away from me. Not Mao Tse-tung and his seven hundred millions, nor all the Queen's men. Cold-blooded. I feel good now. Nor will I have to trample anybody underfoot except my own career. *To hell my career!* It was good while it lasted.

I breathed deep. All I need is time to accomplish the details. The only serious detail is to cover her father. If possible we must get the poor old bastard out of China. That won't be easy because he's the goddamn hostage, but it can be done. If it *cannot* be done, then we must do what we have to do anyway. And leave him to his fate.

I do not believe the fate will be too bad. I don't believe they would do anything to him once she and I are totally beyond their reach and therefore of no further use to them. Pointless. He's a doctor, useful to them. He may be subjected to Struggle, but so are millions of others. The Cultural Revolution cannot last much longer, China cannot afford it. Any price he has to pay is small compared to the alternative. Once we have disappeared he is safe: he is in grave danger as a hostage *only* while we are here, while the Comrades can get at me by getting at her by getting at him. While that situation persists they will be merciless. Therefore in order to make him safe we *must* get out of Hong Kong, whether or not we can get him out of goddamn China.

It was very clear. It was clear to me at 3 A.M. on the Monday morning after the Saturday at Shataukok but it would not be clear to her. No *sir,* not to her. She will break down like she broke down in Canton. Wild frantic fear for her father.

Oh God, Ying. How would I feel if it was my own

father? But it had to be done. Therefore she must not be told—she would be incapable of accommodating it. God knows what she would do. But she would louse it up. The greatest danger would be if the Comrades knew what I was going to do, they would seize him, and her if they could, to make me stay and co-operate. She cannot be told, she would louse it up. Oh God, there was a lot to think about.

Now don't think about it any more tonight. I only need time. Think about Jamaica. It's peaceful there. Like the word "wife." That's a peaceful word. My wife, my wife, just thank God. The bedroom door opened and my wife came out. "Hello, darling," I said. "Why aren't you asleep?"

She looked gaunt. "I was dreaming." She was wide-awake tousled and I loved her very much, I felt reckless calm, almost happy. "What are you doing?"

"Making plans. Come here."

She came and sat down on the edge of the sofa and looked at me, and I wanted to laugh with tears at her, just thank God for her.

"What are we going to do?" she whispered.

I held her tight, then sat up. I said, "Just answer some questions calmly now. We're both tired."

She nodded, tense, red-eyed. I lit a cigarette.

"Your father, he doesn't know about us?"

She shook her head.

"All right," I said. "Now: Would he leave China if he knew the truth, the full story?"

She was looking at me, then she closed her eyes, fists clenched and cried softly, *Oh no! Oh no, I knew you were going to ask that!* She looked at me, eyes shining desperate tearful. *"My father will not leave China! My old father? Why should he leave his country and come to live in Hong Kong? No work! No friends! No home! Why? For me!"* She thumped her breast. "For his daughter who had got into trouble! For me he must give up his life and come here as a criminal! On a snake boat! Risk his life, if they catch him they shoot him! For me my own father *get shot!* Oh no. Not my father—"

My nerves were tight, I had to hang on tight. "But if he knew he was in danger, or *you* were in danger?"

She cried, "Of *course* he would come if he believed that! And risk his *life* in snake boats and then live like

499

a criminal here hiding all the time. And they will catch him in China before he leaves because they are watching him all the time and all because of me!"

I said, "He would be given legal political asylum here."

She cried, "But he will have no *work*, no *friends!* He cannot practice medicine here. And you will have to tell Government everything and you will lose your job! And where will we all be? And he will be a lonely old man with nothing!" She appealed to me desperately. "How can I be so selfish to make my father do that? I have also thought about it, darling! I have thought all about it in my six weeks in China! Not my father!"

It was no good. No good discussing her father with her, not tonight anyway, for Chrissake. I could feel my nerves going again, I stood up. I said as calmly as I could, "I've got to quit the police force anyway, so stop thinking about that!" She opened her mouth to protest, eyes desperate, I said, "Listen to me, Ying! Calm down and don't interrupt!" She blinked and swallowed hard, white-faced. "There's two things you've got to understand immediately. The first is that I have to quit the police force. That is *not* your fault, that's just the rules of the game, and I knew those bloody rules long before you did! I cannot work for the police under pressure from the communists, it would be dangerous and dishonorable. The second thing is this: I'm not going to let even seven hundred million Chinese stop you and me, I don't care if we've got to get the hell out of Timbuktu. That means I've got to make a safe plan pretty damn quick." I shook my finger. "Repeat *safe*. For all of us, *including* your father! I don't know what yet, so don't ask me, just trust me, for Godsake! That brings me to the third point. *We've got to gain time*. And that means we've got to keep them uncertain about whether I have accepted you back because if I didn't love you any more their whole plan falls to pieces. And they won't dare risk that. Now listen carefully."

She nodded white-faced.

"Soon, they are going to contact you to find out how you are getting on with me. They'll be worried about it. You *must* pretend that you are *very* unhappy because you think I do not love you any more. You think I am trying to get rid of you. You think I have got another girl friend somewhere. Say I am being cruel to you. Very selfish. Say anything that a woman would say who is very uncertain of her lover! Do you understand that?" She nodded, desperately uncertain. "And you must *insist* that they give you plenty of time to try to make me love you again."

She was staring at me tremulously. She said, "It is all my fault!"

"Oh Jesus, Ying. *It is not.*"

She cried, *"It is!* Because of me you give up your career! Because of me my father is in danger! I should not have come back here tonight!" She scrambled up, shaking, tearful. "I should have stayed away and told them that you didn't love me any more and then they could do nothing to you!" She clenched her fists, tears running down her white face: "Yes! So I must go away and never come back and we will be safe! Yes! *Never come back!* Never! *Never!*" she shouted, she banged her fist on the table, *"Madness! Of course!"* She threw back her head and banged it down on her fist, shaking, shuddering, crying, *"Never come ba-a-a-ack!"*

I grabbed her shoulders and pulled her up and clutched her tight, she struggled crying to get out of my arms. *"No! Never come back—"* She tried to beat my chest with her fists. *"I must never come back."*

I let her go and slapped her. Once, hard, and there was a shocked silence, tears streaming staring wild-eyed at me gasping, then she tried to pull away from me and I grabbed her tight, then she burst into crying.

I held her tight and I thought my heart would break.

She clung on to me crying, I carried her back to the bedroom, laid her down on the bed. Our bed, I said to her, I remember saying to her, "This is our bed—we will lie in it and you will always come back."

CHAPTER 80

The next day I sent a message to my look-see boat boy at the Yacht Club to take the junk around to Rocky Su's slipway in Aberdeen. That afternoon I drove around there. A lot of the junks were flying the red flag with the five gold stars. I hurried down the narrow concrete path between the clamoring sweating workshops and sweatshops and shacks and huts and cooked-food stalls, chickens, dogs, children, the garbage and the flies and the stench of oil and wood and sea and people, the boat-building, the whirl of saws and the hammering and the yammering and the clattering of Mah-Jongg, I was sweating and I loved every sight and sound of it. This was the Old China, and I loved Aberdeen and oh God I did not want to leave China. Leaving was unreal. I went through a gate in a wooden fence. There was my junk, tied up at the end of the jetty. There were two big deep-sea junks on the slipway, timber, ladders, cables, carpentry gear and mangy dogs and Cantonese music all over the place. I went into Rocky's house, up the wooden stairs to the office, knocked and went in. The sudden air conditioning was bliss. "Hello, Jake!" Rocky said. "How's the junk?"

We went aboard my junk. First we had a quick look around the rigging. He said it looked all right, but I told him to replace all the doubtful ropes, have a good look at the sails. Put her on the slipway, scrape her, two coats of antifoul. I told him about the water in the bilges, to check the stern tubes. Then we started the engines. He revved them and listened, then we went down into the engine room. "They run a bit hot," I said.

He looked at the oil. "They're old engines," he said, "what do you expect?" He wiped his finger along the dipsitck and looked for metal filing in the oil. None.

"How long are they good for?"

He shrugged. "They're okay."

"Would they get me to Manila, say?"

He looked at me. "You want to go to Manila?"

"No," I said. "But for example."

"I'll test them tomorrow," Rocky said. "But sure, why not?"

It was stinking hot down here but I did not want to leave them.

"Take their heads off, Rocky," I said. "New bearings. Rings. If the crankshafts need regrinding, grind them."

"They're okay," Rocky said, "for what you want them for, weekends."

"Do it anyway." I was sweating. "I'm sick of worrying about them."

"All right," Rocky said. "I'll look at them."

"Not just look at them, Rocky. Open them up. How long will it take?" I said. "Everything. Engines, ropes, sails."

"Depends," Rocky said.

"This weekend?" I said.

"It's Tuesday," Rocky said. "Never. Maybe following weekends."

"Definitely following weekends?"

"Depends whether the crankshafts need regrinding. If they need it, big trouble."

Oh Jesus. "You can take two crankshafts out and put them back in ten days, Rocky."

"I suppose so," Rocky said.

"Please, Rocky. Must be by weekend next. I'm taking out a whole party of people." Oh Christ, why hadn't I thought of this while she was away? "And another thing, Rocky." I tried to sound natural. "Can you stow four forty-four gallon drums of diesel in the forward hatches, and put it on the bill?"

"Four? Where are you taking your party?" Rocky joked. "Manila?"

I tried to laugh.

Then I went back through the clamor of Aberdeen, back to the office.

That week the bombs started. At first there were only a few each day, planted in the streets with the poster *"Compatriots Keep Away"* and *"A Gift for Fascist Pigs and Yellow-skinned Running Dogs,"* the homemade bombs of gunpowder and nails and broken glass; then it was scores of bombs every day. In the teeming streets

503

and alleys, bombs planted in the shops, the hotels, in the elevators, on buses and trams and ferries and in the public squares and in mailboxes and parking lots and cinemas and restaurants, bombs planted in children's playgrounds in rag dolls and Donald Duck money boxes, bombs thrown into bus queues and markets and thrown into police stations, bombs laid on the tram tracks and hung on traffic signs.

That week began the time of indiscriminate terror, the screams and the explosions and the hands and arms and legs blown off and children blown to bits and the wails of the ambulances and the screaming of police sirens and the streets cordoned off and the massive traffic jams in the heat and the rain and the fear, and in the communist press they called it Heroic and Glorious and Patriotic and Striking Crushing Blows. And the gas bombs and sulfuric-acid bombs, hurled into the buses at the yellow-skin running dog drivers and conductors and passengers, beat and smash and burn and bomb, and the women and the children screaming scrambling scattering and the communist press hailed it as Traitor-Toppling and Advancing Wave upon Wave. And now in July came the fake bombs among the real ones, and the communists screamed in glee to see whole streets cordoned off and the traffic jams for nothing but a fake bomb. "Trembling mightily for fear of the Thought of Mao Tse-tung, the yellow-skinned running dog police cordoned off the street to the anger and inconvenience of the oppressed masses while the so-called demolition experts coweringly approached the package to find it contained nothing but a snake—" And snakes released on the trams and buses and ferries, and now communist women and schoolgirls screamed in the streets and on the buses that policemen and bus conductors had indecently assaulted them.

And now in July the Glory Strike Struggle Funds began to run out. The Hong Kong—Kowloon All Circles Anti-Persecution Struggle Committee had spent $40 million Hong Kong on the General Strike, and it had failed. And the losses to the communist businesses were $280 million. And the losses to China in foreign exchange were $300 million. And now the Red Guards in Canton and Peking roared that the Hong Kong—Kowloon All Circles Anti-Persecution Struggle Committee must all be returned to China for Struggle for their failures, and the

Macao Chinese Chamber of Commerce said that the Hong Kong—Kowloon All Circles Anti-Persecution Struggle Committee were Revisionist Scabs for failing where Macao had succeeded, and in Peking the government demanded an Inquiry into the Causes of the Failure of the Struggle in Hong Kong and refused to supply any more money to the Glory Strike Fund saying that the Hong Kong—Kowloon All Circles Anti-Persecution Struggle Committee must sell off their luxuries and Redouble Their Struggles and relearn the Thoughts of Mao Tse-tung: and the Hong Kong—Kowloon All Circles Anti-Persecution Struggle Committee went frenzied red for the loss of face and redoubled their Redoubled Struggles, and the order went out to the strikers that they must donate half of their Struggle Pay back to the Glory Strike Struggle Fund, and they would only be paid at all on condition that they threw Glory bombs; and now they instituted a new Glory Dollar Struggle Strike Fund Drive, every Comrade must donate and anybody who does not will perish as a Yellow-skinned Running Dog. And all Comrade employers must donate three Comrade employees to Struggle in the streets. And no shop can sell Motherland Goods unless they place Big Character Protest posters in their windows. And now in July the Hong Kong—Kowloon All Circles Anti-Persecution Struggle Committee distributed leaflets on how to make a bomb; and now there was a new tactic called Striking Back with Redoubled Righteousness, throwing bombs into the crowd which had gathered behind the cordons to watch the police demolish a bomb, and bombs thrown wildly into crowds out of windows and from passing cars. And now in July appeared the Execution Lists signed by the likes of the Traitor-Toppling Tiger-in-Field Onslaught Headquarters, lists of prominent Yellow-skinned Running Dogs Who Must Die, and now in July the order went out to all the communist schools that they must prepare for massive demonstrations during the forthcoming summer school holidays, that all school buildings must be booby-trapped and armed for siege and turned into factories for bombs and all the time the explosions and the blood and the fear and the wail of the ambulances and the running battles in the streets. July was the time of your shirt sticking to the old sweat on your back at midnight, 2 A.M., 4 A.M., dawn, the taste of sweat, dry-mouthed, chain-smoking, the ache in your limbs and the screaming of your nerves in the cacophony of the interrogations and the typewriters and the telexes and telephones and dictaphones and reports and meetings and the dry hunger in your gut because you haven't been home for eighteen hours, for Christ Christ *Christ sake*.

I telephoned Rocky every day to find out the progress on the junk. On Friday he said he had both engines open and the port crankshaft did need regrinding and the starboard cylinders needed reboring. That meant both engine blocks had to come right out and go to a machine shop. "How long?" I demanded.

"Two weeks," Rocky said. "It's hard to get engineers, with the troubles."

"Two *weeks?* I could do the job myself in a week!"

"You try it," Rocky said.

"Do they really need it?"

"Only the starboard engine really needs it. But it's good for a few months. Maybe I should just put them back and we'll wait until something goes wrong?"

Oh Jesus, Jesus.

"No. Do it. But they *must* be back in the boat inside two weeks."

Those weeks were bad. That week we got the green light from Whitehall to raid communist premises. And to use the Army, but for cordon duties only. No cheers went up because nobody knew, except the top; out there in explosions and the running battles in the streets the poor bloody rank and file didn't know anything except the fighting and the sweat and the stink of gas and sweat and blood. I knew, and I did not cheer either. Because I also knew that we were also going to raid communist schools soon.

We were going to raid them in the holidays, when all good schoolchildren should be at home, not fortifying Great Arsenals of the Thought of Mao Tse-tung, not making bombs in the chemistry laboratories, when we could not be accused of Brutally Waging Fascist Atrocities Against Innocent Schoolchildren. We were surely going to raid the schools, and the school holidays were scheduled to begin the last week of July.

That week the police raids on the communist unions began. The dawn raids and the midnight raids, the army trucks and the police trucks rolling suddenly through the streets in the blackness and the soldiers leaping out and running to cordon off the block for the police to move in, axes and blowtorches, the missiles raining down from the upper windows, the bombs and glass and acid flying, the pitched battles on the stairs, down the corridors, through the rooms, across the rooftops, down the fire escapes, the acid and the gunfire and the spears and the booby traps, and a good few Comrades died and a good few policemen too. We knocked over a lot of arsenals, bombs, gunpowder, barrels of gasoline and acid and stacks of spears, missiles, clubs, gas masks. All the buildings were heavily barricaded and booby-trapped with electrocution circuits and acid and explosives. Every building had an extensive first-aid station, one had a full-scale hospital with an operating room. That one also had a full military-operations room for a full-scale guerrilla war for the capture of Hong Kong. That building was so heavily fortified we had to make our entry from the rooftops by helicopters. We got a lot of information from all of them.

I went on every raid, with my S.B. squad. The running scrambling crashing fighting searching. And after all the smoke had cleared and the dead and injured had been carried away, we stayed on, searching and ransacking. And all the time the unreality. The unreality of thinking, reacting, fighting like a policeman, rejoicing like a policeman in what he found, and all the time knowing I was very nearly not a policeman any more. This time in two weeks policemen would be looking for me. And I could not believe it, in the running fighting. But when the smoke had cleared and we got down to it, it was real all right. It was real back in the office making the reports; it was real at the meetings with the director and O.C. British Forces and the political advisers. It was real in the waiting. Waiting for the Christ knows what. Waiting for the Comrades to contact me. Waiting for her to telephone. The loneliness. The fighting and the work work work was nothing: it was the waiting and the loneliness of decision that was bad.

When I woke up it was very bad. If she had been there it would have been better, I needed her very badly when I woke up. But she was not there: we all slept when we could, when we could no longer work. Mostly she slept in her room. Every day she telephoned me.

I do not want to remember the lurch in my gut when I picked up the telephone and heard the strain in her voice. "How are you?" "I am well, and you?" "I'm *all right*." It was our code, it meant that nothing had happened yet, that her contact had not yet contacted her. I hoped wildly that we had already arrested the bastard or shot him in one of our raids. Her name had not been any piece of evidence we had found. It was the first thing I looked for.

"When can I see you?"

"Is anything wrong?"

"No. I just need to see you."

"I need you too."

Oh God, I needed her. To hold, to feel her breathing next to me when I tried to sleep, but most of all to believe in. She was all I had to believe in, to hold on to, all the rest was unreal ruins. I was all she had to believe in, too. We had talked some of it out in our few times together, lying in my arms on the bed, gaunt, nerves screaming. She did not know what to believe, except in me. I had only told her that I had a plan that I could not divulge to her yet, that I knew what I was doing, that we were safe for the time being.

She said, "You must not blame China for this. It is the local hotheads. Every country has those."

"Peking is not behind them any more," I said. "She has to say she is, but she isn't."

She did not want to talk about it. She did not want to know if I was on the raids. She did not want to talk about what was happening at school. I knew what was happening at school. She only said, "Will the schools be raided too?"

"No," I said.

She breathed deep.

I said slowly, deliberately, "Because we do not believe anything worthwhile will come of it. We will only end up fighting with children."

She did not say anything, just lay there, eyes closed, white-faced. She said, "What are we going to do?"

Oh God, if only I could have told her. I said, "We have plenty of time. We are the safest two people in Hong Kong at this moment, because the Comrades are not going to hurt us. We are too valuable to them. They're going to treat us with kid gloves."

She lay there, eyes closed, tense.

"And when the time runs out?"

"It won't run out. They don't want information about what's happening now. That's chicken feed. They want me for the long term. They won't touch us for a long time. Probably not until we're married. They won't do anything to frighten me off marrying you."

But time was running out. In ten days' time the school holidays would start. In eleven days' time there would be the first school raid. The Comrades could start on me today, if they were fools, for information about our next raid. They were getting desperate. She said, from far away, eyes closed, "Then we cannot get married."

"Of course we're getting married."

She lay there, white-faced: "How can we get married if that means you will become a spy against your own country? That is a terrible thing."

I said, "I know what I'm doing. This is what I'm trained for."

"But what will you *do?* When they demand information?"

"They won't do that for a long time. I'm not a fool; for every move there's a counter-move. I know my business, Ying."

She breathed deep and it quivered.

"But . . . will you give the information, or not?"

I lay back. If I said yes, she would say it was terrible, and blame herself. If I said no, she would say, What about my father?

"You must rely on me to know my business, Ying. We will not discuss it any more."

She said, and she looked at me, eyes soft-hard exhausted demanding wet, "What about my father, Jake?"

I looked at her and I wanted to shout for love and fear. "Ying? No harm is going to come to your father from anything that you and I do. I promise you that."

She stared at me. Then her eyes filled up, and she clenched her fists and she clenched her teeth and whispered, "Oh *tell* me! *Tell me tell me tell me!*"

Oh God. I took her, rigid shaking in my arms and held her tight, *Oh Ying.*

"I will be able to tell you in ten days. I promise you. Just trust me for ten days."

She lay rigid, trying hard to control herself.

" 'For every move there's a counter-move.' Oh Jake, you don't know how it frightens me to hear you say things like that." She lay there. She didn't look at me. "In ten days the school holidays start. Supposing there are demonstrations?"

I said carefully, "Demonstrations by schoolchildren are the least of our worries."

She looked at me. "Well it's not the least of mine! I don't want my children fighting policemen!"

Oh Jesus. I said, "Tear gas will keep them indoors."

She hesitated, then breathed deep and said, "What if the children throw bombs?"

"They won't."

She stared at me incredulously. Then she lay back and closed her eyes.

"Oh God," she said.

I could not resist the question. "Are they making bombs?"

She lay there. Her fist clenched on her stomach. "I don't teach chemistry."

"Are they?" I said.

She breathed deep.

"No," she said.

Oh God, I was even pleased that she lied.

"Ying?"

She breathed deep. "Yes?"

I said, "If there are any demonstrations by schoolchildren, you will *not* take part. If you are ordered to do so you will refuse."

She turned to stare at me. Then her eyes widened.

"How can I refuse? How can I let my classes go out into the street to fight policemen"—she closed her eyes quaveringly and changed it—"to demonstrate, without me to look after them? To—stop them getting into trouble. . . ." She looked at me then closed her eyes. "Oh, you don't under*stand*."

"I think I do. This is my profession."

She glared at me, tearful, exhausted: "You always think you do but sometimes you *don't* darling!" She pointed, "Those are *my* children! I've taught them since they were so big! They're only ten, twelve, fourteen years old! They're *decent* children from *decent* families! And you say I must send them out into the street alone to be butchered—"

"Nobody's going to butcher schoolchildren! And *decent* schoolchildren from *decent* families *don't* demonstrate in the streets attacking decent policemen who're trying to maintain the peace—"

She stared at me, white-faced. Then she fell back. "Oh, you don't understand. There is no choice in the matter—"

I got up on my elbow. "I do understand, Ying! I know more about what's happening in this town than you do. I know all about the orders of the Hong Kong–Kowloon All Circles Anti-fucking-Persecution Committee and the so-called Education Anti-Persecution Committee. And if all teachers were like you and set the right example there would *be* no demonstrations by schoolchildren! And you are *not going to participate— do you understand that?* All we need is you in *jail* for three years for riotous assembly! Do you understand that?"

She lay back, staring at me.

"Three years in jail." I glared at her. "What will that be like! What will happen to us then?—*and* your father!"

She lay there. Then she closed her wet eyes.

"You don't understand. If we refuse, the Struggle Squads come—"

"I don't care if Mao Tse-tung himself comes! If there are any demonstrations you walk *right* out of that school and come straight here and lock the door and telephone me! *Do you understand that!"*

She stared at me, then closed her eyes.

"Yes. Yes, I understand that."

I lay back. My mouth was dry. I lay there, feeling my heart beat.

"What if they try to force me?"

"They *won't* try to force you, Ying! You're their bait, their hostage. They don't want to frighten me with that sort of thing. They want you to *marry* me."

She lay there, only the sound of her breathing.

"Yes," she said. "I see."

She was staring at the ceiling. Oh God, I wished I believed it all. I did believe it, it was elementary technique, but their espionage network was all shot to hell by our police raids, who the hell was in charge of her and why the hell had he not contacted her yet? If we had already arrested the bastard then Christ knows what Comrade thug with no brains between his ears might find himself in charge of her. And fuck it up by throwing his weight around before somebody responsible higher up told him to cool it. Oh God, don't let that happen. She said, lying there, "And you still want to marry me?"

Oh God. "Yes. Of course."

She said, eyes closed, "All you have to do is leave me now. And you are free."

Oh, my lover.

"Not so," I said, "because they would still get at me. By threatening to expose me to my own authorities."

She breathed deep. "And after we are married, what will you do, darling?"

I took a big breath. "Trust me to know what I am doing."

She said, eyes closed, *"I'm scared.* And I'm so frightened for my father—"

I held her tight.

"Jake?" She breathed deep and it quavered all the way in. "Please don't let them raid the schools."

CHAPTER 81

I could not tell her. She would not have stood for it, nor understood it, her nerves could not have stood it. She would have broken down for fear for her father: she would have run away. She believed in me, that we did have time, she believed that I had a plan; pale, dry-eyed uptight sick-in-her-guts she clung to and believed in that because she had to; but she would not have believed the truth. All I could tell her was that we were going out on the junk for the weekend. I lay in the dark, listening to her breathing, trying not to think, thinking.

It *is* the only way. There can be no half-measures.

You cannot go to your own police force and confess because they will launch a full-scale investigation and Comrades will grab her father. This way you only lose your career. Nor can you play wait-and-see, on the principle that for every move there's a counter-move. The textbooks are full of the nerves-of-steel boys who played it by ear, who said that for every move there is a counter-move. You run out of counter-moves. Like you run out of time. Oh God yes, this is the only way.

To protect her. Her father. You. Special Branch. Cut and get the hell out of it where they cannot touch you. But she will be incapable of believing that, because of her father. She will believe it eventually, but not in seven days' time, when it starts. You can do nothing else for her old man. What could you do? Get him out of China? He wouldn't come unless he knew the facts, and how would he be told? By letter delivered by Messrs. Vacations in Happiness and Tranquillity's *foki*? He is under surveillance. If that letter was seized by the Comrades it would be all over for him. And even if he got the letter, would he agree? And how would he get out from under surveillance? And even if Messrs. Vacations in Happiness and Tranquillity *did* get him onto the long road down to Hong Kong, what the hell are his chances? And if they caught him? The risk is unthinkable. Only by us getting the hell out of their reach will he be safe. I sincerely believe that. But oh God, I wish I could convince her of that. If only she knew. Then I could sleep now. Then we would not have to use the boat.

If I could tell her we could go by air. Just get out to that airport next Friday night and fly, fly away. Europe. Jamaica. But it's impossible. How could I trick her into getting onto a goddamn aircraft? I couldn't forcibly carry her on. I could not drug her and carry her on. Sure as hell she wouldn't get on of her own accord and leave her father to his fate. But she does not suspect the junk. Nor do they. They will not follow the junk. She will think, they will think, that we're only going out for the weekend. The junk is the only safe way.

That junk has never been so safe. Those Gardiners will go forever now. Please God no typhoons. No storms. July is too early for typhoons. Like hell it is, but there won't be any. We could steam clear to San Francisco on those two old Gardiners now. All they've got to last is six days. Six hundred miles at an average of seven knots, ninety-three hours, four and a half days and we're in the Philippines. Two hours after leaving Hong Kong we're in international waters and we won't even *see* a Chinese gunboat. And even if we do they can't touch us, in international waters. Nor can they touch us in the International Lane, leaving Hong Kong. All right maybe, the International Lane wouldn't stop the sonsabitches, but why should they see us? In the dark. By the time it's daylight we'll be sixty miles out. The worst we'll encounter way out there is a Comrade fishing junk. A rake in front of their bows with a Sterling submachine gun will stop the most ardent Comrade fisherman. For Christ's sake, there won't be any shooting. Stop worrying about shooting sixty goddamn miles out in international waters.

I lay in the dark, staring at the ceiling, thinking, trying not to think, trying to go to sleep. If only I could have told her.

The last Monday before the school holidays began, Rocky telephoned me to tell me the junk was ready. I left the office at 7 P.M. I drove up Garden Road to the supermarket. It did not seem real. I bought three weeks' supply of hard rations, canned food. I had made out a list. Then I drove on to Aberdeen. It did not seem real, all the way. I stashed the food below, under the saloon's floorboards, checked the water, tested the engines, the fuel tanks, the drums of fuel Rocky had stowed in the hatches, I paid him and gave his *foki* ten dollars to take the boat back to the Yacht Club.

It was almost dark now, the sun a big red glow in the east against the forest of masts, the lights twinkling on the junks. It did not seem real that I would never come back. That I was almost not a policeman any more, never would be again. Then it was very real indeed again and I felt my nerves cringe again and a big ache in my throat.

She did not come that night. She had telephoned and said she was exhausted and going straight back to her room to sleep. I was glad, she needed to sleep. Oh, to sleep. Tonight I must sleep too. Tomorrow night and the next and the next I must sleep, I have to be very awake on Friday. And Saturday and Sunday and Monday.

I got home at midnight and sat at the dining table and wrote a new will. That did not bother me. Then I started the letter to the commissioner of police.

I had been drafting it in my head for days, I thought I had it all figured out but it was difficult to begin. I was getting very emotional. It was dead quiet, the black night outside, windows closed, only the faint hum of the air-conditioner. I got the whiskey bottle and a glass. This is it, I thought. This is the end of a life. I started to write.

I enormously regret that I have to quit my service in this manner, that I cannot make this confession in person and make myself immediately available for the lengthy questioning you will want to submit me to. However I undertake that when I am in a place of safety I will make myself available for your interrogations and answer all questions faithfully. I hasten to assure you at the outset, however, that despite the story set out below, I have never disclosed any official information of any kind to any unauthorized person. I equally regret having to desert my colleagues at this difficult time, when they need all the help they can get. However, were I to remain at my post any longer I would be in dereliction of duty, because I am now a security risk, and I would also be placing an innocent person, who is in China, in grave danger.

I proceed now to set out the facts to the best of my recollection . . .

CHAPTER 82

There were no storms over the South China Sea all the rest of that last week. That last Thursday night I worked very late, finishing my Daily Situation Report; at 2 A.M. there were no clouds. She slept with me that night, already asleep when I got home; and Mad Dog thumped his tail at me, stretched flat out beside her on the floor. Oh God, Mad Dog! What about you?

Oh God. I hadn't thought of him. I closed my eyes and tried to refuse to think about Mad Dog. She could not take him. Quarantine and airplanes? Oh God, no it could not be done. Oh God, Mad Dog, what about *you?*

And I closed my eyes to Mad Dog. I took two sleeping pills. Tonight I had to sleep. I had already made my excuses for not attending the director's 6 A.M. meeting tomorrow. I had said I was feeling sick. I was indeed sick, sick in my guts and I could not afford to look at Mad Dog lying there thumping his tail at me adoringly. I got undressed and I lay down beside her.

When I woke she was already gone. I woke with a start, I could hear the rain. I hurried to the window. It was falling in thick furls, hammering on the patio, I could only just make out Kowloon across the harbor. Sky black. Ten o'clock. Oh Jesus! I dashed to the telephone. The directory pages shook in my hands. "Royal Observatory," the voice said.

"What's the forecast for today?"

He said, "Heavy showers, thundery at times, some sunny periods in the afternoon."

Thank God! "You call this a shower?"

"A cloudburst."

Oh thank God. "What about tomorrow?"

"It is too early to forecast tomorrow."

"But what do you *think?* Please, I'm going sailing." My heart was thudding.

He hesitated. "The indications are fair."

I breathed out. "Thank you very much. Good-by."

"I hope you enjoy your sailing," he said stiffly.

My nerves cringed for sleep. I felt sick in my guts. I did not want to go, oh God I did not want to go. My legs felt spongy, weak. I wished she were here. Oh God just to stay here, fall down on the bed in her arms and stay here safe safe safe and sleep sleep sleep. I picked up the telephone and dialed the office. "Dermot," I said, "I'm sorry I'm late, I'm going to see a doctor."

"What's wrong?"

"Nothing. I just haven't been sleeping, I need something."

"All right," Dermot said. "Don't burst a blood vessel, I want you alive."

Then I forced myself to eat two eggs. I put the letter to the commissioner in my jacket. It was still raining hard. The sky was dark overhead but there were some clear patches over Kowloon. I had to remember to write checks for my bills. Then I drove into Central, to Ian Nicholson's office. I talked him into prescribing some powerful sleeping pills, some tranquilizers, and Benzedrine. He also prescribed a tonic.

When I got outside it was only raining a little. There were black clouds and a mist-shroud on the Peak, but overhead it was clearing. The air was cooler and the buildings and the narrow streets looked washed and clean, and I loved every narrow crowded street and coolie. I went back to headquarters.

There was a great deal of work to do and I knew I could not do it all. Dermot asked me how I was, I told him I might have to knock off early. He said, "You've got to look after yourself, you're no good to man or beast if you're so uptight you can't sleep." I told my inspectors I did not want to be disturbed unless Chariman Mao himself called. I tried to work. At lunchtime it started to rain hard again. I telephoned the observatory, but they said it was just another cloudburst. There was a big riot in North Point. At two o'clock she telephoned me, and my heart thudded in my ears. She sounded very strained. She said, Well, the schools had broken up, the holidays had begun, did I still want to go on the boat in view of the rain?

"Yes." I could feel my voice shake. "Definitely. We both need it."

"All right," she said.

I said loudly, "Don't bring Mad Dog."

She was astonished. *"Why?"*

Oh God, my Mad Dog. I said, "I want to be sure we both get a rest. You know what he's like."

She said, "But he loves it so much He's no trouble!" Oh please.

"Please," I said, "Not this time. That's final. I just could not stand him this weekend."

I wrote a letter to the SPCA. I listed the animals to be found at her address: one dog, called Mad Dog; one mouse, called Puku. At my address: one cockatoo, called Percy; one aquarium of assorted tropical fish; one hamster. I enclosed a check for one hundred Hong Kong dollars for their maintenance pending resettlement. My eyes were burning. Oh my Mad Dog. She would break her heart over Mad Dog, and so would I. But it was impossible. I put the SPCA letter into the commissioner's envelope. I wrote a postscript to the commissioner:

I enclose an important letter to the SPCA asking them to care for certain pets left behind by myself and Miss Tsang. Please be so good as to have it delivered soonest. I am sending it through you as I am sure you would not wish anybody to know of this situation before you do.

Then I cleared my desk. I was leaving many things undone and I did not care any more. Then I locked my door, unlocked my safe and took out my Sterling submachine gun. I had carried it on every raid. I disassembled it, thrust the pieces in my briefcase. I put the phial of knockout gas in my pocket. Then I shoved the rest of my files into the safe and locked it. I was sweating.

Then I left. I dropped my safe-keys at Front Desk, signed out, and walked out. It was as easy as that. It was four o'clock. I did not say good-by to anybody. Maybe I would write later. I did not feel anything as I walked out of Special Branch. But as I walked out of the building, and across the long compound, I felt the big ache start in my throat. It was raining only a little but the sky was very black.

CHAPTER 83

I laid the pieces of the Sterling in the bottom of the haversack. I put my pistol holster on against my skin and put a loose sport shirt on over it. I changed into shorts and tennis shoes. Then I wrapped the passports, hers and mine, in a plastic bag with my traveler's checks and tucked them into the bottom of the haversack. Then I started on the wardrobe.

I took five pairs of her panties, three bras, one slip. My hands were shaking. I took four dresses, two summer and two winter, rolled them up into a tight wad and stuffed them in. Two pairs of shoes. A carton of Tampax. Two cardigans. Some ribbons, her nail file, a hairbrush. I looked at the wardrobe, then at the haversack.

"That's it, Ying. That's your lot."

Then I started on my own clothes. Four shirts, underpants, socks, one pair of shoes. My ski anorak. For if it stormed. The haversack was nearly full. A suit, I should take a suit. I picked the best one, rolled it up, it would not go in the haversack. I slung out the anorak and two shirts and I could just stuff the suit in. That was it. No more.

My mouth was dry and I was sweating despite the air-conditioner. That's it. I took the letter to the commissioner of police out of my jacket and put it in my trouser pocket. I looked around the room. A whole life left behind.

"That's it," I said. "That's life."

I went to the kitchen, took the new bottle of whiskey and two cold beers. There was plenty of beer on the junk. Then I opened a bottle of San Miguel. My hands were shaking. I took four big swallows right down hard and for once in my life it did not make things seem any better, it swelled at the ache in my throat. Then I went out onto the patio, to Percy. "Hello," Percy said. His yellow comb flicked up straight. He bounced up and down aggressively on his perch, then he leaned up against the bars to be scratched.

"Hello, Percy," I said. "Hello, old man."

"Hello," Percy said, "tut tut tut."

I scratched his neck through the bars and he hooked his head right under so I could get at his chin and the ache in my throat was bad.

"I'm sorry to leave you, Percy. I really am sorry."

"Tut tut tut," Percy said.

I took a big trembling breath. "You'll be all right, Percy," I said. "The SPCA will come and fetch you on Monday and you'll go to a fine home, old man. A home with children who'll think you're no end of fun and scratch you all day."

Percy didn't say anything. I was scratching his chin and back at the same time and that was Percy's idea of a wonderful time.

"Okay, Percy," I said. My throat was thick. "I'm going to give you a whole pile of seed."

I filled his water and seed bins. I carried his cage inside. Then I fed the hamsters and the fish. There was the sound of a key and Ying opened the door. "Hello!"

"Hello," she said guiltily.

Mad Dog bounded into the room, delighted with the world, tongue slopping and tail beating. I stared at him. She looked strained. She said, "I'm sorry, darling, but he knew we were going on the boat and he looked at me with such eyes, he knows."

Oh God. I looked at him. He was sitting by the haversack quivering with anticipation, tongue slavering, thumping his tail at me to ingratiate himself. *Oh God, Mad Dog, you sentence yourself to death!* I didn't know what to do. I took a big aching breath.

"All right," I said. "All right, Mad Dog." I wanted to get her out of the flat before she noticed anything missing, I picked up the haversack. "Can you carry these bottles?"

"Have you fed Percy?"

"Yes."

"Good-by, Percy," she said. She looked pale and tired. Mad Dog was quivering at the door. "All right," I said, "let's go." The ache in my throat was suddenly very bad, I did not want to look at the penthouse.

She looked at me. "What's the matter, darling?"

"Nothing," I said. My eyes were burning.

"You're so white."

I said, "I need a rest, that's all. So do you. We'll have a good time on the boat."

"Yes," she said. "It'll be good for you."

"Good-by, Percy," I said.

"Good-by," Percy said.

CHAPTER 84

It had almost stopped raining but the sky was very black. She sat apart from me, pent, face white and exhausted. I was shaky, it did not seem real. That I will never drive this car again, see these Wanchai streets. It was hot, the windshield wipers going, sweating. "Ying?" I only said it because I loved her and I wanted to reach her. She looked at me. Her eyes were gaunt, my throat felt thick.

"Nothing," I said. "I love you, that's all. Everything is going to be all right."

She smiled at me. She wanted to humor me, not ask how, but she could not keep the question out of her voice. "Is it, darling?"

"I promise you. Nothing bad is going to happen." I could feel my tears burning, it was all catching up on me, I wanted to cry it out: *We're going to live in the sun where there's bright blue sea and no goddamn politics and we'll have a house and another Mad Dog and another Percy I promise you darling and you'll have your own garden and all the flowers you want I promise you*—"Everything is going to be all right." I loved her so much and I wanted to justify what I was doing to her. "I know what I'm doing."

She looked at me, pale, trying to look happy for my sake. She hesitated, then said, "Will you tell me on the boat?" I knew she cut off, "We can't go on like this." Oh Jesus, I desperately wanted her to be happy today because tomorrow when she woke up it was going to be so terrible for her.

"Yes," I said. "Tomorrow. I promise."

I drove along the Wanchai waterfront, toward Central

521

to mail the letter to the commissioner of police. There was the harbor, the junks, and the sampans, I drove that way because I wanted to see it but now I did not want to look at it. I did not want to look at anything. It started to rain again. I looked in the rear-view mirror. It was impossible to say if anybody was following us. But nobody would be following us.

It was fine seeping China rain now. In the west there was a red-orange-black glow, the sea was black. I was frightened of that red-black. But it was too late now. I stopped the car opposite the post office. "One moment," I said.

I hurried across the street. Suddenly it started raining harder, slanting down. I got to the mailbox, pulled out the letter. My heart was thudding. I rammed it into the mailbox. For a second I stood and I did not look at anything. I looked up into the rain. It beat down on my face.

It did not matter, the black did not matter, the rain, the wind, the Comrades, the car that was maybe following us. Nothing mattered any more, I had mailed the letter. There was no turning back now. Just her and me. The rain felt clean. We were on our own now.

I crossed the road back to the car, got in. I was trembling.

"Why did you stand in the rain, darling?" she said.

"Because it felt clean."

I said, "Open a beer please."

"While you're driving?"

"Yes."

I drove back toward Wanchai and the Yacht Club. It rained all the way. It was very hot and I was sweating. I pressed my fingers to my eyes and breathed deep.

Mad Dog took one bound out the door and galloped across the parking lot and took off, ears flying. We loaded the gear into a sampan. It was raining harder now and I did not care. She sat under her umbrella and I let the rain fall on me as the sampan-woman took us out to the junk and I wanted to say, "Let the rain fall on you, feel this China rain."

We chugged through the dark rain in the sampan. Mad Dog swam behind. It rained all the way out to the junk.

We carried the bags down below. Ying was doing something in the galley, I stuffed the haversack under

522

the bunk. All the extra food was stashed away, she would not find that. I was shaky again now. I went back up on deck. Mad Dog was milling in the water, wanting to come aboard. Oh Christ, Mad Dog. I looked at him. Swim away, Mad Dog! I leaned down over the side, grabbed his collar, and swung him up aboard. Then I started the engines.

"Untie the ropes, please," I said to the sampan-woman.

The rain was beating on the glass of the wheelhouse. It was very hot. I pressed my fingers to my eyes and breathed deep. Then I called down the hatch to her and my voice sounded loud.

"Pour me a beer please, darling. And come up."

The sampan-woman shouted from up forward in the rain, "Untied, firstborn."

"Thank you," I shouted. She came back to the wheelhouse dripping. I gave her two dollars. She climbed down into her sampan.

I shoved both gear levers into forward.

CHAPTER 85

The engines went *doem-doem-doem*. I went through the mouth of the big stone typhoon-breakwater, the rainy lights of Kowloon beyond. I did not want to look at them. Then I opened up both throttles wider . and I felt the powerful surge and my mouth was dry and my hands felt shaky, the sweat running off me. I wanted to get the hell away from the Yacht Club. I did not want to see the magnificent harbor in the rain, Hong Kong Hong Kong Hong Kong. I opened both throttles full.

"This is it," I said.

Mad Dog thumped his tail at me. Sitting there dripping, quivering, he put his ears back and looked at me with adoration.

"Oh Mad Dog. What have I got to do to you?"

I shouted down the hatch into the saloon, "Are you coming up?"

"I'm just making some coffee."

"Please come up."

She came up the ladder with her mug of coffee.

"What's the matter, darling?"

"Nothing," I said.

I wiped my wrist across my eyes. I said, "When you're not with me I don't have anything until you come back."

The rain had stopped when we got into the East Lamma Channel but the sky was very black, no stars. To port was Deep Water Bay, the lights along the beach front. I could see the stern lights of some junks ahead. I drank the beer slowly, I had a long night ahead. And tomorrow. I would have to get some sleep tomorrow. If she could take the wheel. She would have to take the wheel. No, she won't have to, I can keep going on Benzedrine tomorrow. And tomorrow night. Maybe I could get some sleep tonight when we anchor off Po Toi. Two hours. I could even afford four hours. If we leave Po Toi Island at 2 A.M. we'll be forty miles out by dawn easily and China's maritime belt is only twelve. No. How would I wake up? No, I could not sleep at Po Toi, I wouldn't go to sleep anyway. Just take it easy on the beer.

There was some breeze coming into the wheelhouse now and I felt the sweat on me begin to dry. My mouth was dry, no saliva. We had passed the lights of Repulse Bay far away to port and now we were passing the lights of Stanley Village. Po Toi was dead ahead, four miles away. Beyond Po Toi, China waters except for the International Shipping Lane.

Ten miles beyond Po Toi, on the International Shipping Lane, the communist Lema Islands. With their gunboats. And their P.T. patrol boats. And their cannon. And their radar.

We anchored in the bay of Po Toi Island. It is uninhabited. Tomorrow if the sun shone the water would be bright blue clear and you would see the stony bottom, and the fish, and in the early morning she would be over the side down there, naked and goggled and satiny silky long-legged, her long black hair streaming out behind her swimming underwater like a seal looking for the fish, and Mad Dog swimming frantically after her trying to stick his head under water also, oh God.

And I wanted to cry out, *"It's going to be the same again I promise you, in a better place!"* I said, "Eat. You must eat, Ying."

"I have." She was very tired. She tried to eat some more, to please me. My throat felt thick, I was not hungry either, but I forced myself to eat because I would not be able to leave the wheel for eight, ten hours. I said, "I'll make you some hot milk, that'll help you to sleep."

She shook her head. "No thank you, darling, it's too hot for milk."

"You're having some," I said. I got up and went to the galley.

"I'll make it," she said.

"I'll make it." I poured the milk into the pot. She had her back to me. I pulled out the phial of sleeping pills, dropped four into the milk. My hands were shaky again. I stirred it, waiting for it to heat, then poured it into a mug. "Here. Drink it."

I washed the things while she drank the milk to please me. I went up on deck to see the sky. It was still black, no stars. I felt the breeze, from the south. It's nothing, I said, just a breeze. I would not be putting the sails up until tomorrow, and then only as auxiliaries to the Gardiners. Those Gardiners are perfect. No moon. They would still see my navigation lights from the Lemas. But they woud think I was just a fishing junk. They can't stop you anyway, I said, in the International Shipping Lane. The hell they can't, those bastards think they can do anything. But they won't. Why should they? For Christ's sake, stop thinking about it. The Lema Islands are the least of your worries. Tomorrow when she wakes up. For Christ's sake, don't think about that, there's no point thinking about that. I went down below. God, it was unreal. She was still sitting at the table, sipping her milk. "Hello, darling," she said. Trying to sound cheerful.

"How're you feeing?" I said.

"I am a bit tired."

"We'll go to bed soon."

"You've had a bad time too."

"Not so bad." I tried to smile. "It's my line of business, remember."

She said, "Do you really know what to do?"

"Yes," I said. I felt my chest flutter with a kind

525

of laugh. It was relief. That I was doing what I knew I had to do, the only thing for her and us, and right here and now I was anchored off Po Toi doing it, there was no turning back now, the decisions were over. No turning back. I said, "I'll tell you tomorrow. Just sleep, my lover. And trust me."

She said earnestly but her voice was slow, exhausted, "Will it take you a long time to tell me?"

"Yes," I said. "Not tonight. We're both too tired."

She breathed deep, and closed her eyes. "I feel beautiful. I know I'll sleep tonight. I have never felt so relaxed."

"You are beautiful," I said.

"Darling, I'm sorry I'm such a nuisance."

"You're not a nuisance," I said. "I love you."

"Yes I am. I thought maybe you would say I'm too much of a nuisance, too dangerous. And leave me."

"I could never leave you, Ying," I said. "You're not endangering me."

She said dreamily, "Aren't I really, darling? You're so clever and you're a policeman and I love you so I believe you. You're so beautiful."

"You're beautiful," I said.

"Am I really? I feel beautiful. I really think I must go to bed now, darling."

"Come," I said.

I took her by the hand and she heaved herself up. I led her through to the aft cabin. She sat down heavily on the bed, in a lump.

"I can undress myself, darling." She threw back her head to pull herself together.

She sat there in a lump, I took off her blouse and brassiere. And I thought I had never loved her so much. I put my arms around her and she held me dreamily. Mad Dog came snuffling around happily jealous, beating his tail. Then I tipped her over backward and she lay there. I unclipped her skirt. "Lift up," I whispered, and she sighed and lifted her buttocks with great effort and I peeled her pants down off her lovely legs. I looked at her lying there naked flat out drugged, almost asleep. I put my face against her soft belly, her smooth belly softness against my face. "You need a shave, darling," she said dreamily.

I picked her up and put her on the bed properly.

"Good night," I said. I felt shaky.

"Good night," she whispered.

I lowered the mosquito net around her. She looked very beautiful. I pulled the haversack out from under the bunk.

"Come on, Mad Dog," I whispered. My voice was thick and I did not want to look at him. He came amiably, sweeping his tail. I looked back at her lying flat out, naked, fast asleep under the mosquito net. Then I locked the cabin door behind me.

I gave her half an hour to get really deep asleep. I sat at the table in the saloon, chain-smoking. I looked at Mad Dog. He sat, looking up at me adoringly. My eyes burned.

"Oh, Mad Dog! Why did she bring you?"

He put back his ears and thumped his tail twice. *"Oh why did she bring you, boy!"*

I wiped my eyes with my wrist.

"You'd have been all right, Mad Dog, boy. You'd have pined, but you'd have found somebody else to love."

He thumped his tail happily.

"Oh, Mad Dog! Why won't you just swim like hell back to Hong Kong, why won't you have the sense to do that!" I shook his head gently and my eyes were full and he thumped his tail adoringly.

"Oh God, boy, I'm sorry. I love you as much as she does. You're a great dog, Mad Dog. You're not much to look at but you're a great dog, boy. But you see, boy, I couldn't take you ashore and leave you on this island. Because you'd just die of thirst, boy. You'd just die of thirst boy, and that's worse, isn't it?"

He thumped his tail.

Oh God . . . I got up and poured myself a brandy. One brandy. I needed it badly. He watched me. I took a big sip. I sat down and took his head. I wiped my eyes roughly, looked at him. "But, boy? Actually I don't think the SPCA would have found a home for you, fellow. Because you're no oil painting, and I think they would probably have put you to sleep also, boy." I shook his head gently and I had a great ache in my throat. "So you see, maybe it was meant to be like this, boy. Maybe it was."

I wiped my eyes and he thumped his tail.

"You had a good life, boy. You had a swim every

527

day, didn't you? That's pretty good for a mad dog. And she saved you from a dog stew, didn't she, boy?"

He was looking at me adoringly. The ache in my throat was very bad. "All right, boy," I said, "you won't know anything about it. Not a thing." I got up and pulled the little phial of knockout gas out of my pocket. My hands were shaking and my eyes were full of tears. He watched me with interest. I sat down again and I scratched his head with one hand so he closed his eyes and I took a big quivering breath and I held the phial to his nose, and I closed my eyes and pressed the plunger down and scrambled backward to get away from the gas.

He fell in a heap. I stood well off, waiting for the gas to clear. The tears were running down my face. He was out cold, breathing lightly. And I wanted to break down. Then I pulled out my Smith and Wesson and fitted the silencer. I felt like a bloody murderer. I stuck the gun into my belt and I picked him up, and I was crying.

I rowed ashore with him in the dinghy. I took the spade we had used when we planted the pine trees. I carried him across the beach and up the hill, panting, looking for a good place. I had first thought to bury him at sea like the old sea-dog he was, but I did not want the crabs to eat him. I dug him a grave. Sweating, the tears running down my face. I laid him beside the grave and pulled out the gun before I could hesitate, and I was crying. I put the muzzle against his head, and took a big quivering breath and closed my eyes.

"God I'm sorry, boy!"

And I hesitated once.

And I could not pull the trigger.

I looked at him lying there by his grave, his long floppy ears and his tongue hanging out and his big paws spread-eagle and his happy tail flopped out, and his chest breathing, and the tears were running down my face and my hand shaking and the great sick crying in my guts, and oh God I could not pull the trigger. I crouched there, eyes closed, shaking; then I stood up.

"All right, Mad Dog. You win. We'll just do the best we can. We'll cross the bridges as we come to them."

And I picked him up and I stumbled back down the

hill to the beach with him. I put him in the dinghy and rowed back to the junk.

I laid him under the table, out of the way. I knew I had done the wrong thing, but I had a tearful laugh in my chest. I poured myself a stiff brandy and knocked it back. I lit a cigarette and inhaled it deep, quivering, eyes closed.

"All right."

I went to the haversack and pulled out the Sterling. It gleamed shiny gray-black. I screwed it back together and tested the safety. Then I clipped the big magazine on. I felt my Smith and Wesson under my arm.

All-bloody-right.

I climbed back up to the wheelhouse. I laid the Stering behind the wheel. I looked all around. Way astern were the lights of Hong Kong, that was all. I looked up at the sky. Still black, no stars. I was sweating, tearful. I opened the port throttle a little, then pressed the starter, released the decompressor, and she took, *doem-doem-doem-doem*. She sounded very loud, filling the night. Then I started the starboard engine. I wiped my hands on my shirt. I switched on the navigation lights. Then I went forward and heaved up the anchor. My mouth was dry and my heart thudded from the exertion and my legs felt trembly.

I eased both gear levers into forward and felt the screws take, then I swung the wheel hard to starboard and the bows came around, and I opened the throttles wider.

I took her around the dark tip of Po Toi at quarter throttle. Beyond was just black China Sea, I could not make out any horizon. I opened the throttles, to half, then three quarters, then full, *doem-doem-doem-doem-doem*. I saw the lights marking the Western Approaches to the International Lane. I wiped my hands on my trousers. My mouth was dry and I was sweating hard. I wished I had a drink. It was eleven o'clock P.M.

CHAPTER 86

I could see the lights of the Lema Islands, maybe six, seven miles ahead on the starboard bow. I was doing about seven knots in the International Shipping Lane. I would pass the Lemas in about an hour. I could see some fishing junks' lights way off on my port bow, maybe half a dozen, trawling. I looked astern, the faraway lights of Hong Kong made a dull silhouette of the Peak, the lights reflected up into the clouds. Maybe tomorrow or next month I would think about those lights and regret them, but not now, all I wanted now was to get the hell out of them and past the Lemas. One hour and I would be past the terrifying sonsabitches. I looked at them through the binoculars—I could not make out anything except the lights, no buildings yet. In an hour I would know. If they were going to send out a P.T. boat I would see it in an hour at the most.

I wiped my lips, they tasted salty. Those fishing junks over there, how do the Comrades know I'm not one of them? I was glad of those junks. Without the binoculars everything was very black, just the pinpricks of the faraway lights. Thank God the sea was flat. I wish I had a lookout on the bows. Just a lookout. Tomorrow night she will look out. Oh God, tomorrow night. Stop worrying about tomorrow night, tomorrow night is going to be easy. It's all over except for half, three quarters of an hour. I lit another cigarette, it tasted of nothing but dry salty raspness. The top of my shorts was wet with sweat. God, I needed a drink. A drink of anything, I was a fool not to bring a bottle of water up here with me. I was wide awake, dry-eyed salty tense. I wished I had a lookout but really I did not need one. Any vessel would have lights. I wedged the wheel.

I hurried down the steps into the saloon, to the refrigerator. I snapped the cap off a cold San Mig, and grabbed a bottle of water. Down here the noise of the engines was much louder than up at the wheel. I

530

unlocked the cabin door and looked in. She was flat out on her back under the mosquito net. I was sweating. I hurried back up the steps to the wheel.

I checked the compass. I was well inside the International Lane. International law said the lane was five miles off the Lemas and I was at least seven off, but I gave her a little port. I checked the lights through the binoculars.

There was nothing to do but wait. I put the beer to my salty mouth and sipped. I could feel the heavy lines under my eyes and my eyes felt old and dry. I was calmer now. I lit a cigarette and inhaled it hard and after the beer it tasted like food.

I looked at my watch. Another twenty minutes.

It started to rain again.

It was very black in the rain. I cut back the engines, down. I could not see the lights of the Lemas through the rain. It came down, beating on the glass, on the deckhead, I could hardly hear the engines. Jesus, I wished I had a lookout. Sweating. I could taste my sweat. I could not see the lights of the fishing junks, I could not see the lights of Hong Kong astern. I steered her by the compass. My fingers wet the cigarette. God I hated this, not being able to see. Maybe I was doing four knots. I hated it, feverish. If there was an unlighted boat. The rain was coming down in furls now, with gusts sweeping, beating. I cut the engines down further, to maybe three knots. Oh God, it felt very bad not to be able to see the sea. But I was holding the compass-bearing without any difficulty against the gusts and there was no current. I looked at my watch. Eleven twenty-five. I did not know just how far away from the Lemas I was because I had changed speed. I tried to work it out in my head and my mind fumbled with the figures in the dark.

The rain began to let up. It was eleven forty-five.

Then I saw the lights again.

I watched the lights through the binoculars. They trembled. I had opened all the wheelhouse windows wide. My mouth was dry, the water made no difference to my mouth. The lights were much clearer now. The rain was all gone. I had the engines back to seven knots maybe.

The rain had cleared the air, the Lema lighthouse was very clear. I felt the wateriness in my guts. Sweating. I breathed deep, I felt my chest quiver. The binoculars were shaking, my arm ached from holding them. I looked astern. The lights of Hong Kong were misty, it was raining back there, a cloudburst. Lemas' lights were well on my starboard bow now.

I could make out the lighthouse very clearly now and some of the white of the buildings directly under lights. I could not be sure of the jetty. I thought I could see the lights of two MGBs, motor gunboats, tied up. Those were the bastards. Oh God, those were the bastards. Now was the time.

Soon now was the time. Soon soon. If they were going to challenge me, now was about the god-awful time. Any time now. Flash me, signal me from the lighthouse, then the MGBs. No hope against the MGBs. No show at all against those MGB bastards. Flat-hulled, thirty-five knots, they'd catch any goddamn boat. My breath quivered, the sweat on my eyelids ran round the eyepieces of the binoculars, I wiped my face on my wet shirt. Sick, sick hollow ache. Oh God, to get past these lights. Oh God, I am so nearly past them. Midnight. Half an hour more. Half an hour and I'll be three, four miles past these lights, please God. Please God. If they haven't flashed me in ten minutes they won't flash me at all and in half an hour I'll be to hell and gone past these terrible lights, please God. My arm trembled from holding the binoculars, I had to change arms. I looked at my watch, twenty-one minutes past midnight. Twenty past midnight and already those terrible Lema lights were well on my beam, oh God God thank you. I was grinning, tearful-shaky. At twenty-five minutes past midnight, when I was good and past the Lema lights, they flashed me.

Flashed me and suddenly my heart was racing thudding, I jerked and rammed both throttles full, *doemdoemdoemdoem*—hands shaking heart thudding white, I swung the binoculars back on the lighthouse—*dot dot dot dash dot dot dash dash dash*—my mind scrambled to read it above the thudding of my heart although I knew what it would say: *Stop your vessel—stop your vessel*—I grabbed the wheel to make it go faster, engines going *doemdoemdoem* with my heart, I swung the binoculars back on the lighthouse, they were still flashing the Morse. And the sick fear in my guts, solid raging fear *Oh Jesus Christ and Mary*—I thought wildly of turning around and heading flat out back to Hong Kong, I looked wildly astern and goddamn Waglan was way astern, and I would have to run right back past those terrible Lema lights, their god-awful MGBs would catch up in twenty minutes, *there was no going back, for Godsake, no no no going back*—and God knew I would swing around now and turn back flat out and shoot it out with the Sterling all the Christerrible way if I could get us out of this if I could get her away if there was any goddamn chance at all but there's no chance because those MGBs'll catch me in fifteen minutes, for Godsake, the only chance is to go flat out straight on and ignore those signals and maybe to God they'll think I'm just a fishing junk, if I was a fishing junk I wouldn't read that terrible signal—please God they'll think I'm a fishing junk, I *must* be a fishing junk, *why* should they think I'm not a fishing junk unless I obey that signal—please God they've got no right to stop me in the International Lane please God it's just some ignorant night-shift corporal throwing the Thoughts of Chairman Mao around at anything that moves. The sweat like a fever. Not yet the raging fury of fear when you'll scream roar charge fight kill and not care what happens or who you tear apart murder kill just so long you protect your mate your lover your dearest person, not yet that wild animal fear, it was all too slow-moving yet for that; the *doem-doem-doem* of the engines and the *sshh* of the sea and the tremble of the binoculars and the sweat running off me, it was god-awful heart-thudding terrible slow-motion hoping fear, willing willing willing. Willing the boat to go for Christsake faster, and oh Christ it was so slow, eight eight eight knots watching the lights of Lema and all the time the solid waiting fear watching for the MGBs. I could not read the flashing now, it was too fast for me and I turned the shaking binoculars down to look at the MGBs. I still could not make them out properly, too low in the water. Then I saw them move.

They moved, I stared at them through the binoculars. Going astern, off the jetty. The lighthouse was still flashing, *Stop your vessel* again. I closed my eyes and lowered the binoculars. My hands were weak on the wheel. Heart thudding. I wiped the sweat off my face on my shoulders. I looked at the compass, I tried to register the reading, it took a long moment. My breathing was quivering. Both throttles flat out. Nothing I could do. Nothing, just keep going flat out. In the hope of what? I could not outrun them. In the hope of bluffing them when they came alongside. God I'm shaking. Too late to try to turn about and run. This is it. I wiped the sweat off my hands on my sides. Weak weak weak, get sick hollow. I looked through the binoculars. The MGBs had swung around astern and now they were headed out to sea. I could only just make them out. Six, maybe seven miles, abaft my starboard beam. Maybe fifteen minutes, at thirty-odd knots, that's how long it would take them. Fifteen minutes. That's all we've got. Maybe that's all of the life we've got left. Unless a miracle happens. Fifteen minutes. Unless I fight. You can't fight two China MGBs with their cannon. Two fucking great cannons against a wooden junk versus one Sterling against steel hulls that can do thirty-five knots? Blow you clean out of the China Sea. And her with it. And *her. Oh God, not her.* Anything but her. I'd charge the whole China fleet for her but not if I'm going to draw one shot at her.

I lowered the binoculars, wiped my face on my sleeve, pressed my eyes. Nothing I could do. Except there was still the chance I could bluff my way through it. Every chance! *We're in the International Lane*. It *must* be just a routine check. I was well in the International Lane, they had no right to board me. Sick in my guts, strengthless. The engines were going *doemdoemdoem*, flat out, vibrating underfoot. The wheel was good and steady. She was a good boat, she would take us to anywhere. Oh God, to anywhere. Just to live and love and be together, anywhere. San Francisco, Jamaica, Barcelona. And *just live*. And love, a place of our own, a roof and a curtain and a light in the window unafraid for when I come home. And walking on the beach in the sunset and sitting on a park bench and the smell of the grass and the sun on her soft skin and the smile on her mouth and the shine in her eyes, and the knowledge of her, just the knowledge of being together and happy and free, and a packet of peanuts and an ice cream and a bottle of beer, walking hand in hand, and a news-reel and a ride on the top of an omnibus and a pub somewhere, anywhere. And the theaters and museums and art galleries, and the moonlight on the sea and the sound of her feet and the look of her asleep and the feel of her breathing next to me safe in the night, *Oh God anywhere. Please God help me now.* Sweating, shaking. I tried to pray constructively but all I could think was Please God and her lying down there un-conscious and what I had done to her. She had not conspired to run away, she had not conspired to spy on anybody, she had not done anything. Unconscious, defenseless and I was steaming her into Christ knows what and there was nothing *nothing* I could do but keep steaming in the International Lane. Not turn about not run not fight not shoot it out, they can do thirty-five knots to my goddamn eight, there was nothing I could do but keep to the International Shipping Lane and bluff it out, my only hope was the International Lane, *they had no right to board me in the lane!* I looked through the binoculars. They were well off the Lemas now, headed into the lane.

I stopped watching them. They were still too small and there was nothing I could do about it. Except sick-in-my-guts pray. In ten minutes they would not be so small, they would be right godterrible alongside. Ten more minutes. It is a long time to wait. It is a long time to wait holding a steering wheel at eight knots waiting for the communists to run you down. If only I was waiting behind a machine gun. If I could fight. Fight fight fight shoot it out kill the bastards fight for her life and yours, for love fight and shoot clenched-toothed sweating hating fiercely hate-filled roaring murderous reckless roar and charge the sonsabitches as is a man's right against any man who tries to destroy his love his woman his lover his unborn children his life—*oh Jesus Christ to fight!* Not stand here holding this wheel watching waiting for the bastards to come and take me without a fight—

I wedged the wheel and clattered down below. Mad Dog was still out cold. I unlocked the cabin door and looked at her. My breath was quivering, I felt the tears. I lifted up the mosquito net.

Oh *God,* to lie down beside her. Just lie down beside her now and hold her in my arms and feel her safe, alive, breathing, beautiful, my lover my darling my dearest person. To lie down and sleep, sleep and know that tomorrow and the next day and forever she will be here mine safe together. Lying there, not knowing what I'd done to her, not knowing what was happening to her out there. I knelt down by the bunk and put my face on her neck, lightly so as not to wake her and kissed her shoulder and face and hair, the soft smoothness of her and the feel of her breathing, and I tasted my own tears on her skin.

"I love you. Just remember that. For all our days."

I got up, I covered her with a sheet. I did not want any sonofabitch seeing her naked. I wanted to dress her but there was not time, I could not leave the wheel any longer.

"All right, darling," I said.

I locked the door. I put the key in my pocket. Then I clattered back up to the wheelhouse. Sweating shaky hating now.

The MGBs were flashing me now. They were maybe two miles abaft my starboard beam. *Stop your vessel.* Jesus, you bastards. I felt for the Smith and Wesson, I picked up the machine gun, checked it. It shook in my hands. I put it down, wiped the sweat off my face. I could see the sonsabitches clearly now through the binoculars and Jesus I hated them and I was frightened of them. How many times had they flashed me, while I was down below? Then came the big thud of their cannon.

The *boom* of the cannon in the night, I started, shocked, heart thudding, then came the big crash in the sea in front of me and the plume of black and white sea. *"All right,"* I bellowed, *"all-fucking-right!"* I lunged for the throttles shocked outraged and yanked them both back. *"All right!"* I bellowed—I grabbed the binoculars and stared shaking sweating heart-thudding, the junk had heaved right down to one knot, the MGBs were less than a mile off cutting down on me, they had a big sign in red characters painted across the bridge, I could see the gun crew at the cannon, *Jesus, I hated the bastards!* I stared at them hating shaking sweating heart-thudding shocked and the bastards could see I had cut my speed right down for them, they were maybe twelve hundred yards off me now, and then I saw the big puff of smoke from the cannon and I flung myself flat and I heard the shell crack into the sea ahead. I lay there panting gasping whimpering *Jesus, you bastards, oh Jesus Christ,* then I scrambled across the deck and grabbed up the Sterling and scrambled to the starboard door, panting sweating hate-filled. The nearest MGB was five hundred yards off now, the other going to cut across my bows and block off the port side, I rammed the muzzle out through the door and lay there hating shaking tearful waiting. Then they hailed me in English through the loudspeaker, *"Standby for boarding! Standby for boarding! Any resistance will be met with force!"*

I lay, shaking sweating weepy. I could see the sonofabitch with the loudspeaker on the bridge and the gun crew ready. Oh Jesus. Oh *Jesus!* They were still shouting over the loudspeaker. I pressed my eyes hard against the crook of my arm and took a big shuddering breath. Then I tipped the Sterling out into the black sea and it disappeared in a splash. All right. They weren't going to have the excuse of the Sterling as well.

I stood up, shaking hating. Their spotlight was flashing over the wheelhouse. *All-fucking-right!* I stood at the wheelhouse door, hands on hips, outraged.

"Do you bloody mind!" I bellowed in English. *"What's the meaning of this! Turn that bloody light out!"*

They kept the light on me, I shielded my eyes. They were fifty yards off.

"Turn that bloody light out!" It was anger I was shaking with now. Another light swept the length of the boat, a lot of orders in Chinese. I stood there, shaking, sweating, hating. They came alongside, reversed engines, six marines jumped aboard and tied the junk up to the MGB. There was a row of marines covering me with carbines. The big red characters painted across the bridge read *Seize Mao Tse-tung's Thought and Surge Upward!* *"Where's your commanding officer?"* I bellowed in English.

A man stepped down onto the junk, I could not tell his rank by any insignia. He said in English, "this vessel is under arrest."

I shouted, *"You'll be under arrest when your government hears about this! What do you mean by firing at me!"*

"You failed to obey orders to stop!"

"I cannot read Morse, you tried to kill me!"

He said, "You are Superintendent Ja-kob Mak-ah-dam. You are under arrest."

"For what offense?" I shouted.

"For entering China waters illegally."

"Bullshit!" I shouted. *"I am in the International Lane!"*

"You are under arrest."

Three marines entered the wheelhouse. I flung past them and lunged at the saloon hatch and blocked it, panting, shaking. All eyes were on me; they were crouched and ready. I panted full of fight, in Cantonese, shaking, "My fiancée is asleep down there! Now listen here, Officer! I am armed, as a policeman I am entitled to be armed. I am going cruising for the weekend in international waters as I am perfectly entitled to do by international law! I am perfectly innocent of your charges and I'm not having your men invading my fiancée's privacy!"

He was a little round-faced sonofabitch and I hated him so much I believed it.

He said, "Yes. Put your hands on your head."

I knew for hate-filled certain now the bastards had orders not to touch me, not to mark me unless absolutely necessary, certainly not to shoot me. I hated the sonsabitches and I took a deep breath and tried to keep the hate and shake out of my voice.

"You, Officer, firstborn—I know you are only obeying orders and that this is only a routine inspection." My voice shook, sweat on my mouth. "But you alarmed me with your gunfire, which was unnecessary. Nonetheless you were obeying routine orders and I apologize for my anger. You may search my boat if that is what you want, though I formally protest. And when I return to Hong Kong I will lodge a most vehement complaint. But you must understand, as an honorable Comrade of the People's Republic of China, that I will not allow anybody to enter my fiancée's cabin until she is dressed." I was shaking, panting, forcing the words and I hated them so much this was the most important bloody thing, she was absolutely innocent and no bastard was going in there while I still had it in me to block the way, my voice shook and I could feel the fierce tearful hate and by Christ I would murder any sonofabitch who tried to go breaking in there; I said, "Agree?" I started to say "understand" and I changed it in my mouth to "agree" and I felt myself choke.

"Agree," the officer said. "Give me your gun."

I hated them, great shaky hate and I knew for vicious sure the bastards dared not shoot me.

"Certainly not! The gun is the property of Her Majesty the Queen! You have absolutely no right to board me and try to disarm me in international waters and disgrace my fiancée!" I glared at them trying not to pant. They were unnerved, guns ready. Then my brain reeled red-black. "Shoot!" I bellowed at the marines and they jerked. *Come on down I'll wake her up for the big brave soldiers of the People's Liberation Army who arrest innocent people in international waters. I'm turning my back now so shoot!*" and I turned shaking hate-filled furious and clattered down the stairs, and they did not shoot. There was an order and the three marines were coming down after me, the clatter of their boots, then suddenly a great crashing jolt on my neck and I saw black stars of rage, I roared and lashed out and there was nothing in the world but weight and arms all over me, I tried to thrash the bastards off me and my arms were wrenched away from me and I felt the sudden steel snap of the handcuffs, I bucked and fought but the bastards still held me. I bucked upright and in a hate-filled thrashing flash I saw the officer bastard kick in the cabin door and more marines clattering down the stairs, and *Jesus Christ!*

I was on the deck of the MGB when they got her up topside of my junk. She had a dress on and she was very groggy and I shouted at her but they got me out of sight.

539

CHAPTER 87

They towed my junk in to Lemas, and put me in a cabin behind the bridge of the MGB for about an hour. The porthole was battened down, I could see nothing of outside. They did not ask me any questions and they did not answer any. They brought me some green tea and two packets of my cigarettes. Two marines sat in the cabin with me. I demanded to see the commanding officer, I demanded to know what was happening to her, I demanded a lot of things. They just did not answer me. I paced up and down the cabin, raging, sweating. Then I felt the engines maneuvering, and I knew we were putting out to sea again. We went for less than an hour. Then we were docking. They took me out onto a concrete jetty. Then I saw the searchlights up in the mountains and I knew I was on the China side of Shataukok.

Shataukok.

They took me in a vehicle through the quiet streets, to the Public Security Bureau offices. Into a cell. After twenty minutes they took me into an office. There was one man behind the desk. I was blinking from the light, he stood up and extended his right hand:

"Hello, Jake," he said.

I stared at him, my heart thudding in my ears.

"Chester Wu," I said.

He took my hand warmly, grinning, round-faced, he really looked pleased to see me; he said in his perfect Oxford English, "Who else did you expect to interview a Hong Kong policeman in Kwangtung province? Sit down, old man."

I stood there. All I could think was: *"Poetic justice.*

"Poetic justice," I said.

Chester Wu laughed, he was even blushing at little. Christ he was disarming. "You knew I was in charge in this area. Where would they send me, goddamn Tibet? Surely your boys have seen me through their telescopes?"

Jesus Christ I was shaky disarmed exhausted, frightened, but Christ knew I was glad it was Chester Wu.

"Yes. And your cheerful radio broadcasts."

He laughed chubbily as if I had congratulated him on some good university prank.

"And how is old Hong Kong?"

I felt for my cigarettes. I wasn't going to offer the bastard one. "The City of Imperial Decadence Run by White-skinned Pigs and Yellow-skinned Running Dogs?" I said in Cantonese. "You know very well how it goes." I was trying not to sound relieved.

He looked a little hurt, then he said, "Okay, Jake, I don't blame you." He looked at me, then leaned forward earnestly. "Look, Jake, I could sit here and ask you bullshit roundabout questions about what happened to old so-and-so and how's old bloody so-and-so to try to win your grateful confidence, but as it happens I was really asking you, one man to another—how's old Hong Kong? I spent half my life there—"

And oh God I was so relieved it was Chester I had to force myself to keep my voice hard. "Hong Kong is fine, Chester! Police morale is fine! There's the usual number of fucking people having the usual number of adulterous love affairs—get that down on your hidden tape recorder for what it's worth! Anything else, Chester?"

He sat back, looking hurt.

"All right, Jake, you're tired." And I almost felt bad that I had treated him badly. "Let's get down to business."

I clenched my fists on his desk, "The only business is what the hell you mean by arresting me in international waters and what the hell's happened to Ying!"

He said, "Now calm down, Jake! I know you're uptight but for Godsake bear with me! We're both in the same bloody awful game so let's for Christ's sake take it easy on each other."

My heart was thudding. He looked at my kindly. He said, "Now let me say this at the outset, Jake. That unless something unforeseen happens—as long as the decision rests in my hands and not higher up . . . you will not be detained in China."

My heart was thudding in my ears, I felt weak, I

hated and distrusted the bastard but I dearly wanted to trust him.

"And what about Ying?" I could feel myself white, hanging on his words like I was meant to do.

Chester Wu looked at me, reasonably.

"That depends, Jake," he said. "On my report. I'm sure you know all about reports. We're all in the same bloody awful game."

He said earnestly, "Do you love her?" And I wanted to be frank, honest, man-to-man with the bastard exactly like he meant me to be, *thank God for Chester Wu not some Red Guard sonofabitch.* I held on tight and kept a flat face, "You know the answer to that. If you've gone to this trouble to get me here."

He said calmly, naïvely, and for a wild moment I believed he did not know everything, "We didn't go to any trouble, Jake. You were in China waters."

"Bull*shit!*"

He said, "You *were,* Jake. China's territorial waters embrace the whole of Hong Kong and environs, including the so-called International Lane, which is only tolerated, not legally recognized."

I breathed deep. "Oh, yes?"

"Where were you going, Jake?"

I said so vehemently I believed it, *"For a cruise, for Chrissake!* I wanted to get out on the open sea! I'm entitled to go out on the high seas for a few days if I want!"

"Did you advise Dermot?"

"Yes! Check if you goddamn can!"

He said soberly, "Why didn't you obey our Morse signals?"

"Because I've forgotten all the Morse I goddamn knew, I haven't used it for years!" I glared at him shaking. "Can *you* still read it? I didn't dream for one moment your god-awful lighthouse was signaling me!"

He said quietly, "We were watching for you, Jake."

I tried to look astonished and I could feel my heart. *"Why* in heavens name?"

He said, "Don't bullshit me, Jake."

He said, "Bullshit, Jake. In the middle of the night?"

"Sure! It's great at night! I wanted to get out as

542

quick as possible because I have to be back in the office by Monday morning!"

He smiled. "What's wrong with Hong Kong's two hundred odd islands for your weekends?"

I pointed out the window. "Listen, Chester. You know what your boys are doing in Hong Kong! I've been working to a bloody standstill. I'm *sick* of fucking Hong Kong! I wanted to get *right* away for two days. So I couldn't *see* goddamn Hong Kong! That's *why*, Chester!"

He said, "And the girl and the dog drugged?"

"She wasn't *drugged!* I gave her two sleeping pills because she hasn't been sleeping well, that's all, I wanted her to zonk out! I gave the dog one in his food because I was sick of him barking his fucking head off in the night. I've given him a pill before today."

"Why hasn't she been sleeping well, Jake?"

I sat back. I had stopped shaking now.

"Because," I said wearily, "she is worried sick about the political situation, that's why. She's a good communist but she's had the misfortune to fall in love with me and I'm a cop and there's a bloody civil war on over there."

He said, "What specifically is she worried about?"

I said irritably, "Just that! Wouldn't you be? Of *course* she's worried about our affair leaking out. *I'm* worried too. There'd be hell to pay if my authorities found out. And she's just had a trip to China to rub it in."

"What's she told you about her trip?" he said.

I leaned across the table at him. "That girl is a good Chinese patriot, she would never say anything against her beloved China, that's one of the *many* things I admire about her! So you can leave her out of your little black book, Chester! If you want to know she said she was most impressed by her trip, the Cultural Revolution was an extraordinarily successful exercise in political awareness. Et cetera, et cetera!"

He looked friendly, interested.

"And didn't you pick her brains to see what you could find out?"

I looked at him, exasperated. I knew I was doing a good job of it.

"Of course I asked her about her trip, Chester. She's my woman, I missed her, I'm interested in China anyway. But I did *not* question her for my job. The *last* thing I'm likely to do is mix her up in my job, they're a bit too close for comfort. Is this what you fucking kidnapped me for? For God's sake, she's an ordinary bloody schoolteacher, you expect me to squeeze from her— the Thoughts of Mao Tse-tung? I *know* the Thoughts of Mao Tse-tung backward, I'm something of an expert of China's history remember!"

"Cut out the bullshit, Jake."

"Oh Jesus," I said. "There are none so deaf as those who will not hear."

He tried a shot in the dark. "What about the letter?"

I stared at him. "What bloody letter?"

"The letter you wrote before you left. Making your excuses for not being in the office on Monday. Because you'd be hotfoot to Manila."

I stared at him.

"Oh *that* letter! Oh I'm sorry." I shook my head at him. "No, Chester." I smiled at him. "Chester? I was *not* going to Manila. What for? I'm successful in my career and I want to stay that way. I love Hong Kong. It may surprise you to hear it but I also love China. And I think the communists are the best thing that happened to China—I said that in my book! I'm a policeman doing my job, that's all."

He grinned at me, man to man.

"Not bad, Jake. But you were running away."

I shook my head, exasperated. "From what, pray?"

"We'll ask the questions, Jake."

"Then ask them! Don't tell me! Look, go to my flat. You'll find my parrot, my clothes, my books—"

He said, "All that diesel on board? All that food?"

"I always carry plenty of diesel and food—"

He smiled. "Jake, Jake. You stocked up that boat this week. And had the engines overhauled, I can give you the dates."

"So bloody what? Listen, Chester: I like deep-sea sailing. The diesel and food is for emergencies."

He said, "What about the passports?"

I felt myself go white.

"What bloody passports?"

He opened his drawer.

"These."

I stared white-faced.

"A pretty good forgery," he said. "We didn't know you'd been to Macao. Why the passports?"

I said shakily, "Just for emergency. If the Red Guards came marching over the Shamchun and Hong Kong fell I wanted to be able to get her out with me. Listen, Chester: She knew nothing about that passport!"

"Bullshit, Jake."

"She *didn't!*"

He knew he had softened me. "Like she told you that we knew all about you two."

I stared at him, trying to look nonplussed, but I knew I wasn't doing a good job any more. "She did not, for Chrissake!"

He said kindly, "Do you want to get home, Jake?"

I just looked at him, I hated the sonofabitch. Trying not to shake. "Do you want her to be safe?"

I looked at him, I knew all about it, what was coming now but my heart thudded faster. "Go on," I said.

He said, "We could keep you prisoner here indefinitely, you know. Forever."

"On what goddamn charge?"

He shrugged. He didn't need a charge. "Entering China waters illegally. As a spy."

I said, "Only Ian Fleming would think that one up!"

"Or we could shoot you. And her. As a spy."

Jesus, I hated the bastard. They weren't going to bloody shoot either of us, they had better things for us to do. "Go on." I tried to sound weary.

He said, "You're a valuable man to us, Jake."

I knew that. I waited.

"So valuable that we may decide to keep you here in the People's Republic indefinitely for—debriefing? You could tell us an awful lot about what's happening in the force. And especially about Special Branch. S.B. is of great interest to us." He looked at me, he wasn't trying the "old boy" bit any more. "The debriefing would take a long time. Then we would have to check it all out to see if you had told us the truth, that would take even longer. Then? Of course, prison. As a spy. Twenty years? Probably life. Unless you were sentenced to death." He nodded at me. "As for her. Well, prison anyway."

I knew they weren't going to shoot or imprison me, they needed me in Hong Kong to work for them but I shouted, *"She's innocent!"*

He shook his head. "I'm not going to argue with you, there's too much to do. There's an alternative. At a price."

I waited, my heart thudding, this was it.

He said, "We will let you return to Hong Kong. Of course, you will be debriefed first, tell us everything you know. But we will let you return to your job in Hong Kong as if nothing had happened."

I had known it was coming but I had to try to keep the relief out of my voice. "Get on to the price."

He smiled.

"You know it, Jake, you're in the business. The price is information. Past, present, and future. I think you'll accept."

I said, heart thudding, "And what about her? You'll get *nothing* from me unless she comes back with me safe and sound! *Now listen to me, Chester*"—I shook my finger at him—"that's for absolute sure! She comes back with me and you leave her alone!"

I was hate-filled, full of fight. He smiled at me, "Have you quite finished laying down the law, Jake?"

"No! And another thing!" I shook my finger at him. "You better make it snappy! Don't think you can fuck around and dangle carrots! Because they're expecting me back in that office on Monday morning sharp and if I'm not there they'll start looking for me. And they'll find out all about it and then I'll be *no fucking use whatever to you!* So you better get us out of here or you're wasting your time! And *you'll* get *fuck-all information from me unless she goes back with me tomorrow!*"

He smirked.

"Jake? They may call you Somebody-up-There-Likes-Me McAdam, but you're not made of steel. Look at you. You're a shuddering wreck. You know as well as I do that there isn't a man alive who can't be made to talk these days, this isn't World War II old chap, this is World War III."

My heart was thudding, Jesus I hated the bastard. He said, "Who do you think you're kidding, Jake? You're in the business, you wouldn't let her go back if you were in my position, would you now? She's our security, old chap. That you keep your bargain. That you keep the information flowing. That you don't feed us false information to mislead us. Because"—he held up his

546

finger—"you know what will happen to her if you don't keep the bargain."

My ears were ringing, sick fury and fear in my guts. "You're diabolical."

He shrugged patiently.

"Yes, well, espionage is a diabolical business I'm afraid. Ask the CIA. Ask your pukka MI5. All right, old man, no sense being rude with each other. And as for you personally—"

I shouted, *"As for me personally you'll get nothing out of me unless that woman comes back with me safe and sound!"* I crashed my fist on the table and I wanted to crash right over it and grab the bastard's throat. "Listen, Chester, I've also got a few cards to play! *You need me, remember!* When I get back there I could fuck your whole plan up if I turned my back on that woman, if I decided to wash my hands of her. And there's not a damn thing you could do about it except bust me with my own authorities! Or if I had a nervous breakdown and told my authorities myself; I'm bloody near a nervous wreck already—*it's in your own interest to let her go back!* And if she doesn't there's *no fucking bargain!"*

He shouted *"Guards!"* and the door burst open, I swung on the bastards and they seized me by both arms, I tried to fling them off but they had me. He said quietly, "Jake, we have a lot to get through. All I have to do to get your co-operation is bring Ying-ling in here and have you watch the guards work her over, as they say in the classics."

He looked at me, I glared at him, panting.

"Now I want your co-operation, and I know I can get it very easily so I'm not putting you through that physical third-degree stuff. But I'll throw the whole book at you if I have to, including Ying-ling. So co-operate, Jake. I'll tell you what we're going to do. First"—he held up a finger—"we'll debrief you, you'll tell us everything you know: if you don't we'll just work Ying-ling over till you do. Then, having debriefed you, we'll send you back to Hong Kong to work for us, Ying-ling stays here as security—the hostage. But listen to this, Jake! He held up his finger brightly. "There's a bonus in it for you. After you've been working for us in Hong Kong for a while, *if* you've done a good job and kept the bargain" —he paused—"we will let Ying-ling come back to you!"

I shouted at him, desperate, *"If I give you informa-tion now I'm a dead duck under the Official Secrets Act so you've got all the fucking hold on me you need already so let her go with me now!"* The guards jerked me. He shook his head at me.

"A bad try, Jake, we're not naïve, you would just run away with her."

I jerked the guards. *"I won't run, for Christsake! The MI5 would find me wherever I ran to! I don't want to spend the rest of my life as a fugitive from my own people! My only hope is to stay on the job and work for you!"* The guards were holding my arms tight, I was desperate, if the bastards didn't let her go with me she was dead dead dead because on Monday the commis-sioner of police would get my letter, I shouted, *"Let her go with me or there's no bargain! You'll get nothing from me if I rot here till Kingdom Come—nothing!"*

"We'll see, Jake." He picked up the telephone. "Bring the girl in—"

I shouted wildly, *"Lay one finger on her—"*

"And you'll do what, Jake? I'll tell you what: You'll talk."

"She's innocent! She's a good communist!"

"She's a *rotten* communist, Jake. It's people like her that the Cultural Revolution is all about. We have no time for her kind in China except for their hostage value, in which case she's a veritable godsend, old man."

I shouted, *"She's a much better communist than you'll ever be! Just give her back and you'll have all the in-formation you want, I promise you."*

"I'll get all the information I want anyway, I promise you, Jake."

There was a rap on the door, I jerked around wild-eyed heart-thudding terrified.

"Well, here she is," he said. "I suppose we'd better handcuff you." The guards wrenched my wrists forward and he snapped the cuffs on. I wrenched around wildly, the door opened and there she stood, between two guards, and I felt my guts lurch. She was ashen, hand-cuffed and a big white dunce cap on her head, she stared ashen at me. They brought her in. My heart was pound-ing sick. "Ying, I'm sorry—"

"Hello," she said. She looked ridiculous, ashamed,

frightened, exhausted and I loved her so much I would do anything.

"Leave her alone, for Chrissake!"

Chester looked at me inquiringly. "Will you—we . . ." He waved his hand.

"Yes," I shouted. I would do anything.

"Are we on the same wavelength old man?"

"Yes!"

He held up his hands to her mouth. Just a bunch of fives for starters, old man, just a few front teeth—"

I thought I'd go mad, I wrenched at the guards, *"Leave her alone, I've said I agree—"*

He held his fist at her mouth still, looking at me. "But you do bugger around so, old man, telling me what you will and won't do. We must get on to the same wavelength, old man," he said and he drew back his fist and her eyes widened, then she cringed her face away and the guard grabbed her chin and twisted her face back to Chester and her eyes were screwed up and I roared in outrage and wrenched at my guards, and he hit her. Hit her once flat out in the nose—just her gasp and the loud crash of his fist and the splotch of blood and her head jolted and the dunce cap flew off and she sagged and I was bellowing struggling wild. Her head sagged bloody, Chester lifted her bloody face, the blood was running from her nose and gasping mouth and her beautiful eyes were streaming screwed up cringing for the second blow, he stuck his thumb between her lips and pushed them up all bloody and said, "Okay, old man, teeth still intact," and I was bellowing, *"You fucking barbarian!"*

He held up his fist again, "Are we on the same wavelength, old man?"

"Yes!" I bellowed. *"Yes, you fucking barbarian!"*

He lowered his fist. "All right, old man. Take her out," he said.

They walked her out, she was stumbling, head down, face streaming blood and I was wild outraged shaking, all my days I will remember her face cringing away from that blow and the smash and splash of blood. *"Jesus Christ, you bastard!"* I shouted.

He said, "Now sit down, Jake! And calm down!"

"You bastards." The guards shoved me down into the chair and held me there, panting shaking outraged. He sat down.

"You see what I mean, Jake? And what you saw"—he shook his head—"was absolutely *no*thing compared to what we will do, Jake. Good God, old man, that was just one smack in the snoot, we've both done worse to our prisoners under interrogation, haven't we?" I was shaking, sick fury in my guts. He said, "Now just let me finish what I was saying. As regards you personally"—he held up a finger as if nothing had happened—"if you fail to keep the bargain once you are back in Hong Kong, we will of course blow the whole story to your authorities. And that means you will go to jail for, say, twenty years under your Official Secrets Act."

I just stared at the bastard, shaking, hating him, I did not care a damn about the Official Secrets Act now. He took a breath. "Ying-ling stays, as the hostage. If you fail to keep the bargain, we'll take it out on her. We'll keep you well informed of how she's faring, with evidence to prove it."

"You bastard," I whispered.

"In fact," he said brightly, "We'll keep her right here in the Shamchun Valley; *this* side, of course. You'll only be twenty-odd miles apart, as the crow flies, think of that. So near, and yet so far." He smiled at me. "In fact we're going to arrange for you to *see* her!—through the fence of course. So that you'll be able to see we mean business."

I wanted to howl a howl of rage and grief grief grief.

"In fact," he said, "we'll arrange for you to pop over onto this side occasionally, we like to see our chaps from time to time for a bit of debriefing. And on those occasions," he said brightly, "we'll even allow the two of you to be—alone for a while."

I whispered, shaking, "Jesus Christ, you diabolical bastard."

He sat back, looked at me. He knew he had broken me. He let it hang. Then he leaned forward.

"Jake . . . would you like her to go back with you to Hong Kong tomorrow night?" Suddenly my heart was thudding loud with wild hope, I opened my eyes and stared. "Would you like that?" He was smiling earnestly.

Heart hammering, wild hope and joy in my guts.

"Christ, what is this, Chester?"

"Answer my question, Jake, like a good chap."

550

"Of course!"

"Jake," he said earnestly, man to man, "maybe I can let her go back with you."

"Oh Christ, Chester! . . ."

"It's up to you," he said. "And me, of course."

I tried to keep from shaking and all I wanted to do was plead with him, thank him and plead with him. He said, "I may see my way clear to letting her go back with you. If you co-operate entirely. Will you?"

I closed my eyes, the wild hammering of relief and gratitude. I wanted to shout *yes yes yes!* and thank him, tell him anything to get him to give me this, wild relief and joy, exactly like he had meant me to feel; it was basic technique: first terrify your victim, then shock him, then make him desperate, then offer to relent and win his gratitude. And he'll do anything for you. Textbook technique. For a textbook case. "Will you co-operate?" Chester said. I put my fingers to my eyes and pressed and heard my breath quiver against my hands.

"Yes," I said. I wanted to shout *yes please please*, like I was intended. I breathed deep, hating the bastard, and it quivered. I said, "How do I know you'll keep your bargain?"

He smiled: "You haven't much choice have you, Jake, old chap?" he said. "You're in no position to bargain, are you? You've seen what we can do to get the information." He smiled at me. "You must cooperate, fully. Because if you don't"—he held up his finger amiably—"she stays! As the hostage. And we'll get the information anyway, except it'll take an hour or two longer, while we work her over."

I was shaking. Oh God I was frightened of that.

"I don't believe you. You're dangling a carrot. Tell me why you're letting her come back."

He said, "I'll ask the questions, Jake. But I'll tell you. Because it suits our purpose. Having her there with you will keep you on the straight and narrow. Make you less inclined to run to your authorities and make a clean breast. And we'll be better able to watch you like hawks. We'll be in almost daily contact with you!" He smiled. "We'll also insist on you marrying her, of course. As soon as your divorce is through. No more of this immoral love-nest stuff in a Wanchai penthouse, old man, that won't do at all for a superintendent in Special

Branch. We want you nice and respectably settled in a nice block of government B-grade flats. With a nice circle of government friends." He smiled. "That's not such a hardship, is it?"

I tried to keep from closing my eyes and saying *yes yes for Christsake!*

He said, "We'll also insist that you re-establish your social life. You've been a social dropout for a long time now, old chap, since things started going wrong with Catherine. That's not good. You've lost a lot of your valuable contacts, with His Excellency for example, and the Old Man and all those priceless A-grade mob. What about all those valuable dinner parties where you pick up all those interesting bits of scandal? You *must* get back into that lot. Get back in the swing, old chap. And report to us of course. Ying'll be a great asset, old man, a wonderful hostess. As soon as you're settled down together you're going to start throwing a lot of dinner parties, to get back in the swing. We'll check your invitation list." He smiled. "We'll give you a reasonable expense account, of course, so you can do it properly."

I was shaking, but with gratitude, for Ying. The rest wouldn't happen because on Monday the Old Man would have my letter, but I said, *"You can stick your goddamn expense account!"*

He sighed: "There you go again, old man! You'll do as you're bloody *told*, old man!"

I said, "On one condition. She goes back *right now!* You smuggle her across Chung Ying Street right now back into British territory, then I'll co-operate—"

"Jesus Christ!" He sat back. "All right, she's *not* going back *at all!* She stays as the hostage!" He grabbed up the telephone: *"Send the girl in—"*

"No!" I was shaking. "Leave her alone! I'll co-operate!"

He looked at me angrily. "I'm going to give her another bunch of fives, to impress it upon you—"

"No! I'll co-operate!"

He sat back. "Absolutely? No more telling me what you will and won't do?"

"Yes." I was shaking. "Provided she comes back with me."

He looked at me.

"That depends," he said, "on you. And me."

CHAPTER 88

On Saturday morning Chester Wu sent for a doctor to keep us going. He only had another thirty-six hours to work on me and he needed my brain sharp. The doctor was a young woman, I was probably the first European she had treated, she blushed when she took my pulse. Chester said, "Give him something to keep him awake and alert until tomorrow night." She gave me two pills and Chester made her search my mouth to ensure I had swallowed them. She gave Chester some pills too. She said she would come back every four hours. I said to her in Cantonese, "My girl has been brutally hit in the face, please go and see her."

And Chester said in English, "That's been done, relax for Christ's sake." He was getting irritable with the lack of sleep. It was very hot and his fan did not help much. My skin was oily, my shirt stuck. I had asked if I could have a shower, to waste time, and he said, *Don't try to waste time, Jake!* There was plenty of green tea and cigarettes and he had a jar of instant coffee. Once he sent out for some cool drinks, and his *foki* came back with Seven-Up, and two slabs of Cadbury's chocolate. He sent for food and it was good pork and green vegetables but I could not eat. He said, "Eat, for Christ's sake! I've got to keep your damned strength up!"

The giving of information was easy, I did not care about that any more. Except trying to waste time so that I gave as little as possible in the time available. I did not care any more about who or what I betrayed to protect her: the desperately important thing now was that the basards let her go back with me, the desperate solid fear was that if they did not, if they kept her as the hostage, in a few days she would be finished. Because on Monday the commissioner of police would get my letter. And I would be arrested and the game would

553

be up. And that would be Ying's lot if she were still here as the hostage. Anything could happen to her. And I would never see her again. Never never never see her again, never again my love, my woman, my dearest person. I do not make excuses, for I admit again loud and clear that I did not care any more as long as I protected her. Is there a man who can say, "Take my love now and do your worst to her, before my eyes, banish her from me into the vastness of China but nonetheless I will save my honor, I will not violate my oaths of office at any price." If there are such men I believe they have said it only in times of catastrophic war, and not in the name of the rotten, stinking buy-and-sell and blackmail of politics.

I talked. He was very efficient, he had a lot of facts in his head and in the files in front of him. He worked very fast and some very efficient typists, who I never saw, transcribed the tapes as we went along. He had a relay of assistants who came in and listened, took over some questioning but Chester Wu stayed all the time. He knew I would not dare lie, for fear of what would happen to her when any lie was later discovered. If I had had the guts, if I had not had the fear for her, I could have done Hong Kong a lot of good by feeding him a lot of false information. Disinformation, as it's called in the trade. But I dared not. I only lied in denying that I knew certain answers. He knew I had only been back in Special Branch for five months, and that gave me a bit of cover; he knew that in intelligence the left hand does not know what the right is doing and that gave me a bit of cover. I managed to avoid disclosing about half of my own informers and I learned that a few of them were doubles. I wasted as much time as I dared, to save something of the wreck of my life.

I answered the bastard, for fear for her. I answered him all that Saturday, and all that night, and the hate and the fear and the young woman doctor who came every few hours kept us going; I saw the sunrise over China through Chester Wu's window, shining in my eyes, and I thought my heart would break for love of her and wild relief that she was coming back.

CHAPTER 89

At noon on Sunday Chester knocked off. He had got most of what he wanted out of me, he went to sleep it off and his assistants took over. I was wide awake under the Benzedrine, but I could feel my heart and the drag under my eyes. At eight o'clock Chester Wu came back and took over.

He had the Confession with him, and a photographer to photograph me signing it. The Confession was not worth anything but it would make good reading in the *Red Flag* and the Hong Kong left-wing press if they needed it; it went something like this: *I, Jacob McAdam* et cetera *thoroughly disillusioned with the fascist imperialist exploitations and atrocities of the fascist British Imperial thugs and their yellow-skinned running dogs who are hand in glove with the warmongering imperialist American aggressors and the revisionists of the Soviet Union and the lackeys of them all, the bandits of Chiang Kai-shek* et cetera *and having been armed with the Invincible Thought of Mao Tse-tung* et cetera *hereby freely, and voluntarily and repenting* et cetera *announce that I have made a clean breast of my errors and the festering information at my disposal to the authorities of the glorious People's Republic of China in the hopes that by so doing I can make amends and thereafter help to carry high the Great Red Banner of Mao Tse-tung's Thought* et cetera, et cetera. . . . It would fool nobody but it would make good face in the Red newspapers. I said, "Jesus, I expected something more sophisticated from you."

"Sign it, old man. Just a spot of grist for the publicity wallahs. It may be some consolation one day, if you're ever stupid enough to let us down, to know that while you're languishing in a British prison you'll be a hero in China. There'll be protest demonstrations outside the British High Commission in Peking demanding your release. Even another good riot in Hong Kong, all for you. We'll probably name a street after you somewhere. We're very good to our martyrs." He smiled at me brightly. "And as for Ying-ling, she'll be a national hero too, as the stalwart communist martyr girl who made you see the light."

I said, "I'm not signing that fucking thing until Ying and I are back in British waters."

He sighed irritably, and rang his bell. "Bring the girl in," he sighed and I felt my heart turn white.

"All right," I said.

"There's a good chap," Chester said. He sat down beside me and put his hand on my shoulder. "Now sign, and we'll both say cheese to the camera.

"Cheese," Chester said and the flashbulb went.

"You didn't say cheese!" he said. "All right. It's a somber moment, I suppose. Now a few of you and me shaking hands under the Chairman's portrait."

"Get stuffed," I said.

"Guard!" Chester shouted.

"You fucking bastard," I said.

Chester grabbed my right hand warmly. "Say that with a smile."

"Cheese!" and the flashbulb went blinding bright.

After the pictures he checked over any loose ends. He had read all the transcripts of his tapes. He made me initial every page. The last of the Benzedrine was wearing off now and I could feel my nerves really going. I did not care about anything any more, all I wanted to do was lie down and sleep. He sent out for a cold bottle of Snowflake beer, then said, "I don't suppose you better have any after all that Benzedrine, you look gone in. And you've still got to drive that boat of yours."

I closed my eyes. "For Christ's sake, Chester, let us go now."

He said, "Mind if I go ahead? Pity, I think we both deserve a little something. To celebrate."

He rang for the lady doctor.

"Can my friend have a beer after all that Benzedrine, Comrade? How's his heart?"

"No," the lady doctor said. "His heart is very good but no alcohol, it will be a strain on him."

"Sorry, old chap," Chester said in English, "perhaps

you should change your doctor? Give him another Benzedrine," he said in Cantonese.

"Last time," the lady doctor said. "He is very strained."

"You hear that, old chap? Strained. Must look after yourself when you get back."

I could feel my chest hammering under the new Benzedrine. He proceeded to tell me a few things about how we would operate. My nerves were almost gone, all I wanted to do was get Ying the hell out of it. He said that mostly any important debriefing would be done aboard my junk at appointed islands. I would be told where to go on weekends, anchor, and a Chinese fishing junk would come alongside, et cetera. I said yes, yes. It would not happen because tomorrow morning the commissioner would have my letter and Chester's game would be up. *Up, your game's almost up up, fuck you, Chester!* If such meetings happened at all it would be in collaboration with the Hong Kong police and MI5 with me as a double agent, feeding Chester disinformation. I did not know or care what was going to happen to me tomorrow under the Official Secrets Act, I did not believe I would go to prison because I had only talked under duress, what they would probably do is use me for disinformation for as long as they could, but all I cared about was getting her the hell out of here. Chester was in a good mood now, enjoying his cold Snowflake and I said yes, yes, and my nerves were screaming. At about ten o'clock that Sunday night he said, "Well, I guess that's about it, Jake, old man. Nothing more to do but wish you bon voyage and say here's to a long and fruitful relationship!"

I wanted to say *Get fucked*. I breathed deep and felt it quiver all the way. I said,

"Can we please go now?"

He looked at me, very good-humored, " 'We,' old man?"

I stared at him through the sudden raging thudding fear.

" 'We'?" he said.

I wanted to roar it in terror, *"Ying and I!"*

He sat back. "Oh I'm *sorry*, old man! *She's* not going for a while."

I stared at him through the terror, then the wild rage came through, I wanted to bound up across the desk and seize the basttard by the throat and strangle throttle kill him kill him kill him, I was standing shaking sick fury—

"What do you mean?"

I did not hear the guards, I only felt them grab my arms, I flung around and roared at the top of my lungs, the outrage and rage to fight and roar and kill—*"What do you mean!"* and they had me in wild fighting arm locks and a third had a half nelson on me and there was nothing in the world but the raging heart-thudding rage to fight and throw them off and kill kill kill, *What do you mean!* and they wrenched my head bent right over down over Chester's desk, paralyzed, gasping and he was saying through the roaring raging in my chest and the wild fighting grief—"Now calm down, Jake! She *not* going with you—she's *staying* as the hostage as I originally said—to ensure that you co-operate—that you don't try to run away with her or break down like a good Boy Scout and confess all to your authorities—we don't *trust* you yet, Jake!—we're not fools—you might try anything—like disinformation—she stays as the hostage till we trust you. At least until you get your divorce. Then she comes back to you if you've proved reliable and we move on to Plan Two. That's the marriage, Jake. Furthermore, we don't want Catherine finding out about her, Jake, do we? Catherine's been very sticky over this divorce, we don't want any of her private eyes digging into Ying's past, do we now? We *don't* want coming out in your divorce that your mistress used to be a *communist schoolmistress*, what would your police force say about *that!* That would really blow everything for all of us—they wouldn't let you stay in Special Branch if *that* came out, *would* they—?"

And the wild grief and rage and terror screaming, the wild grief grief grief and rage and fury the speechless paralyzing pressing on my neck and the wild grief.

"Now calm down, Jake," he said.

CHAPTER 90

It was about midnight when I saw her. They were about to take me back to the launch. He told me to sit down at the table in his office. I heard her footsteps down the passage. The door opened and there were two guards, and there, between them, she was. I got up from the table, shaking. "Ying!"

She stared at me, pale, wide-eyed, her face was a little swollen, she tried to smile. "Hello," she said.

"Sit *down*, old man," Chester said. I flung his arm aside and strode for her and the two guards jerked her back and thrust their hands on my chest, glaring, and I was trembling in rage, I wanted to hit them with all my might, she was staring at me, pale, gaunt, held tight by the elbows, Chester grabbed my right arm. "Sit down, Jake!"

"Get your flunkies out of here! Get them out!"

"Sit down first!"

"Get them out! Before I go mad!" I sat down, shaking, I hated them with all my sick heart. *"Now get them out of here before I go berserk."*

"All right," he said to the flunkies in Cantonese, "wait outside." She stood there. Chester took her arm. "Now come and sit down, my dear."

He led her to the table, she was shaking, she kept her big eyes on me. She sat down shakily and tried to smile at me. Chester turned and walked to the window and looked out. "Hello," she said and I thought my heart would break. I could not believe what was happening, I was shaking with grief and shock and outrage and the tears were running down my face. "Hello, my love," I said, and I heard my voice choke.

"Please don't worry," I said.

Her eyes were full of tears, holding them back, she closed her eyes and nodded, yes, and tried to smile with her swollen mouth, oh God—

"Listen." I took her hands across the table and they

were clammy and I wanted to howl my rage and grief and fight. "Everything is going to be all right—" I lied, I lied. Oh God and Jesus Christ I could not but lie to her for grief, for love, for love and grief grief grief, oh God and Jesus Christ our farewell did not even have the dignity of truth and privacy, to look into her eyes and say Good-by, good-by forever my greatest love, my only love, my lover my woman my mate, good-by darling. My throat was choked, I held her hands tight and squeezed them and I said, "I am sorry, Ying. I am sorry I got you in this. I have explained to them that you are absolutely innocent."

She had her eyes closed, the tears were running down her swollen face, she nodded once then opened her wet dark eyes and looked at me, and I knew she knew, and my heart heaved and I wanted to cry out and clutch her tight and howl, her eyes said she knew that I was lying, that this was good-by, good-by, her eyes were big desperate urgent trying to tell me, and her swollen lips mouthed the words so Chester Wu would not hear, *"Good-by, my darling,"* and I put my hand up over her mouth to cry to her *No no not yet it's not the end yet not while we're both alive I'll find a way!* and she closed her eyes and pressed her swollen mouth on my palm and kissed it and she sobbed out loud once into my hand and I wanted to howl my love and hate and grief, *Good-by, darling* she cried into my hand, I lifted her chin and the tears were running down my face and she held my wrist and cried silently shaking into my palm and she kissed my palm and I could feel the words *good-by good-by*, "Ying?" and she sat there straight, head up, eyes closed, holding my hand against her face. *"Ying?"* I said and she opened her eyes and my throat was choked and I whispered to her, *I'll find a way,* and she put her fingertip on my mouth to stop me, to stop me making a promise I could not fulfill and the tears were running down her face and her eyes were crying out to me, *Don't say anything my love* and I wanted to shout *I'll find a way!* and Chester Wu said, "No whispering!" and I said aloud, *"I will, Ying,"* and I wanted to bellow and shake the whole building down, she took a big breath and it quivered and she said, "Will you look after Mad Dog?" and I felt my heart crunch and I said, "Yes, of course."

"And Percy," she said.

I nodded yes yes yes.

She was crying. She looked at me, tears running and she tilted back her head and her chin trembled as she tried to sound controlled. "And the sunrise. Think of me in the sunrise. And I will also—"

I thought my heart would break.

"All right," Chester Wu said. He came up to the table and held his finger up at me. "No trouble now, Jake, the guards are right outside." She looked at me and her face was white and wet and her hair hung straight black and she tried to hold the tears.

"Good-by," she said.

And I wanted to howl my rage and grief and roar *It's not good-by as long as I'm alive!* and I grabbed her and clutched her tight against me and I cried, "Good-by, my love, but it's not good-by," and I was so desperate I really meant it.

"Of course it's not," Chester said. "It's only *au revoir.*" Then the guards were coming into the room through my tears, she whispered against me holding me tight, "At least we'll be seeing the same sun," and she held me tight once and then she turned out of my arms and two guards gripped me tight, she had her back to me, head down and her long black hair to me and I heard her sob out loud and she was walking out of the room and the guards were holding me and I tried to shout and it came out, *"Not only the same sun! It will never be good-by!"* and she did not answer and she was gone.

CHAPTER 91

Then they took me back to the Lemas on the MGB. They put me aboard my junk under guards, dressed as fishermen. Mad Dog was overjoyed to see me. Then a big junk towed mine back up the International Lane. At Po Toi it cast off but a guard took my wheel. The big junk escorted mine up the Lamma Channel, back past the lights of Repulse Bay. It seemed a long long time since I had left, it was as if I was remembering the lights all over again and they meant only grief, for that long ago, she had seen these lights, many times, from this deck, where was she now? The guard pointed toward Aberdeen and said "Go." Then they swung about back toward the International Lane, and I was on my own and it was quiet, just the *putt putt* of their engines and Mad Dog thumping his tail on the deck at me.

I stood at the wheel and drifted in neutral and I did not care if I went on the rocks, and the tears were running down my face, and the wild desperate cry in my heart. Maybe I drifted for ten minutes. It started to rain again. Then I put her into gear and opened the throttles a little. It rained all the way and I could not see properly for the rain and the tears in my eyes and I did not care.

I did not take her to my buoy at the Yacht Club, I just dropped anchor. I did not care what happened to the boat any more. I lowered the dinghy and I climbed down into it, holding Mad Dog. The rain came down and I did not care about that either, Mad Dog wanted to jump over and swim ashore and I just held him tight against me. Then I rowed ashore in the black rain.

Then I drove back to the penthouse in Wanchai. It was raining and very quiet all the way, and every street shouted *Ying!* at me.

I let myself into the flat and turned on the lights and Percy said "Hello!" Everything was there, just there. Percy and the fish and Mad Dog beating his tail about the flat, tongue slopping happily unworried, expecting her to come in the door any moment. And her portrait I had painted, on the wall, and the things she had bought from China Products in the kitchen, and our room, the double bed still unmade from the last time we had slept in it together on Thursday night, and her things on her bedside table, her hair clips and her China Products alarm clock and the Chairman Mao ashtray and the half-empty packet of Red Victory cigarettes and in the bathroom her red China Products towel and her spare toothbrush and her Elizabeth Arden bath salts and in the cupboard were her things, her dresses and her panties and her brassieres and her stockings and her shoes, oh good

God Jesus and Mary. It wes unreal and I wanted to shout
that it was all unreal *unreal* UNREAL! *Oh good God and
Jesus no!* Nobody was going to touch her things, nobody
was going to take her things away from me, they were
my things of my woman and they are going to stay
with me until she came back, for when she came back,
I would get her back, somehow somewhere somewhen
I would get her *back, back back back. I'll get her back!*
and I slumped down on the bed and held my face in
my clenched fists shaking.

After a long time I got up. I did not know what time
it was except that it was very nearly dawn. I went to
the front door and Mad Dog tried to scramble through
ahead of me and I pushed him back and he looked up
at me desperately. I rode down in the elevator to the
underground garage and drove out through the hot empty
streets of Wanchai, to headquarters. There were a lot
of lights burning in Special Branch but nobody looked up
as I walked down the passage to my office. There was
a pile of memos on my desk and files in my in-basket.
I did not care what had happened. I locked the door
behind me and I sat down and I picked up the telephone,
it shook in my hand but it was not fear, it was grief.
I dialed Dermot, the director, on his bedside line, it
rang three times and he answered. I said, and my voice
was shaking:

"Dermot, you got to come down to the office immediately. I've got a lot to tell you."

"For Chrissake," Dermot said. "Won't it keep?"

"No," I said. "It's a confession. By me."

"By *you?*" Dermot said.

"And I need your help!"

I slammed down the telephone and I held my head
and I was crying, not crying for anything about Dermot
and this office, I was crying for grief.

I got up, then I went to the window. The gray was
just beginning to turn pink out there. Across the Mountains of Nine Dragons. All I knew was that I was waiting
watching for the sun to rise over the Mountains of Nine
Dragons and all there was now was the crying inside
and I could do nothing except stand and look and love
and cry and hate and vow and rage and cry for grief
grief grief: the sun came up very slowly and I was seeing
it and not seeing it come up over the mountains,
through my tears, all I was seeing was Ying-ling over

there other side those mountains, just there and far away, somewhere, where, where was she going, going anywhere, anywhere into the red vastness of the sunrise over the Mountains of Nine Dragons, *Ying Ying Ying,* her, she, my love, riding now in some vehicle into that sunrise going I knew not where, into the vastness of one quarter of mankind, into that red Red sunrise and are you also seeing it, my love? Oh Jesus Christ and Mary and then the whole east was riotously invincibly red, oh dear Jesus Christ have love and mercy, and I knew it was all a lie. Knew that all the Queen's horses and all the Queen's men would not and could not get other side that sunrise and the great swelling cry and howl of grief came up my throat, oh God oh God oh God and I cried out at the sunrise but I knew it was a lie:

Not only the same sun, my love!

Keep Up With The
BESTSELLERS!

_____ 80409 LOOKING FOR MR. GOODBAR, Judith Rossner $1.95

_____ 80720 CURTAIN, Agatha Christie $1.95

_____ 80676 TALES OF POWER, Carlos Castaneda $1.95

_____ 80588 FOREVER, Judy Blume $1.75

_____ 80675 THE MASTERS AFFAIR, Burt Hirschfeld $1.95

_____ 80445 SECRETS, Burt Hirschfeld $1.95

_____ 78835 THE PIRATE, Harold Robbins $1.95

_____ 80763 WEEP IN THE SUN, Jeanne Wilson $1.95

_____ 80762 THE PRESIDENT'S MISTRESS, Patrick Anderson $1.95

_____ 80751 JULIA, Peter Straub $1.95

_____ 80723 SEVEN MEN OF GASCONY, R. F. Delderfield $1.95

Available at bookstores everywhere, or order direct from the publisher.

POCKET BOOKS
Department FB-2
1 West 39th Street
New York, N.Y. 10018

Please send me the books I have checked above. I am
enclosing $_____ (please add 35¢ to cover postage and
handling). Send check or money order—no cash or C.O.D.'s
please.

NAME_____

ADDRESS_____

CITY_____STATE/ZIP_____

FB-2

POCKET BOOKS

Keep Up With The BESTSELLERS!

_____ 80432 CONVERSATIONS WITH KENNEDY, Benjamin Bradlee $1.95

_____ 80176 THE TOTAL WOMAN, Marabel Morgan $1.95

_____ 80270 TOTAL FITNESS, Laurence E. Morehouse, Ph.D. and Leonard Gross $1.95

_____ 80600 est: 4 DAYS TO MAKE YOUR LIFE WORK, William Greene $1.95

_____ 80446 NICE GUYS FINISH LAST, Leo Durocher with Ed Linn $1.95

_____ 80468 TOILET TRAINING IN LESS THAN A DAY, Nathan Azrin, Ph.D. and Richard M. Foxx, Ph.D. $1.95

_____ 80979 RUNNING FOR PRESIDENT, Martin Schram $1.95

Available at bookstores everywhere, or order direct from the publisher.

POCKET BOOKS
Department NFB-2
1 West 39th Street
New York, N.Y. 10018

Please send me the books I have checked above. I am enclosing $_____(please add 35¢ to cover postage and handling). Send check or money order—no cash or C.O.D.'s please.

NAME_____

ADDRESS_____

CITY_____STATE/ZIP_____

NFB-2

POCKET BOOKS

Carlos Castaneda

With TALES OF POWER now available in a Pocket Book edition, one of the most popular authors of the twentieth century completes his journey into sorcery.

"We are incredibly fortunate to have Carlos Castaneda's books..."
—*The New York Times Book Review*

_____	80676	TALES OF POWER	$1.95
_____	80498	THE TEACHINGS OF DON JUAN	$1.95
_____	80424	JOURNEY TO IXTLAN	$1.95
_____	80497	A SEPARATE REALITY	$1.95

Available at bookstores everywhere, or order direct from the publisher.

POCKET BOOKS
Department CC-1
1 West 39th Street
New York, N.Y. 10018

Please send me the books I have checked above. I am enclosing $_____ (please add 35¢ to cover postage and handling). Send check or money order—no cash or C.O.D.'s please.

NAME_____

ADDRESS_____

CITY _____ STATE/ZIP_____

CC-1

POCKET BOOKS

R. F. DELDERFIELD

Sweeping Sagas of Romance and Adventure

_____ 78777 GIVE US THIS DAY $1.95

_____ 78923 GOD IS AN ENGLISHMAN $1.95

_____ 78554 THEIRS WAS THE KINGDOM $1.50

_____ 78616 TO SERVE THEM ALL MY DAYS $1.75

_____ 80277 THE AVENUE GOES TO WAR $2.25

_____ 78862 DIANA $1.95

_____ 80278 THE DREAMING SUBURB $1.95

_____ 78981 FAREWELL THE TRANQUIL MIND $1.95

_____ 78869 THE GREEN GAUNTLET $1.95

_____ 78672 LONG SUMMER DAY $1.50

_____ 78979 MR. SERMON $1.75

_____ 78673 POST OF HONOR $1.50

_____ 78959 RETURN JOURNEY $1.95

_____ 78977 TOO FEW FOR DRUMS $1.50

Available at bookstores everywhere, or order direct from the publisher.

POCKET BOOKS
Department RFD
1 West 39th Street
New York, N.Y. 10018

Please send me the books I have checked above. I am
enclosing $_____ (please add 35¢ to cover postage and
handling). Send check or money order—no cash or C.O.D.'s
please.

NAME_____

ADDRESS_____

CITY_____ STATE/ZIP_____

RFD

POCKET BOOKS